The Jazz Fiction Anthology

THE

Jazz Fiction

ANTHOLOGY

EDITED BY

Sascha Feinstein & David Rife

INDIANA UNIVERSITY PRESS

Bloomington & Indianapolis

This book is a publication of

Indiana University Press
601 North Morton Street
Bloomington, IN 47404-3797 USA

www.iupress.indiana.edu

Telephone orders 800-842-6796
Fax orders 812-855-7931
Orders by e-mail iuporder@indiana.edu

The paper used in this publication meets the minimum requirements of American National Standard for Information Sciences—Permanence of Paper for Printed Library Materials, ANSI Z39.48-1984.

Manufactured in the United States of America

Library of Congress Cataloging-in-Publication Data

The jazz fiction anthology / edited by
Sascha Feinstein and David Rife.
p. cm.
ISBN 978-0-253-35381-8 (cloth : alk. paper) —
ISBN 978-0-253-22137-7 (pbk. : alk. paper) 1.
Short stories. 2. Jazz in literature. I. Feinstein,
Sascha, date– II. Rife, David. III. Rife, David, date-
PN6120.2J37 2009
808.83'1—dc22

2009021879

1 2 3 4 5 14 13 12 11 10 09

for our mutual chums

Bill Ford, Gary Hafer, and G. W. Hawkes

Contents

· *Introduction* · *ix*

1 Don Asher, "The Barrier" · *1*

2 James Baldwin, "Sonny's Blues" · *17*

3 Toni Cade Bambara, "Medley" · *49*

4 Amiri Baraka, "Norman's Date" · *66*

5 Amiri Baraka, "The Screamers" · *78*

6 Frank London Brown, "Singing Dinah's Song" · *85*

7 Michelle Cliff, "A Woman Who Plays Trumpet Is Deported" · *91*

8 Wanda Coleman, "Jazz at Twelve" · *97*

9 Julio Cortázar, "Bix Beiderbecke" · *107*

10 Julio Cortázar, "The Pursuer" · *115*

11 Kiki DeLancey, "Swingtime" · *166*

12 Ralph Ellison, "A Coupla Scalped Indians" · *177*

13 Rudolph Fisher, "Common Meter" · *190*

14 Sam Greenlee, "Blues for Little Prez" · *205*

15 David Huddle, *Tenorman: A Novella* · *214*

16 Langston Hughes, "The Blues I'm Playing" · *283*

17 Langston Hughes, "Old Ghost Revives Atavistic Memories in a Lady of the DAR" · *298*

18 Phil Kawana, "Dead Jazz Guys" · *301*

19 Yusef Komunyakaa, "Buddy's Monologue" · *313*

20 Ellen Jordis Lewis, "Miss Brown to You" · *318*

21 William Henry Lewis, "Rossonian Days" · *324*

22 John McCluskey, Jr., "Lush Life" · *340*

23 Bill Moody, "Child's Play" · *357*

24 James Reed, "The Shrimp Peel Gig" · *369*

25 Josef Škvorecký, "The End of Bull Mácha" · *385*

26 Terry Southern, "You're Too Hip, Baby" · *404*

27 Julian Street, "The Jazz Baby" · *415*

28 Boris Vian, "'Round About Close to Midnight" · *447*

29 Eudora Welty, "Powerhouse" · *452*

30 John Edgar Wideman, "The Silence of Thelonious Monk" · *464*

31 Xu Xi, "Jazz Wife" · *475*

32 Richard Yates, "A Really Good Jazz Piano" · *482*

· *Authors' Biographies* · *501*

· *Acknowledgments* · *505*

Introduction

When the names of famous jazz musicians are evoked, music—more than biography—invariably comes to mind. The case with jazz fiction, however, is quite different: since language can only translate music inexactly, most stories influenced by jazz celebrate the near-magical capacity of the music to impact human behavior in all of its impressive variety. In turn, the actions of characters and the descriptions of landscapes provide metaphoric ways to consider the essence of music. What fiction *can* do, in other words, is recreate the ambiance of jazz and, even more important, dramatize the lives of players and listeners in ways that allow us to reconsider the music beyond its sheer aesthetic power. The best jazz fiction raises the reader's consciousness about such important matters related to the music as race and, almost always, the struggle for acceptance within society.

Eager to make connections between jazz and literature, many scholars resort to the cultural truism that jazz, being native to America, must therefore be inextricably connected to American literature. Stories like Langston Hughes's "The Blues I'm Playing," which is governed by the struggle between European and American aesthetics, lend credence to such an argument. But just as jazz has become a more international music, so has jazz fiction expanded beyond such a nationalistic constriction. In concert with the American contributions, the international voices in this anthology speak eloquently to the universality of jazz and its capacity to influence relationships—from married couples and lovers to siblings and even casual friends. In short, considering the stunning assortment of short fictions responding to jazz over the last hundred years, one can only conclude that the importance of American identity is subordinate to the more expansive—and infinitely more significant—question of the humanity behind the music and its capacity to shape human behavior.

Consider, for example, the most famous jazz short story ever written—James Baldwin's "Sonny's Blues"—in conjunction with Baldwin's own struggles with personal identity. In 1961, the late oral historian Studs Terkel interviewed Baldwin, who had just published a series of reflections titled *Nobody Knows My Name.* The interview began with a recording of Bessie Smith singing "Back Water Blues," and Terkel's first question typifies his dual interest in art and the life of the artist: "As you listen to this record of Bessie Smith, Jim, what is your feeling?" Baldwin replied: "The first time I heard this record was in Europe, and under very different circumstances than I had ever listened to Bessie in New York. What struck me was the fact she was singing, as you say, about a disaster, which had almost killed her, and she accepted it and was going beyond it. The *fantastic* understatement in it. It is the way I want to write. . . ." Terkel then urged Baldwin to elaborate on the matter by quoting passages from *Nobody Knows My Name,* including this one: "It was Bessie Smith, through her tone and her cadence, who helped me to dig back to the way I myself must have spoken when I was a pickaninny, and to remember the things I had seen and felt. I had buried them very deep." Baldwin went on to say that he "was ashamed of the life in the Negro church, ashamed of my father, ashamed of the blues, ashamed of jazz, and, of course, ashamed of watermelon: all of these stereotypes that the country inflicts on Negroes." But Bessie Smith's bravery, Baldwin explained, enabled him "to dig back" to find a more authentic black identity and a more natural speech: "I had to find out what I had been like in the beginning in order, just technically as a writer, to re-create Negro speech."

The story of Baldwin turning to Bessie Smith while isolated in the snowy mountains of Switzerland has been told numerous times, though few connect this personal revelation with the issues raised in "Sonny's Blues." When the story's narrator hears of his brother Sonny's intention to play jazz, he reacts the way Baldwin would have prior to his Bessie Smith epiphany: "It seemed—beneath him, somehow. I had never thought about it before, had never been forced to, but I suppose I had always put jazz musicians in a class with what Daddy called 'good time people.'" Both brothers struggle—from radically different perspectives —with dramatic issues of identity involving family, society, and race, and it is jazz that enables their deepest response to these profound issues. In other words, the abstraction of music unlocked for them the concrete realities of their lives. By story's end, as Sonny digs "all the way back" into his life and origins, his piano solo allows his brother to experience a revelation very much akin to Baldwin's listening to Bessie Smith: "I seemed to hear with what burning he had made it his, with what burning we had yet to make it ours, how we could cease lamenting. Freedom lurked around us and I understood, at last, that he could help us to be free if we would listen, that we would never be free until we did."

The effect of jazz on Eudora Welty's fiction was undeniably different, though equally compelling. Like other fiction writers, she understood that words cannot impact the soul in the same way as sound; given her position as a white southern woman, she also fully recognized that she could never experience the same sense of identification inspired by jazz. But just as Baldwin introduces jazz to define personal identity in "Sonny's Blues," so Welty embraces the music in "Powerhouse"—arguably the second-most famous jazz story—in order to disclose the sensibility of an artist alienated from his transient locations. Of the origins of "Powerhouse," Welty said that she "wrote it in one night after I'd been to a concert and dance in Jackson [Mississippi] where Fats Waller played. I tried to write my idea of the life of the traveling artist and performer—not Fats Waller himself, but any artist—in the alien world and tried to put it in the words and plot suggested by the music I'd been listening to. It was a daring attempt for a writer like me—as daring as it was to write about the murderer of Medgar Evers on *that* night—and I'm not qualified to write about music or performers. But trying it pleased me then, and it still does please me." Unlike the jazz that brought James Baldwin as well as his characters closer to their essential selves, the music Welty heard provided her with characters, a plot, and a theme, all of which together allowed her to imagine lives utterly unlike her own.

In the best jazz fiction, we learn from the epiphanic experiences of the men and women moved by the music—not just the musicians, obviously, but those who encounter jazz in clubs, on car radios, at concerts, and through stereo speakers. Some jazz stories provide insight into the mind and soul of jazz musicians, but more often they focus on the ambiance of jazz and the power it has to shape human behavior. Such stories, like Terkel's fascination and respect for the lives behind the music, engender character as a way of humanizing art and thus expanding the power and meaning of jazz.

The Jazz Fiction Anthology attempts to present the most definitive selection ever published, but it is by no means the first. In 1948, Charles Harvey edited *Jazz Parody: Anthology of Jazz Fiction,* which included a foreword by Charles Delaunay, several fine jazz photographs by Bill Gottlieb, and about a dozen prose pieces of very mixed quality. Decades later, Chris Parker edited a collection of previously unpublished jazz stories and poems, *B Flat, Bebop, Scat* (1986), but that work vanished before it could cross the ocean to the United States. In 1993, Art Lange and Nathaniel Mackey attempted to represent the entire panoply of jazz-related literature in *Moment's Notice: Jazz in Poetry & Prose;* five years later, John Harvey published *Blue Lightning,* which contains eighteen previously unpublished stories with some musical connection; about a third of these contain interest for the reader of jazz- and blues-inspired fiction. More recently, Robert J. Randisi edited an anthology of jazz-related mystery fiction titled *Murder . . . and All That Jazz* (2004); apart from Bill Moody's "Child's Play," the jazz dimension in most of these stories is negligible.

Two important anthologies of jazz fiction, however, must be acknowledged: *Hot and Cool: Jazz Short Stories,* edited by Marcella Breton, and *From Blues to Bop: A Collection of Jazz Fiction,* edited by Richard Albert. Each appeared in 1990, contained about twenty stories, and soon went out of print. Both editors also made significant contributions to jazz research, Breton by compiling a bibliography of jazz stories for *African American* Review (1992) and Albert by publishing *An Annotated Bibliography of Jazz Fiction and Jazz Fiction Criticism* (1996). Their groundbreaking work is gratefully acknowledged in David Rife's *Jazz Fiction: A History and Comprehensive Reader's Guide* (2008), which features nearly 700 works by more than 500 authors.

All three anthologies—those by Albert and Breton, and this current collection—include James Baldwin's "Sonny's Blues" and Eudora

Welty's "Powerhouse." But after this inevitable overlap, more significant differences emerge. While five other works in Breton's collection also appear in these pages, *The Jazz Fiction Anthology* includes additional works by Langston Hughes and Amiri Baraka, a different story by Josef Škvorecký (the one he himself claims to be his best work of jazz fiction), and new translations of Julio Cortázar (whose unfinished story, "Bix Beiderbecke," has never before been anthologized). In fact, a third of the stories in the present collection had not been published and another two or three had not been translated when Albert's and Breton's books appeared.

The Jazz Fiction Anthology differs even more from Albert's, partly because we have opted not to include novel excerpts. Obviously, strong arguments can be made for either editorial choice. For us, the decision was relatively easy: apart from the fact that the excerpt option would provide a surfeit of riches (and thus, too, a surfeit of pages), we felt it would interfere with the integrity of the novel's form. Nevertheless, we'd like to recognize at least a handful of jazz-related novels, especially Dorothy Baker's *Young Man with a Horn* (if only for historical reasons), Stanley Crouch's *Don't the Moon Look Lonesome,* John Clellon Holmes's *The Horn,* Jack Kerouac's *On the Road,* Bart Schneider's *Blue Bossa,* and Rafi Zabor's *The Bear Comes Home.* Those using this text for courses may wish to supplement its stories with a longer work such as those listed above—though we *have* included two novellas: David Huddle's *Tenorman* (subtitled *A Novella* and previously published as an independent book) and Julio Cortázar's "The Pursuer" (almost as long, freshly translated, and proclaimed by its author the ultimate achievement in jazz fiction).

Writers of jazz fiction have not been saddled with the same stereotypical hipster imagery as jazz poets (black berets, smoky coffeehouses, dope, bongos), and blessedly so. Performances of jazz fiction never became a fad, as poetry-read-to-jazz did beginning in the late 1950s. As a result, jazz fiction has pretty much eluded heated literary debates concerning definition: fiction about jazz versus jazz-like prose. As the variety of this anthology suggests, we don't believe one point of view should negate the other. Is the style of Baldwin's "Sonny Blues" or Richard Yates's "A Really Good Jazz Piano" any "jazzier" than that in their other stories? No. On the other hand, could one argue that the marvelous, free-wheeling style of Cortázar's "Bix Beiderbecke" reflects his impression of Beiderbecke's music ("spinning and spinning a web . . . until everything ended with a shower of swearwords and a backward leap")? Absolutely. And one could make similar arguments for stylistic constructions in Rudolph Fisher's "Common Meter," the dialogue in Eudora Welty's "Powerhouse," Xu Xi's "Jazz Wife," and other stories in which the writers seem to be appropriating certain properties of the music to their own prose. When Sam Greenlee said, "Although I don't always write about jazz, my writing *is* jazz," he could have been referring to the sensibility that created such stories as those mentioned above. And while jazz fiction has never achieved the kind of popularity that jazz poetry did as performance art, a number of people have read their fiction to jazz accompaniment: Frank London Brown was among the earliest, and William Henry Lewis is among the most recent. For that matter, Yusef Komunyakaa's "Buddy's Monologue" cries out for a dramatic presentation.

As previously noted, anthologies and studies of jazz fiction frequently emphasize American dominance, with one critic bluntly stating: "Jazz fiction is uniquely American." While no one can deny the evolution of jazz on U.S. soil and the wealth of work written by Americans, the music has influenced writers from around the globe, and we've tried to suggest that breadth with stories by several international writers: Michelle Cliff, Julio Cortázar, Phil Kawana, Josef Škvorecký, Boris Vian, and Xu Xi. As for the overall order, we've opted to anthologize the works alphabetically by author, partly to make it easier on readers thumbing the text to find a particular story, but also to negate any sense of hierarchy among the authors or the works. The only tempting alternative was to present the stories chronologically, in which case they would have appeared like this:

1922 Julian Street, "The Jazz Baby"
1930 Rudolph Fisher, "Common Meter"
1934 Langston Hughes, "The Blues I'm Playing"
1941 Eudora Welty, "Powerhouse"
1948 Boris Vian, "'Round About Close to Midnight"
1949 Langston Hughes, "Old Ghost Revives Atavistic Memories in a Lady of the DAR"

1953[1] Josef Škvorecký, "The End of Bull Mácha"
1956 Ralph Ellison, "A Coupla Scalped Indians"
1957 James Baldwin, "Sonny's Blues"
1958 Richard Yates, "A Really Good Jazz Piano"
1963 Amiri Baraka, "The Screamers"
1963 Frank London Brown, "Singing Dinah's Song"
1963 Terry Southern, "You're Too Hip, Baby"
1967 Julio Cortázar, "The Pursuer"
1973 Sam Greenlee, "Blues for Little Prez"
1977 Toni Cade Bambara, "Medley"
1983 Amiri Baraka, "Norman's Date"
1984[2] Julio Cortázar, "Bix Beiderbecke"
1985 Don Asher, "The Barrier"
1990 Michelle Cliff, "A Woman Who Plays Trumpet Is Deported"
1990 John McCluskey, "Lush Life"
1995 David Huddle, *Tenorman: A Novella*
1996 Phil Kawana, "Dead Jazz Guys"
1997 James Reed, "The Shrimp Peel Gig"
1997 John Edgar Wideman, "The Silence of Thelonious Monk"
1999 Yusef Komunyakaa, "Buddy's Monologue"
2001 Wanda Coleman, "Jazz at Twelve"
2002 Kiki DeLancey, "Swingtime"
2002 William Henry Lewis, "Rossonian Days"
2003 Ellen Jordis Lewis, "Miss Brown to You"
2003 Xu Xi, "Jazz Wife"
2004 Bill Moody, "Child's Play"

Considered in this order, the stories invite engaging conversations on a range of topics, including race, diction, and the evolution of jazz styles.

In his introduction to *Jazz Parody* from 1948, Charles Harvey wrote: "Jazz criticism has been a failure; it is just a fiction. Let us, therefore, refresh ourselves by reading these stories which have no pretensions to be anything other than fiction." Sixty years later, we can adjust his view in important ways. For one, the body of criticism has been substantiated by important critical writers from the second half of the twentieth century. For another, reading jazz fiction should not be a mere escape from the re-

1. Although written in 1953, this piece did not appear in print until 2002.
2. An unfinished work found among the author's papers. The date is an educated guess.

alities of the music or the humanity of those who play and listen; in fact, it should do the opposite. Synesthesia should be thrilling. As Baldwin said in 1976 about his experiences in Switzerland—alone, writing his first novel, and spinning LPs by Bessie Smith and Fats Waller—"When I realized that music rather than American literature was really my language, I was no longer afraid. And then I could write."

The Jazz Fiction Anthology

1

The Barrier

Don Asher

By the late 1940s I knew the blacks had something I was in dire need of, and I was young and intrepid and naive enough to go looking for it.

From 52nd to 140th Street the winds of change were blowing strong. The convulsions of black-rebellion music exploding out of the theaters and cafés of Harlem had startled white musicians, turned us around; the music was angry, blazing, ferocious—yet always under a tight edge of control. "It's a rogue boat heading for the New World," a black Boston drummer told me, "and Bird and Diz are the navigators."

I'd become aware of a widening chasm separating the levels of rhythmic propulsion achieved by white and black musicians. The former's playing was more even-keeled, linear, lacking the sudden dips and spurts, the coiled-spring tension-and-release and unexpected displacement of meter that sent the beat slamming and teetering down the tracks like a highballing express, generating incredible excitement. I was convinced there was something basic and vital that came easily to them and hard to us. I'd noticed, too, that at integrated jam sessions blacks and whites tended to call different tunes. When I'd suggested "Have You Met Miss Jones?" at an after-hours club, a black had scoffed good-naturedly, "That's one of your white-boy tunes." A similar judgment was passed on Gershwin's "A Foggy Day." Blacks leaned toward tunes with relaxed, more fluid structures—"Willow Weep For Me," "Georgia on My Mind"—written as often by white as black composers. "Willow's more leisurely and doesn't sweat," a black bass player said, "you got time to climb inside it, feel its bones, poke your way around. Your average Caucasian tune is boxy, four-squared, forces you into corners."

Other blacks I talked to found the whole subject of racial-genetic orientation distasteful, awakening the old we-got-rhythm stereotypes and images of grinning darkies dancing for pennies on southern street corners. "All you got to remember when you're blowing," a black drummer told me, "is one simple thing: Rice Krispies. Snap, crackle, pop." A tenor sax player I worked with at a Worcester Turnpike club was at once more specific and expansive: "Dancing and singing and lovemaking and making music have no more to do with color than making mudpies or building snowmen. Music's color blind. Absolutely. Ofay players occasionally pull my sleeve, talkin' about their whiteness closing them off from certain secrets of the trade. Listen to me: *there ain't no secrets.* We all came out of the same alley. How you play has to do with who you listened to when you were coming up, who you hung out with and picked up on. Gershwin picked up on the Harlem rent-party players and wrote himself *Porgy and Bess.* There's a new young cat, concert player, Andre Watts, darker 'n me, plays Brahms and Chopin like their breath is inside him."

I was unpersuaded and would make many pilgrimages in the coming years to the ghetto clubs and after-hours joints (where passing remarks dropped on an ofay could be coolly withering and edged with menace: *You from somewhere else and lost your way, Jim, or just slummin'? . . . Hey, lemme ast you somethin'—the buckles on the shoes means you're queer, right?*), tracking the elusive secret, searching out the passion and sensibility of the black man. Hoping for a miracle of transmutation.

My first stop: the New World, north of 110th Street.

Harlem was beginning to put on a hostile face for the Caucasian *turistas.* The years when affluent whites could pass a flavorful evening slumming in the district's cafés and restaurants were nearing an end. Making the rounds of the celebrated places I'd read of and been told about—Savoy Ballroom, Smalls' Paradise, Apollo Theater, Royal Roost, and Minton's Playhouse with its faded awning and dingy wall mirrors, where the musical rebellion had ignited in the early Forties—I was an easy target for frisky young Harlem bloods, easy to pick out for reasons beyond my whiteness.

"Look how slick this boy looks in his green sky. That chapeau come from Switzerland, right?" (I was nineteen and affecting a spruce kelly-green alpine hat.)

"I guess. Originally . . . "

"What you call a mountain hat."

"Alpine, yes."

"Now what might a elegant lid like that be worth would you say in the current market?"

"Stop cappin' on the boy, Clarence, he's just around to hear the sounds."

"Well now, if he wants to dwell in our sunshine he got to come out of the shade . . . "

A half-formed sense of vulnerability told me it was time to cut out.

"The hat came out of a trash bin. I doubt you could get four bits for it. See you guys . . . " I waved off amicably and headed across the street—solemn dark faces keeping vigil above me, gazing down from lighted brick-framed windows—to the storefront café from which music crackled and charged through the open door into the mild evening like a snarl of high-tension wires.

What I heard inside was something fierce, uncompromising and beautiful, an abrasive fiery sound that ran roughshod through all previously decreed rhythmic and harmonic structures. Here were the fabled "cutting sessions" I'd been told about—initiation rites which were in effect pitched battles, mostly black on black, for whites were still chary of joining the fray. Musicians spoke of "taking" one another, were scornful of outsiders and waited eagerly to ambush anyone who arrived with a burgeoning reputation. *Jump, chump, or I'll burn you up, you don't know nothin'.* After a few nights I began to understand that these sessions served as pressure cookers in which one earned recognition and esteem. Reputations could be made, reinforced or savaged in the course of one scorching set, and amateurs and imposters got weeded out in a hurry; in the annealing process the music tightened up, grew leaner, more sublime.

I asked about the policy of sitting in and was told, anyone can, but you better be able to fly real good or they'll shoot you down, burn you up. And watching night after night in the close-packed, churning clubs

I saw how awesome the firepower was onstage, how efficiently those without strong wings were cut down. These were schooled, confident, nerveless musicians who had found within themselves a core of calm enabling them to adjust to the roaring tempos and turbulent patterns, a cool and secret site from which to launch their blazing cascades of notes. They had done battle in a thousand sessions, knew their horns inside out and could not be fazed by key or tempo. Nor did they show any mercy, constantly raising the ante, calling unconventional tunes with swift-changing harmonies in strange keys at tempos so blistering you either soared or went down in flames. I suffered in vicarious misery with a pianist who sat with his hands in his lap throughout a tune kicked off at a vicious tempo, then quietly rose and retreated with a foolish downcast smile and pitiful squaring of shoulders that was like an attempt to pull a tattered threadbare cloak of dignity about himself. That was it, you either measured up or slunk away. It didn't take me but a minute to realize I was nowhere near ready for this league; they were lying in wait for the likes of me. If you don't have the price of admission, stay out of the hall. I began to suspect that the skills required for entry—so deeply ingrained in the Negro experience of despair, anger and struggle—might lie forever beyond my reach.

Chastened, I returned to Boston, where I was studying at the Berklee College of Music while supporting myself playing occasional gigs with Rudy Yellin's Society Orchestra, and continued my search in the black after-hours clubs of eastern Massachusetts; here the music would be less convulsive and searing, the animus more manageable.

For a young white traversing the urban ghettos during the Fifties a horn case was often a talisman of safe passage.

"What you got in there, man?"

"Alto sax. On my way to a session."

"Oh? Where at?"

Possessing no such identifying badge and looking the way I did (a turnpike barmaid had once remarked behind my back, "The breath my seven-year-old uses to blow out her birthday candles would bowl him over"), I improvised: a sheaf of music manuscript paper under my arm, or an empty battered clarinet case I'd found discarded in a union-hall trash can. Often I came directly from a gig in my tux; this could prove an advantage—smoothing the rites of passage—or (more likely) a liability, depending on the character of the district I was passing through. I usually took the precaution of removing my bow tie and wearing a beat-up raincoat over the soup and fish.

Colleagues at Berklee steered me to Coffee John's, an after-hours place on lower Massachusetts Avenue. The doors opened around ten, but the real action didn't get under way until after midnight when musicians began dropping by from work to drink and jam. A dingy narrow corridor of a room lined with scarred wooden booths facing a small cramped stage.

Guileless, fortified by an instinctive faith in my own inviolability and the holiness of my cause, I sauntered one night into a maelstrom of turbulent sound and close-together black faces, white teeth, hands holding cups and glasses of coffee laced with rye and gin; a low-pitched jumble of voices beneath the music's pulse, the square patch of dance floor packed with weaving bodies. For the better part of a week I hung out (when I told my white friends where I'd been until four in the morning they blanched), standing alone at the beer-and-wine bar, which shut down by law at one o'clock and was separated from the main room by a shoulder-high partition, listening to the music and watching the dancers, ignored but for an occasional curious or indifferent stare, a half-frown etched in a questioning glance. On a Sunday night I asked if I could sit in. The music was strong and gutty but within my ken. I knew most of the tunes; the tempos seemed comfortable. I sensed that one or two of the pianists could play rings around me, but the rings were concentric and not all that wide. I felt I wouldn't be embarrassed as I would have been at the incandescent Harlem sessions.

The trumpet player nominally in charge of the session nodded (I learned later that many of the participating musicians were out of work, that a handful of key players were paid a few dollars a night for their midnight-to-four AM stints) and the pianist, Lonnie, slid off the stool and leaned against a booth, hands in pockets, his stony gaze sliding past my shoulder. I fiddled with the stool's height, inadvertently lowering it, then spinning it up a few revolutions, hearing mocking, skeptical voices behind me: "Already I don't like the looks of this" and "What's this peckerwood gonna do, tune it?" and "Come back, Lonnie, all's forgiven."

"'Blue Skies' okay?" the trumpet player said.

"Sure."

"One flat, you got four bars. 'Bout here," he said, snapping his thumb and middle finger in a lazy circle.

The rhythm falling in behind me was jagged and looser than it had sounded from the floor, looser than I was accustomed to—bass and drums glancing off the beat, churning and slipping around it, rather than hammering it down four-square like spikes in a railbed. Several times I felt the meter sliding out from under my fingers. When this occurred the bass player steadied into a fundamental four-to-the-bar stroll, laying groundwork beneath me; at the same time I experienced the childhood sensation of being effortlessly lifted up on his shoulders (as an uncle had once hoisted me on a summer morning so I could see the parade unfolding down Worcester's main street). The dancers, I noticed uneasily, were drifting off the floor, some shaking their heads. "I don't get it," I heard someone say. I struggled through two more tunes, hands cramping and sweat dropping off my chin onto the keys until the board was slick as an ice rink. The dancers never returned.

The bass player, whose name was Lucius, a slim greying man with high cheekbones and a burgundy cast to his skin, took me aside after the set. "You want a honest critique?" he said and continued even as I nodded earnestly, mopping my face. "The dancers was off balance, that's why they deserted, they couldn't pat their feet right or make their proper moves. You was playing rhythmic enough, don't misapprehend me, but it was too straight-ahead and ricky-tick, if you catch my drift. We're used to a wider beat, space and margin to move around in. It's like a woman sashaying down a wide alleyway swinging her hips and buns, used to plenty of leeway so's she won't bruise herself on the walls, you picture it? Now that alleyway suddenly *narrows* on her and this fine bitch is getting bruised, *hurting,* so naturally she's going to cut out. What you got to do is listen to me and the iron and skins more intensely . . ."

I knew what he meant, sort of. Whether I could do anything about it was another matter. The twin legacies I had to overcome were my white upbringing and a two-year stretch playing businessman's-bounce show tunes, horas, and Viennese waltzes with a clam-and-chowder society band.

I don't know why they kept letting me sit in; it must have taken guts, or simpleness, on my part to ask. Perhaps they were flattered by my interest in their music and derived satisfaction from the role reversal at a time when there were no black teachers in the public schools; or they may have found amusement in the spectacle of Master Charles getting turned on, picking their brains, trying to dwell in their sunshine—tolerant of me because I was just a skinny, earnest, funny-ass kid and not too obvious a nigger lover.

I became aware of a grudging cordiality as I poked my head in each night just after twelve bells. "Here comes the gopher in the watermelon patch" (Nestor, the bartender) and "Where's the sergeant-at-arms? Who let this white trash in?" As I made my way up to the stand a gruff, good-natured raillery followed me. "Better be wearin' your asbestos vest, boy . . . This paddy's gonna get his feathers clipped again . . . What's he gonna play for us tonight, 'Ol' Man Ribber' or 'Short'nin' Bread'?"

There was a beautiful tawny-skinned singer who occasionally sat in. She worked in a show bar on Columbus Avenue and would arrive after one-thirty in a luxurious leather coat, a silver tiara riding a towering knot of blue-black hair, eyes liquid and glittering with the night. Her name was Jonella; a chain smoker with a rich deep grainy voice (which was *why* she smoked, she insisted, to retain that *timbre*), she was always a little stoned, or seemed so to me, saying funny unconnected things, her luminous heavy-lidded eyes looking at you and sliding past you at the same time.

"Don't bust your conk, baby," she'd say to me, apropos of nothing, "everything's gonna be everything."

One night after I'd backed her for a set she introduced the musicians, inventing names she didn't know or remember ("On drums, in lavender trunks and green bathrobe, weighing in at one sixty-four and three-eighths, Rufus Funk, Jr."), and when it came my turn—"Let's give this slick boy on piano whose name I'll think of in a minute a hand for comin' across town and filling in so capably. He's all by his lonesome, innocent and taking care of business, so all you scroungy-ass chicks out there keep your hands off him, hear?" The crowd snickered and guffawed, enjoying the banter.

Off the stand, blowing plumes of smoke over my shoulder, she said, "You starting to get it, baby. You only got one main obstacle to surmount as I see it, which is that when I grew up tapping my feet and clapping my hands, singing 'Shadrach' and 'Swing Low Sweet Chariot' in my uncle's church you were singing 'Rock of Ages' and 'God Bless America.' But don't pay it too much mind," she advised, her liquid eyes gliding past me, "'cause one of these days you're gonna score a touchdown and fifty thousand people'll be watching the game."

She had a cousin or half brother, Wesley—both were vague about the relationship—with the same distracted opaline gaze. Wesley washed cars during the day and came to Coffee John's every night, sometimes sitting in on conga drum or beating a woodblock with a drumstick during Latin tunes. He spent a lot of time in the men's room, and when he wasn't there or on the stand he flitted genially up and down the line of booths, stopping to chat and sample a spiked coffee. In regard to me, he gave generously of his counsel.

"What this boy should do is spend some nights at the Arcady Lounge over on Huntington, observe how those ace bitches synchronizes their hips and butts to the drummer's accents—that's where he'll learn to swing."

"Now what would you know about swing, Wesley?" someone chimed in disdainfully. "You couldn't swing a Mickey Mouse watch on a rubber band."

"I'm sayin' the ec-*dysiasts* is where it's at—those righteous ebon girls wriggling their saucy dusters!" Wesley exclaimed, eyes widening and gleaming in opalescent splendor. "Couple nights at the Arcady that beat'll begin to sink in like a pile driver. Can't help but happen!"

The next time I saw him he'd forgotten the ecdysiasts; New York City was where I should go to pursue my education. "If the boy's serious in his endeavor"—the discussions seemed always to be directed past or lobbed over me, as if my presence were an obstacle to be circumvented—"he's got to earn his credits. The only place to pick up that final diploma is the University of the Streets of New York."

"The Apple is cool," someone else observed somberly, "but rotten at the co'."

"I've already been," I said. "It's rough."

"It's where you got to go to pick up the pearls," Wesley continued, unheeding.

"You got to slog through some heavy mud to get to them pearls," the other said, dubious.

"There's nothin' *new,* man," a third interjected. "There's nothin' new! You don't have to set foot off your back porch. Just hang out, pick up an' get nervous like the rest of us."

"In that town," Wesley said with a touch of awe in his voice, "without the proper credits you can't even cross 125th Street, never mind Fifth Avenue."

I no longer felt the need to carry manuscript paper or an empty clarinet case with me, and had ceased standing alone at the bar; in the crowded cozy booths my jug became communal, alternating with the pints and half pints of my colleagues. On the bruised upright (that was treated lovingly, tuned once a month) I was starting to get it, at least some nights I thought I was (*It* is as hard to define as pornography, but I know it when I hear it), assimilating the displaced, driving rhythms and crackling improvisational patterns, sharpening my ear and expanding my repertoire. My fondest dream was that the Coffee John's regulars would one night rise en masse as I came off the stand, shouting, "The blue-eyed devil plays black!" From Lucius and Everett, a massive older pianist with a wild tangle of snow-flecked hair and a rollicking bravura stride style reminiscent of Fats Waller's, I was discovering what "time" meant—the *quality* of the beat, just as timbre is the quality of the tone—and learning to function at very fast and very slow tempos. At slow tempos the beat has to *swell,* Lucius told me, and passed on the concept of his friend, the fiery West Coast pianist, Hampton Hawes: "It's like taking yourself a mouthful of good wine, swishing it around, savoring it before you let it go down; the swallow is that beat finally dropping." On up-tempos Everett showed me how to stay loose and relaxed by visualizing myself riding a train "rocketing along at a good clip, ninety miles an hour or more, but it doesn't trouble you 'cause you're sitting there cool and collected, your body swaying and rocking naturally with the train's pulse, which is the drums and bass. You don't need to be stomping your feet and getting all cramped up and over-excited." He suggested I listen to some old piano-roll rags and gave me a list of recordings. "That's where everything comes out of. Get that feeling down and it'll open an alley up the middle of your style wide enough for a moose to swing in. Inside the same eight bars there's sass, there's ecstasy, there's heartbreak. And listen to the Iowa boy, Beiderbecke, the cornet on 'I'm Comin' Virginia.' Same thing." (I listened. Bix's horn, rising from a morass of tubas, banjos and trap drums, rang like a carillon in the mountains, lonely, sorrowful and piercing. And those old rags that made my scalp tingle and triggered a grainy current down my backbone—what was there in them, even the jaunty ones, that left such a residue of sadness and ache?)

But the supreme lesson I was beginning to absorb—and it's an abstract and elusive one—is that *time* should be as "natural as a heartbeat pumping pure fresh blood into a tune."

There were occasional nights when the clientele turned over or out-of-town musicians dropped by, and the attitude toward me could change as swiftly as the sky on a March day. As soon as I walked in I could feel, like a radio's hum before the sound begins, a tension rise in the room, the friendly or incurious looks of the previous weeks suddenly vigilant and somber. When I sat in a standard tune would be called in a strange key at a murderous tempo—much faster than the regulars would ever kick it off. An unmistakable chill, unsheathed daggers on the stand. I couldn't help but remember what had befallen musicians with suspect credentials at the ferocious Harlem sessions, where the take-charge players had showed no mercy, ambushing newcomers and forcing them to retire in disgrace. I floundered badly through a headlong "Perdido"—the conclusion greeted out front by embarrassed silence, broken by an angry voice I recognized as Jonella's. "Raise off the boy, Biggie, you don't need to show all those feathers." The intent was plain: Master Charles lured into the deep end of the pool before being blown out of the water.

If you didn't bring your cleats, stay off the field.

Jonella slipped an arm around my shoulder as I came off the stand, sweat-soaked and confused. "Don't pay those uppity dudes any mind, baby. They'll be pickin' trash out of the gutter while you're riding the elephant down the main street, just wait 'n' see. Everything's gonna be everything."

It was a sobering reminder that despite the previous air of geniality and counsel, the barrier was still there and always would be—made up of divergent experiences, temperament, attitudes—a skin-thin membrane but tough and impervious as sheet metal.

Gun-shy, licking my wounds, I stayed off the stand for a few nights. Then, with no sign of the marauders' return, I wandered gingerly back, testing the water. On a Friday, a week after my humbling, I had a good night, winning accolades for my solos, and only Jonella's absence prevented my sense of triumph and renewed self-esteem from being complete. When she came in a little later, I said, "I scored a touchdown, baby, you didn't even see the game."

She regarded me in her glancing sidelong way. "You're not only beginning to play colored, you're talkin' colored."

"Well, you right."

Her look turned reproachful. "Now don't you go cappin' on me with that nigger talk. You be respectful."

"Jonella, listen, I respect you more than anyone I know."

Something cunning infiltrated her expression. The tapering face with its yellowish-mauve tinge, glistening red mouth and luminous eyes was like an exotic African flower, and my heart slammed in my throat. She grinned at me then—an audacious, violent smile—gave her shoulders a brief wild shake and pivoting regally in her satin dress and spike heels, sashayed away down the line of booths.

She didn't seem to belong to anyone. She usually arrived alone and left alone—unless it was with her cousin (or half brother) Wesley—and was no longer working at the Columbus Avenue show bar; I had dropped by to see her early one night and found the place shuttered. Lacking the courage of my infatuation I never asked to see her home, wherever it was. There was no way I was going to leave the club with her; not in 1952 on the outskirts of Dorchester at four in the morning weighing 130 pounds in a winter overcoat.

But she was right, the rhythms and idioms of the black culture were permeating my speech patterns as well as the texture of my playing. "Ain't that a bitch," I might say, registering surprise, wonder or delight. I no longer departed, I "cut out." "A nickel" was five dollars, and "a dime" ten. I wore a "sky" or "lid," not a hat. Someone trying to get my attention was "pulling my coat," and a musician playing strong and confidently with an element of grandstanding was "showing feathers" or "fluffing out his feathers"; if I were greatly impressed by his performance I "wigged." With reference to women, "ace broad" or "fine bitch" were expressions of the highest approbation, but Charles had better be careful in what context and with what inflection he flaunted the argot.

One night I had my first taste of pot. ("Tea," "Mary Jane," and "shit" were the prevailing expressions then.) I don't know how I'd avoided it for so long—except that its use was nowhere near as universal as it would become a decade later. I knew Wesley and others were lighting up in the john—I had been present once or twice when a joint was being passed around—and this night, by whim, or an accident of timing, I was included. "Try some of this Panama Red," Wesley said casually as the joint came back to him from a youth in a tattersall vest. I'd wondered off and on about the sensation and saw no reason not to indulge; it would be a sociable gesture as well as a new experience, akin to accepting a passed-around jug in the booths and taking a pull without wiping the neck. "It's truly evil shit, señor," Tattersall Vest said in a choked voice. I had watched enough musicians smoke to know what to do. The joint had a rich powerful aroma, a piney fragrance. I took several deep pulls, holding the smoke in my lungs as long as I could. When I left the toilet I felt a languorous buzz in one ear as if a somnolent and not particularly bothersome fly had lodged there; and moments later an airy drifting lightness as if my brains had come unmoored and were floating gravity-free around my skull like flakes in a paperweight globe. Well, I thought leisurely, this shit is a gas. I don't know how long I stood by the stage listening to the music, all soft peaks and hollows, watching through a trembling blue smoke haze the congenial clusters of Coffee John's regulars, brothers all (ace boon coons), smoking and jiving and sipping their spiked coffee. Lucius was beckoning me back to the stand. Grinning loosely, confidently (someone told me later), I spun the vacated stool up and up—for some reason it was imperative that I assume a commanding position over the board; it took a long time to reach its summit. The trumpet player, Hardy, called "Black and Blue" and began snapping his fingers in a soft staccato crack, his hand tracing blurred ovals before my eyes. I played a four-bar intro, notes slipping effortlessly off my fingers (long-stemmed flowers trailing from a crystal vase). Innumerable languid choruses drifted by, brass and reeds soloing. Someone poked me in the back: my turn. I broke out and away (a limber colt), chords stacking neatly beneath my left hand like rubber coits, the right hand fleet, darting, venturous. After what seemed a half dozen choruses I reined in (not wanting to show too many feathers), looking around for one of the horns to reenter. "Keep goin'," Hardy said. "Enough, six choruses, don't wanna hog," I told him. Hardy was smiling down at me in a puzzled, half-frowning way. "You ain't even reached the bridge of your first yet."

I remember little else of the evening, only of sauntering down the long corridor of booths—the gritty linoleum floor oddly soft and yielding as if I were walking on blankets or cork—a close-up gallery of faces gleaming at me like dark ivory through the sifting lavender smoke. I seemed to be taking a sinuous path, wandering unwillingly from booth to booth, my shoulders thumping against the wooden supports; it was like promenading the deck of a rolling ship without the accompanying sensation of vertigo. As I lurched for the door someone opened it for me, then someone else was hugging me, someone who smelled like a whole backyard of gardenias; a warm, faintly disappointing embrace, though, one of fraternity rather than romance. "Baby, you feelin' awright?"

"I'm cool," I told Jonella. "Everything's everythin'."

"Had hisself some o' Wesley's Panama Red," a disembodied voice said as the throbbing pumping music propelled me out the door like a giant hand pushing at my back.

I recall getting in my car and a wall of honking horns behind me, then rolling weightlessly from window to window in the deep swaying back seat of a taxi. I woke at 2:30 the next afternoon in my room on Fairfield Street feeling unanchored, my extremities—fingers, toes, ears—numb and tingling as if I'd been out on a freezing day underdressed and was just beginning to thaw. I drank something cold and metallic-tasting from a juice jar in the refrigerator, dressed and caught a bus to Massachusetts Avenue to look for my Studebaker. It took me an hour and a half, starting at Coffee John's and roaming in widening concentric circles, under sober observation from upper-story windows, the framed faces as fixed, doleful and expressionless as those in old sepia photographs. The car was parked five blocks west of the club. The right rear wheel was up on the curb and the headlights were burning; a ticket under the wiper flapped in a gusting wind. The key was still in the ignition. I got in, shut off the lights and tried to start the motor, noticing two youths watching from the opposite curb. It whirred thinly, coughed, tubercular . . . faded. I waited a half minute and tried again: a feeble complaint, another quiet cough, and she died like a dog. The two observers were crossing the street toward me, one tall and slim with a thin fuzz of mustache, wearing a poplin jacket; the other was much smaller and lighter-skinned, a plumpish baby face tucked in the hood of a bulky gray sweat shirt. I rolled down the window and asked where the nearest gas station was.

"Got yourself some trouble, huh?" the tall youth said. "Why don't we take us a peek under the hood."

Maybe like Wesley he worked with cars; black kids, I thought, seemed to know a lot about cars. I got out and lifted the hood, propping it on its stick.

The two silently inclined their heads, inspecting the innards. "Hard to say," the tall boy said after a moment.

"Where's the nearest station?" I asked again.

"Oh, there's nothing for a ways around here," the tall boy said. He stuck his hands in his poplin jacket, regarding me in an unhurried thoughtful manner.

"We could use money for ciggies," the other said in a piping voice that matched his face, the light brown eyes limpid, vacuous, trusting, hands folded into the gray pouch of his sweat shirt.

"I . . . didn't bring my wallet," I said truthfully, shivering a little though it wasn't that cold, wishing I had brought my empty clarinet case for show.

"Any kind of change will do," the tall boy said reasonably.

"I only brought bus fare, some quarters . . . " I fumbled in my pants pocket.

"That'll get it," the tall boy said, holding out a soft palm as pink as a frosted wafer.

I looked around me, at the afternoon shadows darkening the brick buildings, the sun hanging wan and thin, a pale disc pasted on the rim of the November sky; a gust of wind blew dry papers along the gutter. I played the coins carefully into the pink palm. "I'm a musician," I blurted and knew immediately it was a mistake.

"Oh?" The tall boy pocketed the change. "Where at do you play?"

"Coffee John's. Actually I just sit in nights whenever—"

"Where's that at?" The tall youth's eyes had rolled leisurely upward and away, the mouth compressed and rubbery.

"Over on Mass. Avenue, maybe five blocks—"

"What d'you play?" the small boy asked, respectful.

"Piano," I said, which was my second mistake.

The small boy brought something out of the pouch of his sweat shirt, pressed a thumb to it—there was a faint whirring sound—and drew it carefully along the back of my right hand; I thought I heard a soft tearing, like tissue paper parting. Both youths were racing down the street then, yards apart; the small plump boy surprisingly swift, outdistancing the other. The surrounding buildings were now completely in shadow and a piercing chill had fallen over the street. With a sigh I dropped my eyes. There was a thin red line across the knuckles, the skin parted delicately like paper. I reclined against the fender of the car, watching the blood suddenly bloom, incredibly bright, bubbling and winking like a ruby chain in artificial light.

The wind had risen; it had grown colder. I was glancing listlessly toward both intersections and around at the silent, darkening buildings, wondering which way to turn or go, or whether to go anywhere at all, when a car stopped in the middle of the street. "What's up, man, what's the problem?"

It was Wesley, poking his head out the window of a faded green Chevy, the whites of his eyes flaring as they fixed on the blood-soaked handkerchief. Everett was in the passenger seat beside him. They pulled over to the curb and got out.

Everett took my hand in his and gently peeled back the clotted cloth; I felt nothing.

Wesley's breath expelled as if he'd been punched in the chest. "Oh, man, who did you like that?"

"Couple kids. I thought they were going to help . . . " I motioned my head vaguely in the direction they had fled.

"You jus' never knows any more, all these weirdies cruisin' the avenues. Why jus' last week I was over Huntington comin' out of—"

"Stop the damn jabbering and let's *go,*" Everett said, "we got to get this nigger to a doctor."

Riding between them, my legs cushioned by Everett's massive thighs—a fat man's inadvertent caress—a tangle of emotions swept in on me. Bewilderment and wonder that the locus of the music that was my breath and heartbeat should also be the source of animosity and venom. It would take courage to venture to this part of town again; the barrier had been raised a notch, made more forbidding, fortified with steel . . . But even as the pain took hold of my hand with the car's jounce and rattle, my spirits began to lift, a small glow of assurance warmed me as Everett's words echoed far back in my mind . . . *Let's go, we got to get this nigger to a doctor.* Within the urgency, the humorous play and idiom, was a suggestion of alliance, kinship, acceptance: I had made it a little way through the barrier.

I turned to Wesley. "That was some powerful Panama Red last night."

Wesley nodded solemnly. "I can dig it."

*

A thin white scar remains, riding the ridge of the knuckles like a badge of initiation, an emblem of battle.

I never scored the big touchdown, never made it all the way through to the other side—none of us whiteys do—but ten years later, when I was house pianist at the *hungry i* in San Francisco, a middle-aged black man approached me in the bar following an entr'acte medley of Duke Ellington tunes. He said he had enjoyed the music and that I must have grown up or spent a lot of time around Harlem to play like that. I told him I had been born and bred in eastern Massachusetts. "Okay," he said, "but somewhere along the line you must've eaten some okra and sweet potato pie."

2

Sonny's Blues

James Baldwin

I read about it in the paper, in the subway, on my way to work. I read it, and I couldn't believe it, and I read it again. Then perhaps I just stared at it, at the newsprint spelling out his name, spelling out the story. I stared at it in the swinging lights of the subway car, and in the faces and bodies of the people, and in my own face, trapped in the darkness which roared outside.

It was not to be believed and I kept telling myself that, as I walked from the subway station to the high school. And at the same time I couldn't doubt it. I was scared, scared for Sonny. He became real to me again. A great block of ice got settled in my belly and kept melting there slowly all day long, while I taught my classes algebra. It was a special kind of ice. It kept melting, sending trickles of ice water all up and down my veins, but it never got less. Sometimes it hardened and seemed to expand until I felt my guts were going to come spilling out or that I was going to choke or scream. This would always be at a moment when I was remembering some specific thing Sonny had once said or done.

When he was about as old as the boys in my classes his face had been bright and open, there was a lot of copper in it; and he'd had wonderfully direct brown eyes, and great gentleness and privacy. I wondered what he looked like now. He had been picked up, the evening before, in a raid on an apartment downtown, for peddling and using heroin.

I couldn't believe it: but what I mean by that is that I couldn't find any room for it anywhere inside me. I had kept it outside me for a long time. I hadn't wanted to know. I had had suspicions, but I didn't name them, I kept putting them away. I told myself that Sonny was wild, but he wasn't crazy. And he'd always been a good boy, he hadn't ever turned hard or evil or disrespectful, the way kids can, so quick, so quick, especially in Harlem. I didn't want to believe that I'd ever see my brother going down, coming to nothing, all that light in his face gone out, in the condition I'd already seen so many others. Yet it had happened and here I was, talking about algebra to a lot of boys who might, every one of them for all I knew, be popping off needles every time they went to the head. Maybe it did more for them than algebra could.

I was sure that the first time Sonny had ever had horse, he couldn't have been much older than these boys were now. These boys, now, were living as we'd been living then, they were growing up with a rush and their heads bumped abruptly against the low ceiling of their actual possibilities. They were filled with rage. All they really knew were two darknesses, the darkness of their lives, which was now closing in on them, and the darkness of the movies, which had blinded them to that other darkness, and in which they now, vindictively, dreamed, at once more together than they were at any other time, and more alone.

When the last bell rang, the last class ended, I let out my breath. It seemed I'd been holding it for all that time. My clothes were wet—I may have looked as though I'd been sitting in a steam bath, all dressed up, all afternoon. I sat alone in the classroom a long time. I listened to the boys outside, downstairs, shouting and cursing and laughing. Their laughter struck me for perhaps the first time. It was not the joyous laughter which—God knows why—one associates with children. It was mocking and insular, its intent was to denigrate. It was disenchanted, and in this, also, lay the authority of their curses. Perhaps I was listening to them because I was thinking about my brother and in them I heard my brother. And myself.

One boy was whistling a tune, at once very complicated and very simple, it seemed to be pouring out of him as though he were a bird, and it sounded very cool and moving through all that harsh, bright air, only just holding its own through all those other sounds.

I stood up and walked over to the window and looked down into the courtyard. It was the beginning of the spring and the sap was rising in the boys. A teacher passed through them every now and again, quickly, as though he or she couldn't wait to get out of that courtyard, to get those boys out of their sight and off their minds. I started collecting my stuff. I thought I'd better get home and talk to Isabel.

The courtyard was almost deserted by the time I got downstairs. I saw this boy standing in the shadow of a doorway, looking just like Sonny. I almost called his name. Then I saw that it wasn't Sonny, but somebody we used to know, a boy from around our block. He'd been Sonny's friend. He'd never been mine, having been too young for me, and, anyway, I'd never liked him. And now, even though he was a grown-up man, he still hung around that block, still spent hours on the street corners, was always high and raggy. I used to run into him from time to time and he'd often work around to asking me for a quarter or fifty cents. He always had some real good excuse, too, and I always gave it to him, I don't know why.

But now, abruptly, I hated him. I couldn't stand the way he looked at me, partly like a dog, partly like a cunning child. I wanted to ask him what the hell he was doing in the school courtyard.

He sort of shuffled over to me, and he said, "I see you got the papers. So you already know about it."

"You mean about Sonny? Yes, I already know about it. How come they didn't get you?"

He grinned. It made him repulsive and it also brought to mind what he'd looked like as a kid. "I wasn't there. I stay away from them people."

"Good for you." I offered him a cigarette and I watched him through the smoke. "You come all the way down here just to tell me about Sonny?"

"That's right." He was sort of shaking his head and his eyes looked strange, as though they were about to cross. The bright sun deadened his damp dark brown skin and it made his eyes look yellow and showed up the dirt in his kinked hair. He smelled funky. I moved a little away from him and I said, "Well, thanks. But I already know about it and I got to get home."

"I'll walk you a little ways," he said. We started walking. There were a couple of kids still loitering in the courtyard and one of them said goodnight to me and looked strangely at the boy beside me.

"What're you going to do?" he asked me. "I mean, about Sonny?"

"Look. I haven't seen Sonny for over a year, I'm not sure I'm going to do anything. Anyway, what the hell *can* I do?"

"That's right," he said quickly, "ain't nothing you can do. Can't much help old Sonny no more, I guess."

It was what I was thinking and so it seemed to me he had no right to say it.

"I'm surprised at Sonny, though," he went on—he had a funny way of talking, he looked straight ahead as though he were talking to himself—"I thought Sonny was a smart boy, I thought he was too smart to get hung."

"I guess he thought so too," I said sharply, "and that's how he got hung. And how about you? You're pretty goddamn smart, I bet."

Then he looked directly at me, just for a minute. "I ain't smart," he said. "If I was smart, I'd have reached for a pistol a long time ago."

"Look. Don't tell *me* your sad story, if it was up to me, I'd give you one." Then I felt guilty—guilty, probably, for never having supposed that the poor bastard *had* a story of his own, much less a sad one, and I asked, quickly, "What's going to happen to him now?"

He didn't answer this. He was off by himself some place.

"Funny thing," he said, and from his tone we might have been discussing the quickest way to get to Brooklyn, "when I saw the papers this morning, the first thing I asked myself was if I had anything to do with it. I felt sort of responsible."

I began to listen more carefully. The subway station was on the corner, just before us, and I stopped. He stopped, too. We were in front of a bar and he ducked slightly, peering in, but whoever he was looking for didn't seem to be there. The juke box was blasting away with something black and bouncy and I half watched the barmaid as she danced her way from the juke box to her place behind the bar. And I watched her face as she laughingly responded to something someone said to her, still keeping time to the music. When she smiled one saw the little girl, one sensed the doomed, still-struggling woman beneath the battered face of the semi-whore.

"I never *give* Sonny nothing," the boy said finally, "but a long time ago I come to school high and Sonny asked me how it felt." He paused, I couldn't bear to watch him, I watched the barmaid, and I listened to the music which seemed to be causing the pavement to shake. "I told him it felt great." The music stopped, the barmaid paused and watched the juke box until the music began again. "It did."

All this was carrying me some place I didn't want to go. I certainly didn't want to know how it felt. It filled everything, the people, the houses, the music, the dark, quicksilver barmaid, with menace; and this menace was their reality.

"What's going to happen to him now?" I asked again.

"They'll send him away some place and they'll try to cure him." He shook his head. "Maybe he'll even think he's kicked the habit. Then they'll let him loose"—he gestured, throwing his cigarette into the gutter. "That's all."

"What do you mean, that's *all*?"

But I knew what he meant.

"I *mean,* that's *all.*" He turned his head and looked at me, pulling down the corners of his mouth. "Don't you know what I mean?" he asked, softly.

"How the hell *would* I know what you mean?" I almost whispered it, I don't know why.

"That's right," he said to the air, "how would *he* know what I mean?" He turned toward me again, patient and calm, and yet I somehow felt him shaking, shaking as though he were going to fall apart. I felt that ice in my guts again, the dread I'd felt all afternoon; and again I watched the barmaid, moving about the bar, washing glasses, and singing. "Listen. They'll let him out and then it'll just start all over again. That's what I mean."

"You mean—they'll let him out. And then he'll just start working his way back in again. You mean he'll never kick the habit. Is that what you mean?"

"That's right," he said, cheerfully. "*You* see what I mean."

"Tell me," I said at last, "why does he want to die? He must want to die, he's killing himself, why does he want to die?"

He looked at me in surprise. He licked his lips. "He don't want to die. He wants to live. Don't nobody want to die, ever."

Then I wanted to ask him—too many things. He could not have answered, or if he had, I could not have borne the answers. I started walking. "Well, I guess it's none of my business."

"It's going to be rough on old Sonny," he said. We reached the subway station. "This is your station?" he asked. I nodded. I took one step down. "Damn!" he said, suddenly. I looked up at him. He grinned again. "Damn it if I didn't leave all my money home. You ain't got a dollar on you, have you? Just for a couple of days, is all."

All at once something inside gave and threatened to come pouring out of me. I didn't hate him any more. I felt that in another moment I'd start crying like a child.

"Sure," I said. "Don't sweat." I looked in my wallet and didn't have a dollar, I only had a five. "Here," I said. "That hold you?"

He didn't look at it—he didn't want to look at it. A terrible, closed look came over his face, as though he were keeping the number on the bill a secret from him and me. "Thanks," he said, and now he was dying to see me go. "Don't worry about Sonny. Maybe I'll write him or something."

"Sure," I said. "You do that. So long."

"Be seeing you," he said. I went on down the steps.

And I didn't write Sonny or send him anything for a long time. When I finally did, it was just after my little girl died, he wrote me back a letter which made me feel like a bastard.

Here's what he said:

> Dear brother,
>
> You don't know how much I needed to hear from you. I wanted to write you many a time but I dug how much I must have hurt you and so I didn't write. But now I feel like a man who's been trying to climb up out of some deep, real deep and funky hole and just saw the sun up there, outside. I got to get outside.
>
> I can't tell you much about how I got here. I mean I don't know how to tell you. I guess I was afraid of something or I was trying to escape from something and you know I have never been very strong in the head (smile). I'm glad Mama and Daddy are dead and can't see what's happened to their son and I swear if I'd known what I was doing I would never have hurt you so, you and a lot of other fine people who were nice to me and who believed in me.
>
> I don't want you to think it had anything to do with me being a musician. It's more than that. Or maybe less than that. I can't get anything straight in my head down here and I try not to think about what's

> going to happen to me when I get outside again. Sometime I think I'm going to flip and *never* get outside and sometime I think I'll come straight back. I tell you one thing, though, I'd rather blow my brains out than go through this again. But that's what they all say so they tell me. If I tell you when I'm coming to New York and if you could meet me, I sure would appreciate it. Give my love to Isabel and the kids and I was sure sorry to hear about little Gracie. I wish I could be like Mama and say the Lord's will be done, but I don't know it seems to me that trouble is the one thing that never does get stopped and I don't know what good it does to blame it on the Lord. But maybe it does some good if you believe it.
>
> Your brother,
> Sonny

Then I kept in constant touch with him and I sent him whatever I could and I went to meet him when he came back to New York. When I saw him many things I thought I had forgotten came flooding back to me. This was because I had begun, finally, to wonder about Sonny, about the life that Sonny lived inside. This life, whatever it was, had made him older and thinner and it had deepened the distant stillness in which he had always moved. He looked very unlike my baby brother. Yet, when he smiled, when we shook hands, the baby brother I'd never known looked out from the depths of his private life, like an animal waiting to be coaxed into the light.

"How you been keeping?" he asked me.

"All right. And you?"

"Just fine." He was smiling all over his face. "It's good to see you again."

"It's good to see you."

The seven years' difference in our ages lay between us like a chasm: I wondered if these years would ever operate between us as a bridge. I was remembering, and it made it hard to catch my breath, that I had been there when he was born; and I had heard the first words he had ever spoken. When he started to walk, he walked from our mother straight to me. I caught him just before he fell when he took the first steps he ever took in this world.

"How's Isabel?"

"Just fine. She's dying to see you."

"And the boys?"

"They're fine, too. They're anxious to see their uncle."

"Oh, come on. You know they don't remember me."

"Are you kidding? Of course they remember you."

He grinned again. We got into a taxi. We had a lot to say to each other, far too much to know how to begin.

As the taxi began to move, I asked, "You still want to go to India?"

He laughed. "You still remember that. Hell, no. This place is Indian enough for me."

"It used to belong to them," I said.

And he laughed again. "They damn sure knew what they were doing when they got rid of it."

Years ago, when he was around fourteen, he'd been all hipped on the idea of going to India. He read books about people sitting on rocks, naked, in all kinds of weather, but mostly bad, naturally, and walking barefoot through hot coals and arriving at wisdom. I used to say that it sounded to me as though they were getting away from wisdom as fast as they could. I think he sort of looked down on me for that.

"Do you mind," he asked, "if we have the driver drive alongside the park? On the west side—I haven't seen the city in so long."

"Of course not," I said. I was afraid that I might sound as though I were humoring him, but I hoped he wouldn't take it that way.

So we drove along, between the green of the park and the stony, lifeless elegance of hotels and apartment buildings, toward the vivid, killing streets of our childhood. These streets hadn't changed, though housing projects jutted up out of them now like rocks in the middle of a boiling sea. Most of the houses in which we had grown up had vanished, as had the stores from which we had stolen, the basements in which we had first tried sex, the rooftops from which we had hurled tin cans and bricks. But houses exactly like the houses of our past yet dominated the landscape, boys exactly like the boys we once had been found themselves smothering in these houses, came down into the streets for light and air and found themselves encircled by disaster. Some escaped the trap, most didn't. Those who got out always left something of themselves behind, as some animals amputate a leg and leave it in the trap. It might be said, perhaps, that I had escaped, after all, I was a school teacher; or that Sonny had, he hadn't lived in Harlem for years. Yet, as the cab moved uptown through streets which seemed, with a rush, to darken with dark people, and as I covertly studied Sonny's face, it came to me that what we both were seeking through our separate cab windows was that part of ourselves which had been left behind. It's always at the hour of trouble and confrontation that the missing member aches.

We hit 110th Street and started rolling up Lenox Avenue. And I'd known this avenue all my life, but it seemed to me again, as it had seemed on the day I'd first heard about Sonny's trouble, filled with a hidden menace which was its very breath of life.

"We almost there," said Sonny.

"Almost." We were both too nervous to say anything more.

We live in a housing project. It hasn't been up long. A few days after it was up it seemed uninhabitably new, now, of course, it's already rundown. It looks like a parody of the good, clean, faceless life—God knows the people who live in it do their best to make it a parody. The beat-looking grass lying around isn't enough to make their lives green, the hedges will never hold out the streets, and they know it. The big windows fool no one, they aren't big enough to make space out of no space. They don't bother with the windows, they watch the TV screen instead. The playground is most popular with the children who don't play at jacks, or skip rope, or roller skate, or swing, and they can be found in it after dark. We moved in partly because it's not too far from where I teach, and partly for the kids; but it's really just like the houses in which Sonny and I grew up. The same things happen, they'll have the same things to remember. The moment Sonny and I started into the house I had the feeling that I was simply bringing him back into the danger he had almost died trying to escape.

Sonny has never been talkative. So I don't know why I was sure he'd be dying to talk to me when supper was over the first night. Everything went fine, the oldest boy remembered him, and the youngest boy liked him, and Sonny had remembered to bring something for each of them; and Isabel, who is really much nicer than I am, more open and giving, had gone to a lot of trouble about dinner and was genuinely glad to see him. And she's always been able to tease Sonny in a way that I haven't. It was nice to see her face so vivid again and to hear her laugh and watch her make Sonny laugh. She wasn't, or, anyway, she didn't seem to be, at all uneasy or embarrassed. She chatted as though there were no subject which had to be avoided and she got Sonny past his first, faint stiffness.

And thank God she was there, for I was filled with that icy dread again. Everything I did seemed awkward to me, and everything I said sounded freighted with hidden meaning. I was trying to remember everything I'd heard about dope addiction and I couldn't help watching Sonny for signs. I wasn't doing it out of malice. I was trying to find out something about my brother. I was dying to hear him tell me he was safe.

"Safe!" my father grunted, whenever Mama suggested trying to move to a neighborhood which might be safer for children. "Safe, hell! Ain't no place safe for kids, nor nobody."

He always went on like this, but he wasn't, ever, really as bad as he sounded, not even on weekends, when he got drunk. As a matter of fact, he was always on the lookout for "something a little better," but he died before he found it. He died suddenly, during a drunken weekend in the middle of the war when Sonny was fifteen. He and Sonny hadn't ever got on too well. And this was partly because Sonny was the apple of his father's eye. It was because he loved Sonny so much and was frightened for him, that he was always fighting with him. It doesn't do any good to fight with Sonny. Sonny just moves back, inside himself, where he can't be reached. But the principal reason that they never hit it off is that they were so much alike. Daddy was big and rough and loud-talking, just the opposite of Sonny, but they both had—that same privacy.

Mama tried to tell me something about this, just after Daddy died. I was home on leave from the army.

This was the last time I ever saw my mother alive. Just the same, this picture gets all mixed up in my mind with pictures I had of her when she was younger. The way I always see her is the way she used to be on a Sunday afternoon, say, when the old folks were talking after the big Sunday dinner. I always see her wearing pale blue. She'd be sitting on the sofa. And my father would be sitting in the easy chair, not far from her. And the living room would be full of church folks and relatives. There they sit, in chairs all around the living room, and the night is creeping up outside, but nobody knows it yet. You can see the darkness growing against the windowpanes and you hear the street noises every now and again, or maybe the jangling beat of a tambourine from one of the churches close by, but it's real quiet in the room. For a moment nobody's talking, but every face looks darkening, like the sky outside. And my mother rocks a little from the waist, and my father's eyes are closed. Everyone is looking at something a child can't see. For a minute they've forgotten the children. Maybe a kid is lying on the rug, half asleep. Maybe somebody's got a kid in his lap and is absent-mindedly stroking the kid's head. Maybe there's a kid, quiet and big-eyed, curled up in a big chair in the corner. The silence, the darkness coming, and the darkness in the faces frightens the child obscurely. He hopes that the hand which strokes his forehead will never stop—will never die. He hopes that there will never come a time when the old folks won't be sitting around the living room, talking about where they've come from, and what they've seen, and what's happened to them and their kinfolk.

But something deep and watchful in the child knows that this is bound to end, is already ending. In a moment someone will get up and turn on the light. Then the old folks will remember the children and they won't talk any more that day. And when light fills the room, the child is filled with darkness. He knows that every time this happens he's moved just a little closer to that darkness outside. The darkness outside is what the old folks have been talking about. It's what they've come from. It's what they endure. The child knows that they won't talk any more because if he knows too much about what's happened to them, he'll know too much too soon, about what's going to happen to *him*.

The last time I talked to my mother, I remember I was restless. I wanted to get out and see Isabel. We weren't married then and we had a lot to straighten out between us.

There Mama sat, in black, by the window. She was humming an old church song. *Lord, you brought me from a long ways off.* Sonny was out somewhere. Mama kept watching the streets.

"I don't know," she said, "if I'll ever see you again, after you go off from here. But I hope you'll remember the things I tried to teach you."

"Don't talk like that," I said, and smiled. "You'll be here a long time yet."

She smiled, too, but she said nothing. She was quiet for a long time. And I said, "Mama, don't you worry about nothing. I'll be writing all the time, and you be getting the checks. . . . "

"I want to talk to you about your brother," she said, suddenly. "If anything happens to me he ain't going to have nobody to look out for him."

"Mama," I said, "ain't nothing going to happen to you or Sonny. Sonny's all right. He's a good boy and he's got good sense."

"It ain't a question of his being a good boy," Mama said, "nor of his having good sense. It ain't only the bad ones, nor yet the dumb ones that gets sucked under." She stopped, looking at me. "Your Daddy once had a brother," she said, and she smiled in a way that made me feel she was in pain. "You didn't never know that, did you?"

"No," I said, "I never knew that," and I watched her face.

"Oh, yes," she said, "your Daddy had a brother." She looked out of the window again. "I know you never saw your Daddy cry. But *I* did—many a time, through all these years."

I asked her, "What happened to his brother? How come nobody's ever talked about him?"

This was the first time I ever saw my mother look old.

"His brother got killed," she said, "when he was just a little younger than you are now. I knew him. He was a fine boy. He was maybe a little full of the devil, but he didn't mean nobody no harm."

Then she stopped and the room was silent, exactly as it had sometimes been on those Sunday afternoons. Mama kept looking out into the streets.

"He used to have a job in the mill," she said, "and, like all young folks, he just liked to perform on Saturday nights. Saturday nights, him and your father would drift around to different places, go to dances and things like that, or just sit around with people they knew, and your father's brother would sing, he had a fine voice, and play along with himself on his guitar. Well, this particular Saturday night, him and your father was coming home from some place, and they were both a little drunk and there was a moon that night, it was bright like day. Your father's brother was feeling kind of good, and he was whistling to himself, and he had his guitar slung over his shoulder. They was coming down a hill and beneath them was a road that turned off from the highway. Well, your father's brother, being always kind of frisky, decided to run down this hill, and he did, with that guitar banging and clanging behind him, and he ran across the road, and he was making water behind a tree. And your father was sort of amused at him and he was still coming down the hill, kind of slow. Then he heard a car motor and that same minute his brother stepped from behind the tree, into the road, in the moonlight. And he started to cross the road. And your father started to run down the hill, he says he don't know why. This car was full of white men. They was all drunk, and when they seen your father's brother they let out a great whoop and holler and they aimed the car straight at him. They was having fun, they just wanted to scare him, the way they do sometimes, you know. But they was drunk. And I guess the boy, being drunk, too, and scared, kind of lost his head. By the time he jumped it was too late. Your father says he heard his brother scream when the car rolled over him, and he heard the wood of that guitar when it give, and he heard them strings go flying, and he heard them white men shouting, and the car kept on a-going and it ain't stopped till this day. And, time your father got down the hill, his brother weren't nothing but blood and pulp."

Tears were gleaming on my mother's face. There wasn't anything I could say.

"He never mentioned it," she said, "because I never let him mention it before you children. Your Daddy was like a crazy man that night and for many a night thereafter. He says he never in his life seen anything as dark as that road after the lights of that car had gone away. Weren't nothing, weren't nobody on that road, just your Daddy and his brother and that busted guitar. Oh, yes. Your Daddy never did really get right again. Till the day he died he weren't sure but that every white man he saw was the man that killed his brother."

She stopped and took out her handkerchief and dried her eyes and looked at me.

"I ain't telling you all this," she said, "to make you scared or bitter or to make you hate nobody. I'm telling you this because you got a brother. And the world ain't changed."

I guess I didn't want to believe this. I guess she saw this in my face. She turned away from me, toward the window again, searching those streets.

"But I praise my Redeemer," she said at last, "that He called your Daddy home before me. I ain't saying it to throw no flowers at myself, but, I declare, it keeps me from feeling too cast down to know I helped your father get safely through this world. Your father always acted like he was the roughest, strongest man on earth. And everybody took him to be like that. But if he hadn't had *me* there—to see his tears!"

She was crying again. Still, I couldn't move. I said, "Lord, Lord, Mama, I didn't know it was like that."

"Oh, honey," she said, "there's a lot that you don't know. But you are going to find it out." She stood up from the window and came over to me. "You got to hold on to your brother," she said, "and don't let him fall, no matter what it looks like is happening to him and no matter how evil you gets with him. You going to be evil with him many a time. But don't you forget what I told you, you hear?"

"I won't forget," I said. "Don't you worry, I won't forget. I won't let nothing happen to Sonny."

My mother smiled as though she were amused at something she saw in my face. Then, "You may not be able to stop nothing from happening. But you got to let him know you's *there.*"

Two days later I was married, and then I was gone. And I had a lot of things on my mind and I pretty well forgot my promise to Mama until I got shipped home on a special furlough for her funeral.

And, after the funeral, with just Sonny and me alone in the empty kitchen, I tried to find out something about him.

"What do you want to do?" I asked him.

"I'm going to be a musician," he said.

For he had graduated, in the time I had been away, from dancing to the juke box to finding out who was playing what, and what they were doing with it, and he had bought himself a set of drums.

"You mean, you want to be a drummer?" I somehow had the feeling that being a drummer might be all right for other people but not for my brother Sonny.

"I don't think," he said, looking at me very gravely, "that I'll ever be a good drummer. But I think I can play a piano."

I frowned. I'd never played the role of the older brother quite so seriously before, had scarcely ever, in fact, *asked* Sonny a damn thing. I sensed myself in the presence of something I didn't really know how to handle, didn't understand. So I made my frown a little deeper as I asked: "What kind of musician do you want to be?"

He grinned. "How many kinds do you think there are?"

"Be *serious,*" I said.

He laughed, throwing his head back, and then looked at me. "I am serious."

"Well, then, for Christ's sake, stop kidding around and answer a serious question. I mean, do you want to be a concert pianist, you want to play classical music and all that, or—or what?" Long before I finished he was laughing again. "For Christ's *sake,* Sonny!"

He sobered, but with difficulty. "I'm sorry. But you sound so—*scared!*" and he was off again.

"Well, you may think it's funny now, baby, but it's not going to be so funny when you have to make your living at it, let me tell you *that.*" I was furious because I knew he was laughing at me and I didn't know why.

"No," he said, very sober now, and afraid, perhaps, that he'd hurt me, "I don't want to be a classical pianist. That isn't what interests me. I mean"—he paused, looking hard at me, as though his eyes would help me to understand, and then gestured helplessly, as though perhaps his hand would help—"I mean, I'll have a lot of studying to do, and I'll have to study everything, but, I mean, I want to play *with*—jazz musicians." He stopped. "I want to play jazz," he said.

Well, the word had never before sounded as heavy, as real, as it sounded that afternoon in Sonny's mouth. I just looked at him and I was probably frowning a real frown by this time. I simply couldn't see why on earth he'd want to spend his time hanging around nightclubs, clowning around on bandstands, while people pushed each other around a dance floor. It seemed—beneath him, somehow. I had never thought about it before, had never been forced to, but I suppose I had always put jazz musicians in a class with what Daddy called "good-time people."

"Are you *serious*?"

"Hell, yes, I'm serious."

He looked more helpless than ever, and annoyed, and deeply hurt.

I suggested, helpfully: "You mean—like Louis Armstrong?"

His face closed as though I'd struck him. "No. I'm not talking about none of that old-time, down home crap."

"Well, look, Sonny, I'm sorry, don't get mad. I just don't altogether get it, that's all. Name somebody—you know, a jazz musician you admire."

"Bird."

"Who?"

"Bird! Charlie Parker! Don't they teach you nothing in the goddamn army?"

I lit a cigarette. I was surprised and then a little amused to discover that I was trembling. "I've been out of touch," I said. "You'll have to be patient with me. Now. Who's this Parker character?"

"He's just one of the greatest jazz musicians alive," said Sonny, sullenly, his hands in his pockets, his back to me. "Maybe *the* greatest," he added, bitterly, "that's probably why *you* never heard of him."

"All right," I said, "I'm ignorant. I'm sorry. I'll go out and buy all the cat's records right away, all right?"

"It don't," said Sonny, with dignity, "make any difference to me. I don't care what you listen to. Don't do me no favors."

I was beginning to realize that I'd never seen him so upset before. With another part of my mind I was thinking that this would probably turn out to be one of those things kids go through and that I shouldn't make it seem important by pushing it too hard. Still, I didn't think it would do any harm to ask: "Doesn't all this take a lot of time? Can you make a living at it?"

He turned back to me and half leaned, half sat, on the kitchen table. "Everything takes time," he said, "and—well, yes, sure, I can make a living at it. But what I don't seem to be able to make you understand is that it's the only thing I want to do."

"Well, Sonny," I said gently, "you know people can't always do exactly what they *want* to do—"

"*No,* I don't know that," said Sonny, surprising me. "I think people *ought* to do what they want to do, what else are they alive for?"

"You getting to be a big boy," I said desperately, "it's time you started thinking about your future."

"I'm thinking about my future," said Sonny, grimly. "I think about it all the time."

I gave up. I decided, if he didn't change his mind, that we could always talk about it later. "In the meantime," I said, "you got to finish school." We had already decided that he'd have to move in with Isabel and her folks. I knew this wasn't the ideal arrangement because Isabel's folks are inclined to be dicty and they hadn't especially wanted Isabel to marry me. But I didn't know what else to do. "And we have to get you fixed up at Isabel's."

There was a long silence. He moved from the kitchen table to the window. "That's a terrible idea. You know it yourself."

"Do you have a *better* idea?"

He just walked up and down the kitchen for a minute. He was as tall as I was. He had started to shave. I suddenly had the feeling that I didn't know him at all.

He stopped at the kitchen table and picked up my cigarettes. Looking at me with a kind of mocking, amused defiance, he put one between his lips. "You mind?"

"You smoking already?"

He lit the cigarette and nodded, watching me through the smoke. "I just wanted to see if I'd have the courage to smoke in front of you." He grinned and blew a great cloud of smoke to the ceiling. "It was easy." He looked at my face. "Come on, now. I bet you was smoking at my age, tell the truth."

I didn't say anything but the truth was on my face, and he laughed. But now there was something very strained in his laugh. "Sure. And I bet that ain't all you was doing."

He was frightening me a little. "Cut the crap," I said. "We already decided that you was going to go and live at Isabel's. Now what's got into you all of a sudden?"

"*You* decided it," he pointed out. "*I* didn't decide nothing." He stopped in front of me, leaning against the stove, arms loosely folded. "Look, brother. I don't want to stay in Harlem no more, I really don't." He was very earnest. He looked at me, then over toward the kitchen window. There was something in his eyes I'd never seen before, some thoughtfulness, some worry all his own. He rubbed the muscle of one arm. "It's time I was getting out of here."

"Where do you want to *go*, Sonny?"

"I want to join the army. Or the navy, I don't care. If I say I'm old enough, they'll believe me."

Then I got mad. It was because I was so scared. "You must be crazy. You goddamn fool, what the hell do you want to go and join the *army* for?"

"I just told you. To get out of Harlem."

"Sonny, you haven't even finished *school.* And if you really want to be a musician, how do you expect to study if you're in the *army*?"

He looked at me, trapped, and in anguish. "There's ways. I might be able to work out some kind of deal. Anyway, I'll have the G.I. Bill when I come out."

"*If* you come out." We stared at each other. "Sonny, please. Be reasonable. I know the setup is far from perfect. But we got to do the best we can."

"I ain't learning nothing in school," he said. "Even when I go." He turned away from me and opened the window and threw his cigarette out into the narrow alley. I watched his back. "At least, I ain't learning nothing you'd want me to learn." He slammed the window so hard I thought the glass would fly out, and turned back to me. "And I'm sick of the stink of these garbage cans!"

"Sonny," I said, "I know how you feel. But if you don't finish school now, you're going to be sorry later that you didn't." I grabbed him by the shoulders. "And you only got another year. It ain't so bad. And I'll come back and I swear I'll help you do *whatever* you want to do. Just try to put up with it till I come back. Will you please do that? For me?"

He didn't answer and he wouldn't look at me.

"Sonny. You hear me?"

He pulled away. "I hear you. But you never hear anything *I* say."

I didn't know what to say to that. He looked out of the window and then back at me. "OK," he said, and sighed. "I'll try."

Then I said, trying to cheer him up a little, "They got a piano at Isabel's. You can practice on it."

And as a matter of fact, it did cheer him up for a minute. "That's right," he said to himself. "I forgot that." His face relaxed a little. But the worry, the thoughtfulness, played on it still, the way shadows play on a face which is staring into the fire.

But I thought I'd never hear the end of that piano. At first, Isabel would write me, saying how nice it was that Sonny was so serious about his music and how, as soon as he came in from school, or wherever he had been when he was supposed to be at school, he went straight to that piano and stayed there until suppertime. And, after supper, he went back to that piano and stayed there until everybody went to bed. He was at the piano all day Saturday and all day Sunday. Then he bought a record player and started playing records. He'd play one record over and over again, all day long sometimes, and he'd improvise along with it on the piano. Or he'd play one section of the record, one chord, one change, one progression, then he'd do it on the piano. Then back to the record. Then back to the piano.

Well, I really don't know how they stood it. Isabel finally confessed that it wasn't like living with a person at all, it was like living with sound. And the sound didn't make any sense to her, didn't make any sense to any of them—naturally. They began, in a way, to be afflicted by this presence that was living in their home. It was as though Sonny were some sort of god, or monster. He moved in an atmosphere which wasn't like theirs at all. They fed him and he ate, he washed himself, he walked in and out of their door; he certainly wasn't nasty or unpleasant or rude. Sonny isn't any of those things; but it was as though he were all wrapped up in some cloud, some fire, some vision all his own; and there wasn't any way to reach him.

At the same time, he wasn't really a man yet, he was still a child, and they had to watch out for him in all kinds of ways. They certainly couldn't throw him out. Neither did they dare to make a great scene about that piano because even they dimly sensed, as I sensed, from so many thousands of miles away, that Sonny was at that piano playing for his life.

But he hadn't been going to school. One day a letter came from the school board and Isabel's mother got it—there had, apparently, been other letters but Sonny had torn them up. This day, when Sonny came in, Isabel's mother showed him the letter and asked where he'd been spending his time. And she finally got it out of him that he'd been down in Greenwich Village, with musicians and other characters, in a white girl's apartment. And this scared her and she started to scream at him and what came up, once she began—though she denies it to this day—was what sacrifices they were making to give Sonny a decent home and how little he appreciated it.

Sonny didn't play the piano that day. By evening, Isabel's mother had calmed down but then there was the old man to deal with, and Isabel herself. Isabel says she did her best to be calm but she broke down and started crying. She says she just watched Sonny's face. She could tell, by watching him, what was happening with him. And what was happening was that they penetrated his cloud, they had reached him. Even if their fingers had been a thousand times more gentle than human fingers ever are, he could hardly help feeling that they had stripped him naked and were spitting on that nakedness. For he also had to see that his presence, that music, which was life or death to him, had been torture for them and that they had endured it, not at all for his sake, but only for mine. And Sonny couldn't take that. He can take it a little better today than he could then but he's still not very good at it and, frankly, I don't know anybody who is.

The silence of the next few days must have been louder than the sound of all the music ever played since time began. One morning, before she went to work, Isabel was in his room for something and she suddenly realized that all of his records were gone. And she knew for certain that he was gone. And he was. He went as far as the navy would carry him. He finally sent me a postcard from some place in Greece and that was the first I knew that Sonny was still alive. I didn't see him any more until we were both back in New York and the war had long been over.

He was a man by then, of course, but I wasn't willing to see it. He came by the house from time to time, but we fought almost every time we met. I didn't like the way he carried himself, loose and dreamlike all the time, and I didn't like his friends, and his music seemed to be merely an excuse for the life he led. It sounded just that weird and disordered.

Then we had a fight, a pretty awful fight, and I didn't see him for months. By and by I looked him up, where he was living, in a furnished room in the Village, and I tried to make it up. But there were lots of other people in the room and Sonny just lay on his bed, and he wouldn't come downstairs with me, and he treated these other people as though they were his family and I weren't. So I got mad and then he got mad, and then I told him that he might just as well be dead as live the way he was living. Then he stood up and he told me not to worry about him any more in life, that he was dead as far as I was concerned. Then he pushed me to the door and the other people looked on as though nothing were happening, and he slammed the door behind me. I stood in the hallway, staring at the door. I heard somebody laugh in the room and then the tears came to my eyes. I started down the steps, whistling to keep from crying, I kept whistling to myself. *You going to need me, baby, one of these cold, rainy days.*

I read about Sonny's trouble in the spring. Little Grace died in the fall. She was a beautiful little girl. But she only lived a little over two years. She died of polio and she suffered. She had a slight fever for a couple of days, but it didn't seem like anything and we just kept her in bed. And we would certainly have called the doctor, but the fever dropped, she seemed to be all right. So we thought it had just been a cold. Then, one day, she was up, playing, Isabel was in the kitchen fixing lunch for the two boys when they'd come in from school, and she heard Grace fall down in the living room. When you have a lot of children you don't always start running when one of them falls, unless they start screaming or something. And, this time, Grace was quiet. Yet, Isabel says that when she heard that *thump* and then that silence, something happened in her to make her afraid. And she ran to the living room and there was little Grace on the floor, all twisted up, and the reason she hadn't screamed was that she couldn't get her breath. And when she did scream, it was the worst sound, Isabel says, that she'd ever heard in all her life, and she still hears it sometimes in her dreams. Isabel will sometimes wake me up with a low, moaning, strangled sound and I have to be quick to awaken her and hold her to me and where Isabel is weeping against me seems a mortal wound.

I think I may have written Sonny the very day that little Grace was buried. I was sitting in the living room in the dark, by myself, and I suddenly thought of Sonny. My trouble made his real.

One Saturday afternoon, when Sonny had been living with us, or, anyway, been in our house, for nearly two weeks I found myself wandering aimlessly about the living room drinking from a can of beer, and trying to work up the courage to search Sonny's room. He was out, he was usually out whenever I was home, and Isabel had taken the children to see their grandparents. Suddenly I was standing still in front of the living room window, watching Seventh Avenue. The idea of searching Sonny's room made me still. I scarcely dared to admit to myself what I'd be searching for. I didn't know what I'd do if I found it. Or if I didn't.

On the sidewalk across from me, near the entrance to a barbecue joint, some people were holding an old-fashioned revival meeting. The barbecue cook, wearing a dirty white apron, his conked hair reddish and metallic in the pale sun and a cigarette between his lips, stood in the doorway, watching them. Kids and older people paused in their errands and stood here, along with some older men and a couple of very tough-looking women who watched everything that happened on the avenue as though they owned it, or were maybe owned by it. Well, they were watching this, too. The revival was being carried on by three sisters in black, and a brother. All they had were their voices and their Bibles and a tambourine. The brother was testifying and while he testified two of the sisters stood together, seeming to say, amen, and the third sister walked around with the tambourine outstretched and a couple of people dropped coins into it. Then the brother's testimony ended and the sister who had been taking up the collection dumped the coins into her palm and transferred them to the pocket of her long black robe. Then she raised both hands, striking the tambourine against the air, and then against one hand, and she started to sing. And the two other sisters and the brother joined in.

It was strange, suddenly, to watch, though I had been seeing these street meetings all my life. So, of course, had everybody else down there. Yet, they paused and watched and listened and I stood still at the window. "*Tis the old ship of Zion,*" they sang, and the sister with the tambourine kept a steady, jangling beat, "*it has rescued many a thousand!*" Not a soul under the sound of their voices was hearing this song for the first time, not one of them had been rescued. Nor had they seen much in the way of rescue work being done around them. Neither did they especially believe in the holiness of the three sisters and the brother, they knew too much about them, knew where they lived, and how. The woman with the tambourine, whose voice dominated the air, whose face was bright with joy, was divided by very little from the woman who stood watching her, a cigarette between her heavy, chapped lips, her hair a cuckoo's nest, her face scarred and swollen from many beatings, and her black eyes glittering like coal. Perhaps they both knew this, which was why, when, as rarely, they addressed each other, they addressed each other as Sister. As the singing filled the air the watching, listening faces underwent a change, the eyes focusing on something within; the music seemed to soothe a poison out of them; and time seemed, nearly, to fall away from the sullen, belligerent, battered faces, as though they were fleeing back to their first condition, while dreaming of their last. The barbecue cook half shook his head and smiled, and dropped his cigarette and disappeared into his joint. A man fumbled in his pockets for change and stood holding it in his hand impatiently, as though he had just remembered a pressing appointment further up the avenue. He looked furious. Then I saw Sonny, standing on the edge of the crowd. He was carrying a wide, flat notebook with a green cover, and it made him look, from where I was standing, almost like a schoolboy. The coppery sun brought out the copper in his skin, he was very faintly smiling, standing very still. Then the singing stopped, the tambourine turned into a collection plate again. The furious man dropped in his coins and vanished, so did a couple of the women, and Sonny dropped some change in the plate, looking directly at the woman with a little smile. He started across the avenue, toward the house. He has a slow, loping walk, something like the way Harlem hipsters walk, only he's imposed on this his own half-beat. I had never really noticed it before.

I stayed at the window, both relieved and apprehensive. As Sonny disappeared from my sight, they began singing again. And they were still singing when his key turned in the lock.

"Hey," he said.

"Hey, yourself. You want some beer?"

"No. Well, maybe." But he came up to the window and stood beside me, looking out. "What a warm voice," he said.

They were singing *If I could only hear my mother pray again!*

"Yes," I said, "and she can sure beat that tambourine."

"But what a terrible song," he said, and laughed. He dropped his notebook on the sofa and disappeared into the kitchen. "Where's Isabel and the kids?"

"I think they went to see their grandparents. You hungry?"

"No." He came back into the living room with his can of beer. "You want to come some place with me tonight?"

I sensed, I don't know how, that I couldn't possibly say no. "Sure. Where?"

He sat down on the sofa and picked up his notebook and started leafing through it. “I’m going to sit in with some fellows in a joint in the Village.”

“You mean, you’re going to play, tonight?”

“That’s right.” He took a swallow of his beer and moved back to the window. He gave me a sidelong look. “If you can stand it.”

“I’ll try,” I said.

He smiled to himself and we both watched as the meeting across the way broke up. The three sisters and the brother, heads bowed, were singing *God be with you till we meet again.* The faces around them were very quiet. Then the song ended. The small crowd dispersed. We watched the three women and the lone man walk slowly up the avenue.

“When she was singing before,” said Sonny, abruptly, “her voice reminded me for a minute of what heroin feels like sometimes—when it’s in your veins. It makes you feel sort of warm and cool at the same time. And distant. And—and sure.” He sipped his beer, very deliberately not looking at me. I watched his face. “It makes you feel—in control. Sometimes you’ve got to have that feeling.”

“Do you?” I sat down slowly in the easy chair.

“Sometimes.” He went to the sofa and picked up his notebook again. “Some people do.”

“In order,” I asked, “to play?” And my voice was very ugly, full of contempt and anger.

“Well”—he looked at me with great, troubled eyes, as though, in fact, he hoped his eyes would tell me things he could never otherwise say—“they *think* so. And *if* they think so—!”

“And what do *you* think?” I asked.

He sat on the sofa and put his can of beer on the floor. “I don’t know,” he said, and I couldn’t be sure if he were answering my question or pursuing his thoughts. His face didn’t tell me. “It’s not so much to *play.* It’s to *stand* it, to be able to make it at all. On any level.” He frowned and smiled: “In order to keep from shaking to pieces.”

“But these friends of yours,” I said, “they seem to shake themselves to pieces pretty goddamn fast.”

“Maybe.” He played with the notebook. And something told me that I should curb my tongue, that Sonny was doing his best to talk, that

I should listen. "But of course you only know the ones that've gone to pieces. Some don't—or at least they haven't *yet* and that's just about all *any* of us can say." He paused. "And then there are some who just live, really, in hell, and they know it and they see what's happening and they go right on. I don't know." He sighed, dropped the notebook, folded his arms. "Some guys, you can tell from the way they play, they on something *all* the time. And you can see that, well, it makes something real for them. But of course," he picked up his beer from the floor and sipped it and put the can down again, "they want to, too, you've got to see that. Even some of them that say they don't—*some,* not all."

"And what about you?" I asked—I couldn't help it. "What about you? Do *you* want to?"

He stood up and walked to the window and remained silent for a long time. Then he sighed. "Me," he said. Then: "While I was downstairs before, on my way here, listening to that woman sing, it struck me all of a sudden how much suffering she must have had to go through—to sing like that. It's *repulsive* to think you have to suffer that much."

I said: "But there's no way not to suffer—is there, Sonny?"

"I believe not," he said and smiled, "but that's never stopped anyone from trying." He looked at me. "Has it?" I realized, with this mocking look, that there stood between us, forever, beyond the power of time or forgiveness, the fact that I had held silence—so long!—when he had needed human speech to help him. He turned back to the window. "No, there's no way not to suffer. But you try all kinds of ways to keep from drowning in it, to keep on top of it, and to make it seem—well, like *you.* Like you did something, all right, and now you're suffering for it. You know?" I said nothing. "Well you know," he said, impatiently, "why *do* people suffer? Maybe it's better to do something to give it a reason, *any* reason."

"But we just agreed," I said, "that there's no way not to suffer. Isn't it better, then, just to—take it?"

"But nobody just takes it," Sonny cried, "that's what I'm telling you! *Everybody* tries not to. You're just hung up on the way some people try—it's not *your* way!"

The hair on my face began to itch, my face felt wet. "That's not true," I said, "that's not true. I don't give a damn what other people do, I don't even care how they suffer. I just care how *you* suffer." And he looked at me. "Please believe me," I said, "I don't want to see you—die—trying not to suffer."

"I won't," he said, flatly, "die trying not to suffer. At least, not any faster than anybody else."

"But there's no need," I said, trying to laugh, "is there? in killing yourself."

I wanted to say more, but I couldn't. I wanted to talk about will power and how life could be—well, beautiful. I wanted to say that it was all within; but was it? or, rather, wasn't that exactly the trouble? And I wanted to promise that I would never fail him again. But it would all have sounded—empty words and lies.

So I made the promise to myself and prayed that I would keep it.

"It's terrible sometimes, inside," he said, "that's what's the trouble. You walk these streets, black and funky and cold, and there's not really a living ass to talk to, and there's nothing shaking, and there's no way of getting it out—that storm inside. You can't talk it and you can't make love with it, and when you finally try to get with it and play it, you realize *nobody's* listening. So *you've* got to listen. You got to find a way to listen."

And then he walked away from the window and sat on the sofa again, as though all the wind had suddenly been knocked out of him. "Sometimes you'll do *anything* to play, even cut your mother's throat." He laughed and looked at me. "Or your brother's." Then he sobered. "Or your own." Then: "Don't worry. I'm all right now and I think I'll be all right. But I can't forget—where I've been. I don't mean just the physical place I've been, I mean where I've *been*. And *what* I've been."

"What have you been, Sonny?" I asked.

He smiled—but sat sideways on the sofa, his elbow resting on the back, his fingers playing with his mouth and chin, not looking at me. "I've been something I didn't recognize, didn't know I could be. Didn't know anybody could be." He stopped, looking inward, looking helplessly young, looking old. "I'm not talking about it now because I feel *guilty* or anything like that—maybe it would be better if I did, I don't know. Anyway, I can't really talk about it. Not to you, not to anybody," and now he turned and faced me. "Sometimes, you know, and it was actually when I was most out of the world, I felt that I was in it, that I was with it, really, and I could play or I didn't really have to *play,* it just came out of me, it was there. And I don't know how I played, thinking about it now, but I know I did awful things, those times, sometimes, to people. Or it wasn't that I *did* anything to them—it was that they weren't real." He picked up the beer can; it was empty; he rolled it between his palms: "And other times—well, I needed a fix, I needed to find a place to lean, I needed to clear a space to *listen*—and I couldn't find it, and I—went crazy, I did terrible things to me, I was terrible *for* me." He began pressing the beer can between his hands, I watched the metal begin to give. It glittered, as he played with it, like a knife, and I was afraid he would cut himself, but I said nothing. "Oh well. I can never tell you. I was all by myself at the bottom of something, stinking and sweating and crying and shaking, and I smelled it, you know? *my* stink, and I thought I'd die if I couldn't get away from it and yet, all the same, I knew that everything I was doing was just locking me in with it. And I didn't know," he paused, still flattening the beer can, "I didn't know, I still *don't* know, something kept telling me that maybe it was good to smell your own stink, but I didn't think that *that* was what I'd been trying to do—and—who can stand it?" and he abruptly dropped the ruined beer can, looking at me with a small, still smile, and then rose, walking to the window as though it were the lodestone rock. I watched his face, he watched the avenue. "I couldn't tell you when Mama died—but the reason I wanted to leave Harlem so bad was to get away from drugs. And then, when I ran away, that's what I was running from—really. When I came back, nothing had changed, *I* hadn't changed, I was just—older." And he stopped, drumming with his fingers on the windowpane. The sun had vanished, soon darkness would fall. I watched his face. "It can come again," he said, almost as though speaking to himself. Then he turned to me. "It can come again," he repeated. "I just want you to know that."

"All right," I said, at last. "So it can come again. All right."

He smiled, but the smile was sorrowful. "I had to try to tell you," he said.

"Yes," I said. "I understand that."

"You're my brother," he said, looking straight at me, and not smiling at all.

"Yes," I repeated, "yes. I understand that."

He turned back to the window, looking out. "All that hatred down there," he said, "all that hatred and misery and love. It's a wonder it doesn't blow the avenue apart."

We went to the only nightclub on a short, dark street, downtown. We squeezed through the narrow, chattering, jam-packed bar to the entrance of the big room, where the bandstand was. And we stood there for a moment, for the lights were very dim in this room and we couldn't see. Then, "Hello, boy," said a voice and an enormous black man, much older than Sonny or myself, erupted out of all that atmospheric lighting and put an arm around Sonny's shoulder. "I been sitting right here," he said, "waiting for you."

He had a big voice, too, and heads in the darkness turned toward us.

Sonny grinned and pulled a little away, and said, "Creole, this is my brother. I told you about him."

Creole shook my hand. "I'm glad to meet you, son," he said, and it was clear that he was glad to meet me *there,* for Sonny's sake. And he smiled, "You got a real musician in *your* family," and he took his arm from Sonny's shoulder and slapped him, lightly, affectionately, with the back of his hand.

"Well. Now I've heard it all," said a voice behind us. This was another musician, and a friend of Sonny's, a coal-black, cheerful-looking man, built close to the ground. He immediately began confiding to me, at the top of his lungs, the most terrible things about Sonny, his teeth gleaming like a lighthouse and his laugh coming up out of him like the beginning of an earthquake. And it turned out that everyone at the bar knew Sonny, or almost everyone; some were musicians, working there, or nearby, or not working, some were simply hangers-on, and some were there to hear Sonny play. I was introduced to all of them and they were all very polite to me. Yet, it was clear that, for them, I was only Sonny's brother. Here, I was in Sonny's world. Or, rather: his kingdom. Here, it was not even a question that his veins bore royal blood.

They were going to play soon and Creole installed me, by myself, at a table in a dark corner. Then I watched them, Creole, and the little black man, and Sonny, and the others, while they horsed around, standing just below the bandstand. The light from the bandstand spilled just a little short of them and, watching them laughing and gesturing and moving about, I had the feeling that they, nevertheless, were being most careful not to step into that circle of light too suddenly: that if they moved into the light too suddenly, without thinking, they would perish in flame. Then, while I watched, one of them, the small, black man, moved into the light and crossed the bandstand and started fooling around with his drums. Then—being funny and being, also, extremely ceremonious—Creole took Sonny by the arm and led him to the piano. A woman's voice called Sonny's name and a few hands started clapping. And Sonny, also being funny and being ceremonious, and so touched, I think, that he could have cried, but neither hiding it nor showing it, riding it like a man, grinned, and put both hands to his heart and bowed from the waist.

Creole then went to the bass fiddle and a lean, very bright-skinned brown man jumped up on the bandstand and picked up his horn. So there they were, and the atmosphere on the bandstand and in the room began to change and tighten. Someone stepped up to the microphone and announced them. Then there were all kinds of murmurs. Some people at the bar shushed others. The waitress ran around, frantically getting in the last orders, guys and chicks got closer to each other, and the lights on the bandstand, on the quartet, turned to a land of indigo. Then they all looked different there. Creole looked about him for the last time, as though he were making certain that all his chickens were in the coop, and then he—jumped and struck the fiddle. And there they were.

All I know about music is that not many people ever really hear it. And even then, on the rare occasions when something opens within, and the music enters, what we mainly hear, or hear corroborated, are personal, private, vanishing evocations. But the man who creates the music is hearing something else, is dealing with the roar rising from the void and imposing order on it as it hits the air. What is evoked in him, then, is of another order, more terrible because it has no words, and triumphant, too, for that same reason. And his triumph, when he triumphs, is ours. I just watched Sonny's face. His face was troubled, he was working hard, but he wasn't with it. And I had the feeling that, in a way, everyone on the bandstand was waiting for him, both waiting for him and pushing him along. But as I began to watch Creole, I realized that it was Creole who held them all back. He had them on a short rein. Up there, keeping the beat with his whole body, wailing on the fiddle, with his eyes half closed, he was listening to everything, but he was listening to Sonny. He was having a dialogue with Sonny. He wanted Sonny to leave the shoreline and strike out for the deep water. He was Sonny's witness that deep water and drowning were not the same thing—he had been there, and he knew. And he wanted Sonny to know. He was waiting for Sonny to do the things on the keys which would let Creole know that Sonny was in the water.

And, while Creole listened, Sonny moved, deep within, exactly like someone in torment. I had never before thought of how awful the relationship must be between the musician and his instrument. He has to fill it, this instrument, with the breath of life, his own. He has to make it do what he wants it to do. And a piano is just a piano. It's made out of so much wood and wires and little hammers and big ones, and ivory. While there's only so much you can do with it, the only way to find this out is to try; to try and make it do everything.

And Sonny hadn't been near a piano for over a year. And he wasn't on much better terms with his life, not the life that stretched before him now. He and the piano stammered, started one way, got scared, stopped; started another way, panicked, marked time, started again; then seemed to have found a direction, panicked again, got stuck. And the face I saw on Sonny I'd never seen before. Everything had been burned out of it, and, at the same time, things usually hidden were being burned in, by the fire and fury of the battle which was occurring in him up there.

Yet, watching Creole's face as they neared the end of the first set, I had the feeling that something had happened, something I hadn't heard. Then they finished, there was scattered applause, and then, without an instant's warning, Creole started into something else, it was almost sardonic, it was *Am I Blue*. And, as though he commanded, Sonny began to play. Something began to happen. And Creole let out the reins. The dry, low, black man said something awful on the drums, Creole answered, and the drums talked back. Then the horn insisted, sweet and high, slightly detached perhaps, and Creole listened, commenting now and then, dry, and driving, beautiful and calm and old. Then they all came together again, and Sonny was part of the family again. I could tell this from his face. He seemed to have found, right there beneath his fingers, a damn brand-new piano. It seemed that he couldn't get over it. Then, for awhile, just being happy with Sonny, they seemed to be agreeing with him that brand-new pianos certainly were a gas.

Then Creole stepped forward to remind them that what they were playing was the blues. He hit something in all of them, he hit something in me, myself, and the music tightened and deepened, apprehension began to beat the air. Creole began to tell us what the blues were all about. They were not about anything very new. He and his boys up there were keeping it new, at the risk of ruin, destruction, madness, and death, in order to find new ways to make us listen. For, while the tale of how we suffer, and how we are delighted, and how we may triumph is never new, it always must be heard. There isn't any other tale to tell, it's the only light we've got in all this darkness.

And this tale, according to that face, that body, those strong hands on those strings, has another aspect in every country, and a new depth in every generation. Listen, Creole seemed to be saying, listen. Now these are Sonny's blues. He made the little black man on the drums know it, and the bright, brown man on the horn. Creole wasn't trying any longer to get Sonny in the water. He was wishing him Godspeed. Then he stepped back, very slowly, filling the air with the immense suggestion that Sonny speak for himself.

Then they all gathered around Sonny and Sonny played. Every now and again one of them seemed to say, amen. Sonny's fingers filled the air with life, his life. But that life contained so many others. And Sonny went all the way back, he really began with the spare, flat statement of the opening phrase of the song. Then he began to make it his. It was very beautiful because it wasn't hurried and it was no longer a lament. I seemed to hear with what burning he had made it his, with what burning we had yet to make it ours, how we could cease lamenting. Freedom lurked around us and I understood, at last, that he could help us to be free if we would listen, that he would never be free until we did. Yet, there was no battle in his face now. I heard what he had gone through, and would continue to go through until he came to rest in earth. He had made it his: that long line, of which we knew only Mama and Daddy. And he was giving it back, as everything must be given back, so that, passing through death, it can live forever. I saw my mother's face again, and felt, for the first time, how the stones of the road she had walked on must have bruised her feet. I saw the moonlit road where my father's brother died. And it brought something else back to me, and carried me past it, I saw my little girl again and felt Isabel's tears again, and I felt my own tears begin to rise. And I was yet aware that this was only a moment, that the world waited outside, as hungry as a tiger, and that trouble stretched above us, longer than the sky.

Then it was over. Creole and Sonny let out their breath, both soaking wet, and grinning. There was a lot of applause and some of it was real. In the dark, the girl came by and I asked her to take drinks to the bandstand. There was a long pause, while they talked up there in the indigo light and after awhile I saw the girl put a Scotch and milk on top of the piano for Sonny. He didn't seem to notice it, but just before they started playing again, he sipped from it and looked toward me, and nodded. Then he put it back on top of the piano. For me, then, as they began to play again, it glowed and shook above my brother's head like the very cup of trembling.

3

Medley

Toni Cade Bambara

I could tell the minute I got in the door and dropped my bag, I wasn't staying. Dishes piled sky-high in the sink looking like some circus act. Glasses all ghosty on the counter. Busted tea bags, curling cantaloupe rinds, white cartons from the Chinamen, green sacks from the deli, and that damn dog creeping up on me for me to wrassle his head or kick him in the ribs one. No, I definitely wasn't staying. Couldn't even figure why I'd come. But picked my way to the hallway anyway till the laundry-stuffed pillowcases stopped me. Larry's bass blocking the view to the bedroom.

"That you, Sweet Pea?"

"No, man, ain't me at all," I say, working my way back to the suitcase and shoving that damn dog out of the way. "See ya round," I holler, the door slamming behind me, cutting off the words abrupt.

*

Quite naturally sitting cross-legged at the club, I embroider a little on the homecoming tale, what with an audience of two crazy women and a fresh bottle of Jack Daniels. Got so I could actually see shonuff toadstools growing in the sink. Cantaloupe seeds sprouting in the muck. A goddamn compost heap breeding near the stove, garbage gardens on the grill.

"Sweet Pea, you oughta hush, cause you can't possibly keep on lying so," Pot Limit's screaming, tears popping from her eyes. "Lawd hold my legs, cause this liar bout to kill me off."

"Never mind about Larry's housekeeping, girl," Sylvia's soothing me, sloshing perfectly good bourbon all over the table. "You can come and stay with me till your house comes through. It'll be like old times at Aunt Merriam's."

I ease back into the booth to wait for the next set. The drummer's fooling with the equipment, tapping the mikes, hoping he's watched, so I watch him. But feeling worried in my mind about Larry, cause I've been through days like that myself. Cold cream caked on my face from the day before, hair matted, bathrobe funky, not a clean pair of drawers to my name. Even the emergency ones, the draggy cotton numbers stuffed way in the back of the drawer under the scented paper gone. And no clean silverware in the box and the last of the paper cups gone, too. Icebox empty cept for a rock of cheese and the lone water jug that ain't even half full that's how anyhow the thing's gone on. And not a clue as to the next step. But then Pot Limit'll come bamming on the door to say So-and-so's in town and can she have the card table for a game. Or Sylvia'll send a funny card inviting herself to dinner and even giving me the menu. Then I zoom through that house like a manic work brigade till me and the place ready for white-glove inspection. But what if somebody or other don't intervene for Larry, I'm thinking.

The drummer's messin round on the cymbals, head cocked to the side, rings sparkling. The other dudes are stepping out from behind the curtain. The piano man playing with the wah-wah doing splashy, breathy science fiction stuff. Sylvia checking me out to make sure I ain't too blue. Blue got hold to me, but I lean forward out of the shadows and babble something about how off the bourbon tastes these days. Hate worryin Sylvia, who is the kind of friend who bleeds at the eyes with your pain. I drain my glass and hum along with the opening riff of the guitar and I keep my eyes strictly off the bass player, whoever he is.

Larry Landers looked more like a bass player than ole Mingus himself. Got these long arms that drape down over the bass like they were grown special for that purpose. Fine, strong hands with long fingers and muscular knuckles, the dimples deep black at the joints. His calluses so other-colored and hard, looked like Larry had swiped his grandmother's tarnished thimbles to play with. He'd move in on that bass like he was going to hump it or something, slide up behind it as he lifted it from the rug, all slinky. He'd become one with the wood. Head dipped down sideways bobbing out the rhythm, feet tapping, legs jiggling, he'd look good. Thing about it, though, ole Larry couldn't play for shit. Couldn't never find the right placement of the notes. Never plucking with enough strength, despite the perfectly capable hands. Either you didn't hear him at all or what you heard was off. The man couldn't play for nuthin is what I'm saying. But Larry Landers was baad in the shower, though.

He'd soap me up and down with them great, fine hands, doing a deep bass walking in the back of his mouth. And I'd just have to sing, though I can't sing to save my life. But we'd have one hellafyin musical time in the shower, lemme tell you. "Green Dolphin Street" never sounded like nuthin till Larry bopped out them changes and actually made me sound good. On "My Funny Valentine" he'd do a whizzing sounding bow thing that made his throat vibrate real sexy and I'd cutesy up the introduction, which is, come to think of it, my favorite part. But the main number when the hot water started running out was "I Feel Like Making Love." That was usually the wind up of our repertoire cause you can imagine what that song can do to you in the shower and all.

Got so we spent a helluva lotta time in the shower. Just as well, cause didn't nobody call Larry for gigs. He a nice man, considerate, generous, baad in the shower, and good taste in music. But he just wasn't nobody's bass player. Knew all the stances, though, the postures, the facial expressions, had the choreography down. And right in the middle of supper he'd get some Ron Carter thing going in his head and hop up from the table to go get the bass. Haul that sucker right in the kitchen and do a number in dumb show, all the playing in his throat, the acting with his hands. But that ain't nuthin. I mean that can't get it. I can impersonate Betty Carter if it comes to that. The arms crooked just so, the fingers popping, the body working, the cap and all, the teeth, authentic. But I got sense enough to know I ain't nobody's singer. Actually, I am a mother, though I'm only just now getting it together. And too, I'm an A-1 manicurist.

Me and my cousin Sinbad come North working our show in cathouses at first. Set up a salon right smack in the middle of Miz Maybry's

Saturday traffic. But that wasn't no kind of life to be bringing my daughter into. So I parked her at a boarding school till I could make some other kind of life. Wasn't no kind of life for Sinbad either, so we quit.

Our first shop was a three-chair affair on Austin. Had a student barber who could do anything—blow-outs, do's, corn rows, weird cuts, afros, press and curl, whatever you wanted. Plus he din't gab you to death. And he always brought his sides and didn't blast em neither. He went on to New York and opened his own shop. Was a boot-black too then, an old dude named James Noughton, had a crooked back and worked at the post office at night, and knew everything about everything, read all the time.

"Whatcha want to know about Marcus Garvey, Sweet Pea?"

If it wasn't Garvey, it was the rackets or the trucking industry or the flora and fauna of Greenland or the planets or how the special effects in the disaster movies were done. One Saturday I asked him to tell me about the war, cause my nephew'd been drafted and it all seemed so wrong to me, our men over there in Nam fighting folks who fighting for the same things we are, to get that blood-sucker off our backs.

Well, what I say that for. Old dude gave us a deep knee bend, straight up eight-credit dissertation on World Wars I and II—the archduke getting offed, Africa cut up like so much cake, Churchill and his cigars, Gabriel Heatter on the radio, Hitler at the Olympics igging Owens, Red Cross doing Bloods dirty refusing donuts and bandages, A. Philip Randolph scaring the white folks to death, Mary McLeod Bethune at the White House, Liberty Bond drives, the Russian front, frostbite of the feet, the Jew stiffs, the gypsies no one mourned . . . the whole johnson. Talked straight through the day, Miz Mary's fish dinner growing cold on the radiator, his one and only customer walking off with one dull shoe. Fell out exhausted, his shoe rag limp in his lap, one arm draped over the left foot platform, the other clutching his heart. Took Sinbad and our cousin Pepper to get the old man home. I stayed with him all night with the ice pack and a fifth of Old Crow. He liked to die.

After while trade picked up and with a better class of folk too. Then me and Sinbad moved to North and Gaylord and called the shop Chez Sinbad. No more winos stumbling in or deadbeats wasting my time talking raunchy shit. The paperboy, the numbers man, the dudes with classier hot stuff coming in on Tuesday mornings only. We did up the place nice. Light globes from a New Orleans whorehouse, Sinbad likes to lie. Brown-and-black-and-silver-striped wallpaper. Lots of mirrors and hanging plants. Them old barber chairs spruced up and called antiques and damn if someone didn't buy one off us for eight hundred, cracked me up.

I cut my schedule down to ten hours in the shop so I could do private sessions with the gamblers and other business men and women who don't like sitting around the shop even though it's comfy, specially my part. Got me a cigar showcase with a marble top for serving coffee in clear glass mugs with heatproof handles too. My ten hours in the shop are spent leisurely. And my twenty hours out are making me a mint. Takes dust to be a mother, don't you know.

It was a perfect schedule once Larry Landers came into my life. He part-timed at a record shop and bartended at Topp's on the days and nights I worked at the shops. That gave us most of Monday and Wednesdays to listen to sides and hit the clubs. Gave me Fridays all to myself to study in the library and wade through them college bulletins and get to the museum and generally chart out a routine for when Debbie and me are a team. Sundays I always drive to Delaware to see her, and Larry detours to D.C. to see his sons. My bankbook started telling me I was soon going to be a full-time mama again and a college girl to boot, if I can ever talk myself into doing a school thing again, old as I am.

Life with Larry was cool. Not just cause he wouldn't hear about me going halves on the bills. But cause he was an easy man to be easy with. He liked talking softly and listening to music. And he liked having folks over for dinner and cards. Larry a real nice man and I liked him a lot. And I liked his friend Hector, who lived in the back of the apartment. Ole moon-face Hector went to school with Larry years ago and is some kind of kin. And they once failed in the funeral business together and I guess those stories of them times kinda keep them friends.

The time they had to put Larry's brother away is their best story, Hector's story really, since Larry got to play a little grief music round the edges. They decided to pass up a church service, since Barn was such a treacherous desperado wouldn't nobody want to preach over his body and wouldn't nobody want to come to hear no lies about the dearly departed untimely ripped or cut down or whatever. So Hector and Larry set up some kind of pop stand awning right at the gravesite, expecting close blood only. But seems the whole town turned out to make sure old evil, hell-raising Barn was truly dead. Dudes straight from the barber chair, the striped ponchos blowing like wings, fuzz and foam on they face and all, lumbering up the hill to the hole taking bets and talking shit, relating how Ole Crazy Barn had shot up the town, shot up the jail, shot up the hospital pursuing some bootlegger who'd come up one keg short of the order. Women from all around come to demand the lid be lifted so they could check for themselves and be sure that Barn was stone cold. No matter how I tried I couldn't think of nobody bad enough to think on when they told the story of the man I'd never met.

Larry and Hector so bent over laughing bout the funeral, I couldn't hardly put the events in proper sequence. But I could surely picture some neighbor lady calling on Larry and Barn's mama reporting how the whole town had turned out for the burying. And the mama snatching up the first black thing she could find to wrap around herself and make an appearance. No use passing up a scene like that. And Larry prancing round the kitchen being his mama. And I'm too stunned to laugh, not at somebody's mama, and somebody's brother dead. But him and Hector laughing to beat the band and I can't help myself.

Thing about it, though, the funeral business stories are Hector's stories and he's not what you'd call a good storyteller. He never gives you the names, so you got all these he's and she's floating around. And he don't believe in giving details, so you got to scramble to paint your own pictures. Toward the end of that particular tale of Barn, all I could picture was the townspeople driving a stake through the dead man's heart, then hurling that coffin into the hole right quick. There was also something in that story about the civil rights workers wanting to make a case cause a white cop had cut Barn down. But looked like Hector didn't have a hold to that part of the story, so I just don't know.

Stories are not Hector's long suit. But he's an absolute artist on windows. Ole Moon-face can wash some windows and make you cry about it too. Makes these smooth little turns out there on that little bitty sill just like he wasn't four stories up without a belt. I'd park myself at the breakfast counter and thread the new curtains on the rods while Hector mixed up the vinegar solution real chef-like. Wring out the rags just so, scrunch up the newspapers into soft wads that make you think of cat's paws. Hector was a cat himself out there on the sill, making these marvelous circles in the glass, rubbing the hardhead spots with a strip of steel wool he had pinned to his overalls.

Hector offered to do my car once. But I put a stop to that after that first time. My windshield so clear and sparkling felt like I was in an accident and heading over the hood, no glass there. But it was a pleasure to have coffee and watch Hector. After while, though, Larry started hinting that the apartment wasn't big enough for four. I agreed, thinking he meant Earl had to go. Come to find Larry meant Hector, which was a real drag. I love to be around people who do whatever it is they do with style and care.

Larry's dog's named Earl P. Jessup Bowers, if you can get ready for that. And I should mention straightaway that I do not like dogs one bit, which is why I was glad when Larry said somebody had to go. Cats are bad enough. Horses are a total drag. By the age of nine I was fed up with all that noble horse this and noble horse that. They got good PR, horses. But I really can't use em. Was a fire once when I was little and some dumb horse almost burnt my daddy up messin around, twisting, snorting, bouncing, rearing up, doing everything but comin on out the barn like even the chickens had sense enough to do. I told my daddy to let that horse's ass burn. Horses be as dumb as cows. Cows just don't have good press agents is all.

I used to like cows when I was real little and needed to hug me something bigger than a goldfish. But don't let it rain, the dumbbells'll fall right in a ditch and you break a plow and shout yourself hoarse trying to get them fools to come up out the ditch. Chipmunks I don't mind when I'm at the breakfast counter with my tea and they're on their side of the glass doing Disney things in the yard. Blue jays are law-and-order birds, thoroughly despicable. And there's one prize fool in my Aunt Merriam's yard I will one day surely kill. He tries to "whip whip whippoorwill" like the Indians do in the Fort This or That movies when they're signaling to each other closing in on George Montgomery but don't never get around to wiping that sucker out. But dogs are one of my favorite hatreds. All the time woofing, bolting down their food, slopping water on the newly waxed linoleum, messin with you when you trying to read, chewin on the slippers.

Earl P. Jessup Bowers was an especial drag. But I could put up with Earl when Hector was around. Once Hector was gone and them windows got cloudy and gritty, I was through. Kicked that dog every chance I got. And after thinking what it meant, how the deal went down, place too small for four and it was Hector not Earl—I started moving up my calendar so I could get out of there. I ain't the kind of lady to press no ultimatum on no man. Like "Choose, me or the dog." That's unattractive. Kicking Hector out was too. An insult to me, once I got to thinking on it. Especially since I got one item on my agenda, making a home for me and my kid. So if anybody should've been given walking papers, should've been me.

Anyway. One day Moody comes waltzing into Chez Sinbad's and tips his hat. He glances at his nails and glances at me. And I figure here is my house in a green corduroy suit. Pot Limit had just read my cards and the jack of diamonds kept coming up on my resource side. Sylvia and me put our heads together and figure it got to be some gambler or hustler who wants his nails done. What other jacks do I know to make my fortune? I'm so positive about Moody, I whip out a postcard from the drawer where I keep the emeries and write my daughter to start packing.

"How much you make a day, Miss Lady?"

"Thursdays are always good for fifty," I lie.

He hands me fifty and glances over at Sinbad, who nods that it's cool. "I'd like my nails done at four-thirty. My place."

"Got a customer at that time, Mr. Moody, and I like to stay reliable. How about five-twenty?"

He smiles a slow smile and glances at Sinbad, who nods again, everything's cool. "Fine," he says. "And do you think you can manage a shave without cutting a person's throat?"

"Mr. Moody, I don't know you well enough to have just cause. And none of your friends have gotten to me yet with that particular proposition. Can't say what I'm prepared to do in the future, but for now I can surely shave you real careful-like."

Moody smiles again, then turns to Sinbad, who says it's cool and he'll give me the address. This look-nod dialogue burns my ass. That's like when you take a dude to lunch and pay the check and the waiter's standing there with *your* money in his paws asking *the dude* was everything all right and later for *you.* Shit. But I take down Moody's address and let the rest roll off me like so much steaming lava. I start packing up my little alligator case—buffer, batteries, clippers, emeries, massager, sifter, arrowroot and cornstarch, clear sealer, magnifying glass, and my own mixture of green and purple pigments.

"Five-twenty ain't five-twenty-one, is it, Miss Lady?"

"Not in my book," I say, swinging my appointment book around so he can see how full it is and how neatly the times are printed in. Course I always fill in phony names case some creep starts pressing me for a session.

For six Thursdays running and two Monday nights, I'm at Moody's bending over them nails with a miner's light strapped to my forehead, the magnifying glass in its stand, nicking just enough of the nails at the sides, tinting just enough with the color so he can mark them cards as he shuffles. Takes an hour to do it proper. Then I sift my talc concoction and brush his hands till they're smooth. Them cards move around so fast in his hands, he can actually tell me he's about to deal from the bottom in the next three moves and I miss it and I'm not new to this. I been a gambler's manicurist for more years than I care to mention. Ten times he'll cut and each time the same fifteen cards in the top cut and each time in exactly the same order. Incredible.

Now, I've known hands. My first husband, for instance. To see them hands work their show in the grandstands, at a circus, in a parade, the pari-mutuels—artistry in action. We met on the train. As a matter of fact, he was trying to burgle my bag. Some story to tell the grandchildren, hunh? I had to get him straight about robbing from folks. I don't play that. Ya gonna steal, hell, steal back some of them millions we got in escrow is my opinion. We spent three good years on the circuit. Then credit cards moved in. Then choke-and-grab muggers killed the whole tradition. He was reduced to a mere shell of his former self, as they say, and took to putting them hands on me. I try not to think on when things went sour. Try not to think about them big slapping hands, only of them working hands. Moody's working hands were something like that, but even better. So I'm impressed and he's impressed. And he pays me fifty and tips me fifty and shuts up when I shave him and keeps his hands off my lovely person.

I'm so excited counting up my bread, moving up the calendar, making impulsive calls to Delaware and the two of us squealing over the wire like a coupla fools, that what Larry got to say about all these goings-on just rolls off my back like so much molten lead.

"Well, who be up there while he got his head in your lap and you squeezing his goddamn blackheads?"

"I don't squeeze his goddamn blackheads, Larry, on account of he don't have no goddamn blackheads. I give him a shave, a steam, and an egg-white face mask. And when I'm through, his face is as smooth as his hands."

"I'll bet," Larry says. That makes me mad cause I expect some kind of respect for my work, which is better than just good.

"And he doesn't have his head in my lap. He's got a whole barbershop set up on his solarium."

"His what?" Larry squinting at me, raising the wooden spoon he stirring the spaghetti with, and I raise the knife I'm chopping the onions with. Thing about it, though, he don't laugh. It's funny as hell to me, but Larry got no sense of humor sometimes, which is too bad cause he's a lotta fun when he's laughing and joking.

"It's not a bedroom. He's got this screened-in sun porch where he raises African violets and—"

"Please, Sweet Pea. Why don't you quit? You think I'm dumb?"

"I'm serious. I'm serious and I'm mad cause I ain't got no reason to lie to you whatever was going on, Larry." He turns back to the pot and I continue working on the sauce and I'm pissed off cause this is silly. "He sits in the barber chair and I shave him and give him a manicure."

"What else you be giving him? A man don't be paying a good-looking woman to come to his house and all and don't—"

"Larry, if you had the dough and felt like it, wouldn't you pay Pot Limit to come read your cards? And couldn't you keep your hands to yourself and she a good-looking woman? And couldn't you see yourself paying Sylvia to come and cook for you and no funny stuff, and she's one of the best-looking women in town?"

Larry cooled out fast. My next shot was to bring up the fact that he was insulting my work. Do I go around saying the women who pass up Bill the bartender and come to him are after his joint? No, cause I respect the fact that Larry Landers mixes the best piña coladas this side of Barbados. And he's flashy with the blender and the glasses and the whole show. He's good and I respect that. But he cooled out so fast I didn't have to bring it up. I don't believe in overkill, besides I like to keep some things in reserve. He cooled out so fast I realized he wasn't really jealous. He was just going through one of them obligatory male numbers, all symbolic, no depth.

Like the time this dude came into the shop to talk some trash and Sinbad got his ass on his shoulders, talking about the dude showed no respect for him cause for all he knew I could be Sinbad's woman. And he arguing that since that ain't the case, what's the deal? I mean why get hot over what if if what if ain't. Men are crazy. Now there is Sinbad, my blood cousin who grew up right in the same house like a brother damn near, putting me through simple-ass changes like that. Who's got time for grand opera and comic strips, I'm trying to make a life for me and my kid. But men are like that. Gorillas, if you know what I mean.

Like at Topp's sometimes. I'll drop in to have a drink with Larry when he's on the bar and then I leave. And maybe some dude'll take it in his head to walk me to the car. That's cool. I lay it out right quick that me and Larry are a we and then we take it from there, just two people gassing in the summer breeze and that's just fine. But don't let some other dude holler over something like "Hey, man, can you handle all that? Why don't you step aside, junior, and let a man . . . " and blah-de-da-de-dah. They can be the best of friends or total strangers just kidding around, but right away they two gorillas pounding on their chest, pounding on their chest and talking over my head, yelling over the tops of cars just like I'm not a person with some say-so in the matter. It's a man-to-man ritual that ain't got nothing to do with me. So I just get in my car and take off and leave them to get it on if they've a mind to. They got it.

But if one of the gorillas is a relative, or a friend of mine, or a nice kinda man I got in mind for one of my friends, I will stick around long enough to shout em down and point out that they are some ugly gorillas and are showing no respect for me and therefore owe me an apology. But if they don't fit into one of them categories, I figure it ain't my place to try to develop them so they can make the leap from gorilla to human. If their own mamas and daddies didn't care whether they turned out to be amoebas or catfish or whatever, it ain't my weight. I got my own weight. I'm a mother. So they got it.

Like I use to tell my daughter's daddy, the key to getting along and living with other folks is to keep clear whose weight is whose. His drinking, for instance, was not my weight. And him waking me up in the night for them long, rambling, ninety-proof monologues bout how the whole world's made up of victims, rescuers, and executioners and I'm the dirty bitch cause I ain't rescuing him fast enough to suit him. Then got so I was the executioner, to hear him tell it. I don't say nuthin cause my philosophy of life and death is this—I'll go when the wagon comes, but I ain't going out behind somebody else's shit. I arranged my priorities long ago when I jumped into my woman stride. Some things I'll go off on. Some things I'll hold my silence and wait it out. Some things I just bump off, cause the best solution to some problems is to just abandon them.

But I struggled with Mac, Debbie's daddy. Talked to his family, his church, AA, hid the bottles, threatened the liquor man, left a good job to play nurse, mistress, kitten, buddy. But then he stopped calling me Dahlin and started calling me Mama. I don't play that. I'm my daughter's mama. So I split. Did my best to sweeten them last few months, but I'd been leaving for a long time.

The silliest thing about all of Larry's grumblings back then was Moody had no eyes for me and vice versa. I just like the money. And I like watching him mess around with the cards. He's exquisite, dazzling, stunning, shuffling, cutting, marking, dealing from the bottom, the middle, the near top. I ain't never seen nothing like it, and I seen a whole lot. The thing that made me mad, though, and made me know Larry Landers wasn't ready to deal with no woman full grown was the way he kept bringing it up, always talking about what he figured was on Moody's mind, like what's on my mind don't count. So I finally did have to use up my reserves and point out to Larry that he was insulting my work and that I would never dream of accusing him of not being a good bartender, of just being another pretty face, like they say.

"You can't tell me he don't have eyes," he kept saying.

"What about my eyes? Don't my eyes count?" I gave it up after a coupla tries. All I know is, Moody wasn't even thinking about me. I was impressed with his work and needed the trade and vice versa.

One time, for instance, I was doing his hands on the solarium and thought I saw a glint of metal up under his jacket. I rearranged myself in the chair so I could work my elbow in there to see if he was carrying heat. I thought I was being cool about it.

"How about keeping your tits on your side of the table, Miss Lady."

I would rather he think anything but that. I would rather he think I was clumsy in my work even. "Wasn't about tits, Moody. I was just trying to see if you had a holster on and was too lazy to ask."

"Would have expected you to. You a straight-up, direct kind of person." He opened his jacket away with the heel of his hand, being careful with his nails. I liked that.

"It's not about you," he said quietly, jerking his chin in the direction of the revolver. "Had to transport some money today and forgot to take it off. Sorry."

I gave myself two demerits. One for the tits, the other for setting up a situation where he wound up telling me something about his comings and goings. I'm too old to be making mistakes like that. So I apologized. Then gave myself two stars. He had a good opinion of me and my work. I did an extra-fine job on his hands that day.

Then the house happened. I had been reading the rental ads and For Sale columns for months and looking at some awful, tacky places. Then one Monday me and Sylvia lucked up on this cute little white-brick job up on a hill away from the street. Lots of light and enough room and not too much yard to kill me off. I paid my money down and rushed them papers through. Got back to Larry's place all excited and found him with his mouth all poked out.

Half grumbling, half proposing, he hinted around that we all should live at his place like a family. Only he didn't quite lay it out plain in case of rejection. And I'll tell you something, I wouldn't want to be no man. Must be hard on the heart always having to get out there, setting yourself up to be possibly shot down, approaching the lady, calling, the invitation, the rap. I don't think I could handle it myself unless everybody was just straight up at all times from day one till the end. I didn't answer Larry's nonproposed proposal cause it didn't come clear to me till after dinner. So I just let my silence carry whatever meaning it will. Ain't nuthin too much changed from the first day he came to get me from my Aunt Merriam's place. My agenda is still to make a home for my girl. Marriage just ain't one of the things on my mind no more, not after two. Got no regrets or bad feelings about them husbands neither. Like the poem says, when you're handed a lemon, make lemonade, honey, make lemonade. That's Gwen Brooks's motto, that's mine too. You get a lemon, well, just make lemonade.

"Going on the road next week," Moody announces one day through the steam towel. "Like you to travel with me, keep my hands in shape. Keep the women off my neck. Check the dudes at my back. Ain't asking you to carry heat or money or put yourself in no danger. But I could use your help." He pauses and I ease my buns into the chair, staring at the steam curling from the towel.

"Wicked schedule though—Mobile, Birmingham, Sarasota Springs, Jacksonville, then Puerto Rico and back. Can pay you two thousand and expenses. You're good, Miss Lady. You're good and you got good sense. And while I don't believe in nothing but my skill and chance, I gotta say you've brought me luck. You a lucky lady, Miss Lady."

He raises his hands and cracks his knuckles and it's like the talking towel has eyes as well cause damn if he ain't checking his cuticles.

"I'll call you later, Moody," I manage to say, mind reeling. With two thousand I can get my stuff out of storage, and buy Debbie a real nice bedroom set, pay tuition at the college too and start my three-credit-at-a-time grind.

Course I never dreamed the week would be so unnerving, exhausting, constantly on my feet, serving drinks, woofing sisters, trying to distract dudes, keeping track of fifty-leven umpteen goings on. Did have to carry the heat on three occasions and had to do helluva lotta driving. Plus was most of the time holed up in the hotel room close to the phone. I had pictured myself lazying on the beach in Florida dreaming up cruises around the world with two matching steamer trunks with the drawers and hangers and stuff. I'd pictured traipsing through the casinos in Puerto Rico ordering chicken salad and coffee liqueur and tipping the croupiers with blue chips. Shit no. Was work. And I sure as hell learned how Moody got his name. Got so we didn't even speak, but I kept those hands in shape and his face smooth and placid. And whether he won, lost, broke even, or got wiped out, I don't even know. He gave me my money and took off for New Orleans. That trip liked to kill me.

*

"You never did say nothing interesting about Moody," Pot Limit says insinuatingly, swinging her legs in from the aisle cause ain't nobody there to snatch so she might as well sit comfortable.

"Yeah, she thought she'd put us off the trail with a rip-roaring tale about Larry's housekeeping."

They slapping five and hunching each other and making a whole lotta noise, spilling Jack Daniels on my turquoise T-straps from Puerto Rico.

Come on, fess up, Sweet Pea," they crooning. "Did you give him some?"

"Ahhh, yawl bitches are tiresome, you know that?"

"Naaw, naaw," say Sylvia, grabbing my arm. "You can tell us. We wantta know all about the trip, specially the nights." She winks at Pot Limit.

"Tell us about this Moody man and his wonderful hands one more time, cept we want to hear how the hands feeel on the flesh, honey." Pot Limit doing a bump and grind in the chair that almost makes me join in the fun, except I'm worried in my mind about Larry Landers.

Just then the piano player comes by and leans over Sylvia, blowing in her ear. And me and Pot Limit mimic the confectionary goings-on. And just as well, cause there's nothin to tell about Moody. It wasn't a movie after all. And in real life the good-looking gambler's got cards on his mind. Just like I got my child on my mind. Onliest thing to say about the trip is I'm five pounds lighter, not a shade darker, but two thousand closer toward my goal.

"Ease up," Sylvia says, interrupting the piano player to fuss over me. Then the drummer comes by and eases in on Pot Limit. And I ease back into the shadows of the booth to think Larry over.

I'm staring at the entrance half expecting Larry to come into Topps, but it's not his night. Then, too, the thing is ended if I'd only know it. Larry the kind of man you're either living with him or you're out. I for one would've liked us to continue, me and Debbie in our place, him and Earl at his. But he got so grumpy the time I said that, I sure wasn't gonna bring it up again. Got grumpy in the shower, too, got so he didn't want to wash my back.

But that last night fore I left for Birmingham, we had us one crazy musical time in the shower. I kept trying to lure him into "Maiden Voyage," which I really can't do without back-up, cause I can't sing all them changes. After while he come out from behind his sulk and did a Jon Lucien combination on vocal and bass, alternating the sections, eight bars of singing words, eight bars of singing bass. It was baad. Then he insisted on doing "I Love You More Today Than Yesterday." And we like to break our arches, stomping out the beat against the shower mat.

The bathroom was all steamy and we had the curtains open so we could see the plants and watch the candles burning. I had bought us a big fat cake of sandalwood soap and it was matching them candles scent for scent. Must've been two o'clock in the morning and looked like the hot water would last forever and ever and ever. Larry finally let go of the love songs, which were making me feel kinda funny cause I thought it was understood that I was splitting, just like he'd always made it clear either I was there or nowhere.

Then we hit on a tune I don't even know the name of cept I like to scat and do my thing Larry calls Swahili wailing. He laid down the most intricate weaving, walking, bopping, strutting bottom to my singing I ever heard. It inspired me. Took that melody and went right on out that shower, them candles bout used up, the fatty soap long since abandoned in the dish, our bodies barely visible in the steamed-up mirrors walling his bathroom. Took that melody right on out the room and out of doors and somewhere out this world. Larry changing instruments fast as I'm changing moods, colors. Took an alto solo and gave me a rest, worked an intro up on the piano playing the chords across my back, drove me all up into the high register while he weaved in and out around my head on a flute sounding like them chilly pipes of the Andes. And I was Yma Sumac for one minute there, up there breathing some rare air and losing my mind, I was so high on just sheer music. Music and water, the healthiest things in the world. And that hot water pounding like it was part of the group with a union card and all. And I could tell that if that bass could've fit in the tub, Larry would've dragged that bad boy in there and played the hell out of them soggy strings once and for all.

I dipped way down and reached way back for snatches of Jelly Roll Morton's "Deep Creek Blues" and Larry so painful, so stinging on the bass, could make you cry. Then I'm racing fast through Bessie and all the other Smith singers, Mildred Bailey, Billie and imitators, Betty Roche, Nat King Cole vintage 46, a little Joe Carroll, King Pleasure, some Babs. Found myself pulling lines out of songs I don't even like, but ransacked songs just for the meaningful lines or two cause I realized we were doing more than just making music together, and it had to be said just how things stood.

Then I was off again and lost Larry somewhere down there doing scales, sound like. And he went back to that first supporting line that had drove me up into the Andes. And he stayed there waiting for me to return and do some more Swahili wailing. But I was elsewhere and liked it out there and ignored the fact that he was aiming for a wind-up of "I Love You More Today Than Yesterday." I sang myself out till all I could ever have left in life was "Brown Baby" to sing to my little girl. Larry stayed on the ground with the same supporting line, and the hot water started getting funny and I knew my time was up. So I came crashing down, jarring the song out of shape, diving back into the melody line and somehow, not even knowing what song each other was doing, we finished up together just as the water turned cold.

4

Norman's Date

Amiri Baraka

Norman comes into the bar and tells me this one night.

Norman always had great stuff to say, about painting and people he knew and Europe. Personalities and marvelous accomplishments. Fashionable stuff, in a way. But one night he comes up with this—it knocked me out.

He's drinking. He's got one hand holding up his very expensive trench coat. He's got a Gauloise dangling outta his mouth. (That's his usual stance.) He says: I met a woman, huh, the other night. Boy! He's talking and puffing the Gauloise, his coat pushed back, a couple of guys and me listening. We got drinks. It's not even late. Nobody's drunk.

Yeh, I'd been at the Five Spot, he says. He's talking like it's real. He's earnest, ya know? I was listening to Monk. And I see this babe standing by the bar digging the music. She's listening, she smiles. She's weaving, she's got a glass. Ya know. I start watchin her.

She's great, man. Great looking. Long and slender and blond. And all dolled up, but with good taste. Even some goddamn jewelry—and I hate jewelry. But on her it looks great, really great. And she spots me after a while. I was playin' it cool, ya know? I thought maybe her ol' man was in the john and coming right back. Shit, didn't want no trouble. The music's great, too. That crazy Monk. And Wilbur. And that goddamn Trane is learning to play Monk's tunes, ya know?

Norman holds up his glass and gestures at us; there were maybe two others and me in our knot. He gestures for drinks all around. He's lighting another Gauloise with the stump he's got in his mouth. He shrugs acknowledgment as we hold up our glasses, saluting him. Norman was a kind of generous guy in a way, but he comes on tough. An ex-captain in the goddamn bombers during the Second World War. He's always got a scowl on his puss. People who don't know him think he's an asshole. A couple of friends of mine, even. They say Norman never invites them to his goddamn parties—the stuck-up elitist bastard. Ya know, Norman was making a little money then. Flying back and forth to Paris. Had regular shows there and a good gallery in New York. Big abstract expressionist canvasses. Big as hell, with the paint soaked in. And you could tell his Rorschach—he had his own style. You could tell a Norman anywhere once you'd seen them.

I got to know him through Frank. He was always jammed up with painters, especially the abstract expressionists—De Kooning, Kline, Guston, Hartigan, and even Rivers. He wasn't abstract, not on canvas anyway. I think Rivers took out his abstraction in the real world. But he would leave half a person out of his paintings. I guess as a kind of tribute to all the money the A.E.'s was making.

Cedar Bar. The early '60s, before Malcolm and hot street shit sent people flying every which way. (A buncha us to Harlem!) But we hung tough then. And bullshit—massive amounts of it got laid down in that joint.

So she looks at me, Norman's saying, right in the eye. Hey, what a look! It went right through me. My pecker started to turn over just a little bit, ya know? This babe was really good looking, no shit!

We're sipping and Norman's a good storyteller. He brings in the whole nuance of the thing. The environmental vibes, so to speak. He describes the woman. He really describes her. She sounds good, like a cross between Brigitte Bardot and Marilyn Monroe. (I think these were his references.) But not "whorish," he says, not at all whorish. Real nice!

Norman's a big square-jawed Jewish guy with a permanently sneering lower lip. It gives him character. But actually, he's a sweet guy in a lotta ways. He'd probably give you his last dime, but he ain't never gonna get to that. No, not his *last* dime, knowing Norman. He knows what's happening and being broke ain't it!

Monk's doing his wild dance. Norman demonstrates. Oh shit! I was laughing. Fuckin Norman, don't dance, please. Just get on with the goddamn story.

And the babe is getting warmer and warmer. I could feel it across the room. Warmer, right there across the room. Through the music and over the people. A not insubstantial volume—is that the term? (We spat that around. Hey, whatever.) But the babe is sending like fuckin heat-rays across the room. And I start thinking . . . I wasn't thinking shit. But the ding-dong is clearly on the move. And we're still fifteen feet apart. And Monk is squatting down and . . . Norman demonstrates again. He comes up and gestures with the glass. Sam bought another round.

When the set's over, she looks away. I say shit, what a fuckin tease. This bitch! But then the fuckin broad turns and looks me right up and down from eyehole to peehole. Yeh, she lays them baby-blue glimmers right on the tip of my pecker. We howled.

How'd you know it was the tip end? Fuckin drunk Basil always got some contentious shit to raise—he's beginning to get a little potted.

Hey, you know where somebody's looking, goddamnit. Norman pretended to be incensed. We laughed.

I said, Basil never had nobody look at his drunken ass. He's too fuckin drunk.

What? What? Basil chugalugged his brew. You wanna see the eye-prints on my ding-a-ling? (Norman made the jerk-off sign.) Everybody almost fell down.

John the bartender comes over, says, What the fuck you guys bull-shittin about now? Goddamn Norman lying about something again?

John, kiss my ass, will ya, Norman said. Give us a fuckin free round and quit buttin in the customers' fuckin conversation.

So then, while she's shooting the heat-rays at my johnson, I start to return it full-up, ya know?

What'd you do, pee? (Basil again.)

Ya prick, shaddup! Let him finish. Go ahead, Norman.

It's crowded as hell in the Five Spot. Hey, where was I? I was getting it in. I'm in the Five Spot every night—Monk and Trane, man. That's bad-bad. Not just bad, but bad-bad!

Yeh, everybody said amen to that. And it was bad, bad-bad. Check the records.

So I start over, says Norman. Yeh, I start over. Not goofy like Basil.

Basil shrugged, chugalugged, and waved for another at John, who was now standing behind the bar cocking an ear. He knew the kind of good stories Norman could tell.

I start over, very cautious and cool. Like I'm moving through the crowd, like maybe I was going to the john or to somebody else's table, right?

Yeh, we encouraged.

And then when it looks like I might pass the table, I turn like slow. Norman gave the No. 1 demo of Valentine: Norman Valentine: eyes squinted sexily, shoulders pulled back, his trench coat hanging over that one arm, ever-present drink in hand. Yeh, we were clapping through our brew. Yeh, like that.

She looked up at me. Maybe she'd never taken her eyes away, I dunno. But when I turned, she caught me again from pecker to soul and back again. Whew.

We *whewed* too. John smirked, but listened even harder. Basil was grinning silently and making funny motions with his body that I decided were cheerleading stunts.

And then I'm standing there over the table, and she's whispering almost, her voice low and soft, like quiet. People all around cackling and howling like they do at intermission. Pushing back and forth. And I'm standing there with this wild-looking woman stroking me through the eyes, down clear to the balls!

Norman was outdoing himself. His metaphors were usually sharp, but maybe this eternal story of boy meets girl (accompanied by T. Sphere Monk) was out. We were getting rapt and dumping beer down us, or whatever. No, I think I was drinking bourbon and soda.

She says, So why you standing there? There's room. I guess I kept staring. You just want to look?

Huh. I dunno if I said huh. I probably did, but she thought it was something else with the cigarette. Hi, I said, and she laughs with that uncanny, quiet, low voice.

Hi, yourself. I was wondering if you were coming over or what. I thought for a while you might be just window shopping.

I laughed and eased into the seat. I sort of held the glass up like a little toast as I sat, and she did the same.

Whatcha drinking? It's always my first statement to any broad, no matter how she looks. She's drinking that goddamn Dubonnet on the rocks. I shoulda . . .

What? Basil snapped out of his slow drunken grin. Dubonnet, for Christ's sake! Who the hell drinks that?

Shaddup, drunk, will ya? I think it was White propped against the bar, at least as drunk as Basil, kibitzing. I wanna hear the goddamn story.

OK, OK. Basil started to order another round, but John was already drawing it. So what happened next, Norman? Goddamnit, this is getting good. And Basil begins to chugalug again.

Yeh, we start talking, ya know? I tell her about me. She said she'd seen some of my work at Castelli's. She tells me she was even at an opening of mine.

Yay, a fuckin art lover! Basil was smirking and White was frowning at him an unserious frown.

She tells me she used to paint when she first came to the Village, but got bored. She worked at an ad agency. She was a model. She even went out to Hollywood.

Yay, Hollywood! White cheered.

Shaddup, drunken bastard, Basil jeered unseriously.

So what's she do then? I wanted to keep the story moving. Stories turn me on, especially from guys like Norman, because you keep waiting for some slip-up so you can tell it's bullshit, or else it's real and you pick up some info.

She says she's thinking about it. She says she saved up some money so she's between careers. She even wanted to play the goddamn violin—took lessons and everything. But nothing.

Anyway, we're getting cozy—Monk comes back out. She keeps on with the Dubonnet and I'm sloshing down bourbon and waters like they're gonna ration the shit the next day. She's purring at me. Asking me about art. Asking me about my life.

She tells me she never married. That she lived with a few guys a couple times, but nothing serious. She's twenty-seven—just my age category. (Norman was thirty-seven then.) And man, once I got close to her, she looked even better. Smooth ivory skin. Pale lips. These blue-gray peepers that seemed like they wanted to change colors. And then Norman chugalugs. And a set of fuckin—he makes a cupping motion —breasts.

Basil and White turned and squinted at Norman at the same time. I was laughing, so it made a little sound of air rushing out between my teeth. We almost said at the same time. *Breasts?*

Wow, after the air, I let out what we all had got simultaneously. Hey, Norman, I've never heard you say "breasts" before. I thought them things upon the ladies' chests was boobs. Or boobies. Ain't that what he calls them?

Right.

Yep.

White and Basil chimed in.

Norman with a goddamn woman with some breasts is hard to take. It was White's most coherent statement of the evening.

There were breasts, lads. And he got another setup from John. John was shaking his head back and forth. Come on, Norman. Don't slow down now. Let's hear about the goddamn breasts, for Christ's sake!

By the end of Monk's set, we were both mellow. We already got the next day planned out. Lunch, a trip to my gallery, a show. More Monk and Trane the next night. Then she says, I think it's time to head in. If we get too drunk we'll only sleep.

It was the desired turning point of the story. All the circle of the narrated-to got closer, and armed with the last free drink, we licked our lips and waited for the next installment. Even Domenick, who was half-listening and half-trying to ignore Norman 'cause he didn't like him, cocked a blatant ear and dragged his eyes off a passing lady-painter's ass.

Yeh, she says that. I hadn't even asked to go to her place. But she just pops out with it—bam! Sleep, hell, hold on. I'm not in a sleepin' mood. Alcohol don't put me to sleep. It just makes me mean. And she laughed that low laugh and her eyes seemed to change colors. Like, like . . .

Like what? I was pressing.

No, let me finish.

Go ahead!

I like that in men, she says. Mean and very physical.

Wow, Basil said. Wow. She said very physical, huh? You shoulda called White.

Shaddup, drunk. Go on, Norman.

You're coming home with me, right? she says.

Hey, you ain't even told us the woman's name, I put in. It just occurred to me. Maybe this was the slip-up, I thought.

He don't wanna tell us her name because he wants to keep a good thing secret, Domenick spoke for the first time, a little ironically and a trifle sour.

Shaddup, Domenick, Basil grinned. You didn't tap nobody on the shoulder when that last fat ass floated by, either. Domenick was cooled out.

Monica. Monica Hess, Norman said straightforwardly.

Oh, a German babe. I came on with some academic shit.

Yeh, I guess, but she didn't press it. She said she'd grown up in a small town in the Midwest—in Ohio, actually. In fact, she comes from a town called Hess, Ohio, named after her fuckin grandfather.

Wow, we howled. That this bastard scored was the general sentiment. A fuckin painter and a rich bitch.

A rich sexy . . .

Beautiful.

Yeh.

Bitch.

Smoke would get in Norman's eyes and he'd squint. And you wouldn't really know sometimes what kind of expression was on his face.

She told me a lot about herself, her childhood. All the different careers. She said she couldn't find a man to satisfy her, either.

Wow, a general wow, came from us. And the anticipation hooked up together like a rope.

To satisfy her? White hunched Basil so sharply that Basil *ugghed* in drunken pantomime like it hurt. It did, but he was too drunk to care.

So you naturally volunteered for that gig, I chuckled.

Yeh. Norman was grinning now, a strange light in his eyes. Yeh, I volunteered alright. On the goddamn spot. My pecker was starting to rise like the fuckin flag on the 4th of July! So we get to her place, ya know? She lives on 4th Avenue.

Hey, you know they're going to call that Park Avenue South in a little while?

Fuck them. White spat. It's 4th Avenue, not no fuckin Park Avenue South!

Fuckin a tweety! Basil wet us with his affirmation.

Come on with the story, Norman. It was Domenick, maybe thinking Norman's ending would be so weak it would give the whole thing up as bullshit. Norman never even looked at him. He rasped at John through the open end of his lips. Buy the loud guy a drink on me.

Where on 4th Ave.?

You know the building that looks like a convent or tourist attraction in an old European village?

Yeh.

By the bookstore, across from the post office.

Yeh. Hey, that's a pretty heavy looking building.

What's the goddamn rent in there?

She says she pays 450 a month.

What? (And this was the early '60s when that was even further out than it is today.)

Four-fifty?

Jeez, what's in the goddamn place?

Hey, it's worth it. The inside of the joint is no quaint shit. It's super modern. (Norman used the French pronunciation so the whole effect was got.) And get this, there's a goddamn doorman inside. But we go around to a back entrance on Broadway she's got a key for. Go to an elevator, and get this—the elevator only stops at her floor.

Everybody was now sufficiently impressed. On the real side.

I pressed. You mean everybody in that joint got their own elevators?

I dunno. She says she dunno either. But she has.

Wow.

So we slide right in and up. The elevator door opens right into her apartment.

Yeh?

And it's laid out gorgeous. Rugs everywhere. Not the wall-to-wall, but different Indian and Persian rugs. Oriental rugs in different parts of a hardwood floor. She's got modern furniture in some rooms, old antiques in others. Glass and leather and plastic shit some places. Wood and easy-chairs other places. The living room is modern. She's got paintings everywhere.

Any of yours?

Yeh, yeh. She had a big orange painting that Castelli sold last year. It's called *Orange Laughter.* But she had a Kline, a Guston, a big De Kooning woman. A fuckin Larry Rivers naked woman.

Like the one he did of Frank with the dangling pecker?

No—it was more modest. Norman was being ironic. Hey, she had a Frankenthaler. A goddamn Rauschenberg. A Jasper Johns.

What the hell is this woman, a goddamn art buyer? Basil.

She's just got money, fool. White.

Art buyers got money.

I said, She told you she *saved* money? Ho ho ho!

No, she's loaded. It's maybe an eight-room apartment. A couple bedrooms, guest room, full kitchen. Books. Records. Big Fisher components. Speakers in all the rooms. She pushed a button and there's a goddamn Morty Feldman piano concerto on.

Fat-ass Morty!

So what happens, man? Shaddup, you guys!

We listen to Morty. We listen to Earl Brown. John Tudor and John Cage. Monk. We drink. We talk. The view is great—great! We lay in front of her goddamn fireplace. She even played some Basie and we danced. We talked and talked. And then we got undressed on the floor. What a body!

Everybody was pushed forward now, heads thrust at Norman like they could see the big pretty breasts and round peachlike behind. The long blond hair draped around her when she let it down, cushioning her head and neck and back, and the downstairs hair yellow too, and the odor coming out of her. Norman almost sung about her like some goose-pimpling eau de cologne called Fuck Me Now Immediately Daddy Do Not Dally Any Further!

So we did it first on the floor. She undressed like her clothes were burning her. But it was sexy, mate, I tell you. And there she was. And in a few seconds—

There were you, I shot in.

Yeh.

Laughter.

And what is there to say about big thighs pulling open of their own accord? And eyes hot as a weird blue stove?

Wow.

A couple hours later, we go again. She's quieter now, but clings real tight. She even dug her nails in my back just a little when the whistle blew.

Yeh, yeh, yeh! We whistled and beat on the chairs.

Yeh, Norman. Tell it. White wobbled.

And then just before we go to sleep—it's about 2 now—she tells me a little saying her mother told her. It went: No matter how much you might get hurt, there's love that can heal you.

Was it good, Norman? Basil smirked.

It was very, very good. Exquisite body. And she knew what she was doing. She knew all the right spots.

No matter how much you might hurt, I repeated, there's love that can heal you.

Yeh, I felt good. Hey, it was heavenly. Heavenly. And then she sang a little song. Some kind of folk tune. Maybe it was European, I dunno. I thought it was Mother Goose or something. No words, just humming and a kind of refrain she repeated.

Hey, man, that sounds great. White had stood up straight to speak. Getting as sober as he could for the official congratulations.

Heavy stuff, young Norman, I added.

Hooray for Norman! Basil sputtered. Not only do people buy his paintings, but he gets to fuck beautiful girls that sing, for Christ's sake! This tickled Domenick.

But then Norman looked at us with another thing in his face and voice. Yeh, it was good. I thought it was beautiful, the fire and all. I even picked her up and carried her and laid her in the big bed.

Hey, that's a line from Frank Yerby, I kibitzed him, admiringly so. Frank Yerby.

Yeh. Norman puffed and puffed on the cigarette now. And John had a big smile, pulling his head up and down slowly, affirming the reality of the tale.

But then I went to the window, finished another bourbon and smoked a Gauloise, and looked down at 4th Avenue.

It was that cool, huh?

Yeh. And after that, I went and lay down beside her. In the little night light, I could still see how beautiful she was, and I thought, Shit, it's my fuckin lucky period. Goddamn. So I lay out. I was painting pretty good. Another show in a couple months. A couple bucks in my pocket. And this fantastic sweet thing next to me in the half-dark.

Wow.

Norman got another drink and pulled himself straight.

Wow.

Yeh, wow, he said, his eyes clouding over like a windshield without a defroster on a suddenly frosty day. And then, about an hour or so later, I guess—I was sleeping—and I dunno, I just felt . . . Something just got in me. Something woke me up.

Uh-huh.

And I open my eyes, raise up a little in bed. My eyes had to get used to the half-dark. But I notice too that Monica is also raised up in bed. Full up. My eyes focus and I can suddenly see her. She's sitting there, man, straight up in bed . . . And she's got a pair of scissors held up in the air! And now she can see that I see her and our eyes meet.

What? It came from all of us at once, and the word just hung a second in the whistling smoke, half-crumpled and half-floated to the floor.

But I could tell—I could see—that Norman wasn't lying. He wasn't. And now he was repeating the last part again, so it could really penetrate.

Yeh, she was sitting there in the dark with a pair of fuckin scissors.

Why? Basil finally asked, almost sober now.

We looked at each other and at Norman.

Norman coughed from the smoke in his face, the cigarette still dangling. His eyes playing over us, convincing us without the least opposition. What you mean, Why? he was saying. How the fuck would I know? I sure as hell wasn't staying around to find out.

We all finally let it go, the caged-up air—the surrogate terror in it, and even an inch of curious delight. Norman's eyes glowed a little and he grinned the grin of the escaped hunter.

A cold glaze replaced his living eyes, and the ice of death came into his face. The cigarette should have dropped, but it was stuck to his bottom lip, even with his mouth hung open.

What's happening? I, the rest of us, looked at Norman, then turned to look over our shoulders. There was a blond woman now standing just inside the bar's entrance.

She began to walk toward us. I thought, Hey, now Norman's slip-up is coming right straight out with the lying shit. But Norman looked ashen. I didn't think a mere lie could do that. We were all starting to grin. I guess it had also occurred to the others too that what Norman had told us was a really well-told lie. And now, here was the chick in person to uncover the lie.

But before our smiles could tumble into place and replace our quizzical stares, Norman's ashen silence transmitted a howl of deep fear to us all. Not light-weight bullshit. So when we looked at the woman striding straight toward us, unnoticed by the rest of the raucous barflies, what we saw made us all believers. Believers forever in all the unknown spaces of terror, the blankness between the stars.

The bitch still had a pair of scissors in her hand. And as she came toward us, she held them up and waved them slowly back and forth, like a wand. But they were covered, even dripping, with very fresh blood.

5

The Screamers

Amiri Baraka

Lynn Hope adjusts his turban under the swishing red green yellow shadow lights. Dots. Suede heaven raining, windows yawning cool summer air, and his musicians watch him grinning, quietly, or high with wine blotches on four-dollar shirts. A yellow girl will not dance with me, nor will Teddy's people, in line to the left of the stage, readying their *Routines*. Haroldeen, the most beautiful, in her pitiful dead sweater. Make it yellow, wish it whole. Lights. Teddy, Sonny Boy, Kenny & Calvin, Scram, a few of Nat's boys jamming long washed handkerchiefs in breast pockets, pushing shirts into homemade cummerbunds, shuffling lightly for any audience.

"The Cross-Over," Deen laughing at us all. And they perform in solemn unison a social tract of love. (With no music till Lynn finishes "macking" with any biglipped Esther screws across the stage. White and green plaid jackets his men wear, and that twisted badge, black turban/on red string conked hair. (OPPRESSORS!) A greasy hipness, downness, nobody in our camp believed (having social-worker mothers and postman fathers; or living squeezed in lightskinned projects with adulterers and proud skinny ladies with soft voices). The theory, the spectrum, this sound baked inside their heads, and still rub sweaty against those lesser lights. Those niggers. Laundromat workers, beauticians, pregnant short-haired jail bait separated all ways from "us," but in this vat we sweated gladly for each other. And rubbed. And Lynn could be a common hero, from whatever side we saw him. Knowing that energy, and its response. That drained silence we had to make with our hands, leaving actual love to Nat or Al or Scram.

He stomped his foot, and waved one hand. The other hung loosely on his horn. And their turbans wove in among those shadows. Lynn's tighter, neater, and bright gorgeous yellow stuck with a green stone. Also, those green sparkling cubes dancing off his pinkies. A-boomp bahba bahba, A-boomp bahba bahba, A-boomp bahba bahba, A-boomp bahba bahba, the turbans sway behind him. And he grins before he lifts the horn, at Deen or drunk Becky, and we search the dark for girls.

Who would I get? (Not anyone who would understand this.) Some light girl who had fallen into bad times and ill-repute for dating Bubbles. And he fixed her later with his child, now she walks Orange St. wiping chocolate from its face. A disgraced white girl who learned to calypso in vocational school. Hence, behind halting speech, a humanity as paltry as her cotton dress. (And the big hats made a line behind her, stroking their erections, hoping for photographs to take down south.) Lynn would oblige. He would make the most perverted hopes sensual and possible. Chanting at that dark crowd. Or some girl, a wino's daughter, with carefully vaselined bow legs would drape her filthy angora against the cardboard corinthian, eyeing past any greediness a white man knows, my soft tyrolean hat, pressed corduroy suit, and "B" sweater. Whatever they meant, finally, to her, valuable shadows barely visible.

Some stuck-up boy with "good" hair. And as a naked display of America, for I meant to her that same oppression. A stunted head of greased glass feathers, orange lips, brown pasted edge to the collar of her dying blouse. The secret perfume of poverty and ignorant desire. Arrogant too, at my disorder, which calls her smile mysterious. Turning to be eaten by the crowd. That mingled foliage of sweat and shadows: *Night Train* was what they swayed to. And smelled each other in The Grind, The Rub, The Slow Drag. From side to side, slow or jerked staccato as their wedding dictated. Big hats bent tight skirts, and some light girls' hair swept the resin on the floor. Respectable ladies put stiff arms on your waist to keep some light between, looking nervously at an ugly friend forever at the music's edge.

I wanted girls like Erselle, whose father sang on television, but my hair was not straight enough, and my father never learned how to drink. Our house sat lonely and large on a half-Italian street, filled with important Negroes. (Though it is rumored they had a son, thin with big eyes, they killed because he was crazy.) Surrounded by the haughty daughters of depressed economic groups. They plotted in their projects for mediocrity, and the neighborhood smelled of their despair. And only the wild or the very poor thrived in Graham's or could be roused by Lynn's histories and rhythms. America had choked the rest, who could sit still for hours under popular songs, or be readied for citizenship by slightly bohemian social workers. They rivaled pure emotion with wind-up record players that pumped Jo Stafford into Home Economics rooms. And these carefully scrubbed children of my parents' friends fattened on their rhythms until they could join the Urban League or Household Finance and hound the poor for their honesty.

I was too quiet to become a murderer, and too used to extravagance for their skinny lyrics. They mentioned neither cocaine nor Bach, which was my reading, and the flaw of that society. I disappeared into the slums, and fell in love with violence, and invented for myself a mysterious economy of need. Hence, I shambled anonymously thru Lloyd's, The Nitecap, The Hi-Spot, and Graham's desiring everything I felt. In a new English overcoat and green hat, scouring that town for my peers. And they were old pinch-faced whores full of snuff and weak dope, celebrity fags with radio programs, mute bass players who loved me, and built the myth of my intelligence. You see, I left America on the first fast boat.

This was Sunday night, and the Baptists were still praying in their "fabulous" churches. Though my father sat listening to the radio, or reading pulp cowboy magazines, which I take in part to be the truest legacy of my spirit. God never had a chance. And I would be walking slowly toward The Graham, not even knowing how to smoke. Willing for any experience, any image, any further separation from where my good grades were sure to lead. Frightened of post offices, lawyer's offices, doctor's cars, the deaths of clean politicians. Or of the imaginary fat man, advertising cemeteries to his "good colored friends." Lynn's screams erased them all, and I thought myself intrepid white commando from the West. Plunged into noise and flesh, and their form become an ethic.

Now Lynn wheeled and hunched himself for another tune. Fast dancers fanned themselves. Couples who practiced during the week talked over their steps. Deen and her dancing clubs readied *avant-garde* routines. Now it was *Harlem Nocturne,* which I whistled loudly one Saturday in a laundromat, and the girl who stuffed in my khakis and stiff underwear asked was I a musician. I met her at Graham's that night and we waved, and I suppose she knew I loved her.

Nocturne was slow and heavy and the serious dancers loosened their ties. The slowly twisting lights made specks of human shadows, the darkness seemed to float around the hall. Any meat you clung to was yours those few minutes without interruption. The length of the music was the only form. And the idea was to press against each other hard, to rub, to shove the hips tight, and gasp at whatever passion. Professionals wore jocks against embarrassment. Amateurs, like myself, after the music stopped, put our hands quickly into our pockets, and retreated into the shadows. It was as meaningful as anything else we knew.

All extremes were popular with that crowd. The singers shouted, the musicians stomped and howled. The dancers ground each other past passion or moved so fast it blurred intelligence. We hated the popular song, and any freedman could tell you if you asked that white people danced jerkily, and were slower than our champions. One style, which developed as Italians showed up with pegs, and our own grace moved toward bellbottom pants to further complicate the cipher, was the honk. The repeated rhythmic figure, a screamed riff, pushed in its insistence past music. It was hatred and frustration, secrecy and despair. It spurted out of the diphthong culture, and reinforced the black cults of emotion. There was no compromise, no dreary sophistication, only the elegance of something that is too ugly to be described, and is diluted only at the agent's peril. All the saxophonists of that world were honkers, Illinois, Gator, Big Jay, Jug, the great sounds of our day. Ethnic historians, actors, priests of the unconscious. That stance spread like fire thru the cabarets and joints of the black cities, so that the sound itself became a basis for thought, and the innovators searched for uglier modes. Illinois would leap and twist his head, scream when he wasn't playing.

Gator would strut up and down the stage, dancing for emphasis, shaking his long gassed hair in his face and coolly mopping it back. Jug, the beautiful horn, would wave back and forth so high we all envied him his connection, or he'd stomp softly to the edge of the stage whispering those raucous threats. Jay first turned the mark around, opened the way further for the completely nihilistic act. McNeeley, the first Dada coon of the age, jumped and stomped and yowled and finally sensed the only other space that form allowed. He fell first on his knees, never releasing the horn, and walked that way across the stage. We hunched together drowning any sound, relying on Jay's contorted face for evidence that there was still music, though none of us needed it now. And then he fell backwards, flat on his back, with both feet stuck up high in the air, and he kicked and thrashed and the horn spat enraged sociologies.

That was the night Hip Charlie, the Baxter Terrace Romeo, got wasted right in front of the place. Snake and four friends mashed him up and left him for the ofays to identify. Also the night I had the gray bells and sat in the Chinese restaurant all night to show them off. Jay had set a social form for the poor, just as Bird and Dizzy proposed it for the middle class. On his back screaming was the Mona Lisa with the mustache, as crude and simple. Jo Stafford could not do it. Bird took the language, and we woke up one Saturday whispering *Ornithology*. Blank verse.

And Newark always had a bad reputation, I mean, everybody could pop their fingers. Was hip. Had walks. Knew all about The Apple. So I suppose when the word got to Lynn what Big Jay had done, he knew all the little down cats were waiting to see him in this town. He knew he had to cook. And he blasted all night, crawled and leaped, then stood at the side of the stand, and watched us while he fixed his sky, wiped his face. Watched us to see how far he'd gone, but he was tired and we weren't, which was not where it was. The girls rocked slowly against the silence of the horns, and big hats pushed each other or made plans for murder. We had not completely come. All sufficiently eaten by Jay's memory, "on his back, kicking his feet in the air, Go-ud Damn!" So he moved cautiously to the edge of the stage, and the gritty Muslims he played with gathered close. It was some mean honking blues, and he made no attempt to hide his intentions. He was breaking bad. "Okay, baby," we all thought. "Go for yourself." I was standing at the back of the hall with one arm behind my back, so the overcoat could hang over in that casual gesture of fashion. Lynn was moving, and the camel walkers were moving in the corners. The fast dancers and practicers making the whole hall dangerous. "Off my suedes, motherfucker." Lynn was trying to move us, and even I did the one step I knew, safe at the back of the hall. The hippies ran for girls. Ugly girls danced with each other. Skippy, who ran the lights, made them move faster in that circle on the ceiling, and darkness raced around the hall. Then Lynn got his riff, that rhythmic figure we knew he would repeat, the honked note that would be his personal evaluation of the world. And he screamed it so the veins in his face stood out like neon. "Uhh, yeh, Uhh, yeh, Uhh, yeh," we all screamed to push him further. So he opened his eyes for a second, and really made his move. He looked over his shoulder at the other turbans, then marched in time with his riff, on his toes across the stage. They followed; he marched across to the other side, repeated, then finally he descended, still screaming, into the crowd, and as the sidemen followed, we made a path for them around the hall. They were strutting, and all their horns held very high, and they were only playing that one scary note. They moved near the back of the hall, chanting and swaying, and passed right in front of me. I had a little cup full of wine a murderer friend of mine made me drink, so I drank it and tossed the cup in the air, then fell in line behind the last wild horn man, strutting like the rest of them. Bubbles and Rogie followed me, and four-eyed Moselle Boyd. And we strutted back and forth pumping our arms, repeating with Lynn Hope, "Yeh, Uhh, Yeh, Uhh." Then everybody fell in behind us, yelling still. There was confusion and stumbling, but there were no real fights. The thing they wanted was right there and easily accessible. No one could stop you from getting in that line. "It's too crowded. It's too many people on the line!" some people yelled. So Lynn thought further, and made to destroy the ghetto. We went out into the lobby and in perfect rhythm down the marble steps. Some musicians laughed, but Lynn and some others kept the note, till the others fell back in. Five or six hundred hopped-up woogies tumbled out into Belmont Avenue. Lynn marched right in the center of the street. Sunday night traffic stopped, and honked. Big Red yelled at a bus driver, "Hey, baby, honk that horn in time or shut it off!" The bus driver cooled it. We screamed and screamed at the clear image of ourselves as we should always be. Ecstatic, completed, involved in a secret communal expression. It would be the form of the sweetest revolution, to hucklebuck into the fallen capital, and let the oppressors lindy hop out. We marched all the way to Spruce, weaving among the stalled cars, laughing at the dazed white men who sat behind the wheels. Then Lynn turned and we strutted back toward the hall. The late show at the National was turning out, and all the big hats there jumped right in our line.

Then the Nabs came, and with them, the fire engines. What was it, a labor riot? Anarchists? A nigger strike? The paddy wagons and cruisers pulled in from both sides, and sticks and billies started flying, heavy streams of water splattering the marchers up and down the street. America's responsible immigrants were doing her light work again. The knives came out, the razors, all the Biggers who would not be bent, counterattacked or came up behind the civil servants smashing at them with coke bottles and aerials. Belmont writhed under the dead economy and splivs floated in the gutters, disappearing under cars. But for a while, before the war had reached its peak, Lynn and his musicians, a few other fools, and I, still marched, screaming thru the maddened crowd. Onto the sidewalk, into the lobby, halfway up the stairs, then we all broke our different ways, to save whatever it was each of us thought we loved.

6

Singing Dinah's Song

Frank London Brown

A Gypsy woman once told me. She said: "Son, beware of the song that will not leave you."

But then I've never liked Gypsy women no way, which is why I was so shook when my buddy Daddy-o did his number the other day. I mean his natural number.

You see, I work at Electronic Masters, Incorporated, and well, we don't make much at this joint although if you know how to talk to the man you might work up to a dollar and a half an hour.

Me, I work on a punch press. This thing cuts steel sheets and molds them into shells for radio and television speakers. Sometimes when I'm in some juice joint listening to Dinah Washington and trying to get myself together, I get to thinking about all that noise that that big ugly punch press makes, and me sweating and scuffing, trying to make my rates, and man I get *eeevil*!

This buddy of mine though, he really went for Dinah Washington; and even though his machine would bang and scream all over the place and all those high-speed drills would whine and cry like a bunch of sanctified soprano church-singers, this fool would be in the middle of all that commotion just singing Dinah Washington's songs to beat the band. One day I went up and asked this fool what in the world was he singing about; and he looked at me and tucked his thumbs behind his shirt collar and said: "Baby, I'm singing Dinah's songs. Ain't that broad mellow?"

Well, I. Really, all I could say was: "Uh, why yes."

And I went back to my machine.

It was one of those real hot days when it happened: about ten-thirty in the morning. I was sweating already. Me and that big ugly scoundrel punch press. Tussling. Lord, I was so beat. I felt like singing Dinah's songs myself. I had even started thinking in rhythm with those presses banging down on that steel: *sh-bang boom bop! Sh, bang boom bop, sh'bang boom bop.* Then all of a sudden:

In walks Daddy-o!

My good buddy. Sharp? You'd better believe it; dark blue single breast, a white on white shirt, and a black and yellow rep tie! Shoes shining like new money. And that pearl gray hat kinda pulled down over one eye. I mean to tell you, that Negro was sharp.

I was way behind on my quota because, you see, fooling around with those machines is *not* no play thing. You just get tired sometimes and fall behind. But I just *had* to slow down to look at my boy.

James, that was his real name. We call him Daddy-o because he's so. I don't know; there just ain't no other name would fit him. Daddy-o's a long, tall, dark cat with hard eyes and a chin that looks like the back end of a brick. Got great big arms and a voice like ten lions. Actually, sometimes Daddy-o scares you.

He walked straight to his machine. Didn't punch his time card or nothing. I called him: "Hey, Daddy-o, you must have had a good one last night. What's happening?"

Do you know that Negro didn't open his mouth?

"Hey, Daddy-o, how come you come strolling in here at ten-thirty? We start at seven-thirty around this place!"

Still no answer.

So this cat walks over to his machine and looks it up and down and turns around and heads straight for the big boss's office. Well, naturally I think Daddy-o's getting ready to quit, so I kind of peeps around my machine so that I can see him better.

He walked to the big boss's office and stopped in front of the door and lit a cigarette smack-dab underneath the "No Smoking" sign. Then he turned around like he had changed his mind about quitting and headed back to his machine. Well, I just started back to work. After all it's none of my business if a man wants to work in his dark blue suit and a white on white shirt with his hat on.

By this time Charlie walked up just as Daddy-o started to stick his hand into the back of the machine.

Charlie liked to busted a blood vessel. "Hey, what the hell are you doing? You want to 'lectrocute yourself?"

Now I don't blame Charlie for hollering. Daddy-o knows that you can get killed sticking your hand in the back of a machine. Everybody in the plant knows that.

Daddy-o acted like he didn't hear Charlie, and he kept right on reaching into the hole. Charlie ran up and snatched Daddy-o's hand back. Daddy-o straightened up, reared back and filled his chest with a thousand pounds of air: one foot behind him and both of those over-sized fists doubled up. Charlie cleared his throat and started feeling around in his smock like he was looking for something, which I don't think he was.

Pretty soon Mr. Grobber, the big boss, walked up. One of the other foremen came up and then a couple of set-up men from another department. They all stood around Daddy-o and he just stood there cool, smoking one of those long filter-tips. He started to smile, like he was bashful. But whenever anyone went near the machine, he filled up with more air and got those big ham-fists ready.

Well after all, Daddy-o was my buddy and I couldn't just let all those folks surround him without doing something, so I turned my machine off and walked over to where they were crowding around him.

"Daddy-o, what's the matter, huh? You mad at somebody, Daddy-o?"

Mr. Grobber said: "James, if you don't feel well, why don't you just go home and come in tomorrow?"

All Daddy-o did was to look slowly around the plant. He looked at each one of us. A lot of the people in the shop stopped working and were looking back at him. Others just kept on working. But he looked at them, kind of smiling, like he had a feeling for each and every one of them.

Then quick like a minute, he spread his legs out, and stretched his arms in front of the machine like it was all he had in this world.

I tried once again to talk to him.

"Aww come on, Daddy-o. Don't be that way."

That Negro's nose started twitching. Then he tried to talk but his breath was short like he had been running or something.

"Ain't nobody getting this machine. I own this machine, baby. This is mine. Ten years! On this machine. Baby, this belongs to me."

"I know it do, Daddy-o. I know it do."

Charlie Wicowycz got mad hearing him say that, so he said, "Damn," and started into Daddy-o. Daddy-o's eyes got big and he drew his arm back and kind of stood on his toes and let out a holler like, like I don't know what.

"Doonnnn't you touch this machiiinnneeeee!"

Naturally Charlie stopped, then he started to snicker and play like he was tickled except his face was as white as a fish belly. I thought I would try, so I touched Daddy-o's arm. It was hard like brick. I let his arm go.

"Daddy-o man, I know how you feel. Let me call your wife so she can come and get you. You'll be all right tomorrow. What's your phone number, Daddy-o? I'll call your wife for you, hear?"

His eyes started twitching and he started blinking like he was trying to keep from crying. Still he was smiling that little baby-faced smile.

"Daddy-o, listen to me. Man, I ain't trying to do nothing to you. Give me your number and your wife will know what to do."

His lips started trembling. Big grown man, standing there with his lips trembling. He opened his mouth. His whole chin started trembling as he started to speak: "Drexel."

I said: "Okay, Drexel. Now Drexel what?"

"*Drexel.*"

"Drexel what else, Daddy-o?"

"Drexel seven-two-three."

"Seven-two-three. What else Daddy-o? Man, I'm trying to help you. I'm going to call your wife. She'll be here in a few minutes. Drexel seven-two-three, what else? What is the rest of your phone number. Daddy-o! I'm talkin' to you!"

"Eight-eight-eight-eight-nine."

"Drexel seven-two-three-eight-nine? That it, Daddy-o?"

Mr. Grabber started walking around scratching his stomach. He stopped in front of Charlie Wicowycz. "Call the police, Charlie."

Charles left.

The other foremen went back to their departments. The setup men followed them. Mr. Grobber, seeing that he was being left alone with Daddy-o, went back to his office.

Daddy-o just stood there smiling.

I ran to the office and called the number he had given me. Daddy-o's wife wasn't home, but a little girl who said that she was Daddy-o's "Babygirl" answered and said that she would tell her mother as soon as she came home from work.

When I walked out of the office, the police were there. I thought about the time I had to wait three hours for the police to get to my house the time somebody broke in and took every stitch I had. One of the cops, a big mean-looking something with ice-water eyes, moved in on Daddy-o with his club out and Daddy-o just shuffled his feet, doubled up his fists and waited for him.

I started talking up for my boy.

"Officer, please don't hurt him. He's just sick. He won't do no harm."

"Who are you? Stay outa."

I tried to explain to him. "Look, Officer, just let me talk to him. I . . . I'm his friend."

"All right. Talk to him. Tell him to get into the wagon."

I touched Daddy-o's arm again. He moved it away, still smiling. I said: "Man, Daddy-o, come on now. Come on, go with me. I know how it is. I know how it is."

He still had that smile. I swear I could have cried.

I started walking, pulling his arm a bit.

"Come on, Daddy-o."

He came along easy, still smiling, and walking with a kind of strut. Looking at each and every one of us like we were his best friends. When we got to the door, he stopped and looked back at his machine. Still smiling. When we got outside, I led him right up to the wagon. The back door was open and it was dark in there. Some dusty light scooted through a little window at the back of the wagon that had a wire grating in it. It didn't look very nice in there. I turned to Daddy-o.

"Come on, Daddy-o. The man said you should get in. Ain't nothing going to git you, Daddy-o. Come on, man. Get in."

I felt like anybody's stoolie.

"Come on, get in."

He started moving with me, then he stopped and looked back at the plant. One of the officers touched his arm. And that's when he did his natural number.

He braced his arms against the door. And started to scream to bust his lungs: "That *is* my machine. I *own*. Me and *this* machine is *blood* kin. Don't none of you somitches touch it. You *heah*? You, you *heah*?"

The water-eyed policeman started to agree with Daddy-o.

"Sure, kid. You *know* it. Lotsa machines. You got lots of 'em."

Daddy-o turned to look at him at the same time his partner gave him a shove. The water-eyed policeman shoved him too. Daddy-o swung at him and missed. When he did that, the water-eyed policeman chunked him right behind the ear and Daddy-o fell back into the wagon. Both policemen grabbed his feet and pushed him past the door and the water-eye slammed it.

They jumped in and started to drive away. Daddy-o was up again and at the window. He was hollering, and his voice got mixed up with the trucks and cars that went by. I watched the wagon huff out of sight and I went back into the plant.

Inside, I got to thinking about how sharp Daddy-o was. I was real proud of that. I caught sight of Daddy-o's machine. You know that thing didn't look right without Daddy-o working on it?

I got to thinking about my machine and how I know that big ugly thing better than I know most live people. Seemed funny to think that it wasn't really mine. It sure *seemed* like mine.

Ol' Daddy-o was sure crazy about Dinah Washington. Last few days that's all he sang: her songs. Like he was singing in place of crying; like being in the plant made him sing those songs and like finally the good buddy couldn't sing hard enough to keep up the dues on his machine and then . . . Really.

You know what? Looking around there thinking about Daddy-o and all, I caught myself singing a song that had been floating around in my head.

It goes: "*I got bad news, baby, and you're the first to know.*"

That's one of Dinah Washington's songs.

7

A Woman Who Plays Trumpet Is Deported

Michelle Cliff

This story is dedicated to the memory of Valaida Snow, trumpet-player, who was liberated—or escaped—from a concentration camp. She weighed sixty-five pounds. She died in 1956 of a cerebral hemorrhage. This was inspired by her story, but it is an imagining.

She came to me in a dream and said: "Girl, you have no idea how tough it was. I remember once Billie Holiday was lying in a field of clover. Just resting. And a breeze came and the pollen from the clover blew all over her and the police came out of nowhere and arrested her for possession.

"And the stuff was red . . . it wasn't even white."

A woman. A black woman. A black woman musician. A black woman musician who plays trumpet. A bitch who blows. A lady trumpet-player. A woman with chops.

It is the thirties. She has been fairly successful. For a woman, black, with an instrument not made of her. Not made of flesh but of metal.

Her father told her he could not afford two instruments for his two children and so she would have to learn her brother's horn.

This woman tucks her horn under her arm and packs a satchel and sets her course. Paris first.

This woman flees to Europe. No, *flee* is not the word. Escape? Not quite right.

She wants to be let alone. She wants them to stop asking for vocals in the middle of a riff. She wants them to stop calling her *novelty, wonder,* chasing after her orchid-colored Mercedes looking for a lift. When her husband gets up to go, she tosses him the keys, tells him to have it washed every now and then, the brass eyeballs polished every now and then—reminds him it's unpaid for and wasn't her idea anyway.

She wants a place to practice her horn, to blow. To blow rings around herself. So she blows the USA and heads out. On a ship.

And this is not one of those I'm travelin'-light-because-my-man-has-gone situations—no, that mess ended a long time before. He belongs in an orchid-colored Mercedes—although he'll probably paint the damn thing gray. It doesn't do for a man to flaunt, he would say, all the while choosing her dresses and fox furs and cocktail rings.

He belongs back there; she doesn't.

The ship is French. Families abound. The breeze from the ocean rosying childish cheeks, as uniformed women stand by, holding shuttlecocks, storybooks, bottles. Women wrapped in tricolor robes sip bouillion. Men slap cues on the shuffle-board court, disks skimming the polished deck. Where—and this is a claim to fame—Josephine Baker once walked her ocelot or leopard or cheetah.

A state of well-being describes these people, everyone is groomed, clean, fed. She is not interested in them, but glad of the calm they convey. She is not interested in looking into their staterooms, or their lives, to hear the sharp word, the slap of a hand across a girl's mouth, the moans of intimacy.

The ship is French. The steward assigned to her, Senegalese.

They seek each other out by night, after the families have retired. They meet in the covered lifeboats. They communicate through her horn and by his silver drum.

He noticed the horn when he came the very first night at sea to turn down her bed. Pointed at it, her. The next morning introduced her to his drum.

The horn is brass. The drum, silver. Metal beaten into memory, history. She traces her hand along the ridges of silver—horse, spear, warrior. Her finger catches the edge of a breast; lingers. The skin drumhead as tight as anything.

In the covered lifeboats by night they converse, dispersing the silence of the deck, charging the air, upsetting the complacency, the well-being that hovers, to return the next day.

Think of this as a reverse middle passage.

Who is to say he is not her people?

Landfall.

She plays in a club in the Quartier Latin. This is not as simple as it sounds. She got to the club through a man who used to wash dishes beside Langston Hughes at Le Grand Due who knew a woman back then who did well who is close to Bricktop who knows the owner of the club. The trumpet player met the man who used to wash dishes who now waits tables at another club. They talked and he said, "I know this woman who may be able to help you." Maybe it was simple, lucky. Anyway, the trumpet player negotiated the chain of acquaintance with grace; got the gig.

The air of the club is blue with smoke. Noise. Voices. Glasses do clink. Matches and lighters flare. The pure green of absinthe grows cloudy as water is added from a yellow ceramic pitcher.

So be it.

She lives in a hotel around the corner from the club, on the Rue de l'Université. There's not much to the room: table, chair, bed, wardrobe, sink. She doesn't spend much time there. She has movement. She walks the length and breadth of the city. Her pumps crunch against the gravel paths in the parks. Her heels click along the edge of the river. All the time her mind is on her music. She is let alone.

She takes her meals at a restaurant called Polidor. Her food is set on a white paper-covered table. The lights are bright. She sits at the side of a glass-fronted room, makes friends with a waitress and practices her French. *Friends* is too strong; they talk. Her horn is swaddled in purple velvet and rests on a chair next to her, next to the wall. Safe.

Of course, people stare occasionally, those to whom she is unfamiliar. Once in a while someone puts a hand to a mouth to whisper to a companion. Okay. No one said these people were perfect. She is tired—too tired—of seeing the gape-mouthed darky advertising *Le*

Joyeux Nègre. Okay? Looming over a square by the Pantheon in all his happy-go-luckiness.

While nearby a Martiniquan hawked *L'Étudiant Noir.*

Joyeux Négritude.

A child points to the top of his *crème brulée* and then at her, smiles. Okay.

But no one calls her nigger. Or asks her to leave. Or asks her to sit away from the window at a darker table in the back by the kitchen, hustling her so each course tumbles into another. *Crudités* into *timbale* into *caramel.*

This place suits her fine.

The piano player longs for a baby part-*Africaine.* She says no. Okay.

They pay her to play. She stays in their hotel. Eats their food in a clean, well-lighted place. Pisses in their toilet.

No strange fruit hanging in the Tuileries.

She lives like this for a while, getting news from home from folks who pass through. Asking, "When you coming back?"

"Man, no need for that."

Noting that America is still TOBA (tough on black asses), lady trumpet players still encouraged to vocalize, she remains. She rents a small apartment on Montparnasse, gets a cat, gives her a name, pays an Algerian woman to keep house.

All is well. For a while.

1940. The club in the Quartier Latin is shut tight. Doors boarded. The poster with her face and horn torn across. No word. No word at all. Just murmurs.

The owner has left the city on a freight. He is not riding the rails. Is not being chased by bad debts. He is standing next to his wife, her mother, their children, next to other women, their husbands, men, their wives, children, mothers-in-law, fathers, fathers-in-law, mothers, friends.

The club is shut. This is what she knows. But rumors and murmurs abound.

The piano player drops by the hotel, leaves a note. She leaves Paris. She heads north.

She gets a gig in Copenhagen, standing in for a sister moving out—simple, lucky—again. Safe. Everyone wore the yellow star there—for a time.

1942. She is walking down a street in Copenhagen. The army of occupation picks her up. Not the whole army—just a couple of kids with machine guns.

So this is how it's done.

She found herself in a line of women. And girls. And little children.

The women spoke in languages she did not understand. Spoke them quietly. From the tone she knew they were encouraging their children. She knows—she who has studied the nuance of sound.

Her horn tucked tight under her armpit. Her only baggage.

The women and girls and little children in front of her and behind her wore layers of clothing. It was a warm day. In places seams clanked. They carried what they could on their persons.

Not all spoke. Some were absolutely silent. Eyes moved into this strange place.

Do you know the work of Beethoven?

She has reached the head of the line and is being addressed by a young man in English. She cannot concentrate. She sweats through the velvet wrapped around her horn. All around her women and girls and little children—from which she is apart, yet of—are being taken in three different directions. And this extraordinary question.

A portrait on a schoolteacher's wall. Of a wiry-haired, beetle-browed man. And he was a colored genius, the teacher told them, and the children shifted in their seats.

Telemann? He wrote some fine pieces for the horn.

The boy has detected the shape of the thing under her arm.

She stares and does not respond. How can she?

The voices of women and girls and little children pierce the summer air as if the sound was being wrenched from their bodies. The sun is bright. Beads of sweat gather at the neck of the young man's tunic.

It should not be hot. It should be drear. Drizzle. Chill. But she knows better. The sun stays bright.

In the distance is a mountain of glass. The light grazes the surface and prisms split into color.

Midden. A word comes to her. The heaps of shells, bones and teeth. Refuse of the Indians. The mound-builders. That place by the river just outside of town—filled with mystery and childhood imaginings.

A midden builds on the boy's table, as women and girls and little children deposit their valuables.

In the distance another midden builds.

Fool of a girl, she told herself. To have thought she had seen it all. Left it—the worst piece of it—behind her. The body burning—ignited by the tar. The laughter and the fire. And her inheriting the horn.

8

Jazz at Twelve

Wanda Coleman

We arrive before the room fills.

We're decades away from Naptown. We're at Billy D's off the Gold Coast in Malibu. We're dressed in our snazziest. Kevin wears the bronze silk tie I bought him for our first anniversary. We are here for the James Ditzi Quintet, Frank Lattimore on drums. Our main reason for coming is Frank's invitation. Frank and Kevin are running buddies. In his day, not too long ago, Frank was known as one of the greatest stickmen alive. Kevin talks about Frank constantly.

What I don't know is Frank's still shooting up.

We look around. It's a wide space. Roughhewn posts and wood floor-to-ceiling make it cozy, covelike, a ritzy pirates' den. The west wall is all glass and wood columns lined with tiny cocktail tables for two off the main room. I pick one in the middle. Kevin prefers the patio deck outside. There are three tables set for adventuresome listeners, but I seem to chill easily of late and prefer sitting inside. Besides, I'm definitely interested in hearing the music full range.

My name is Babe. I'm Kevin's wife.

They play James Ditzi a lot on KJAS. He's hot for the moment. I think that's nice, a guy in his late fifties getting that kind of public relations. Especially a White Guy. What we Blacks do to The Music leaves scant unexplored. But James has his own signature. Not too many new music guitarists get major radio play. In these days of pop-disco-rock, it's tough for jazzniks to draw. They don't teach music appreciation in grade school anymore. A whole generation has grown up without proper ears.

Frank's damned near the same age as James but has had it harder if looks tell. Frank is tall, tan and lanky with restless arms and elegantly fingered hands. He carries himself like a man who schmoozes for a living. The man was already legend where I grew up. Then one day here he is marching into my living room, trailing Kevin. Stumbling yet. High as in cosmic, his blueringed brown irises juiced out at me from under savvy lids. I took one look at him, got instantly evil and hissed at Kevin.

"Don't bring that scroungy nigger in my house unless he's sober."

This motivated Kevin's tall explaining. That night I find out "the world's greatest drummer" works for the same delivery service that's just hired Kevin. He's wowed by the man. When he talks, his hazel eyes spark as if personally tripping with Frank through every boo joint from Harlem to St. Louis. Kevin promises next time Frank will mind his Ps and Qs. He'll see to it. But in the meantime, Frank did this. One time Frank did that. Frank went here-and-there. Frank also played with other greats including bassist Spence Alcohol, and even recorded with "the S.A." on the old Spasmic label. Frank's given Kevin a couple of his mint LPs and a couple of bootlegged vinyls. Sometimes after dinner we fire up and listen. I watch Kevin glow, wishing he could travel backwards in time.

Other reasons I don't like Frank include his cavalier attitude. Like too many musicians of his colored generation he's full of self-hate and self-delusion. It makes him need to indulge his weaknesses—dope and disrespecting women. Plus he's bought the lie that one plays better if one's high. He still conks hair that hasn't had the decency to get gray. And he prefers White women. Blonde if possible. Frank will accept a sistuh when times are hard, but she's got to be fair-skinned. He used to shack with Kevin's mother in the days when she was light enough to pass. Kevin takes after her, but on the olive side, with wavy mink hair slicked back in a foot-long ponytail.

So Frank is the closest thing Kevin's ever had to Daddy.

What I don't know is that in a week or two Spence Alcohol will show up and start to wear the nap off my sofa. He's a honey-skinned bear of a "Black Irishman" who shares Frank's taste in women. He will have just hit the streets, residing at a Hollywood halfway house until his parole officer is placated or until his new lady makes up her mind to marry and support him. He will leave L.A. for Portland in the very near future and will die there before the turn of the century. In the meanwhile, I will make the mistake of thinking Spence is cut out of better rag than Frank. Sometimes I forget the one about birds of like feather. Spence is still strung out also, but doesn't shoot it anymore. He smokes it Vietnamese-style.

Our breath is taken by the mauve and gold sunset. Too-blue water laps the shore at our sand-level window. We watch it recede, lulled into its rhythm. Billy D's is a relatively new place on the booming coast.

They're playing vintage Mr. Ellington softly over the PA.

The waiter comes over. I do rapid calculations and figure that by careful nursing we can make Mr. D's mandatory two-drink minimum. Kevin reads me and smirks. He looks at the waiter.

"We're special guests of Frank's."

The waiter gives back the appropriate grimace then takes our orders for a rum and coke duet.

There's noise at the entrance and James appears followed by his young, black-haired roadie. Lights come on behind Kevin's eyes. One of his not-so-secret ambitions is to be a roadie. Frank's roadie. But Frank's touring days are over, sporadic local gigs his limit. Without a word Kevin goes over to the bandstand, introduces himself, and offers to help set things up. James shakes his hand and accepts. I spy for a beat. Our drinks arrive. I watch the icy dew form on Kevin's glass. I ordered mine without ice. Cold liquids bother me lately, set my teeth on edge.

I don't know I'm pregnant.

Kevin and I are holed up on the upper story of a mid-city four-plex. Our one-bedroom deathtrap rental elicits romantic nods of approval from friends and dread from my parents. It's a funky vermin-ridden cavern owned by a merciless survivor of Treblinka. On the first day of every month I curse the Nazis for having bled the humanity out of her. She insists on cash payment and I insist on receipts. When I put the money in her talons my eyes are invariably drawn to the sea-gray numbers swimming in liver spots, blood warts, moles, assorted scars and blotches.

I work the ten-key punch from nine-to-five for a medical supply outfit. My wage—slave pay—barely keeps us in rent, utilities and food when Kevin doesn't work. When he does, we manage to have a few extras, go out more, dream a little. Of course I see to all the duns. I'm not stingy, just cautious. It's always a bitch on the meatless end of the bone. I worry as I scrimp. But even when things are tight, I make a special effort to budget Kevin pocket money. He'd rather make his own, does when he can, but there are economic limits on unskilled high school grads. At least I've got office and accounting skills. Since we've been together Kevin's rarely kept a job longer than three or four months.

What I don't know is that my rare coin collection will turn up missing in a couple of months. It will be followed by a disappearance of the cash I had hidden in a sealed envelope behind the oranging Modigliani print over the living room couch.

I don't crab about Kevin's smoking habit. He's made several attempts to turn me on, but I seem to have some strange immunity. He's quit trying to educate me into it and either smokes alone or with the guys. Even so, I have no objections to living a little bit outside The Law, just enough to mute survival pressures.

Once in a while Kevin comes up with a kilo of sans. He breaks down the brick of weed, cleans it, and bags it into lids. He keeps a couple of ounces for his personal stash then barters the rest. We burn the cash on clothes, auto repairs and other needs. One time he bought himself a very used electric bass guitar. The last time he bought me an eighteen-carat gold slave bracelet. A year from now I will pawn it at less than a quarter of its worth to buy antibiotics for the baby.

The sun has set in the Pacific. The room is slightly cooler and the waitress is lighting the little red candle lamps on each table. This is the way to groove, I think, in no rush, unconcerned. One thought meandering after another. I watch Kevin clown with James on the bandstand. He admires the electric guitars and mandolin. James laughs as Kevin bows his legs and pretends to strum the mandolin, his eyes skyward, doing his Hendrix imitation. Kevin would sell his soul for the ability to play. But all he can do is admire the talent of others. He's a freak for most kinds of music and likes all of it loud. We have quite a sound system at home, one of those quadrasonic models that makes sound travel around the room, speaker to speaker.

Kevin hates it when I'm cynical about the music business. The chilly fickle industry, which has marginalized me, fails to stem his childlike worship. "Music is my religion," he told me one night as we made love to Pink Floyd.

What I don't know is Kevin's got another habit. He hides his outfit behind the old forty-fives I never play anymore in the bottom of the record cabinet. During a snit of spring fever I will find the cotton balls, the test tube, the syringe and the rubber hose.

When Kevin comes in nights, he's fairly wired. He likes running the streets, so a job making deliveries suits him. He prides himself on having learned every shortcut in Los Angeles. The company he works for is so ramshackle that benefits are minimal. There's no accident or medical insurance coverage, and don't even dare think dental. Kevin drives a funked up little black Dodge Dart. He's put a citizen's band radio in it and spruced it up with mud flaps, a new set of fat gangster whitewalls and chromespoked rims. He plans to have the windows tinted. There's a black and yellow bumper sticker that reads, "Mafia Staff Car."

What we don't know is that three weeks from now we will go to The Pandemonium to see a play by Mtui Sambusa, the Black feminist poet. It's another culturally correct event we'll sacrifice to see at my insistence. I will cry in my seat. Kevin will comfort me. When we exit to the theatre parking lot we will find the window of his Dart smashed. The CB will be ripped out of the dash and the tires will be missing—rims and all. Kevin will talk the parking lot attendant into letting us leave the car there overnight. Spence Alcohol will drive Kevin to the junkyard the next morning for rusted replacement rims and retreads.

I sit at an angle facing the bandstand. I look up and see James Ditzi trailing Kevin to our table. In a funny way, Kevin likes to brag about having me as his wife. I moonlight as a songwriter. Ten years ago I lucked into a musician's workshop and became the hit of their Tuesday night showcase. One of my songs was picked up by a major rhythm-and-blues star who was scouting incognito. Within the year my opus bulleted up the charts and went semi-solid gold. I made a nice piece of coin on the publishing—enough for two years without having to "sweat the man." I thought my career was made. I didn't know about one-hit wonders.

James has heard my name around, he says. He's even had three or four occasions to play jazz renditions of my song, "Too Bad for Me." I smile appropriately ladylike and thank him. He's scared I'm going to reach into my tote and abracadabra lead sheets. But I keep my hands nested around my drink. He relaxes when he sees he's not being hustled. There's a big half laugh, half bark across the room and we look up to see Mr. Spence making his way towards us. He and James Ditzi go all the way back to a one-night stand in Jersey. Kevin makes sure I'm introduced. Spence has heard of me also.

We exchange a bit of loose industry chitchat. Then James goes out back to talk money. Spence goes with him to meet Mr. Billy D, who's enclaved in his very private office. I've heard Mr. D doesn't mingle with us nobodies.

What we don't know is that the weather will be unusual this winter. There will be volcanic action in Hawaii and monsoon-like swells off the coast of Southern California. A few wealthy seaside dwellers will lose their dream homes. A couple of cliff-side mansions will be splashed onto Pacific Coast Highway by heavy rainfall. A couple of sturdy piers will be washed away. Billy D's will be flooded and by Christmas its doors will forever shut.

The rest of the combo shows. Piano is Jefty Lerner, swift, small-boned, and smart in Ben Franks and a three-piece suit. All the men are suited. But Jefty looks like he should be teaching high school English somewhere. Then Robin Roy shows, the very tall, very bulky, cask-chested reedman who reddens when he blows. He looks like James Ditzi's younger, stouter brother. He favors dark solid colors while James is vested under fine pinstripes and a crisp white dress shirt with studs. There's Clark Wiggins, a horn man obviously under the influence of Miles Davis. They begin tuning up and the evening's patrons gradually spill into the room.

Kevin's out of things to do and sits across from me with a mild case of jitters, eager to see Frank. He's started firing cigarettes, one after the other. Every few seconds he turns and scans the room, exit to exit. Early is a word foreign to Frank's vocabulary. The only time he's prompt is when it's time to score.

Becky, Frank's "main squeeze," he likes to call her, shows up. She's a slight but sturdy, freckle-skinned blonde young enough to be Kevin's half-sister. She's riding with her even younger brother. They have to flash IDs before Security allows them to sit. She waves at James then spots

Kevin and comes over to our table to say hello. We've met before and I'm always friendly; nevertheless, she's acutely aware of my prejudice, though no one else seems to notice. She's a dispatcher for the same delivery company employing Frank and Kevin. After pleasantries, Becky steers her brother to a front table near where the drums will sit.

What she doesn't know is that three days from now she'll place a frantic call to Kevin, out of her skull because Frank's been arrested for beating her. Neighbors will have complained and the police will be only too willing to oblige, especially after making note of Frank's new tracks. She's so much in love she will refuse to press charges but they'll hold him on an old drug beef. What I don't know is that I'll be feeling generous enough to reach deep into my emergency stash for Frank's bail.

A pretty brown-skinned woman about my age goes up to James and they rap a bit. She's a singer copping the chops of The Fancy Miss Nancy from frosted fried hairdo to choreographed hand movements. She even mimics that cool, frozen Las Vegas smile. I pray she won't sing "All in Love Is Fair." I'm still in my late Billie Holiday phase, although I'm starting to look more like a slightly pudgy Lena Horne.

Kevin jumps to his feet and rushes across the room. Frank has just come in, lugging one of his drums. He's wearing white work gloves to protect his hands. I wonder how he manages to get all his equipment into that torn-up old Volks. I watch as he lowers the drum, pockets the gloves, and exchanges hand slaps with Kevin. Then I watch as Kevin hoists the drum into its place on the bandstand while Frank watches, smiling.

Becky scurries over and gives Frank a big rub-a-dub hug. He kisses her on the nose then pats her rear as she scoots back to her table. Spence joins them and the room momentarily fills with staccatos of laughter. The S.A. points to the bar where he'll anchor for the evening. Then Kevin and Frank go back outside to finish unloading.

I take out the little leatherette notebook I always carry in my tote. Should a few notes start to kick around inside my head I like to be ready. Or should the opening words of a lyric—or even a refrain—find their way to my mind's ear. I keep my little books of songs ritualistically. I date them and make notes as to when and where they're composed. I'm living for the day when women's music will receive as much attention as men's or dying for the day of my posthumous discovery by some lover of innovative fusion. In the interim, dolor in lieu of fame does. Taking the bus to and from the job does. Relying on someone else to pick up the tab on nights like this does. Living on the edge of Kevin's fear does.

Tune-up ends and serious business begins. Instantly the room is transformed. This could be The Five Spot. This could be Birdland. This could be a maiden voyage on a spaced-out ship into the inner regions of night. Kevin is sitting across from me now. He's giving me his moonful look, the one that tells me I'm beautiful. Whenever he does, I suddenly hear Nat King Cole singing "Angel Eyes."

I feel the words of a lyric forming. Kevin watches, thoughtfully smoking a cigarette as I write. I know there's a joint in the glove compartment for the drive home. I glance ocean-ward from time-to-time and refresh my inspiration in the window light dancing on the tide. The words flow as smoothly as the opening number "Eleanor Rigby."

James dominates the set then gives each artist a little taste. Frank is the essence of mellow and evokes a couple of throaty enthusiastic "yeahs," one of them Kevin's.

The guest, "Miss Fancy" lady vocalist, rises, steps to the bandstand and after a brief introduction, eases her way to the mike. Very sweetly, James chords the opening of "My Funny Valentine." She's not bad at all and, after a significant career move, will someday be a major league contralto. I go fluttery inside and fall into Kevin's orbs as she wrings out my heart.

What I don't know is that soon after the baby arrives Kevin will take his clothes and split.

The third piece is a rephrasing of Wes Montgomery's "Bumpin'" with phenomenally lighter, tighter, yet more complex fingering by James. However, all ears are on Frank Lattimore.

The man on drums steals the attention effortlessly. I see why he doesn't work regularly, besides the dope, which, in this business, never seems to keep anyone of the Bright Persuasion from earning *mucho dinero*. Especially after they confess and repent. Part of Frank's problem is that he isn't repentant enough. The rest is the man's bloody genius. In this town, anything even hinting of excellence is immediately put on ice. Especially if it's one of Us. Frank is the only Negroid on the bandstand.

By the fourth number, "You Are My Sunshine," James decides not to fight it. Frank dominates the ensemble yet gives it back a more cohesive self. He's not greedy and James obviously appreciates this. But I don't really hear James anymore, meaning the guitar specifically. I'm lost in the combined sounds. Totally. Frank has tranced the entire room.

During intermission Frank will be approached by a wealthy young man from Japan. He will offer Frank grand theft dough for private lessons—more scratch than Frank's seen in his entire career. Frank will thank him and say no.

This is not a man playing drums. This is a man caressing a woman. The only woman he's true to. She's as Black as the Congo, as wide as the Atlantic, as glorious and as illusive as heaven promised here-and-now. She is as water rises to tongue the troubled shore with shimmers of foam. She is the heady pungency of fresh after-sex. She is the desolation of being a gifted, recalcitrant stranger in one's native land.

Amen.

What Frank doesn't know is that there's another young woman taking notes that night. She's a reporter for the *Times*. She is pale, ashen blonde, and of lofty attitude. She will pen a rave review tonight. It'll run tomorrow. It will praise every member in the Ditzi group . . . except Frank. He will be mentioned fleetingly as being "on drums." I will read it aloud to Kevin and he will snot up with rage and kick over one of the stereo speakers.

But right now, tonight, my head is bursting as another lyric finds me. I stab my little notebook in swift, ecstatic jabs, caught in the thrall. Now Frank's on the brush, devilishly whisking the skins. Now he kisses the cymbal ever so blithely.

Kevin can't take his eyes off his step-dad. I'm almost amazed into excusing Frank's earthly transgressions. If I weren't so up tight, I'd thank him for reminding me why I love music and the witchery of transforming pain into exquisite loveliness.

Kevin and I share weepy little smiles as the set breaks. We lean into our tiny table and start Frenching as the waiter brings our second round of drinks.

What we don't know is that on the first day of winter, Frank's old VW will be spotted apparently abandoned on a convenience store parking lot after curfew. The great Mr. Lattimore will be found late of an overdose of what most folks will prefer to call heroin. It will be one of those exceptionally bright, smogless, cloud-flecked days we have in this region. I'll stand on the veranda looking out towards the hills of Silver Lake. The baby will be sleeping quietly out back. I'll be listening to one of the old Spence Alcohol cuts featuring Frank Lattimore on drums, grateful Kevin left the music behind.

9

Bix Beiderbecke

Julio Cortázar

I'm a Panamanian woman and I've been living with Bix for a while now.

I write it and move on to the next line. No one's going to believe it; if they believed it, they'd be like me and I don't know anyone like me. Not the same as me, but more or less like me. Maybe that's a good thing because I can write it without caring whether anyone reads it or not, or whether this ends up being torched by the last match of the last cigarette. Or whether it's tossed out, or given to someone to do with as he will; all of that will be left behind, so far behind me and Bix. I write it because I don't have anything else to do and because it's true or it'll seem true to someone like me. There are people like that, I've brushed past them in my life, close up or far away, not everyone's still trapped by what they were taught. Look, Rimbaud said he had fallen in love with a pig, and all the professors think he was a great poet. They probably think it without believing it, because that's what you have to think if you don't want to look bad. But I know he was a great poet and Bix knew it too, even though he never read a line of French and I had to translate Rimbaud for him and he would clutch his head and just sit there thinking, or he'd go to the piano and start playing what's now called "In a Mist," which was his way of saying he understood French poetry because it came to him through Debussy and since everything almost always came to him through music and that was his only way of understanding things he didn't understand when they came to him in other ways, life for example, the nature of what I would call reality and that he only understood in

C major or F-sharp, blowing softly into his cornet or going to the piano and giving birth to "Lost in a Fog," burning his lips with the cigarette forgotten by his spider hands that were spinning webs on the keyboard until everything ended with a shower of swearwords and a backwards leap; I always kept a tube of ointment around to treat his lips, and then we'd kiss, laughing, and he'd start swearing again because it hurt and because the cornet was going to hurt even more in a few hours when he played in The Blue Room, for eighty dollars the night.

Goddamittohell, as Uncle Ramón would say; he always squished words together and made them sound like the lash of a whip on your ass, it's not that it's that hard for me to write because I don't work at it much and this typewriter glides along like the rum that's been gliding me along for hours, everything shows up on a ribbon I can barely see, it's not that I write by sense of touch but I don't even look at the paper, I prefer following my two fingers jumping up and down, my left hand hitting the return bar and moving on to the next line, I have a Tiffany lamp that spills orange, green, blue spots on the paper and on my face and hands; writing is like dancing slowly with Bix in The Phoenix, being part of, being part of what?, being part of the thing that unites us all without anyone knowing they're united and will only be united with the other parts that very night because even if we return to The Phoenix it won't be the same anymore, like the waves on Waikiki one after another for millions of years and not one of them the same as any other, who can say that one wave contains the same number of water-drops as the others, or the same shape or the same happiness or that its crest has the same design or that it breaks the same way on that beach where Bix used to like to sleep and I would smoke while watching him, little and ugly, with that bit of German that stuck to him along with his damn last name and some gestures that came from his father or uncles, the Beiderbeckes with their Christmas tree and Bix's mother's scented cakes, those old memories injected into the soul in the midst of the Midwest, Germans in cowboy shirts and speaking American and more patriotic than Thomas Jefferson. Goddamittohell, as Uncle Ramón would say, Goddamittohell with Germany, that Germany I never heard Bix mention because he was from this side of the world, I never understood why he didn't change his last name like other musicians did, Eddie Lang for example. It struck Bix as immensely funny that my last name was Manzanares, he twisted it round and round when I told him what it meant in Spanish, he shook with laughter and then squeezed me tight and said Linda, Linda Manzanares, Linda *Applegarden, Appletrees, Applefuckingpie,* in the end he settled on *Applepie,* and then he almost always started gobbling me up because there was nothing he liked more than apple pie with beer, he would suck on my nose repeating *Applepie, Applepie,* and I blew it right into his mouth and he jumped back swearing and saying I was disgusting, spitting out the apple pie that I fired right into his mouth, poor thing.

I met Bix around the same time as I met Omar, and my parents, Mamá and Papá (I write Mamá and Papá because it makes me laugh, it's funny to say Mamá and Papá when you think about those hairy beetles who sent me to be raised by the nuns and whipped me silly when I visited on Sundays and forgot a sanitary napkin next to the sink, revolting creature, said Mamá; disgusting, she's going to have to be taught some manners, replied my darling Papá), but at least they had the television at their house and some Sundays I could sit waiting in the living room knowing that Omar would come watch me; my family, charming as always, playing dominoes in the dining room and I would be sitting by myself, waiting for the moment when Omar was announced and I would slip down in the armchair and wait for Omar to come into the foreground again and start talking, watching me, dissimulating with some speech or another, people of Panama, my fellow citizens, anything for the people filling the stadium or the theater because all he really wanted was to watch me and he had to spew the worst nonsense so no one would realize he had come on TV to watch me, I would wait for him stretched out on the couch and he would start talking and his green tiger eyes clawing into me and I would smile at him, Omar, oh Omar, I let him watch me while I pulled my skirt up little by little letting him watch me, showing him everything little by little, not in any rush because Omar was going to be there half an hour spewing nonsense for the other people but I had invented our code, out of every so many words I picked the ones Omar was saying just to me while he clawed into me with his tiger eyes and the muscles on his temples trembled, his hands reaching up as if to grab me, to do to me what I was doing to myself in front of him while he watched me and talked to me. I could see the doorway to the dining room in the mirror and I knew when I had to straighten myself out, lower my skirt, Omar understood because he could see the mirror from the TV too, sometimes Papá or more often Mamá would come in as if they were surprised, or both of them looking at each other and saying my goodness, who would have thought this girl was going to be so interested in politics, I'm going to tell Sister Filotea, it's not good that at her age, Goddamittohell, Uncle Ramón would say from the dining room, you walked out on the game again, it's impossible to play with you people.

Of course Bix couldn't watch me like Omar, in Bix's day there wasn't television but what difference did it make, he showed up the day my Cousin Freddie came back from the States with a stack of jazz records and he started wanting to paw at me until I sent him back to his corner of the ring with a little smack that's hardly worth mentioning, we stayed friends afterwards because he met Rosalía and the three of us would get together in Rosalía's house when I ran away from the nuns and Freddie would give us lectures about traditional jazz, Dixieland and those things, and he played the records for us, no one knew anything about Bix and me, Freddie would talk about him in a whisper, explaining about his life, how he died young, consumed by gin, how that cornet solo in "I'm Coming, Virginia," and Rosalía yeah, yeah, sure, and then Bix like Omar taking advantage of the opportunity to watch me in his way, playing every solo just for me, seeing me through the music just like later on he would see and understand Rimbaud through his piano, him and me alone while Rosalía and Freddie kissed each other in the middle of Paul Whiteman's "Tutti" where Bix only popped in for a moment to watch me from his solo and tell me what he would tell me so many times later on, *Applefucking pie, little Apple pie, sweet Apple pie.*

The two men didn't bother each other, every so many Sundays Omar would come watch me from the TV and Bix, at Rosalía's house; I stole one of the albums from Freddie and listened to it at home alone, Mamá complaining, that music, girl, it sounds like a Negro thing, where's the melody, turn that crap off or I'm going to throw it away, I would hide it in a different place every time and then finally it was like she was getting halfway used to "Jazz Me Blues," and I was listening to precisely that, playing it softly in my room on a terrible record player that Juanita Leca lent me when I heard Papá shouting on the phone to Uncle Ramón and they were talking about Omar, I didn't understand why Papá was getting all worked up, he was talking about the news on the radio, and when I turned it on and found out the helicopter had crashed and they were looking for Omar's body it was like all my blood ran dry, the record with "Jazz Me Blues" was spinning and spinning in silence, I took it off the record player and hugged it and I saw the blank screen of the TV in the mirror and suddenly everything, now he wasn't going to watch me anymore, his eyes would be all smashed to bits, he was never going to watch me ever again. Mamá was sobbing loudly in the living room and I left the record on a table and went outside, I walked back to the convent and into my room and only remembered much later that I had abandoned the record, that Bix wouldn't watch me either if I lost the record and all of a sudden I didn't care if they broke it or threw it out which of course they did right away, those hairy beetles. I didn't care about anything because something happened to me that night that I don't even know myself, it's not that I don't want to write it but I don't know, it's like Omar had taken me with him who knows where, and everything stopped hurting, I think I fell asleep or I dreamed all of this while I was wide awake, suddenly time didn't exist, Omar didn't either, I felt the first warning of my period coming on, the soft pressure that always exasperated me because of the work involved with the towels and all that, but not now, it was as if I understood that Omar had shown me a way, as if he had never been in love with me and instead he was showing me something else, a way to make me understand that Bix was still always there, that only Bix was there now and everything depended on me going to look for him in a way I never went to look for Omar who only watched me through the TV but without anything else, without the things I felt in my chest now, in my belly that was starting to ache more and more, this thing I'm writing without understanding anything and it was as if Omar was showing me the way to get to Bix.

I'm Panamanian and I'm forty years old. I hadn't turned eighteen yet when I found Bix after the stuff I described up above which I'm not going to reread because I know it won't mean much of anything to anyone or almost anyone (I must have written it for that "almost," I suppose, what difference does it make). By then I was already what the hairy beetles (one of them was already dead) would have called a whore, because when I was seventeen and in my last year with the nuns I accepted a date with Pedro from the garage who was around twenty-five but I liked him maybe because he was small like Bix in the photos and I went off to his filthy room carrying one of Bix's albums and I made him put it on while he undressed me, and it was probably a coincidence but right when I started screaming with pain Bix came in with his solo on "Royal Garden Blues" and I kept on screaming but now the pain was turning upside down, it was filling up like with gold, I belonged to Bix at last, that's how it had to be although that idiot Pedro was slobbering all over me, so proud to be banging me right there in his bed and he wanted to start again and I told him fine, but first put the record back on, and he was staring at me like he was thinking I was stupid or half crazy.

I've said I'm Panamanian twice now, it seems like something only someone who was new to typing would do, but repeating it is the only way I can move forward and make it all the way to that town in Ohio or Maryland where Bix and the boys were playing, that's what makes me drug this all up with words just like I drug myself up with other things sometimes, because you're part of all that too and I don't know, I'm telling you as if I was caressing you down there or slowly licking one of your ears, I don't know but I really don't want you to ask questions, I'm not asking you to believe me because I don't either, it's not a question of believing or not believing but of thinking that you don't have to be a hairy beetle and letting things take place on the page just like they're also taking place out on the street or in the room next door. That night I couldn't get close to Bix because there were too many people but the next morning I found him having coffee in the hotel cafeteria looking lost in something that must have interested him on the ceiling, and without asking permission I sat down in the chair in front of him and I put my hand on his and told him, you know, I want you to know, you've been watching me for so long now that I can't stand it anymore. And he lowered his eyes from the ceiling, very slowly, you could feel how his gaze slipped through the air like a trumpet lick and he said, fine, if that's the way it is why don't you have a coffee with me and this time you can watch me.

Freddie had explained to me that Bix had been, I mean he was, a man with problems, although nobody seemed to know a whole lot about what was going on with him, he just wasn't happy and except for the jazz he was all alone, surrounded by lots of people, of course, but alone and drinking more and more. The musicians and other people didn't know if he made do with whores or if it just didn't work for him with women, in the end he had had a type of reformist girlfriend, who everyone placed an enormous amount of trust in, the way you do when you love a friend who's all fucked up and you think this kind of girlfriend is going to save him from who knows what, we must all be idiots. But that was later on, now Bix was going around alone at all the gigs with the band and by five o'clock in the afternoon his eyes were starting to get glassier and glassier, Trum and the others had to keep an eye on him so he wouldn't disappear from the hotel when it was time to work. *Apple pie,* he said to me when I explained my name, it's almost worse than my name, if you get right down to it.

Since he didn't talk much, I had to invent one thing or another and I started mentioning records to him, which were, in the end, the only places he'd been watching me from until now, and I saw he was shaking his head and it didn't always seem like he recognized the names; when I realized why—it was something I had to learn little by little, so difficult not to talk to him about the things I wanted to discuss but he didn't, like the reformist girlfriend for example—, well, that's when I started talking to him about the concert from the previous night and I told him I would go to the next one. *Apple pie,* said Bix, I hope you're not one of those fans who never misses a show, I've never been able to stand that, the same face in the audience more than once makes me lose the will to live, I feel like I almost have to repeat the solos I played yesterday and that's something I'm never going to do. Although you never know, said Bix looking at his empty coffee cup, you never know if one of these days I won't start copying myself, I wouldn't be the first.

"I don't want to be a face for you," I replied sweetly, and it would have made me happy if he'd kicked me under the table. "I'll buy myself wigs, you'll never recognize me."

"Goodbye," said Bix, throwing some coins on the table and turning his back on me.

That night I sat right up next to the stage and I didn't even put a different dress on, I saw him come in behind the others and look at me almost immediately, claw into me with his eyes, and then something strange happened and it's that Bix raised his cornet to his mouth as if he was going to warm it up long before he started playing, and almost in a whisper he played three or four measures of his solo in "Jazz Me Blues." They didn't play that piece that night, it had been just for me and I knew that Bix had forgiven me. I followed him on the tour but without ever approaching him; at the fourth concert he touched me on the shoulder during the break and showed me the bar with a . . . *

Translated by Sandra Kingery

*Incomplete story, with this truncated ending.

10

The Pursuer

Julio Cortázar

In memoriam Ch. P.

Be thou faithful unto death.

APOCALYPSE 2.10

O make me a mask.

DYLAN THOMAS

Dédée called me in the afternoon to tell me Johnny wasn't doing very well, and I went to the hotel right away. Johnny and Dédée have been living in a hotel on Rue Lagrange for a few days, in a room on the fourth floor. A single glance at the door made it clear to me that Johnny was living in the most abject poverty; the window opens out onto a courtyard that's practically black, and you have to keep the light on at one in the afternoon if you want to read the paper or see anyone's face. It's not cold, but I found Johnny wrapped in a blanket, squeezed into a filthy armchair that's shedding pieces of yellowish burlap all over the place. Dédée has aged and the red dress looks terrible on her; it's a dress for work, for the lights of the stage; in that hotel room, it turns into a repulsive type of blood clot.

"Our friend Bruno's as faithful as bad breath," said Johnny by way of greeting, raising his knees until his chin was resting on them. Dédée got me a chair and I reached for a pack of Gauloises. I had a bottle of rum in my pocket, but I didn't want to remove it until I had some idea what was going on. More than anything, I was annoyed by the lamp, its eyeball dangling from the socket on a cord dirty with flies. After looking at it once or twice, and putting my hand out to act as a lampshade, I asked Dédée if we couldn't turn it off and make do with the light from the window. Johnny followed my words and movements with a great distracted attention, like a cat that won't take its eyes off something but is clearly completely focused on something else; is something else. In the end Dédée got up and turned off the light. In what remained, a mixture of gray and black, we recognized one another better. Johnny took one of his large skinny hands out from under the blanket, and I felt the flabby warmth of his flesh. Then Dédée said she was going to make some Nescafé. I was happy to know they at least have a tin of Nescafé. As long as a person has a tin of Nescafé I know they're not in the most dire poverty; they can still hold out a bit longer.

"It's been a while since we've seen each other," I said to Johnny. "At least a month."

"You're always counting time like that," he responded grumpily. "The first of the month, the second, the third, number twenty-one. You, you give everything a number. And that one over there, she does the same thing. Do you know why she's so pissed off? Because I lost the sax. She's right, of course."

"But how could you lose it?" I asked, knowing at the same time that that was the very thing one couldn't ask Johnny.

"In the metro," Johnny said. "To be safer, I put it under my seat. It was wonderful traveling along knowing I had it under my legs, nice and safe."

"He realized when he was climbing the stairs in the hotel," Dédée said, with a slightly hoarse voice. "And I had to go running out like a crazy woman to tell the people at the metro, the police."

Judging by the silence that followed, I knew it had been a waste of time. But Johnny started laughing the way he does, the chuckle emerging from behind his lips and teeth.

"Some poor idiot's probably trying to squeeze a note out of it right now," he said. "It was one of the worst saxes I've ever had; you could tell Doc Rodríguez had played it, its soul was completely deformed. It wasn't really such a terrible instrument, but Rodríguez is capable of wrecking a Stradivarius just by tuning it."

"And you can't get another one?"

"That's what we're trying to find out," Dédée said. "We think Rory Friend has one. The bad thing is that Johnny's contract . . . "

"Johnny's contract," Johnny aped. "What about Johnny's contract? I have to play and that's all there is to it, and I don't have a sax or the money to buy one, and the boys are in the same spot."

That last part isn't true, and all three of us know it. No one's willing to lend Johnny a horn any more, because he loses or wrecks it right away. He lost Louis Rolling's sax in Bordeaux, and that sax Dédée bought him when he got a contract for a tour in England: he stomped and beat on that one until it was in three pieces. Nobody knows how many instruments he's lost, broken or pawned by now. And on every one of them, he played the way I think only a god can play an alto sax, assuming they renounced the lyres and flutes.

"When do you start, Johnny?"

"I don't know. Today, I think, right, Dé?"

"No, the day after tomorrow."

"Everybody knows the dates except me," grumbles Johnny, pulling the blanket up to his ears. "I would have sworn it was tonight and that I had to go rehearse this afternoon."

"Same difference," Dédée said. "The thing is he doesn't have a sax."

"Same difference? It's not the same difference. The day after tomorrow is after tomorrow, and tomorrow is way after today. And today itself is quite a bit after right now, when we're chatting with our friend Bruno and I'd feel a whole lot better if I could forget about time and drink something that would warm me up a bit."

"The water's about to boil, hang on a minute."

"I didn't mean warm from boiling," Johnny said. So I pulled the bottle of rum out and it was like turning on the light, because Johnny opened his mouth wide, amazed, and his teeth started shining, and even Dédée had to smile when she saw him looking so surprised and pleased.

The rum with Nescafé wasn't that bad, and all three of us felt much better after the second drink and a cigarette. By then I'd realized that Johnny was withdrawing little by little and he was still making allusions to time, a subject that's concerned him ever since I've known him. There aren't many other people in the world who're that concerned with everything related to time. It's an obsession, the worst of his obsessions, and there're a lot of them. But he lays it out and explains it with a charm few people can resist. I remembered a rehearsal before a recording session, in Cincinnati, long before coming to Paris, in '49 or '50. Johnny was in great shape back then, and I'd gone to the rehearsal just to hear him and also Miles Davis. Everyone was in the mood to play, they were happy, dressed up (I may remember that because of the contrast, because of how badly dressed and dirty Johnny goes around now), they were playing happily, not at all impatient, and the sound technician was making approving gestures behind his window, like a satisfied baboon. And precisely at that moment, when Johnny seemed to be lost in happiness, all of a sudden he stopped playing and, after throwing a punch at someone, I don't know who, he said: "I've been playing this tomorrow," and most of the boys came to an abrupt stop, two or three of them going on a few extra bars, like a train that takes a while to grind to a halt, and Johnny was hitting himself on the forehead and repeating: "I already played this tomorrow, it's terrible, Miles, I already played this tomorrow," and they couldn't get him past that, and from that point on everything was all messed up, Johnny wasn't in the mood to play, he wanted to leave (to get his fix, the sound technician said, mad as hell), and when I saw him walk out, staggering, his face ashen, I wondered if the whole thing can continue much longer.

"I think I'm going to call Dr. Bernard," Dédée said, sneaking a sideways glance at Johnny, who's taking little sips of rum. "You've got a fever and you're not eating."

"Dr. Bernard's a poor sad fool," Johnny said, licking his glass. "He'll give me some aspirin, and then he'll say he really loves jazz, people like Ray Noble. You get the idea, Bruno. If I had the sax, I'd meet him at the door with some music that would make him bounce right back down all four flights of stairs, hitting his ass on every step."

"In any case, it wouldn't hurt you to take some aspirin," I said, looking at Dédée out of the corner of my eye. "If you want, I'll call him when I leave, so Dédée doesn't have to go out. But look, that contract . . . If you start the day after tomorrow, something can probably be done. And I can try to get a sax from Rory Friend. And worst case scenario . . . The thing is you're going to have to be more careful, Johnny."

"Not today," Johnny said, looking at the bottle of rum. "Tomorrow, when I have the sax. So there's no reason to talk about it right now. Bruno, I keep realizing more and more that time . . . I think music always helps us understand this somewhat. Well, not understand, because the truth of the matter is I don't understand anything. I just realize there's something. Like those dreams, don't you think, when you start to suspect that everything's going to go bad, and you're a little frightened ahead of time; but at the same time you're not at all sure, and maybe everything flips over like a pancake and all of a sudden you're in bed with a beautiful girl and everything's more perfect than perfect."

Dédée's washing the cups and glasses in a corner of the room. I realized they don't even have running water; I see a washtub with pink flowers and a hand basin that makes me think of an embalmed animal. And Johnny keeps on talking with his mouth half covered by the blanket, and he looks embalmed too, with his knees against his chin and his smooth black face that the rum and the fever are starting to dampen more and more.

"I've read a thing or two about this stuff, Bruno. It's strange, and actually really hard . . . I think music helps, you know. Not to understand, because in reality I don't understand anything." He hits himself on the head with his fist. His head sounds like a coconut. "There's nothing inside here, Bruno, nothing that you could say is anything. It doesn't think or understand anything. I've never needed to, to tell you the truth. I start understanding from the eyes on down, and the lower you go, the better I understand. But it's not really understanding, I agree with that."

"Your fever's going to go back up," Dédée scolded from the back of the room.

"Why don't you just shut up? It's true, Bruno. I've never thought about anything, I only realize the things I've thought all of a sudden, but that's not really helpful, is it? What good does it do to realize you've thought something? It doesn't make any difference to the thing if you think it or if someone else does. It's not really that it's me. I just take advantage of what I think, but always afterwards, and that's what I can't stand. And so then it's hard, it's just so hard . . . Any of that rum left?"

I gave him the last few drops right as Dédée was turning the light back on; you could barely see anything in the room. Johnny's sweating, but he's still wrapped in the blanket. He shivers from time to time, making the armchair creak.

"I realized when I was really little, almost as soon as I learned to play the sax. Things were always pretty crappy at home, and they were always going on about debts and mortgages. Do you know what a mortgage is? It must be something awful, because my mom would start yanking her hair out by the roots every time my dad talked about the mortgage, and they'd end up taking swings at each other. I was thirteen . . . but you've already heard all this."

I certainly have heard it, and I've certainly made every effort to get it down correctly and truthfully in the biography I wrote about Johnny.

"That's why time never stopped at home, you know. From one fight to the next, almost without stopping to eat. And to top it all off, religion, oh, you can't even imagine that one. Then the teacher got me a sax, a sax that would've made you die laughing if you saw it, and I think I realized right away: the music took me out of time, although that's nothing more than a way of saying it. If you want to know what I really feel, I think the music put me into time. But then you have to believe that time, this time, doesn't have anything to do with . . . well, with us, if I can say it like that."

I've long since become accustomed to the hallucinations experienced by Johnny, and by those who share his lifestyle, so I listen to him attentively but without worrying too much about what he's saying. I wonder instead about how he got the drugs in Paris. I'll have to ask Dédée, prevent any potential complicity on her part. Johnny's not going to be able to withstand much more in this state. Drugs and poverty just don't mix. I think about the music that's being lost, the dozens of recordings where Johnny could continue leaving that presence of his, that astonishing step forward he's taken, surpassing any other musician. "I've been playing this tomorrow" suddenly makes perfect sense to me, because Johnny's always playing tomorrow and the rest of them are trailing behind him, stuck in the today that he leaps over effortlessly with the first notes of his music.

I'm sensitive enough as a jazz critic to understand my limitations, and I realize that what I'm thinking is on a lower plane than where poor Johnny finds himself, trying to move forward with his incomplete phrases, his sighs, his sudden rages and his tears. He couldn't care less that I think he's a genius, and he's never been vain about the fact that his music is so far beyond what his fellow musicians play. I think, glumly, that he's at the beginning of his sax while I'm forced to settle for the end. He's the mouth and I'm the ear, which is better than saying he's the mouth and I'm . . . Every critic, unfortunately, is the sad ending of something that began as a taste, like a delicacy to be bitten and chewed. And the mouth moves again, Johnny's big tongue greedily recovers a trickle of saliva from his lips. His hands create a drawing in the air.

"Bruno, if you could write it some day . . . Not for me, you understand, what do I care. But it must be nice, I think it's got to be nice. I was telling you that when I started playing when I was a kid, I realized that time would change. I told Jim about it once and he told me everyone feels the same thing, and that when you get lost in thought . . . He said it like that, when you get lost in thought. But that's not it, I don't get lost in thought when I play. I just change places. It's like in an elevator, you're in the elevator talking with people, and you don't feel anything strange, and in the meantime the first floor goes by, the tenth, the twenty-first, and the city stays down there, and you're finishing the sentence you started when you got in, and between the first words and the last, there're fifty-two floors. I realized when I started playing that I was getting into an elevator, but it was an elevator of time, if I can say it like that. It's not that I would forget about the mortgage or about religion. Just that at times like those, the mortgage and religion were like the suit you're not wearing; I know the suit's in the closet, but you can't tell me that the suit exists at that point in time. The suit exists when I put it on, and the mortgage and religion existed when I stopped playing and my mom came in with her hair sticking up all over the place, complaining that I was going to destroy her eardrums with that devil-music."

Dédée brought another cup of Nescafé, but Johnny looks at his empty glass sadly.

"This thing about time is complicated, it grabs onto me from all sides. I've started realizing little by little that time isn't like a bag that gets filled up. I mean, even if you change the stuff that's inside it, there's only so much you can fit in a bag and that's it. See my suitcase, Bruno? You can get two suits and two pairs of shoes in it. Okay, now imagine you empty it and you go to put the two suits and the two pairs of shoes back inside, and you realize that only one suit and one pair of shoes fits. But it gets even better. The best thing is when you realize you can fit a whole store in the suitcase, hundreds and hundreds of suits, like I fit music into time when I'm playing sometimes. Music and what I think about when I ride the metro."

"When you ride the metro."

"Yeah, well, that's the thing," Johnny replied, shrewdly. "The metro's a great invention, Bruno. When you ride the metro you realize everything that could fit in your suitcase. Maybe I didn't lose the sax in the metro, maybe . . . "

He starts laughing, coughs, Dédée looks at him concerned. But he waves his hands around, and he laughs and coughs, mixing everything, shaking himself off underneath the blanket like a chimpanzee. Tears start running down his cheeks and he drinks them, laughing the whole time.

"It's better not to confuse things," he says after a while. "I lost it and that's the end of it. But the metro helped me realize about the trick with the suitcase. Look, this whole idea about things being elastic is very strange, and I feel it all over the place. Everything's elastic, my friend. Things that look solid have an elasticity . . . "

He thinks, concentrating.

". . . an elasticity that's been delayed," he adds surprisingly.

I give a sign of approving admiration. Bravo, Johnny. The man who says he's incapable of thinking. Damn, Johnny. And now I'm really interested in what he's going to say, and he realizes it and looks at me even more shrewdly.

"Do you think I'll be able to get another sax to play the day after tomorrow, Bruno?"

"Yes, but you'll have to be careful."

"Of course, I'll have to be careful."

"A month-long contract," explains poor Dédée. "Two weeks at Rémy's club, two concerts and the records. We could really get back on our feet."

"A month-long contract," Johnny apes, waving his arms wildly. "Rémy's club, two concerts and the records. *Be-bata-bop bop bop, chrrr.* I want to drink drink drink. And to smoke smoke smoke. I especially want to smoke me some smoke."

I offer him a pack of Gauloises, even though I know perfectly well he's thinking of something else. It's gotten dark, the hallway is starting to be full of people coming and going, conversations in Arabic, a song. Dédée's gone out, probably to buy something for dinner. I feel Johnny's hand on my knee.

"She's a good person, she really is. But I'm sick of her. I haven't loved her for a while now, she drives me crazy. But she still excites me, sometimes; she knows how to make love like . . . " he taps his fingers together, like the Italians. "But I need to get away from her, go back to New York. I especially need to go back to New York, Bruno."

"What for? Things are going better for you here than there. I don't mean work, but life itself. It seems like you have more friends here."

"Yeah, there's you and the Countess, and the boys at the club . . . Didn't you ever make love with the Countess, Bruno?"

"No."

"Well, it's something that . . . But I was telling you about the metro, and I don't know why we changed the subject. The metro's a great invention, Bruno. One day, I started feeling something in the metro, afterwards I forgot . . . And then it happened again, two or three days later. And in the end I realized. It's easy to explain, you know, but it's easy because it isn't really the real explanation. The real explanation simply can't be explained. You'd have to take the metro and wait for it to happen to you, even though I think it only happens to me. It's a little bit like that, you know. But honestly, you never made love with the Countess? You have to ask her to get on that gold stool she's got in the corner of her room, next to this really pretty lamp, and then . . . Jesus, this one's back already."

Dédée comes in with a package and looks at Johnny.

"Your fever's up. I called the doctor, he's coming at ten. He said you shouldn't do anything too strenuous."

"Okay, fine, but first I'm going to tell Bruno the thing about the metro. The other day I finally made sense out of what was going on. I started off thinking about my mom, and then Lan and the kids, and of course at that moment I felt like I was walking through the old neighborhood, and I saw the guys' faces, the ones from back then. It wasn't thinking, I suppose I've already told you a bunch of times that I never think; it's like I'm standing on a corner watching the things that I'm thinking go by, but I'm not thinking what I see. Do you get it? Jim says we're all the same, that in general (that's what he says) people don't think on their own. Let's assume that's true. The thing is I took the metro at Saint-Michel and I started thinking about Lan and the kids right away, and I was seeing the neighborhood. I started thinking about them just after I sat down. But at the same time I knew I was in the metro, and I saw that after a minute more or less we were arriving at Odéon and people were getting on and off. Then I kept on thinking about Lan and I saw my mom when she was coming back from picking up groceries, and I started seeing all of them, being with them in a really nice way, like I hadn't felt in a long time. Memories always make me feel kind of sick, but this time I liked thinking about the kids and seeing them. If I start telling you everything I saw you're not going to believe it because it would take a long time. Even though I wouldn't go into every single detail. For example, just to pick one thing, I was seeing Lan in this green dress she would wear when she went over to Club 33 where I used to play with Hamp. I was seeing the dress with its ribbons, a bow, some trim on the sides and a collar . . . Not all at the same time, but in reality, I was walking around Lan's dress and looking at it slowly. And then I looked at their faces, Lan's and the kids', and then I remembered Mike who lived in the room next door, and how Mike had told me a story about some wild horses in Colorado, and he worked on a ranch and he was talking and bragging the way horse breakers do . . . "

"Johnny," Dédée said from her corner.

"The important thing is that I'm only telling you one little part of everything I was thinking and seeing. How long have I been telling you this part?"

"I don't know, let's say like two minutes."

"Let's say like two minutes," apes Johnny. "Two minutes and I've only told you one little part. If I told you everything I saw the kids do, and how Hamp was playing 'Save it, Pretty Mama' and I was listening to every note, get it?, every single note, and Hamp isn't the kind to cut it short, and if I told you I also heard my mom say a very long prayer, where she was talking about cabbages, I think, she was asking forgiveness for my dad and me and she was saying something about cabbages... Well, if I told you that whole thing in detail, more than two minutes would go by, right Bruno?"

"If you really saw and heard all that, a good quarter hour would go by," I told him, laughing.

"A good quarter hour would go by, huh, Bruno. So then tell me how it's possible that I suddenly feel the metro come to a stop and I leave my mom and Lan and all that, and I see we're at Saint-Germain-des-Prés, which is exactly a minute and a half away from Odéon."

I never worry too much about the things Johnny says, but now, with the way he was looking at me, I felt cold.

"Just a minute and a half by your time, and by the time of that one over there," Johnny said, pointing resentfully. "And also the time of the goddamn metro and my watch too. So then, how can it be that I've been thinking a quarter hour, huh, Bruno? How can someone think a quarter hour in a minute and a half? And I swear I hadn't smoked that day, not at all, not even one little puff," he adds, like a kid making excuses. "And it's happened to me again after that. Now it's starting to happen all over the place. But," he adds wisely, "I only realize in the metro because riding the metro is like being inside a clock. The stations are the minutes, you see; it's the time that belongs to you guys, to the present, but I know there's another time, and I've been thinking, thinking..."

He covers his face with his hands and trembles. I should have left already, and I don't know how to go about saying goodbye so Johnny doesn't get upset, because he's terribly touchy with his friends. If he keeps going like this, it's going to make him sick, at least he won't talk about these things with Dédée.

"Bruno, if I could always live in those kinds of moments, or the ones when I'm playing and time also changes... You realize what could happen in a minute and a half... Then people, not just me but that one over there and you and all the boys, would be able to live hundreds of years; if we found the way we could live a thousand times more than we're living now with our clocks and our obsession with minutes and the day after tomorrow . . . "

I smile as best I can, understanding vaguely that he's right, but that what he assumes and what I feel about his assumptions will dissipate just like they always do once I head out the door and focus on my normal life again. Right now, I'm sure that what Johnny's saying doesn't merely derive from the fact that he's half crazy or from the fact that reality escapes him and leaves, in its place, a type of parody that he converts into hope. Everything Johnny tells me at times like this (and Johnny's been telling me and telling everybody these kinds of things for over five years now), you can't just listen and promise yourself you'll think about it again later. As soon as you step outside, as soon as it's your memory that's repeating the words and not Johnny, everything turns into a drug-induced fantasy, a monotonous thievery (because there are other people who say similar things, one hears about similar claims all the time) and after wonder, irritation is born, and for me, at least, I start feeling like Johnny's pulling my leg. But that only happens the next day, not when Johnny's saying it to me, because when he is, I feel like there's something that wants to give way somewhere, a light that wants to turn on, or actually, as if something needed to be broken, ripped apart from stem to stern like inserting a wedge into a log and pounding away on it until the job's done. But Johnny doesn't have the strength to pound away on anything anymore, and I don't even know what kind of hammer I'd need to use to insert a wedge, which I can't imagine either.

So I finally left, but first one of those things that had to happen—either it or something like it—happened: when I was saying goodbye to Dédée and I had my back turned to Johnny, I could feel that something was going on; I saw it in Dédée's eyes and I turned quickly (because maybe I'm a little afraid of Johnny, this angel who's like my brother, this brother who's like my angel) and I saw that Johnny had suddenly shed the blanket he was wrapped in, and I saw him sitting in the armchair completely naked, his legs pulled up and his knees next to his chin, shivering but laughing, naked from head to toe in that filthy armchair.

"It's starting to get hot," Johnny said. "Bruno, look at this cool scar I have between my ribs."

"Cover up," Dédée ordered, embarrassed and not knowing what to say. We know each other pretty well and a naked man is just a naked man, but in any case Dédée felt embarrassed and I didn't know how to act so I wouldn't give the impression that I was shocked by what Johnny was doing. And he knew it and he laughed with his whole huge mouth, keeping his legs obscenely up in the air, his privates hanging off the edge of the chair like a monkey in the zoo, and the skin on his thighs with some odd blemishes that made me feel endlessly disgusted. Then Dédée grabbed the blanket and quickly wrapped him up in it, while Johnny laughed happily.

I said my goodbyes quietly, promising to come back the next day, and Dédée accompanied me to the landing, closing the door so Johnny doesn't hear what she's going to tell me.

"He's been like this ever since we got back from the tour in Belgium. He was playing so good everywhere, and I was really happy."

"I wonder where he could have gotten the drugs," I said, looking her right in the eye.

"I don't know. He's been drinking wine and brandy almost constantly. But he also smoked, although less than he did there . . . "

There is Baltimore and New York, it's three months in the Bellevue psych ward, as well as the long stretch in Camarillo.

"Did Johnny really manage to play well in Belgium, Dédée?"

"Yes, Bruno, I think better than ever. People were going wild, the boys in the band told me so a bunch of times. These strange things would happen all of a sudden, like always with Johnny, but never in front of the audience, luckily. I thought . . . but you can see, now he's worse than ever."

"Worse than in New York? You didn't know him back then."

Dédée isn't stupid, but no woman likes to hear about her man's life before she was part of it, plus she has to put up with him right now and the stuff from before is just words. I don't know how to talk to her about this, and I don't even fully trust her, but in the end I decide to continue.

"I imagine you guys are out of money."

"We have the contract starting the day after tomorrow," Dédée said.

"Do you think he's going to be able to appear in public and record?"

"Sure," Dédée said, a little surprised. "Johnny can play better than ever if Dr. Bernard can get him over the flu. The problem is the sax."

"I'm going to take care of that. Here you go, Dédée. Only . . . It would be better if Johnny didn't find out."

"Bruno . . . "

By waving my hand and starting down the stairs, I stopped Dédée's predictable, useless gratitude. It was easier for me to say it to her once we had four or five steps between us.

"He absolutely can't be doing drugs before the first concert. Let him drink a little but don't give him any money for the rest of it."

Dédée didn't say anything, although I saw how her hands were folding and refolding the bills until she made them disappear. At least I know Dédée doesn't take drugs. Her only complicity in the whole thing would come out of love or fear. If Johnny gets down on his knees, like I saw him do in Chicago, and starts begging her, crying . . . But that's a risk just like all the other risks with Johnny, and for the time being, there'll be money for food and for medicine. Back out on the street, I turned up the collar on my raincoat because it was starting to drizzle, and I breathed in deep until my lungs hurt; I thought Paris smelled like cleanliness, like warm bread. I didn't realize how Johnny's room smelled until now: like Johnny's body sweating beneath the blanket. I went into a café to have a brandy and rinse my mouth, and maybe also my memory that insists over and over on Johnny's words, his stories, his way of seeing what I don't see and deep down don't want to see. I started thinking about the day after tomorrow and it felt like calmness, like a bridge stretching out nicely from the countertop in the bar right into the future.

When you're not too sure about anything, the best thing to do is to create obligations that'll function as life preservers. Two or three days later I thought I had the obligation to find out if the Countess was supplying Johnny Carter with drugs, and I went to her studio in Montparnasse. The Countess really is a Countess and has tons of money that she got from the Count, although they divorced a while ago because of the drugs and other, similar reasons. Her friendship with Johnny comes from New York, probably from the year when Johnny got famous overnight simply because someone gave him the opportunity to get four or five guys together, they liked his style and Johnny could really play the way he wanted for the first time, and he stunned everyone. This isn't the time or place to do jazz criticism, and anyone who's interested can read my book about Johnny and the new postwar style, but I can really say that in '48—let's say until '50—there was some kind of music explosion, but a cold, silent explosion, an explosion where everything remained in its place and there wasn't any shouting or debris, but the crust of convention splintered into millions of pieces and even its champions (in the bands and in the audience) turned something they no longer felt in the same way into a question of self-esteem. Because after Johnny left his mark on the alto sax you can no longer hear previous musicians and think they're the be all and end all; you have to settle for applying that type of veiled resignation that's called historical consciousness, and to say that any one of those musicians used to be wonderful and still is, within-his-context. Johnny made his way through jazz like a hand turning the page, and that was the end of it.

The Countess, who's got ears like a greyhound for everything that's music, always admired Johnny and his friends in the group enormously. I imagine she must have given them a not insignificant sum of money in the days of Club 33, when the majority of the critics were complaining about Johnny's recordings, judging his jazz in accordance with standards that were moldy with age. Probably also around that period the Countess began to sleep with Johnny now and again, and to smoke with him. I've seen them together lots of times before recording sessions or in between acts at the shows, and Johnny seemed enormously happy when he was with the Countess, even though Lan and the kids were waiting for him in some other part of the theatre or at home. But Johnny never had the vaguest idea what it's like to wait for anything, and it doesn't cross his mind that anyone else would be waiting for him either. Even his way of dumping Lan demonstrates what he's like. I saw the postcard he sent her from Rome, after he'd been gone for four months (he got on a plane with two other musicians without Lan knowing anything about it). The postcard showed Romulus and Remus, who Johnny always found really amusing (one of his songs is named after them), and it said: "Waking alone in a multitude of loves," which is a line from Dylan Thomas, who Johnny reads all the time. Johnny's agents in the States arranged to deduct part of his royalties and send them to Lan, who for her part realized pretty quickly that it hadn't been such a bad deal to be liberated from Johnny. Someone told me the Countess also gave Lan money, without Lan knowing where it came from. I'm not surprised because the Countess is preposterously generous and her way of understanding the world is like the omelets she makes in her studio when her friends start showing up in droves; it consists of maintaining a type of permanent omelet that can be filled with different things and sections can be cut off and offered up as needed.

I found the Countess with Marcel Gavoty and Art Boucaya, and they were in fact just talking about the recordings Johnny had made the previous afternoon. When they caught sight of me, they acted as if they were witnessing the appearance of an archangel, the Countess giving me big sloppy kisses until she wore herself out and the guys slapping me on the back in that way bassists and baritone sax players do. I had to take refuge behind an armchair, defending myself as best I could, and all because they found out that I'd provided the magnificent sax with which Johnny had just recorded four or five of his best improvisations. The Countess started going on right away about how Johnny was a dirty rat, and since they were on the outs (she didn't say why), the dirty rat knew full well that the only way he could get the money to go buy a sax would be to ask her forgiveness properly, the way he should. Naturally Johnny hasn't felt like asking her forgiveness since returning to Paris—it seems the fight was in London, two months ago—and because of that no one could know that he lost the damn sax in the metro, etc. When the Countess starts talking, you've got to ask yourself if Dizzy's style hasn't infected her language, because it's an interminable series of variations in the most unexpected registers, until in the end the Countess slaps herself on the thighs, opens her mouth wide and starts laughing as if she were being tickled to death. And then Art Boucaya took the opportunity to tell me about yesterday's session, which I had had to miss because my wife has pneumonia.

"Tica can vouch for it," Art said pointing to the Countess who's squirming with laughter. "Bruno, you can't imagine what it was like until you hear those recordings. If God was anywhere yesterday, you can take my word for it that He was in that damn recording studio where, by the way, it was hotter than a million hell fires all piled up on top of each other. You remember 'Willow Tree,' Marcel?"

"Do I remember," Marcel said. "The idiot asks me if I remember. I'm tattooed with 'Willow Tree' from head to toe."

Tica brought us highballs and we settled in for a chat. In reality we didn't talk much about yesterday's session, because any musician knows these things can't be talked about, but the little bit they told me rekindled a glimmer of hope and I thought maybe my sax would bring Johnny luck. But there was no lack of anecdotes to minimize that hope, like, for example, the fact that Johnny took his shoes off between cuts and walked around the studio barefoot. But on the other hand, he made up with the Countess and promised to come by her studio to have a drink before tonight's show.

"Do you know the girl Johnny's with now?" Tica wanted to know. I described her as succinctly as possible, but Marcel filled in the details the way the French do, with all kinds of nuances and allusions that the Countess fully enjoyed. He didn't make the slightest reference to drugs, even though I'm so apprehensive that I thought I could smell some in Tica's studio, plus Tica laughs the same way I notice Johnny and Art laughing at times, typical of junkies. I wonder how Johnny got the drugs if he was fighting with the Countess; my confidence in Dédée suddenly came crashing down, if I ever really had any confidence in her. In the end they're all the same.

I'm a little bit envious of that equality which brings them closer together and so easily makes them complicit; from my puritanical point of view—I don't need to confess it, anyone who knows me is aware of the fact that I'm horrified by moral ambiguity—they look like sick angels, irritating in their irresponsibility but repaying what others do for them with things like Johnny's recordings and the Countess's generosity. But I'm not admitting everything, and I'd like to force myself to say it: I envy them, I envy Johnny, that Johnny who comes from the other side, although no one knows exactly what that other side is. I envy everything except his pain, which won't be hard for anyone to understand, but even his pain must give him an inkling of something that's denied me. I envy Johnny and at the same time it enrages me that he's destroying himself by squandering his talent, by allowing the stress in his life to make him accumulate all sorts of foolish behaviors. I think if Johnny could straighten out his life, without giving anything up, not even drugs, and if he could be more successful at piloting the plane he's been flying blind for five years now, perhaps he'd end up in the worst possible place, completely insane or dead, but not without reaching the depths he's searching for in his sad monologues *a posteriori,* in his recitation of experiences which are fascinating but only reach the halfway point. And I sustain this belief out of my own personal cowardice, and perhaps deep down I wish Johnny's story would just come to an end once and for all, like a star that bursts into a thousand pieces, leaving all the astronomers dumbfounded for a week, and then afterwards you go to sleep and tomorrow's another day.

It would seem like Johnny suspected everything I was thinking, because he gave me a happy wave when he entered and he came over to sit by my side almost immediately, after kissing the Countess and spinning her through the air, and exchanging a complicated onomatopoeic ritual with her and Art that they all found enormously funny.

"Bruno," Johnny said, settling himself into the best couch, "that horn's the best. These guys can tell you what I got out of it yesterday. Tica was dropping tears as big as light bulbs, and I don't think it's because she owes her hairdresser money, right Tica?"

I wanted to know something more about the session, but Johnny has enough with that quick burst of pride. He almost immediately started talking with Marcel about tonight's program and how good the two of them look in the brand-new gray suits they're going to wear for the show. Johnny's really doing well and you can see he hasn't smoked too much in days; he seems to have the exact dosage he needs to be in the mood to play. And just as I'm thinking that, Johnny places his hand on my shoulder and leans over to say:

"Dédée told me I behaved pretty bad with you the other night."

"Bah, don't even think about it."

"But I do think about it. And if you want my opinion, the truth is I was fabulous. You should feel happy I acted like that with you; I don't do it with just anyone, believe you me. It shows how much I appreciate you. We should go somewhere to talk about stuff. Here . . . " He sticks out his bottom lip, scornful, and laughs, he shrugs, it looks like he's doing a dance on the couch. "Old Bruno. Dédée says I really did behave pretty bad."

"You had the flu. Feeling better?"

"It wasn't the flu. The doctor came, and he started telling me right off that he loves jazz, and that I should go to his house some night to listen to records. Dédée told me you gave her money."

"To help you guys get by until you're paid. How're things looking for tonight?"

"Well, I'm ready to go. I'd play right now if I had the sax, but Dédée insisted on bringing it to the theatre herself. It's a wonderful sax; yesterday I felt like I was making love when I was playing. You should have seen Tica's face when I finished. Were you jealous, Tica?"

And they started laughing hysterically again, and Johnny decided it would be a good idea to run around the studio, expressing his happiness by leaping through the air, and he and Art started dancing without music, raising and lowering their eyebrows to set the beat. It's impossible to get upset with Johnny or with Art; it would be like getting mad at the wind for messing up your hair. In whispers, Tica, Marcel and I exchanged thoughts about that night's show. Marcel is sure that Johnny's going to stage a reprise of his incredible success of 1951, when he came to Paris for the first time. After yesterday he's sure everything's going to come out fine. I'd like to feel just as calm, but in any case I won't be able to do anything except sit in the front of the theatre and listen. At least I've got the peace of mind of knowing that Johnny isn't drugged up like that night in Baltimore. When I said that to Tica, she squeezed my hand like she was about to fall into the water. Art and Johnny went over to the piano, and Art's showing Johnny a new tune, Johnny moves his head and sings along under his breath. They're both extremely elegant in their gray suits, although the weight Johnny's gained lately doesn't look so good.

Tica and I talked about the night in Baltimore, when Johnny had his first breakdown. While we were talking, I looked Tica right in the eye, because I wanted to make sure she understands me, and that she won't give in this time. If Johnny drinks too much brandy or smokes the tiniest little bit, the concert will be a failure and everything'll come crashing down. Paris isn't some provincial club and everybody has his eye on Johnny. And once I'm thinking about it, I can't help but have a bad taste in my mouth, an anger that isn't directed at Johnny or the things that happen to him; no, it's aimed at me and the people surrounding him, the Countess and Marcel, for example. Deep down we're all selfish, under the pretext of helping Johnny what we're doing is saving our idea of him, preparing ourselves for the new pleasures Johnny's going to give us, polishing the statue we all built together and defending it come what may. Johnny's failure would be bad for my book (the English and Italian translations are due out any day now), and things like that probably account for part of the reason why I take care of Johnny. Art and Marcel need him in order to make a living, and the Countess, who knows what the Countess sees in Johnny besides his talent. None of that has anything to do with the other Johnny, and I suddenly realized that maybe that's what Johnny was trying to tell me when he ripped off the blanket and displayed himself naked as a worm: Johnny without his sax, Johnny without money or clothes, Johnny obsessed by something his poor intelligence isn't capable of understanding but which floats slowly through his music, caressing his skin, preparing him perhaps for an unpredictable leap we'll never understand.

And when you think about things like that, you really end up with a bad taste in your mouth, and all the sincerity in the world doesn't offset the sudden discovery that you're just a piece of crap next to a guy like Johnny Carter, who's come over now to drink his brandy on the couch, looking at me with an amused expression. It's time now for us to head over to Pleyel Hall. Let the music save the rest of the night at least, and accomplish one of its worst missions completely: placing a smokescreen right in front of the mirror, erasing us all from the map for a couple of hours.

As usual, tomorrow I'll write a review about tonight's concert for *Jazz Hot.* But here, with this shorthand scribbled on my knee during the breaks, I don't feel the slightest urge to talk like a critic, that is, to make comparative judgments. I know full well that, for me, Johnny has stopped being a jazzman and his musical genius is like a façade, something everyone can come to understand and admire but which conceals something else, and that something else is the only thing that should matter to me, perhaps because it's the only thing that really matters to Johnny.

It's easy to say it, while Johnny's music is still in me. When that cools down . . . Why can't I just behave like him?, why can't I just dive head-first into the wall? I place the words meticulously in front of the reality they're supposed to describe, I shield myself behind considerations and suspicions that are no more than stupid rhetoric. I feel like I understand why prayer instinctively demands that you fall to your knees. The change in position symbolizes the change in tone of voice, in what the voice is going to express, in the expression itself. When I get to the point of discerning that change, things that had seemed arbitrary until just a second earlier are imbued with meaning, they become extraordinarily simple and at the same time they're more profound. Marcel and Art didn't realize yesterday that Johnny wasn't crazy when he removed his shoes in the recording studio. At that moment, Johnny needed to touch the ground with his skin, anchor himself to the earth that his music was reconfirming, not escaping. Because this is something else I feel in Johnny: he doesn't run away from anything, he doesn't take drugs to run away like most junkies, he doesn't play the sax to hide behind a trench made of music, he doesn't spend weeks locked in mental hospitals to feel himself sheltered from the demands he's incapable of withstanding. Even his style, the most authentic thing about him, a style that's worthy of absurd labels without needing any of them, proves that Johnny's art isn't a substitution or a completion. Johnny abandoned the "hot" jazz that was more or less current ten years ago, because that violently erotic language was too passive for him. In his case, desire precedes pleasure and thwarts it, because desire forces him to move forward, look for something new, deny out of hand the simple connections of traditional jazz. I think that's why Johnny isn't overly fond of the blues, where masochism and nostalgia . . . But I already wrote about all this in my book, showing how the renunciation of immediate satisfaction led Johnny to develop a new language which he and other musicians are currently taking as far as it can go. This jazz rejects all easy eroticism, all Wagnerian romanticism, if I can say it like that, occupying an apparently uncommitted space where music achieves absolute freedom, just like a painting released from representation achieves the freedom to be nothing more than a painting. But then, master of a music that doesn't provide easy orgasms or nostalgia, master of a music that I'd like to label metaphysical, Johnny seems to make use of that music to discover himself, to take a bite out of the reality that escapes him day by day. That's where I find the full paradox of his style, its aggressive triumph.

Incapable of satisfying itself, it serves as a continuous incentive, an infinite construction where pleasure doesn't depend on the conclusion but on exploratory reiterations, on the use of facilities that leave behind that which is immediately human without losing humanity. And when, like tonight, Johnny gets lost in the continuous creation of his music, I know full well that he's not escaping anything. Going in search of something can never be an escape, even if we relocate the meeting spot every time; and as for what might be left behind, Johnny ignores it or completely rejects it. The Countess, for example, thinks Johnny's afraid of poverty, without realizing that the only thing Johnny can be afraid of is not finding a pork chop within reach of his knife when he feels like eating one, or a bed when he's sleepy, or a hundred dollars in his wallet when he thinks it would be normal to have a hundred dollars. Johnny doesn't move in a world of abstractions like we do; that's why his music, that admirable music which I heard tonight, doesn't have anything abstract about it. But only he can have a sense of what he's reaped while playing, and he's probably already on to something else, losing himself in some new conjecture or assumption. His conquests are like a dream, he forgets them when the applause awakens him and brings him back, this man who travels such distances, living his quarter hour in a minute and a half.

It would be like going through life tied to a lightning rod in the middle of a thunderstorm and thinking nothing's going to happen. Four or five days later, I met Art Boucaya at the Dupont in the Latin Quarter, and he couldn't wait to start rolling his eyes and tell me the bad news. At first I felt a type of satisfaction that I can't quantify as anything other than mean-spirited, because I had been well aware that the calm couldn't last much longer; but afterwards I thought about the consequences, and my affection for Johnny made my stomach clench; then I had two brandies while Art described what had happened. To summarize, it seems that Delaunay had organized a recording session that afternoon to introduce a new quintet with Johnny as the leader, Art, Marcel Gavoty and a couple of really good Parisian musicians on piano and drums. The thing was supposed to start at three in the afternoon and they planned on having the whole day and part of the night to really get into it and record a few things. And what happened? What happened is that Johnny starts things off by arriving at five, by which time Delaunay was already boiling over with impatience, and after throwing himself into a chair he says he doesn't feel good and that he only came so he wouldn't spoil the day for the boys, but he really doesn't feel like playing.

"Marcel and I tried to convince him to just take it easy for a little while, but he wouldn't stop talking about some fields or something with urns that he had found, and on and on about the urns for half an hour. In the end he started taking all these leaves out of his pockets, he'd picked them up in some park. End result: the floor of the studio looked like the botanical gardens, the employees were wandering back and forth looking miserable, and all of that without recording a single note; just imagine the sound engineer sitting there in his booth smoking for three hours, that's an awful lot for an engineer in Paris.

"In the end, Marcel convinced Johnny that it'd be good to just give it a try; the two of them started playing and the rest of us gradually joined in, mostly just to shake off that exhaustion that comes from not doing anything. I had realized a while earlier that Johnny's right arm was all sort of cramped up, and when he started playing I swear it was a terrible thing to see. His face gray, you know, and some kind of a shudder from time to time; I thought he was going to fall flat on his face at any moment. And then just like that, he lets out a shout, looks at us one by one, very slowly, and asks us what we're waiting for to begin 'Amorous.' You know the one, that tune of Alamo's. So, Delaunay signals the engineer, we all come in as best we can, and Johnny opens his legs, he plants himself like he's on a boat that's pitching, and he takes off playing in a way I swear I've never heard before. For three minutes, until all of a sudden he lets out a squawk capable of destroying the very harmony of the universe, and he goes over to a corner leaving the rest of us right in the middle of it, letting us finish up as best we could.

"But here's the worst of it: when we finished, the first thing Johnny said was that it was all shit, that the recording wasn't worth a damn. Of course, none of us paid any attention to him, not Delaunay or any of the rest of us, because in spite of its faults, Johnny's solo was worth a thousand of the ones you hear on a normal day. Something different, I can't explain it . . . You'll hear it soon enough; as you could guess, Delaunay and the sound technicians sure aren't planning on destroying that recording. But Johnny was insisting like a crazy man, threatening to break the glass to the sound booth if they didn't prove to him that it had been erased. In the end, the engineer showed him something or other and convinced him, and then Johnny proposed that we record 'Streptomicyne,' which came out much better but also much worse, I mean, it's an impeccable record, completely solid, but it doesn't have that incredible thing that Johnny blew on 'Amorous.'"

Sighing, Art finished his beer and looked at me mournfully. I asked him what Johnny did after that, and he told me that after driving them all crazy with his stories about the leaves and the fields full of urns, he refused to go on playing and then stumbled out of the studio. Marcel took the sax away from him so he wouldn't lose it or smash it again, and between him and one of the French guys they got him back to the hotel.

What else can I do except go see him right away? But I put it off until tomorrow anyway. And the next morning I found Johnny in the police report section of the *Figaro,* because during the night it seems Johnny set the hotel room on fire and took off running naked down the hallway. Neither he nor Dédée was hurt, but Johnny's under observation at the hospital. I showed the news to my wife because I thought it might give her something to smile about during her convalescence, and I went straight to the hospital where my press pass didn't help me in the slightest. The most I found out is that Johnny's delirious and that he has enough drugs in his system to drive ten people completely insane. Poor Dédée wasn't able to resist, to convince him to stay clean; all of Johnny's women end up being his accomplices, and I'm completely convinced that the Countess is the one who got him the drugs.

In any case, the thing is I went straight to Delaunay's house to ask him to let me listen to "Amorous" as soon as possible. We'll see if "Amorous" turns out to be poor Johnny's last will and testament; and in that case, my professional duty . . .

But no, not yet. Dédée called five days later to tell me that Johnny's much better and wants to see me. I decided not to reproach her, first of all, because I imagine it's a waste of time, and second because poor Dédée's voice sounds like it's coming out of a cracked teapot. I promised to go right away, and I told her that maybe when Johnny's better we could organize a tour through some of the cities in the interior. I hung up when Dédée started to cry.

Johnny's sitting up in bed, in a room with two other patients who, luckily, are sleeping. Before I can say anything, he's trapped my head with his two huge hands and kissed me over and over on the cheeks and forehead. He's looking terribly haggard, even though he said they give him plenty to eat and he's got an appetite. For the time being, what worries him most is whether the boys are badmouthing him, whether his breakdown caused problems for anyone, and things like that. It's almost pointless to respond because he knows perfectly well that the concerts were cancelled and that that hurts Art, Marcel and the rest of them; but he asks me as if he were thinking that something good, something that would solve everything, had happened in the meantime. And at the same time he's not fooling me, because his supreme indifference is at the heart of this whole thing; Johnny couldn't care less whether everything's gone to hell, and I know him too well not to realize it.

"What do you want me to say, Johnny? Things could have turned out better, but you've got this talent for wrecking things."

"Yeah, I can't deny it," Johnny said tiredly. "And all because of the urns."

I remembered Art's words, and I just kept looking at him.

"Fields full of urns, Bruno. Tons of invisible urns, buried in this enormous field. I was walking around and from time to time I would bump into something. You'll say I dreamed it, huh. That's how it was, look: from time to time I would bump into an urn, until I realized the whole field was full of urns, there were thousands and thousands of them, and every urn was filled with the ashes of a dead person. Then I remember that I bent down and I started digging with my nails until one of the urns was out in the open. That's right, I remember. I remember I thought: 'This one's going to be empty because this one's mine.' But no, it was full of a gray powder just like I know the other ones were even though I hadn't seen them. Then . . . that's when we started recording 'Amorous,' I think."

I managed a discreet glance at his temperature chart. Quite normal; who would have thought? A young doctor stuck his head in, greeting me with a nod and giving Johnny an encouraging, almost sporty sort of wave; he seemed like a nice guy. But Johnny didn't respond, and when the doctor left without coming through the door, I saw that Johnny had his fists clenched.

"That's what they'll never understand," he said. "They're like a monkey with a feather duster, like the girls at the conservatory in Kansas who thought they were playing Chopin, no less. Bruno, in Camarillo they put me in a room with three other people, and in the morning this intern who was so brand spanking clean that it was a pleasure to see him used to come in. He looked like the son of Mr. Kleenex and Mrs. Tampax, he really did. A kind of enormous idiot who would sit by my side and give me encouragement, me, who wanted to die, who wasn't thinking about Lan or anyone else any more. And the worst of it was the guy got offended because I didn't pay any attention to him. He seemed to be waiting for me to sit up in bed, impressed with his white face and his slicked-back hair and his manicured nails, as if he thought I was going to get better like those people who go to Lourdes and throw away their crutches and start dancing on their way out . . .

"Well, that guy and all the other guys at Camarillo were convinced. About what, you want to know? I don't know, I swear, but they were convinced. About what they were, I suppose, about what they're worth, about their degrees. No, it's not that. Some of them were modest enough, they didn't think they were infallible. But even the most modest ones felt certain. That's what really pissed me off, Bruno, *that they felt certain.* Certain about what? You tell me, because even me, a poor idiot with more plagues beneath his skin than the devil himself, even I had enough awareness to feel that everything was like jelly, that everything was shaking all around me, that you only had to pay a little bit of attention, feel a little bit, shut up a little bit, to discover the gaps. In the door, in your bed: gaps. In your hand, in the newspaper, in time, in the air: all full of gaps, everything spongy, everything like a colander straining itself . . . But they were American science, do you get it, Bruno? Their white coats protected them from the gaps; they didn't see anything, they accepted what other people had already seen, they imagined they were seeing too. And naturally they couldn't see the gaps, and they felt very certain of themselves, completely convinced about their prescriptions, their injections, their damn psychoanalysis, their you-shouldn't-smoke and their you-shouldn't-drink . . . Oh, when I was finally able to demand to be moved, get on the train, look out the window at how everything was traveling backwards, getting torn to pieces, I don't know if you've seen how the landscape starts breaking apart when you watch it float off back into the distance . . . "

We're smoking Gauloises. They've given Johnny permission to drink a little brandy and smoke eight to ten cigarettes. But you can tell it's just his body that's smoking, that he's off somewhere else almost as if he were refusing to climb up out of the pit. I wonder what he's seen, what he's felt these last days. I don't want to upset him, but if he were to start talking on his own . . . We smoke, silently, and sometimes Johnny stretches out his arm and runs his fingers over my face, as if to identify me. Then he plays with his wristwatch, he looks at it affectionately.

"The thing is that they think they're smart," he says suddenly. "They think they're smart because they've gathered a ton of books together and gobbled them all up. It makes me laugh, because in reality they're good kids and they go around convinced that what they're studying and what they're doing is hard and profound. It's the same in the circus, Bruno, and among us it's the same too. People assume that certain things are the hardest, and that's why they applaud for trapeze artists or for me. I don't know what they think, that being a good musician tears you to pieces, or that the trapeze artist rips out his tendons every time he makes a move. In reality the stuff that's really hard is something else entirely, all those things people think they can do all the time. Looking, for example, or understanding a dog or a cat. These are the things that are hard, really hard. Last night all of a sudden I decided to look at myself in this little mirror, and I tell you it was so incredibly hard that I almost threw myself out of bed. Imagine you're looking at yourself; just that alone is enough to give you the chills for half an hour. That guy isn't really me, I immediately felt clearly that that wasn't me, I caught that guy by surprise, out of the corner of my eye and I knew it wasn't me. That's what I felt, and when you feel something . . . But it's like at Palm Beach, one wave is followed by the next and then the next . . . You've barely felt something and then the next one comes along, the words come . . . No, it's not the words, it's what's inside the words, that type of glue, that drool. And the drool comes and it covers you, and it convinces you that the guy in the mirror is you. Of course, you can't help but see it. It's me, my hair, this scar. And people don't realize that the only thing they're accepting is the drool, and that's why they think it's so easy to look at themselves in the mirror. Or to cut a slice of bread with a knife. Have you ever cut a slice of bread with a knife?"

"Yeah, that's happened pretty often," I said, amused.

"And you didn't think anything of it. I can't, Bruno. One night I threw everything so far away that the knife almost took out the eye of the Japanese guy at the next table. It was in Los Angeles; it caused such an enormous commotion . . . When I explained it to them, they arrested me. Even though the whole thing seemed so simple to explain. That's when I met Dr. Christie. A wonderful guy, even though me and doctors . . ."

He moved his hand through the air, touching it all over, leaving it as if marked by the passage of his hand. He smiles. I have the feeling he's alone, completely alone. I feel hollow beside him. If Johnny decided to move his hand through me, he'd cut me like butter, like smoke. Maybe that's why he sometimes brushes my face with his fingers, cautiously.

"You've got the loaf of bread there, on the tablecloth," says Johnny, looking at the air. "It's a solid thing, there's no denying it, it smells great and the color's beautiful. It's not me, it's different, outside of me. But if I touch it, if I reach out my fingers and grasp it, then there's something that changes, don't you think? The bread's outside of me, but I touch it with my fingers, I feel it, I feel like it's the world, but if I can touch it and feel it, then you can't really say it's something else, can you?"

"That, my friend, is a question that very many men with very long beards have been racking their brains over for thousands of years."

"With bread, it happens during the day," Johnny murmurs, covering his face. "And I'm brave enough to touch it, to cut it in two, to stick it in my mouth. Nothing happens, I know; that's the terrible part. Do you realize how terrible it is that nothing happens? You can cut bread, you stick a knife right into it, and everything goes on just like before. I don't understand, Bruno."

I was beginning to get concerned about Johnny's face, his excitement. It's become more and more difficult to get him to talk about jazz, his memories, his plans, bring him back to reality. (To reality; as soon as I write it, it makes me feel sick. Johnny's right, this can't be reality, it's not possible that being a jazz critic is reality, because if it is, someone's pulling our leg. But at the same time we can't keep humoring Johnny like this because we'll all end up going crazy.)

He's fallen asleep now, or at least he's closed his eyes and is pretending to be asleep. Once again I realize how difficult it is to know what he's doing, what Johnny *is*. If he's asleep, if he's pretending to sleep, if he believes he's sleeping. You're much further outside Johnny than you are with any other friend. No one can be more vulgar, more common, more tied to the circumstances of a poor life; accessible on all sides, apparently. He's no exception, apparently. Anybody can be like Johnny, as long as he accepts being a poor sick devil, addicted and lacking willpower and full of poetry and talent. Apparently. For me, having spent my life admiring geniuses, the Picassos, the Einsteins, the whole damn list anyone can come up with in a minute (and Gandhi, and Chaplin, and Stravinsky), I'm as prepared as anyone to admit that these geniuses go around with their heads in the clouds and that you shouldn't be surprised by anything they do. They're different, there's no two ways about it. But in Johnny's case, the difference is secret, irritating in its mysteriousness, because there's no explanation for it. Johnny isn't a genius, he hasn't discovered anything, he plays jazz like a few thousand other Negro and white musicians do, and even though he does it better than any of them, you've got to admit that it depends a little on the audience's preferences, fashion, the times, in short. Panassié, for example, believes that Johnny simply isn't any good, and although we believe the one who simply isn't any good is Panassié, in any case these are matters that're open to discussion. All of this proves that Johnny isn't anything special, but as soon as I think it, I ask myself if there isn't something in Johnny that is most definitely special (which he's more unaware of than anyone). I'm sure he'd get a good laugh out of it if anyone told him that. I pretty much know how he thinks, how he lives these things. I say how he lives these things, because Johnny . . . But that's not what I wanted to talk about, what I wanted to explain to myself is that the distance between Johnny and us has no explanation, it isn't based on explainable differences. And it seems to me he's the first one to pay the consequences for that, it affects him as much as it affects us. It makes you want to say right off that Johnny is like an angel among men, until basic honesty forces you to swallow the phrase, cleverly turning it on its head, and recognizing that perhaps what's going on is that Johnny is a man among angels, a reality amidst the unreality of the rest of us. And maybe that's why Johnny touches my face with his fingers and makes me feel so unhappy, so transparent, so insignificant with my good health, my house, my wife, my prestige. My prestige, above all. Above all my prestige.

But it's the same as always, I left the hospital and as soon as I was back out in the world, in time, in everything I have to do, the tables had spun softly through the air and had flipped over. Poor Johnny, so outside of reality. (It's the truth, it's the truth. It's easier for me to believe it's the truth now that I'm in a café and two hours away from my visit to the hospital, more than all that stuff I wrote earlier, trying as hard as I could to force myself to be at least a little bit decent with myself.)

Luckily the thing with the fire turned out okay, because as could have been guessed the Countess has been up to her old tricks so the thing with the fire would turn out okay. Dédée and Art Boucaya came to see me at the paper, and the three of us went to Vix to listen to the now famous—although still secret—recording of "Amorous." In the taxi Dédée told me, without really wanting to, how the Countess had resolved the whole situation Johnny had gotten himself into with the fire, which really hadn't gone much beyond a singed mattress and the terrible scare it caused all the Algerians who live in the hotel on Rue Lagrange. The fine (already paid), another hotel (already arranged by Tica), and Johnny's convalescing in a huge and very lovely bed, drinking milk by the bucketful and reading the *Paris Match* and *The New Yorker* as well as his famous (and filthy) paperback of Dylan Thomas poems covered in penciled notations.

After this news and a brandy at the corner café, we settled into the recording studio to listen to "Amorous" and "Streptomicyne." Art asked them to turn off the lights and he stretched out on the floor to listen better. And then Johnny came in and his music moved through us, across our faces, he came in there with us even though he's in his hotel and in bed, and he swept us with his music for a quarter hour. I understand why he's enraged by the idea that they're going to release "Amorous," because anyone can find its faults, the perfectly perceptible squawks that accompany the ends of some phrases and especially the wild final descent, that brief muffled note that reminds me of a heart being broken, a knife slicing into a loaf of bread (and there he was, talking about bread just a few days ago). But on the other hand Johnny would miss what is for us terribly beautiful, the anxiety trying to break free during that improvisation, full of escapes in every direction, questions, desperate motion. Johnny can't understand (because what he sees as a failure strikes us as a new path, or at the very least the sign pointing to a new path), but "Amorous" will remain one of the greatest moments in jazz history. The artist within him will go wild with rage every time he hears this parody of his desire, of everything he wanted to be able to say while he was fighting, staggering, saliva running from his mouth alongside the music, more alone than ever when confronted by that which he's pursuing, which continues to flee him no matter how much he pursues it. It's curious, I needed to hear this, although everything was already converging on this, on "Amorous," in order to realize that Johnny isn't a victim, he isn't being pursued like everyone believes, as I myself implied in my biography (the English edition, by the way, just came out and it's selling like Coca-Cola). Now I know it's not like that, Johnny pursues instead of being pursued, the difficulties in his life all stem from being the hunter, not from being the animal that's being chased to ground. No one can know what it is that Johnny pursues, but it's like that, it's there, in "Amorous," in the drugs, in his absurd speeches about so many things, in his relapses, in that little Dylan Thomas book, in the whole poor devil that is Johnny and that enlarges him and converts him into a living absurdity, into a hunter without arms and without legs, into a hare that's running after a tiger that's sleeping. And I find myself forced to say that in the end "Amorous" made me want to vomit, as if that could free me of him, of everything in him that runs against me and against everyone, that shapeless black mass without hands and without feet, that crazed chimp who runs his fingers over my face and smiles at me with pity.

Art and Dédée don't see (I don't think they want to see) beyond the formal beauty of "Amorous." Dédée even prefers "Streptomicyne," where Johnny improvises with his usual ease, with what the audience takes to be perfection and I believe is in Johnny actually distraction, letting the music take off, being elsewhere. Once we were outside I asked Dédée about their plans, and she told me that as soon as Johnny can leave the hotel (the police are preventing it for now) a new label is going to record everything he wants, and the pay's decent. Art maintains that Johnny's full of wonderful ideas, and that he and Marcel Gavoty are going to "work up" the new stuff with Johnny, although after the last few weeks, one can see that Art isn't so sure about it, and I also found out on the side that he's been talking with his agent about returning to New York as soon as possible. Which I more than understand, poor guy.

"Tica's really helping out," Dédée said resentfully. "Of course, it's all so easy for her. She always arrives at the last minute, and she doesn't have to do anything except open her purse and fix everything. Me, on the other hand . . . "

Art and I looked at each other. What're we supposed to say to her? Women spend their lives circling around Johnny and guys like Johnny. It's not surprising, you don't have to be a woman to feel attracted to Johnny. The hard thing is to circle around him without losing your distance, like a good satellite, like a good critic. Art wasn't in Baltimore back then, but I remember when I first met Johnny, when he was living with Lan and the kids. It was sad to see Lan. But after dealing with Johnny for a while, accepting little by little his mastery over his music, his daytime nightmares, his inconceivable explanations about things that never happened, his sudden displays of affection, then one understood why Lan looked like that and how it was impossible for her to live with Johnny and look any other way at the same time. Tica's another story: she escapes him by being promiscuous and living the good life, plus she's got the dollar by the balls, which is even better than having a machine gun, at least that's what Art Boucaya says when he's feeling resentful of Tica or when his head hurts.

"Come as soon as you can," pleaded Dédée. "He likes talking to you."

I would have liked to lecture her about the fire (about the cause of the fire, which she must have been involved in) but it would be as useless as telling Johnny himself that he needs to become an upstanding citizen. For the time being everything's going well, and it's curious (it's disconcerting) that as soon as things start going well on Johnny's end, I feel immensely pleased. I'm not innocent enough to believe it's nothing more than a friendly reaction. It's more like a postponement, a breather. I don't need to look for explanations when I feel it as clearly as I can feel the nose on my face. It makes me mad to be the only one who feels this, who suffers from it all the time. It makes me mad that Art Boucaya, Tica and Dédée don't realize that every time Johnny suffers, goes to jail, wants to kill himself, sets a mattress on fire or runs naked through the hallway of a hotel, he's paying something for them, he's dying for them. Without knowing it, and not like the people who give long speeches from death row or write books to denounce the evils of humanity or play the piano with the air of someone who's cleansing the world of sin. Without knowing it, poor saxophonist, and with everything about that word that's ridiculous, that's insignificant, that signifies just one more among so many other poor saxophonists.

The bad thing is that if I keep on going like this I'm going to end up writing more about myself than about Johnny. I'm beginning to remind myself of some kind of missionary and I don't like that at all. While I was returning home I was thinking, with the cynicism necessary to regain confidence, that in my book about Johnny I only mention the pathological side of his personality discreetly, in passing. I didn't think it was necessary to explain to people that Johnny believes he's walking through fields full of urns, or that pictures move when he looks at them; these are, after all, ghosts of the drugs and will disappear when he finishes treatment for his addictions. But you could say that Johnny leaves me those ghosts as a pledge, he places them in my pocket as if they were handkerchiefs until it's time to take them back. And I think I'm the only one who puts up with them, lives with them and fears them; and no one knows that, not even Johnny. You can't confess things like that to Johnny, the way you might confess them to a really great man, to a teacher before whom we choose to humble ourselves in exchange for a piece of advice. What is this world that I have to shoulder like a burden? What kind of missionary am I? There isn't the slightest hint of greatness in Johnny; I've known it ever since I first met him, ever since I began to admire him. This hasn't surprised me for a while now, although in the beginning I found this lack of greatness disturbing, perhaps because it's a dimension one isn't prepared to assign to the first person who comes along, especially to a jazzman. I don't know why (I don't *know* why) at one point I thought there was in Johnny a greatness that he disproves day after day (or that we disprove, which isn't the same thing really; because, let's be honest, within Johnny there's something like the ghost of another Johnny who might have been, and that other Johnny is full of greatness; you notice, in the ghost, the lack of that dimension, which it nevertheless negatively evokes and contains).

I say this because the attempts Johnny has made to change his life, from his failed suicide attempt to the drugs, are the ones you would expect from someone as lacking in greatness as he is. I think this makes me admire him even more, because he's really a chimpanzee who wants to learn how to read, a poor fellow who runs face first into walls, and isn't convinced, and starts all over again.

Oh, but if the chimpanzee starts reading some day, what a massive upheaval, what chaos, what a save-yourself-if-you-can, but first of all, get out of my way. It's terrible to see a man without the slightest hint of greatness throw himself against the wall like this. He denounces every one of us with the impact his bones make, he rips us to shreds with his first line of music. (Martyrs, heroes, fine: you know what to expect from them. But Johnny!)

Sequences. I don't know how to say it any better, it's something like the notion that terrible or idiotic sequences suddenly come together in a person's life, without knowing what law beyond the official statutes determines that a certain phone call is going to be immediately followed by the arrival of our sister who lives in Auvergne, or that the milk's going to boil over, or that, glancing out the balcony, we're going to catch a glimpse of a kid being run over by a car. Just like on soccer teams and boards of directors, it would seem that destiny always names some substitute in case the regulars fail. And that's why this morning, when I'm still surrounded by the pleasant knowledge that Johnny Carter was doing better and was happy, I get an urgent phone call at the paper: it's Tica calling, and the news is that Bee, Lan and Johnny's youngest daughter, just died in Chicago, and of course Johnny's going crazy, and it would be good if I could go give his friends a hand.

I went back up the stairs of some hotel—there've been so many stairs in my friendship with Johnny—to find Tica having tea, Dédée soaking a towel, Art, Delaunay and Pepe Ramírez who're quietly discussing the latest news about Lester Young, and Johnny motionless in bed, a towel on his forehead and a perfectly tranquil, almost scornful countenance. I immediately hid the sympathetic expression I had prepared, simply giving Johnny's hand a firm squeeze, lighting a cigarette and waiting.

"It hurts me right here, Bruno," Johnny said after a while, touching the spot conventionally associated with the heart. "Bruno, she was like a little white stone in my hand. And I'm nothing more than a poor yellow horse, and no one, no one, can wipe the tears from my eyes."

All this said solemnly, almost recited, and Tica looking at Art, and the two of them exchanging gestures encouraging understanding and indulgence, taking advantage of the fact that Johnny has his face covered with the wet towel and can't see them. Personally I'm sickened by cheap phrases, but everything Johnny said, in addition to the fact that I feel like I've read it somewhere, sounds to me like a mask he put on before talking, as hollow as that, as useless as that. Dédée came in with another towel and switched them, and in between I managed to catch a glimpse of Johnny's face and I saw it was ash gray, his mouth twisted and his eyes squeezed shut until they're a mass of wrinkles. And as always with Johnny, things took place differently than expected, and Pepe Ramírez, who doesn't know him all that well, is still feeling affected by the shock and perhaps the scandal, because after a while Johnny sat up in bed and began spouting insults, slowly, chewing each word over, and then letting it loose like a spinning top insulting the people responsible for the "Amorous" recording, without looking at anyone but pinning us all down like bugs on cardboard, needing nothing more than the incredible obscenity of his words, and he was insulting everyone from "Amorous" like that for two minutes, starting with Art and Delaunay, continuing on through me (although I . . .) and ending up with Dédée, in the name of Jesus Christ our Lord and the fucking whore who gave birth to each and every one of them without exception. And that in the end, that and the thing about the little white stone, was the funeral oration for Bee, dead of pneumonia in Chicago.

Two empty weeks will pass; tons of work, newspaper articles, visits here and there—a good summary of the life of a critic, that man who can only live by depending on other people, on news and on distant decisions. Speaking of which, one night Tica, Baby Lennox and I will find ourselves in the Café de Flore, very happily humming "Out of Nowhere" and talking about a piano solo by Billy Taylor who all three of us think is good, especially Baby Lennox who's dressed in Saint-Germain-des-Prés style and you should see how it looks on her. Baby will observe

Johnny's arrival with the rapture only a twenty year old could muster, and Johnny will look at her without seeing her and will keep on going, until he's seated at another table, completely drunk or asleep. I'll feel Tica's hand on my knee.

"See, he smoked again last night. Or this afternoon. That woman . . . "

I answered without really wanting to get into it that Dédée's no guiltier than anyone else, including her since she's smoked with Johnny dozens of times and will do it again the first time she gets it into her head. I'll feel a strong urge to leave and be alone, like always happens when it's impossible to get close to Johnny, to be with him and take his side. I'll see him making drawings on the table with his finger, keep on staring at the waiter who's asking him what he wants to drink, and finally Johnny'll draw a type of arrow in the air and he'll hold it up with both hands as if it weighed a ton, and at the other tables the people will begin to become very discreetly amused, the way they get at the Flore. Then Tica'll say: "Shit," she'll go to Johnny's table, and after saying something to the waiter, she'll start talking into Johnny's ear. It goes without saying that Baby will insist on entrusting me with her most cherished hopes, but I'll tell her vaguely that Johnny needs to be left alone that night and that good girls go to bed early, and if possible with a jazz critic. Baby will laugh nicely, her hand will caress my hair, and afterwards we'll sit and watch the girl who coats her face in white lead and uses green make-up on her eyes and even her mouth. Baby'll say it doesn't look so bad on her, and I'll ask her to quietly sing me one of those blues tunes that's making her famous in London and Stockholm. And afterward we'll go back to "Out of Nowhere," which is pursuing us endlessly tonight like a dog that's also made of white lead and green eyes.

Two of the guys from Johnny's new quintet will show up, and I'll take advantage of the opportunity to ask them how things went tonight; that's how I'll find out that Johnny was barely able to play, but that what he did manage to play was worth all of John Lewis's ideas put together, assuming that Lewis is capable of having any ideas because, like one of the guys said, the only thing he always has on hand are enough notes to cover a gap, which isn't the same thing. And in the meantime I'll wonder just how much Johnny, and especially the audience that believes in Johnny, is going to be able to withstand. The guys won't accept a beer, Baby and I'll be alone again, and I'll end up giving in to her questions and explaining to Baby, who really deserves her nickname, why Johnny's sick and finished, why the guys from the quintet are more fed up every day, why things are going to explode one of these days like they've already exploded in San Francisco, in Baltimore and in New York a half dozen times.

Other musicians who play in the area will come in, and some of them will go to Johnny's table and they'll say hi to him but he'll look at them as if he's far away, with a horribly idiotic face, his eyes damp and meek, his mouth incapable of containing the spittle that shines on his lips. It'll be fun to observe Tica's and Baby's two-part dealings: Tica resorting to her power over men to keep them away from Johnny with a quick explanation and a smile, Baby whispering in my ear about all her admiration for Johnny and how good it'd be to take him to a clinic to be treated for his addictions, and all that simply because she's like a bitch in heat and would like to go to bed with Johnny this very night, something that is incidentally impossible as far as I can see, which makes me quite happy. Just like ever since I've known her, I'll think about how nice it would be to be able to caress Baby's thighs and I'll be one step away from suggesting that we go have a drink someplace quieter (she won't want to and deep down I won't either, because that other table will keep us chained and unhappy right here) until suddenly, without any warning of what's going to happen, we'll see Johnny get up slowly, look at us and recognize us, come toward us—let's say toward me, because it's not about Baby—and when he reaches the table he'll bend over a little bit as if it were the most natural thing in the world, like someone who's going to take a french fry from a plate, and we'll see him kneel down in front of me, he'll get on his knees as if it were the most natural thing in the world and he'll look me right in the eye, and I'll see that he's crying, and I'll know without words that Johnny's crying for little Bee.

My reaction's so natural: I wanted to pick Johnny up, keep him from making a fool of himself, and in the end I'm the one who makes a fool of himself because there's nothing more pitiful than a man making an effort to move another man who's just fine where he is, who's perfectly comfortable in whatever position he feels like adopting, so the customers at the Flore, who don't get upset about little things, didn't look upon me very kindly, even though the majority of them didn't know that that Negro kneeling down there is Johnny Carter; they looked at me like people would look at someone who climbs up onto an altar and starts tugging on Jesus to remove him from the cross. The first one to reproach me for it was Johnny, he was crying silently, and he raised his eyes and looked at me, and between that and the customers' obvious disapproval I had no choice but to sit back down again in front of Johnny, feeling worse than him, wanting to be anywhere except in that chair in front of Johnny on his knees.

The rest wasn't so bad, although I don't know how many centuries went by before anyone moved, before the tears stopped running down Johnny's face, before his eyes stopped staring into my own while I tried to offer him a cigarette, to light one for myself, to give Baby a sign that I understood since she was, it seems to me, about to run out or start crying in turn. As always, it was Tica who fixed the whole mess, sitting down at our table very calmly, pulling a chair over next to Johnny and putting her hand on his shoulder, without forcing him, until in the end Johnny straightened out a little bit and progressed from that nightmare to the more appropriate posture of a sitting friend, simply raising his knees a few centimeters and allowing the very acceptable comfort of a chair between his rear end and the floor (I was going to say "and the cross," this really is contagious). People got tired of looking at Johnny, he got tired of crying, and we got tired of feeling like shit. I suddenly understood the affection some painters have for chairs; any of the chairs at the Flore now struck me as an object of unexpected wonder, a flower, a perfume, the perfect instrument to bestow order and honor on any of the city's inhabitants.

Johnny took out a handkerchief and apologized without being too insistent about it, and Tica ordered a double espresso and made him drink it. Baby was wonderful: suddenly renouncing all her stupidity surrounding Johnny, she began humming "Mamie's Blues" without giving the impression of doing it on purpose, and Johnny looked at her and smiled, and it seemed to me that both Tica and I thought at the same time that the image of Bee was disappearing little by little from the depths of Johnny's eyes, and that Johnny once again accepted the idea of returning to our side for a while, accompanying us until the next time he tried to take flight. As always, as soon as I stopped feeling like shit, my superiority over Johnny allowed me to treat him indulgently, talking a little bit about everything without getting into things that were too personal (it would have been awful to see Johnny slip down in the chair, once again . . .), and luckily Tica and Baby were behaving like angels and the last hour had involved such a turn-over in clientele at the Flore that the customers at one in the morning didn't even suspect what had just happened, although in reality not too much had happened if you really think about it. Baby was the first to leave (Baby's a studious girl: by nine a.m., she'll be practicing with Fred Callender for a recording session in the afternoon) and Tica finished off her third glass of brandy and offered to drive us home. Then Johnny said no, he wanted to keep talking with me, and Tica thought that was good and she left, but not without buying everyone a round first, like a Countess should. And Johnny and I had a glass of chartreuse, since these weaknesses are permitted among friends, and we started walking down Saint-Germain-des-Prés because Johnny insisted it'll do him good to walk and I'm not the type to abandon a friend in these kinds of circumstances.

We go along Rue de l'Abbaye to Place de Furstenberg, which reminds Johnny dangerously of a toy theater that his godfather seems to have given him when he was eight. I attempt to lead him over toward Rue Jacob because I'm afraid the memories will bring Bee back to him, but you could say Johnny has closed that chapter for the remainder of the evening. He's walking along peacefully, without hesitation (I've seen him stumbling down the street on other occasions, and not because he's drunk; something in his reflexes just isn't working right) and the heat of the night and the silence of the streets does us both good. We smoke Gauloises, we let ourselves be drawn toward the river, and in front of one of the bookseller's tin shacks on Quai de Conti some memory or other or some student's whistling brings a Vivaldi melody to our mouths and we both start singing it with a great deal of feeling and enthusiasm, and Johnny says that if he had his sax he'd spend the night playing Vivaldi, which I find exaggerated.

"Well, I'd play a little Bach and Charles Ives too," Johnny says, obligingly. "I don't know why the French don't like Charles Ives. Do you know his stuff? The one about the leopard, you really should know the one about the leopard. *A leopard . . .*"

And in his weak tenor voice he sings at length about the leopard, and it goes without saying that a lot of what he sings isn't Ives at all, which Johnny doesn't care about as long as he's sure he's singing something good. In the end we sit on the wall along the river, opposite Rue Gît-le-Coeur and we smoke another cigarette because it's a beautiful night and after a while the tobacco will make us go have a beer in a café and Johnny and I like that in advance. I almost don't pay any attention when he mentions my book for the first time, because he goes back to talking about Charles Ives right away and how much fun he had incorporating many of Ives's tunes into his records, without anyone realizing (not even Ives himself, I suppose), but after a while I start thinking about the business about the book and I try to get him back onto the subject.

"Oh, I read a few pages," Johnny says. "At Tica's thing they were talking a lot about your book but I didn't even understand the title. Yesterday Art brought me the English version and then I made sense out of a few things. It's good, your book."

I adopt the attitude that's expected in these situations, combining an air of offhanded modesty with a certain amount of interest, as if his opinion might reveal to me—me, the author—the truth about my book.

"It's like in a mirror," says Johnny. "At first I thought reading what someone writes about you would be more or less like looking at yourself, and not in a mirror either. I admire writers a lot, the things they say are incredible. That whole thing about the origins of bebop . . . "

"Well, all I did was literally transcribe what you told me in Baltimore," I say, defending myself without knowing from what.

"Right, and it's all there, but in reality it's like in a mirror," Johnny insists.

"So what else do you want? Mirrors reflect reality."

"There are things missing, Bruno," says Johnny. "You know a lot more than me, but I think there are things that're missing."

"Things you forgot to tell me then," I respond, really annoyed. This uncivilized monkey is capable of . . .

(Better have a talk with Delaunay, it would be a real shame if some reckless statement were to ruin a sincere critical work that . . . *Lan's red dress, for example,* Johnny's saying. And in any case, take advantage of anything new that comes out tonight and incorporate it into the next edition; that wouldn't be bad. *It kind of stank,* Johnny's saying, *and that's the only thing that's worth a damn on that record.* Yes, listen carefully and proceed quickly, because in other people's hands these possible denials could have regrettable consequences. *And the urn in the middle, the big-*

gest one, full of some dust that was almost blue, Johnny's saying, *just like this compact my sister used to have.* As long as he doesn't get beyond the hallucinations, the worst thing would be if he denied the background ideas, the aesthetic system that's been praised . . . *And plus "cool" isn't at all what you wrote,* Johnny's saying. Pay attention.)

"What do you mean it's not what I wrote? It's fine that things change, Johnny, but less than six months ago you . . . "

"Six months ago," says Johnny, getting down off the river wall and putting his elbows on it so he could rest his chin on his hands. "Six months. Oh, Bruno, I could really jam now if the boys were here . . . And by the way: what you wrote about the sax and sex is really ingenious, great play on words. *Six months ago. Six, sax, sex.* Positively charming, Bruno. Damn you, Bruno."

I'm not going to start explaining to him that his mental age doesn't permit him to understand that that innocent play on words supports an entire theoretical system that's quite profound (Leonard Feather thought it was exactly right when I explained it to him in New York) and that the paraeroticism of jazz has been evolving since the time of the washboard, etc. It's the same as always, suddenly I'm pleased to be able to think that critics are much more necessary than I myself am prepared to recognize (in private, within these pages) because the creators, from the composers all the way down to Johnny and passing through the whole damn series of them, are incapable of extrapolating the full dialectical consequences of their work, postulating the underlying principles and the transcendence of what they're writing or improvising. I've got to remember this when I'm feeling depressed and sorry for myself because I'm nothing more than a critic. *And the name of the star is called Wormwood,* Johnny's saying, and I suddenly hear his other voice, the voice when he's . . . how can I say this, how do I describe Johnny when he's outside of himself, all alone again, off in another world? I get down off the river wall, concerned; I look closely at him. And the name of the star is called Wormwood, there's nothing you can do about it.

"And the name of the star is called Wormwood," says Johnny, talking into his hands. "And their dead bodies shall lie in the street of the great city. Six months ago."

Even if no one sees me, even if no one knows, I shrug my shoulders up toward the stars (the name of the star is called Wormwood). We're back to the same old thing: "I've been playing this tomorrow." The name of the star is called Wormwood and their dead bodies shall lie in the street six months ago. In the street of the great city. Off in another world, far away. And me bearing grudges, just because he didn't want to tell me anything else about my book, and I really didn't get to learn what he thinks about the book that thousands and thousands of fans are reading in two languages (three pretty soon, and they're already talking about a Spanish edition. I guess they do play something besides the tango in Buenos Aires).

"It was a beautiful dress," Johnny says. "You can't even imagine what Lan looked like in it, but it'd be better if I told you over a whisky, if you have any money. Dédée only left me three hundred francs."

He laughs mockingly, looking at the Seine. As if he didn't know how to get drinks and drugs. He starts telling me Dédée's a really good person (and nothing about the book) and that she does it out of the goodness of her heart, but luckily he's got his friend Bruno (who wrote a book, but nothing about that) and the best thing would be to go sit in a café in the Arab Quarter, where they leave you alone as long as they see you belong somewhat to the star called Wormwood (that's what I'm thinking, we're going in by Saint-Sévérin and it's two in the morning, the time when my wife tends to wake up and rehearse everything she's going to say to me in the morning along with her café au lait). That's how things go with Johnny, that's how we drink a terrible cheap brandy, that's how we double our dosage and feel so happy. But about the book, nothing, only his sister's swan-shaped compact, the star, little bits of things that are passed off as little bits of sentences, little bits of glances, little bits of smiles, like drops of spittle on the table, stuck to the edge of the glass (Johnny's glass). Yes, there are times when I wish he were dead. I suppose lots of people would think the same thing if they were in my shoes. But how do I resign myself to the fact that Johnny'll die, taking with him what he doesn't want to say to me tonight, that after his death he'll continue hunting, continue being off in another world (I don't know how to write all this any more) even if his death gives me peace, a promotion at the university, the authority that comes from undisputed publications and well organized burials.

From time to time, Johnny interrupts his long drum roll on the table, looks at me, makes an incomprehensible gesture and goes back to drumming. The owner of the café knows us from when we used to come in with an Arab guitarist. Ben Aifa would have liked to have gone to bed a while ago, we're the only people left in the grimy café that smells of *ají* and greasy meat pies. I'm practically collapsing with exhaustion too but the anger keeps me going, a muted rage that isn't directed at Johnny, it's more like when you make love all afternoon and you feel the need for a shower, wanting the soap and water to remove everything that's starting to turn rancid, starting to display too clearly what was, in the beginning . . . And Johnny's beating a stubborn rhythm on the tabletop, and at times he sings softly, almost without looking at me. He might very well never offer up another commentary on my book. Things lead him from place to place, tomorrow it could be some woman, some new problem to deal with, a trip. The most prudent thing would be to get the English edition away from him on the sly, talk with Dédée and ask her to do this favor in exchange for all of yours. This worry, this near rage, it's absurd. There was no reason to expect any enthusiasm on Johnny's part; the truth is it had never occurred to me to think he might read the book. I know perfectly well that the book doesn't tell the truth about Johnny (it doesn't lie either), but it's limited to Johnny's music. Out of discretion, out of kindness, I didn't want to put everything on display: his incurable schizophrenia, the sordid undercurrent of drugs, the promiscuity of that pitiful life. My goal was to show the essential contours, putting the emphasis where it really belonged, Johnny's incomparable art. What else could I say? But perhaps it's precisely there where he's waiting for me, lying in wait for something like always, crouching down, prepared to give one of his absurd leaps where we all end up getting hurt. And that's where he may be waiting for me, waiting for me in order to deny all the aesthetic principles I've used to create the ultimate explanation of his music, the great theory of contemporary jazz that has afforded me so much acclaim in so many places.

To be completely honest, what do I care about his life? The only thing I worry about is whether he'll let himself get carried away by the type of behavior I'm not capable of participating in (let's say I choose not to participate in) and end up denying the conclusions in my book. Or that he'll let it slip out publicly that my affirmations are false, that his music is something else entirely.

"Hey, a while ago you said there were things missing in my book."

(Pay attention now.)

"That things are missing, Bruno? Oh, yeah, I said there were things missing. Look, it's not only Lan's red dress. There's . . . Do you think there really are urns, Bruno? I saw them again last night, a huge field, but they weren't so buried this time. Some of them had inscriptions and drawings on them, there were giants with helmets like in the movies, and huge clubs in their hands. It's terrible to walk around among all those urns and know there isn't anybody else, I'm the only one who walks around them, searching. Don't worry, Bruno, it doesn't matter that you forgot to put all that in there. But, Bruno," and he raises a finger that isn't trembling, "what you forgot about is me."

"Come on, Johnny."

"Me, Bruno, me. And it's not your fault that you couldn't write what I can't play. When you tell people that my true biography is on my records, I know you really mean it and it sounds good too, but it's not true. And if I myself haven't been able to play like I should, play what I really am . . . no one can ask you for miracles, Bruno. It's hot in here, let's go."

I follow him out onto the street, and we wander a little ways until a white cat meows at us in an alleyway and Johnny's there petting it a long time. Well, that's enough now; in Place Saint-Michel, I can get a cab to take him to the hotel and I'll go home. In the end it wasn't so terrible; for a little while there I was afraid that Johnny had elaborated a type of anti-theory to my book, and that he was going to try it out on me before releasing it all over the place full speed ahead. Poor Johnny petting a white cat. Deep down the only thing he really said is that no one knows anything about anyone else, which isn't news to anybody. All biographies assume that and continue onward, what the hell. Let's go, Johnny, let's go home, it's late.

"Don't think it's only that," says Johnny, straightening up suddenly as if he knew what I was thinking. "There's God, my friend. You sure didn't get that one right."

"Let's go, Johnny, let's go home, it's late."

"There's what you and people like you, my friend, call God. A tube of toothpaste in the morning, they call that God. Garbage cans, they call that God. The fear of kicking the bucket, they call that God. And you had the nerve to mix me up in all that crap, you wrote that my childhood, and my family, and who knows what ancestral inheritance . . . A whole heap of rotten eggs and you clucking around right in the middle of them, very happy with your God. I don't want your God, he's never been mine."

"The only thing I said was that Negro music . . . "

"I don't want your God," Johnny repeats. "Why'd you make me accept Him in your book? I don't know if there's a God, I play my music, I create my God, I don't need your inventions, you can leave all that for Mahalia Jackson and the Pope, and you take that part out of your book right now."

"If you insist," I say, to say something. "In the second edition."

"I'm as alone as this cat is, much more alone because I know it and he doesn't. Damn thing, he's digging his claws into my hand. Well, jazz isn't only music, I'm not only Johnny Carter."

"That's precisely what I was trying to say when I wrote that sometimes you play like . . . "

"Like it's raining up my ass," Johnny says, and it's the first time all night that I feel him get enraged. "I can't say anything, you immediately translate it into your dirty language. If you see angels when I play, that's not my fault. If other people open their mouths and say I've reached perfection, that's not my fault. And that's the worst part, that's what you really forgot to say in your book, Bruno: it's that I'm not worth a damn, that what I play and what people applaud me for isn't worth a damn, it truly isn't worth a damn."

Strange modesty, really, at this time of night. This Johnny . . .

"How can I explain it to you?" yells Johnny, putting his hands on my shoulders, shaking me back and forth. ("Quiet down out there!" someone shouts from a window.) "It isn't a question of more music or less music, it's something else . . . For example, it's the difference between Bee being dead and Bee still being alive. What I play is Bee dead, you know, while what I want, what I want . . . And that's why I smash the sax sometimes and people think I lost control because I'm drunk. Of course the truth is I'm always drunk when I do it, because a sax really does cost a lot of money."

"Let's go this way. I'm going to get you a cab to take you back to the hotel."

"You're just a bundle of goodness, aren't you, Bruno," says Johnny, mockingly. "Our friend Bruno jots down everything you say to him in his notebook, everything except the important stuff. I never thought you could be so wrong until Art gave me the book. At first I thought you were talking about someone else, Ronnie or Marcel, and then Johnny this and Johnny that, which means it was about me and I was wondering but is that me?, and there I am again in Baltimore, and at Birdland, and that my style . . . Listen," he adds almost coldly, "it's not that I don't realize you wrote a book for the public. That's fine and everything you say about my way of playing and feeling jazz seems perfectly okay to me. What do we need to keep talking about your book for? Some garbage in the Seine, that straw that's floating along the dock, that's your book. And I'm that other straw, and you're that bottle that's bobbing along over there. Bruno, I'm going to die without finding . . . without . . . "

I grab onto him by his arms, lean him against the river wall. He's sinking into the same delirium as always, muttering parts of words, spitting.

"Without finding . . . " he repeats. "Without finding . . . "

"What did you want to find, brother?" I ask. "People shouldn't ask for the impossible, what you've found would be enough for . . . "

"For you, I know," Johnny says bitterly. "For Art, for Dédée, for Lan . . . You don't know how . . . Yes, sometimes the door started to open . . . Look at those two straws, they found each other, they're dancing for each other . . . It's pretty, huh . . . It started to open . . . Time . . . I've already told you, I think, that this stuff about time . . . Bruno, I've spent my life looking for that door to finally open in my music. Just anything, a crack . . . I remember in New York, one night . . . A red dress. Yes, red, and it looked great on her. So, one night we were with Miles and Hal . . . we'd been going over the same stuff for an hour I think, just us, so happy . . . Miles played something so beautiful that it almost knocks me off my chair, and then I was off, I closed my eyes, and I was flying. Bruno, I swear to you I was flying . . . I could hear myself as if it was from very far away but inside myself, beside myself, someone was standing . . . Not exactly someone . . . Look at that bottle, it's amazing the way it bobs along . . . It wasn't someone, just that you look for comparisons . . . It was the belief, the connection, the way it is in our dreams sometimes, don't you think?, when everything's resolved, Lan and the girls are waiting for you with a turkey in the oven, you're driving along and don't hit a single red light, everything glides along as smooth as a billiard ball. And what was by my side was just like me but not taking up any space, without being in New York, and especially without time, without later . . . without later having . . . For a while there wasn't anything but forever . . . And I didn't know it was a lie, that it happened because I was lost in the music, and that as soon as I stopped playing, because after all I had to let poor Hal come in and quench his desire for the piano at some point, at that very instant I would fall head first back into myself . . . "

He cries softly, rubbing his eyes with his dirty hands. I don't know what to do anymore, it's so late, the damp is coming up off the river, we're both going to catch cold.

"I think I wanted to swim without water," Johnny murmurs. "I think I wanted to have Lan's red dress but without Lan. And Bee's dead, Bruno. I think you're right, your book's really good."

"Come on, Johnny, I'm not planning on getting offended about what you don't like about it."

"It's not that, your book's good because . . . because it doesn't have any urns, Bruno. It's like what Satchmo plays, so clean, so pure. Don't you think that what Satch plays is like a birthday or a good deed? We . . . I tell you I wanted to swim without water. I thought . . . but only an idiot . . . I thought that one day I was going to find something else. I wasn't satisfied, I thought the good things, Lan's red dress, and even Bee, were like mousetraps, I don't know how to explain it any other way . . . Traps created in order to make people conform, you know, so we say everything's fine. Bruno, I think that Lan and jazz, yes, even jazz, were like ads in a magazine, pretty things so I'd be satisfied like you are because you have Paris and your wife and your job . . . I had my sax . . . and my sex, like the book says. Everything I needed. Traps, my friend . . . because it can't be right that there's nothing else, it can't be right that we're that close, that stuck on the other side of the door . . . "

"The only thing that matters is giving as much of yourself as you possibly can," I say, feeling insurmountably stupid.

"And winning *Down Beat*'s poll every year, of course," agrees Johnny. "Of course, of course. Of course."

I move him toward the square little by little. Luckily there's a cab on the corner.

"More than anything, I don't accept your God," Johnny murmurs. "Don't give me that, I won't accept it. And even if He really is on the other side of the door, I don't give a damn. There's no merit in making it through the door if He opens it for you. Kicking the door down, now that would have merit. Beating it down, coming all over it, pissing on that door day in and day out. That time in New York I think I opened the door with my music, but then I stopped playing and so He, damn Him, He shut it right in my face, just because I've never prayed to Him, because I'm never going to pray to Him, because I don't want to have anything to do with that doorman, that uniformed lackey who opens doors in exchange for a tip, that . . . "

Poor Johnny, then he goes and complains that one doesn't include these things in a book. Three o'clock in the morning, *madre mía.*

Tica went back to New York, Johnny went back to New York (without Dédée, now all set up with Louis Perron, who's a promising trombonist). Baby Lennox went back to New York. It wasn't a very exciting season in Paris and I missed my friends. My book about Johnny was selling really well all over, and of course Sammy Pretzal was now talking about a possible adaptation for Hollywood, which is always interesting when you consider the relationship between the franc and the dollar. My wife was still furious about my thing with Baby Lennox, nothing too serious otherwise, after all Baby's decidedly promiscuous and any intelligent woman should understand that these things don't compromise the conjugal equilibrium, plus Baby was already gone, she went back to New York with Johnny, finally affording herself the pleasure of getting into the same boat with him. She'd be doing drugs with Johnny now, lost like him, poor girl. And "Amorous" just came out in Paris, right when the second edition of my book was going to press and they were talking about translating it into German. I thought a lot about possible modifications for the second edition. Celebrated to the extent my profession allows, I wondered whether it wasn't necessary to show my subject's personality in a different light. I talked about it a few times with Delaunay and with Hodeir, but they didn't really know what advice to give me because they thought the book was great and people liked it the way it was. I thought I could sense that the two of them were afraid I would infect the book with literariness, ultimately distorting it with nuances that had little or nothing to do with Johnny's music, at least the way we all understood it. I thought the opinion of authorities in the field (and my personal decision, it would be ridiculous to deny it at this stage of the game) justified leaving the second edition as it was. The meticulous perusal of the trade magazines from the States (four articles on Johnny, news about another suicide attempt, this time with tincture of iodine, a pumped stomach and three weeks in the hospital, playing in Baltimore again as if nothing had happened) made me feel much calmer, besides the pain that these regrettable relapses caused me. Johnny hadn't said a single compromising word about my book. Example (in *Stomping Around,* a music magazine from Chicago, Teddy Rogers's interview with Johnny): "Have you read what Bruno V . . . wrote about you in Paris?" "Yes. It's very good." "Nothing else to say about the book?" "Nothing, except that it's very good. Bruno's a great guy." It remained to be seen what Johnny might say when he was drunk or drugged up, but at least there weren't any rumors that he was denying anything. I decided not to change the second edition, to continue presenting Johnny like he was deep down: a poor fool of barely mediocre intelligence, gifted like so many musicians, so many chess players and so many poets with the ability to create wonderful things without having the slightest awareness (at the most, the pride of a boxer who knows he's strong) about the dimensions of his work. Everything encouraged me to leave that portrait of Johnny as it was; there's no point in creating conflict with an audience that's looking for a lot of jazz but no musical or psychological analysis, nothing that's not momentary and clearly delineated satisfaction, hands clapping to the beat, faces slackening blissfully, music traveling through their skin, mixing with their blood and respiration, and that's enough, no profound discourse.

First the telegrams came (to Delaunay, to me, by the afternoon they were already releasing their idiotic commentaries in the papers); twenty days later I got a letter from Baby Lennox, who hadn't forgotten me. "They treated him great at Bellevue and I went to pick him up when he got out. We were living in Mike Russolo's apartment, he's on tour in Norway. Johnny was doing really good, and even though he didn't want to play in public he agreed to do some recordings with the guys from Club 28. Since it's you, I can tell you that in reality he was very weak" (I can imagine what Baby meant to imply with this, after our little adventure in Paris) "and the way he breathed and moaned at night scared me.

The only thing that consoles me," Baby added sweetly, "is that he died happy and without knowing what was coming. He was watching TV and all of a sudden he just fell to the floor. They told me it was instantaneous." From which you could deduce that Baby hadn't been there, and that's how it was because we later found out that Johnny was living at Tica's and had spent five days with her, worried and depressed, talking about giving up jazz, moving to Mexico and working in the fields (everyone gets that urge at some point in their lives, it's almost boring), and Tica was watching over him and doing everything possible to calm him down and make him think about the future (that's what Tica said later on, as if she or Johnny had ever had the slightest idea about the future). In the middle of this TV program that Johnny found really funny, he started to cough; all of a sudden he doubled over sharply, etc. I'm not so sure that his death was as instantaneous as Tica told the police (trying to get out of the terrible jam that having Johnny die in her apartment had gotten her into, with the drugs at arm's reach, some of poor Tica's previous difficulties, and the not completely convincing results of the autopsy. You can just imagine everything a doctor would find in Johnny's liver and lungs). "You don't want to know how much his death hurt me, although I could tell you other things," our dear Baby added sweetly, "but some time when I feel more up to it I'll write you or tell you in person (it looks like Rogers wants to sign me for Paris and Berlin) everything you need to know, since you were Johnny's best friend." And after an entire page dedicated to insulting Tica, who if you believed her was not only responsible for Johnny's death but the attack on Pearl Harbor and the Black Plague, poor little Baby concluded: "Before I forget, one day in Bellevue he kept asking for you. He was all confused and thought you were in New York and didn't want to come see him, he was always talking about some fields full of things, and afterward he would call for you and even swear at you, poor thing. You know what fevers are like. Tica told Bob Carey that Johnny's last words were something like: 'Oh, make me a mask,' but you can imagine that at that moment . . . " I certainly could imagine it. "He'd gotten really fat," Baby added at the end of her letter, "and when he walked, he had to gasp for air." Those were the details that were to be expected from someone as sensitive as Baby Lennox.

All of this coincided with the release of the second edition of my book, but luckily I had time to add a note about his death, typed up in nothing flat, and a photograph of the funeral where you could see lots of famous jazzmen. In that way, the biography became, in a manner of speaking, complete. Perhaps I shouldn't be the one to say that, but naturally I'm speaking from a purely aesthetic point of view. They're already talking about a new translation, into Swedish or Norwegian, I think. My wife's just thrilled with the news.

Translated by Sandra Kingery

11

Swingtime

Kiki DeLancey

When he was home, things were different. From time to time he'd blow in. Then there'd be this traveling road show. It would travel right into our house. He'd come in, and a great sweep of breath and wind would gather in around him. It would seem to sweep right on in with him, not carrying him, not following him, but part and parcel with him. It was like the clothes he was wearing, like his arms swinging and his legs striding. This great sweep of wind and excitement just went with him. Like his eyes looking around, like his voice going out. They all went along with him. Then there'd be noise, there'd be people. People setting things up and taking things down. Doors slamming, people getting things ready, people sitting at long tables outside, eating cheese and olives. People playing music. There was always music, coming from ten places at once. There was always a guy with a trombone, blowing a string of notes to himself, and a choppy guitar in the next room, and people shouting, crazy laughing and clapping. There'd be a lot of them, his band, I guess, or else musicians who just knew him, whom he invited to his house while he was out on the road; and when he showed up, they showed up. People who wanted to play with him, maybe. People who wanted something from him, money, a commitment to play, or just his autograph. He'd set up tables, there were always tables set up. There was a constant meal going on. There were always people sitting down and eating, at all times. They were mostly dark-haired, a lot of them talking, cussing, and laughing, in an Americanized Greek, or in their harsh and twisted English. It was their twisted, musician-style English. They had a funny way of talking. They'd all use funny words, funny to listen to. Not intended for kids, maybe, but them not having any other way of talking. Women would be with them. They'd be in these big, bouncy dresses they wore then, or else in those short capri pants, with their hair done up, but never quite to the extent of my mother. Never quite as elegantly or as complex as my mother. None of these women ever came there on their own, either. They never came there on their own merits. They always came with one of these guys, one of these musicians, or wannabes, or big mouths, which all of these guys all were.

And my father would be in the middle of everything. He'd be sitting at the long table, at the long table set up outside on the brick patio Perseus had made, under the arbor, under the grapevines with the grapes dripping down; and he'd just be sitting there, not at the head of the table or anything, just at some seat or there in the middle. He'd be leaning back in his chair, with his arms loose, in short sleeves, one of those soft, cotton knit, short-sleeved shirts with buttons, and his arms hanging maybe loosely straight down his sides, straight down the sides of the armless chair, or resting lightly on his knees; and his knees would be loose, his legs stretched out kind of loose in front of him, his knees jiggling maybe, popping and tapping around to whatever rhythm he had going inside at the time. He'd wear these loose, light-colored pants; these soft looking, almost flimsy, fine-colored trousers, flipping around a bit as he tapped with his legs, and cowboy boots. He almost always wore cowboy boots. Other times he'd sit absolutely still, just relaxed, leaned back, listening closely to what somebody was saying close to his ear, or just sort of watching everybody, watching and listening to everyone and seeing what was going on, seeing over them and leaning back in one of the same, uniform straight-backed chairs, the rush-seated chairs. Then you might see him walking around the house, and the noise would be going, music coming from everywhere, from a radio, or radios, and a record player in the dining room, and one in the living room, and somebody playing real loud now on the clarinet, and the piano, and somebody beating hard on the dining room table with the palms of his hands; and him walking through it, shouting out to people, "Go after it, boy!" Not ever singing, not playing along, but yelling out at them, or telling jokes, or on the phone screaming that he couldn't be there on that day, they'd better get that straight. Get that straight. And then walking through the halls, slamming through the kitchen, dragging out boxes of wine, carrying out platters of food, and talking to the cook, never yelling at her; always sweet to her, always kind to the yardman Perseus, always patiently telling him what needed done, always softly talking to the maids and cooks and cleaners.

Somewhere in this mix was my mother. She'd be around him, even when she wasn't exactly sitting or standing near him; even if she was in the other room, she'd be doing something that was going to take her over to where he was, or starting something in motion that would bring him over to where she was. She was getting things going, setting in motion whatever it was going to take. She'd use me for this, too. "None of these other bitches had a boy in them," she'd say. She'd push me forward. What could I do but stand there. "Jules here is just like his father," she'd say. "Manly in every way. Just like his stud of a father. Inside that quiet exterior is a growing he-man. A dynamo. Behind that weak chin is a font of determination. Inside that sunken chest is the heart of a lion. Inside that ugly boy is an ugly man."

My father would hear this. He'd come into the room. "No shit, either," he'd say. He'd always go for it. He'd always take hold and go for it. "This is one tough son of a bitch," he'd say. "One ugly, tough bastard." Then would come the football. Then I'd feel the football, crammed into my stomach. It always appeared from somewhere. It always appeared in his hand, passed there by her, probably, by her, I guess, if I think about it, shoved hard into my stomach. And there in the living room, with the tables shoved back, I'd slam into him. Or moved outside, hauled outside by the shoulders of my shirt, I'd crouch down and run at him. You closed your eyes after awhile. After doing this, after being through it before, you closed your eyes. You closed your eyes and just ran forward, and he would come. He would be standing there, maybe even running toward you too, ready to meet you. He'd always be ready to catch you. He must have run, too. He must have run right at you, or the impact wouldn't have been so hard. The impact couldn't have been so sudden, so heavy, and so encompassing, with the big weight of him, the enormous and solid weight of all that mass, all that muscle and gristle grinding over you, bearing down on you, crushing down on you, into the hot tearing grass of the yard. "Jules, Jules, Jules," somewhere they'd be chanting. You'd open your eyes into the grass, the ball shoved up into your throat, spit and probably blood dripping down around the brown leather and making a little course, working its way down onto a blade of the bent grass to collect in a tiny pool right under your eyes, right in front of the line of vision of your own watering eyes, with your breath hot in the grass, and your face so close in the grass, so pressed down and weighted down in the grass that you had to re-breathe with each gasp the same stink, the same hot breath you'd just expelled, and in your ears then the laughing cry of a dozen voices, of a score of voices, chanting for you, "Jules—Jules—Jules—Jules."

Then of course you'd come upon them in halls, in corridors, and in rooms. Not that you wanted to. Not that you tried to. Not that you didn't plan every blasted step you took in that house so that you wouldn't. "She's taking a bath," you'd say to yourself. And he—he's on the phone with some promoter, some agent on the East Coast. Mrs. Leshon is in the kitchen. Mrs. Leshon is in the kitchen. They won't do it with Mrs. Leshon standing in there watching them. Not even them, with Mrs. Leshon standing there watching them. Not even them. So then it was all clear for you, and you'd go cautiously into the kitchen. You'd go every step with ears open, eyes open, cautiously proceeding and listening for the warning sounds you knew. Then you'd push through the kitchen door, it would swing breathlessly closed behind you, and there they'd be. There they'd be, and you trapped there with them; you trapped there alone with them, in the corner between the door hinges and the wall ovens, and them, unaware, hushed, even silent, over against the sink, her with her hands ripping through his hair, tearing at his hair, and him silent, panting, staring, pushing her face back, pushing with his big huge hands her face back, and back, until it was all the way back, with his arms bulging, his arms in the thin cotton shirt flexed and rigid. He was pinning her head back. He was holding her head back. She was fighting. She was struggling. Her limbs were meeting him, crawling along his flesh, legs and arms in deliberate, muscular battle: a battle not of resistance, not of her attempt to resist, but of her utter and single-mindedly complete attempt to destroy: to win: to come up against him and somehow win. It was impossible to tell whether this was a fight or an attempt at sex. His hands were enormous, and backed with large, round veins. Her hands were long, with long red nails.

That was him and her. Between her and me, it was different than that. She was my mother. She was nice to me. So she didn't have hair, steel-gray hair tied back in a bun, or wear a long dark dress down to her ankles, or something, or steal me rolls from the bakery like his mother did for him, or harp the old man into getting me music lessons. She didn't do those things, but she was nice to me. She played tiddlywinks with me, with these little, small, thin chips, like poker chips, plastic chips, only smaller, and thin, and light blue and pink. And she made up nicknames for me, little names. Jules.

You say to yourself, I'm going to go back and remember this stuff, and you wouldn't think, would you, a guy thinking through things, just for his own sake, just for his own peace of mind's sake, would tell lies. A guy thinking like that, for himself only, would tell nothing but the absolute truth. Nobody can hear. Nobody can see. Why would you think of anything, or use words about anything that weren't the very true words? Words that weren't the very accurate and most reasonable words? You go over things, and it jabs you. You think of things, and why would you even do it? Why would you go to the trouble in the first place of thinking through and intentionally rethinking and reliving everything anyway? Because it's all already contained in you. If it wasn't contained in you already, inside you like you were a neat and smooth and impermeable capsule, if it wasn't in there, then you couldn't think about it anyway. You can't go back and try to remember something unless you already remember it. You remember it anyway. It happened to you once, and it's in your mind already. So why would you do that, why would you make yourself go back and reconstruct and face all those things? When you think of most of them, they twist in you. They hurt. You're forced, maybe against your own will, to smooth them, to ease them, or they won't go by at all. But some of them, some of them when you see them, when you rethink them, you see that for once you really were right. You really were shortchanged. You really were better. You really were more deserving. You really were innocent. You really were deserving of better. You really were misused. You really were manipulated. You really were treated unfairly. Then you feel a little better. It cools you down. Then you can say to yourself, they really didn't do right by me. It really wasn't right. It really wasn't. Then, there you are.

Fame and fortune: isn't that why you go to New York? That's why he went to New York. That's why he left Peter's. Playing at Peter's every night, jumping around, singing, and women coming after him, and money pouring into Peter's pockets, and some into his, the overflow coming into his, and into his bands', was pretty good. There was local fame in that. There was some sort of money in that. Localized fame and localized money. But in New York, at that time, there were big clubs. A different kind of club. Famous places. Places that, when you played there, got reviews. You got reviews, and stories about you were published in the big newspapers, so droves of people would pile out to see you. Droves of people would start buying the records. They'd start knowing you by name.

Somehow he got this record deal, of course. That was the start of it, that enabled him to go up there. Somehow, they heard of him down there, in Peter's. They heard about him, or sent somebody down there to check him out personally, or by accident somebody happened to hear him, the right, the one right person happened to hear him. So they called him up, they telephoned or telegraphed and had him come up. They named him Mickey Coffee and his Roadhouse Crew. And the band, they wanted the band. They thought the band was hot. Jazz bands, in those days, weren't put together off the street. In those days, people didn't grow up hearing that kind of music. Outside of where he came from, I don't think it was played at all. The other people that came from there too, and Mickey Coffee, were the people that invented it, and who played it, and it kind of belonged to them. So he brought the whole band with him, in a big old car that one of the guys owned, the clarinet player I think owned. And in it was the five or six guys, and instruments in cases, his trumpet in a case and the clarinet and trombone and guitar, whatever all they were playing in the band in those days. Between them all, maybe, a suitcase full of clothes. Between them all, maybe, three clean shirts.

They were set up to play at one of those big clubs. The very first night they were in town they were playing up on a real stage, the first time they'd played on an elevated stage in a club, a big stage, about two feet up off the floor. With a stage entrance, so you didn't have to walk through the crowd, and all the pulling women, to get on stage. And curtains, on the side at least. Curtains that maybe weren't closed, but that you could come out from behind. When you walked onto the stage, you could make an entrance. You could make a real entrance, from behind these curtains. You could jump out, leap or parade out from the side of them, and there you were, blowing already, and the place coming down already, coming down around you, so the noise, the laughter, the shouts that were coming maybe from the audience, maybe from the band, were all falling in place, all landing in a kind of rhythm, right around the music, and so that the shouts and the honking horns and the screaming piano were all the song: the notes, and the rhythms, and the strange voices all winding together and spiraling over that stage into the most amazing sound that ever lifted you out of your skin, and everybody else that was in there out of their skins. Everybody that was in there just rose up at once, rose up in their seats, raised up their hands, their arms, and their hearts rose. Their hearts rose. And that was just your entrance.

The second day they were in town, whoever was in charge of all this, the producer you'd call him today, decided what songs Mickey Coffee and the band were going to record. He'd been out to the club to hear them the first night, and he wrote down what he wanted to record. That's how they recorded about eight sides, maybe only six sides, their first recordings. About six sides, one right after the other, cut right there in the studio, from start to finish, one time through apiece. At night they were back in the club, playing from midnight till four, with drinking and yelling and hollering going on all around them. It was pandemonium, in those days. The way they played inspired it, and the people were ready for it, too. They were more than ready for something. The band was a whirlwind up there, wild was the word for it, and they filled everybody who happened to be in there with electricity. It was electrifying. He was electrifying. That trumpet would scream. It would scream. And he'd sing, too, of course. He'd sing real soft, these kind of dirty words, suggestive kind of words in those songs. He didn't really say anything dirty; I mean, he didn't use actual words. He'd just take the words, the ordinary words, and he'd touch them in such a way, touch them as they came out, with his lips, with his mouth, that they shocked you. They tortured you. And prohibition was over. The Depression, you know, "The Depression," and everything. Everyone wanted something. They all wanted something. They wanted to scream and stomp. Mickey came up in the middle of it. He came up singing and wiggling his shoulders. He'd sing soft and wiggle his shoulders. Wriggle them, which was not really done in those days. A singer might sway, might hold onto the mike stand and drift back and forth a little bit. To wriggle, to stomp, was very unusual. I'm not saying he was the only one. I'm not saying he was even the first one. Somebody might have done it before. Somebody else might have been the first one. I don't know who, but there's always somebody. There's always somebody who was there ahead of you. That doesn't take away from what Mickey did. That wriggling, a sort of shivering, was bizarre, was very exciting to some people. Like the electricity of that music was hitting him too, and he was trying to resist it, and trying to ignore it, but part of it showed through. Just a little bit of it showed irresistibly through. He was trying to suppress it, but he couldn't suppress it. He was trying to be a regular guy, a decent and respectable person, but that music, that electricity, and the power of his own voice were too much for anybody to bear. He was caught in the middle of it, just like all the rest of them.

Then the first record came out, and in a couple of weeks he was playing in a real club. The real thing, this time. That first joint was just a joint, it turned out. This was the real thing. It was called The Venue. You were in one of the top spots, right there. It wasn't the only one; I'm saying there were other top clubs in a city that size, but none of them were any higher up than this one. It had red carpet, and a great big black bar, a black lacquer bar, with big, chrome, art deco lamps built along the walls, into the walls from floor to ceiling every thirty feet. And the place was crammed with tables, just crammed with tables. Crammed with customers, all drunk, drinking, dancing, packed into space, and all going out the next day, whenever they were sober, and buying his record.

So maybe the first date they only cut two sides, because it was right after that, that summer, they went back in and cut the next two sides. They cut two more sides. First they covered some Crosby song that was big in the movies, and then that's when they recorded the first song he wrote, or the first song that he wrote that got to be recorded. It was called "Shivers Up My Spine," and for a long time after that it was his trademark. His first trademark song. He had a lot of them, because he was around for a long time. Every ten years or so, there'd be another one, but that was the first one, and the one he wrote himself. "Shivers Up My Spine."

Shivers up their spines. And down again. Down again, all the way. He'd sing real low, and slow. The band would play the intro, kind of upbeat but nothing real catchy, and he'd sing, come in singing quietly, in this pent-up, controlled kind of voice, in his low register (which wasn't that low), almost in a hoarse whisper, like he could just barely keep it in. That came across to you. Out of the record, or from the stage. You could hear that. You could hear all that pent-up energy, all that controlled, fearsome, just barely controlled primitive drive. He was keeping it down, he was holding onto it somehow, but it was under there, he was telling you. I'm an animal, he was telling you. I'm a goddamn animal. Then they would break, and the band would go nuts. They'd tear up. They'd tear up, the loudest and most freewheeling kind of jazz you ever heard, whirling around your head, nothing but madness set free, madness that was nothing but the beautiful raw power of the human race, the whole human race, with that barely nameable naked trumpet screaming from the exact center of it. It was almost an unnamable, unrecognizable sound. You almost couldn't tell it was a trumpet. Not an animal, because it was too beautiful for that, too artful for that, but not a man. Not like the voice of any man who'd ever lived. Not like the voice of any man anyone'd ever heard before.

Immediately the babes set on him. The dishes, they called them then. Dishes, or maybe chicks, they would have called them in the band. They set on him, and they never laid off again. Never really, ever again. They hadn't really done that to him when he'd been starting out at Peter's. They hadn't done that to him at all back then. Maybe because he didn't have a record out. Having a record out makes you seem like a star to people, even if it's your first or second record, and not very many people have bought it yet. Maybe it's because he didn't do the shivering at Peter's. He wrote the song in the big car, in the corner of the old velveteen back seat on the way into town. They could have just liked that song real well, and the way he learned to sing it, to pronounce the word, the words, "your lips" that were in the song, that were in the chorus and that he'd repeat about a hundred times before they did the end. That had a big effect on people. The way he pronounced them did. There was the word, "Full." It was the word, "beautiful," and he'd sing "beauty—" and stop: pause. Then he'd say it: "Full." The way he would wind his mouth around it. The way his breath would explode along his tongue. That just twisted them up. It twisted everybody up. He did that shivering. He did that wriggling. Just subtly. Just barely there, you know. He looked better, too. He gained about ten pounds, maybe fifteen pounds, and it did him a world of good. He was just hitting his middle twenties, he was right in there in his middle twenties then, and when he put that weight on he looked a lot more like a grown man, and less like a young kid. There was the name change, too, from Michael Kafes to Mickey Coffee. Maybe there was something about the name that they liked.

Another simpler reason is that the women at home knew him. They'd grown up with him, a lot of them did, so he was nothing special to them. That made it harder to hear that thing under his voice that was saying, I'm the first guy in the world ever to be like me. The women at home knew his wife, too. They knew he had a kid. In New York the kid was more than a thousand miles away, the wife too, and that was just like being not married at all. To him it was, anyway. To him, he was completely married and completely not married at the same time. He could talk to his wife on the phone, go pick up some girl for lunch, stop by the post office and mail home some money on the way back to the hotel with her on his arm, the girl, tell her it was for his mother and show her that it even had his mother's name written on the envelope, while she'd sort of wiggle with satisfaction; then go on up the elevator, with his face in her blouse, walk calmly down the hall, open up his room, ball her for an hour, call downstairs for coffee and a newspaper, read the paper and drink coffee, lie back down and get it again, walk her downstairs and pay for her cab, meet a couple guys from the band, tell them to start the first set tonight with the new song, buy everybody dinner, show the pictures of his kid to the cashier, go down to The Venue and stroll around, kissing women every ten feet and listening to the early band, play till two, go backstage and bang some fan who sneaked in back there and was waiting for him behind some curtains when he went by, some forty-year-old, beautiful, married, drunk woman, drink at the bar while they rubbed up against him, then playing again, playing music, making the high terrible trumpet shrieks and going up in smoke and flames.

Records. Clubs. Movies. Shorts. He did all this. Whatever there was to be done, whatever could be done, in those days, he did. His clarinet player had quit, and gone home to his family, and he hired a new fellow that he met in New York, a Greek fellow, who had been playing clarinet in a bouzouki band for the locals. His name was Hermes Spyrtos. They called him Jack Herman. That was the luckiest thing in the world. There was something about Jack Herman, something in him, that knew what my father was going to do. He'd put the end of the clarinet in his mouth, the black, oblique mouthpiece in his mouth. The song would start. Jack'd be tootling along, nothing special, kind of keeping up with everybody while my dad would come in with the vocals, give them the silky whispering thing, maybe a little of the be-bop singing he'd been picking up there in the city, the fast singing he'd been hearing down 52nd Street; they'd work their way to the break, the trumpet solo would strike up, a big virile shout like it always did, and then, bam, that clarinet would be right there, would wrap itself so tightly around the trumpet, climb up on its back, rip right up full-speed with it, almost past it, almost but never exactly past it: always right along with it, the same syncopation, the same instant drops and curls, and the rebounds, and the rises, impossibly tight but absolutely free, absolutely wild, and never the same way twice. Never the same way twice. They read each other's impulses. They knew the way the other guy was going to go, didn't guess it, didn't think about it, just went ahead with it and there they were, both always getting there at the same time, both always in the same place at the same time. Then the vocal would pick up again, and Herman, Hermes, would pitter-patter out, sort of slip back out, so you didn't even notice, you didn't notice, back in there with the trombone and piano and the bass, back in there somewhere behind the soft shy singing, until the end would come, and man, the dam would break, the wild gruesome motivating spirit that was there, that made them what they were up together on the stage would lash around and bind them, and they'd be off, colliding, owning it, not controlling it but of it, being it, then smash, it would all be over. They always ended like that, just, smash, and done. Crash, and silence. They did that live, every night. They did that live, fifty times every night.

12

A Coupla Scalped Indians

Ralph Ellison

They had a small, loud-playing band and as we moved through the trees I could hear the notes of the horns bursting like bright metallic bubbles against the sky. It was a faraway and sparklike sound, shooting through the late afternoon quiet of the hill; very clear now and definitely music, band music. I was relieved. I had been hearing it for several minutes as we moved through the woods, but the pain down there had made all my senses so deceptively sharp that I had decided that the sound was simply a musical ringing in my ears. But now I was doubly sure, for Buster stopped and looked at me, squinching up his eyes with his head cocked to one side. He was wearing a blue cloth headband with a turkey feather stuck over his ear, and I could see it flutter in the breeze.

"You hear what I hear, man?" he said.

"I *been* hearing it," I said.

"Damn! We better haul it outa these woods so we can see something. Why didn't you say something to a man?"

We moved again, hurrying along until suddenly we were out of the woods, standing at a point of the hill where the path dropped down to the town, our eyes searching. It was close to sundown and below me I could see the red clay of the path cutting through the woods and moving past a white lightning-blasted tree to join the river road, and the narrow road shifting past Aunt Mackie's old shack, and on, beyond the road and the shack, I could see the dull mysterious movement of the river. The horns were blasting brighter now, though still far away, sounding like somebody flipping bright handfuls of new small change against the sky. I listened and followed the river swiftly with my eyes as it wound through the trees and on past the buildings and houses of the town—until there, there at the farther edge of the town, past the tall smokestack and the great silver sphere of the gas storage tower, floated the tent, spread white and cloudlike with its bright ropes of fluttering flags.

That's when we started running. It was a dogtrotting Indian run, because we were both wearing packs and were tired from the tests we had been taking in the woods and in Indian Lake. But now the bright blare of the horns made us forget our tiredness and pain and we bounded down the path like young goats in the twilight; our army-surplus mess kits and canteens rattling against us.

"We late, man," Buster said. "I told you we was gon fool around and be late. But naw, you had to cook that damn sage hen with mud on him just like it says in the book. We coulda barbecued a damn elephant while we was waiting for a tough sucker like that to get done . . . "

His voice grumbled on like a trombone with a big, fat pot-shaped mute stuck in it and I ran on without answering. We had tried to take the cooking test by using a sage hen instead of a chicken because Buster said Indians didn't eat chicken. So we'd taken time to flush a sage hen and kill him with a slingshot. Besides, he was the one who insisted that we try the running endurance test, the swimming test, *and* the cooking test all in one day. Sure it had taken time. I knew it would take time, especially with our having no scoutmaster. We didn't even have a troop, only the *Boy Scout's Handbook* that Buster had found, and—as we'd figured—our hardest problem had been working out the tests for ourselves. He had no right to argue anyway, since he'd beaten me in all the tests—although I'd passed them too. And he was the one who insisted that we start taking them today, even though we were both still sore and wearing our bandages, and I was still carrying some of the catgut stitches around in me. I had wanted to wait a few days until I was healed, but Mister Know-it-all Buster challenged me by saying that a real stud Indian could take the tests even right after the doctor had just finished sewing on him. So, since we were more interested in being *Indian* scouts than simply *Boy* Scouts, here I was running toward the spring carnival instead of being already there. I wondered how Buster knew so much about what an Indian would do, anyway. We certainly hadn't read anything about what the doctor had done to us. He'd probably made it up, and I had let him urge me into going to the woods even though I had to slip out of the house. The doctor had told Miss Janey (she's the lady who takes care of me) to keep me quiet for a few days and she dead-aimed to do it. You would've thought from the way she carried on that she was the one who had the operation—only that's one kind of operation no woman ever gets to brag about.

Anyway, Buster and me had been in the woods and now we were plunging down the hill through the fast-falling dark to the carnival. I had begun to throb and the bandage was chafing, but as we rounded a curve I could see the tent and the flares and the gathering crowd. There was a breeze coming up the hill against us now and I could almost smell that cotton candy, the hamburgers, and the kerosene smell of the flares. We stopped to rest and Buster stood very straight and pointed down below, making a big sweep with his arm like an Indian chief in the movies when he's up on a hill telling his braves and the Great Spirit that he's getting ready to attack a wagon train.

"Heap big . . . teepee . . . down yonder," he said in Indian talk. "Smoke signal say . . . Blackfeet . . . make . . . heap much . . . stink, buck-dancing in tennis shoes!"

"Ugh," I said, bowing my suddenly war-bonneted head. "Ugh!"

Buster swept his arm from east to west, his face impassive. "Smoke medicine say . . . heap . . . *big* stink! Hot toe jam!" He struck his palm with his fist, and I looked at his puffed-out cheeks and giggled.

"Smoke medicine say you tell heap big lie," I said. "Let's get on down there."

We ran past some trees, Buster's canteen jangling. Around us it was quiet except for the roosting birds.

"Man," I said, "you making as much noise as a team of mules in full harness. Don't no Indian scout make all that racket when he runs."

"No scout-um now," he said. "Me go make heap much pow-wow at stinky-dog carnival!"

"Yeah, but you'll get yourself scalped, making all that noise in the woods," I said. "Those other Indians don't give a damn 'bout no carnival—what does a carnival mean to them? They'll scalp the hell outa you!"

"Scalp?" he said, talking colored now. "Hell, man—that damn doctor scalped me last week. Damn near took my whole head off!"

I almost fell with laughing. "Have mercy, Lord," I laughed. "We're just a couple poor scalped Indians!"

Buster stumbled about, grabbing a tree for support. The doctor had said that it would make us men and Buster had said, hell, he was a man already—what he wanted was to be an Indian. We hadn't thought about it making us scalped ones.

"You right, man," Buster said. "Since he done scalped so much of my head away, I must be crazy as a fool. That's why I'm in such a hurry to get down yonder with the other crazy folks. I want to be right in the middle of 'em when they really start raising hell."

"Oh, you'll be there, Chief Baldhead," I said.

He looked at me blankly. "What you think ole Doc done with our scalps?"

"Made him a tripe stew, man."

"You nuts," Buster said. "He probably used 'em for fish bait."

"He did, I'm going to sue him for one trillion, zillion dollars, cash," I said.

"Maybe he gave 'em to ole Aunt Mackie, man. I bet with them she could work up some out*rageous* spells!"

"Man," I said, suddenly shivering, "don't talk about that old woman, she's evil."

"Hell, everybody's so scared of her. I just wish she'd mess with me or my daddy, I'd fix her."

I said nothing—I was afraid. For though I had seen the old woman about town all my life, she remained to me like the moon, mysterious in her very familiarity; and in the sound of her name there was terror.

Ho' Aunt Mackie, talker-with-spirits, prophetess-of-disaster, odd-dweller-alone in a riverside shack surrounded by sunflowers, morning-glories, and strange magical weeds (Yao, as Buster, during our Indian phase, would have put it, Yao!); *Old Aunt Mackie, wizen-faced walker-with-a-stick, shrill-voiced ranter in the night, round-eyed malicious one, given to dramatic trances and fiery flights of rage; Aunt Mackie, preacher of wild sermons on the busy streets of the town, hot-voiced chaser of children, snuff-dipper, visionary; wearer of greasy headrags, wrinkled gingham aprons, and old men's shoes; Aunt Mackie, nobody's sister but still Aunt Mackie to us all* (Ho, Yao!); *teller of fortunes, concocter of powerful, body-rending spells*

(Yah, Yao!); *Aunt Mackie, the remote one though always seen about us; night-consulted adviser to farmers on crops and cattle* (Yao!); *herb-healer, root-doctor, and town-confounding oracle to wildcat drillers seeking oil in the earth*—(Yaaaah-Ho!). It was all there in her name and before her name I shivered. Once uttered, for me the palaver was finished; I resigned it to Buster, the tough one.

Even some of the grown folks, both black and white, were afraid of Aunt Mackie, and all the kids except Buster. Buster lived on the outskirts of the town and was as unimpressed by Aunt Mackie as by the truant officer and others whom the rest of us regarded with awe. And because I was his buddy I was ashamed of my fear.

Usually I had extra courage when I was with him. Like the time two years before when we had gone into the woods with only our slingshots, a piece of fatback, and a skillet and had lived three days on the rabbits we killed and the wild berries we picked and the ears of corn we raided from farmers' fields. We slept each rolled in his quilt, and in the night Buster had told bright stories of the world we'd find when we were grown-up and gone from hometown and family. I had no family, only Miss Janey, who took me after my mother died (I didn't know my father), so that getting away always appealed to me, and the coming time of which Buster liked to talk loomed in the darkness around me, rich with pastel promise. And although we heard a bear go lumbering through the woods nearby and the eerie howling of a coyote in the dark, yes, and had been swept by the soft swift flight of an owl, Buster was unafraid and I had grown brave in the grace of his courage.

But to me Aunt Mackie was a threat of a different order, and I paid her the respect of fear.

"Listen to those horns," Buster said. And now the sound came through the trees like colored marbles glinting in the summer sun.

We ran again. And now keeping pace with Buster I felt good; for I meant to be there too, at the carnival; right in the middle of all that confusion and sweating and laughing and all the strange sights to see.

"Listen to 'em, now, man," Buster said. "Those fools is starting to shout 'Amazing Grace' on those horns. Let's step on the gas!"

The scene danced below us as we ran. Suddenly there was a towering Ferris wheel revolving slowly out of the dark, its red and blue lights glowing like drops of dew dazzling a big spider web when you see it in the early morning. And we heard the beckoning blare of the band now shot through with the small, insistent, buckshot voices of the barkers.

"Listen to that trombone, man," I said.

"Sounds like he's playing the dozens with the whole wide world."

"What's he saying, Buster?"

"He's saying. 'Ya'll's mamas don't wear 'em. Is strictly without 'em. Don't know nothing 'bout 'em . . . "

"Don't know about what, man?"

"Draw's, fool; he's talking 'bout draw's!"

"How you know, man?"

"I hear him talking, don't I?"

"Sure, but you been scalped, remember? You crazy. How he know about those people's mamas?" I said.

"Says he saw 'em with his great big ole eye."

"Damn! He must be a Peeping Tom. How about those other horns?"

"Now that there tuba's saying:

They don't play 'em, I know they don't.
They don't play 'em, I know they won't.
They just don't play no nasty dirty twelves . . . "

"Man, you *are* a scalped-headed fool. How about that trumpet?"

"Him? That fool's a soldier, he's really signifying. Saying,

So ya'll don't play 'em, hey?
So ya'll won't play 'em, hey?
Well pat your feet and clap your hands,
'Cause I'm going to play 'em to the promised land . . .

"Man, the white folks know what that fool is signifying on that horn they'd run him clear on out the world. Trumpet's got a real *nasty* mouth."

"Why you call him a soldier, man?" I said.

"'Cause he's slipping 'em in the twelves and choosing 'em, all at the same time. Talking 'bout they mamas and offering to fight 'em. Now he ain't like that ole clarinet; clarinet so sweet-talking he just *eases* you in the dozens."

"Say, Buster," I said, seriously now. "You know, we gotta stop cussing and playing the dozens if we're going to be Boy Scouts. Those white boys don't play that mess."

"You doggone right they don't," he said, the turkey feather vibrating above his ear. "Those guys can't take it, man. Besides, who wants to be just like them? Me, *I'm* gon be a scout and play the twelves too! You have to, with some of these old jokers we know. You don't know what to say when they start teasing you, you never have no peace. You have to outtalk 'em, outrun 'em, or outfight 'em and I don't aim to be running and fighting all the time. N'mind those white boys."

We moved on through the growing dark. Already I could see a few stars and suddenly there was the moon. It emerged bladelike from behind a thin veil of cloud, just as I heard a new sound and looked about me with quick uneasiness. Off to our left I heard a dog, a big one. I slowed, seeing the outlines of a picket fence and the odd-shaped shadows that lurked in Aunt Mackie's yard.

"What's the matter, man?" Buster said.

"Listen," I said. "That's Aunt Mackie's dog. Last year I was passing here and he sneaked up and bit me through the fence when I wasn't even thinking about him . . . "

"Hush, man," Buster whispered, "I hear the son-of-a-bitch back in there now. You leave him to me."

We moved by inches now, hearing the dog barking in the dark. Then we were going past and he was throwing his heavy body against the fence, straining at his chain. We hesitated, Buster's hand on my arm. I undid my heavy canteen belt and held it, suddenly light in my fingers. In my right I gripped the hatchet which I'd brought along.

"We'd better go back and take the other path," I whispered.

"Just stand still, man," Buster said.

The dog hit the fence again, barking hoarsely; and in the interval following the echoing crash I could hear the distant music of the band.

"Come on," I said. "Let's go round."

"Hell, no! We're going straight! I ain't letting no damn dog scare me, Aunt Mackie or no Aunt Mackie. Come on!"

Trembling, I moved with him toward the roaring dog, then felt him stop again, and I could hear him removing his pack and taking out something wrapped in paper.

"Here," he said. "You take my stuff and come on."

I took his gear and went behind him, hearing his voice suddenly hot with fear and anger saying, "Here, you 'gator-mouthed egg-sucker, see how you like this sage hen," just as I tripped over the straps of his pack and went down. Then I was crawling frantically, trying to untangle myself and hearing the dog growling as he crunched something in his jaws. "Eat it, you buzzard," Buster was saying, "see if you tough as he is," as I tried to stand, stumbling and sending an old cooking range crashing in the dark. Part of the fence was gone and in my panic I had crawled into the yard. Now I could hear the dog bark threateningly and leap the length of his chain toward me, then back to the sage hen; toward me, a swift leaping form snatched backward by the heavy chain, turning to mouth savagely on the mangled bird. Moving away, I floundered over the stove and pieces of crating, against giant sunflower stalks, trying to get back to Buster, when I saw the lighted window and realized that I had crawled to the very shack itself. That's when I pressed against the weathered-satin side of the shack and came erect. And there, framed by the window in the lamp-lit room, I saw the woman.

A brown naked woman, whose black hair hung beneath her shoulders. I could see the long graceful curve of her back as she moved in some sort of slow dance, bending forward and back, her arms and body moving as though gathering in something which I couldn't see but which she drew to her with pleasure; a young, girlish body with slender, well-rounded hips. *But who?* flashed through my mind as I heard Buster's *Hey, man; where'd you go? You done run out on me?* from back in the dark. And I willed to move, to hurry away—but in that instant she chose to pick up a glass from a wobbly old round white table and to drink, turning slowly as she stood with backward-tilted head, slowly turning in the lamplight and drinking slowly as she turned, slowly; until I could see the full-faced glowing of her feminine form.

And I was frozen there, watching the uneven movement of her breasts beneath the glistening course of the liquid, spilling down her body in twin streams drawn by the easy tiding of her breathing. Then the glass came down and my knees flowed beneath me like water. The air seemed to explode soundlessly. I shook my head but she, the image, would not go away and I wanted suddenly to laugh wildly and to scream.

For above the smooth shoulders of the girlish form I saw the wrinkled face of old Aunt Mackie.

Now, I had never seen a naked woman before, only very little girls or once or twice a skinny one my own age, who looked like a boy with the boy part missing. And even though I'd seen a few calendar drawings they were not alive like this, nor images of someone you'd thought familiar through having seen them passing through the streets of the town; nor like this inconsistent, with wrinkled face mismatched with glowing form. So that mixed with my fear of punishment for peeping there was added the terror of her mystery. And yet I could not move away. I was fascinated, hearing the growling dog and feeling a warm pain grow beneath my bandage—along with the newly risen terror that this deceptive old woman could cause me to feel this way, that she could be so young beneath her old baggy clothes.

She was dancing again now, still unaware of my eyes, the lamplight playing on her body as she swayed and enfolded the air or invisible ghosts or whatever it was within her arms. Each time she moved, her hair, which was black as night now that it was no longer hidden beneath a greasy headrag, swung heavily about her shoulders. And as she moved to the side I could see the gentle tossing of her breasts beneath her upraised arms. *It just can't be,* I thought, *it just can't,* and moved closer, determined to see and to know. But I had forgotten the hatchet in my hand until it struck the side of the house and I saw her turn quickly toward the window, her face evil as she swayed. I was rigid as stone, hearing the growling dog mangling the bird and knowing that I should run even as she moved toward the window, her shadow flying before her, her hair now wild as snakes writhing on a dead tree during a springtime flood. Then I could hear Buster's hoarse-voiced *Hey, man! Where in hell are you?* even as she pointed at me and screamed, sending me moving backward, and I was aware of the sickle-shaped moon flying like a lightning flash as I fell, still gripping my hatchet, and struck my head in the dark.

When I started out of it someone was holding me and I lay in light and looked up to see her face above me. Then it all flooded swiftly back and I was aware again of the contrast between smooth body and wrinkled face and experienced a sudden warm yet painful thrill. She held me close. Her breath came to me, sweetly alcoholic as she mumbled something about "Little devil, lips that touch wine shall never touch mine! That's what I told him, understand me? Never," she said loudly. "You understand?"

"Yes, ma'm . . ."

"Never, never, NEVER!"

"No, ma'm," I said, seeing her study me with narrowed eyes.

"You young but you younguns understand, devilish as you is. What you doing messing round in my yard?"

"I got lost," I said. "I was coming from taking some Boy Scout tests and I was trying to get by your dog."

"So that's what I heard," she said. "He bite you?"

"No, ma'm."

"Corse not, he don't bite on the new moon. No, I think you come in my yard to spy on me."

"No, ma'm, I didn't," I said. "I just happened to see the light when I was stumbling around trying to find my way."

"You got a pretty big hatchet there," she said, looking down at my hand. "What you plan to do with it?"

"It's a kind of Boy Scout ax," I said. "I used it to come through the woods . . ."

She looked at me dubiously. "So," she said, "you're a heavy hatchet man and you stopped to peep. Well, what I want to know is, is you a drinking man? Have your lips ever touched wine?"

"Wine? No, ma'm."

"So you ain't a drinking man, but do you belong to church?"

"Yes, ma'm."

"And have you been saved and ain't no backslider?"

"Yessum."

"Well," she said, pursing her lips, "I guess you can kiss me."

"MA'M?"

"That's what I said. You passed all the tests and you was peeping in my window . . ."

She was holding me there on a cot, her arms around me as though I were a three-year-old, smiling like a girl. I could see her fine white teeth and the long hairs on her chin and it was like a bad dream. "You peeped," she said, "now you got to do the rest. I said kiss me, or I'll fix you . . ."

I saw her face come close and felt her warm breath and closed my eyes, trying to force myself. *It's just like kissing some sweaty woman at church,* I told myself, *some friend of Miss Janey's.* But it didn't help and I could feel her drawing me and I found her lips with mine. It was dry and firm and winey and I could hear her sigh. "Again," she said, and once more my lips found hers. And suddenly she drew me to her and I could feel her breasts soft against me as once more she sighed.

"That was a nice boy," she said, her voice kind, and I opened my eyes. "That's enough now, you're both too young and too old, but you're brave. A regular li'l chocolate hero."

And now she moved and I realized for the first time that my hand had found its way to her breast. I moved it guiltily, my face flaming as she stood.

"You're a good brave boy," she said, looking at me from deep in her eyes, "but you forget what happened here tonight."

I sat up as she stood looking down upon me with a mysterious smile. And I could see her body up close now, in the dim yellow light; see the surprising silkiness of black hair mixed here and there with gray, and suddenly I was crying and hating myself for the compelling need. I looked at my hatchet lying on the floor now and wondered how she'd gotten me into the shack as the tears blurred my eyes.

"What's the matter, boy?" she said. And I had no words to answer.

"What's the matter, I say!"

"I'm hurting in my operation," I said desperately, knowing that my tears were too complicated to put into any words I knew.

"Operation? Where?"

I looked away.

"Where you hurting, boy?" she demanded.

I looked into her eyes and they seemed to flood through me, until reluctantly I pointed toward my pain.

"Open it, so's I can see," she said. "You know I'm a healer, don't you?"

I bowed my head, still hesitating.

"Well open it then. How'm I going to see with all those clothes on you?"

My face burned like fire now and the pain seemed to ease as a dampness grew beneath the bandage. But she would not be denied and I undid myself and saw a red stain on the gauze. I lay there ashamed to raise my eyes.

"Hmmmmmmm," she said. "A fishing worm with a headache!" And I couldn't believe my ears. Then she was looking into my eyes and grinning.

"Pruned," she cackled in her high, old woman's voice, "pruned. Boy, you have been pruned. I'm a doctor but no tree surgeon—no, lay still a second."

She paused and I saw her hand come forward, three claw-like fingers taking me gently as she examined the bandage.

And I was both ashamed and angry and now I stared at her out of a quick resentment and a defiant pride. *I'm a man,* I said within myself, *Just the same I am a man!* But I could only stare at her face briefly as she looked at me with a gleam in her eyes. Then my eyes fell and I forced myself to look boldly at her now, very brown in the lamplight, with all the complicated apparatus within the globular curvatures of flesh and vessel exposed to my eyes. I was filled then with a deeper sense of the mystery of it too, for now it was as though the nakedness was nothing more than another veil; much like the old baggy dresses she always wore. Then across the curvature of her stomach I saw a long, puckered crescent-shaped scar.

"How old are you, boy?" she said, her eyes suddenly round.

"Eleven," I said. And it was as though I had fired a shot.

"Eleven! Git out of here," she screamed, stumbling backward, her eyes wide upon me as she felt for the glass on the table to drink. Then she snatched an old gray robe from a chair, fumbling for the tie cord which wasn't there. I moved, my eyes upon her as I knelt for my hatchet, and felt the pain come sharp. Then I straightened, trying to arrange my knickers.

"You go now, you little rascal," she said. "Hurry and git out of here. And if I ever hear of you saying anything about me I'll fix your daddy and your mammy too. I'll fix 'em, you hear?"

"Yes, ma'm," I said, feeling that I had suddenly lost the courage of my manhood, now that my bandage was hidden and her secret body gone behind her old gray robe. But how could she fix my father when I didn't have one? Or my mother, when she was dead?

I moved, backing out of the door into the dark. Then she slammed the door and I saw the light grow intense in the window and there was her face looking out at me and I could not tell if she frowned or smiled, but in the glow of the lamp the wrinkles were not there. I stumbled over the packs now and gathered them up, leaving.

This time the dog raised up, huge in the dark, his green eyes glowing as he gave me a low disinterested growl. *Buster really must have fixed you,* I thought. *But where'd he go?* Then I was past the fence into the road.

I wanted to run but was afraid of starting the pain again, and as I moved I kept seeing her as she'd appeared with her back turned toward me, the sweet undrunken movements that she made. It had been like someone dancing by herself and yet like praying without kneeling down. Then she had turned, exposing her familiar face. I moved faster now and suddenly all my senses seemed to sing alive. I heard a night bird's song; the lucid call of a quail arose. And from off to my right in the river there came the leap of a moon-mad fish and I could see the spray arch up and away. There was wisteria in the air and the scent of moonflowers. And now moving through the dark I recalled the warm, intriguing smell of her body and suddenly, with the shout of the carnival coming to me again, the whole thing became thin and dreamlike. The images flowed in my mind, became shadowy; no part was left to fit another. But still there was my pain and here was I, running through the dark toward the small, loud-playing band. It was real, I knew, and I stopped in the path and looked back, seeing the black outlines of the shack and the thin moon above. Behind the shack the hill arose with the shadowy woods and I knew the lake was still hidden there, reflecting the moon. All was real.

And for a moment I felt much older, as though I had lived swiftly long years into the future and had been as swiftly pushed back again. I tried to remember how it had been when I kissed her, but on my lips my tongue found only the faintest trace of wine. But for that it was gone, and I thought forever, except the memory of the scraggly hairs on her chin. Then I was again aware of the imperious calling of the horns and moved again toward the carnival. Where was that other scalped Indian; where had Buster gone?

13

Common Meter

Rudolph Fisher

The Arcadia, on Harlem's Lenox Avenue, is "The World's Largest and Finest Ballroom—Admission Eighty-Five Cents." Jazz is its holy spirit, which moves it continuously from nine till two every night. Observe above the brilliant entrance this legend in white fire:

TWO—ORCHESTRAS—TWO

Below this in red:

FESS BAXTER'S FIREMEN

Alongside in blue:

BUS WILLIAMS' BLUE DEVILS

Still lower in gold:

HEAR THEM OUTPLAY EACH OTHER

So much outside. Inside, a blazing lobby, flanked by marble stairways. Upstairs, an enormous dance hall the length of a city block. Low ceilings blushing pink with rows of inverted dome lights. A broad dancing area, bounded on three sides by a wide soft-carpeted promenade, on the fourth by an ample platform accommodating the two orchestras.

People. Flesh. A fly-thick jam of dancers on the floor, grimly jostling each other; a milling herd of thirsty-eyed boys, moving slowly, searchingly over the carpeted promenade; a congregation of languid girls, lounging in rows of easy chairs here and there, bodies and faces unconcerned, dark eyes furtively alert. A restless multitude of empty, romance-hungry lives.

Bus Williams' jolly round brown face beamed down on the crowd as he directed his popular hit—"*She's Still My Baby*":

> You take her out to walk
> And give her baby-talk,
> But talk or walk, walk or talk—
> She's still my baby!

But the cheese-colored countenance of Fessenden Baxter, his professional rival, who with his orchestra occupied the adjacent half of the platform, was totally oblivious to "*She's Still My Baby.*"

Baxter had just caught sight of a girl, and catching sight of girls was one of his special accomplishments. Unbelief, wonder, amazement registered in turn on his blunt, bright features. He passed a hand over his straightened brown hair and bent to Perry Parker, his trumpetist.

"P.P., do you see what I see, or is it only the gin?"

"Both of us had the gin," said P.P., "so both of us sees the same thing."

"Judas Priest! Look at that figure, boy!"

"Never was no good at figures," said P.P.

"I've got to get me an armful of that baby."

"Lay off, papa," advised P.P.

"What do you mean, lay off?"

"Lay off. You and your boy got enough to fight over already, ain't you?"

"My boy?"

"Your boy, Bus."

"You mean that's Bus Williams' folks?"

"No lie. Miss Jean Ambrose, lord. The newest hostess. Bus got her the job."

Fess Baxter's eyes followed the girl. "Oh, he got her the job, did he?—Well, I'm going to fix it so she won't need any job. Woman like that's got no business working anywhere."

"Gin," murmured P.P.

"Gin hell," said Baxter. "Gunpowder wouldn't make a mama look as good as that."

"Gunpowder wouldn't make you look so damn good, either."

"You hold the cat's tail," suggested Baxter.

"I'm tryin' to save yours," said P.P.

"Save your breath for that horn."

"Maybe," P.P. insisted, "she ain't so possible as she looks."

"Huh. They can all be taught."

"I've seen some that couldn't."

"Oh you have?—Well, P.P., my boy, remember, that's you."

*

Beyond the brass rail that limited the rectangular dance area at one lateral extreme there were many small round tables and clusters of chairs. Bus Williams and the youngest hostess occupied one of these tables while Fess Baxter's Firemen strutted their stuff.

Bus ignored the tall glass before him, apparently endeavoring to drain the girl's beauty with his eyes; a useless effort, since it lessened neither her loveliness nor his thirst. Indeed the more he looked the less able was he to stop looking. Oblivious, the girl was engrossed in the crowd. Her amber skin grew clearer and the roses imprisoned in it brighter as her merry black eyes danced over the jostling company.

"Think you'll like it?" he asked.

"Like it?" She was a child of Harlem and she spoke its language. "Boy, I'm having the time of my life. Imagine getting paid for this!"

"You ought to get a bonus for beauty."

"Nice time to think of that—after I'm hired."

"You look like a full course dinner—and I'm starved."

"Hold the personalities, papa."

"No stuff. Wish I could raise a loan on you. Baby—what a roll I'd tote."

"Thanks. Try that big farmer over there hootin' it with Sister Fullbosom. Boy, what a sideshow they'd make!"

"Yea. But what I'm lookin' for is a leadin' lady."

"Yea? I got a picture of any lady leadin' you anywhere."

"You could, Jean."

"Be yourself, brother."

"I ain't bein' nobody else."

"Well, be somebody else, then."

"Remember the orphanage?"

"Time, papa. Stay out of my past."

"Sure—if you let me into your future."

"Speaking of the orphanage—?"

"You wouldn't know it now. They got new buildings all over the place."

"Somehow that fails to thrill me."

"You always were a knockout, even in those days. You had the prettiest hair of any of the girls out there—and the sassiest hip-switch."

"Look at Fred and Adele Astaire over there. How long they been doing blackface?"

"I used to watch you even then. Know what I used to say?"

"Yea. 'Toot-a-toot-toot' on a bugle."

"That ain't all. I used to say to myself, 'Boy, when that sister grows up, I'm going to—'"

Her eyes grew suddenly onyx and stopped him like an abruptly reversed traffic signal.

"What's the matter?" he said.

She smiled and began nibbling the straw in her glass.

"What's the matter, Jean?"

"Nothing, Innocence. Nothing. Your boy plays a devilish one-step, doesn't he?"

"Say. You think I'm jivin', don't you?"

"No, darling. I think you're selling insurance."

"Think I'm gettin' previous, just because I got you the job."

"Funny, I never have much luck with jobs."

"Well, I don't care what you think, I'm going to say it."

"Let's dance."

"I used to say to myself, 'When that kid grows up, I'm going to ask her to marry me.'"

She called his bluff. "Well, I'm grown up."

"Marry me, will you, Jean?"

Her eyes relented a little in admiration of his audacity. Rarely did a sober aspirant have the courage to mention marriage.

"You're good, Bus. I mean, you're good."

"Every guy ain't a wolf, you know, Jean."

"No. Some are just ordinary meat-hounds."

From the change in his face she saw the depth of the thrust, saw pain where she had anticipated chagrin.

"Let's dance," she suggested again, a little more gently.

*

They had hardly begun when the number ended, and Fess Baxter stood before them, an ingratiating grin on his Swiss-cheese-colored face.

"Your turn, young fellow," he said to Bus.

"Thoughtful of you, reminding me," said Bus. "This is Mr. Baxter, Miss Ambrose."

"It's always been one of my ambitions," said Baxter, "to dance with a sure-enough angel."

"Just what I'd like to see you doin'," grinned Bus.

"Start up your stuff and watch us," said Baxter. "Step on it, brother. You're holding up traffic."

"Hope you get pinched for speedin'," said Bus, departing.

The Blue Devils were in good form tonight, were really "bearing down" on their blues. Bus, their leader, however, was only going through the motions, waving his baton idly. His eyes followed Jean and Baxter, and it was nothing to his credit that the jazz maintained its spirit. Occasionally he lost the pair: a brace of young wild birds double-timed through the forest, miraculously avoiding the trees; an extremely ardent couple, welded together, did a decidedly localized mess-around; that gigantic black farmer whom Jean had pointed out sashayed into the line of vision, swung about, backed off, being fancy. . . .

Abruptly, as if someone had caught and held his right arm, Bus's baton halted above his head. His men kept on playing under the impulse of their own momentum, but Bus was a creature apart. Slowly his baton drooped, like the crest of a proud bird, beaten. His eyes died on their object and all his features sagged. On the floor forty feet away, amid the surrounding clot of dancers, Jean and Baxter had stopped moving and were standing perfectly still. The girl had clasped her partner close around the shoulders with both arms. Her face was buried in his chest.

Baxter, who was facing the platform, looked up and saw Bus staring. He drew the girl closer, grinned, and shut one eye.

They stood so a moment or an hour till Bus dragged his eyes away. Automatically he resumed beating time. Every moment or so his baton wavered, slowed, and hurried to catch up. The blues were very low-down, the nakedest of jazz, a series of periodic wails against a background of steady, slow rhythm, each pounding pulse descending inevitably, like leaden strokes of fate. Bus found himself singing the words of this grief-stricken lamentation:

Trouble—trouble has followed me all my days,
Trouble—trouble has followed me all my days—
Seems like trouble's gonna follow me always.

The mob demanded an encore, a mob that knew its blues and liked them blue. Bus complied. Each refrain became bluer as it was caught up by a different voice: the wailing clarinet, the weeping C sax, the moaning B-flat sax, the trombone, and Bus's own plaintive tenor:

Baby—baby—my baby's gone away.
Baby—baby—my baby's gone away—
Seems like baby—my baby's gone to stay.

Presently the thing beat itself out, and Bus turned to acknowledge applause. He broke a bow off in half. Directly before the platform stood Jean alone, looking up at him.

He jumped down. "Dance?"

"No. Listen. You know what I said at the table?"

"At the table?"

"About—wolves?"

"Oh—that—?"

"Yea. I didn't mean anything personal. Honest, I didn't." Her eyes besought his. "You didn't think I meant anything personal, did you?"

"'Course not," he laughed. "I know now you didn't mean anything." He laughed again. "Neither one of us meant anything."

With a wry little smile, he watched her slip off through the crowd.

*

From his side of the platform Bus overheard Fess Baxter talking to Perry Parker. Baxter had a custom of talking while he conducted, the jazz serving to blanket his words. The blanket was not quite heavy enough tonight.

"P.P., old pooter, she fell."

Parker was resting while the C sax took the lead. "She did?"

"No lie. She says, 'You don't leave me any time for cash customers.'"

"Yea?"

"Yea. And I says, 'I'm a cash customer, baby. Just name your price.'"

Instantly Bus was across the platform and at him, clutched him by the collar, bent him back over the edge of the platform; and it was clear from the look in Bus's eyes that he wasn't just being playful.

"Name her!"

"Hey—what the hell you doin'!"

"Name her or I'll drop you and jump in your face. I swear to—"

"Nellie!" gurgled Fessenden Baxter.

"Nellie who—damn it?"

"Nellie—Gray!"

"All right then!"

Baxter found himself again erect with dizzy suddenness.

The music had stopped, for the players had momentarily lost their breath. Baxter swore and impelled his men into action, surreptitiously adjusting his ruffled plumage.

The crowd had an idea what it was all about and many good-naturedly derided the victim as they passed:

"'Smatter, Fess? Goin' for toe-dancin'?"

"Nice back-dive, papa, but this ain't no swimmin' pool."

Curry, the large, bald, yellow manager, also had an idea what it was all about and lost no time accosting Bus.

"Tryin' to start somethin'?"

"No. Tryin' to stop somethin'."

"Well, if you gonna stop it with your hands, stop it outside. I ain't got no permit for prize fights in here—'Course, if you guys can't get on together I can maybe struggle along without one of y' till I find somebody."

Bus said nothing.

"Listen. You birds fight it out with them jazz sticks, y' hear? Them's your weapons. Nex' Monday night's the jazz contest. You'll find out who's the best man next Monday night. Might win more'n a lovin' cup. And y' might lose more. Get me?"

He stood looking sleekly sarcastic a moment, then went to give Baxter like counsel.

*

Rumor spread through the Arcadia's regulars as night succeeded night.

A pair of buddies retired to the men's room to share a half-pint of gin. One said to the other between gulps:

"Lord today! Ain't them two roosters bearin' down on the jazz!"

"No lie. They mussa had some this same licker."

"Licker hell. Ain't you heard 'bout it?"

"'Bout what?"

"They fightin', Oscar, fightin'."

"Gimme that bottle 'fo' you swaller it. Fightin'? What you mean, fightin'?"

"Fightin' over that new mama."

"The honey-dew?"

"Right. They can't use knives and they can't use knucks. And so they got to fight it out with jazz."

"Yea? Hell of a way to fight."

"That's the only way they'd be any fight. Bus Williams'd knock that yaller boy's can off in a scrap."

"I know it. Y'ought-a-seen him grab him las' night."

"I did. They tell me she promised it to the one 'at wins this cup nex' Monday night."

"Yea? Wisht I knowed some music."

"Sho-nuff sheba all right. I got a long shout with her last night, papa, an' she's got ever'thing!"

"Too damn easy on the eyes. Women like that ain't no good 'cep'n to start trouble."

"She sho' could start it for me. I'd 'a' been dancin' with her yet, but my two bitses give out. Spent two hard-earned bucks dancin' with her, too."

"Shuh! Might as well th'ow yo' money in the street. What you git dancin' with them hostesses?"

"You right there, brother. All I got out o' that one was two dollars worth o' disappointment."

Two girl friends, lounging in adjacent easy chairs, discussed the situation.

"I can't see what she's got so much more'n anybody else."

"Me neither. I could look a lot better'n that if I didn't have to work all day."

"No lie. Scrubbin' floors never made no bathin' beauties."

"I heard Fess Baxter jivin' her while they was dancin'. He's got a line, no stuff."

"He'd never catch me with it."

"No, dearie. He's got two good eyes too, y'know."

"Maybe that's why he couldn't see you flaggin' 'im."

"Be yourself, sister. He says to her, 'Baby, when the boss hands me that cup—'"

"Hates hisself, don't he?"

"'When the boss hands me that cup,' he says, 'I'm gonna put it right in your arms.'"

"Yea. And I suppose he goes with the cup."

"So she laughs and says, 'Think you can beat him?' So he says, 'Beat him? Huh, that bozo couldn't play a hand organ.'"

"He don't mean her no good though, this Baxter."

"How do you know?"

"A kack like that never means a woman no good. The other one ast her to step off with him."

"What!"

"Etta Pipp heard him. They was drinkin' and she was at the next table."

"Well, ain't that somethin'! Ast her to step off with him! What'd she say?"

"Etta couldn't hear no more."

"Jus' goes to show ya. What chance has a honest workin' girl got?"

Bus confided in Tappen, his drummer.

"Tap," he said, "ain't it funny how a woman always seems to fall for a wolf?"

"No lie," Tap agreed. "When a guy gets too deep, he's long-gone."

"How do you account for it, Tap?"

"I don't. I jes' play 'em light. When I feel it gettin' heavy—boy, I run like hell."

"Tap, what would you do if you fell for a girl and saw her neckin' another guy?"

"I wouldn't fall," said Tappen, "so I wouldn't have to do nothin'."

"Well, but s'posin' you did?"

"Well, if she was my girl, I'd knock the can off both of 'em."

"S'posin' she wasn't your girl?"

"Well, if she wasn't my girl, it wouldn't be none of my business."

"Yeah, but a guy kind o' hates to see an old friend gettin' jived."

"Stay out, papa. Only way to protect yourself."

"S'posin' you didn't want to protect yourself? S'posin' you wanted to protect the woman?"

"Hmph! Who ever heard of a woman needin' protection?"

*

"Ladies and gentlemen!" sang Curry to the tense crowd that gorged the Arcadia. "Tonight is the night of the only contest of its kind in recorded history! On my left, Mr. Bus Williams, chief of the Blue Devils. On my right, Mr. Fessenden Baxter, leader of the Firemen. On this stand, the solid gold loving-cup. The winner will claim the jazz championship of the world!"

"And the sweet mama, too, how 'bout it?" called a wag.

"Each outfit will play three numbers: a one-step, a fox-trot, and a blues number. With this stop watch which you see in my hand, I will time your applause after each number. The leader receiving the longest total applause wins the loving-cup!"

"Yea—and some lovin'-up wid it!"

"I will now toss a coin to see who plays the first number!"

"Toss it out here!"

"Bus Williams's Blue Devils, ladies and gentlemen, will play the first number!"

Bus's philosophy of jazz held tone to be merely the vehicle of rhythm. He spent much time devising new rhythmic patterns with which to vary his presentations. Accordingly he depended largely on Tappen, his master percussionist, who knew every rhythmic monkeyshine with which to delight a gaping throng.

Bus had conceived the present piece as a chase, in which an agile clarinet eluded impetuous and turbulent traps. The other instruments were to be observers, chorusing their excitement while they urged the principals on.

From the moment the piece started something was obviously wrong. The clarinet was elusive enough, but its agility was without purpose. Nothing pursued it. People stopped dancing in the middle of the number and turned puzzled faces toward the platform. The trap drummer was going through the motions faithfully but to no avail. His traps were voiceless, emitted mere shadows of sound. He was a deaf mute making a speech.

Brief, perfunctory, disappointed applause rose and fell at the number's end. Curry announced its duration:

"Fifteen seconds flat!"

Fess Baxter, with great gusto, leaped to his post.

"The Firemen will play their first number!"

Bus was consulting Tappen.

"For the love o' Pete, Tap—?"

"Love o' hell. Look a' here."

Bus looked—first at the trap drum, then at the bass; snapped them with a finger, thumped them with his knuckles. There was almost no sound; each drum-sheet was dead, lax instead of taut, and the cause was immediately clear: each bore a short curved knife cut following its edge a brief distance, a wound unnoticeable at a glance, but fatal to the instrument.

Bus looked at Tappen, Tappen looked at Bus.

"The cream-colored son of a buzzard!"

Fess Baxter, gleeful and oblivious, was directing a whirlwind number, sweeping the crowd about the floor at an exciting, exhausting pace, distorting, expanding, etherealizing their emotions with swift-changing dissonances. Contrary to Bus Williams's philosophy, Baxter considered rhythm a mere rack upon which to hang his tonal tricks. The present piece was dizzy with sudden disharmonies, unexpected twists of phrase, successive false resolutions. Incidentally, however, there was nothing wrong with Baxter's drums.

Boiling over, Bus would have started for him, but Tappen grabbed his coat.

"Hold it, papa. That's a sure way to lose. Maybe we can choke him yet."

"Yea—?"

"I'll play the wood. And I still got cymbals and sandpaper."

"Yea—and a triangle. Hell of a lot o' good they are."

"Can't quit," said Tappen.

"Well," said Bus.

Baxter's number ended in a furor.

"Three minutes and twenty seconds!" bellowed Curry as the applause eventually died out.

Bus began his second number, a foxtrot. In the midst of it he saw Jean dancing, beseeching him with bewildered dismay in her eyes, a look that at once crushed and crazed him. Tappen rapped on the rim of his trap drum, tapped his triangle, stamped the pedal that clapped the cymbals, but the result was a toneless and hollow clatter, a weightless noise that bounced back from the multitude instead of penetrating into it. The players also, distracted by the loss, were operating far below par, and not all their leader's frantic false enthusiasm could compensate for the gaping absence of bass. The very spine had been ripped out of their music, and Tappen's desperate efforts were but the hopeless flutterings of a stricken, limp, pulseless heart.

"Forty-five seconds!" Curry announced. "Making a total so far of one minute flat for the Blue Devils! The Firemen will now play their second number!"

The Firemen's foxtrot was Baxter's rearrangement of Burleigh's "Jean, My Jean," and Baxter, riding his present advantage hard, stressed all that he had put into it of tonal ingenuity. The thing was delirious with strange harmonies, iridescent with odd color-changes, and its very flamboyance, its musical fine-writing and conceits delighted the dancers.

But it failed to delight Jean Ambrose, whom by its title it was intended to flatter. She rushed to Bus.

"What is it?" She was a-quiver.

"Drums gone. Somebody cut the pigskin the last minute."

"What? Somebody? Who?"

"Cut 'em with a knife close to the rim."

"Cut? He cut—? Oh, Bus!"

She flashed Baxter a look that would have crumpled his assurance had he seen it. "Can't you—Listen." She was at once wild and calm. "It's the bass. You got to have—I know! Make 'em stamp their feet! Your boys, I mean. That'll do it. All of 'em. Turn the blues into a shout."

"Yea? Gee. Maybe—"

"Try it! You've got to win this thing."

An uproar that seemed endless greeted Baxter's version of "Jean." The girl, back out on the floor, managed to smile as Baxter acknowledged the acclaim by gesturing toward her.

"The present score, ladies and gentlemen, is—for the Blue Devils, one minute even; for the Firemen, six minutes and thirty seconds! The Devils will now play their last number!" Curry's intonation of "last" moved the mob to laughter.

Into that laughter Bus grimly led his men like a captain leading his command into fire. He had chosen the parent of blues songs, the old "St. Louis Blues," and he adduced every device that had ever adorned that classic. Clarinets wailed, saxophones moaned, trumpets wept wretchedly, trombones laughed bitterly, even the great bass horn sobbed dismally from the depths. And so perfectly did the misery in the music express the actual despair of the situation that the crowd was caught from the start. Soon dancers closed their eyes, forgot their jostling neighbors, lost themselves bodily in the easy sway of that slow, fateful measure, vaguely aware that some quality hitherto lost had at last been found. They were too wholly absorbed to note just how that quality had been found: that every player softly dropped his heel where each bass-drum beat would have come, giving each major impulse a body and breadth that no drum could have achieved. Zoom-zoom-zoom-zoom. It was not a mere sound; it was a vibrant throb that took hold of the crowd and rocked it.

They had been rocked thus before, this multitude. Two hundred years ago they had swayed to that same slow fateful measure, lifting their lamentation to heaven, pounding the earth with their feet, seeking the mercy of a new God through the medium of an old rhythm, zoom-zoom. They had rocked so a thousand years ago in a city whose walls were jungle, forfending the wrath of a terrible black God who spoke in storm and pestilence, had swayed and wailed to that same slow period, beaten on a wild boar's skin stretched over the end of a hollow tree trunk. Zoom-zoom-zoom-zoom. Not a sound but an emotion that laid hold on their bodies and swung them into the past. Blues—low-down blues indeed—blues that reached their souls' depths.

But slowly the color changed. Each player allowed his heel to drop less and less softly. Solo parts faded out, and the orchestra began to gather power as a whole. The rhythm persisted, the unfaltering common meter of blues, but the blueness itself, the sorrow, the despair, began to give way to hope. Ere long hope came to the verge of realization—mounted it—rose above it. The deep and regular impulses now vibrated like nearing thunder, a mighty, inescapable, all-embracing dominance, stressed by the contrast of wind-tone; an all-pervading atmosphere through which soared wild-winged birds. Rapturously, rhapsodically, the number rose to madness and, at the height of its madness, burst into sudden silence.

Illusion broke. Dancers awoke, dropped to reality with a jolt. Suddenly the crowd appreciated that Bus Williams had returned to form, had put on a comeback, had struck off a masterpiece. And the crowd showed its appreciation. It applauded its palms sore.

Curry's suspense-ridden announcement ended:

"Total—for the Blue Devils, seven minutes and forty seconds! For the Firemen, six minutes and thirty seconds! Maybe that wasn't the Devils' last number after all! The Firemen will play their last number!"

It was needless for Baxter to attempt the depths and heights just attained by Bus Williams's Blue Devils. His speed, his subordination of rhythm to tone, his exotic coloring, all were useless in a low-down blues song. The crowd, moreover, had nestled upon the broad, sustaining bosom of a shout. Nothing else warmed them. The end of Baxter's last piece left them chilled and unsatisfied.

But if Baxter realized that he was beaten, his attitude failed to reveal it. Even when the major volume of applause died out in a few seconds, he maintained his self-assured grin. The reason was soon apparent: although the audience as a whole had stopped applauding, two small groups of assiduous handclappers, one at either extreme of the dancing area, kept up a diminutive, violent clatter.

Again Bus and Tappen exchanged sardonic stares.

"Damn' if he ain't paid somebody to clap!"

Only the threatening hisses and boos of the majority terminated this clatter, whereupon Curry summed up:

"For Bus Williams's Blue Devils—seven minutes and forty seconds! For Fess Baxter's Firemen—eight minutes flat!"

He presented Baxter the loving-cup amid a hubbub of murmurs, handclaps, shouts, and hisses that drowned whatever he said. Then the hubbub hushed. Baxter was assisting Jean Ambrose to the platform. With a bow and a flourish he handed the girl the cup.

She held it for a moment in both arms, uncertain, hesitant. But there was nothing uncertain or hesitant in the mob's reaction. Feeble applause was overwhelmed in a deluge of disapprobation. Cries of "Crooked!" "Don't take it!" "Crown the cheat!" "He stole it!" stood out. Tappen put his finger in the slit in his trap drum, ripped it to a gash, held up the mutilated instrument, and cried, "Look what he done to my traps!" A few hardboiled ruffians close to the platform moved menacingly toward the victor. "Grab 'im! Knock his can off!"

Jean's uncertainty abruptly vanished. She wheeled with the trophy in close embrace and sailed across the platform toward the defeated Bus Williams. She smiled into his astonished face and thrust the cup into his arms.

"Hot damn, mama! That's the time!" cried a jubilant voice from the floor, and instantly the gathering storm of menace broke into a cloudburst of delight. That romance-hungry multitude saw Bus Williams throw his baton into the air and gather the girl and the loving-cup into his arms. And they went utterly wild—laughed, shouted, yelled and whistled till the walls of the Arcadia bulged.

Jazz emerged as the mad noise subsided: Bus Williams's Blue Devils playing "*She's Still My Baby.*"

14

Blues for Little Prez

Sam Greenlee

The garbage collectors found Little Prez in the alley near Six-trey, OD'd away, layin' there cool and stiff, the tools of his burglar trade beside him and the shit for his fix there, too. He'd run across some of that almost pure smack only the rich white folks can get nowadays stuck behind a real Picasso drawing in a Sandburg Village townhouse on the North Side. Didn' pull no capers usually on the North Side 'cause rippin' off white folks was a one-way ticket to the slam, but he turned on all the afternoon before with some junkies he knew lived in Old Town, turnin' on, noddin' an' diggin' teevee an' the nex' mornin' everybody was gone an' no smack aroun' when he woke up an' he needed a fix quick so he walked over to the Village an' dug a back-door with a lock jus' beggin' to be picked. So he slid in through the sci-fi electronic computerized plastic kitchen that could do everything except fuck an' cook food you could taste, past the big color console TV sittin' squat an' fat like some bloated Buddha gon' wrong diggin' him with its big charcoal-grey cyclops eye, an' on past the little brother Sony TV in the bedroom 'cause any Pig seein' a nigger walkin' down North State Street with a idiot box was gon' jack you up for sure. Dug a cassette recorder good enough for a fix, but the real score after he emptied all the dresser drawers on the floor looking for a stash of cash was a fancy wrist watch good enough for the first fix of the day an' he could stick it in his pocket, an' then he dug the picture wasn' hangin' right in the way junkies have of focusin' in on jus' one thing an' foun' the package taped behind it and stuck it in his pocket when he heard a noise before he could check it out. He slid on back out the kitchen door of the white man's pad like his momma been doin' for more years than Little Prez been livin'. On out into the eye-blinkin' hard hot sun cuttin' through his shades like razor blades an' lettin' him know once more that daylight and junkies ain' no match. On down into the dank damp tube of the subway feelin' more like home where no daylight an' no eyeball burnin' sun could come. Bought two Hershey bars in the vending machine on the platform, his junkie juices flowing in his mouth askin' for some sugar, an' he tried to cool his junkie nerves jumpin' up and down his spine like grasshoppers up a long stalk of ragweed in a Woodlawn vacant lot where he used to play an' catch grasshoppers and make 'em spit tobacco an' tell ladybirds to fly away home 'cause they pad was on fire an' he didn' ever step on ants 'cause that would make it rain an' when it rained he'd have to stay in his funky crib in the middle of the rats and roaches an' the sound of the soap opera down the hall dealin' with silly-ass so-called hangups of jive-ass white folks whose ghost-white voices walked into the room an' took over. Tol' his grasshopper nerves to cool it an' his monkey to take a vacation 'cause he was gon' turn on soon as he hustled that fancy-ass watch layin' in his pocket nex' to his long unused dick 'cause smack been for a longtime his only ol' lady. Was sniffin' an' scratchin' but bein' cool with it 'cause they might be a undercover pig sittin' in the subway car waitin' to jack up some junkie 'cause he didn' have nothin' else to do an' it was easier than messin' with some beret-wearin' gangbanger who didn' give a shit an' might kick some pig's ass or worse an', shit, he sure wished the pigs would get off his back but he been cool since the last time he got out of the slam in Joliet an' he was stoolin' for the pigs now and so they let him alone an' even laid a lid on him now an' then when he said somethin' they wanted to hear, but right now he was out of his 'hood an' some motherfuckin' rookie lookin' for a promotion an' didn' know Little Prez might bust him or even rip him off 'cause the quickest way for a honky pig cop to get a promotion in Chicago was to off a nigger. So he wished the damn train would get him the hell on back to the South Side where he belonged an' he could get him a fix an' all his hangups take a vacation along with his monkey, an' all the time he had the best smack he ever had in his pocket but he forgot about it like everything else when he needed a fix, jus' thinkin' how much he needed to turn on an' how good he be feelin' after he shoot up an' all the down things be movin' in his head while he noddin'. The

El came on up out of the tube and the sunlight hit him across his eyes right through his shades as hard as a pig from the Southwes' Side hatin' niggers an' hungup an' evil 'cause one of his neighbors sold his crib to a nigger jus' three blocks away an' even though the pig pumped a full magazine of buckshot in through the nigger's picture window they jus' boarded it over an' now they was "for sale" signs all over the block an' nex' thing you know they be takin' over his neighborhood an' he moved twice already gettin' away from niggers. Little Prez knew how to read all that shit in a honky pig's face, an' how much shit the pig gon' make him take an' how much smilin' sometimes didn' do no good 'cause a lot of them pigs got they kicks stompin' niggers.

Little Prez got off at Fifty-fifth, glad he was back in his own 'hood, an' he hustled the watch to a barber for 35 bills, bought his shit, hurried to his crib an' knew he could make a thing out of his make 'cause his monkey not buggin' him too much. Let himself into his funky-junky pad with jus' a mattress on the floor an' a table an' a refrigerator (didn' usually have nothin' in it, the only thing in the crib worth anything the stereo an' color teevee). He dug sittin' an' noddin' diggin' TV with the sound off an' his earphones on, diggin' the sounds an' watchin' TV without havin' to listen to them screechy tacky voices sounding like somebody scratchin' his fingernails across a blackboard when he high. He had a small white enamel sterilizer he ripped off from an abortionist one time an' that was a good score 'cause he foun' two shoeboxes full of cash an' he didn' have to steal nothin' for months after that caper. Little Prez dug he was a different kind of junkie shootin' up with sterile needles and the only tracks in his arms was when he turned on someplace else with some junkie friends or when he was too strung-out to wait for the red light to go on the sterilizer. But he was scared of dirty needles; his momma aways tol' him 'bout germs an' shit, an' he knew a lotta junkies got wasted from hepatitis an' shit from turnin' on with dirty needles. He turned on the TV without no sound to that soap opera always had somebody black on it talkin' to white folks all the time, an' Little Prez used to make up what they talkin' about between nods diggin' the sounds on his headphones. Then he took his time puttin' on a stack o' sounds: Prez, Stitt, Jug, Trane an' a old Wardell outa print nowadays an' he tol' everybody it was one of his "collector's items." He had some of the new sounds an' dug 'em, but when he was turned on he mainly listened to the sounds that was the sounds in the streets when he first got out there in 'em. He put the records on the box then started gettin' his make together diggin' Prez during his first administration winnin' the election for all-time in front of that bad-ass Basie band. He put the needle in the sterilizer. "Rock-à-Bye Basie," diggin' Earl Warren doin' a few Johnny Hodges type bars, then Prez fatter-toned than usual, the band riffin' so bad behind him, an' then Sweets blowin' like he invented the Harmon mute. Little Prez hummin' along with 'em everyone of 'em and the band too, an' not missin' a note, gettin' the make ready, careful like he was gettin' his horn together in some funky backstage like Prez gettin' ready to blow. The red light went on an' tol' him the needle was ready, an' he got the rest of the make together while Prez was doin' trippin'-type things on "Taxi War Dance." Took out the needle and the tablespoon with the handle bent over double, made up over an alcohol lamp, Prez wailin' now, bootin' the band an' they talkin' to each other, Prez an' the brass section, an' Prez, four bars each an' them cats could say more in four bars than some of these young dudes in four sides. Herschel Evans blowin' now, deeper-toned than Prez, earthy sound like he had to keep his feet planted on the ground 'cause Prez always wantin' to fly, big fat sound no reed squeak, sound soundin' like it an' Herschel the same thing with the rhythm section rock-steady an' swingin' behind him. Whole band riffin' now an' Little Prez puttin' the rubber hose roun' his pipestem arm, flexin' his fist an' lookin' for a collapsed vein to show, gettin' uptight now 'cause it so close an', shit, where was the motherfucker, the needle ready an' Prez sayin' things an' the earphones right there, shit, where was it, wantin' to put it in his arm an' beggin' for pussy he knew he wasn' gonna get, never as bad as waitin' for that vein to show an' give him a target for the clean dickhead of his needle, an' one showed an' he hit it an' slow slow makin' it last shot up an' pulled the needle out, still proud an' hard even when empty an' his own dick never been like that even when he was a stud an' hustlin' a stable of four of the finest whores on the South Side. He put the dick/needle in the sterilizer, put on the earphones an' waited for the flash, better than any orgasm he ever had an' didn' miss anymore 'cause he had all the sex he needed every day in Miss Skag an' it hit him an' he moaned an' Prez blowin' "D. B. Blues" an' Little Prez layin' there an' noddin' an' diggin' Lester, his man, President of all the tenor men.

II

We called him Little Prez 'cause he dug Lester so much. Could scat all Prez's solos note for note in the right key standin' there near the basketball backboard in McCosh playground, his hands shoulder high, holdin' an imaginary tenor like Prez downstage at the Regal Theater blowin' with that bootin' Basie band behind him, Jo Jones kickin' on drums, Freddie Green rockin' steady an' Walter Page walkin' strong, the brass bright an' bitin' punctuatin' the saxophone riffs, an' Prez would start out with his tenor hangin' low an' like it gettin' good to him comin' up slow 'til it shoulder-high an' him steppin' in place in time like it so good he can't stan' still an' the band kickin' twelve-bar ass behind him, an' we could see an' hear all that on a sunny day when bored with basketball, an' Little Prez doin' his thing. Was a little nigger, Little Prez, with a head too big for his scrawny body, lookin' skinny even under all those clothes his momma made him wear to keep him from catchin' cold but didn' work too well he was always sniffin', even in the summertime. Little Prez couldn' do nothin' but rap, was the Rap Master of the 'hood. Couldn' fight like Tampy, play basketball like Raby, football like Fuzz, run like C. B., hit a softball like Junior. Couldn' sing, dance, drink, fuck, steal, play games, hunt rats. Wasn' dumb or smart in school, didn' have a fine momma with a sharp boyfrien' with a big Cadillac or Lincoln. Couldn' do shit but rap, lie an' signify. Could play the dozens for days, talk about your momma bad enough to make you cry, run off 42 verses without repeatin' hisself. Sing-say the "Signifyin' Monkey" like nobody else. Couldn' do nothin' else 'cep rap an' he could rap like the real Prez blew, an' when Little Prez got big everybody knew he was gonna blow tenor too an' he would walk down to the pawnshop near Cottage Grove an' dig the horns in the barred window, mostly old beatup Martins and Selmers, but sometimes one or two lookin' bran' new, left by some strungout junky musician. Cheated on his lunch money, delivered the *Tribune* in the mornin's, sold the *Defender* an' the *Courier* on Fridays, hauled groceries from Kroger's in his wagon, an' finally he had the bread an' got his Selmer, walked out with it in the case on down Sixty-third in a crablike shuffle jus' like Prez, an' everybody said if Little Prez could blow like he talked he'd be a bitch. He dug every tenor goin', dug Jug offin' everybody every Saturday afternoon at Al Benson's Battle of the Bands at the Pershing. Dug E. Parker McDougal an' Johnny Griffin still blowin' with the DuSable High School band before Hamp came through. Dug Dexter an' heard the cats in the playgroun' tryin' to put down Prez to the tune o' "Dexter's Deck"; "My name's Dexter, outblow Lester anyday . . . " and he laughed. Dug Jug an' Stitt, Wardell, Lockjaw an' Gator Tail, Quinichette, the vice pres, Ike Quebec, Ben Webster. Dug 'em at the Parkway, Savoy, Pershing, White City an' the Regal. In the Propeller Lounge, Blue Note, Bee Hive an' the Sutherland. Saw 'em come and disappear, saw 'em early an' saw 'em late, saw 'em try to imitate the President, an' Little Prez tried to deal with somethin' we didn't know: that Little Prez couldn' blow. All them sounds and notes and things runnin' roun' in his head and he couldn' bring 'em out through his horn. Wore a black porkpie like Prez, sometimes tossed his head in that faggot put-on like Prez, drank good Gordon's gin, wore eight-sided dark green tea glasses, big bold-look ties, pin-stripe double-breasted box-back suits like Prez. Lived, ate, slept Prez but couldn' blow like Prez. Practiced six, eight, 10 hours a day, treated his horn better than his momma, shaved his reeds, soaked his reeds, changed his mouthpiece, oiled his keys, polished the brass, an' Prez blew his nose better than Little Prez blew his horn. Couldn' deal with it, wouldn' deal with it, didn' want to deal with it 'cause he knew it was a lie 'cause his momma tol' him, his preacher tol' him, teacher tol' him, everybody tol' him hard work and sacrifice would suffice. Didn' know, couldn' know the only people really believed in the Protestant work ethic was black folks, didn' know even though he'd grown up in a black Baptist church what a Protestant Ethic was, jus' believed if you wanted somethin' bad enough and worked long enough and hard enough you had to get it, couldn' quit it, had to get it. If you worked hard enough you had to get it and didn', couldn' dig that the people worked hardest had the least. . . . An' all the time Little Prez blowin' an' not knowin' he doin' the right thing for the wrong reasons. Blowin' with visions of Cadillacs dancin' in his head, long an' lavender an' full o' chicks with hydramatic hips, a closet full of clothes an' enough shoes to change everyday for a month an' not wear the same pair twice. Didn' know, wouldn' know, couldn' know music ain' got nothin' to do with them kinda things. Didn' even stop to think Prez didn' have them kinda things, sittin' in a cheap hotel on Broadway lookin' at Birdland through gin-glazed eyes, diggin' all his imitators and emulators draggin' down all the bread for blowin' the shit he'd discarded 20 years before, an' all of 'em white boys.

So Little Prez blew ugly 'cause his head was ugly and he never knew the reason why. Tried everything twice and then once more 'til one day he discovered Smack. Started out sniffin' and found everything turned soft and warm, the hard edges roundin' off an' the sounds, smells and taste becomin' somethin' else, an' when he blew he sounded jus' like Prez—to hisself. Started out sniffin', then skinpoppin' an' had to put away his horn to go out in the streets to support his habit. Started snatchin' pocketbooks 'til a welfare mother with her check jus' cashed and five hungry kids to feed kicked his ass an' almos' held him 'til the pigs got there. Ran some whores on Sixty-third and Cottage 'til the shit turned him too greedy and impotent and one day he had to make a choice between a fix an' a payoff and the pig he tried to stall busted him and he spent his first time in the slam and dug he could get all the shit he needed long as he had some bread, and between his momma and hustlin' his ass inside to guards and/or cons he was cool and wasn' even in a hurry to get out, but by the time he got out he'd had a full course in Breaking and Entering, an' now he was a full-time junkie and part-time thief, but the dream never deferred 'cause nex' week he was gon' renew his union card, get a band together, cut a record and blow everybody's mind. Spent time twice in the slam an' went to Lexington three times, not to kick his habit but reduce it when it got too expensive to support. An' you could see him on a corner on Six-trey noddin' his junkie nod and blowin' tenor sounds inside his head loud enough to drown out the racket of the El on its way between Cottage Grove and King Drive, which usta be South Park in his before-junkie days.

III

Little Prez sat up straight out of his nod like he was havin' a bad dream he couldn't remember. The box was still playin' the last record over and over. It was almos' dark outside, the sun comin' pale an' weak down the airshaft and crawlin' into his funky room on weak wino knees. He got up quick an' turned on the lights; big, bright, naked bulb 'cause he was afraid of the dark. A drag for a rip-off junkie, afraid of the dark 'cause the dark is when he had to work, slippin' down alleys in the dark into dark houses an' workin' with not much light, checkin' out whatever would bring the most bread with the least work: portable TV sets, watches an' jewelry and men's suits, if they wasn' too big or too small, but money the bes' 'cause you didn' get ripped off five-to-one by a fence or worse than that if you had to hustle somethin' quick on the streets. Move through the dark pad hopin' you was right they was no dog in it an' no silent burglar alarm, but even so knew no pigs would be in no hurry to answer an alarm from a nigger's home. Check out the bedroom first an' dump all the stuff from the drawers on the floor an' mos' times they was cash in there somewhere 'cause even credit-card niggers didn' really trust banks and usually had a stash somewhere in the pad. It was a drag havin' to work in the dark with the shadows long an' always lookin' like they movin' an' furniture sittin' there lookin' like people, so he always had to turn on before he went inside to keep from climbin' the walls. He got his shit together, his burglar tools in a attaché case—he thought that was cool puttin' rip-off tools in a attaché case of good pigskin he'd ripped off from a pad in Pill Hill but he usually worked Woodlawn where he grew up 'cause the pigs didn' give a damn and the folks lived there couldn' afford to buy and train them big man-eating dogs them saditty niggers had roun' the house an' he laughed like hell everytime he read 'bout one of them big motherfuckers turnin' on his owner. He was waitin' for the sterilizer to turn on the red light an' reached in his pocket and pulled out the envelope he forgot he had and opened it up and they was ten packets looked like horse an' he opened one, wet his finger, dipped it in and tasted an' it was smack, tasted like good shit an' he almos' sat down and cried. Thought 'bout stayin' home an' turnin' on but he'd cased the job for a month an' he decided to do it and took one lid of the new stuff to turn on with before he went inside the pad he had staked out.

IV

He stood listening, in the dark alley not far from Six-trey. Good place for a rip-off an' he'd pulled four capers there in a year, only one dog, old and half-blind down at the other end o' the block and barked at everything including the El, so nobody paid him any mind. Had lived a whole history in Woodlawn alleys: ripped-off his first sweet potato from a store on Six-trey and cooked it over a fire in the alley; shot his first basketball and missed; smoked his first cigarette, his first joint, felt his first tit, drank his first wine, had his first fight, an' lost, had his first fuck leanin' against a garage, sniffed his first horse and pulled his first B & E caper in alleys near Six-trey. Couldn' keep away, an' his momma still lived on Eberhart an' kep' a $20 bill in a sugar bowl so he wouldn' rip off her TV when he was uptight for a fix. Little Prez moved deeper into the shadows, madeup an' hit himself. Took loose the rubber tubing an' waited for the flash an' the white folks' almos' pure horse galloped through his thin junkie veins an' smacked his ass for the las' time, the horse too pure, too white for the black junkie's heart an' they foun' him the nex' day, OD'd away. No more Prez for Little Prez, his horn in its case in the closet. No more dreams of standing in the spotlight in eight-sided dark green tea glasses, his horn held high nex' to his right shoulder. No more rip-offs an' no more monkeys to feed an' somewhere on the South Side a little black kid saved his pennies to buy a horn so he could blow just like Trane.

15

Tenorman: A Novella

David Huddle

I

When Carnes got out of the hospital in Stockholm, we offered him the horn of his choice, the studio of his dreams, and luxurious support for as long as he stayed clean. At the time, Carnes was 59 years old, but he looked closer to seventy. During the worst winter of his life, a couple of days before somebody checked him into the hospital, he had hocked his old horn. When we talked to him, he still vividly remembered having almost died on the streets of Gőteborg. He was ready to consider what we had to offer him.

The first condition of our agreement was that he had to move back to the States—we wanted him in the Washington area, within driving distance of the museum's main office. He wasn't eager to come back to "Ol' Virginny," as he put it, but our deal must have seemed like his own customized version of paradise: a comfortable place to live; whatever he wanted in the way of food, clothes, books, records, and so on; along with an ideal working circumstance and all the time he wanted to spend with this replacement tenor he had asked for.

He already had that horn on his wish list, a Selmer Mark VI, vintage 1957, that Getz had played for a couple of years and that some private collector in Stockholm had picked up and let Carnes try out one afternoon some years back. How much of the American taxpayers' money we had to pay for that saxophone is still a confidential matter.

Carnes wondered if he could live in his studio. "I want to hole up for a while, gentlemen. I just want to stay put." We couldn't have asked for a better inclination on his part.

So we found a large duplex in Chevy Chase and had half of it fixed up just as he described it, a small kitchen with a big window that looked out onto a backyard garden, a neat little living area with a waterbed for his bad back, and a first-rate stereo—he didn't necessarily want big speakers or a powerful amplifier, but he did ask for "the best sound you gentlemen can get for me." And he did accept a CD player after we told him it would be easier to obtain the recordings he wanted on CD rather than on vinyl. But no TV, no wet bar, and not much in the way of art. We gave him the tour late one afternoon when the light was angling in through the windows. "Feels fine, gentlemen," he said, walking around and touching things, plunking a few keys on the piano.

There was no shortage of young musicians who wanted a chance to spend time around Carnes, to study with him, as it were. We turned away lots of them who'd just heard about our project, people whose names you probably would know if you listen seriously to jazz. Carnes was this living landmark of the music, an artist already of forty years' consequence, who had reached the apex of his genius here at the end of his life. We had our pick of the New York prodigies, the kids who'd been brought along by Wynton Marsalis and his dad. Our grant provided money to pay musicians top wages just to be available to Carnes when he wished for their assistance in his composing, his arranging, his noodling around in his art.

So when Carnes said, "Send me in that piano man," Cody Jones, our gifted twenty-two-year-old pianist, presented himself at the studio door. Then Carnes and Cody could work on a piece as long as the old man wanted to. If Carnes decided they needed a bassist, they summoned Wil Stanfield, who appeared with his instrument, pleased to have been called and eager to jam with Carnes. Ditto with Curtis Wells, our Juilliard dropout drummer. And so on. Wynton himself came down from New York occasionally and sent word in to the old man that he was available; Carnes appreciated that and always asked him to step right in. He liked Wynton, respected what he'd done for jazz. The two of them spent as much time talking as they did playing music.

When he had tired them out—he himself was apparently indefatigable—Carnes thanked the young musicians, laconically advised them to stay away from drugs, drink, and loose women; raised a gnarled old hand; and told them "later." Then he played to himself and to the empty studio for another hour, or two hours, or all night if he wanted. Some nights—or early mornings—he set down his compositions or made notes for them, a kind of scoring only he seemed to understand. But usually he relied on his memory and set down nothing. He did exactly what he wanted to, and whatever it was, it suited us. We videotaped and recorded everything he did, every sound he made. Except for when he went to the bathroom. We could have done that, too, if we'd wanted; Carnes didn't care about the recording and video-taping part of the project; he seemed happy doing what he was doing, living inside his music.

We didn't talk about it much among ourselves, but I know that most of us on the team were pretty proud of what we'd done, rescuing this wonderful old guy, bringing him home to the U.S.A., nourishing his work and preserving it for posterity. If it hadn't been for us and our project, Carnes most likely would have been sleeping on a steam vent in Gőteborg. Or been frozen to death and locked up in some morgue drawer in Stockholm, waiting for next-of-kin to send for the body.

A significant part of our project was that Sony-CBS provided us with state-of-the-art equipment. They let us use this amazing machinery; the stuff in our studio half of the duplex was huge—we'd had to knock down a couple of walls to make room for it—but our cameras took up so little room in Carnes's apartment and were so unobtrusive that he seldom took note of them.

Our musicologists and recording specialists worked on editing and assembling the work of the old tenorman—including random observations he made in conversations with the younger musicians and with Wynton—into archives and professional recordings. The income from these recordings would go into his estate; there would be more than enough to provide comfortably for generations of the old man's heirs, if he had any.

Carnes didn't like talking too much business with us. He said he just wanted to work. And we made it so that he didn't have to bother himself with any of the petty matters of preserving and marketing his work. He simply did what he pleased and asked for whatever he wanted—which, given the infinite possibilities available to him, wasn't really very much. What he asked for we brought to him, almost instantly.

For a while our only difficulty was that the old man had developed a taste for fresh fruit and sometimes wanted it at odd hours. Finally, we worked out a deal with one of the grocery suppliers in the D.C. area. Every morning they sent over their truck and let us select the best of their fruit, which came from all over the world.

Carnes told our musical historian that, from about the age of ten on, this was the cleanest year of his life. Coffee was his only vice. At night, an hour or two before he went to bed, he drank tea while he listened to his stereo. In those late hours, he favored the recordings of Ben Webster and Coleman Hawkins. "My old pals," he called them. "Gents," he'd say, "I'm gonna spend a little time with the Hawk now," and of course we'd clear out for him.

He liked listening to his records by himself. And of course what he played was of interest to our people, too. We kept track of his choices and matched them against the compositions he was producing during those months. A couple of our more scholarly team members were fascinated with that aspect of his *creative process,* a term, incidentally, that never failed to bring a droll expression onto Carnes's face whenever somebody used it around him. "My process," he'd repeat after one of our guys and draw his mouth down and kind of grin.

Why we didn't anticipate that the old guy might wish the company of a woman none of us knew. In retrospect, it astonishes us that we didn't, though our having no women on our team probably had a lot to do with it. Most of us had wives or girlfriends or partners, but for some reason we figured a working genius didn't need a significant other.

Historically, Carnes had never had anything to do with women musicians—not that there had been that many female instrumentalists in jazz in his day. Years before, he had been quoted as saying he didn't like to work with singers, male or female, because just about the time he knew where he was going with his solo, the singer would be ready to pick up the vocal again. But of course he'd had a couple of wives and plenty of girlfriends. So we should have anticipated how he'd be—opposite sex-wise—when he came clean.

About this matter of a woman, we were stupid—there wasn't one of us who wouldn't admit it.

Months had passed. We were all fond of Carnes. He was a dear guy, and he seemed to like most of our team members. Something that impressed him was that everybody on the project knew his music—we could remind him of a tune he'd recorded with Ray Brown and Tommy Flanagan in 1959, when he might not remember anything more than the way the notes came to him through his embouchure and his fingers when he picked up his horn.

Something else that seemed to please him secretly was how much all of us on the Project respected him. He'd had years of getting used to dealing with people who knew him as just a guy in a band and wouldn't have dreamed he was a major American artist. Now with us, he had to beg us to stop calling him "sir" and "Mr. Carnes." "'Ed,'" he'd say, "I want you to call me 'Ed.' And don't say 'sir' to me. I *work* for a living." But it was evident that he appreciated the way we honored him with our manners. We weren't putting on an act for him; we were on the Project because we loved the music of Edgar DeWeese Carnes.

"Gentlemen, you've been awfully good to me. I don't deny that for a minute. I'm not complaining here. And I don't want you to think I'm pulling out a surprise. This isn't anything I thought of when we first talked about our arrangement. It's something that came to me this past week—because I'm getting somewhere in my music. I had to play for my living, so I couldn't ever sit back and think about it, make one thing build onto the next. So if this is a surprise, it's a surprise to me, too. But what it comes down to is that I need something very similar to a girlfriend.

"I don't mean I want you to go out and get me some woman off the street. And I don't mean I want you to find me some pretty widow out of the church choir. I just need the company of an *interesting* woman. You know what I mean? Hard for me to explain to you what that is, if you don't know already. But somebody I can talk to. Not necessarily about music. But she'd have to know something about that, too. Don't want some tone-deaf Marylou in here trying to tell me about current events. I swear I don't know how to tell you. I'd go out and find her myself, except I know I'd find some other things while I was at it. Won't do for me to be going to the clubs looking for company. You gentlemen have to go out and find her for me, and I don't even know how to tell you what she looks like."

Who could blame Carnes for what he wanted? We understood his request perfectly well, but we weren't sure how to go about granting it. No one on our staff could quite imagine himself going out to the jazz clubs in search of female companionship for our man.

Cody Jones threw back his head and laughed out loud when someone asked him what he thought. "I think it's time for a party is what I think," Cody said.

"Good idea," our director said when he heard Cody's suggestion. "Henry," he said to me, "I think you need to make the arrangements for a party where Mr. Carnes might meet someone who interests him."

I knew, of course, that if this party were a success, my director would receive full credit for it and that if it flopped, I would be held responsible. I had no quarrel with that. From my first day of working with this director, I had understood the nature of being his assistant. Nevertheless, the racial complication made the assignment difficult: a thirty-five-year-old white guy throwing a party where a sixty-year-old black guy would enjoy himself.

As a child growing up in Welch, West Virginia, I took piano lessons until my teacher confided to my father that he was wasting his money on my musical future. I hold a B.A. in government studies from the University of Virginia and an M.A. in Fine Arts Management from American University. My wife and I live in a raised ranch in Fairfax, Virginia, in a neighborhood that is 95 percent white. No more than three or four black people have attended any social gathering to which I have been invited.

My relationship with jazz has been informed by my paranoiac intuition that blacks despise whites, coupled with my yearning to know how blacks suffer their lives with such grace. I've had very few black friends. The night after my boss informed me that I was to be responsible for it, I dreamed about this party—a sort of sixties vision of blacks and whites and Asians and Native Americans all talking intensely and eating and laughing and dancing and enjoying each other's company, the whole undulating panorama shimmering in extravagant colors. The background music was Carnes's "Scandinavian Suite." Carnes himself—elegantly dressed, ebullient, garrulous, and utterly charming—was at the center of the gathering, surrounded by women of various ethnic backgrounds.

Acting as his translator, with Carnes's arm draped across my shoulder, I communicated his witty and inscrutable observations to these women. My dream did not provide me with an explanation for why Carnes needed a translator.

I cannot imitate his speech patterns. He grew up in Buffalo, New York, and since he'd dropped out of high school, his language wasn't quite up to the level of his intellectual development; nevertheless, in his own way he was quite an articulate man.

"A party, huh?" Carnes said when I went in at breakfast to tell him that we were thinking of having a gathering in his honor and that we would like to have his thoughts about what kind of party it should be. "You thinking about having it here or somewhere else? You don't know? Well, Henry, I'll tell you, around here is pretty familiar to me.

"Some years ago I went to this reception for Mr. Ellington at an embassy in Brussels, Belgium. That place scared me so bad I had to drink every little glass of champagne I could lift off those little trays they were passing by us. I disgraced myself before I ever got to say hello to that man who had meant everything that mattered to me. I had so much to ask Mr. Ellington, questions I'd been saving up to ask him. My one chance to talk with him, and there I was so drunk that when I stumbled up to speak, he turned away from me, turned his back on me. I won't ever forget that.

"But aside from me being a drunk anyway, I blame it on all those pictures on the wall, those cold floors, bright lights, and nowhere to sit down.

"If you can get one of these boys here who's got his own place in town, somebody who wouldn't mind having a party at his house, why that might be nice. I'd like there to be a sofa where I can sit down and not have to be spitting in people's faces when I talk to them. If the talk gets just right, why then I don't miss Mr. Booze so much.

"You know I come from a family of quick-tempered people on both sides. My mother and my father, especially when they were young, it didn't take anything to get them riled up. They'd start saying things they'd know they were going to regret. To their own children they'd say what you wouldn't whisper to a yard dog barking at you from under somebody's front porch. They knew better; they just did it anyway.

"So I was like that, too, I learned from them—I had it in me anyway. When I was a young man, my temper was a crazy thing ready to fly out of my head any minute.

"I did temper things, too, used to try to hit people, even though I was the world's worst fighter. Then I'd have a drink to calm myself down. What I told myself was, I'll have this drink, then I won't be so mad anymore. That much of it was right; I'd forget about what I was mad about and who I was mad at. But then I'd get mad at somebody else over something they said, and I'd be drunk by then and not making any sense.

"Good thing my mother and father let me learn how to play a horn. I wasn't cut out to be a boxer, I'll tell you that much. I hit this bass player one time, a kid named Herman Drexler from Rochester, hit him right in the mouth with my fist. Herman Drexler wiped off his mouth and looked at his hand to see if he was bleeding. He saw he was, then he popped me one right in the forehead. It knocked me back about ten feet before I went down to the floor. I'd never been hit like that. Herman walked up and looked down at me and said, 'I would have hit you in the mouth except you wouldn't be able to play." I said, 'Thank you, Herman, I appreciate that.' And I did. He and I played that night in the same band again, both of us paying special attention to what we were telling each other in the music. And we didn't play bad, either. But I never did hit anybody again after that. Herman taught me. It's easy to learn not to hit anybody compared to what it takes to learn not to drink anymore. I still want a drink every day. I just don't want one worse than I do want one. Sometimes it's close between want and don't want.

"Only thing I've still got with me that I want to hold on to now is playing this horn. Everything else, it's okay with me for it to be gone. Especially drinking. I hope it stays gone."

Carnes is a relatively small man, five foot ten or so, with a substantial belly. He keeps his hair short, and he doesn't have much of it anyway. Most of his scalp has a polished look to it. His skin is various shades of reddish brown, like stained oak, his face somewhere between medium and light brown and his hands very light skinned. His hands are surprisingly small.

"Hands like these," he says, holding them up for exhibition, "I should be playing alto." He puts his hands on his knees. "But I don't like the upper register, don't like the sound of it. On tenor, I have to sacrifice some of the low notes, that low B-flat, unless I just have to have it. My hands are strong, but these fingers don't stretch the way a tenorman's ought to." He wiggles the little finger of his left hand and laughs when Bob Fulton, one of our technical people, leans forward to get a close look at that treasure of a pinky of his.

"Got my mother's hands." Carnes shakes his head. "What'd I get from my father? No, he wasn't any kind of a musician—everybody guesses that he must have been. But here's how he was. Anywhere we went where somebody was playing an instrument or singing, my father would stop and listen. He would be quiet, and he wouldn't pay any attention to us when we tried to hurry him along. Two old white women playing violin duets in a shopping mall, my father would find a bench, sit there, and listen half the afternoon. Salvation Army band playing in their overcoats on a corner, my father would stand in the snow, listening, listening. College boy strumming a banjo on his landlady's porch, kitchen help practicing their harmony while they take a break in the alley, church choir running through Sunday's hymns on a Thursday night, it didn't matter, my father stopped and listened. Sometimes we'd just have to leave him sitting or standing where he was and come back later.

"Thing about it is, I don't really know what my father was hearing. He didn't tap his foot, he didn't nod his head, he didn't smile or frown, he didn't even applaud when the song was finished and everybody else was clapping their hands. He'd sit and wait for what else was going to be played. My father had this infinite patience. But he almost never talked about the music, never explained why he listened to it like that.

"Except this one time, after we'd come home from downtown Buffalo. I was pestering him about why he'd stood around listening to this hammering dulcimer player outside a music store. I was about twelve years old then; I'd been playing in my school band for about a year. I thought I was hot stuff on that old banged-up school-band saxophone. 'Daddy,' I said, 'why you even listening to that old hillbilly music, la-te-da-te-da?'

"He looked over his glasses at me—he was a schoolteacher and had a way of looking at you when he wanted to. 'It's what a human being has inside,' he said. 'I know I don't know as much about music as you do, but I also know that when I hear somebody playing—not on the radio or on a record but right there themselves—I have to listen to it. I know I need to do that.'

"My father was quiet a while, looking at me. I didn't have anything to say back to him, either, because I was so surprised he'd explained anything to me about it. I hadn't expected him to answer me on that topic because he never had before when I'd pestered him. 'I couldn't say that there's much in this world that I know for sure, but I do know that.' His voice was real low like he might have been telling me something, or maybe he just needed to say something out loud. 'I know I need to listen when somebody plays. And I never heard any kind of music that somebody played that I didn't think, All right, a man may be a bad thing, but at least he has that inside him.'

"When I think back about him now, I don't ever remember him humming or whistling or singing in church or any of those things. My father was a nonmusical man, if you can feature such a creature—ha! But music meant more to him than it does to most people." Carnes shook his head. "I guess I didn't have much choice but to pick up a horn and stick with it," he said. And even as he was talking, I was aware of how his words were being recorded. I could envision the text, the black alphabet spinning out into the future on the white page of a book that would be published not so many years from when we were just sitting there talking at his little kitchen table.

That was the first time our project ever seemed to me like some very subtle thievery or embezzlement we were practicing, with Carnes the victim.

II

"I don't think that's the case at all," Marianne told me. The evening after my conversation with Carnes about his father, she and I were talking over coffee and dessert at Bottelli's, where we had met for dinner.

"You saved this man, not merely from obscurity but also from an ignominious death. He's better off than he ever has been, the people who appreciate his music are delighted to have him still playing, and you're doing work you love. Tell me who's being hurt by this project. Even the taxpayers ought to be happy to have their dollars supporting an artist instead of a general or a politician." She doesn't add "a bureaucrat," and I appreciate that.

My wife teaches law at Georgetown. In a woman a shade over six feet tall, whose eyes are that blazing blue of a romantic, a fanatic, a seer, Marianne's common sense is disconcerting.

Thin, pale, and discriminating in her wardrobe but eschewing makeup or any attention to her dark hair beyond washing and brushing it, she is not someone you expect to speak to you like the proverbial old farmer leaning on the barnyard fence.

The first time I saw her—on the other side of a D.C. apartment dining room at a party—I fantasized a woman who'd walk up to me and say, "Do you have plans for this weekend? And by the way, what is your name?" Three minutes later I glanced at her again and imagined the same woman walking up to ask if I had yet taken Jesus for my personal savior.

Her appearance suggests the irrational—I suspect that it's her height even more than her eyes. You expect her to be reckless, flagrantly disregardful of convention, some variety of a missionary or ideological extremist. You remark that woman as the dangerous one, the one you'd follow against your better judgment.

What Marianne did say that evening, when I finally located someone who would introduce us, was, "I have to go home now. Paper due tomorrow in Intellectual Properties." (She was a student in those days.) "Very pleased to make your acquaintance." Then she shook hands with me, hello and good-bye all at the same time, with a hand neither warm nor cold, but very slender, very pale. Brief and formal as my initial encounter with Marianne Stettler was, she nevertheless gave me the flicker of a conspiratorial look. The next day and the day after that, I was hearing her voice and remembering her lifted eyebrows, her high forehead.

Three days after the party, I went to a lot of trouble to get her phone number and called her up. We don't—either of us—understand what she saw in me that made her agree to go out with me. Whatever personal trait it was must also have been the same quality that eventually persuaded her to marry me. We guess it was my conversational ability, or rather the fact that I listened to her when her peers seemed to be listening to the person they thought she was.

I still have the power to hear Marianne with a more exact understanding than most of her acquaintances, so that when she needs to be heard, she counts on my doing that for her.

Other aspects of our relationship are—to our sorrow—less dependable. After the first months of our marriage, the two of us discovered ourselves to be sexually fastidious. Rarely now do we find ourselves in the mood at the same time, though we each have mournfully admitted to the other that we'd be better off if we had more sex. It's just that neither of us can stand merely to accommodate the other—or to be merely accommodated by the other. We'd probably have divorced years ago except for our mutually confessed suspicion that other lovers would find our finicky ways much less tolerable than we do. Thus our incompatibility has become a cruel form of compatibility.

In the natural pause of our waiter's warming our cups with fresh coffee, I decided to shift the topic of conversation to what was really on my mind. "Mr. Carnes has requested female company," I told Marianne. Then I watched her face to see what it would tell me before she delivered a spoken response. There came the thinnest of smiles—a teasing acknowledgment that any idiots should have anticipated that sooner or later Carnes would have wanted female company.

"I—want—a—woman!" Marianne gleefully whisper-shouted. She was referring to that Fellini movie where the boy-hero's uncle climbs a tree and shouts, again and again, forlornly, out into the desolate landscape. "I want a woman!" is a landmark reference for Marianne and me, a dramatic metaphor for something we understand to account for what happens in the world that we find of interest. She and I were intensely interested in all sorts of sexual behavior; we passed through a phase of regularly watching nature programs on TV, just to inform ourselves of the mating procedures of animals, birds, insects, reptiles, and so on. We found it somewhat reassuring that there was nothing about watching monkeys or arctic foxes do it that made us want to do it.

As a result of our informal research, Marianne and I have convinced ourselves that almost every human couple we know has its difficulties;

almost every individual of our acquaintance seems to us, when we really think about it, painfully isolated. As dreadful as our own circumstance is, we count ourselves better off than most.

Marianne's tone shifted to sarcasm. "Haven't you guys ever listened to his music?"

Of course I asked her what she meant.

"What do I mean?" Marianne drummed her slender fingers on the tablecloth, smiling toward the ceiling, as if addressing a guardian angel who certainly wouldn't have had to ask her what she meant. "Maybe you can't hear it because you're guys! Maybe that's why I can hear it, even though it's not my kind of music, and I've never met the man."

Here Marianne turned a droll face toward me because she felt that I should have made some occasion for her personally to meet the man whose music has commanded the last several years of my professional energies. It isn't that I don't want her to meet Carnes; it is merely the case that all of us involved in the project have taken pains not to parade him in front of our friends and relatives.

It occurred to me that in our considering Carnes such a prize, perhaps we have denied him the acquaintance of people he might very well enjoy meeting—like Marianne. I knew that most of my colleagues' wives and girlfriends thought of him exactly as Marianne did, as a quaint, little old black man whom they'd like to shake hands with just to satisfy some mild curiosity. My colleagues and I had confided to each other that our wives and girlfriends didn't love the music. Thus our informal agreement not to bring them in to meet him. And we didn't expect them to love the music. Either you loved it or you didn't, we told each other.

Sitting comfortably with my wife in Bottelli's, it also occurred to me that it is men who love what Carnes plays, men who are devoted to him.

"Let me just say," Marianne said, "that that time you played all those Carnes tapes for me, I had this fleeting notion that if music could unhook a bra, a good many of Mr. Carnes's female listeners would experience a sudden loosening of their undergarments."

When I asked why she hadn't told me what she thought at the time I'd played the tapes for her, she merely smiled and shrugged.

"So does that account for why you were less than enthusiastic about his music?" I asked her.

The little wrinkle that appeared between Marianne's eyebrows told me that she was taking the question seriously. "Maybe it does," she said, toying with her coffee spoon. "I didn't think it through at the time, but here's how it must be. As a woman, you sense that you're the *object* of that music. The crudest example I can think of would be if you walk by a construction site in the city and suddenly you're the object of the whistling and hooting and leering of a bunch of workers sitting around with their lunch pails and their cigarettes. You have a choice of walking on or confronting the bastards or stopping to try to embarrass them with a friendly chat. The least complicated response is to keep walking.

"So that's how, if you're a woman, you might decide to respond to Carnes's music, even though it's very polite, very elegant, very seductive. It's not construction workers in hard hats; it's male models in tuxedos, leaning over and whispering softly into your ear, asking if they can fetch you any little thing. But the issue is exactly the same. A woman might decide, as I instinctively decided, to take note of that music but just not to get involved. Because that's the least complicated way for a woman to deal with what she's hearing. But there must also be the woman who says to herself, 'Hey, this stuff is gorgeous, and it's all for me. I have to listen to this man play. I don't have any choice.'"

"So a man and a woman listening to Carnes play would hear two different tunes, even though they'd be listening to the same sounds at the same time?"

Marianne shrugged and sipped the last of her coffee. "It's not a point I'd want to argue in court," she said. "It's just what I think right now. How are you guys going to find him some female company?" she asked. "Got any pimps on the staff?"

Talking with Marianne can, at any moment, turn into an adventure. In spite of our years of marriage, in spite of our understanding of each other in certain areas of thought and feeling, I find that I can't depend on my estimates of our conversational relationship. I may think that she and I are in perfect accord—as we usually are—when beneath our literal words we are actually carrying on an old argument. I may think that I am setting forth a proposition that she will certainly, vehemently reject, only to discover that in fact I am expressing thoughts she has been keeping to herself for months. "Wait a minute," I will plead. "Are we arguing or agreeing?"

"Both. Neither. Whatever," she will say and kiss me on one cheek while pretending to slap me on the other. In such moments, though they are metaphysically disconcerting and though I never tell her so, Marianne is utterly charming.

"We are going to give a party in Mr. Carnes's honor," I told her. "You are finally going to meet the man himself."

"I'll wear two bras," she said. "Or else no bra at all." I could tell that the idea of a party for Carnes had exhilarated Marianne.

I saw that we had achieved one of those remarkable episodes of mood synchronization, but I had to remind myself that it wouldn't last until we got home—or even, for that matter, until we reached the lot behind Bottelli's, where our separate cars were parked.

III

Cody Jones had driven the old man up to Baltimore to shop. For Carnes, they'd purchased a deep maroon suede blazer, a matching tie designed to look like a work of art, a custom-fitted pair of black flannel pants, a white tab-collar shirt, and a pair of cordovan-and-white wing-tip shoes. Thus the unkempt genius of our project studio had been transmogrified into the trim and brilliant young man-of-the-world of his 1963 publicity photos. Freshly barbered and shaved, he walked into that party with a swagger and glide I'd never seen before.

"Here he is," Marianne whispered—we were standing arm in arm—and this was the first time she'd ever seen him. She might not have consciously decided to do so, but she began moving us in his direction.

Others in the room were apparently similarly affected by our resplendent guest of honor. When we came up to him, we were joining a cluster of well-wishers. Carnes stood at the center, shaking hands with strangers and embracing old friends. "Very pleased, very pleased," he was saying, ". . . nice of the Stanfields to open their home to this old expatriate reprobate."

Because Marianne is so tall—a couple of inches taller than me—people in crowds generally make way for her. When Carnes turned our way, he exaggerated how far he had to lean back to look up into her face. She'd chosen a short black velvet sheath of a dress that accentuated her greyhound thinness. She wore no makeup, but she'd brushed her hair into uncommon shininess and she'd worn her white-gold earrings with the matching necklace that seemed to be pulling the room's light toward her pale face and slender neck.

"Well now," rumbled Carnes, his ordinary voice deepened to a rich baritone. "I believe I am just about to meet the Countess of Verticality. You must be Henry's wife; I see him clutching onto your elbow like he has to keep you from floating away from us. Eddie Carnes, your highness. Very pleased to meet you."

"Do you really think of yourself as an expatriate, Mr. Carnes?" Marianne asked as she withdrew her hand from his.

Carnes's eyebrows lifted; he put his hands in his pockets and leaned back on his heels, looking slowly from one to the other of the men and women clustered around him.

Wil Stanfield approached the group, accompanied by a woman who caught and held Carnes's attention. She had lightly freckled skin the color of a ginger cookie, and she wore a strand of pearls with a yellow silk blouse. Her straightened hair had been dyed a dark red and extravagantly swirled up and around her head. When she came up to us, Carnes addressed her. "What do you think, young lady? Am I an expatriate?"

The look this not-especially-young woman gave Carnes was something like a smile—Marianne later explained to me that it was a smile with *background,* an expression that told Carnes she had lived through too much for smiling to be a simple matter but that, in deference to him and out of general politeness, she would try to participate in the occasion he had just constructed. Her face also seemed to instruct him that he could get by with only so much of this kind of behavior with her. She spoke in a low voice. "Well, Mr. Carnes, when was the last time you felt at home?"

He snorted, as if half-amused and half-insulted by her counter question. "Last time I felt at home," he mused and shook his head. The look he then gave the woman became steady, though I can't say what I thought

Carnes meant to convey to her, perhaps that he recognized her good sense and that he was certain the two of them understood each other.

"You're Wil Stanfield's cousin, aren't you?" he said, reaching for her hand.

She nodded. Not conventionally pretty, she was a woman Marianne and I probably would have remarked even if she hadn't been noticed by Carnes. Her silk blouse and straight skirt set off her figure. There was a proud way she held her head that made me understand why she went to such trouble to have her hair styled up off her neck.

"Thelma Watkins."

She nodded again, or rather bowed her head toward Carnes. "You know my name?"

Carnes nodded at Wil Stanfield, flashed a smile, and held onto Thelma Watkins's hand. "He mentioned you a couple of times. Said he thinks a lot of you, said you helped him through the difficulties of his former life." Again, Carnes snorted, meaning, I supposed, that such difficulties were familiar to him. Then he blinked and widened his eyes. "Sometimes I pay attention to what my good men tell me. Selective attention, I guess you'd call it. Can I freshen your drink, Ms. Watkins? I already see that I'm going to have to invent my own ginger ale because none of these thoughtful boys can seem to discover it for me."

The two of them walked away from us, toward the Stanfields' kitchen. "Why don't one of you boys put on a record for this party?" Carnes waved at Curtis Wells and Cody Jones, who were taking an inventory of Wil Stanfield's CD collection.

"Does he have that Art Tatum/Ben Webster you all played for me the other day? I'd like for Mr. Tatum and Mr. Webster to help me talk to this young lady." Though his voice was pitched low, it carried across the room.

With her head slightly bowed, Thelma Watkins walked beside him. I couldn't tell if that was from her embarrassment at Carnes's display of interest or from smiling to herself and wishing to hide it. Though his fingers must have been touching the back of her arm, she and Carnes kept a decorous distance from each other. But there already seemed to be a strand of intimacy between them.

"Quick work," sighed Marianne. I knew she wished she had held more of Carnes's attention—I knew she had expected to hold more of his attention. But then she brightened and turned to me. "But I helped, didn't I? I was the one who asked the question that got them going!" The tension that had informed her posture and voice had been replaced with a loosey-goosey exuberance. I left her in the company of Curtis Wells and his girlfriend while I went to refill our drinks.

Later, when we talked it over, Marianne and I agreed that Carnes's meeting with Thelma Watkins at the party had what we called *dramatic content.* Anyone carefully observing it would have remarked it as an event of significance. Soon afterward, the rooms of the house filled to capacity; in the resulting body-to-body intimacy, the party took on such a generous spirit that it actually resembled my absurd dream of a multicultural paradise.

I'd had the good luck to accept Curtis Wells's suggestion to hire his girlfriend's father as our caterer. This Mr. Willaford was a genius of barbecuing pork, seasoning potato salad, and serving country cooking as a stylish cocktail buffet. Early in the evening the mayor of Washington dropped by to meet and to chat with Carnes, but to all the musicians' relief, she had to hurry away to another social engagement.

All this while, circulating through the rooms, speaking with one guest and another, Carnes showed himself to be aware of Thelma Watkins, to be "in touch" with her, as if they carried tiny wireless communication devices. In Carnes it wasn't difficult to see the signs of this connection; he seemed to want it to be visible. However, Ms. Watkins was subtle to the point of inscrutability. Marianne claims to have observed plenty of evidence of Ms. Watkins' interest in our guest of honor—Ms. Watkins was usually in the same room as Carnes and she usually was at least partially turned toward him. But I noticed nothing special in her behavior. Of course everyone was drawn toward Carnes, everyone seemed to be keeping an eye on him.

The surprise of the evening was the appearance of Wynton and his brother Branford—apparently willing to give up their commitment for the sake of this evening's celebration—who were dramatically presented by Wil Stanfield when he opened the set of double doors to his music studio (they had been closed until this moment). The distinguished siblings held their instruments ready and immediately launched a duet of Carnes's signature tune, "Buffalo Stampede." They riffed through it once with astonishing alacrity, then finished so abruptly that for a shocked moment the whole house rang with silence. Carnes himself broke it by cracking his hands together in loud applause.

Whether or not Carnes knew that the Marsalis brothers were going to appear as they did, he acted as if he had rehearsed the whole thing with them. He and Cody Jones stepped into the studio. Carnes's horn was already assembled and ready for him on a stand. Cody took the piano bench; Curtis Wells mounted the waiting set of drums; Wil Stanfield took up his bass; and after some tuning and murmuring with each other, the little band broke into another familiar Carnes tune, "Midnight Sunrise."

Live jazz so intoxicates me that I become happy, childish, and downright stupefied. The energy of the music that the Marsalis/Carnes combo played that evening plugged directly into some socket of my sensibility. Carnes and Wynton and Branford traded more and more intricate eight-bar solos, then the three of them riffed in varying patterns of harmony, unison, and counterpoint, as if they'd practiced these numbers for months when the fact was they were probably playing them—inventing them!—together for the first time ever.

Marianne is the only person to whom I've ever tried to explain my feelings about live jazz. The metaphor I chose was a field I played in as a child, a field that had the power to make me feel happy. Actually, this was a hillside meadow, sowed in alfalfa and occasionally cut and bailed. In the middle of it was an area where I could stand and look out over our little town of Welch, West Virginia, about half a mile away. For the one who stood right there, the landscape held ten thousand extremely vivid details; it could be considered for hours, and some of it could be held in mind for many days at a time, but since it could never be completely absorbed, it was permanently fresh and interesting. The field held me and me alone in its enormous palm. When I had studied the vista until my head was filled with it, I lay down in the alfalfa and gave myself over to the breeze and the sunlight. A freedom came into me. I felt my life to be so rich with possibility that whatever I wished would drift my way as surely as the clouds sailed across the sky.

A similar exhilaration came over me as I listened to Carnes and his supporting musicians. Though I lost my awareness of the party, Marianne stayed alert to what was happening. She told me later that about halfway through the third number, just as Carnes was about to finish his solo in "Cat's Cradle," Thelma Watkins slid away from her place in the audience and walked back through a swinging door into the kitchen. Unless she meant to signal to Carnes that she had no use for his music, I couldn't imagine why she would have done such a thing. Marianne, though, had considered Ms. Watkins's behavior and thought she understood it.

"It's just what I was telling you, Henry. I'm sure your genius's music doesn't have the same effect on men, but a woman has to choose whether she's going to submit to it or not. And I can imagine what it would be like if Carnes had focused in on me the way he did that woman. When I saw her leave the room, it broke a spell that was starting to work on me. I'd been standing there beside you—and I knew you'd 'lifted off' the way you do when one of your old jazz guys picks up a horn and starts to play. You were up there in the zone, and I was thinking that now I understood the power that music has over you. I had started entertaining this fantasy of walking right up front, right up in front of Carnes, and just standing there with my arms wide open—like, Did you call, sir? Well, here I am. I'd been thinking, What would he do if I walked up there like that? I was thinking of it as a kind of joke.

"But I understand this now: It wasn't just some silly little joke that occurred to me and wasn't some random fantasy that just appeared in my brain out of nowhere. In this case, I'll bet that almost every woman there was feeling the same impulse. It's physiological! I'll bet if you had the right kind of equipment, you could track it scientifically, the places in his music where Carnes sends out his message: *Come to me, all you ladies.*"

"So in your view, Marianne, Thelma Watkins chose to retreat to the kitchen when the signal Carnes was sending her was a directive to come to the front of the crowd? Should we interpret her retreat as a signal to him that she isn't interested in him?"

"You're a man. I shouldn't have expected you to understand."

"All you have to do is explain it to me."

"No self-respecting woman wants to respond to a general effort at seduction. Sure, girls threw their underpants at Elvis, but somewhere around the age seventeen, you begin to understand that it isn't in your best interests to behave like that. You want the man who wants you to be wanting only you, not a whole roomful of females. You learn to discern just how individualized a man's desire for you is."

"So Thelma Watkins found Carnes's mating signal a bit too generic for her taste."

"That's a crude way to put it."

"But that's what you mean, isn't it?"

"Approximately."

In my circulating through the party on my own, I managed to find an opportunity to quiz Wil Stanfield about Ms. Watkins. When he talked about his cousin, it was evident that he looked up to her, that in his eyes she was a heroine.

For the past twenty years, Thelma Stanfield Watkins had been an English teacher at Mount Vernon High School in Washington. She was as much a legend locally as Carnes was in the world of jazz. She taught the college preparatory sections of senior English. If a young black man or woman at Mount Vernon had hopes of gaining admission to a college, he or she was placed in one of Ms. Watkins's classes, and he or she had to make the grade under Ms. Watkins. The grade was a B; when she gave a student at least a B (and not a B–), she designated the student as a candidate for college.

All up and down the East Coast, college-admissions officers had come to understand and to respect Thelma Watkins's standard of grading. College football and basketball coaches knew about her to the extent that when they talked with an athlete from Mount Vernon—a high school with a longstanding reputation of graduating fine athletes—they knew to ask what grade in English the recruit expected or hoped to receive from Ms. Watkins.

Some weeks later I learned from Wil Stanfield that Thelma had been married for twelve years to Nelson Watkins, a white man, a journalist, who had gradually come to treat her badly because of her refusal to have his children. Watkins's bad treatment of Thelma had been mostly in the form of psychological abuse. Thelma's refusal to have his children had originally been intuitive, but over the course of some years had become a matter of conviction: Watkins wanted to father children with black blood so as to outrage his old-South family—and particularly his father who was the mayor of Six Mile, South Carolina. Wil told me that Thelma had wanted children, and at first had even wanted Watkins's children, but not on those terms.

Thelma's truncated marriage to Watkins had left her childless and more than usually skeptical of men. The experience hadn't improved her view of the white race either, Stanfield told me, though he supposed that because she was a teacher, she was accustomed to battling prejudice, within herself as well as in the world around her. "She's not bitter," he explained to me, "but if she didn't fight it so hard, she would be."

These things and more Marianne and I later came to know about Thelma Watkins. At the party at Wil Stanfield's home, we witnessed a kind of romantic maneuvering between her and Carnes that we recognized as elegant, even poignant, in its restraint, its wariness, its being so deeply informed by the complex personal histories of both would-be lovers.

A couple of days after the party, I had occasion to ask Carnes if he had taken note of Ms. Watkins's leaving the room during his solo in "Cat's Cradle."

He chuckled. "When I saw her step back into that kitchen, I knew she and I had us a little something. I had thought maybe we did—I hoped we did—but until then, I didn't know it for sure."

IV

My notes indicate that a week after the party in Carnes's honor, Whitney Ballston, our historical consultant, made the following observation in an informal discussion at the Project's main office: "It's like somebody else, like another human being entirely. There are no precedents anywhere in all of Mr. Carnes's recordings for this 'enlarged' sound or these bizarre composition patterns, or even for the energy in his playing right now. There's even a new way he's using silence, letting half or three quarters of a phrase stand and then picking it up out of nowhere as if he'd been playing a whole sequence of notes in his mind without putting them through the horn. Yesterday I asked him if he'd changed mouthpieces or the weight of his reed or anything like that, and he just laughed at me."

Phil Hughes, our chief recording engineer, then spoke as follows: "I'm wondering if maybe we ought not to call in a medical team and let them have a go at the old guy—I mean just to get some data on these phenomena. Hell, I don't mean that there's anything *wrong* with him. Ha ha."

Hughes's assistant, Billy Steele, an Eastman dropout and would-be tenorman, shook his head and told us that Carnes had sent Cody Jones out to buy him some new records; he had instructed Cody to buy him anything he could find by Glenn Gould or Vladimir Horowitz. "The man has been listening to the piano sonatas of Alessandro Scarlatti," Billy said in the mock voice of a classical-station radio announcer. "I didn't sign up for this job to have to spend half the evening listening to goddamn Scarlatti. That is one above-average-dead dude," Billy added sadly.

The singular aspect of Carnes's altered sonic personality, as far as I was concerned, was how little contact with Thelma Watkins it was based upon. At the party, when she had said her thank-you's and good-bye's, Carnes had walked Ms. Watkins to her car. The two of them had stood out there talking for maybe five minutes—Marianne had pulled aside a curtain, and I had joined her there in the foyer to catch a glimpse of that sidewalk scene. Of course we couldn't hear what they said to each other, but we do know that their good night was formalized by a handshake and a belly laugh from Carnes that we heard from where we stood in the house—but not a kiss, not even a peck on the cheek.

Following the party, there had been one call, made by Carnes from his apartment phone, in which he had asked Ms. Watkins if she might consider having dinner with him, and she had said yes, but not until Friday after next—she had term papers from her seniors that were going to take up all of her time that coming weekend. He had been surprisingly cheerful in agreeing to wait so long to see her.

The philosophical question that nagged me was how a major artist like Carnes could be so profoundly affected by a woman with whom he'd exchanged fewer than five hundred words, seen no more than a couple of hours, and been intimate with only to the extent of having shaken her hand twice. Was great art really so fickle as that?

Yes seemed to be the obvious answer, and since Carnes's encounter with Thelma Watkins evidently demonstrated a fickleness of profound proportion, incumbent upon those of us involved in the project, it seemed to me, was the duty to explicate his experience as intelligently as possible.

We have been taught—or somehow learned—to perceive significant change in an artist's work as resulting from momentously traumatic life experiences. Eddie Carnes met a high-school teacher at a party and shook hands good night with her; within a week, his work had changed as drastically as Picasso's movement from the "rose period" into cubism.

The practical question that nagged me was to what extent our project should involve itself with Carnes's—to phrase it crudely—love life.

Our initial agreement with Carnes was that the Project had the right to record, in aural, visual, and printed media, everything he did, everything he said, every note he played. At the time he signed the agreement—with a shaking hand but a grand flourish nevertheless—Carnes had refused even to discuss those provisions: "No problem, gentlemen," he had said. "No problem whatsoever. I just want to play my horn. And if you gentlemen want to listen in, why bless you, be my guest."

Admittedly, Carnes had changed a great deal since the day he affixed his signature to that document. Nevertheless, we were legally—if not ethically—entitled to scrutinize whatever exchanges he might have with Thelma Watkins. Indeed, we had recorded the phone call Carnes made to Ms. Watkins to ask her out to dinner, though it had not been our intention to eavesdrop on that particular conversation; our equipment had simply routinely picked it up.

However, it was not simple routine that had me pocketing the cassette of that afternoon's phone calls and taking it home with me to play for Marianne. Though I recognized this overnight borrowing of the tape as an act of questionable integrity, I needed Marianne's advice as to how to proceed at this crucial point in the Project's history. Congress was again threatening to cut the Endowment's budget, and my director was heavily involved in lobbying for his projects. The last thing he needed to know was that the Carnes Project was about to face a *romantic* problem. If push came to shove, as it might in a few months when the renewal of the Endowment's funding came up in the House, my director needed to be able to blame any errors of judgment on someone else—and in the case of the Carnes Project, that someone else was me.

Such was my thinking when I brought the recording home with me.

There is a look Marianne takes on in her professional clothing that I must say I appreciate a great deal, though I recognize that primness is a dominant theme in female attorneys' fashions. "A nun with style, that's how I'm supposed to look," Marianne has complained to me on those occasions when I have accompanied her to Taft's Corners to shop for the blazers, flannel skirts, and high-collared blouses that she is expected to wear in her office and her classroom at Georgetown Law School.

Nevertheless, we both enjoy the stuffy luxuriousness of those clothes, the understated tailoring, the subtle blending of dark and darker strands of wool, the fine texture of silk and pinpoint oxford.

Around our house, though, when she comes home from the office, Marianne will frequently untuck and unbutton her blouse, will slide down and step out of her panty hose, and will sit with her feet up and her flannel skirt any old which way. Such disarray is her momentary rebellion against the strictures of her life. When she first began doing it, we were both a little surprised at how the look aroused me.

"Slatternly is apparently what I go for," I confessed to her. "What can I say?" I said.

However, consistent with our erotic history, we also discovered that in this hour of my arousal, Marianne was in the opposite state, a kind of romantic trough. She was tired and almost always at least partially angry—usually at a male colleague or a male student who had attempted some male form of bullying with her. I give Marianne credit; she had, in the past, made an effort to accommodate my desire for her during our cocktail hour, but for both of us the results had been disheartening.

So I have come to witness Marianne's quotidian dishevelment with a kind of esthetic detachment—as if I were watching a film by Truffaut in which a classically tall, thin, initially impeccable woman loosens her clothing, then sits with one foot on the floor, the other on the coffee table, her skirt at midthigh, and raises her bourbon and soda to the camera. "To the male gender—may it continue to self-destruct!" Marianne ordinarily follows her customary toast with a snort and a guffaw.

This particular evening I had the tape cued and waiting for her so that when we had settled ourselves with our drinks in the living room, all Marianne had to listen to was Carnes's phone conversation with Thelma Watkins, which, to be perfectly frank, sounded comically—embarrassingly—decorous: "*. . . and I was just wondering if you might like to have dinner with me. . . .*"

"*Well, Mr. Carnes, I'm very flattered that . . .*"

I clicked off the machine and waited for her response. Apparently, it had been an unusually exhausting day for Marianne. She lay with both her feet resting on the sofa back, and she set the cold bottom of her glass in the center of her forehead. With her eyes closed like that, she was silent for such a while that I thought perhaps she had drifted into a nap. However, I waited her out—as over the years I have learned to do in order to make occasions for her to speak with absolute candidness. When she finally did speak, my mind had been wandering back through the archives of the history of Marianne and Henry. What she said snapped me back to the issue at hand.

"Henry, I can give you professional advice about what to do in this matter. That's the easy part. Talk to Carnes himself. Tell him what your thinking is, tell him you want to be able to demonstrate some crucial issues about the nature of the artistic process. Tell him no one's ever been able to look carefully at the way a relationship affects an artist. Blah, blah, blah. My guess is that Carnes will tell you he doesn't mind your boys carrying on business as usual.

"You'd probably also want to ask his advice on how to present the matter to Ms. Watkins. She's not likely to be enthusiastic about having her personal life incorporated into the official history of Eddie Carnes and his music. And you'll have to be scrupulous in observing whatever limitations she wants to impose on your taping.

"But I think you and I both had better recognize that we have a personal interest in what's happening with Eddie Carnes. Don't you think we'd better admit that to ourselves and each other? I've been thinking about it ever since we peeked at them out the window at that party. It was no mystery why you might want to keep an eye on them—part of your crazy job and all that—but I wondered what I was doing, spying on them like some dame in a James Bond movie. It disturbed me even more when I thought about it. Don't we want something out of those two people, Henry? Don't we want them to do something for us? Or don't we want what's happening between them to do something about what's not happening between us?"

Characteristic of Marianne's serious conversational style, she had refined her phrasing into an exactness that suited her. It was a quality that made her a strong attorney and an excellent law professor. She was quiet then, and I was, too, for a long while. "Yes," I said. "Yes, I see that now."

Marianne lifted her glass off her forehead and turned to face me. "Professionally, I advise you not to bring home any more tapes." Her eyes held mine for such a length of time that I came to understand what she wanted me to understand.

"But you'll understand if I choose to disregard your advice?"

"Personally, yes, I'll understand that. I was your wife before I became a lawyer. I expect I'll be your wife when I finish being a lawyer."

"And you'll understand if I happen to bring home a tape every now and then?"

She turned her face back toward the ceiling and placed the bottom of her cold glass back on her forehead. "I can get through the rest of my life without anything changing much one way or the other. I'm inclined to be a cheerful person, as you know. But I have this dread that one morning when I'm eighty years old, I'm going to wake up and realize that I've been a prisoner. I'm going to look over at you and see that you've been a prisoner, too, for years!—and that maybe we could have done something different that would have made us happier. Sometimes I think you and I traded the promise of our whole lives for what we had those first few months we were married."

"This is what people do," I said. "This is what happens. It isn't as if we don't have very rewarding lives; it isn't as if we don't enjoy each other."

Marianne sighed. "Yes, I know you're right, Henry. I'm okay, as you very well know, and I know you're fine, too. I don't mean to be whining, and I know part of it is just that it's been a long day, and my skull feels like it's going into labor. But part of this negative fantasy of mine is that after you and I have waked up and realized that we've been prisoners, the nurse or somebody is going to come in and tell us, 'Oh yeah, I forgot to tell you, you guys have been in constant pain all this time.' And then it's going to hit us, years and years of pain that we haven't even known we were experiencing. I see us both just howling."

"Yes. Maybe so," I said. "Maybe that's just how it'll be."

V

I did in fact have a talk with Carnes in which I subtly attempted to convey to him that, unless he requested otherwise, we would continue our audio- and video-taping as we had been doing all along. To this day, I do not know if he understood me and gave me tacit permission to carry on or if I simply imagined his understanding and agreement while actually he was in his own world so completely that I would have had to shout into his face to get the issue across to him.

"Henry, your boys don't get in my way. I appreciate that. I appreciate that a lot." He was impatient to talk about the tape from the party, of the impromptu combo with the Marsalis brothers, to which he had been listening and about which he was excited. "Wouldn't mind for that to go into the stores," he said. "First time the five of us ever played together. Definitely something happening in those tunes. You don't hear that except when the musicians get excited about what they're hearing from each other. It's rough here and there—I like that anyway—but anybody cares about the music isn't going to be bothered. On 'Coldest Blues,' that Branford was sailing. I'd heard that Wynton's brother could play, but nobody said he could get up there like that. I even heard that those two didn't get along anymore, but I'm here to testify that their *horns* still get along just fine."

Never really unsociable, Carnes had always been generous in answering questions or trying to provide information to us. When we talked with him, we always had a sense that he was trying to give as much of himself to us as he could. But he was also a man who gave plenty of signals when it was time for a conversation to be over. Talking privately with him in the past, I had experienced a steadily increasing awareness of his desire to get back to his music. Now, even though I'd been with him for more than an hour, he seemed to want me to stay with him there in his little kitchen and to keep the conversation going.

"That white Zulu wife of yours, Henry, what did she think of that music that night? I snuck a peek at her; she looked like she was digging it; then I glanced again, and her face told me she had dropped in on the wrong planet. So I stopped looking. Somebody like her can make me lose the changes. She say anything to you? Look like she definitely had her thoughts."

"Marianne doesn't quite know what to make of jazz, Eddie," I told him. I went on to tell him of her parents' desire for Marianne to have a practical education and a financially rewarding career. "They were determined that she not be 'tracked' into the arts just because of her gender. So they kept her from being warped one way, but the background they gave her was warped in the other direction. She never really even had a chance to hear jazz until she and I got married," I told him.

"Women." He shook his head. "I give 'em my life, but they don't even know it. I keep on telling them my story; they don't listen. Or else they hearing me better than I think they are. Maybe they hearing more than I'm telling. I don't know." The grin he gave me was classically rueful. "What do you think, Henry?"

It shocked me that he would ask what I thought. So far as I could recall, I hadn't ever seen Carnes in a questioning mode. I had come to expect him to be self-contained. He certainly wasn't a conversational bully, he wasn't insensitive, and he even seemed to be a good listener whenever anyone told him something. But at this moment I couldn't remember his ever having asked anybody a question.

"I'm not a musician, Eddie," I told him. "Or an artist of any kind. So I don't tell my story. I have to depend on guys like you to do my telling for me."

"Well, then, you in a sad way, son!" He laughed long and loud. "You let me do your telling for you, you talking about what you might not want credit for." Then, as he sat gazing at me in a very friendly and companionable way, his face changed. He turned toward that kitchen window of his that he spent ordinarily so much time staring out of. I began to have that old feeling of his wanting the conversation to be over. I stood up and stretched. I told him that I probably ought to get back to the office. I told him I'd see what I could do about getting the tape of the party combo moving toward some kind of commercial production.

"What do you think we ought to call the record, Eddie?" It wasn't really a serious question. I was already standing at the door, and I was looking for a light tone to finish up our talk.

"What should we call it?" Carnes mused. "'Back to the Kitchen'? Something like that? I don't know. I'll ask that schoolteacher what she thinks we ought to call it. She and I going out on the town Friday night. I'll ask her what she thinks and let you know."

When I left him, Carnes seemed to have perked himself up with the thought of his forthcoming evening with Thelma Watkins.

VI

There are ways to persuade yourself that you're not really responsible for what you're doing. Government employees know this better than people in most other professions.

The recording system in Carnes's studio and living quarters had been in place and working so long that he didn't think about it anymore, and we didn't give it much attention, either. The equipment simply kept cranking out these cassettes, which one of the Project's interns labeled and filed each morning. For it to be otherwise, someone would have to make a conscious decision to stop the procedure and turn off the equipment.

That Friday, nobody noticed anything special about what Carnes was up to, and that sly old man was successful in keeping his high spirits muted to such an extent that no one thought to tease him about his date that evening. But all day I was intensely aware of both his schedule and his mood—his glee seemed obvious to me, but I wasn't about to say anything to anybody else about it. And that evening I was the last one to leave the Project offices. Naturally, I checked to see that the taping equipment was on as usual. My guess—indeed, my hope!—was that Carnes never gave the slightest thought to the likelihood that his evening with Thelma Watkins would be recorded.

Marianne and I were scheduled for dinner out that night; she, however, called me at home to say that she needed another couple of hours at her office—she was presenting a paper on child-support guidelines at a legal educators' meeting next week. She sounded tired. We agreed we'd order pizza instead of going out. She was pleased that I wanted to wait to eat until she came home.

I'm not one of those men who's comfortable around the house by himself. It's just never been something I liked very much. I wander around, looking out this window and that, channel grazing on the TV, reading a bit of a magazine or maybe a review in the *Post* that I didn't get to that morning. I open the refrigerator and stare at the contents before I decide that I don't really want anything to eat.

If Marianne's home, I don't have a problem. I talk with her or I just sit with her—that's okay with me, being quiet while she reads—or the two of us watch TV. She's pretty calm around the house, at least she is when I'm there. Maybe she'd say the same thing about me—I must seem to her to be perfectly comfortable at home. Because that's what I am when she's in the house with me. I've never mentioned to her how antsy I am around there when she's not home. Probably I hadn't thought much about it before.

I found myself in the bedroom, standing in front of her dresser, staring into her lingerie drawer. I picked out a slip that I liked her to wear—though I'd never told her as much—very lacy and light in my hands when I unfolded it. When I held it up to the light, it was the gauzy ghost of Marianne.

I tried to imagine Marianne at home without anybody around. Surely she wouldn't do the weird routines that I found myself doing. I smiled at the idea of her opening up my underwear drawer and holding my T-shirts up to the light. Men and women are unaccountably different in their inclinations; how clearly in that moment I could see! I fixed Marianne's things as I thought I'd found them and closed the drawer, meaning, I think, to head downstairs, to pour myself a drink, and to discipline myself into reading something worthwhile.

I couldn't remember ever having thought about Marianne by herself. Plenty of times I'd imagined her in her car, driving to work or driving home or driving on trips. I'd thought about her traveling, sitting in airports, riding in taxis into other cities, always moving toward some kind of activity or group of people. Maybe when she'd been away on business trips, I'd even imagined her in hotel rooms by herself—but in that case I think I usually envisioned her calling me or calling her parents in Fredericksburg or showering and dressing to go out to dinner with her colleagues.

Why was I finding it so difficult to think about her just killing time at home, just being alone, the way I was right then? The oddest notion came to me: What difference would it make how tall Marianne was if she was home by herself? Or how blue her eyes were? Or what she looked like at all? Or how smart she was? Who would care about any of that? Even she herself wouldn't be concerned about those qualities of hers that meant so much to those of us who knew and loved her.

So then the question was, What *would* matter about her? What would be the part of herself that determined what she would do and how she would feel in that circumstance?

Did one person ever get to see what really mattered about another person?

I didn't know.

Part of what was wrong here was that I didn't like thinking about Marianne being in a circumstance that I myself was finding somewhat unpleasant at the moment. But I couldn't seem to put my finger on exactly why the idea of Marianne alone caused me such discomfort.

Sitting halfway down our staircase—just because that's where I'd stopped to sit—I almost wept at the idea or the image, whatever. Of course I didn't take myself seriously. In the past, occasionally, I'd had experiences like this, when I seemed about to be overwhelmed by powerful emotions triggered by something slight. When I cleared my head, I was certain I'd be able to focus perfectly well on Marianne's being by herself.

Carnes on the other hand was someone I'd gotten so used to thinking of as being by himself that I had trouble envisioning him being *connected*—to Thelma Watkins or to anyone else—the way I was connected to Marianne. And I wondered why that was the case. Was it because he was a musician or an artist? Did I ordinarily think of artists as being alone? Was it because Carnes was black that I so easily isolated him in my mind.

I remembered a conversation about race Carnes had had with Robin Stone, a young white tenorman who had come by the studio some months before to pay his respects. "I'll tell you what I think the basic difference is," Carnes had told Stone. "You have to think about being white about ten percent of your time, and I have to think about being black about ninety percent of mine. Everything else is pretty much the same—but that's still a pretty big difference."

This memory and these thoughts seemed about to get the best of me. I felt as guilty as if I'd been a member of the Ku Klux Klan for all these years and suddenly seen how odious it had all been. So far as I could figure it, Carnes's race had nothing to do with the ease with which I could imagine him being by himself. He was simply a man who, in the months of my acquaintance with him, stood alone in the world. Nevertheless, I felt terrible.

"Henry, what in God's name are you doing? Have you gone to bed at nine o'clock? I thought we were going to order pizza."

I was so happy Marianne had finally come home that I wasn't as embarrassed as I probably should have been about being curled up in our bed with all my clothes still on. "I just got bored without you here to talk to, darling." I threw off the covers and nearly leaped out of the bed to give her a hug. "I thought I'd take a nap while I waited for you. So I'd be good company for you when you got here."

My mood changed so drastically and so rapidly that I became almost too silly to manage ordering the pizza. Though her day had been long and extremely abrasive, Marianne was charmed by my antics. There is a reluctant smile that comes to her face that is very dear to me, that inspires me to perform like a trained bear for her, my ultimate goal being to provoke her to put her hands on her hips and say, "Now, stop it, Henry, just stop it," as she tries (and fails) to force her expression into a frown. At bedtime, we were very affectionate with each other. In my estimation, we came very close to igniting the old carnal kindling.

VII

Timing is the secret to most issues of human relations. I suspected that I had picked up this notion from Carnes, who loved to wink at you and say, "Timing," if he had played something especially well, or on the occasion of any sort of achievement. But his one-word philosophy, or perhaps theology, also applied to failures—from dropping a glass to botching a glissando—in which case, he would shrug and shake his head and say, "Timing."

In this case, the issue was the timing of Marianne's and my hearing the tapes of Carnes's evening with Ms. Watkins—there were three cassettes, which meant there had been plenty to record. At the Project offices the next day, they had gone unheard, so far as I knew. Carnes had successfully kept his morning-after behavior sufficiently ordinary to avoid reminding anyone he'd been out the previous night. I had no idea what had transpired that evening or what Carnes's plans were for seeing Ms. Watkins again. But I knew the exact drawer in our library and the exact place in that drawer where the tapes were stored. I waited a couple of days before I found an occasion to remove them and slide them into my leather portfolio case.

I had decided against overtly announcing to Marianne what I intended to do; I had no wish to challenge her scruples—professional or otherwise—by making her decide far in advance whether or not we would hear these tapes. Instead I felt I had carried out a peripheral communication with her on the topic. I suspect that about 75 percent of what transpires between husbands and wives takes this form. Neither person actually says, "I'm going bowling tonight," or "I'm going to buy that dress I told you about," or "We'll be having Swiss Steak for dinner," but the information makes its way from one brain to the other by way of the intricate nuances that spouses have learned to send to and receive from each other.

I had asked Marianne if she had any particular plans for this Wednesday evening—and she had said no. In another conversation I had mentioned to her a raucous exuberance that had suddenly appeared in Carnes's playing—squeaks and squawks of a sort that he had eschewed his entire career up until now. And in still another exchange, this one at breakfast that very morning, I had asked Marianne if she thought Ms. Watkins was actively looking for companionship in the same way that Carnes was.

Marianne had thought about it a moment before answering. "Well, maybe not in exactly the same way. Women are not generally as goal oriented as men are, as you know, but I expect that somewhere in her consciousness there's that old, familiar biological voice whispering to her."

"You mean 'yes'?"

She sipped her coffee, leveling a stare at me over the edge of her cup. "Not exactly," she said before rising to go finish dressing for work.

So at dinner with her that evening, I suspected that at least on some level of consciousness, Marianne knew I had brought home these tapes, and I felt as antsy as Carnes must have felt the afternoon before he went out with Ms. Watkins. I must have been somewhat less successful about disguising my true state of being because as we were clearing the table, Marianne remarked, "What is it with you, Henry? You act like a kid who's planning to slip out his bedroom window after midnight."

Rather than answer her—and therefore verbalize the issues—I simply went to the dining room chair where I had put down my portfolio case, extracted the tapes, brought them back to the kitchen, and plunked the cassettes on the white countertop beside our gathering of dirty dishes. Marianne looked at them only a moment before turning her eyes to my face. We said nothing more during the several minutes it took for her to wash the dishes and me to dry them. When I glanced at her, Marianne slightly tightened her lips, a more-than-adequate communication of her feelings.

Our kitchen received extraordinary attention from the two of us that evening. We attended to the most minute details of tidiness. When there was nothing else we could do, short of pulling out the refrigerator and dusting behind it, we marched into the living room. Picking up a copy of *Family Advocate,* Marianne took her seat in one of my grandmother's high-backed wing chairs. I carried the tapes to the stereo and fast-forwarded the first one to about the point where I guessed Carnes's evening would have begun, then I had to listen a bit and fast-forward it a bit more to reach a point where I thought we should begin.

Carnes's studio and apartment microphones were voice-, or noise-, activated, a characteristic that was noticeable on the tape only when he wasn't holding a normal conversation, or playing his saxophone, or even noodling around on the piano, which he was inclined to do in the early stages of his compositions. Those phenomena it picked up and recorded with astonishing clarity and fidelity. The tiny mobile mikes we had installed in his jacket pockets were slightly more problematic, but then fidelity wasn't really an issue for what they picked up. When I finally did start the first tape and sit down to listen, Marianne and I exchanged glances. Now and then one or the other of us would inhale sharply, or say something out loud. A couple of times Marianne raised her finger to her lips to shush me, and more than once one of us would try to talk to the other while the tape was playing.

"*Yeah, I guess this is the place*" was the observation that cued me to begin the tape. It was followed by the slamming of the car door, presumably behind Carnes as he turned toward Ms. Watkins's house or apartment, and by the muted cadence of his footsteps. There was a background noise that rose in pitch as Carnes's footsteps changed their pace and pitch—apparently from his climbing a short flight of steps. I informed Marianne that the noise was the rumbling of Carnes's belly. "He's anxious," I told her.

No trace of a smile came to Marianne's lips.

Carnes both knocked and rang a doorbell; still there was a bit of a wait—during which Carnes paced inside a hallway or foyer—before a door unlocked and opened. *"Good evening, Mr. Carnes. I thought perhaps you might have trouble finding—"*

He interrupted her. *"Ed, or Eddie, please, Ms. Watkins, or I guess I mean Thelma, unless you'd rather I didn't call you by your first—"*

"No, it's fine, I mean—" There were some door-locking noises followed by feet shuffling, then making their way back down the short flight of steps.

"Well, then, we should—"

"Ed?"

"Or Eddie. Whichever. Thelma."

"Yes, Thelma."

Carnes cleared his throat. *"This car's what they give me whenever I want to go anywhere, Thelma. They give me this driver, too. I guess they think*

I can't drive. Maybe I can't, I don't know. Been a long time. My license ran out when I lived in Sweden. Anyway, if it was my car I was coming to pick you up in, it wouldn't be this one. Here you go."

Apparently he shut the door on Ms. Watkins while she was asking him what sort of a car he would have picked her up in if it had been his own.

"Timing," he muttered to himself while he walked around to the other door. I could see him shaking his head and taking on his rueful expression. *"Do better,"* he instructed himself as he opened the door on his side.

"I guess it would be one of those Saabs. I got to liking those cars when I was over there. I think I wrecked one of them one night. Meant to be backing up and drove it right into somebody's front porch. But if I ever get me another car, it'll be a Saab, dark red, and leather seats, with one of those new stereos makes you think you in a studio when you're driving along. That's what I'd bring to your door, Thelma."

"Nice car. That would be a nice car, Ed." She would be nodding at him, encouragingly. *"*Eddie *maybe. Try* Eddie *and see if it sounds all right. Ed makes me think I need to sit up straight."*

*"*Eddie *makes me think I need to send you to the principal's office. Should we go back to* Mr. Carnes*?"*

"Oh, no, mercy, let's don't go back to that, Thelma. I'll see if I can get along with Ed. Sitting up a little straighter won't hurt me. Just don't send me down to that principal's office." The two of them laughed as if this were the most amusing occasion of their adult lives.

At this point Marianne said, "Why are we listening to this, Henry? I know I'm the one who said we wanted to. Did I say why we wanted to? They're so—I don't know what they are. But this embarrasses me."

I knew that Marianne didn't want or need an answer from me. I nodded at her. I knew she understood that I, too, was painfully conflicted about what we were doing. And I took note of the fact that, in spite of her protest, she hadn't actually asked me to turn off the tape. I said nothing.

"So you're a teacher. Wil says that even when you were a little girl and his family came to visit yours, you liked to correct his English."

Ms. Watkins laughed sociably. *"Yes, I did like that—Mother let me get by with it because I was an only child, and she thought it wouldn't harm Wil anyway. I did love improving my little cousin Wil. Perhaps you have noticed that Wil speaks a very clear standard English; he has used that ability to his advantage, and he has his cousin to thank for it."*

"I didn't finish high school."

"I know that, Ed."

There was a lengthy pause before Carnes spoke again. *"How you going to keep from correcting my English? We got a whole dinner to get through, just the two of us."*

Again there was that polite laugh from Ms. Watkins, but within it there was a note of warmth, so clearly present that Marianne and I widened our eyes at each other to remark it. I could just see Ms. Watkins—I think I began to think of her as Thelma in exactly this moment—reaching over and patting his hand as she spoke, and Carnes's clasping her hand and holding onto it.

"Ed, my cousin says that he has personally known only one or two persons in the world as intelligent as you are. I don't know if you know just how devoted to you my cousin is; to be around you, he'd be happy just to stand by your side all day and hand you toothpicks when you needed them."

"Maybe you better set him straight, just like in the old days."

This time the note her laugh sounded was one of sorrow, an almost harmonic response to the humorously rueful tone of Carnes's voice. *"One thing I have learned. My cousin's judgment of people is very precise. Perhaps he has told you about my former husband, the little-beloved Nelson Watkins? When I took that man to meet Wil, Wil hadn't been around him five minutes before he took me aside and said, 'Cuz, I know he's being nice to you, but that man will do you some harm. Don't trust him.' I'm sorry to say that I told my little cousin to relax, to try to put his racism aside and to look at Nelson for what he was. If I had listened to Wil then, I'd have saved myself fifteen years of trouble. Fifteen long years of trouble."* And now Thelma's laugh sounded the bitter joy of saying good-bye to the trouble.

"So this is where you're taking me to dinner? Well, I'm very flattered. I've heard it's just the place."

"I don't know anything about it." The car door slammed, and there was a pause with some pacing while Carnes came around to Thelma's side to open her door. *"I just asked Cody Jones. He eats out a lot, knows all the fancy places. Cody said this was where I should take you."*

There followed a bit of murmuring, pacing, door opening, maneuvering, and then a background noise of voices, clinking glasses, and silverware. Carnes was apparently expected at this place because he and Thelma were seated very quickly—for days afterward Marianne and I tried to guess which restaurant it might have been, but we couldn't even come up with a likely possibility. They began studying their menus right away, which was interesting because Carnes immediately asked Thelma to pick out what he should eat. *"I never could order anything I wanted from a restaurant menu. I gave up on that years ago. What looks great to me on the menu isn't what I want when they set it in front of me. Been that way since I was a kid."*

Thelma ordered a Chateaubriand for the two of them, and she persuaded Carnes to try a bottle of sparkling cider. When it came, she proposed a toast: *"To music."*

The clinking of their glasses was followed by a significant pause, during which I knew that, just as I was, Marianne was struggling to envision the nature of the interaction between Carnes and Thelma. It struck me then how such moments as these determined individual destinies. One of them could have seen in the other's slight relaxing of facial muscles a significant opening up of the self, could have sensed the other's offering of vast resources of intrigue and understanding. One of them could have decided—intelligently or stupidly—that the other would be endlessly engaging.

VIII

"Mr. Carnes—Ed. I'm sorry. Let me start over again. Ed. I appreciate your taking me out. This is a rare occasion for me, and I understand that you, too, haven't had much of a social life either since you've been here in the Washington area. I'm curious about the man whose shadow my cousin has decided to stand in as long as you'll let him. I wonder if you'd mind telling me about yourself."

"You already know more than most people do."

"I do know some things. Wil has told me a lot."

"I told you some, too, Thelma. The other night when the boys and I were playing at the party. I told you all the really important stuff right then. Told you so much you had to step back in the kitchen."

"I'm not a musician, Ed. Am I blushing? Well, maybe I did notice how intensely you were playing. But I didn't have any way to know what I was hearing, or what you might have wanted me to hear. Listening to you with those people all around me, I felt uncomfortable. That's why I had to leave the room. I needed to sit down by myself for a minute. I could still hear you from in there. As I say, I'm not a musician. All the family talent for music went to Wil. But even if I could have understood what you were playing, I'd still like to hear what you'd choose to tell me face to face like this. In plain English, as we say. Whatever you want me to know."

"What I want you to know?"

"Yes."

"What I want you to know, and I can't use my horn to tell it to you. Well now. Do you give your students this kind of assignment?"

"No, Ed." Her voice was very soft. *"This is an assignment for a grown-up."*

Their waiter came to serve them something—salad, I supposed—the interlude of which would give him time to gather his thoughts. I understood what must have been perfectly evident to Carnes: His future was about to be determined by what he told this woman. I found myself weirdly cheering him on: *Talk for your life, Eddie!* I nearly said out loud.

"Thelma, I'll take you at your word and tell you what I can. It may not be anything you want to hear. In a few weeks I'll be sixty-one years old. I'm a drunk who has the good luck not to be drinking right now. But I'm not to be trusted in that regard—I don't trust myself, which is why I'm keeping myself away from my old pal Mr. Booze right now.

"I'm somebody who always wanted to be close to somebody—always wanted to be close to a woman, I should go ahead and say, because that's how it's been. When I was little, I was what they used to call a mama's boy, but my mama was a schoolteacher, and so she had work to do. She used to have to run me out of the house, I hung around her so close. So all my life I did a lot of chasing women. Trying to get back in that house and hang around with Mama, you know. Then when one of these women seemed like she wanted

to let me hang around her all the time, I had to run myself out of the house. Wanted to hang around with Mama but didn't know how to do it. Couldn't let myself be close to anybody.

"I don't know why that was the way things went; it just was. With the result being what you see sitting right here in front of you, somebody so totally by himself he wants to break your heart every time he picks up a horn. Anybody who hears me—man or woman—I want them to be thinking, 'Man, that Eddie Carnes, he must be the one I've been wanting to meet all my life. That Eddie Carnes must be a man with a hundred-and-ten-percent platinum soul.' Fact is, over the years, plenty of people—men and women—have stepped forward to try to give me exactly what my horn told them I wanted. 'I accept your adoration,' *I say,* 'but it's not quite enough. I have to have more.' *So then I stash away that little offering of adoration and go on playing, trying to build up this store of love, trying to warehouse what people are so kind as to bring me.*

"There's got to be something on the other side of that. I have to tell you the truth. I'm a lot better musician than I deserve to be, and I think there has to be some kind of reason for that. I'm not even close to religious, but I can't believe that I got born into this world with the privilege of being able to play beautiful music just to be able to get a lot of people to testify that they think I have a beautiful soul.

"If it don't come out to more than that, then music ain't what I think it is. And all those people whose music I love so much just threw their lives away. If it don't come out to more than that, then all music is is what you hear at the grocery store, some bunch of union-scale fiddle players sawing on a Beatles song to make you buy more margarine.

"Here's a little story for you, Thelma, a little story for the two of us, since you asked me to tell you whatever I wanted to about myself, and I'm taking you up on your dare, I'm accepting your invitation.

"In my sixth grade, there was this thing that started at recess with somebody rolling down a hillside. I don't remember who it was, or even if it was a boy or a girl. It doesn't matter. Somebody else saw it and went rolling down, too. Soon enough, all of us boys and girls, or at least a lot of us, began rolling down in turns.

"It must have been springtime, because that's the weather I remember, some sweetness in the air and just warm enough to take your jacket off after you'd rolled down the hill a couple of times. The slope was right at the edge

of the schoolyard, so it felt like we were doing something away from school, something private, just among ourselves. The teachers didn't have anything to do with it, you know what I mean?

"One afternoon, a boy rolled into a girl—I seem to have in mind that it was James Blair rolling into Marilyn Scott—and the two of them commenced tussling and giggling. When they stopped rolling down at the bottom of the hill, they picked themselves up, walked back up the hill, and repeated the whole thing.

"Soon enough, the rest of us were imitating them. It had this boy-girl requirement to it that wasn't like anything else we did. The pairs of us just clicked into place, like each one of us had been waiting through those first six grades of school to make a move on that particular girl or that particular boy. After a while what had been just some children rolling down the hill had evolved into coeducational wrestling matches with a rolling component to them.

"I don't think many of us knew what we were doing. But we damn sure knew we liked it and meant to keep on doing it. It was sort of a competition, girls versus boys, but it was also like a project you had to work on with each other; you had to cooperate. I mean it was strange. It was like playing and it was like fighting, which we understood well enough. But there was this new dimension to it. To make it work—to make it feel good—we needed each other, and we had to admit to each other that we needed each other. We had a couple of days of recesses to work on it and refine the procedure, as it were.

"It got to be our passion. Kids from the other grades would come out and watch us, but we had claimed the hill, and we didn't let anybody do it except just us sixth-graders who had been in on it from the start. It was wild out there. Girls stopped worrying about whether or not their dresses came up. Boys' shirts started coming off. People's clothes got ripped.

"You can figure out what would have happened. Just about the time things were about to go completely out of control, our teacher, Miss Whitt, and our principal, Mr. Jackson, made us stop. When we stayed and tried to do it after school, on our own time, a couple of us got paddled the next day; a couple more of us were sent home. No matter how much we wanted to do our thing out there, we had no choice but to give it up.

"That's the outside of that story. The inside of it is what happened between me and Diana Childress. Diana was tall and skinny—the way a lot of girls are at that age—and she had the darkest skin of anybody in my

sixth-grade class. Her mother was Haitian. She had this proper little accent whenever she said anything, which wasn't that often. Maybe it was just quiet-person's accent, I don't know. Anyway, she was mostly a fierce and silent girl. I think that's what I liked most about Diana, that fierceness that seemed like it could break out of her any moment, though I don't remember her ever losing her temper.

"She wore white socks and bright blue and yellow cotton dresses, ironed very nicely I guess by her mama, with the skirt hemmed to just below her knees. Diana kept her hair done up just so and held her head in this prideful way. Scary enough to make us boys keep our distance. But I'll confess that I'd had my eye on that girl ever since she came to our school in third grade. Maybe I thought I saw her looking at me, too, not often but just every now and then.

"When that time came, in the rolling down the playground hillside, when the boys and girls paired off the way we did, it didn't take half a second for Diana and me to find each other. She was just there in front of me, or I was there in front of her, like we had known all along that something like this was going to happen. We had hold of each other's shoulders; we were glaring into each other's faces. Then we were just gone down that hillside. Just gone!

"I can see us now as clearly as if somebody had taken a home movie of us, Diana Childress and Eddie Carnes rolling down the hill at recess, wrestling and grunting and maybe laughing, I don't know. Soon as we got to the bottom, we were up and running to the top and grabbing hold of each other by the shoulders and arms and falling down to the ground and rolling down the hill again.

"All we ever had to say to each other was 'Get up, fool!' or 'Like this, try it like this!' or 'Hurry!' It was like she and I had this desperate errand we had to carry out, again and again.

"When it was over, I mean to tell you, it was all over. Diana and I were not the ones who got paddled or the ones who got sent home to tell our parents what we'd been up to. Compared to the others in our class, we were probably among the least indecent. I don't remember Diana's dresses coming up very much because her mama had hemmed them all down so low anyway. And I certainly kept my shirt on, didn't even dream of taking it off. But maybe it would have been better if we had been among the punished ones. Because we were definitely among the casualties.

"Over the years Mister Negative has come to visit me plenty of times—and I know I don't have to tell you about it because you ain't been attending no lifetime tea party yourself—but I'd put down the end of that hillside wrestling as one of my alltime saddest things.

"It wasn't even how terrible I felt just by myself. It was how I knew Diana felt. We didn't talk about it—couldn't really talk about it, didn't have the words even for ourselves, let alone for each other. But when I'd look at her in class or out at recess by the swings or wherever, I just knew what we'd lost. I could feel it in my body, and I could see it in Diana's body. Diminished is what we were! Less than we had been!

"Glaring at each other, wrestling, going at each other, and working with each other all at the same time—teeth and elbows and legs and bellies and all our muscles—we had been glorious!

"Then they took it away.

"Or we lost it. I don't know. We were just children.

"But I have to tell you, Thelma. That rolling down the hill with Diana Childress was the thing for me. It beat the hell out of hanging around the dining room table trying to get Mama's attention. If somebody came up to me right this minute and said, 'Eddie, you'll have to give up sex for the rest of your life, but you can go back to rolling down the hillside of Thibault Elementary School of Buffalo, New York, with Diana Childress whenever you want to,' I'd say, 'You got yourself a deal.'

"Nobody was ever so there with me as that girl—nothing but the naked truth of her present in those blazing eyes and flared nostrils and hard little shoulders and arms. She and I wanted to rip each other's insides out and crawl up inside each other. Our bodies were these huge stones that we were striking against each other, making fiery sparks all around ourselves, trying to kill each other and bring each other back to life all at the same time. Anything I ever had with anybody after that—friendship or love or sex or whatever—was never more than just—" Carnes cleared his throat and went on. *"I guess I just talked myself out of your good graces, didn't I, Thelma? I didn't know it was going to come out like that. Happens when you try to improvise outside the changes. Got to go where it takes you. Sorry. Guess I'm just wasting your time, huh?*

"But it's better that you know. No matter what the song is, my song has two parts to it. The first part is that I rolled down the hill with Diana

Childress. The second part is that they made us stop rolling down the hill. No matter what you hear me playing, that's what I'm playing. 'Song in Two Parts,' by Eddie Carnes."

IX

"What boys and girls did together, Ed, wasn't anything I knew about in sixth grade. I was one of those slow-to-mature girls. I wore glasses, read three and four books a day, got straight A's, didn't see what there was about boys, especially sixth-grade boys, that could hold anybody's attention.

"Though they were fifteen years apart in age, both my parents grew up right here in Washington, graduated from Howard, then took government jobs. So we lived in a nice neighborhood, we had nice things, and everybody treated us with respect. We were all three light skinned and very proper people. I couldn't help thinking I was better than most of the kids at my school, because they treated me like I was better than they were. They very politely left me alone except to ask for my help with their homework or for an answer on a quiz. Until I went to college, I didn't have any friends, didn't even know what it felt like to have a close friend.

"I was a very serious child, and I loved my parents. I know that sounds simpleminded, but, really, it was the single most important thing in my life when I was growing up. Maybe most kids love their parents, but the difference was that I knew I loved mine. I was an only child. They treated me like I was their reason for being in this world.

"That age difference between my father and my mother was something I was very aware of when I was growing up. It was as if my father had come from another world. He was very handsome, very well dressed. He wore dark suits and ties and these beautiful starched white shirts. Wing-tip shoes that he shined every morning. When he retired from the Treasury Department, he was a GS-14, quite a position for a black man to hold at that time. Everything he did, every word he spoke, was very deliberate, very thought out. And he adored me.

"It's taken me years to know how unusual a man he was, how disciplined he must have had to be. He was formal with my mother but very thoughtful. Even when just the three of us were having dinner on a weeknight, he waited for her and held her chair to seat her at the dinner table. To any questions she asked him about even the slightest little thing, he gave her very complete answers. Her frustration with him was sometimes evident to me, but I never saw my father lose control of himself. I never saw him act other than kindly to my mother. I was the witness to my father's devotion to my mother.

"She is still alive—just turned seventy and in very good health, thank you. But it's not as easy for me to see her objectively and describe her as it is him. My father died eleven years ago this August; I have a very settled view of him, a kind of official portrait, every detail of which I hold vividly in mind, because it never changes.

"My mother and I still have a lot going on between us. Even today—even though I'm old enough to have grandchildren—I still feel my mother wanting me to do this, not wanting me to do that. I don't ask her what she thinks, and she rarely tells me; nevertheless, I don't ever make an important decision without considering what her opinion of it would be. Even having dinner with you here tonight, Ed, yes, it's true. And I won't tell you what I imagine my mother's opinion of you would be. But let's just say—"

Here the first tape abruptly ended. I was ready to sit and talk a bit with Marianne before starting up the second one, but when I kept sitting still in the silence, Marianne gave me an impatient look. "More?" I asked her.

"What do you think?" I thought her tone was more brittle than the occasion called for. Nevertheless, I walked over, changed the cassettes, and started up the tape number two.

"—don't want to make her sound so bad. She had—and still has—the kind of pretensions that a lot of well-to-do white ladies of her day had. Not that many black women can afford to have the view of life she holds. At the same time, she's an extremely kind and decent person. Though she occasionally resented the bond between my father and me, she has never been anything other than considerate of me.

"She was a young woman of uncommon beauty.

"From the time she turned fourteen, people stared at her. People—white and black—treated her like royalty. Strangers expected her to be a famous

singer or movie star just because she had such a remarkable face. So from early on in her life, it must have been very hard for her not to think of herself as a privileged person. She was privileged.

"You see, most of us have the experience of wanting more than we actually get—that's just the natural circumstance for most human beings. But my mother always had more than she wanted—more love, more attention, more praise, more success. She was always turning away things that other people would have killed for—especially the attentions of men.

"When she was growing up, she had her pick of what she used to call the eligible bachelors. She chose my father, who was older but nevertheless eligible and so desirable that he was beyond everybody else's wildest dreams. But my mother must not have seen him as anything more than she deserved. After all, in choosing him, she had had to give up a number of handsome, charming, successful young men. There was no way for her to see him other than as one among many. Modest as she tried to be, my mother could see my father only as the lucky one and herself as the one who had, however willingly, sacrificed many other possibilities for his sake.

"The informing image of my childhood is seeing my mother smile shyly at someone who has approached her, taking my father's arm, and turning her face toward his suit jacket—shielding herself from some unwanted attention by demonstrating that she was the wife of this dignified and formidable older man. My mother turned away from the attention people offered her all the time: I was aware of that from earliest childhood.

"I wish I could say that's all there is to it.

"At that time—1958, 1959, I think it would have been—my mother was a research officer at Health, Education, and Welfare. Her job was to gather statistics from all over the country and to help prepare statistical reports on the nation's schools. Her boss was a white man named Anthony Pritchett, for whom she'd worked from her first day of government service.

"Anthony Pritchett had a passionate commitment to racial integration; he had worked his way up in the bureaucracy to an associate directorship; and like just about everybody else, he thought the world of my mother. He was a bachelor with an Ivy League education, a very witty and stylish man, the kind of person who's attracted to Washington and who usually does very well here. Over the years he'd become a friend of my parents. He'd come to our house for dinner, or else he'd take us out to dinner. Almost always he'd

have some very articulate date, never a beautiful woman but always somebody with a lot of personality, somebody who'd impress you with her bright way of talking."

Marianne caught my eye and nodded at me. I started to ask her what she meant, but I didn't want to interfere with what Thelma was telling.

"Though he never said so and though he obviously respected the man, I'm pretty certain my father had decided that Anthony Pritchett was homosexual. There was a certain amount of putting up with Mr. Pritchett that we all three understood we had to do because he was my mother's boss and because he was somebody who really was doing a lot 'for colored people.' Anthony Pritchett needed to present himself in Washington society as somebody who had Negro friends. We served that function for him—even I was aware of it—though of course he was extremely thoughtful of us, more thoughtful than he would have been if we'd been white.

"Anthony Pritchett owned a dark green Mercedes convertible, just about the most elegant car in all of Washington, maybe in all of the country in those days. He kept it polished on the outside and immaculate on the inside. It was this aspect of our friendship with him that my father and I agreed we most appreciated, getting to ride in that lovely car when he took us out to dinner.

"One day I came home from school early—there was a teacher's meeting one Friday afternoon that I had forgotten to tell my mother about—and that green Mercedes was parked about a block and a half away from our house. That was the year I had begun riding city buses home by myself. I hadn't seen my coming home a couple of hours early as a problem; I had my own house key; I was used to letting myself in the house early and waiting an hour or two for my mother to come home. She'd worked out an arrangement with Mr. Pritchett regularly to take work home with her so that she could come home early to be with me. I'd simply have to wait for her a bit longer than I usually did.

"Walking down the street from the bus stop to my house, I passed that green Mercedes, and I said to myself, 'Oh, that's Mr. Pritchett's car.' Seeing it made me happy, reminding me of the way my father always shook his head and grinned politely at Mr. Pritchett about how pretty his car was whenever it was parked in our driveway.

"The closer I got to home, the more reluctant I became to go on. By the time I turned the corner and could see our house, my feet were dragging, and

my whole body felt heavy, as if somebody had opened it up and dumped in a load of wet cement. But my brain still wasn't accepting the message. I kept walking, slower and slower.

"Nobody was home—no lights were on in our living room, as there would have been if either of my parents was there. The curtains in the upstairs bedrooms were slightly open, as we kept them during the day when we were not there. My father's car was not in the driveway. I was seeing exactly what I should have been seeing. This was where I lived. Here was where I was going to cross the street and walk up the driveway and go around to the back door. . . .

"But I wasn't able to make the turn. My body kept me walking on past the house. As I remember it now, my mind was even sort of protesting, saying, Hey, what are you doing? What's wrong with you? Where are you going?

"I kept staring back even after I had walked past it, and here is what haunts me still. A curtain moved in my parents' bedroom, as if someone had been standing there watching me walk past and wanted to keep an eye out for where I was going. I'm almost certain I saw the slightest little move of that curtain, as if someone had hooked it back with a finger. But even a moment afterwards, I was wondering if I had actually seen it.

"If a little thing like that happens, something that can't leave any evidence, then it's just so easy to doubt it. Worse still, somewhere along the line I also began doubting that the Mercedes I had passed by a couple of blocks back was Mr. Pritchett's car, or even that I passed a green Mercedes convertible.

"Nothing ever happened to confirm or deny what some essential part of me was pretty certain had happened, that Mr. Pritchett had brought my mother home and that they had taken some trouble to disguise the fact that they were in our house together.

"I walked down the street a couple of blocks to a park where my father had often taken me as a small child. There were swings there, seesaws, crude merry-go-rounds, and structures for little kids to climb. It probably wasn't safe for me to be there by myself, but I wasn't thinking about that—or wasn't, really, thinking about anything. Something seemed to have switched my brain off, except for the part of it I needed to move my body around. I fooled around aimlessly for a while in the completely empty playground. Then I sat in a

swing with my book bag in my lap until it was the usual time for me to be walking home. Then I walked home.

"When I unlocked the back door and stepped inside our kitchen, I could feel my life—my old life—tugging on me. Something inside me was desperately struggling to take up just where I'd left off and sit down at the kitchen table with a glass of milk and half a dozen Fig Newtons and get started on my math homework. The whole kitchen seemed to be telling me that that's what I should do, just wipe out of my mind Mr. Pritchett's car and the moving curtain, just pick up my life and go on with it.

"So I spread out all my stuff on the table and even took a glass down from the cabinet. But I couldn't let go of what I thought I'd seen. Even though the weather was warm enough—it was early fall—I'd picked up a little chill from being out on that playground all that time. And so I told myself that I'd just walk around the house a bit until I warmed up. What I did, of course, was walk straight upstairs to my parents' bedroom and check it out.

"Nothing was different—not the bed, my parents' dressers and bedside tables, their clothes in their closet, not the slightest little thing. I even stepped over to the window where I thought I'd seen the curtain move. I stood there and hooked it with my finger. Nothing in that room told me that there'd been anybody there since early that morning.

"In the hallway, something turned me toward what we called the sewing room, though the only sewing my mother had done in there in my whole lifetime was fixing a button back onto the sleeve of my father's suit jacket. It wasn't a room that any of the three of us ever had a reason to enter. Since we always kept the door closed, I went for long periods of time forgetting that it was even a part of our house.

"Ed, I've already told you I was a naive child. I possessed only the vaguest notions of what sex was all about or of how most grown-up men and women conducted themselves. We had no TV. We almost never went to the movies—when we took family outings, we went to cultural or educational events. The books I read were on the order of Anne of Green Gables and Little Women. How my parents talked, how my parents dressed, what my parents ate, and how my parents behaved with each other and with me—those were the topics in which I had expertise. But something made me walk into that room where the instant I stepped inside I knew that my mother had been with Mr. Pritchett not more than an hour before. It was warm in there, and there was

a scent that I understood as if a scientist had dissected it for me: my mother's bath soap and Mr. Pritchett's cologne.

"Afternoon sunlight streamed through the window while I stood there in a kind of trance.

"When I heard—or rather sensed—my mother's footsteps walking up the driveway toward the back door, I slipped out of the sewing room and down the hall to the bathroom. As I knew she would, my mother called to me, and I shouted back to her that I was in the bathroom. After a while, I flushed the toilet and washed my hands and came downstairs. She was waiting for me, just as I knew she would be—it's uncanny how well kids and their parents know each other, and mine and I knew each other about ten times better than most. She was sitting at the kitchen table, looking over my sheet of math problems while she waited for the water to boil for her after-work cup of tea."

For a few moments Carnes and Thelma were beset with waiters clearing their table, asking them how their meal had been, offering them coffee and a chance to see the dessert menu. But Thelma began speaking again so soon that I understood she felt some urgency about finishing her story.

"My mother and I talked—and even argued a bit—exactly the way we always did in that ninety minutes or so we had to ourselves, between her coming home and my father's coming. It was an afternoon similar to hundreds of previous afternoons we'd spent together, nothing different.

"Except that I was pretending I knew nothing whatsoever about what I thought I knew about. And my mother, almost certainly, was pretending that she hadn't done anything unusual earlier that day. Sometimes, when I think about this part of that day, it disturbs me more than any of it. My mother and I were each putting on an act for the other. My mother might even have seen me walking past the house and known that I suspected her of something wrong. Maybe we each knew that the other knew something. Whatever was the case, my mother revealed nothing in what she said to me or in how she behaved in my presence.

"She did such a good job of carrying out our usual conversational ritual that I began to doubt all of it again, despite what the sewing room had so clearly told me. A smell is the easiest thing in the world to imagine, I told myself. And just before bedtime that evening, I found a moment when I could

peek into that room without my parents knowing it. It was cool in there by then, and it smelled the way it always did, kind of dank and inhospitable. With the overhead light on, the old sofa in there looked like the last place in the world you'd want to sit down. My mother and Mr. Pritchett couldn't possibly have gone in there. They couldn't possibly have come to our house that afternoon. My mother couldn't possibly have gone into her own bedroom, hooked back the curtain with her finger to watch me walking past the house and staring back at it on my way to the playground. I had made it all up in my mind.

"If I am understanding you correctly, Ed, you are telling me that your life was powerfully affected by something you came to know in the act of rolling down the hillside with your classmate Diana Childress. It was a certainty of experience that served as a kind of reference point for your later experiences with the opposite sex.

"What I think I mean for you to understand from my little story is that the opposite was—is—the case with me. Essentially, I came not to know something—or I came to unknow something. A permanent piece of doubt was installed into my perception of how men and women behave with each other.

"With every couple I have ever known or seen or read about, I have suspected one of them of having betrayed the other. But it can't even be as simple as that: I even have to doubt my suspicion because I could have been completely wrong about my mother.

"Either way it was, I have this dreadful understanding of her. If she had an affair with Anthony Pritchett, I know what her thoughts and feelings must have been—I don't condemn her for it, though I know it would have crushed my father if he had found out about it. On the other hand, if nothing ever happened between my mother and Mr. Pritchett, I understand that perfectly well, too. She loved my father, I don't doubt that."

Carnes spoke up, which surprised both Marianne and me: He had been silent for such a length of time. *"Why don't you ask your mama? She'd probably tell you. Maybe she even wants you to know."*

Thelma didn't answer him right away. When she did speak, it was evident that she was thinking hard about the question: *"If she did have an affair with Anthony Pritchett, I can't stand to know it—and I can't stand for her to know that I know it. The other would be fine—if she didn't have the affair. I would have no problem with that. But I can't take a chance by asking her. It's a doubt that I can't do without, however debilitating it may have been for me. However debilitating it may be."*

There was another long pause before Carnes spoke again, his voice grainy, a soft rasp: *"So here we are."*

"Here we are. Here we are, indeed. With what we have brought with us."

X

"Death by Chocolate okay with you? I think I'd have to order it no matter what it was."

"Death by Chocolate is fine with me, Ed. I'm sure it'll be good. You go ahead and order it and ask them to bring us two forks. But holding hands on a first date is not a good idea. My mother offered me that advice in 1964. She said it leads to what comes next—and to what comes after that."

"Ah yes, your mother. But we know about her, don't we? And what comes next is just a sweet little glide of these educated fingers down the inside of your arm. Like this."

"Why, Eddie, I'm surprised at you. I'm going to have to send you down to that principal's office after all. Are you forgetting about all this luggage we brought with us to the restaurant?"

"I told you a story. You told me a story. You ever been to the opera, Thelma? Way they do it there, the tenor sings his solo, the soprano sings hers, and then they sing the duet. That's where we are right now. I sang, you sang; now it's time for us to sing."

"Well, sir, I have indeed been to the opera—just enough to know how the opera always turns out. So if we're going to sing a duet, it's not going to be that same old one, the well-known my-place-or-your-place-and-please-let's-hurry-up-before-you-find-out-something-terrible-about-me-or-I-find-out-something-horrible-about-you. Besides that, I listened to your story. Did you listen to mine?"

"You telling me you don't trust me?"

"I'm telling you I don't trust you just like you told me no matter what I do, I can't live up to that skinny little girl you rolled down the hill with in sixth grade."

Marianne responded to this remark of Thelma's with a quick exclamatory pulling down of her chin.

"I don't think you understand, Thelma. We told each other those things. Takes all the harm out to tell it."

"On the contrary. It puts all the harm right up here on the table so that we can examine it carefully."

"So all right. So all right. I see you saying you don't trust me or yourself or even old Mr. Love himself. I see that, all right. I'm not running away from it. You running away from a skinny little thing like Diana Childress?"

There were a couple of beats of silence before Thelma answered. *"No, Ed, I'm not running away. And I know you aren't. But that doesn't mean we have to run in the other direction, either."*

"Just tell me what direction we running in, lady. That's all I want to know."

"Well, sir, I hate to tell you, but we're not running. At least I'm not. I don't know in what direction we're moving, but I know I'm taking my time."

"Long as we getting there, I don't mind the speed."

"May not be any there. May not even be any we."

"You too hard, lady. You just too damn difficult!"

"You give up?"

"No."

"Then my level of difficulty must not be beyond your abilities."

"So tell me what comes next. I got it straight what doesn't come next. What does?"

"You and your driver take me home. You walk me to my door, where we may have, if we choose, a very pleasant good-night kiss. Then your driver takes you home."

"Then what?"

"Then I'm going to call you in a week or two and invite you out to dinner."

"You taking me out to dinner?"

"If you accept my invitation. That's how we do things these days. You take me out; I take you out."

"So all right. Then what?"

"Then I will probably ask you to tell me something else about yourself."

"'Nother story?"

As Carnes clearly was, I was a bit exasperated with Thelma, too.

"Another story, yes. And then if you ask me to, I might tell you one, too."

"All right. All right. How long does this go on?"

"How long does what go on?"

"Going out. Trading stories."

"Going out I don't know about. Trading stories I think has to keep going. When I don't want to hear what you have to tell me or when you don't want to hear what I have to tell you, then our friendship will, as they say, have reached a natural conclusion."

"How about if I just play my horn for you?"

"I would like that very much, but I'm afraid that when I ask you, you're still going to have to tell me about yourself. If I were a musician, we could use our instruments to communicate with each other. Since I'm not, you're still going to have to talk to me. I need your words, sir."

"This might not work out, Thelma. I might run out of words."

"Yes, that's right, it might not work out. You might run out of wanting to hear what I have to tell you, too."

"Or you might."

"Or I might."

"Be simpler for us just to go to my house and hit the sheets. Get up in the morning and take inventory."

"No, that would be far too complicated for me. Maybe if we were young and didn't know very much, we could do that and not be harmed by it. I'm not going to be combing the knots out of my hair in your bathroom mirror in the morning, I'm sorry. We're too mature to behave like that, Ed. We have to do something else."

"No end to the penalties of old age."

"No end to the penalties. Yes, that's right."

Carnes and Thelma were laughing and apparently getting up from their table when Marianne suddenly stood up and walked over to the stereo to turn it off. "I'm ashamed of myself for having listened to that."

I shrugged, but she wasn't paying any attention to me. She strode back to the wing chair and flounced down. "No, I'm not at all ashamed of myself for having listened to it," she said. Then she flashed her eyes at me as if I'd accused her of having done something terrible. "She's a very refreshing woman. You and I both could learn something from her, Henry."

"And not from him?"

"In this situation, he's your classic testosterone-motivated male. She, on the other hand, is worth paying attention to. She's just as romantic as women have always been, but she's taken charge of her biological destiny. She's insisting on the value of intelligence and mutual personal inquiry and revelation as legitimate elements of courtship."

Marianne paused a moment, as if she were gathering her thoughts, her energy—even her anger—to go on. But then something in her face changed completely. She was looking at me as if she had been pulled into a trance that permitted her to see straight through my skull. "So what do you think, Henry?" she asked, her voice much softer. "What are they going to do?"

"You're asking me what they're going to do?" I really was taken aback. "It's perfectly evident that they're going to do exactly what Thelma said they were going to do. She's asserted herself. She's taken charge. She's a smart lady, and she's already explained to him why she's wary. Carnes has got himself a goodnight kiss coming. That's it."

"Maybe."

"Maybe?"

"Things go the way they go, Henry. I know this from my single-women colleagues, who can talk enlightened sexual politics all day long, then go out that night, and the next morning find themselves waking up in bed beside some flaming pig of a guy they can't for the life of them figure out how they ended up with. Thelma likes Carnes. That's pretty clear. And she gave a whole lot of herself away to him when she told him that story."

"So?"

"So anything can happen. They're on the way back to her place. Getting out of the car, he can ask her if he should tell the driver not to wait for him, he'll get a cab back. She might hear something in his voice, might see something in his face that persuades her she ought to let him come in with her."

I couldn't see how she was getting such notions from the conversation we'd just heard. She was not inclined to indulge herself in romantic fantasies. I was baffled by her. "So if you really want to know what happens, Marianne, go back over there and switch on the machine. We have the rest of this tape to listen to and even another one after that."

"No."

"What do you mean, 'No'?"

"We have to take it from here, Henry."

I had to think about that. I definitely had to think about that. I gave her a very quizzical look.

She stood up and switched off the lamp beside her chair.

XI

"Carnes wouldn't know how to respond if Thelma said, 'Yes, go ahead and let your driver go home,'" I told Marianne while she was arranging the pillows and bedcovers. I had already made myself comfortable on my side of the bed.

"Maybe Carnes has known all along that Thelma needs company just as much as he does." Marianne leaned over to turn her bedside light out, then settled herself in with her hip just touching mine. "Men don't usually know the difference between being horny and being lonely, but Carnes knew enough to ask you guys at the Project to find him some female companionship; so maybe he knows that if he waits for the right moment and says exactly the right thing in exactly the right tone of voice, it'll happen for them. She'll smile and look down and say, 'You can come in for a little while, Mr. Carnes.'"

"Ed."

Marianne laughed softly. "Ed."

"This is something you want to happen?"

She thought a moment. In spite of the dark, I thought she might have given me a small smile. "We're not necessarily talking sex here. I just don't want some silly obstacle denying them what they might be for each other."

"Like?"

"Like fear, pride, clumsiness, too much aggression on his part, too much caution on hers, asininity—"

"Bad timing?"

"Bad timing. Yes, certainly. You know how it is at the movies, Henry. You want the man and the woman to get together, to live happily."

"Even if you and your man have gotten together but not lived happily."

"Yes. Even if. Or if you and your woman have not lived happily, then maybe you're even more desperate about wanting it to happen for the movie couple. You want to walk out of that theater knowing that at least those people worked it out. If they got hold of what you don't have, then maybe it's at least worthwhile to keep on going with your life because eventually you might find the way for you and your sad old lady or your mean old man to take hold of it. You want to see it happen. We want to see it happen, don't we?"

"Yes," I said. "We want to see it happen. We're not talking sex, but we are talking biology, ontogeny recapitulating ontology, whatever." Then we were both quiet for a while, the two of us just lying beside each other and thinking to ourselves, before I went on. "So, let's just say Carnes does make it inside Thelma's front door? What happens next? How does it go?"

"You tell it, Henry."

"Why do I have to tell it?"

"There are two of us here, aren't there? I've gotten us from listening to the tape in the living room to lying here in the bed, talking with each other. You have no idea how much willpower that took. I can't go on. You take hold of the story. I'm exhausted."

"Amusing," I said, though I wasn't certain I understood her.

I decided to make the effort. It was cozy there with her, floating our voices up through the dark toward the ceiling. "Carnes comes in. They're standing there just inside the door. Thelma turns on some lights. He looks around. 'Nice,' he says. Meaning that he's intimidated by how tastefully she has furnished these rooms."

"So she glances back at her stereo," says Marianne, "and says, 'I'd put on some music, but I'd probably pick exactly what you'd hate to hear.' Meaning that he should relax, she has insecurities of her own."

"So Carnes would hear that in her voice," I say. "He'd hear that right off. He'd walk over and say, 'Let me pick something.' He'd immediately feel like he had a chance to be at ease with her."

"And she'd consider slipping off her heels, but then she'd have second thoughts about that, about maybe giving away too much too soon. So she'd keep her shoes on, but she'd ask him if he wanted anything to drink."

"He'd say, 'Tea, if you have it. Nothing if you don't.'"

"Yes. Yes. That's just the way he says things." Marianne's pleasure was such that my body could actually register it humming in her body beside me. "And of course Thelma's got a selection of teas that would keep the emperor of China happy. She tells him all the kinds of tea that she has."

"Which tickles him and makes him want to tease her."

"'What in the name of heaven are you going to do with all that tea, lady?' he'd say in that booming voice of his."

"And she'd blush a little in spite of herself."

"Yes, I expect she would."

"Have we seen her blush?"

"Well, we haven't, but we know what she'd look like anyway, don't we?"

"Yes, yes. All right. And does he blush? Does Carnes blush?"

"Seems unlikely, doesn't it? But he must do something. Obviously he gets embarrassed."

"Yes, he does."

"So she fixes tea, and he picks out a record. It's an old stereo. One of those big cratelike pieces of furniture like they used to sell at Sears. But it's in good shape. And she has plenty of records he's interested in. He picks a Sarah Vaughan that he knows has Miles playing the solos on."

"So the water's on, and the record starts. And Carnes is standing there in her living room. Thelma comes in and stands there, the two of them looking at each other and smiling, half out of politeness and half out of being pleased with themselves. So who says what next?"

"She does. She says, 'Sit down, Ed.'"

"And he's watching her eyes to see where she wants him to sit."

"It's the sofa."

"You're exactly right. It's the sofa."

Marianne and I are almost sitting up in the bed we're so wide awake. The story is humming right along. "They sit right down," I say.

XII

Edgar Carnes, 61

Composer

Edgar DeWeese Carnes, a jazz musician whose compositions have recently come to be viewed as classics, died at his home yesterday, of an apparent heart attack. He was 61.

Born in Buffalo, New York, Mr. Carnes had resided in Chevy Chase, Maryland, for the past year and a half. After a number of years of residence in Gőteborg, Sweden, Mr. Carnes had associated himself with the American Music Recovery Program sponsored by the National Endowment for the Arts in collaboration with the Smithsonian Institution. Among Mr. Carnes's notable compositions are "Scandinavian Suite," "Coldest Blues," "Hope in One Pocket," "Lady of Pain," and "Buffalo Stampede."

Eschewing the showmanship that brought so many of his peers into the public spotlight, Mr. Carnes, who was universally known as "Eddie," was considered primarily a musician's musician. The late Stan Getz said of him that his compositions were passionate, intricately conceived, deeply informed by both the jazz and classical traditions, and almost impossible to play well without the highest level of instrumental accomplishment.

Joe Henderson, a contemporary of Mr. Carnes's, spoke of their experience at the Village clubs in the mid-1960s: "When Eddie played those songs of his, there was a quality of revelation about them, as if he'd found something absolutely new between the cracks of what we were playing and writing in those days; he played his own pieces so sweetly they sounded familiar even though you'd never before heard them or anything quite like them."

Wynton Marsalis, a personal friend of the deceased, is currently producing a recording of Mr. Carnes's music that he hopes will enhance Mr. Carnes's reputation. "Eddie Carnes was an artist of absolute integrity," Mr. Marsalis said in a telephone interview this morning. "His songs were so advanced that you didn't know what you were hearing unless you had a good deal of musical education. Eddie wasn't trying to be ahead of his time; he just naturally was. And his playing was so intensely emotional that a lot of musicians backed away from it. But he seemed unaware of his public reputation—or the lack of it; he just played his horn and put together his tunes. Many of Eddie's pieces weren't even scored until recently, and these are tunes that people like Johnny Griffin and Sonny Stitt have been playing for years. Eddie Carnes was a one-of-a-kind jazzman, an example to all of us of somebody who never compromised his music."

Asked once why he had never played in the big bands that made the reputations of so many of his peers, Mr. Carnes explained, "My ears couldn't take in all those sounds at once. I tried sitting in a few times with the Clouds of Joy out in Kansas City. It felt like I had gone to the corner of hell they reserved especially for us jazzmen: I heard horns coming down out of the ceiling and coming up out of the floor. Only way I could stand it was by ingesting most of a fifth of Johnnie Walker. And then I couldn't read the charts, and nobody wanted me up on the stand anyway. I love every bit of Mr. Ellington's work, and I used to buy his records just as soon as they came out, but it still makes me nervous to listen to almost any other big band but his."

Henry McKernan, spokesperson for the National Endowment's Carnes Project, expressed "the sorrow and disappointment we all feel when the career of a major artist is unexpectedly cut short. Eddie Carnes was working right up until a few hours before he died. All of us here at the Project had grown immensely fond of the man. He was shy and considerate, a wonderful storyteller and late-night raconteur. It was a privilege being associated with Eddie Carnes. We're certain that his reputation will continue growing now that the Endowment and the Smithsonian can make his music more generally available than it has been. The truly sad part of it," Mr. McKernan explained, "is that Eddie had just recently begun moving in a new direction. We had all been excited listening to this new work and trying to anticipate where he was headed with it. We have enough of it on tape to know that it might have given him compositions of major consequence. As it is, we'll just have to guess what he might have done with this new material. He has left us more than enough to listen to and to appreciate for many years to come."

Mr. Carnes's first marriage, to Louise Campbell, also of Buffalo, New York, ended in a divorce. Their daughter, Constance, died in an auto accident in 1979. Mr. Carnes's second marriage, to Elizabeth Krőnen, of Stockholm, Sweden, also ended in a divorce. He is survived by a brother, Dr. Ellis Carnes, of San Diego, California.

XIII

NATIONAL ENDOWMENT FOR THE ARTS
WASHINGTON, D.C. 20506
American Music Recovery Program
The Carnes Project
CONFIDENTIAL MEMORANDUM

Date: November 13, 1994
To: Robert Smallwood, Director
The National Endowment for the Arts
From: Henry McKernan, Project Director
American Music Recovery Program
Subject: The Future of the Carnes Project

Inasmuch as Mr. Carnes's death has unexpectedly altered the status of this project, our discussion of its future must begin immediately. Like every Project Director, I am intensely aware of the pressure on you to justify each of the Endowment's programs. An obvious response to the death of Mr. Carnes, from the public, the executive office, and the Congress, will be to advocate wrapping up this project as soon as possible.

Therefore it is with special urgency that I make this appeal to you to support my request for extended funding of the Carnes Project through the end of FY97.

Although it was clear from the beginning that Mr. Carnes was an unacknowledged major figure in the development of jazz from the mid-fifties through the late sixties, the Carnes Project has opened the possibility—and indeed now the necessity—of completely redefining his place in American music. Not only were we able to recover many of his unrecorded compositions from the seventies and eighties, we have also taken into our archives a virtual deluge of new material. Though this may be a somewhat exaggerated comparison, it is as if John Keats had been granted an additional five years of good health and ideal working conditions: the nature and scope of the achievement has been enlarged almost beyond our capacity to imagine it.

Ironically enough, by taking responsibility for Mr. Carnes's artistic life, the Endowment has implicitly accepted responsibility for Mr. Carnes's posterity. Had we not granted Mr. Carnes these months of being able to give maximum attention to his art, we would, to put it bluntly, have had a great deal less work to accomplish. As it is, we are now responsible for seeing to it that the history of American music gives Mr. Carnes his due place, a place that will be overwhelmingly informed by what he accomplished under our sponsorship.

We can only speculate about the final evaluation of Eddie Carnes's overall career, but the unofficial consensus of those of us who have worked on the Project is that the work of his nineteen months with us is two or three times more significant than what he accomplished in the previous forty-some years of his working life. By virtue of our work on the Carnes Project, the Endowment can take pride in having contributed significantly to the evolution of American music. Though we should probably not make any public claims to this effect, with Eddie Carnes we actually succeeded in entering the creative process of a major American artist. Surely we can present these positive aspects of our work in such a way as to enhance our funding possibilities for FY96 and FY97.

There being no precedent for the Carnes Project, it is essential that the Endowment now carry out a reckoning with what it actually means for it (and us) to become intimately involved with an individual artist. With Mr. Carnes, we were able to observe and to record the daily life of a creative genius working at the height of his powers. We have the artist's shorthand notation of a major composition, we have recordings of his improvisational studies for that composition, we have recordings of his ideas about the composition as he discussed them with other musicians. We know whom he talked with and what advice those persons offered. We know what Mr. Carnes ate for lunch on the day he finished the piece, as well as what music he listened to each evening as he worked on it, what time he went to bed, and what time he waked up. We even know whether or not he shaved on the days when he composed its most essential elements. The nature of artistic work has never been so visible, has never been so accessible to those of us who value it. The labor of sorting through our archival materials and carrying out the appropriate disposition of recordings and documents has just begun. More significantly, it is now possible for us to consider how the theoretical potential of this vast body of material might be explored. What can these documents and recordings tell us about creativity? About genius? About inspiration? In processing the Carnes materials, we may find that we must function as scientists and artists as well as librarians.

We officers of the Endowment must also begin to address certain unanticipated issues related to sponsoring and studying artistic endeavor. In our initial planning stages, we gave a great deal of discussion to the matter of Mr. Carnes's personal well-being. I take some pride in knowing that we did everything possible to make him feel at home here at Project Headquarters. We have every reason to believe that his last months were among the happiest of Mr. Carnes's life. The exuberance and wit of his last compositions and recordings will testify to his high spirits during his final days.

However, another "personal" dimension of this project must also be considered in our deliberations over the future of the American Music Recovery Program—the personal lives of our own officers. To set it forth candidly, my own private life has been severely altered because of my emotional involvement with Mr. Carnes and his music. Eddie Carnes's death has plunged me more deeply than ever into the work of the Project. At the suggestion of my wife, I've taken an apartment within walking distance of Project Headquarters, and though I find this arrangement convenient, I am somewhat dismayed at the extent to which the Project has taken over my life.

Some months ago, I had a dream in which I served as Carnes's translator; although the dream was absurd in most respects, I believe it accurately signaled a kind of responsibility that has settled upon me as a result of my directing the Carnes Project. Whether or not I am the right person to be his "translator" is beside the point—and one of the most troubling things my wife said to me in our last conversation was that Eddie Carnes never intended his music for bureaucrats like me. Whether or not that's true, I am the person responsible for delivering to the world what Eddie Carnes had to say to it in the final months of his life. I have accepted that assignment.

A lesson I have taken from Mr. Carnes is that you have to, as he put it, "take what comes to you and go with it." Eddie Carnes came into my life. He came into it much more profoundly than I ever intended for him to do so. Although he was a man whose experience was utterly different from mine, knowing him as I came to know him was a rare privilege. I have no choice now but to "go with it."

I know that matters of funding beyond the immediate fiscal year are problematic, but I will be greatly reassured if I can know that I have your support in my request to sustain the Carnes Project at least through FY97. I must point out that perverse as it may seem, Carnes's death offers us an opportunity for rallying support for the Project. The occasion has brought forth attention from the media, and it has focused sentiment in the jazz community. Relevant, too, is the familiar phenomenon of living artists who are largely ignored by the public but who become both popular and important after their deaths. Timing is crucial, and this may be the ideal time to request extended funding for the Carnes Project. Should you need further information or assistance from me in drafting up the documents to support our request, please contact me immediately. I'm eager to help in any way possible, and I'm available to you at almost any hour of the day.

Many thanks for your consideration of this request. I look forward to receiving your timely reply.

XIV

I have very little right to speak about Ed Carnes. My acquaintance with the man was extremely limited. We met at a party; we talked a while; we enjoyed each other's company sufficiently for him to extend an invitation to me to have an evening out with him and for me to accept his invitation. We had a very pleasant dinner, during which we exchanged stories of our childhoods, our growing up.

As you might imagine, our lives were very different—though perhaps that difference was more of an opportunity than it was an obstacle to our friendship.

I was intrigued with Mr. Carnes; I "liked" him—as my students would put it. I wished to see more of him. And my sense of Ed Carnes was one of his trying to journey toward me. On both occasions when I was with him, I had the impression that he was making an effort to find out about me, to understand me, to see the world from my point of view, to be close to me.

In the one evening we spent in each other's company, when I asked him to speak about himself, he obliged me with such candidness that I could hardly help but be touched by him. And so I responded by speaking to him as openly as I possibly could about my own childhood and growing up. I surprised myself with what I was willing to tell him—though perhaps I saw it as a more significant revelation than he did. At any rate, I would say that he and I had a meaningful exchange of—what should I call it?—personal information about each other.

So there's that: Ed Carnes was willing to try to become close to another person—and from my limited experience, I'd say that's a rare quality in a man.

After he had taken me out for dinner, and we'd gotten into that car that the Endowment provided for him, Ed gave me a mischievous look and asked if I would mind if we stopped by a little club where some friends of his were playing. He explained that he had not been in a club for a number of years and that until now he'd been afraid to enter one again because of his drinking. He knew that in that atmosphere the temptation to drink would be too much for him. But he thought that my being with him that night would protect him.

If I had said no, I'm certain that he'd have understood. After all, I had been under the impression that our evening was nearly over. He knew that I was ready to go home, say thank you and good night to him. He knew that I was tired and that I had had an exhausting week at school. But he was asking me to do something for him, something that was important to him. I wanted him to know that I cared that much about him. I said all right, I could probably stay out another hour or so and not fall asleep on him.

So he had his driver take us to Blues Alley, where David Murray was playing with some other musicians; Marcus Roberts was the young man playing piano—Ed was very excited about him. I don't remember the others.

From the car to the door of Blues Alley, holding onto Ed's arm, I had a reassuring sense of being with him, being close to him. Once we were inside the door of that place, with that beery smell and all that noise and smoke, I felt him just drift away from me. I withdrew my hand from his arm very soon after we were inside, but I don't think he noticed. He reminded me of some of my students who can be very attentive in my classroom but who become completely different human beings once they step out into that hallway.

Of course Ed was welcomed like a long-lost brother by the musicians who saw him come in. It wasn't more than a half hour before they sent his driver back outside to bring in Ed's saxophone, which just happened to be in the trunk of the car. I wondered if he hadn't deliberately set me up for this situation. Apparently, he had hoped I'd agree to go with him to Blues Alley, and apparently he had hoped he would be invited to play with the band. Though he wasn't entirely innocent, he also wasn't guilty of outright trickery either.

Excitement just spread through the whole place when they started whispering, "Eddie Carnes is going to play with the band." I felt it all around me—by that time we were sitting at a table where his friends had made room for us. I no longer felt on equal footing with him, but I was still in touch with Ed enough to know that he was very excited, too, in spite of his efforts to sit there nonchalantly.

He walked up to the bandstand, unpacked and assembled his instrument, then sat down and gave me a steady look that I think he meant to convey that he intended this occasion to be a kind of present to me, a gift. It took quite a bit of concentration for me to understand his intentions because even if he had been Duke Ellington himself, returned from the dead, I wouldn't have wanted to hear him play in such a noisy, bad-smelling place at that hour of the night. I could hardly catch my breath for the smoke. There was so much noise that the only way you could communicate with anyone was by screaming into his or her ear. But this was something Ed was doing for me. I tried chanting it to myself as I sat there among the many people who worshipped him: Ed Carnes is doing this for me.

When they started playing, the crowd quieted down immediately. Even I felt a shiver of anticipation, or maybe just nervousness, pass through me. They had chosen a very bluesy tune—one of Ed's compositions, I think—which they played so slowly, it was almost a ballad. Then Ed stood up to take his solo at the microphone.

At that moment I divided into two separate people. Part of me felt the intensity and the delicacy of his playing—and I really could perceive a beauty coming out of his horn that I had never before experienced, what I would prefer to call a *glory* of sound, except that I doubt Ed would have liked such a spiritual word for the earthy way he was playing.

The other part of me was just objectively witnessing the whole performance. That part of me was seeing a man who was forever out of my reach—a man who *had* to remain distant from me because that person existed only when he was playing his saxophone.

I'd say this other—disengaged—part of me was cold and calculating except that this is also the part of me that had tears coming to my eyes. Because that *judging* part of myself was making me understand what I was hearing: Ed Carnes was calling to me, asking me so very sweetly to come to him. To come to him there in the song. To *stay* there with him in the song.

At the same time, his playing was telling me, You can never be here with me, you can never touch me here in this song, this is mine and mine alone.

While I was sitting there at his table with his friends and admirers, listening to his music, this question came to me: What can you do with a man like that?

The answer came, too, very quickly: Nothing.

I had no choice. It was as if someone had opened up a door on a long, empty hallway that led into deeper and deeper darkness and then asked me if I wanted to enter. My answer was just so clearly, so overwhelmingly *no!*—I had to stand up from that table. I had to leave that place.

Of course I made my manners as best I could. I explained to Ed's friends that I wasn't feeling well, that rather than interrupt him in the middle of something that obviously meant a great deal to him, I would call a cab and go home on my own. I assured everyone that I would be fine.

My friends tell me I am not a worldly person. Perhaps if I had been more accustomed to the world of music—of jazz, of Blues Alley—I might not have been such a coward in the face of what I understood about Ed Carnes. I might have had the courage to enter that dark hallway, or I might have loved his music so much that I would have been willing to struggle futilely for the rest of my life—or the rest of his—to be close to him.

Regret was what gave me my last glimpse of Ed. I had been thinking to myself, Why can't you be the kind of person who can be here for him? All he wants is for you to be here for him.

As I made my way back through that crowd of drinkers and jazz fans at Blues Alley, I had been chiding myself, How can you be so prideful as to walk away from this man?

Just before I walked out to the coatroom, I turned to see if Ed was noticing that I was leaving. He wasn't. He was standing up there at the microphone with sweat broken out all across his forehead and his forehead wrinkled up into these deep lines with his eyes squeezed shut. Just for the moment of my seeing him like that, I thought that his saxophone looked like an instrument of torture that had been attached—against his will—to his poor mouth. He seemed to be straining to push it away from himself.

The effort Ed was making to produce that gorgeous sound was perfectly visible on his face. The music his horn was playing was telling the world how much he longed to be close to somebody—but his eyes were shut! They were shut so tightly that he couldn't possibly have seen another human being, even one who might have been standing close enough to breathe on him, let alone one who was all the way across a room full of people, waving her hand at him, trying to tell him goodbye.

16

The Blues I'm Playing

Langston Hughes

I

Oceola Jones, pianist, studied under Philippe in Paris. Mrs. Dora Ellsworth paid her bills. The bills included a little apartment on the Left Bank and a grand piano. Twice a year Mrs. Ellsworth came over from New York and spent part of her time with Oceola in the little apartment. The rest of her time abroad she usually spent at Biarritz or Juan les Pins, where she would see the new canvases of Antonio Bas, young Spanish painter who also enjoyed the patronage of Mrs. Ellsworth. Bas and Oceola, the woman thought, both had genius. And whether they had genius or not, she loved them, and took good care of them.

Poor dear lady, she had no children of her own. Her husband was dead. And she had no interest in life now save art, and the young people who created art. She was very rich, and it gave her pleasure to share her richness with beauty. Except that she was sometimes confused as to where beauty lay—in the youngsters or in what they made, in the creators or the creation. Mrs. Ellsworth had been known to help charming young people who wrote terrible poems, blue-eyed young men who painted awful pictures. And she once turned down a garlic-smelling soprano-singing girl who, a few years later, had all the critics in New York at her feet. The girl was so sallow. And she really needed a bath, or at least a mouthwash, on the day when Mrs. Ellsworth went to hear her sing at an East Side settlement house. Mrs. Ellsworth had sent a small check and let it go at that—since, however, living to regret bitterly her lack of musical acumen in the face of garlic.

About Oceola, though, there had been no doubt. The Negro girl had been highly recommended to her by Ormond Hunter, the music critic, who often went to Harlem to hear the church concerts there, and had thus listened twice to Oceola's playing.

"A most amazing tone," he had told Mrs. Ellsworth, knowing her interest in the young and unusual. "A flare for the piano such as I have seldom encountered. All she needs is training—finish, polish, a repertoire."

"Where is she?" asked Mrs. Ellsworth at once. "I will hear her play."

By the hardest, Oceola was found. By the hardest, an appointment was made for her to come to East 63rd Street and play for Mrs. Ellsworth. Oceola had said she was busy every day. It seemed that she had pupils, rehearsed a church choir, and played almost nightly for colored house parties or dances. She made quite a good deal of money. She wasn't tremendously interested, it seemed, in going way downtown to play for some elderly lady she had never heard of, even if the request did come from the white critic, Ormond Hunter, via the pastor of the church whose choir she rehearsed and to which Mr. Hunter's maid belonged.

It was finally arranged, however. And one afternoon, promptly on time, black Miss Oceola Jones rang the doorbell of white Mrs. Dora Ellsworth's gray stone house just off Madison. A butler who actually wore brass buttons opened the door, and she was shown upstairs to the music room. (The butler had been warned of her coming.) Ormond Hunter was already there, and they shook hands. In a moment, Mrs. Ellsworth came in, a tall stately gray-haired lady in black with a scarf that sort of floated behind her. She was tremendously intrigued at meeting Oceola, never having had before amongst all her artists a black one. And she was greatly impressed that Ormond Hunter should have recommended the girl. She began right away, treating her as a protégée; that is, she began asking her a great many questions she would not dare ask anyone else at first meeting, except a protégée. She asked her how old she was and where her mother and father were and how she made her living and whose music she liked best to play and was she married and would she take one lump or two in her tea, with lemon or cream?

After tea, Oceola played. She played the Rachmaninoff *Prelude in C Sharp Minor.* She played from the Liszt *Études.* She played the *St. Louis Blues.* She played Ravel's *Pavanne pour une Enfante Défunte.* And then she said she had to go. She was playing that night for a dance in Brooklyn for the benefit of the Urban League.

Mrs. Ellsworth and Ormond Hunter breathed, "How lovely!"

Mrs. Ellsworth said, "I am quite overcome, my dear. You play so beautifully." She went on further to say, "You must let me help you. Who is your teacher?"

"I have none now," Oceola replied. "I teach pupils myself. Don't have time anymore to study—nor money either."

"But you must have time," said Mrs. Ellsworth, "and money, also. Come back to see me on Tuesday. We will arrange it, my dear."

And when the girl had gone, she turned to Ormond Hunter for advice on piano teachers to instruct those who already had genius, and need only to be developed.

II

Then began one of the most interesting periods in Mrs. Ellsworth's whole experience in aiding the arts. The period of Oceola. For the Negro girl, as time went on, began to occupy a greater and greater place in Mrs. Ellsworth's interests, to take up more and more of her time, and to use up more and more of her money. Not that Oceola ever asked for money, but Mrs. Ellsworth herself seemed to keep thinking of so much more Oceola needed.

At first it was hard to get Oceola to need anything. Mrs. Ellsworth had the feeling that the girl mistrusted her generosity, and Oceola did—for she had never met anybody interested in pure art before. Just to be given things for *art's sake* seemed suspicious to Oceola.

That first Tuesday, when the colored girl came back at Mrs. Ellsworth's request, she answered the white woman's questions with a why-look in her eyes.

"Don't think I'm being personal, dear," said Mrs. Ellsworth, "but I must know your background in order to help you. Now, tell me . . . "

Oceola wondered why on earth the woman wanted to help her. However, since Mrs. Ellsworth seemed interested in her life's history, she brought it forth so as not to hinder the progress of the afternoon, for she wanted to get back to Harlem by six o'clock.

Born in Mobile in 1903. Yes, m'am, she was older than she looked. Papa had a band, that is her stepfather. Used to play for all the lodge turnouts, picnics, dances, barbecues. You could get the best roast pig in the world in Mobile. Her mother used to play the organ in church, and when the deacons bought a piano after the big revival her mama played that, too. Oceola played by ear for a long while until her mother taught her notes. Oceola played an organ, also, and a cornet.

"My, my," said Mrs. Ellsworth.

"Yes, m'am," said Oceola. She had played and practiced on lots of instruments in the South before her stepfather died. She always went to band rehearsals with him.

"And where was your father, dear?" asked Mrs. Ellsworth.

"My stepfather had the band," replied Oceola. Her mother left off playing in the church to go with him traveling in Billy Kersands' Minstrels. He had the biggest mouth in the world, Kersands did, and used to let Oceola put both her hands in it at a time and stretch it. Well, she and her mama and steppapa settled down in Houston. Sometimes her parents had jobs and sometimes they didn't. Often they were hungry, but Oceola went to school and had a regular piano teacher, an old German woman, who gave her what technique she had today.

"A fine old teacher," said Oceola. "She used to teach me half the time for nothing. God bless her."

"Yes," said Mrs. Ellsworth. "She gave you an excellent foundation."

"Sure did. But my steppapa died, got cut, and after that Mama didn't have no more use for Houston so we moved to St. Louis. Mama got a job playing for the movies in a Market Street theater, and I played for a church choir, and saved some money and went to Wilberforce. Studied piano there, too. Played for all the college dances. Graduated. Came to New York and heard Rachmaninoff and was crazy about him. Then Mama died, so I'm keeping the little flat myself. One room is rented out."

"Is she nice?" asked Mrs. Ellsworth, "your roomer?"

"It's not a she," said Oceola. "He's a man. I hate women roomers."

"Oh!" said Mrs. Ellsworth. "I should think all roomers would be terrible."

"He's right nice," said Oceola. "Name's Pete Williams."

"What does he do?" asked Mrs. Ellsworth.

"A Pullman porter," replied Oceola, "but he's saving money to go to Med school. He's a smart fellow."

But it turned out later that he wasn't paying Oceola any rent.

That afternoon, when Mrs. Ellsworth announced that she had made her an appointment with one of the best piano teachers in New York, the black girl seemed pleased. She recognized the name. But how, she wondered, would she find time for study, with her pupils and her choir, and all. When Mrs. Ellsworth said that she would cover her *entire* living expenses, Oceola's eyes were full of that why-look, as though she didn't believe it.

"I have faith in your art, dear," said Mrs. Ellsworth, at parting. But to prove it quickly, she sat down that very evening and sent Oceola the first monthly check so that she would no longer have to take in pupils or drill choirs or play at house parties. And so Oceola would have faith in art, too.

That night Mrs. Ellsworth called up Ormond Hunter and told him what she had done. And she asked if Mr. Hunter's maid knew Oceola, and if she supposed that that man rooming with her was anything to her. Ormond Hunter said he would inquire.

Before going to bed, Mrs. Ellsworth told her housekeeper to order a book called "Nigger Heaven" on the morrow, and also anything else Brentano's had about Harlem. She made a mental note that she must go up there sometime, for she had never yet seen that dark section of New York; and now that she had a Negro protégée, she really ought to know something about it. Mrs. Ellsworth couldn't recall ever having known a single Negro before in her whole life, so she found Oceola fascinating. And just as black as she herself was white.

Mrs. Ellsworth began to think in bed about what gowns would look best on Oceola. Her protégée would have to be well-dressed. She wondered, too, what sort of a place the girl lived in. And who that man was who lived with her. She began to think that really Oceola ought to have a place to herself. It didn't seem quite respectable. . . .

When she woke up in the morning, she called her car and went by her dressmaker's. She asked the good woman what kind of colors looked well with black; not black fabrics, but a black skin.

"I have a little friend to fit out," she said.

"A *black* friend?" said the dressmaker.

"A black friend," said Mrs. Ellsworth.

III

Some days later Ormond Hunter reported on what his maid knew about Oceola. It seemed that the two belonged to the same church, and although the maid did not know Oceola very well, she knew what everybody said about her in the church. Yes, indeedy! Oceola were a right nice girl, for sure, but it certainly were a shame she were giving all her money to that man what stayed with her and what she was practically putting through college so he could be a doctor.

"Why," gasped Mrs. Ellsworth, "the poor child is being preyed upon."

"It seems to me so," said Ormond Hunter.

"I must get her out of Harlem," said Mrs. Ellsworth, "at once. I believe it's worse than Chinatown."

"She might be in a more artistic atmosphere," agreed Ormond Hunter. "And with her career launched, she probably won't want that man anyhow."

"She won't need him," said Mrs. Ellsworth. "She will have her art."

But Mrs. Ellsworth decided that in order to increase the rapprochement between art and Oceola, something should be done now, at once. She asked the girl to come down to see her the next day, and when it was time to go home, the white woman said, "I have a half-hour before dinner. I'll drive you up. You know I've never been to Harlem."

"All right," said Oceola. "That's nice of you."

But she didn't suggest the white lady's coming in, when they drew up before a rather sad-looking apartment house on 134th Street. Mrs. Ellsworth had to ask could she come in.

"I live on the fifth floor," said Oceola, "and there isn't any elevator."

"It doesn't matter, dear," said the white woman, for she meant to see the inside of this girl's life, elevator or no elevator.

The apartment was just as she thought it would be. After all, she had read Thomas Burke on Limehouse. And here was just one more of those holes in the wall even if it was five stories high. The windows looked down on slums. There were only four rooms, small as maids' rooms, all of them. An upright piano almost filled the parlor. Oceola slept in the dining room. The roomer slept in the bed-chamber beyond the kitchen.

"Where is he, darling?"

"He runs on the road all summer," said the girl. "He's in and out."

"But how do you breathe in here?" asked Mrs. Ellsworth. "It's so small. You must have more space for your soul, dear. And for a grand piano. Now in the Village . . . "

"I do right well here," said Oceola.

"But in the Village where so many nice artists live we can get . . . "

"But I don't want to move yet. I promised my roomer he could stay till fall."

"Why till fall?"

"He's going to Meharry then."

"To marry?"

"Meharry, yes m'am. That's a colored Medicine school in Nashville."

"Colored? Is it good?"

"Well, it's cheap," said Oceola. "After he goes, I don't mind moving."

"But I wanted to see you settled before I go away for the summer."

"When you come back is all right. I can do till then."

"Art is long," reminded Mrs. Ellsworth, "and time is fleeting, my dear."

"Yes, m'am," said Oceola, "but I gets nervous if I start worrying about time."

So Mrs. Ellsworth went off to Bar Harbor for the season, and left the man with Oceola.

IV

That was some years ago. Eventually art and Mrs. Ellsworth triumphed. Oceola moved out of Harlem. She lived in Gay Street west of Washington Square where she met Genevieve Taggard, and Ernestine Evans, and two or three sculptors, and a cat painter who was also a protégée of Mrs. Ellsworth. She spent her days practicing, playing for friends of her patron, going to concerts, and reading books about music. She no longer had pupils or rehearsed the choir, but she still loved to play for Harlem house parties—for nothing—now that she no longer needed the money, out of sheer love of jazz. This rather disturbed Mrs. Ellsworth, who still believed in art of the old school, portraits that really and truly looked like people, poems about nature, music that had soul in it, not syncopation. And she felt the dignity of art. Was it in keeping with genius, she wondered, for Oceola to have a studio full of white and colored people every Saturday night (some of them actually drinking gin *from bottles*) and dancing to the most tomtom-like music she had ever heard coming out of a grand piano? She wished she could lift Oceola up bodily and take her away from all that, for art's sake.

So in the spring, Mrs. Ellsworth organized weekends in the upstate mountains where she had a little lodge and where Oceola could look from the high places at the stars, and fill her soul with the vastness of the eternal, and forget about jazz. Mrs. Ellsworth really began to hate jazz—especially on a grand piano.

If there were a lot of guests at the lodge, as there sometimes were, Mrs. Ellsworth might share the bed with Oceola. Then she would read aloud Tennyson or Browning before turning out the light, aware all the time of the electric strength of that brown-black body beside her, and of the deep drowsy voice asking what the poems were about. And then Mrs. Ellsworth would feel very motherly toward this dark girl whom she had taken under her wing on the wonderful road of art, to nurture and love until she became a great interpreter of the piano. At such times the elderly white woman was glad her late husband's money, so well invested, furnished her with a large surplus to devote to the needs of her protégées, especially to Oceola, the blackest—and most interesting of all.

Why the most interesting?

Mrs. Ellsworth didn't know, unless it was that Oceola really was talented, terribly alive, and that she looked like nothing Mrs. Ellsworth had ever been near before. Such a rich velvet black, and such a hard young body! The teacher of the piano raved about her strength.

"She can stand a great career," the teacher said. "She has everything for it."

"Yes," agreed Mrs. Ellsworth, thinking, however, of the Pullman porter at Meharry, "but she must learn to sublimate her soul."

So for two years then, Oceola lived abroad at Mrs. Ellsworth's expense. She studied with Philippe, had the little apartment on the Left Bank, and learned about Debussy's African background. She met many black Algerian and French West Indian students, too, and listened to their interminable arguments, ranging from Garvey to Picasso to Spengler to Jean Cocteau, and thought they all must be crazy. Why did they or anybody argue so much about life or art? Oceola merely lived—and loved it. Only the Marxian students seemed sound to her for they, at least, wanted people to have enough to eat. That was important, Oceola thought, remembering, as she did, her own sometimes hungry years. But the rest of the controversies, as far as she could fathom, were based on air.

Oceola hated most artists, too, and the word *art* in French or English. If you wanted to play the piano or paint pictures or write books, go ahead! But why talk so much about it? Montparnasse was worse in that respect than the Village. And as for the cultured Negroes who were always saying art would break down color lines, art could save the race and prevent lynchings! "Bunk!" said Oceola. "My ma and pa were both artists when it came to making music, and the white folks ran them out of town for being dressed up in Alabama. And look at the Jews! Every other artist in the world's a Jew, and still folks hate them."

She thought of Mrs. Ellsworth (dear soul in New York), who never made uncomplimentary remarks about Negroes, but frequently did about Jews. Of little Menuhin she would say, for instance, "He's a *genius*—not a Jew," hating to admit his ancestry.

In Paris, Oceola especially loved the West Indian ballrooms where the black colonials danced the beguine. And she liked the entertainers at Bricktop's. Sometimes late at night there, Oceola would take the piano and beat out a blues for Brick and the assembled guests. In her playing of Negro folk music, Oceola never doctored it up, or filled it full of classical runs, or fancy falsities. In the blues she made the bass notes throb like tomtoms, the trebles cry like little flutes, so deep in the earth and so high in the sky that they understood everything. And when the nightclub crowd would get up and dance to her blues, and Bricktop would yell, "Hey! Hey!" Oceola felt as happy as if she were performing a Chopin étude for the nicely gloved Oh's and Ah'ers in a Crillon salon.

Music, to Oceola, demanded movement and expression, dancing and living to go with it. She liked to teach, when she had the choir, the singing of those rhythmical Negro spirituals that possessed the power to pull colored folks out of their seats in the amen corner and make them prance and shout in the aisles for Jesus. She never liked those fashionable colored churches where shouting and movement were discouraged and looked down upon, and where New England hymns instead of spirituals were sung. Oceola's background was too well-grounded in Mobile, and Billy Kersands' Minstrels, and the Sanctified churches where religion was a joy, to stare mystically over the top of a grand piano like white folks and imagine that Beethoven had nothing to do with life, or that Schubert's love songs were only sublimations.

Whenever Mrs. Ellsworth came to Paris, she and Oceola spent hours listening to symphonies and string quartettes and pianists. Oceola enjoyed concerts, but seldom felt, like her patron, that she was floating on clouds of bliss. Mrs. Ellsworth insisted, however, that Oceola's spirit was too moved for words at such times—therefore she understood why the dear child kept quiet. Mrs. Ellsworth herself was often too moved for words, but never by pieces like Ravel's *Bolero* (which Oceola played on the phonograph as a dance record) or any of the compositions of *les Six*.

What Oceola really enjoyed most with Mrs. Ellsworth was not going to concerts, but going for trips on the little river boats in the Seine; or riding out to old chateaux in her patron's hired Renault; or to Versailles, and listening to the aging white lady talk about the romantic history of France, the wars and uprising, the loves and intrigues of princes and kings and queens, about guillotines and lace handkerchiefs, snuff boxes and daggers. For Mrs. Ellsworth had loved France as a girl, and had made a study of its life and lore. Once she used to sing simple little French songs rather well, too. And she always regretted that her husband never understood the lovely words—or even tried to understand them.

Oceola learned the accompaniments for all the songs Mrs. Ellsworth knew and sometimes they tried them over together. The middle-aged white woman loved to sing when the colored girl played, and she even tried spirituals. Often, when she stayed at the little Paris apartment, Oceola would go into the kitchen and cook something good for late supper, maybe an oyster soup, or fried apples and bacon. And sometimes Oceola had pigs' feet.

"There's nothing quite so good as a pig's foot," said Oceola, "after playing all day."

"Then you must have pigs' feet," agreed Mrs. Ellsworth.

And all this while Oceola's development at the piano blossomed into perfection. Her tone became a singing wonder and her interpretations warm and individual. She gave a concert in Paris, one in Brussels and another in Berlin. She got the press notices all pianists crave. She had her picture in lots of European papers. And she came home to New York a year after the stock market crashed and nobody had any money—except folks like Mrs. Ellsworth who had so much it would be hard to ever lose it all.

Oceola's one-time Pullman porter, now a coming doctor, was graduating from Meharry that spring. Mrs. Ellsworth saw her dark protégée go South to attend his graduation with tears in her eyes. She thought that by now music would be enough, after all those years under the best teachers, but alas, Oceola was not yet sublimated, even by Philippe. She wanted to see Pete.

Oceola returned North to prepare for her New York concert in the fall. She wrote Mrs. Ellsworth at Bar Harbor that her doctor boyfriend was putting in one more summer on the railroad, then in the autumn he would intern at Atlanta. And Oceola said that he had asked her to marry him. Lord, she was happy!

It was a long time before she heard from Mrs. Ellsworth. When the letter came, it was full of long paragraphs about the beautiful music Oceola had within her power to give the world. Instead, she wanted to marry and be burdened with children! Oh, my dear, my dear!

Oceola, when she read it, thought she had done pretty well knowing Pete this long and not having children. But she wrote back that she didn't see why children and music couldn't go together. Anyway, during the present Depression, it was pretty hard for a beginning artist like herself to book a concert tour—so she might just as well be married awhile. Pete, on his last run in from St. Louis, had suggested that they have the wedding Christmas in the South. "And he's impatient, at that. He needs me."

This time Mrs. Ellsworth didn't answer by letter at all. She was back in town in late September. In November, Oceola played at Town Hall. The critics were kind, but they didn't go wild. Mrs. Ellsworth swore it was because of Pete's influence on her protégée.

"But he was in Atlanta," Oceola said.

"His spirit was here," Mrs. Ellsworth insisted. "All the time you were playing on that stage, he was here, the monster! Taking you out of yourself, taking you away from the piano."

"Why, he wasn't," said Oceola. "He was watching an operation in Atlanta."

But from then on, things didn't go well between her and her patron. The white lady grew distinctly cold when she received Oceola in her beautiful drawing room among the jade vases and amber cups worth thousands of dollars. When Oceola would have to wait there for Mrs. Ellsworth, she was afraid to move for fear she might knock something over—that would take ten years of a Harlemite's wages to replace, if broken.

Over the teacups, the aging Mrs. Ellsworth did not talk any longer about the concert tour she had once thought she might finance for Oceola, if no recognized bureau took it up. Instead, she spoke of that something she believed Oceola's fingers had lost since her return from Europe. And she wondered why anyone insisted on living in Harlem.

"I've been away from my own people so long," said the girl, "I want to live right in the middle of them again."

Why, Mrs. Ellsworth wondered further, did Oceola, at her last concert in a Harlem church, not stick to the classical items listed on the program. Why did she insert one of her own variations on the spirituals, a syncopated variation from the Sanctified church, that made an old colored lady rise up and cry out from her pew, "Glory to God this evenin'! Yes! Hallelujah! Whooo-oo!" right at the concert? Which seemed most undignified to Mrs. Ellsworth, and unworthy of the teachings of Philippe. And furthermore, why was Pete coming up to New York for Thanksgiving? And who had sent him the money to come?

"Me," said Oceola. "He doesn't make anything interning."

"Well," said Mrs. Ellsworth, "I don't think much of him." But Oceola didn't seem to care what Mrs. Ellsworth thought, for she made no defense.

Thanksgiving evening, in bed, together in a Harlem apartment, Pete and Oceola talked about their wedding to come. They would have a big one in a church with lots of music. And Pete would give her a ring. And she would have on a white dress, light and fluffy, not silk. "I hate silk," she said. "I hate expensive things." (She thought of her mother being buried in a cotton dress, for they were all broke when she died. Mother would have been glad about her marriage.) "Pete," Oceola said, hugging him in the dark, "let's live in Atlanta, where there are lots of colored people, like us."

"What about Mrs. Ellsworth?" Pete asked. "She coming down to Atlanta for our wedding?"

"I don't know," said Oceola.

"I hope not, 'cause if she stops at one of them big hotels, I won't have you going to the back door to see her. That's one thing I hate about the South—where there're white people, you have to go to the back door."

"Maybe she can stay with us," said Oceola. "I wouldn't mind."

"I'll be damned," said Pete. "You want to get lynched?"

But it happened that Mrs. Ellsworth didn't care to attend the wedding, anyway. When she saw how love had triumphed over art, she decided she could no longer influence Oceola's life. The period of Oceola was over. She would send checks, occasionally, if the girl needed them, besides, of course, something beautiful for the wedding, but that would be all. These things she told her the week after Thanksgiving.

"And Oceola, my dear, I've decided to spend the whole winter in Europe. I sail on December eighteenth. Christmas—while you are marrying—I shall be in Paris with my precious Antonio Bas. In January, he has an exhibition of oils in Madrid. And in the spring, a new young poet is going over whom I want to visit Florence, to really know Florence. A charming white-haired boy from Omaha whose soul has been crushed in the West. I want to try to help him. He, my dear, is one of the few people who live for their art—and nothing else. . . . Ah, such a beautiful life! . . . You will come and play for me once before I sail?"

"Yes, Mrs. Ellsworth," said Oceola, genuinely sorry that the end had come. Why did white folks think you could live on nothing but art? Strange! Too strange! Too strange!

V

The Persian vases in the music room were filled with long-stemmed lilies that night when Oceola Jones came down from Harlem for the last time to play for Mrs. Dora Ellsworth. Mrs. Ellsworth had on a gown of black velvet and a collar of pearls about her neck. She was very kind and gentle to Oceola, as one would be to a child who has done a great wrong but doesn't know any better. But to the black girl from Harlem, she looked very cold and white, and her grand piano seemed like the biggest and heaviest in the world—as Oceola sat down to play it with the technique for which Mrs. Ellsworth had paid.

As the rich and aging white woman listened to the great roll of Beethoven sonatas and to the sea and moonlight of the Chopin nocturnes, as she watched the swaying dark strong shoulders of Oceola Jones, she began to reproach the girl aloud for running away from art and music, for burying herself in Atlanta and love—love for a man unworthy of lacing her boot straps, as Mrs. Ellsworth put it.

"You could shake the stars with your music, Oceola. Depression or no Depression, I could make you great. And yet you propose to dig a grave for yourself. Art is bigger than love."

"I believe you, Mrs. Ellsworth," said Oceola, not turning away from the piano. "But being married won't keep me from making tours, or being an artist."

"Yes, it will," said Mrs. Ellsworth. "He'll take all the music out of you."

"No, he won't," said Oceola.

"You don't know, child," said Mrs. Ellsworth, "what men are like."

"Yes, I do," said Oceola simply. And her fingers began to wander slowly up and down the keyboard, flowing into the soft and lazy syncopation of a Negro blues, a blues that deepened and grew into rollicking jazz, then into an earth-throbbing rhythm that shook the lilies in the Persian vases of Mrs. Ellsworth's music room. Louder than the voice of the white woman who cried that Oceola was deserting beauty, deserting her real self, deserting her hope in life, the flood of wild syncopation filled the house, then sank into the slow and singing blues with which it had begun.

The girl at the piano heard the white woman saying, "Is this what I spent thousands of dollars to teach you?"

"No," said Oceola simply. "This is mine. . . . Listen!. . . . How sad and gay it is. Blue and happy—laughing and crying. . . . How white like you and black like me. . . . How much like a man. . . . And how like a woman. . . . Warm as Pete's mouth. . . . These are the blues. . . . I'm playing."

Mrs. Ellsworth sat very still in her chair looking at the lilies trembling delicately in the priceless Persian vases, while Oceola made the bass notes throb like tomtoms deep in the earth.

O, if I could holler

sang the blues,

Like a mountain jack,
I'd go up on de mountain

sang the blues,

And call my baby back.

"And I," said Mrs. Ellsworth rising from her chair, "would stand looking at the stars."

17

Old Ghost Revives Atavistic Memories in a Lady of the DAR

Langston Hughes

It had been a delightful afternoon, the tea delicious, the cinnamon toast just right, and the agenda had gone off very well except that sometime or other at the very end, although it was not on the agenda, the Negro question had come up again to disturb the ladies of the D.A.R. Mrs. G. Leighton Palmer regretted that, as usual, some of the Daughters had become excited, even shrill. But the gavel of their President finally managed to restore gentility.

After the last guest had gone, Mrs. Palmer opened wider the French windows in her music room to let in a little Washington air to rid the room of the cigarette smoke in which fortunately only two of the ladies indulged.

"Ah, well," sighed Mrs. G. Leighton Palmer, "some old girls insist on trying to be young girls. Smoking is perhaps all right for debutantes, since it's now a female fashion, but—"

Her sentence ended in mid-air because, just as she turned away from the windows, Mrs. Palmer saw a ghost slip onto the piano stool.

"Whoever in the world are you?" she gasped, stopping in her tracks.

"Old Ghost," the unwanted musician answered, striking a low rumbling chord on the piano.

"Of whom?" cried Mrs. Palmer.

"Blind Boone," said the ghost, putting the soft pedal on.

"A Negro?" asked Mrs. Palmer.

"Indeed he was," answered Old Ghost, "and a great artist in his day."

"Paderewski has played on that piano," said Mrs. Palmer. "In my husband's day we had only great musicians in our home—and no Negroes."

"I know," said Old Ghost. "That's why I am here now."

"Leave my house at once," cried Mrs. Palmer, "or I will have you ejected!"

"Ejected? No one can eject a wraith," said Old Ghost. "I'm a poltergeist."

"I do not care what you are," said Mrs. Palmer. "It is against our rules to have a Negro on the agenda. Go at once."

"Not at once," said Old Ghost. "I must practice my scales."

"Such impudence," cried Mrs. Palmer. "I'll ring for George."

"If you want George to continue in your service," said Old Ghost, "as he has lo these many years, you had better not ring. George might be amazed, especially since he once heard Blind Boone in his youth and might remember this tune."

"I trust you are finished now," said Mrs. Palmer as the last silver note died away.

"Not yet, but soon," said Old Ghost. "In fact, as soon as I have rendered a bit of boogie a la Hazel Scott."

"Don't mention that name," cried Mrs. Palmer. "It was she who precipitated the discussion today that so agitated our ladies. Hazel shall never play in Constitution Hall. Never! Never! Personally I did not object to Marion Anderson, who really sings spirituals as beautifully as my late cook. But Hazel! Boogie woogie! Now you! No! Get out! Out! Get out."

"Froggy Bottom," said Old Ghost, tapping his right heel on the Persian rug and letting go with a fast eight-to-the-bar.

"Oh!" gasped Mrs. Palmer. "Oh!" Suddenly she began to dance, to boogie and, as the music modulated, even to be-bop—for ghosts have strange powers over persons still on an earthly plane. Old Ghost with his rhythms revived atavistic memories in Mrs. G. Leighton Palmer that were now taking modern choreographic forms. Even her vocabulary acquired a new phrase. "Ah, do it, daddy!"

"Hucklebuck!" cried Old Ghost

As he disappeared Mrs. Palmer's ancient carcass squatted in one final scoop and swished like a duck, "Hucklebuck, baby! Hucklebuck!"

18

Dead Jazz Guys

Phil Kawana

Lee and Mike first met in the public library. Mike was sitting cross-legged on the floor leafing through a biography of Miles Davis when he was hit on the back of the neck by a large volume on George Bernard Shaw that had somehow worked its way free of Lee's arms.

"Oh, I'm terribly sorry. Are you alright?" Lee said, squatting down to retrieve the errant tome.

"Yeah, yeah, I'm okay," Mike muttered as he handed the book back to her. He looked up. Lee was wearing pale blue jeans, a white shirt buttoned to the collar, and a dark embroidered waistcoat. Straw-blonde hair tumbled down to just below either shoulder, framing a face that would have been strikingly pretty, were it not for a faint scar running down the right side of her jaw and disappearing beneath the shirt. She was slim, and looked to be in her early twenties. Lee smiled apologetically, and it was only then that Mike noticed that she wore no make-up. "You could try some lighter reading, though."

Lee's smile broadened a little, and for a brief moment her eyes dropped. "Miles Davis?" she asked, nodding to the book he had dropped in his lap.

"Mmm. I've just started listening to his stuff. I got given a CD of his not long ago."

"Which one? I quite like his music."

"*Doo Bop.*"

"Right. That was his last one. He died before it came out."

Mike nodded. He already knew this by reading the liner notes, but was quite happy to keep talking. There was a pause of a few seconds, and Lee looked as if she was about to move on.

"Are you into Shaw?" he asked.

"No, not really. I'm just picking some books up for my father."

"Oh."

"Um, anyway, sorry about that."

"That's okay."

Lee stood, smiled again, then carried on down the aisle. Mike watched her go. She held herself tall and erect, and just before she disappeared she flicked a lock of hair back over her shoulder and half turned her head to glance at him. For a brief moment their eyes met. Mike smiled, and Lee nodded slightly, then was gone.

When he got back to his flat, Mike slipped *Doo Bop* on the stereo, turned the volume up, and went into the bathroom. He looked at himself in the mirror for several minutes. By the colour of his skin and the structure of his face, he looked more like a Native American than a Māori. High cheekbones and dark eyes—legacy of his part-Samoan mother—over a straight nose, all painted a smooth and flawless coffee brown. He had a frame custom-made for an athletic build, but had inherited his parents' tendency to fat, which meant he had to work hard to keep himself looking good.

"And I do look good," he tried to assure himself. He wasn't feeling quite that confident. In his mind was a picture of Lee, cool and collected and dressed with casual money. Not wealth, but definitely middle class. He tugged a little irritably at his tatty flannel shirt. He hoped the slacker look was going to stay in for a while longer. He wondered what she had thought of his hair. His hair was very short on top, shaved to the scalp at the back and sides, leaving a topknot that was ordered into twelve thin dreadlocks, reaching down to below his shoulder blades. "Oh well," he sighed, and went to find something to eat.

The following day, dole day, Mike decided to treat himself to a couple of cream buns for lunch. He was standing at the counter of the bakery waiting to be served when he heard a voice addressing him.

"I hope I didn't leave any bruises yesterday."

Lee was standing next to him. She had a friend with her, a girl about the same age, shorter and with dark hair and bright green eyes. The friend wore too much make-up, and by the forced neatness of the dress she wore, Mike guessed that she probably worked either in a pharmacy or a bookstore. She looked at Mike, and then at Lee with the faintest dropping of her jaw.

"Hi," said Mike as casually as he could. "I think I survived okay."

Lee was about to say something else when the woman behind the counter loudly asked who was next. Mike turned and paid for his cream buns and a small bottle of orange juice. He could hear Lee's friend whispering, but couldn't quite make out what it was she was saying. As he turned around again, Lee was giving her friend a swift elbow in the ribs. She looked up and caught his eye. "We were going to have lunch in the park," she said.

Mike had planned on going straight home, but a flirt like this was too good to pass up. "Yeah, so was I," he lied.

"Mind if we join you?" Lee asked as she nudged her friend towards the counter to pay for their food.

"Sure, no problem."

"That's if, ah . . . "

"Nah, no problem."

"Oh, good." There was a pause as they both glanced over to the friend. "Janice and I eat there every Thursday."

"Yeah?"

"In summer. When it's not raining."

Janice returned just in time to prevent a second awkward silence. As they left the bakery, Mike held the door open for the other two. Lee walked straight through and waited on the pavement outside. Janice glanced up at Mike with an amused smirk.

It was a five minute walk to the park. For the first minute the three of them walked quietly, Lee in the middle. Mike could feel Janice looking at him two or three times.

"My name's Lee, by the way," said Lee. "And this is Janice."

"Mike. Mike Arapeta."

"Hi, Mike."

"Hello, Mike," Janice said. Her voice had a slight nasal tone to it that immediately irritated Mike. He hoped she wouldn't turn out to be too talkative.

"Hi," Mike answered. He began to feel self-conscious. He had on the same clothes he had been wearing in the library the day before, while Lee was in an expensive-looking navy jacket over a white polo neck, tan trousers and an expensive leather belt. Mike glanced around the street, hoping they wouldn't run into anyone he knew.

"So, what do you do, Mike?" Janice asked.

Mike was about to mumble "not very much" when Lee spoke. "He collects books on George Bernard Shaw." Janice uttered a little grunt of surprise and looked at Mike with renewed interest. "Janice works at Shandy's Hair. Spends all her working life finding out what everyone else is doing." Lee and Mike both laughed. "I was telling her last night that I had met someone with fabulous hair that she really should have seen."

"Where did you get it done?" Janice interrupted.

"Most of it I did myself," Mike replied. "A friend helped me put the dreads in."

"Really?" Janice sounded a little put out. "It looks good."

"Thanks."

They reached the small park and sat down on some concrete edging that surrounded a bed of brilliantly coloured petunias.

"I did Lee's hair," Janice said between bites of custard square.

"You did a nice job. It looks nice."

"Thank you," Lee and Janice both said at the same time. Lee watched as Mike took his first bite of the cream bun and washed it down with a gulp of orange juice. "You don't really look like a cream bun eater."

"I'm not, normally," Mike said, carefully wiping some cream from the corner of his mouth with the back of one hand. He was looking at her shoes as he spoke, still feeling a bit too shy to look at her directly. Brown Doc Martens. "Just now and then. You know, monthly sugar fix."

"Yeah. For me it's chocolates. So what do you normally eat? No, wait. Let me guess." Mike shot a quick look at her as she paused. There was a hint of pink tongue pressing against her teeth. "Chicken?"

"No. Fish and rice, mostly. Some chicken."

"Oh God, you're not a tofu muncher are you?" Janice asked with a giggle.

"Yeah, sometimes." Her tone annoyed him, and he looked squarely at her until she backed off, trying to lose herself behind the remains of her custard square. "I like to eat healthily." He looked down at the bun in his hand, half finished and oozing cream and sugar. "Most of the time."

"It's fun to be naughty every now and then," Lee said. Somehow she had moved along the edging a little, and her knee briefly pressed against Mike's. He looked up at her again, and this time she caught his eye and held it. He could feel adrenalin starting to move through him, and he leaned forward on his knees so that they wouldn't notice if he started to get hard. Lee kept gazing at him.

"Are you a Rastafarian?" Janice asked.

"Rastas are vegetarian," Mike said without looking at her. His attention was still fixed on Lee. "Proper Rastas, anyway."

"It's just that I wondered, you know, your dreadlocks . . . "

"I like dreads," Mike stated, "that's all."

"You almost look Indian," Lee said, "like that guy in *Last of the Mohicans.*"

"Daniel Day Lewis' brother?" Janice asked, a degree of puzzlement in her voice.

"No," Lee said with a sexy smirk. "Magua, the evil one. Are you evil, Mike?"

"No. Just a little naughty from time to time."

"Like I said, it's fun to be naughty every now and then."

Janice stood and waited for several seconds for Lee to do likewise. When it became obvious that Lee was going to stay where she was, Janice said, "We were going to go to Underground, to check out that jacket . . . "

"I haven't finished my lunch yet," said Lee, impassively.

"I've got to be back at work in fifteen minutes!"

"You go. I'll catch up with you later."

"Lee!" The exasperation in Janice's voice made it even more nasal. "Lee! C'mon!"

Lee sighed. “Oh, alright then.” She stood slowly. Janice started to walk away, but Lee paused, looking down at Mike, who was now feeling safe enough to sit upright and look back at her. “What are you doing tonight, Mike?”

“Dunno. Taking you out somewhere?”

“Sounds good to me. Where shall I meet you?”

“Lee!” called Janice impatiently.

“How about here at seven? We can work out what to do from there.”

“You’re on.” She ambled off slowly to join Janice. As she went she called back over her shoulder, “I’ll try and lose the hairdresser!”

Mike nodded. He watched as they slowly lost themselves amongst the early afternoon shoppers, Janice obviously grumpy. “Yee ha,” Mike said softly to himself, then swallowed the last of the orange juice and tossed his rubbish into a nearby bin.

He was back at the park at ten minutes to seven that evening, clad in baggy black trousers and matching shirt. He had tied his dreads together at the nape of his neck with a bright red band. He wandered back and forwards past the petunia bed, glancing at his reflection in the showroom window across the street. “Naughty” is what she had said, and it was how he had dressed. He had never been out with a *real* Pākehā before. He had gone out with a couple of girls, Joy and Helena, but they had been raised in the same state house area as he had, and were nothing like Lee. He didn’t really know what to expect, but it seemed she liked a bit of an edge. So he had dressed like a hood.

A hood with cash. Mike wished he had thought to borrow his cousin’s car. He felt in his pocket. He had one hundred and fifty dollars on him. It was all the money he had. In one hand he was carrying a small box of Belgian chocolates.

Lee drove up in a white BMW at five minutes past seven. The passenger window whispered open, allowing the muted sound of a trumpet to escape from the interior of the car. Lee leaned across the front seat. “I hope I haven’t kept you waiting.”

“No, I only just got here.”

“Great. Hop in.” She opened the door for him and he got in. She turned the music down and they pulled out into the traffic. “Miles Davis," she said, waving a finger briefly at the stereo. "One of his earlier recordings."

"Nice. I, ah, bought you some chocolate."

"Thank you."

"They're Belgian."

"Yum. Just put it on the back seat, will you?"

Mike looked at Lee. Again, she didn't seem to be wearing any make-up, but the scar on her jaw was so faint now, he wouldn't have spotted it if he hadn't already known it was there. She was wearing the navy jacket again, but Mike could not tell what she had on beneath it. A quick glance down revealed a white mini. Her legs were tanned and muscular. He looked up to see that she was watching him.

"Like?"

"Yes," he said, a little embarrassed. "You look good."

"Thank you, Michael."

"Actually, it's Michele. My grandfather's name. He was an Italian."

"Italian?"

"Yeah, came over here to escape Mussolini."

"You don't look very Italian."

"I'm only a quarter. Half Māori, quarter Italian, quarter Samoan. What a mixture, huh?" The two of them laughed. Lee swept some hair away from her face.

"You have got Italian style, though. You look great." Her gaze lingered on him just a little longer than it needed to. Mike smiled nervously. Lee continued, chatting away breezily as if they had known each other for years. "My family's Dutch, mostly. There's a bit of Danish and a bit of Irish in there somewhere too."

"What's your last name?"

Lee laughed. "Didn't I tell you? Promise not to laugh?"

"Why? What is it?"

"Roelofs. Lee Roelofs. It was a real pain in the ass at school."

"I bet."

Lee put on a deep voice. "Hey Lee, wanna *roll-off* this? Way-hey!" They stopped at traffic lights, and Lee leaned forward to turn the music up a little. "The car belongs to my father. He's not allowed to drive any more, so I get it whenever I want."

"Cool. It's a nice car."

"Mmm." The lights changed to green, and Lee slipped the BMW into drive. "Dad had a stroke, did I say?" Her voice was a little sad, but she shrugged her shoulders and smiled across at Mike. "So, where should we go? Have you eaten? I'm hungry."

"No, not yet." His fingers flicked along the edge of the money in his pocket, hoping she wouldn't suggest somewhere expensive.

"Well, how about Thai?" Lee said. "There's a great Thai takeaways just down here a little further, they do a fabulous chili beef."

Mike wondered if he was being patronized. Had she guessed he was almost broke? Lee noticed his expression, smiled and put a hand on his knee. "I'm a chili freak, and they have the best in town. What do you think?"

"Sounds alright to me," Mike said. He was very conscious of her hand.

"Great, let's go." She lifted her hand off. "Dad was born and raised in Indonesia, and we were brought up on Asian food. I don't think I had steak, egg and chips until I was at high school."

"That was just about all my father lived on."

"Him and about ninety-five percent of the male population of the country." Lee pulled the car over as she spoke, and parked outside the Thai place. It was dingy and unappealing, but the food was as good as she had said. They ate leaning against the car.

"What kind of music do you like, apart from Miles Davis?" Mike asked as they got back into the car.

"Oh, all sorts. Anything but polkas and new age drivel. What about you?"

Mike shrugged. "Jazz, reggae—surprise, surprise—techno stuff."

"Have you ever listened to Kraftwerk?"

"I've heard *of* them. Never listened *to* them, though."

"You want to?" She looked at Mike, her eyebrows raised slightly. "I've got a few of their CDs at home, and it's still a bit early to go anywhere."

"Would your folks . . . "

"I don't live at home," she said with a shake of her head. "They bought me a place on the Parade. Great view, right next to the beach. Privileges of an only child."

"Yeah, okay then."

Lee's place was a fourth floor apartment that had an unobstructed view out across the harbour. Mike stood and looked out of the glass sliding door that opened on to a small balcony. Lee was hunting through a six foot high compact disc rack, looking for her copy of *Trans Europe Express.* She let out an exclamation of triumph when she located it.

"Here we go," she said as she put it on. "Go out on to the terrace if you want, I'll get us a drink. What'll you have? Vodka, rum or wine's all I've got at the moment. There might be some orange juice in the fridge."

"Vodka and orange, if you've got it. Just straight vodka's okay though."

"Coming up." Lee disappeared into the kitchen. She joined Mike out on the terrace a few minutes later. She handed him a tumbler of vodka and orange. The sky over the harbour was a pale blue, just beginning to develop the darker hues of twilight. "Here you go. Great view, huh? I really like it out here. It's brilliant when it's dark."

"I bet. Thanks." He took a sip. She had mixed it strong. "What do you do for a living?"

"A bit of this, a bit of that, a lot of sponging off Dad." She leaned against the railings and regarded him. There was a gentle breeze that blew her hair behind her. "You must think I'm a spoilt little rich girl."

"It's good work if you can get it," he smiled and lifted his glass again. "Cheers."

Lee lifted her glass of wine in reply, and sipped from it slowly. "I'm glad I ran into you today"

"Are you?" Mike wondered if now was the time.

"Yes," Lee said, and held eye contact for several seconds. She tossed back the rest of her wine and started inside, beckoning Mike to follow her. "When I described you to Janice, she thought you're probably a drug dealer. Are you, Mike?"

"No." He felt like he was being made fun of, and wondered what was going on inside her head. She looked a little disappointed. "Would you like me to be?"

Lee just smiled. "I've got some hash and some ecstasy stashed away if you'd like?"

"Ecstasy's a bit too yuppie for me."

Lee laughed and poured them both another drink. "Maybe later then. I used the last of the orange juice before, I'm afraid. Is it okay straight?"

"Fine."

"Good," she said as she handed him a second glass of vodka. "So what do *you* do to make your way?"

"Officially I'm a government statistic. Unofficially I do bone-carving."

"Really? Do you sell them locally?"

"I've got a cousin in Taupo, he sells them to tourists up there. I send them up there, and he brings me down some cash once a month. Under the table."

They sat on a settee that faced out over the harbour. Kraftwerk pulsed from speakers in each corner of the room. Lee turned sideways and leaned back against the arm of the settee. She looked at Mike over the rim of her wine glass. Her jacket slipped open, and Mike realized the white mini was a high-necked one-piece dress. Lee eased her legs up onto the seat so that they pressed against his thigh. Slowly, cautiously, Mike reached down and began to gently stroke her shins.

"That feels nice," she said and straightened out her legs over his. She kicked her shoes off over the end of the settee. "Keep going."

Mike put his drink down on an end table, and then ran his hands slowly up and down her calves. Lee nestled down in the seat, purring happily and closing her eyes. Mike had to almost turn around to reach her feet, which he massaged gently. When he turned back towards her, Lee's eyes were open again. He slid his hands up past her knees, over the outer sides of her thighs until the tips of his fingers stopped just inside the hem of her dress. Lee reached back over her head, placing her drink on the table behind her. Her lips parted, and she reached out to touch Mike's neck. She slipped her fingers under his shirt and on to his chest. Her hands were warm and soft. "You have nice skin," Lee said.

Mike eased his fingers out from her dress and slid them up her sides, underneath her jacket, leaning forward as he went. Soon he was lying, half behind her, his hands gently touching her back, his nose against her cheek. He could feel her breath against his cheek, and her hands clasping behind his neck to pull him closer to her. He slid his lips along Lee's jaw to her ear, tugged softly at her earlobe. "I want you," she whispered.

They kissed, slowly at first, nuzzling and nibbling at each other's lips, but as the passion built, they quickly began to explore mouth, teeth, tongue. Lee wriggled her way on top of Mike, took his hands in hers and pulled him up off the settee. She held him close and whispered softly. "I had an accident when I was a kid. There are still scars . . . "

Mike understood her choice of clothes then. He held her lightly by the waist and kissed her. "It's okay."

Afterwards, as they lay tired and content in the shadows, Mike found himself thinking about jazz. Exploration, experimentation, exultation. It seemed the perfect accompaniment for the moment. He padded through to the stereo, hunted through the rack until he found a disc by John Coltrane and Don Cherry. He slipped it into the player and stood in the semi-darkness, listening. Dead jazz guys, electronically resurrected to perform their musical miracles just for him and Lee. He wondered how long a dead man could play. Notes slithered through the room and out across the water like a mirrored cobra, flexing and twisting, reflecting back the lights of the city. Mike pondered whether it was all doomed to just fade away with the dawn of the living. He went back into the bedroom. Lee was lying across the bed like a reclining ivory sculpture.

"You're beautiful," he said.

Lee sat up, hugged her legs to her chest and rested her chin on her knees. Her eyes followed him as he sat next to her. "Can I ask a personal question?" she asked.

"Sure."

"You ever slept with a Pākehā before?"

"No. Believe it or not."

"I believe it."

"Do you think that's strange?"

"I don't know. No, probably not. I've never slept with someone I hadn't been seeing for months before, so I guess . . . "

"Yeah, I suppose."

Lee let go of her legs, shuffled over and kissed Mike again. She rested one hand on the back of his head, fingers twisting through his dreadlocks. "Do you want to stay the night?"

"Yeah."

"Good. I'd like that."

In the darkness, they touched something together, the edges of a fantasy. At some time they would have to awake, return to the deadness of the everyday, enshrouded by elevator music. But for now, angels arose from the grave to serenade them. From the lounge, John Coltrane's saxophone and Don Cherry's trumpet writhed and danced around each other. Supple, sinewy and alive.

19

Buddy's Monologue

Yusef Komunyakaa

THE SCENE: Semi-dark corridor of the Insane Asylum of Louisiana.
THE TIME: Circa 1915. A late afternoon.
THE CHARACTERS: *Charles Buddy Bolden, Mister Sebe Bradham, an attendant. Charles Buddy Bolden, who played cornet, and apparently "went crazy," is a legendary figure in the early history of jazz in New Orleans.*

Buddy Bolden plays "Funky Butt" for two or three minutes before the curtain opens. He continues to play, with his back to the audience. He stops blowing and turns around, obviously annoyed. Speaking to Sebe Bradham, an attendant, an imaginary character, whom he addresses throughout the piece, Bolden says:

Mister Sebe, the horn was just sitting there. Sitting there like the cornet I found in the street back in New Orleans. Begging to be played. Believe me, Mister Sebe, I fought with myself before I took it. I walked three solid miles. Yeah, I walked three miles in a circle, before I unlatched the case. *(Pause.)* This is nothing like my horn. No siree. This thing's too light, and it ain't hardly broken in yet. Ain't kissed sorrow. *(He turns to the window again, playing the same tune. He stops, turns, and takes a few steps toward the imaginary Bradham, doubling over with a piercing laugh. The laughter grows slowly into a near-whimpering sound. He assumes a stern composure. He extends the horn, and he quickly pulls it back, holding it behind his back as he speaks.)* I had me some women back then. Yeah. Carving contests. Seeing who outdid who. Things like that are just second nature. Same way I blew my horn. I played "Don't Go 'Way Nobody" like I made love. *(Pause.)* How did I get here? Did someone steal the sweatband from my hat? Huh? Did someone put a lizard's tongue under my mattress? Tell me that. Did someone sprinkle salt on my doorsteps? Why can't I stop touching things? Love to handle dreams and things. *(Shrugs.)* They don't talk back. Can't, can they? *(Pause.)* Women heard my silver cornet all over town. I blew from a real strong muscle. The heart's almost as strong. I blew because I didn't know anything else. There's no other way. Not for me. *(Pause.)* Lord, Robichaux. John could never figure me out. I'd carve him seven ways to the four winds. Low-down. I'd put muscle behind everything I blew. *(Pause.)* Sometimes I didn't know what I wanted to play because it hadn't been thought of. Not before I played it. I just played. I had to. It was like a pound of maggot-meat inside my head. Notes. And more notes. They were always coming. Growing. Getting fatter. Making more and more sense. Making no sense. Notes no one ever blew before. Like lice on a red rose. *(Pause.)* I'd make that cornet shout. Yessiree. Those street hawkers in the French Market—I talked their talk. Hawkers up and down Rampart, up and down Conti. Hawkers singing old rags, bottles, and bones. I blew those cries. I could blow a whore's moan. I could blow a good woman's moan. I blew for Hattie. I blew what I knew and what I didn't. I'd blow "The House Got Ready" four ways to the wind. Up and down, and all the way 'round. Anywhere. Nowhere. There. *(Pointing to his head.)* Here. Lovers. Other men's women. Back-door women who wanted a back-door man. *(Pause.)* We always ended up nowhere. Anna Bartholomen and Ella. Two good-timing two-timers. On North Liberty and Conti, selling herself for pocket change. Emma. Emma Thorton, trying to go somewhere on her looks. She lived on Josephine. That's right. I was on First, a few blocks 'round the corner. Yessiree. That's history. Last time I saw her she was performing in Lincoln Park with Remer's Vaudeville. Some kinda shuck-and-jive fuss. You know. All this helped to dethrone The King. *(Pause.)* You can go and look up Alphonse Picou and ask him. I could almost hold a note half the night. I'd squeeze it out till it was a drop of blood in my brain. Women would holler. They'd roll their hips like a Model-T Ford. Night wave. Blue and black. My sound reached the water and traveled Uptown. Everybody came to hear me. That's right. I played low-down blues. I blew what I lived and saw. What I hadn't seen or dreamt, I still blew it. *(Pause.)* Was that silver cornet my punishment? Was I doomed when I first raised it to my lips? Huh? Was I, doctor—Mister Sebe? *(Pause.)* Doctor, I had me some women. Good and bad. They fought to carry my horn, but I'd just hand them my coat and hat. Yeah, they did. Sure did. *(Falsetto.)* Let me have his horn. No, no, no. I wanta carry Buddy's cornet. No, I got his piece. *(Normal voice.)* Ha! I carried my own goddamn horn. Nobody touched my horn! *(Pause.)* I loved only three women. Only three in my whole life. Only three. Cora—my sister. Alice—my mama. And Hattie—my heart. *(Pause.)* I hate Buddy Bolden. I hate his no-good guts! *(He slaps himself across the face. He freezes.)* Okay. Okay, Mister Sebe, I won't do that anymore. I promise. *(Crossing his heart.)* I cross my heart and I hope to die. I promise. But sometimes a man comes to hate himself. You know. Don't you, Mister Sebe, you know, right? *(Pause.)* My sister and my mama drove Hattie and me apart. Hattie's gone. Long gone. My son's gone also. They could be in hell for all I know. *(Pause.)* Now, Hattie, she was a sweet woman. Stole my heart and I never got it back. I was never all here *(pointing to his head)* after we broke up. Nora, my second wife, my girl's mama, she was another story. She never could fit into Hattie's shoes. And she always knew, too. *(Pause.)* Berenedine, my girl, lost too. Loss? How can you measure loss, doctor? *(Pause.)* Come here. Come on, doctor. Look into my eyes. *(Buddy leans forward, and then pulls back.)* That's right. All I could do was blow my brains out—my silver horn. I polished it like a woman's leg. *(Pause.)* Devil's music? No sir. I know. The devil's music could never be so bittersweet. I played day and night. Night and day. Sunny and rainy. Uptown and downtown. But I never played no devil's music anywhere anytime. Not me. Horn shiny as a woman's leg. I blew wide open. Up-tempo. That scream lodged in the back of the throat, it had to get out somehow. But still sweet and easy. Honky-tonk my foot. I had an ear. Could read too. Go and ask Louis and Willie Cornish, if you don't believe me. Ask Red. Ask Cornelius Tillman. Ask Zue. Ask Ray Lopez. And Brock. Ask Henry Zeno. Ask God knows who. Ask 'em all. And don't forget to ask 'em how sweet I blew on that cylinder we cut. *(Pause.)* Sometimes a man can be broken by what his mouth won't say, right? What the horn told me to blow. I've forgotten. Eyes behind these eyes you look into and see nothing. World inside my head. Someplace the women could never get to. Not but one. That Hattie. Lord, Lord.

(Points to his head.) This door was even closed off to mama and Cora. It was no place at all. No room. Nora, I think, felt it. Somewhere. Somehow. Scared her to death. *(Pause.)* Hattie cried when we made love. She'd just cry. Make love and cry. Not moan, mind you. Really shed tears. I tried to play that cry. Over and over, I tried. That sound. Sometimes after we made love I'd play for her. Just for Hattie—so soft I could hardly hear myself blowing. She'd be crying and I'd be playing. Notes. Terminals inside a lock. Doors to unlock. Doors inside the head. Doors. Flesh doors and wooden doors. *(Pause.)* I craved a new skin to crawl into. My color was wrong. I was wrong. All my friends were wrong. The music we played was wrong. The woman I loved was wrong. We were all wrong. Born wrong. *(Pause.)* Now I touch things. I walk in circles and touch things. In straight lines and touch things. Love to handle things. Things don't talk back. Can't. They just are. They can't talk back, can they, doctor. Mister Sebe? *(Pause.)* I got scared of the horn. It didn't have in it what my mind wanted to make it do. It betrayed me. It did. I just couldn't make the sound I had in my head. It hurt like hell. Awful. I felt the sound it couldn't make. Didn't make. Do you understand? Do you really? How can you understand, when I don't? *(Pause.)* Clem was in my place that night. Frankie Dusen said, "We don't need you no more, Buddy." I just fell into pieces. Frankie, of all people: he had listened to me like a mockingbird. But did I stand there and poor-mouth? Did I beg? Did I crawl? No, I didn't. I just walked out. Grabbed myself up into an empty bag and walked out. Yessiree, I did. Sometimes you have to holler. Nobody hollered King Bolden. Not a soul. Not a living goddamn soul. *(Pause.)* If someone had, I don't know what I would've done. *(Half-singing, half-talking.)* "Make me a pallet on the floor, make me a pallet on the floor, make it soft, make it low, so your sweet man will never know." Goofer dust? Never know. Whiskey? Never know. Women? Maybe so. *(Bolden raises his horn to his lips, blowing a note or two.)* I don't care if you call Big Bradford in here, Mister Sebe. I just don't care. I don't care about the white jacket or Big Bradford. *(Bolden shakes his head. He reluctantly lets the cornet fall to the floor, turning on his heels and walking back toward the window. The attendant walks on stage and picks up the cornet and walks off stage. Bolden never notices Bradham; he continues talking.)* I was blowing. The sun was setting. Blowing. Setting. Setting and blowing. I was blowing and it had almost set. Now it's stopped. I was making the sun set,

Doctor. Setting in the east. In the west. Nowhere to set. The sun was going home. I was blowing and the sun was taking me home. *(The curtain starts to close slowly. Bolden continues talking.)* Now it's gone. Home to Jesus. No sun. No sun in here. Gone. Long gone. I was blowing. Blowing. The sun was setting. I was going home. *(A very distant-sounding cornet plays "Get Out of Here and Go on Home" very softly and otherworldly for about thirty seconds. Then there's one loud blast on the cornet. Abrupt silence.)*

20

Miss Brown to You

Ellen Jordis Lewis

You knew the end of the breath was coming but you didn't know when. That note, the one that blew at you with a warm subway rush, the melting, heavy sigh of promise and regret. The one I heard in dreams when I was Sleepytime Gal and on nights when I couldn't admit I was tired and he played Trouble in Mind. That note said when it was through, I'd have to remember American History, my blue notebook, and all the other homework I hadn't done. I wanted it to last forever.

✳

My mother, whose chicken legs I got, would have cut a rug all night.

✳

To the audience before the first set, Stomp said "Well, alright." He'd start hammering with the foot. He closed his eyes and blew hard. Then when the band got going, they'd all raise their horns like elephants making a salute to the elephant god. They always did that at the best parts. Feet going, cheeks blowing, horns waving, you couldn't help but look up and pray.

The photos on the wall, from 1920, 1930, all the way up to now, showed that salute, the drummer and bass player with a look on their faces like someone had just told a dirty joke. There were women with dark lips smiling, and smoke everywhere. Everyone in those pictures was famous, because someone would pull me over to say, "See him? That's Sidney Bechet. I played with him."

Stomp installed me at one of the rickety wood tables in the back, with an open tab on Shirley Temples. He sometimes looked over to make sure my head was down, doing homework. When he introduced a song, he said a little history about it, and then sometimes segued into, "Speaking of history, I think Miss Brown over there happens to know some. What did you learn today, Miss Brown?" And I had to tell something about Suffragettes or the American Revolution. I supposed the same thing was happening at dinner tables all around the country.

*

She sang to me, no matter what she was saying. "What do you think we're having tonight, Miss Brown?"

"Black-eyed peas?"

"Hm. Black-eyed peas need forks to be eaten, and I don't see forks on that table."

"Hooray for black-eyed peas," I'd say, going for the cutlery drawer.

"They need forks and we need forks." She'd slide past me on linoleum, her little Totes slippers whispering along like Herbie's drums when he took the brushes to them. I called out "Zanzibar Shuffle" when I was still in diapers, apparently; if Stomp ever called her anything else, I can't remember.

She would see me off to the school bus. Stomp would yawn and start his day sometime while I was gone, and when I opened the door at dinnertime, they'd both be there, like it was me coming home from work to my kids. There'd be a record going or the tape machine playing some old jams. They liked it loud. Sometimes the door would already be open and they'd be dancing, not embarrassed at all that their music was dancing its own way down the hallway to the other apartments.

She chopped carrots at the dining room table while I did my homework. She said, "Make sure your father remarries."

When she died, I revised the promise and made a pact with her ghost: He wouldn't have to remarry. I'd never leave Stomp, no matter what. He'd always be able to count on me. Lovable, huggable Evelyn Brown. Miss Brown to you.

*

After the gig, George, the piano player, hauled me up on his lap. He said, "My dear, we've got to stop meeting this way."

"Tickle the ivories, tickle the ivories," I cooed. Then he was all over my ribs so I couldn't stand it, and I squealed and squirmed down to the floor.

"Ah!" His hands shot out and I ran around the table to Herbie, the drummer.

"Show me your long division," he said. I got my notebook and we went through it line by line, with a drumstick showing our place. I explained it to Herbie and how I got what I did, and he nodded, and said "uhm hmm," never once contradicting me.

They drank smoky, dark liquor in tumblers. It made them get sad and happy all at once. They'd talk about dead guys and the funny things the dead guys used to do, like swim the Seine in Paris in the middle of the night or bringing the whole band except the piano to practice in graveyards after getting evicted for all that noise.

During our long walk up Fifth Avenue, we waved and nodded to doormen who, at four in the morning, welcomed us like royalty. The whole wide street seemed to be only for us. Mica in the pavement glittered in the lamplight. I skipped along, playing soccer with the stones, not stepping on a single crack. It was magical and quiet, broken only once in a while when the air was cleaved by a lone euphoric taxi soaring to points downtown. Darkness in the park called to us across the street, beyond the avenue's width of asphalt that protected us from total wildness. By the time we got to 110th street, I was stumbling like a drunk.

*

In the middle of the night I woke up and went to the kitchen. Stomp was sitting at the table, a tumbler set on the red checked cloth. "Miss Brown, did you know I could find the beat in her arguing? Bum buh buh bum bum buh bum . . ." He hit the table. "You goddamn deadbeat liar! She rhymed when she was angry too, yes, she did. And she had no idea. It took the life out of me to keep from smiling. But couldn't stay angry at her when she was giving me so much music."

*

"You slept through it." Humiliated at the parent-teacher conference.

"They'll live." He tapped his hand on the kitchen table. "Plus, I got an A student here. They don't need to talk to me."

"They were wondering where you were. I was sitting there and they had to call and hear your bleary old voice."

"They probably gave your time to some problem kids who need it."

"What about the problem parents?"

"Oh, Miss Brown." He tried to hug me and I tore away.

"You don't care. I don't have a future in anything except sitting in bars."

"Come here. We'll figure it out."

"You don't care. You couldn't even come to school to find out." I ran to the door. My hand was on the knob. I was wearing flip flops, Bugs Bunny pajama bottoms and a t-shirt with Max Roach on it. There was no way I could go out looking like this.

"You go do what you need to do."

Great. Any other father would have a fit if his daughter threatened to go out in this neighborhood at night, outfit aside. Not mine. Go right ahead, honey, don't let the door slam behind you. I grabbed a fistful of change from the bowl and slammed the door.

60 blocks later, I saw Herbie leaning against the building. "You need a smoke?" he asked.

Grateful for the opportunity, I said no.

He motioned to the stoop, and we sat. Women with glittering dresses laughed by, clutching their men. I noticed their feet—perfectly clean toes painted red, bound by translucent nylon.

"Marge got me when we were playing together on the Mississippi Princess. See, you can't go anywhere else when you're on a boat." He took a drag and let it out in a long stream. "She had me trapped, and she knew it. So she didn't do anything, see? She ignored me. She made me go to her." He looked at me. "She also taught me about arguing. You have a difference with someone you love, you got to go away. But then you come back, see? It's true, you leave, but you need to come back before too long."

I nodded.

"Just like I got to go back in there." He motioned toward the club door. "You have bus money?"

"Yeah." I had the money I was going to go in there and get drunk with. I might as well use it for bus fare home. Go home and clean my toes.

*

I can't remember what happened first, but George stopped grabbing me around the waist and I started listening to The Who. I would go over to my friend Suzi's house and I would try to get her brothers to talk to me. We went to Suzi's room and listened to records. We turned the volume up and sang along. We shaved our legs, turned orange with self tanner, and wrecked our hair with permanents.

Stomp and I started having the same things for dinner: spaghetti, frozen trays. Mornings, the evidence was still there.

He was at the kitchen table with a tumbler one night when I opened the door, swinging a jacket that belonged to a boy that I'd met too early in life to appreciate, and he said the problem with hope was memory. "You want to keep your hopes one step ahead of your memories. You want to keep the good days happening tomorrow. But the time comes when you have more memories."

*

The smoke enveloped me like arms. Welcome home from college, it said. The clarinet riffs stroked my hair. Herbie's drumbeats kissed my cheek. How long had it been? No time at all, seemed like. Tumblers half-filled with sweet brown liquor, swizzle stick, and a cherry sat in their places on the old tables. The photos on the wall were brown and happy. A little more faded, maybe. And the guys onstage were still playing like the men and ladies in the photos were real, right there in front of them.

I took one of the empty tables in the back, and Stomp put his foot down harder when he saw me. He was smiling as he blew, and I waited for the elephant salute. George had just started a solo, and the crowd was rapt. His hands scampered over the keys like bad children; it looked like he was hunched over them to keep them from getting away.

Then I noticed something was missing. None of the musicians had feet. Not George, not Herbie, not the trumpet player, not Stomp. The feet were gone, but you could still hear them laying the beat. The crowd cheered at the end of George's solo, and seemed not to notice the musicians seemed to be floating. Was this some sort of magician's trick they were doing, some sort of sad way to lure a crowd? Maybe it was a joke. They launched into "After You've Gone" and became clear—transparent—straight through up to their knees. Stomp hadn't told me about this new act. Mirrors, maybe.

They were invisible up to their shoulders when the salute came for the finale. Up, up went the horns, and blew straight at me with a sound I'll never forget. I looked up at the gleam flashing in the lights, the instruments suspended in air, playing themselves, before they too disappeared and left an empty stage.

Some of the audience disappeared too. A few hours later, the entire club was gone, floor, chairs, walls, stage, roof, and all. They say it happened gradually, but I know that I barely escaped.

21

Rossonian Days

William Henry Lewis

for Ernest Holliman, Earl McAdams, who carried the old way, and Nathanael Fareed Mahluli, who brings the new.

You hearing, but you ain't listening.

MY NANA, DOROTHY HOLLIMAN

The memory of things gone is important to the jazz musician.
Things like the old folks singing in the moonlight
in the backyard on a hot night . . .

DUKE ELLINGTON

Listen. This happens for just a moment. The car is headed north, to Denver. That's where the gig is. The band is from Kansas City. West by south, through Pueblo, and every dirty-snow mile of Route 87, stretching north by west. This kind of traveling never takes the short way. More road than anybody wants. Not much else to see. The fields will be gray for months. Land slips from the road, rolls in swells of rye and hay across the plain to the Front Range.

The car is long and the wheels are wide. Front grille stout like America itself. The car is a Lincoln, rides like horsehair across bass strings.

No curves to this car, only rounded right angles—suggestion of flair, but nothing is small time here.

No two-tone paint job. All black. Six coats of pure gloss. Shine for days. Tinted glass. Chrome nothing more than nuance. More power switches than anybody will ever use: EZ drive *power* steering. *Power* windows. *Power* locks. *Power* antenna. *Power* seats. What don't got *power,* the car don't *need.* The whole deal—chrome trim sidewalls to suicide doors—holds more class than most will get from getting in. You don't drive it. *Ride* it. The Lincoln Continental four-door convertible: chariot for the *re*birth of the cool.

Inside, everybody's got room without anybody's last nerve being worked over. The bass is strapped to the roof; horns and drums packed like china; clothes for tonight rest on instrument cases. The worries ride up front, steaming the windows.

> *Call back to memories less rich but more grand, like Milt Hinton snapshots that didn't make print: Ellington, asleep in a cashmere topcoat, fedora brim angled across the bridge of his nose, head at rest on Strayhorn's shoulder. Missouri is outside. They glide through the dusk of the Midwest, "Lush Life" drifting on AM, night coming on.*
>
> *In another image—maybe Ohio this time—Duke at work, writing in the small spot of a car lamp. Harry Carney sawing logs, shoulder to Duke's shoulder. Too many road gigs were cats filling a car like the last boxcar headed north: Sweet Pea, Monster, Snooky, all the rest, blessings on the stand, but all the same, smelly-sock brothers filling space where, if the Duke is on, a Black-and-Tan Fantasy is always birthing. Not all of his rides smooth, but you know the elders always wander the hard way first.*
>
> *Call back to days of try. Edward Kennedy Ellington: Duke before there was Wayne, regent of a tight backseat, sounds making themselves on pages under dim light, no hambone room. Outside, it was always night, dark in the heartland, where brothers wasn't safe after dark. You ain't been blue 'til you had that Mood Indigo. Ride a million miles through Columbus, Des Moines, Peoria, Tulsa, Vidor, Lincoln, just to enter the Cotton Club through the front door. . . . Hambone, hambone, where you been?*

Somebody before now played this road—someone heard by some or maybe never whispered—so drive this Lincoln like holding the family photographs, and when it rolls in, brother, stride right.

It is some time after the turn of the year: say it's 1965 or a year later, maybe years earlier. There's no stick to this moment, but it will echo. Don't need a year to know this story is old. The trip has been made by many: like making good time in a '31 Hudson from Baton Rouge to Chitown. Been in moments like this, riding with hay discs strapped to the slatboards of a flatbed International Harvester bound for Macon. Been up to and down from Ft. Worth for a summer of Saturday nights. Skylark was the ride in those days. Chickory, pork chops, grits, a skillet of cornbread cooling in the pantry every morning. In and out of icehouses of all sorts, sometimes even those for *Whites Only*. Been asked back to and booed out of every juke joint on the Chitlin Circuit, southern route that splits the cats who are *down* from those who ain't, and *if you miss the A train, you have missed the quickest way to Harlem.*

No matter the year, it is winter. The plains are a hard, gray-brown bed nobody wants; there is the long road following the Front Range of the Rockies. For long breaths the road is lost in angry wind and tired snow, and the only thing that keeps the car on track is the tenor player at the wheel, working through Moody's "Tin Tin Deo," Afro-Latino jam, up from beneath the underdog's fatback jawbone. A downbeat thick like adobo sauce to go with that *arroz con pollo;* the band chanting . . . *oh, tin tin deo* . . . and now the conga is in it . . . *oh, tin tin deo* . . . cowbell, crisp like momma's catfish . . . *oh, tin tin deo, oh, tin tin deo* . . . a four-four swing gone East Harlem *bebop,* the rhythm something you know, but the rattle is new: stick on a can, good groove under the Lexington Avenue local, 104th Street.

Long after the tune leaves his humming, the tenor thinks he still hears it . . . *oh, tin tin deo* . . . on his last breath, from the backseat, deep in somebody's chest or fifty miles back. Wind keeps rhythm. White sky stained gray like old bone. The fields empty. More snow coming. Bourbon is passed from backseat to front, and somebody says if there's a God out in all of that, he best be blowin' for us. Then all is quiet.

Not much to say once you hear the call. A body has been waiting a long time for that call, through the passage of centuries, through all the rent-party nights and ten-cent coffee hours. Time was when days were three shifts: Some of one spent sleeping and practicing, most of two spent working or looking for work. Word spreads down the Santa Fe line, an ad cut from the *Kansas City Call,* letter from a cousin in Pueblo, an auntie in the parlor with the phone pressed to the radio: a "jazz-endorsed" P.S.A. from W-VBA, the disc jockey calling out from far away, late night, low and steady, like a talking drum across the bend of the savannah's horizon:

> *Are there any musicians left out there? Here's this from the Rossonian Auditorium, Denver's best kept secret: Management would like to remind you there's always a stage for great talent at the Rossonian. Maybe you have got a talent that we would want to showcase. Perhaps you're the next swinging sensation, ready to strike it big back East. Go East, young man, but swing in the West! Give us a call—Albion six eight six seven—tell us your name and address and let us know what your talent is: horn, piano, vocals? Have you got a band? Call soon, Albion six eight six seven, or write us, Management, The Rossonian Auditorium, two six four zero Welton, Denver, Colorado. Tell us what you can do . . .*

Many places are right for moments like this, but the moments are fewer than the places. Where it's at is now: the band, the car, the road, and where all three will stop. Kansas City is gone for now. The gig is at The Rossonian. In Denver. On Five Points. Where Welton meets Washington. Come night, the people are there, roasting ribs and frying catfish, domino games in front rooms, Cadillacs angled to the curbs like Chris-Crafts. Five Points, where it has been and is. It's not Beale Street or 18th and Vine, but it wants to be.

The Saturday-night local headliner is bound to pack it tighter than the mickeys allow anyplace else. Nobody has a care, except for showing up and showing out their hard-earned, store-bought clothes, ones that won't do Sunday morning, but do it right on Saturday night. Can't roll up to *that* scene in some small-money ride. Nobody will take the scene for serious. These days, cats are pulling out their best jive; everybody who's nobody is hustlin'. *Everybody can blow a horn, son, but what can you do?* So drive the Points in the soft-top Lincoln Continental *convertible,* shag top shiny in a stingy man's winter. Drive up in some sorry vehicle, that's what folks remember.

They remember Andy Kirk and Mary Lou Williams—*when you hear the saxes ride, what's the thing that makes them glide? It's the lady who swings the band!* Basie and Jimmy Rushing. They remember Charlie Parker. But Bird didn't need no car to break out of K.C. Mary and Andy floated in style through the West with the Twelve Clouds of Joy. And Elders are quick to say *ain't nobody worth a damn come out of Missouri since the thirties . . .*

But it is 1960, give or take some years back or forward, and the arrangement of players doesn't matter—a piano man, tenor and trumpet players, drums, double-bass man, maybe a trombone, maybe a singer—no one knows their names.

> *It doesn't matter, but everything matters: Bebop has died, Straight-Ahead Jazz is dying. The small traveling band ain't long for this road. Long-playing records play the hits—what's popular spinning on records for less than any five-piece group driving state to state. They not gonna like you out west because you Sonny Rollins, son, they gonna like you 'cause they heard your record was on the tops of the Billboard and Down Beat lists. Or maybe you got an angle: Dave Brubeck and Chet Baker blowin' Blues like the brothers, but their Blues ain't about paying the bills. Only a few will rise off the highways and land on wax.*

Make that no nevermind. *This* car is headed for a gig. There are highways full of these long, black cars, carrying the best jazz nobody's ever heard. To hear it *live:* another breakdown chorus, Basie swinging "April in Paris" "*one more time . . .*" a third reprise, volta, groove—call it what you want, it swings just the same—"*jus' one more, once . . .*"

Music from the marrow. At clubs a rung above juke joint; velvet-draped lounge or speakeasy; intimate auditorium, backlit in blue. No need for a name, just a love for Blues, a four-four swing tapping your toe—*hit that jive, jack, put it in your pocket til I get back.* The show: Standards spill like laughter, one into the next; the piano man is running through "Twinkle Toes"; the tenor is just sitting down; the trumpet man sips on his sour mash and picks lint from his sleeve; the drummer's got a new suit: Ivy-League cut, iridescent green rust shimmers when his brushes ease across the snare, left stick teasing the cymbal like a pastor's blessing. Late night makes early morning, the glow of early morning shows through the skylight, stars like embers through the wire glass. A third set beginning, lights low, dim footers set brown skin glowing. Folks look younger than they ever have or ever will.

> *Play on, Brother, play on, it don't matter that tomorrow is a workday or a Sunday or another sack o' woe day, play on, because right now everything is right.*

No record or radio catches that. But it's hits that are selling now, not that *better-get-it-in-your-soul* music, all its mothers and fathers sold off to new owners. It's the sixties. Just forty years gone since they lynched 617. Red Summer's strange fruit rots slowly in our gut. We get silent. We learn the ulcers we bear. Or we forget. But you know the Emmett Till Blues. Where's your singing now? Just a whistle get you dead.

> *This is a voice stowed in the Middle Passage. Call looking for Response. After the chain and yoke, there were weeks of dark quiet, the wash of seawater against the ship's bow. Inside, a song of rot breathing head to foot, row over row. This was a voice that sang Benin, Ibo, Fang, Hausa. This is a voice that learned Georgia, Louisiana, Tennessee, South Carolina, all the Dixon below Mason. This is a voice that learned cotton, tobacco, and sugarcane. This is a voice that almost unlearned itself.*
>
> *No more drums, no elders' words. They beat you if you speak out or refuse the labor. They hunt you when you run. They listen for the bell welded around your neck, smell you out with hounds when you run from the noose. Not much music in hose spray or last snap of rope, jolt of cord and spine; that razor quick like fire and fierce between the legs. No voice in that night.*

But Coltrane preaches "Alabama," so listen: People been hanging from trees; Elders gone north and west and back again; Harlem, Detroit, Chicago, burnt: northern lights when they told you only Mississippi was burning. And who sang the Oklahoma Blues? Tulsa, 1921: that fire fierce but silenced. No news carried that. That's our death, people: no story, no wire, no radio, no voice, no ear, no report, no Call and Response to know that people out here are living and dying. Nobody to sing their Blues. Nobody to hear it wail.

Listen. You got to listen: 'Trane's Blues. Four girls, baptized with bombs. Bessie Smith, a story we forgot. The ghost whistle of Emmett Till cups the street corner of every young Black man's dreams. People going broke on northern city Blues, and their voice, only thing they ever owned for sure, sold for the price of a record.

Soon enough, they don't want to hear no "Strange Fruit," Sing us "Body and Soul," Billie, they cheer. Smile and sweat through "Body and Soul" for the money thing. Soon enough, change chimes in Brothers' pants pockets as they easy step the sunny side of Lenox Avenue; Billie Holiday all but gone, another echo in the alley.

The road and the soundless miles are for the singers and players, heard and unheard. They all want the voice; they travel. Once they've heard the voice it will never leave them alone. They travel. Most will never hear it, but they travel. This is the road jazz folk play. Have played. Been playing. Been played by. Will play for.

I let a song go out of my heart
It was the sweetest melody
I know I lost heaven,
'cause you were the song

Before King's English. Before written word, there was story, in song and wail, drumbeat, hambone, and sandshoe, the hot breath of mothers birthing field-to-factory generations. Thick and light, the sound moved as the people did, on to East St. Louis, on to South Detroit and Cleveland, to Chi-town, where Brothers blew that hard, Midway city, get-ol'-man-Hawk-out-my-draws bop.

On north and east, to Philly, and of course the City, the Village, 52nd Street, and 125th Street, Harlem, Mecca at Lenox Ave, nothing small in Smalls' Paradise, where anybody on the move was moving. On out westward: Austin, Lincoln, Denver, K.C.—all the gigs before, in between, and after—all the way out to the Pacific, that high-tone, low-key, California-here-we-come land of give up the gravy.

Just one night, one good jam in Denver—tear up the Rossonian—and the skate to the West Coast was smooth.

After that, return to the South slow and easy, like nobody's ancestors ever left it. A stroll on Beale. Cakewalk down Rampart.

After that, leave it, freer than any freedom train headed north.
After that, to The City. The road will lead to The City.
After that, only Ancestors and Elders know . . .

Some kind of way, the trip will be made. There are so many cities, all too far from Kansas City, but the trip will be made. Phone rings, the gig is on. Denver. The Rossonian. Down in Five Points. The Rossonian: two sets, one night, a hundred heads, five-spot to get in, two drinks to stay, a quarter take of the door. Fill the place—management is happy, band is happy, and like that, the Rudy Van Gelder is the call from Englewood Cliffs, just across the Hudson, where the studio is still buzzing from when Miles Davis's Quintet was the Word.

So the trip will be made: three days, two nights. Head out Route 24 after a half day's shift, roll past Topeka, already lit in the winter early dusk of the Plains, pass through Kandorado as the blue bowl of late night pours its last stars across the West; make Pueblo for the late set at the Blossom Heath. Two encores milk gas money for the trip—*nice work if you can get it.* Sleep off last night's drunk until just before new day's dark, then a biscuit, coffee, corn liquor, junk, or smack. Here comes Denver. The Rossonian: oasis in jazz nowhere on the way to jazz somewhere. Someday soon, stompin' at The Savoy.

And after the gig is swung, tired or no, never mind hangover, no time for a strung-out morning, the Lincoln will make fast back to Kansas City, the small low-money gigs, the stormy Monday job, the life that always expects the empty-handed return.

So the phone rings, for the bassist, the drummer, the singer, the piano man; maybe a vibraphone player—but maybe they ain't ready for the vibes out in the Mile High, not yet, and this ain't the time for testing new waters.

The phone rings for the horn players—the sax, trumpet, trombone, whichever horns, any of them are waiting for that phone to ring. Everybody wants that *taste,* like what Cannonball and Nat got on the grill out in California. Monk fixing on which suit coat to wear—dark or light—while the car is running and the photographer is waiting. Ain't we all been waiting for *that* phone to ring? Cannonball Adderley filling seats like it was summer Bible school. Mercy, mercy, mercy. Dizzy blowing that horn easy as waxing the Cadillac: L.A. smooth, beret, goatee, horn-rims, and herringbone. Ivy-League cut suit, fresh bed, dry martini, *salt peanuts, salt peanuts.*

> *Go get some. Don't bring no soft sound. There are few chances, one or two big moments. Many misses. The young cats, they got good at hitting the target, notes all dressed up and in line, so on top of technique, the soul got blowed out. They miss. Those Brothers will rattle some walls with a few records, but come five years, those cats are quiet, waiting on that phone. They missed.*
>
> *The phone didn't have to ring for Satchmo, who never missed. Not Charlie, who was blessed with more jam than he could jive. Not Bessie, who was hit enough to bring it back black and blue—beautiful like that until she couldn't bring no more. Not Prez or Johnnie, who didn't know what slow was. Not Billie, who didn't know what "no" was and gave her soul to encores and needles. Not Ella, who never knew an off note. Not Milt, who gave "Bags' Groove" to the grooveless. Not Chet, who gave to music and no one else. Not Nina, who got more sugar in her bowl, her well-deep voice the middle of whatever best and worst day anybody ever lived through. Not even Clifford, who lived through one car wreck only to be taken in another before he was twenty-seven. Not even thirty yet, and he needed no phone to ring. He already swung with strings, just like Charlie Parker.*

The phone rings for the rooftop and boiler-room players. The brother running scales on his lunch hour. Down by the river-side. With mute when it's late. A bus-ride hum. Not yet twenty, but a lifetime waiting on that phone. Sometimes it rings. They pick it up. They say yes. They travel.

The bag is packed, shirt's been pressed for weeks, instrument oiled, shoes shined—chamois across alligator pumps, matchstick to clean each wingtip hole. The savings is cracked—quarters and singles from days of pinching for days of playing. The landlord is dodged. Never mind the bills. The bossman is conned: *. . . you see, I just gotta see my Auntie Berthene, up over in Denver, else she likely to up and die fore this time next week.*

And somebody will always be left behind. A woman, a man, maybe large-eyed children, but somebody's left on the porch, in the day's first light. They wonder what makes *this* time the time when it's the *Big Time*?

What makes it different from the last Big Time? St. Louis: gone for three days. Or Memphis: gone for a week and come back with half the world dragged out in between. Somebody will be left. Somebody is always left. But nobody will remember after the record deal is signed and the reel-to-reel is playing back "If I Were a Bell," take two. Gin gimlets all around. Someone will tell the story about Ben Webster trying out the tenor when the piano had no luck in it for him. *In a mellow tone* from that day on. It will feel like that; your story will be told down the ages. When that new sound comes, everyone will know the name on the album—bookings sticking at Birdland, Leonard Feather calling for a *Down Beat* feature—and nobody will never, ever be left alone again. Whoever it is that's left behind, that's the promise left on their lips as night air makes their embrace stiff.

Inside the Lincoln it's quiet cool. Nobody looks at anyone else. Snows still coming. The sax player drives the car quietly now, changes and progressions silent secrets to an inner hum of his head. The drummer is almost asleep, slumped against the passenger window as he syncopates finger taps between the hushed beats of passing fenceposts. The trumpet player works a soft-scat to the high C he's never hit. The piano man has blank paper at the ready. The singer low-moans spirituals that got her through the ten-hour days of working somebody else's clothes against a washboard. *Joshua fit the battle of Jericho, Jericho, Jericho . . .*

The bassist rubs a matchstick, pushing it to spark, pulling back before the rasp springs to fire. The car is full with the quiet of knowing. Some kind of way, they know some sound is going to roll up the highway and reclaim the song-breath of Blackfolk.

Each looks from the car, feeling like the voice isn't in the horn, or the hands, or the head, but lost somewhere out in this land and sky, way out west, vaulting farther than the road will go. Listen out there for the Call, dropped by some ancestor rushing west or north, when making music first felt like some step-and-fetch shuffle. Mommas wait years for a voice like this. Some fathers leave home looking for it and never come back.

> *This voice something like some thing drifting in the summer air of childhood days, caught and lost in sun-glare. It's wind lingering in the branches of the boabab just before rain covers the savannah. An Elder whispering. A mother's sigh carried on the wind, the rasp of*

> *callused hands across burlap bags when the cotton is high. It's Biloxi crickets, never seen but heard, in want of wet and hot, loud for days even in winter, through the cold, hard bright of day, out here, on the winter-bare spine of the Rockies—miles of dry and nothing—where crickets echo only in imagining.*

The tight air waits for any sound, and when the bass player strikes his match, everyone is startled. Wait for it: brass stopper and snare skin, bass string strained, sevenths and discordant ninths sustained on the high registers of the ivories. *I let a song go out of my heart.* Nothing is captured: not time, rushing past the Lincoln, come and gone, down the road fast, like it's the car—not the passing of seconds or minutes—pushing the hours; not this vast rusted-out bowl of land spilling from the Rockies; not the wail of prairie birdsong, ringing like something forgotten, impossible in March, not here, not now, not this road.

> *I let a song go out of my heart*
> *Believe me, darlin', when I say*
> *I won't know sweet music,*
> *until you return someday*

The music of open air is waiting. The Blues has done its sliding, the Bebop's been straight and never narrow, and still here's that yearning, like the songs were so many grapes to be plucked and rolled around in the mouth. Driving from gig to gig, all fixed life loses itself for want of that fresh new groove. Everyone wants the sound we haven't heard yet. Since we were children we wanted that song to fit in somewhere between the first jumble of quarter note and half rest and the last few miles before the gig; measure after measure of notes. And that sound is taunting, take me in.

> *. . . child, take me in, roll me in your mouth, under your hands; pull me from blank space and empty air and make me beautiful: love me. Begin the Beguine. I am a Love Supreme. I am the song you've always wanted, so love me.*

It is hours before the Rossonian. Night has already covered Missouri. The wind and snow are dropping off, and it's near dusk in Colorado. Sun so low it lies sideways into the frost on the windows. The Rockies are all but gone, last light like a bright wick on Pikes Peak.

The Pueblo gig has been swung, is now only another last night, and this is the hour when all feels still; air cups the cold without wind, martins roost on the powerlines, and that long road from Kansas City is lost in the swirl of snow wake. All that road going, long and hard, not because the distance is great or the time is slow, but because the trip is not new.

There is no company but the crackle of prairie air across radio waves and a worry of what Denver holds in store: an old town, maybe a new night; fresh start, worn body; maybe a different crowd. The same women in different dresses, the men in their one good suit. Another night of promises never spoken. To the body: *Please, no more, no more up and down the road and in and out of the Blues.* To the people: *Tonight, on this one night, we truly are glad to be here.* To whoever was left last night: *You know I'm working all this for you, baby.* To the nameless body at the end of this night: *You know I'm working all this for you, baby.* To the bottle: *You know I'm working all this for you.* To the smack, the junk, the horse, the krik-krak monkey, five-and-dime-sho'-nuff-right-on-time-feeling, *you know I'm working all this for you.* The horn, the strings, to the drums, those piano keys, and the run that's coming tonight, its gonna be tonight, it's *gotta* be tonight, because it needed to be tonight for the past five years, *you know I'm working all this for you.*

It takes the heart all day to find its beat for the big night. Soon as the gear is packed out of the Colorado Springs Club—even though there's a night to be had in the Springs—the hands start twitching with want for the next night. Where's that song? Waiting on a song to come: For all of the sound in the world, Colorado Springs the night before the Rossonian is a world of too much quiet. Soon it will be provin' time. Hands, be still.

Heart, be loud.

Denver will rise out of the plain. The road will soon pull the band down Colorado Boulevard, past homes where maids and yardmen work toward tonight. *Begin the Beguine.*

The streets will rush toward Five Points, a turn into the alley, the rise of stairs to stagedoor from the cobblestones. An open door and a taste of Rossonian air. Breathe once, let out the long road coming. Wait a moment. No breathing, in or out. The quiet room. Step to the empty stand.

Imagine walls lit from the floor. Imagine arched alcoves vaulting into a dome the color of any night full of lovers. Night in Tunisia.

Imagine calls of the ancients, taking their rest above the balcony. Hear the drums, the voices. Somewhere voices call across grasslands. Imagine a room with doors all directions, not just north. Now inhale, take in the thick, dark air of from here to who knows what's next.

In one of those long-mile hours they wondered, *Why this long trip? Why have we gone all this way to have so little?* We have come this far, through many beginnings and endings, and rebirths, to this: No more to show than we had before we began. We been down this road, but what of this long life and no voice?

We "wonder as we wander," and maybe we make it big at the end of this moment we've been driving to. If we don't make it, we'll steal away until we do, and if we do, we'll be playing for the money and the name, but someday, somewhere down this road, or the road to L.A. or the road to New York, somebody's going to say, boy, you got to use the back door; boy, smile that big-lip grin for the camera; boy, you real lucky to get even ten percent of the take at the door . . .

Then we remember why the Call and Response die a bit each day. When that happens, will we look out to the flat, barren horizon, still voiceless like now, still driving to that next chance, and cry, what craziness brought us here?

But anybody who's played up and down these roads will tell you that something touched them sent them flowing, somebody spoke to them, dipped them in Call and Response.

It could have been Basie, or Big Joe Turner, shouting the Blues down Vine Street, "Kansas City Blues" swung in a low key, "Black-and-Tan Fantasy," or havin' it bad and that ain't being good, but it didn't have to be. The sound that says *play me* came before mouth to mouthpiece or stick to high hat.

It was Momma singing "Get Away Jordan" in the backyard or it was a frontroom evening full of her momma's stories.

It was Daddy's comin-home whistle and Sunday-stroll scrape of wingtips on porch steps.

It was the late-night laughter of an uncle back home from Up South, on the road, looking for one night's meal and one good year of work.

It was a grade-school teacher, short on smiles, long on the blackboard screech and scratch sharp through the chalk haze and radiator knock.

It was the wind-heavy sigh before summer storms.

The early-evening call of the Icee man in mid-July, a joyful echo gone too soon after childhood.

A reverend at an all-Sunday service full of Tennessee heat. Every spiritual almost forgotten. Every low bellow. Each high wail of every Elder come and gone. It was somebody testifyin'. Like a whole tentful of folks bearing witness in the middle of some South Carolina field.

Getting ready to take the stand, one of these musicians will tingle with a remembrance of childhood and fantasy afternoons. And of long Sundays. The Rossonian audience will remember Sundays, too. Right then, before the blowing begins, something mighty spiritual will happen. *Come Sunday.* Whether it's song or sermon, or both being the same, the people will come from the offices, the factories, the markets, and the fields, where song and sermon were born. All will remember how that reverend had it together: everybody's story in one Sunday afternoon.

And that remembrance feels like taking the stand.

It will be hot like the August of '23; only Elders speak of that. The congregation has waited all day for the sermon. Men's Sunday-white collars ringed with sweat; talcum the women dusted above their bosoms gone in that first hour, when the organist broke into "Old Landmark."

Children have dozed, stirred, and fallen off again to the heat of high summer. Tithe plate's been passed around enough so that everybody's given, even the one deacon who's passed more plates than he ever helped fill. The choir's turned itself out, rising from "In the Upper Room" to "He Saved My Soul," and now, after the sun has pushed its dust-heavy beams from the back of the church to the front, they are tired. Everybody's tired. Been tired since before last Sunday. Since before the church was built, burnt, and rebuilt. Before runaway prayer meetings. Before men came with Bible and whip. Been tired.

The Rossonian audience will be waiting. The band will soon be giving in to that next moment of happening. It's like that for the reverend, too, and as he steps to the stand, afternoon sun angles through the transoms, shafts of light burning on his lectern like a signal fire. He walks with the step of wise griot women. His brow is furrowed, his blood is quick. He smiles at young ones and nods to the Elders, and then starts in with *my brothers and sisters, we come too far to stop singin now . . .*

This is when stories mix: traveling band from far away taking the stand, hard-working people stepping out to be graced with music, and the air of that room many times graced itself. This could be Zion Baptist or Minton's, back in Kansas City. There's something to be heard. The Word will be played. This is the language many know but few can speak.

. . . a Love Supreme, a Love Supreme, a Love Supreme, a Love Supreme, a Love Supreme, a Love Supreme, a Love Supreme, a Love Supreme, a Love Supreme . . .

Soon it will be time for you to take the stand. Time's come to blow, that's the real time, when the lights lose their glare, faces in the crowd spring from smoke-dark into the footlights; the band is in the groove, *sho' nuff,* but they sound mono while the jam that's buzzing in your head is all *stereo.* Hi-fi. Good-to-the-wood, down-to-the-wax groove. And you heard it from way off, like back into the bridge of the second song in the first set, when "Cherokee" was busted out like anybody who's somebody from Kansas City would swing it.

From way off, you wanted that groove, you heard the jam coming, like before anybody took the stand, before the Lincoln pulled to the Rossonian stage door, open like any drumming circle in a Congo square, sanctuary from all roads long and tired, from the long way north and the width of the Midwest.

By the time you feel it, the jam has been at work from way back, *music back to your momma,* when hand slap and downbeat filled southern evenings, drums or *Weary Blues* cotton-picking song, rising into the heat-faded poplar and pollen-heavy pine that divided plantations;

still farther, on the slow spine of the Blue Ridge or rippling above turtle wake in some South Carolina swamp, where many had run and few masters were greedy enough to follow. Back then and there, you might have heard drums and song drifting from the Dismal Swamp and the Big Thicket, places unlivable, but more livable than living chained with iron, with the bloody knuckle from cotton husk, with a new God and *His* words, with a hard-handed driver called silence.

To get here from there, remember the songs of Elders now gone. Take Duke's hand through the "Money Jungle." *Steal away, steal away,* follow Harriet Tubman from the swamp, from prayer meetings, from memories of tame and kalimba chime, follow Sojourner Truth on the railroad that runs only north and west, catch the train, it's Underground, it's straight ahead, the A Train, Coltrane's Blue Train, it's the only train, *follow the Drinking Gourd, follow the Drinking Gourd.*

And from there to here came the groove that fills your head. A sound that needs no reason to be, no story, no event, no particular year. Just the knowledge that somebody may be out there, just beyond where you begin to hear your song drift past hearing, out to where there's a brother or a sister in the audience, down the block, in the next state, on that next plantation plot; maybe nobody you love, but somebody who came from where your people came from, and with just an utterance there may be an answer back, like any *right-on, praise-the-lord-pass-the-peas, I-heard-that,* call-and-response, because out there, they know that yes:

> *this voice comes from somebody, and it tells the story of who I am, who my people are, day by day, and no matter joy or the Weary Blues, I will lift my sound to the evening air—across tired miles, across rivers I've known, across the sea I never knew could bring so much dark to light, across the bones of my Elders—because I know that somebody out there will hear it, nod their head, answer back, knowing the same pain, the same Middle Passage, many other passages from then to now, and can know a great many things, but need know only that this is a voice, it is blowing to the world, it is bold, it is strong, it knows no yoke, no money, no god, but knows a way. It is my language. It is the story. It pushes against the hard morning of yet another day, and it is mine. It is mine.*

22

Lush Life

John McCluskey, Jr.

Dayton, Ohio
Late September, 1955

Behind the dance hall the first of the car doors were banging shut, motors starting up, and from somewhere—a backyard, an alley—dogs barked. The band's bus was parked at one darkened corner of the parking lot. Empty, it was a mute and hulking barn at this hour. Along its side in slanted, bold-red letters was painted a sign: Earl Ferguson and America's Greatest Band.

Suddenly, the back door to the dance hall swung open and loud laughter rushed out on a thick pillow of cigarette smoke. Ahead of others, two men in suits—the taller one in plaids and the other in stripes—walked quickly, talking, smoking. They stopped at a convertible, a dark-red Buick Dynaflow, dew already sprouting across its canvas top. Other men, all members of the band, in twos or threes, would come up, slap each other's backs, share a joke or two, then drift toward the bus. In the light over the back door, moths played.

The shorter man, Billy Cox, took off his glasses, fogged the lens twice, then cleaned them with his polka-dot silk square. He reached a hand toward Tommy, the bassist, approaching.

"I'm gone say see y'all further up the road in Cleveland," Tommy said. "But after a night like tonight, it's gone be one hell of a struggle to tear ourselves from this town. Am I right about that, Billy C.?"

Tommy laughed, gold tooth showing, and patted his impeccable "do." More than once it had been said that Tommy sweated ice water. With his face dry, hair in place, tie straightened after three hours of furious work, no one could doubt it now.

Tommy spoke again, this time stern, wide-legged and gesturing grandly. "Just you two don't get high and dry off into some damn ditch." His usual farewell slid toward a cackle. Billy waved him off.

In the Scout Car, as the Dynaflow was called, Billy and Earl Ferguson would drive through the night to the next date. Throughout the night, they would stay at least an hour or so ahead of the bus. They would breakfast and be nearly asleep by the time the bus pulled into the same hotel parking lot, the men emerging, looking stunned from a fitful sleep on a noisy bus.

From a nearby car, a woman's throaty laugh lit up the night. They turned to see Pretty Horace leaning into a car, the passenger's side, smoothing down the back edges of his hair and rolling his rump as he ran his game.

"Man, stop your lying!" came her voice. She, too, was toying with the ends of her hair, dyed bright red and glowing in that light. Her friend from the driver's seat, with nothing better to do perhaps, leaned to hear, to signify, her face round as the moon's.

Moving with a pickpocket's stealth and slow grin spreading, Poo moved up to the driver's side of the car and whispered something. The driver jerked back, then gave him her best attention, smiling. One hand to her throat, she moistened her lips, glistened a smile.

In unison, Billy and Earl shook their heads while watching it all. Billy slid one hand down a lapel, pulled a cigarette from the corner of his mouth. "Some of the boys gone make a long night of this one."

Earl nodded. "Some mean mistreaters fixing to hit that bus late and do a whole lot of shucking, man."

Yes, some would dare the bus's deadline by tipping into an after-hours party, by following some smiling woman home. The rules were simple, however: if you missed the bus and could not make practice the next day, you were fined fifty dollars. If you missed the date because you missed the bus or train, you were fired. Daring these, you could seek adventure that broke the monotony of long road trips. You could bring stories that released bubbles of laughter throughout an overheated and smoke-filled bus.

Cars were rolling out of the side parking lot and, passing members of the band, the drivers honked in appreciation. Earl bowed slowly and waved an arm wide and high toward his men, some still walking out of the back door of the dance hall. Then he embraced Billy, mugged, and pointed to Billy's chest as if branding there all the credit for a magnificent night. After all, they had done Basie and Ellington to perfection. Their own original tunes had been wonders to behold. From the very beginning the audience had been with them and danced and danced, heads bobbing and shoulders rocking, cheering every solo. The dancers had fun on the stairstep of every melody; hugging tightly, they did the slow grind to the promise of every ballad. Now they thanked the band again with the toot of their horns, shouts, and the wave of their hands.

Within an hour, the bus would start up, all the equipment packed and stored below. Then it would roll slowly out of the parking lot. Some of the men would already be snoring. By the outskirts of town, a car might catch up to it, tires squealing as the car rocked to a stop. One of the men—usually McTee or "Rabbit" Ousley, as myth might have it—would climb out and blow a kiss to some grinning woman behind the wheel and strut onto the bus like some wide-legged conqueror. The doors to the bus would close behind him, sealing his stories from any verification and sealing the band against the long, long night.

But it was the Dynaflow, Earl and Billy inside, pulling away first. They would leave before these tales of triumph, outright lies about quick and furious love in a drafty backroom or tales of a young wife whispering "run! run!" and the scramble for a window after the husband's key slid into the lock downstairs. Yes, before all that Earl and Billy would pull from the parking lot and start away, slow at first, like they had all the time in the world.

Well before the edge of town, they would have checked for cigarettes, surely and from some magical place on a side street, a jukebox blaring and the smell of fried chicken meeting them at the door with its judas-hole, they would find their coffee in Mason jars, coffee heavily sugared and creamed, and steaming chicken sandwiches wrapped neatly in waxed paper. Older women, who would do double duty at Sunday church dinners, would smile and wipe their hands on their aprons. And, bless them, these good and prodigal sons with conked hair. Then, moving toward the door, Billy and Earl would be greeted by achingly beautiful women with late-night joy lacing their hoarse voices. Billy and Earl would take turns joking and pulling each other away, then, outside and laughing, climb back into the car for the journey through the night.

For the first few minutes, the lights of Dayton thinning, used car lots and a roller rink as outposts, they were silent before nervous energy swept over them. It was that unsettling bath of exhaustion and exuberance, rising to a tingle at the base of the neck, so familiar at the end of a performance. With Earl at the wheel, they began to harmonize and scat their way through "Take the A Train," "One O'clock Jump," and their own wonderful collaboration, "October Mellow." In this way they would ride for a while. They would sing in ragged breaths before they gave out in laughter. The radio might go on, and there would be mostly the crackle of static, or, faintly, a late-night gospel concert with harmonies rising and falling, like a prayer song tossed to the wind. Stray cars would rush past in the next lane, headed back toward Dayton. They passed a trailer groaning under its load, one or two squat Fords, then settled back. The night's first chapter was closed behind them with the noise from the motor, with smears of light.

Like a sudden tree in the car's lights, a sign sprouted and announced the city limits of Springfield.

Billy started nodding as if answering some ancient question. "Springfield got more fine women than they got in two St. Louises or five New Orleans, I'm here to tell you."

"Wake up, Billy. Find me a place with women finer than they got in St. Louis or New Orleans or Harlem—think I'm gone let Harlem slide?—find me such a place and you got a easy one hundred bill in your hand and I'll be in heaven. I'm talking serious now."

Billy snorted, sitting up straight and shaking his head. "I ain't hardly sleeping. Just remembering it all. See, I ain't been through here since 1952, but I can call some preacher's daughter right now—brown skin and about yeah-tall—yeah, at this very hour. Lord, she would be so fine that you and me both would run up the side of a mountain and holler like a mountain jack."

The Earl blew a smoke ring and watched its rise; maybe it would halo the rear-view mirror. "Well, okay, I'll take your word for it now, but if we're ever back through here, I definitely want to stop and see if these women are as pretty as you say."

"They pretty, they mamas pretty, they grandmamas pretty. . . . "

Earl laughed his high-pitched laugh. "You get crazier every day, Billy Cox." He pushed the accelerator, slamming them deeper into their seats.

Earl leveled off at sixty and for minutes was content to enjoy the regular beat of the wheels hitting the seams across the pavement, pa-poom, pa-poom, pa-poom. It was the next stretch of road, ten miles outside of Springfield, that they truly sensed the flatness of the place. In the darkness there were no distant hills promising contour variety, or perspective. Fields to the left? Woods to the right? They were silent for a minute or so. Crackling music flared up once again from the radio, then died.

"What do you think of the new boy's work tonight?" Billy asked.

"Who, 'Big City'? Not bad, man. Not bad at all." Earl snapped his fingers. "He's swinging more now. Matter of fact, he's driving the entire trumpet section, Big Joe included. You get the prize on that one, you brought him in. I remember you kept saying he could play the sweetest ballads, could curl up inside something like Strayhorn's 'Daydream' as easy as a cat curl up on a bed."

Billy nodded and looked out the side window. "I knew he had it in him the first time I heard him. His problem was hanging around Kansas City too long with that little jive band and just playing careful music. Sometimes you can't tell what's on the inside—just fast or slow, just hard or soft, just mean or laughing sweet. Can't never tell with some. But I had that feeling, know what I'm saying? Had the feeling that if we cut him loose, let him roam a little taste, that he could be all them combinations, that he could be what a tune needed him to be."

Earl tossed a cigarette stub out the window. He remembered the night he had met young Harold. The band was on break, and Harold walked up slowly, head down. The trumpet player had been nervous in his too-tight suit. Earl had later confided to Billy that he looked like he had just come in from plowing a corn field and that if he joined the band he would have to learn how to dress, to coordinate the colors of his ties and suits, shine his shoes. When you joined the Ferguson band, you joined class. Style was more than your sound. It was your walk, the way you sat during the solos by others, the way you met the night. Earl had promptly nicknamed him 'Big City.'

"He said meeting you was like meeting God," Billy had said the next morning over hash browns and lukewarm coffee.

Earl smiled now. He was not God, true. He did know that among bandleaders roaming with their groups across this country, he was one of the best. He knew, too, that soft-spoken Billy Cox, five years younger, was the best composer in the business, period. Together they worked an easy magic. Few could weave sounds the way they could, few could get twelve voices, twelve rambunctious personalities, to shout or moan as one. And with it all was the trademark sound: the perfect blend of brass and reeds. Basie might have a stronger reed section, with the force of a melodic hurricane; Ellington, a brass section with bite and unmatchable brightness. But they had the blend. Within the first few notes you knew that it was Earl Ferguson's band and nobody else's. Now and then players would leave to join other caravans inching across the continent, but the sound, their mix, stayed the same.

The scattered lights of Springfield were far behind them now, merged to a dull electric glow in the rearview mirror. And out from the town there were only occasional lights along State Route 42, one or two on front porches, lights bathing narrow, weathered and wooded fronts, wood swings perfectly still in that time. Tightly-closed shutters, silences inside. Both tried to imagine the front of the houses at noon—children pushing the porch swing? a dog napping in the shade nearby? clothes flapping on a line running from behind the house? Gone suddenly, a blur to pinpoint, then out.

From a pocket Billy had taken out a matchbook. A few chord progressions had been scribbled on the inside cover. Then drawing out a small lined tablet from beneath the seat, he quickly drew a bass staff and started humming.

"You got something going?" Earl asked.

"I think, yeah. A little light something, you know, like bright light and springtime and whatnot."

Earl tapped the wheel lightly with the palm of his free hand. "Toss in a small woman's bouncy walk, and I might get excited with you."

"Well, help me then. This time you use the woman—tight yellow skirt, right?—and I'll use the light, the light of mid-May, and when they don't work together I think we'll both know."

"Solid. What you got so far?"

Billy did not answer. He kept a finger to his ear, staring from the matchbook cover to the tablet. Earl let it run. You don't interrupt when the idea is so young.

More often than not, Billy and Earl brought opposites, or, at least, unlikely combinations together. One of the band's more popular numbers, a blues, was the result of Billy's meditations on the richly perfumed arms of a large and fleshy woman, arms tightly holding a man who mistook her short laugh for joy. To this, Earl had brought the memory of a rainy night and a long soft moan carried on the wind, something heard from the end of an alley. They used only the colors and sounds from these images, and only later when the songs were fully arranged did the smell and the touch and the smell of them sweep in. There had been other songs which resolved the contrasts, the differences, between the drone of a distant train and an empty glass of gin, a lipstick print at its rim, fingerprints around it. A baby's whimpering and a man grinning as he counted a night's big take from the poker table, painted bright red fingernails tapping lightly down a lover's arm and the cold of a lonely apartment. How much did the dancing couples, those whispering and holding close as second skins or those bouncing and whirling tirelessly feel these things, too? Or did they bring something entirely different to the rhythms, something of their own?

Earl and Billy had talked about this many times. They had concluded that it was enough to bring contexts to dreams, to strengthen those who listened and danced. And there were those moments, magical, alive, when the dance hall was torn from the night and whirled, spinning like a top, a half mile from heaven.

Billy started whistling and tapping his thigh. Then he hummed a fragment of a song loudly.

Earl was nodding. "Nice. Already I can hear Slick Harry taking off with Ousley just under him with the alto. In triplets? Let's see, go through it again right quick."

Again Billy hummed and Earl brought in high triplets, nervous wings snagged to the thread of the melody, lifting the piece toward brightness. They stopped, and Billy, smiling now, worked quickly, a draftsman on fire, adding another line or two, crossing out, scribbling notes. He would look up to follow the front edges of the car's lights then away to the darkness and back to the page.

"Listen up." Billy gave the next lines flats predominating, while offering harsh counterpoint to the first two lines and snatching the song away from a tender playfulness for a moment. He scratched his chin and nodded. Pointed to the darkness.

"This is what I got so far." And he sang the line in a strong tenor voice, his melody now seeming to double the notes from the last line, though the rhythm did not vary. It was the kind of thing Art Tatum might do with "Tea for Two" or something equally simple. The song moved swiftly from a lyrical indulgence to a catch-me-if-you-can show of speed.

"Watch it now," Earl said, "or they will figure us for one of those beboppers." He chuckled. The woman in his mind walked faster, traffic about her thickened, the streets sent up jarring sounds. Those would be trumpets, probably. Surroundings leaned in. Trombones and tenor saxophones playing in the lowest octaves announced their possibilities.

Earl offered a line of his own. His woman walked quickly up the steps of a brownstone. In. Common enough sequence, but no surprise there. Whatever prompted it, though, was fleeting. Gone. Then he said, "Okay, forget mine for now. Let's stay with what you got."

Billy shrugged and marked off another staff, then glanced again to the match cover. He let out a long, low whistle. "Now we come to the bridge."

"This is when we need a piano, Earl. I bet the closest one to here is probably some ole beat-up thing in one of these country churches out here. Or something sitting in the front parlor of one of these farmer's houses and the farmer's daughter playing 'Jingle Bells' after bringing in the eggs."

Hip and arrogant city was in their laughter, of funky cafés where fights might break out and beer bottles fly as the piano man bobbed and weaved, keeping time on scarred pianos that leaned and offered sticky keys in the lowest and highest octaves.

Then the Earl of Ferguson told the story of a piano search years before Billy had joined the band. With two other men in the car and barely an hour east of St. Louis when the puzzle of a chord progression struck with the force of a deep stomach cramp. Spotting one light shining in the wilderness, a small neon sign shining over a door, he ordered the car stopped. Trotting up, Earl noticed the sign blink off. He banged on the door, the hinges straining from each blow. Nobody turned off a sign in his face. The door swung open and up stepped an evil-looking, red-haired farmer in overalls, a man big enough to fill the doorway.

"I said to this giant, 'Quick, I got to get on your piano.' Not 'I got to find your toilet' or 'I got to use your phone,' but 'I got to use your piano.'" He shook his head as he laughed now.

"That giant rocked on his heels like I had punched him square in the chest. He left just enough room for me to squeeze in and sure enough there was a raggedy piano in the corner of his place.

"P. M. had enough sense to offer to buy some of the man's good whiskey while I'm sitting there playing and trying to figure out the good chord. P. M. always did have good common sense. Most folks try to remember what just happened, but Past already on what's happening next. I'm forgetting you never knew P. M. The guys called him Past Midnight because he was so dark-skinned. The shadow of a shadow. Next thing they calling him Past, then one day Rabbit showed up calling him P. M., and it stuck. His real name was Wiley Reed, and he was one of the best alto players in the world."

He paused now, glanced out his side window. "Anyway, he showed his class that night. The giant steady looking around suspicious-like at first. I mean, he didn't know us from Adam, didn't know how many more of us was waiting outside to rush in and turn out the joint. But he loosened up and took his mess of keys out and go to his cabinet. I'm just playing away because this is the greatest song of my life, don't care if it is in some country roadhouse way out in Plumb Nelly. I'm cussing, too, Billy, because this song is giving me fits, do you hear me? It just wouldn't let me go. All I wanted was to make it through the bridge. I figured the rest would come soon as I'm back in the car.

"Well, P. M. and the man making small talk, and Leon trying to get slick on everybody and tipping over to get him a few packs of Old Golds. I'm checking all this, see, and closing in on something solid and oh-so-sweet and hearing the big guy go on and on about getting home because his wife already thinking he's sniffing around the new waitress—I remember that part clear as I'm sitting here—when, boom! Leon open up the closet, a mop and a jug of moonshine fell out and this woman inside trying to button up her blouse. She give a scream like she done seen the boogieman. All hell commence to break loose. Next thing you know Leon backing off and telling the woman he ain't meant no harm, just trying to get some cigarettes, he lie. Big Boy running over and telling me we got to take our whiskey and go, song or no song. I look up and two white guys running down the steps from just over our heads, one of them holding some cards in his hands. The other one run to the telephone like he reporting a robbery. I mean from the outside it's just a little-bitty place on the side of the road but inside all kinds of shit going on. Well, I found the chords I wanted, did a quick run-through and called out to the fellows to haul ass. If some man's wife or some woman's man don't come in there shooting up the place, then the sheriff might raid the place for all-night gambling. Either way, we lose."

Earl was laughing now. A light rain had started to fall just as he ended his tale. The windshield wipers clicked rhythmically, the bump of the road seemed a grace note: *Bachoo-choo, bachoo-choo.*

"Never know when you get the tune down right. Go too early and you pluck it raw. Go too late and you got rotten fruit." Earl coughed. "Don't go at all and you put a bad hurt on yourself."

From across the highway, a rabbit darted toward them, then cut away. Earl had turned the car just slightly before straightening it without letting up on the accelerator.

"Almost had us one dead rabbit."

Billy did not answer. He was tapping his pencil on the tablet. Up ahead and to the east they would discover the electric glow of Columbus. Beyond that they would have three more hours before Cleveland and breakfast at the Majestic Hotel on Carnegie Avenue. There might be a new singer or two waiting to try out with the band. Who knows? Somebody—another Billy or Sassy Sarah—might get lucky and ride back with them to New York, her life changed forever. Some young woman, prettier than she would ever know, would otherwise be serving up beef stew or spareribs in some tiny smoky place on Cedar Avenue, notes running through her head or thoughts of a sickly mother and two children she and her husband were trying to feed. How many times Billy and Earl had seen it, how many times they had heard the hope there, the sweat mustaches sprouting, the need to escape the routine nights. It was common ground. They had all been there, falling to sleep in clothes that smelled of cigarette smoke, the world a place of slow mornings with traffic starting and a door slamming, a baby crying and an "oh, goddam, one more funky morning, but I'm alive to see it through anyhow."

There was a bump beneath the car. "You clipped something for sure that time, sportey-odey."

"All kinds of stuff out here at night," Earl said. "They like the warm road. Coons, possums, snakes, cows."

"Cows?"

"Yeah, cows." Billy had lit a cigarette. Earl tapped the end of the fresh one he had just placed in his mouth, and Billy reached to light it. "Thanks. Don't tell me you done forgot that cow we nicked on the road to Saratoga Springs."

Yes, yes, Billy remembered. "Cow must have thought we was the Midnight Special, much noise as I was making trying to scare him off the road. Probably just out to get him a little side action in the next field." The car had knocked it to one knee before it struggled back up and, in the rearview mirror, slipped into the darkness.

They were quiet for long moments. After music, after hours, different thoughts could struggle to life. If there was an uneasiness earlier, swift terror could strike them in the darkest hours before dawn. They could grow suddenly uneasy in the silences. They could sense it together like a bone-deep chill starting. For now. Billy pushed the wing shut on his side, rolled his window up another inch.

In a small town just west of Columbus, they passed a café, the lone light in that stretch. A man behind a long counter—white apron, white T-shirt—was scrubbing the counter and talking with a customer. He stopped his work to make a point, head moving from side to side. The customer nodded. Another man stood over a table at the window, dunking a donut. With his free hand, he waved as the car passed. Surprised, Earl honked once, then turned to glance back.

"That back there reminds me of something."

"Huh?"

"That man right back there waving. You didn't see him? Standing back there, waving at us and probably every car coming through here this late."

"Don't tell me you want to get some food," Billy said. "Hell, Earl, I thought those chicken sandwiches and pound cake . . . "

"No, no. That ain't what I'm thinking. Had a guy in the band by the name of Boonie years ago, way before you joined the band. Boonie could play him some mean trombone. I'm here to tell you. Fact, he could play trumpet and cornet, too. Probably would have played the tuba, if I would have asked him to. Like you, he was the master of horns. Anyway, something happened—could have been bad gin or something else nobody will ever know about. He just snapped, and they found him one morning standing on a corner cussing at folks and swearing up and down that he was the Governor of Africa. They took him to the jailhouse first, then the crazy house. They didn't keep him there long, six, seven months maybe.

"I went up to see him, way out in the country, Billy, you know where they put those places. Well, just past the gate was this man, and he waved at me when I first came in, and, while I was walking around with Boonie, he waved a couple more times. At first, I thought he was just part of the staff because he was all over the place. But then I noticed he's wearing the same kind of clothes as Boonie. And he keeps smiling, you know? By the time I left, he was back out by the gate and waving again. It didn't take me long to figure out that all he had to do was wave at whatever was new and moving by. Like that man back there waving at the night."

Billy only glanced at him, then looked back to his notebook. Earl shook his head and chuckled. "Governor of Africa, can you beat that? Boonie was lucky, though; I mean, the way he wound up. He never got his chops back after he got out. He worked around a little, then finally left the Life. He got a foundry job and raised his family in Detroit. Others ain't been so lucky."

Earl glanced ahead to more lights, showing up through the rain. He knew some who entered the hospitals, never to emerge. And many, too many, died before the age of 50. Just last March, young "Bird" Parker had died in New York, not yet 35. He whose notes surprised like shooting stars. Playing this music could be as risky as working in a steel mill or coal mine. But what were the choices? What could he do about it, leader of some? Perhaps only show them a lesson or two through his example. Now he did limit himself to one large and long drink per night—one part scotch and three parts water—from an oversized coffee mug. Soon he would cut down on his cigarettes. Beyond that he let the rules pronounce the purpose: you needed a clear head and a sound body to play the music he lived for.

Their talk of work and women—the incomplete song still a bright ribbon over their heads—pulled them well beyond the glow of Columbus. Coffee and sandwiches finished, they were down to three cigarettes each and figured there was nothing open between Columbus and Cleveland. Billy took over at the wheel. Twenty miles or so north of Columbus, they neared a car in trouble at the side of the road. The hood was up and in the swath of the front headlights was a man—very young, thin, white—kneeling at the back tire.

"Keep going, Billy. That cracker'll get help."

Billy slowed. "Well, Earl, it won't hurt . . . "

Earl stared at him, hard. "You getting soft-hearted on me? That boy could be the Klan, see? You remember what happened to the Purnell band down in Tennessee just last month? Huh, remember that stuff? Got beat up by a bunch of rednecks, one of them getting his nose broke, and they still winding up in jail for disturbing the peace and impersonating a band? No, let him get help from his own kind."

Billy pulled the car off the road. "He's just a kid, Earl."

"You go without me, then." He watched Billy leave, then quickly felt under his seat.

Earl could hear him ask, "Need a hand?"

"Sure do," the boy said loudly. "If you got a jack on you, we can do this in no time."

Beneath his seat in the Dynaflow, Earl had found the gun wrapped in a towel. He opened the glove compartment and placed it inside, unwrapping the towel and leaving the small door open. He began to hum the new song slowly, softly, watching his friend, smiling Billy, trusting Billy, help a stranger.

Billy brought the jack from their trunk and set it up. He could smell alcohol on the boy, and, straightening up, he saw a girl in the car sip from a flask. Neither could have been older than eighteen. She was trying to hum something, missing, then tried again.

"Dumb me out here without a jack, I swear," the boy said. Billy only nodded as they set the jack under the frame.

The boy called the girl out of the car, and she stood apart shyly, both hands holding up the collar of her light coat.

"Your friend back there under the weather?" the boy asked.

"He just don't need the exercise," Billy said. "How about her? She feeling all right?"

The boy looked up in surprise, then he smiled. "No, she all right. She don't need no exercise either." He leaned closer to Billy as they pulled off the wheel and started to set the spare. "'Course, me and her just about exercised out." Then he laughed "Whoo-ee!"

The tire was on now, and the boy was tightening the lugs. "Pretty nice car you got back there. You a undertaker or a preacher?"

"No, neither one. I'm a musician."

The boy whistled low. "Musicians make enough for a car like that? I need to learn me some music. You get to travel a lot and see them big-city women and all like that?"

"Sure do."

The boy glanced at the girl and said loudly. "'Course, a man could go all over the world and never find a woman sweet as my Josie there."

Her hair needed a brush, her dress was wrinkled, and her shoes were old and run-over. She was plain and drunk. In the morning she might be in the choir of a tiny church and by evening making biscuits to the staccato of radio news broadcasts. Billy was folding up the jack and turning away.

"Ain't she about the prettiest doggone thing a man could ever see?"

"I know how you feel, sport. I got one just as sweet back in New York."

Billy walked away and waved good-bye with his back turned. He slammed the trunk closed, then settled behind the wheel. He pulled the car back onto the highway.

Earl was whistling. "Feel better?" he asked, not looking up.

"What's that for?" Billy pointed to the gun.

"I thought about cleaning it. Ain't been cleaned in a year." Then: "My daddy told me once that it takes more than a smile and a good heart to get through this world. Told me sometimes you can reach out a helping hand and get it chopped off."

Billy was shivering. "Hide it, Earl. Please."

"Okay, okay. Look, while you were playing the Good Samaritan with Jethro back there, I finished the song. Listen up, youngblood."

Earl hummed through the opening key, stretching the note, then moved through the bright afternoon of the melody, repeated the line in the thinning light of its early evening. The song soon lifted to the bridge, a vivid golden stairstep on which to linger briefly. Then the return to the opening line that suggested new possibilities: the smell of a pine forest after a rain, a meadow, too, a deer or two frozen on one edge. There was a street, glistening, a small oil slick catching dull rainbows and a stranger's laughter like a bright coin spinning at their feet. Yes, all of that.

The small and proud woman walking, her hips working against yellow wool, had been lost to Earl. She would return, surely, to move through another song, walking to a different rhythm. For now, she had brought Earl excited to Billy's first thoughts. Provided a spirit. Together, they hummed the song through, speeding it up, slowing. Each time, they tried different harmonies—the bass stronger here, the trombones higher there. Most of the parts had been worked through by the time they noticed the hills near Medina taking shape.

"Got it," Billy said, finally. He slapped the wheel with relief.

"It's nice," Earl said.

"Think the people will like it?" Billy asked.

Earl yawned and looked out the window. Maybe he could get twenty minutes or so of sleep before they touched the edges of the city. "You worry too much, Billy. 'Course they gone like it. They got no choice. We did the best we could. We'll run through it this afternoon, do it again in Pittsburgh, and maybe have it ready by the time we hit Philly. Can't you just hear Big City's solo already?" He settled back, eyes closed.

Cars, trees, corn fields just harvested were explosions of dull colors. Signs placed one hundred feet apart, a shaving cream ad, suddenly claimed Billy's attention. *The big blue tube's / Just like Louise / You get a thrill / From every squeeze.* He laughed aloud, then started whistling as the car roared into a stretch of light fog. Billy leaned forward, his head almost touching the windshield. He stiffened.

"Earl, wake up. I got something to tell you."

"Let it slide. Tell me over grits and coffee." Earl kept his eyes closed.

"No, it can't wait. It happened back there in Dayton. I just now remembered. You know on that second break? Well, I stepped outside to get a little air, take a smoke, you understand. A couple folk stroll past and tell me how much they like our playing, so I'm talking with them awhile and then I see this woman—short with a red wig and she standing off to the side. She look up every now and then like she want to come over and say something. But she wait until nobody's around and she walk over real quick-like. Something about her made me think about a bird hopping, then resting, hopping some more. She told me she really like the music, like some of the songs really get a hold of her. . . . "

Earl opened one eye. "Yeah, and she just want to take a cute little man like you home to make music to her all the time."

"No, no, no. Nothing like that, but you better believe I was hoping for some action."

Forehead still to the windshield, Billy fumbled for words, worked a hand like he was flagging down a car. "No, she's smiling but not smiling, if you know what I mean. We talk about a lot of things, then she gets down to the thing she really wanted to talk about, I figure. She told me about her baby. She told me about hearing her baby screaming one day and she rush from her ironing and found him in the next room bleeding. He fell on a stick or glass or something, cut his belly, and blood going every which way. Said her son's belly was thin, like a balloon, but not going down when it's poked. She put her hand there, she said, and could feel each beat of the heart. Every time the heart beat, more blood would spurt out between her fingers. She screamed for help, screamed for her neighbors next door, just screamed and screamed. Blood was all over her, too, she said, but she never saw that until later. All she could do is tell her child not to die and press on that thin belly. And pray and pray, even after he in the ambulance. She told me that baby was all she got in this world."

Billy shook his head slowly. "What could I say to all that? Here I go outside for some fresh air and a draw or two on my Lucky Strikes. She brings me this story when I want to know whether my shoes are shined, my front still holding up, or whether some big-legged woman want to pull me home with her. I touched her on the shoulder, was all I could do. She told me the baby lived, and she smiled this dopey smile. Then she left."

Earl's eyes were closed. He waved his hand as if shooing a fly from his forehead. "It's this music we play, Billy. It opens people up, makes them give up secrets. Better than whiskey or dope for that. It don't kill you, and you can't piss it away. You can whistle it the next day in new places. You can loan it to strangers, and they thank you for it."

Then he shrugged. "It's what keeps us going all night."

Sitting back, fog thinning, Billy nodded and started back whistling. Before long they would sight the giant mills pumping smoke into the grey morning. At Lakewood Billy might swing closer to the grey and glassy Erie. Then he would pick up speed and head toward the eastside, through a world raging to light outside their windows. Finally, they would gain Carnegie Avenue and weave their way among the early church traffic. They would find the Majestic Hotel, breakfast, and attempt to sleep, two wizards before the band.

23

Child's Play

Bill Moody

Wilson Childs stood as always, flat footed, eyes shut, the tenor saxophone held straight out in front of him, his left foot barely tapping out the tempo, and blew the first two notes of "Stella by Starlight." He let them hang in the air, waiting for the answering chord from the pianist, then frowned as he realized the drummer had missed his count. He gave an inward sigh and without looking back, he could feel the whole rhythm section scuffling to find the groove, glancing at each other with questioning looks—was it me?—trying to settle in before eight bars had gone by.

Wilson looked out over the crowd. Even the few people paying attention didn't know anything was wrong. The rest continued their conversations and laughter over the din of blenders, coffee machines, and drink orders shouted by jeans-clad waitresses, who were probably students at Berkeley. It never changed, Wilson Childs thought, except now, the club was smoke free.

They were in yet another reincarnation of the Jazz Workshop on Broadway, nestled in the North Beach mix of sex shops and tittie bars, Italian bakeries and coffee shops, just a short walk from Columbus Avenue and City Lights Bookstore.

Wilson played with the melody, turning it inside out, waiting for a sign that somebody knew where one was. Finally, Dean James, the youngish pianist, laid down the chords and everybody found it and settled down. Wilson decided to give it to Dean for his show of taking charge first. He nodded toward him and took the horn out of his mouth.

He gave the drummer a look but he was paying attention to the music now and not the blonde in the short skirt, her long legs crossed, gazing at him from her perch on a high stool at the bar.

Wilson folded his hands across the horn and sighed again, remembering another time at the Jazz Workshop, years ago, when the whole place was blue with smoke and the bar was crowded with musicians catching Wilson Childs and Quincy Simmons on an off Monday night. Miles had been there, too, Wilson remembered, talking to some guy at the bar, getting ready for his opening at the Blackhawk and, Wilson knew, scouting him. Wilson was the hot young tenor player then. Big things were expected of him, but now they were gone, as surely as Quincy Simmons was gone.

The word was on the street. Coltrane had left Miles to form his own group, and Miles was looking for a replacement.

Wilson caught Miles glancing at him once and smiled as Quincy Simmons spun out three choruses on the Monk tune, "Well, You Needn't." During the bass solo, Miles passed the bandstand and in that gravely voice said, "Hey, Childs, I'll call you."

But Miles had not called, not that night, not ever after what happened later that night.

Now, Wilson tipped his head to the left, listening to Dean's last sixteen bars, put the horn back in his mouth playing like, oh shit give me this thing, turning Stella into a whore. He played four choruses that made the whole band shake their heads and then took it out. The rest of the set went okay and was acknowledged by a few real listeners. Wilson set his horn down and made for the tiny band room in back. Except for Dean, who he tapped on the shoulder, Wilson ignored the rhythm section.

He stepped out the back door into the little alleyway and lit a cigarette, thinking again about Quincy Simmons, wondering what had happened to him. Was he really dead? He'd seen the notice in a small jazz magazine—what was it, ten years ago?—but he'd never believed it. He let his mind drift back to that earlier night at the Workshop in 1961.

The band was smoking and Wilson was sorry Miles had left early. Wilson and Quincy had left in Quincy's car, headed for Bop City, see who was around, maybe play a little when the cops pulled them over.

"Oh shit," Wilson said, tapping the baggy of grass in his coat pocket. "I can't handle this."

"Put it under the seat, man," Quincy said, checking the rearview mirror. "It's probably nothing."

But it wasn't nothing. The cops eyed the saxophone case, got them both out of the car and searched the car. The cop found the baggy under the front seat and held it up happily. "Well, well," he said, glancing at Wilson. "Whatta we have here?"

The cop was young, younger than Wilson but white and this was San Francisco. He stood by, his hand resting on his gun, seemingly uneasy about the whole thing.

"This yours?" the young cop asked Wilson.

Wilson sighed. He didn't need a bust, not now, not with his record. But before he could answer, Quincy cut in, "It's mine," he said. "Just holding for a friend."

Wilson looked at Quincy, tried to tell him to shut up with his eyes but Quincy wouldn't stop. "He's got nothing to do with it, Officer. He didn't even know I had it."

"Sure," the cop said. "Am I going to find anything else?" He stepped back, put his hand on his gun.

Quincy sighed. "Yes. Under the driver's seat."

The young cop looked from Quincy to Wilson and made a quick decision. "Cuff him," he told his partner, who bent Quincy over the hood of the car and locked the cuffs on his wrists.

His eyes on Wilson, the cop reached under the seat, felt around and came up with a gun. "Well, well," he said, smiling. He held it up for his partner and Wilson to see. "Looks like I did have a probable cause, huh?"

Wilson didn't have to act surprised. He just stood, frozen to the spot and said nothing. It was a small gun, one of those short barrel kind he'd seen in movies hundreds of times.

"You drive?" the young cop asked turning his attention back to Wilson. Wilson nodded. "License?" Wilson took out his wallet and showed the cop. He studied it for a moment and handed it back. "Okay, because I'm a nice guy, I'm going to give you a break. You can drive your partner's car home. I'm not going to find anything else in the car, am I?"

"No," Wilson said, his eyes moving quickly to Quincy, who was already in the police car, staring at Wilson. "Can I talk to him for a minute. I need to ask him who he wants me to call."

"Yeah, go ahead." He nodded for his partner to open the door. While they conferred, Wilson leaned in to Quincy.

"Man, what the fuck you doing with a gun? Why you want to do this?"

Quincy smiled. "No big thing, man. You don't need a bust now. Next week you'll be with Miles. Just get me out, okay."

"Okay, let's go," the young cop said, brushing Wilson back and shutting the door of the police car.

"I got it covered," Wilson said to Quincy. "Don't worry."

Then Wilson Childs stood on the curb, watching the police car drive away.

But it didn't go the way they thought. Quincy Simmons' previous record was brought up and an overzealous D.A. decided to apply the screws and Quincy was remanded to county jail, bail pending, while the gun was checked out, facing maybe a year if they pushed it. By then, the gun was traced to a convenience store robbery and Quincy had more to explain than he ever could.

Wilson visited him once, sitting across from him, separated by the thick glass, talking on the phones. "You okay, man?" Wilson said, sickened to see Quincy in the jail house jump suit. Wilson knew what it was like. He'd been there himself.

"Yeah. P.D. says they'll give me a week to get my shit together after the arraignment, but I might be looking at a year, six months if I'm lucky."

Wilson closed his eyes and gripped the phone. "Look, man, I can tell them, it was . . ."

Quincy cut him off. "No, you wait for that call from Miles, just do the gig. You don't need this shit now. You hear me?"

Wilson nodded, knowing he should ignore Quincy, step up and let them know they had the wrong man, but he didn't, and there was nothing he could do about the gun. Quincy did manage a release but never turned up for sentencing.

Wilson never saw him again. He was just gone, disappeared, dropped off and out of sight.

The rumors flowed, but nobody knew for sure and Wilson lived with it every day of his life for the past twenty years, haunted by his own failure. Some years later a story turned up in one of the jazz magazines that Quincy Simmons had died, but Wilson didn't believe it. He just couldn't.

Wilson put out his cigarette and had started back inside when he ran into Dean.

"Oh, there you are," Dean said. "Did you hear? Some guy at the bar told me."

"Hear what?"

"Quincy Simmons. They found him."

Wilson played through the rest of the night in a fog, just going through the motions. He couldn't keep his mind off Quincy Simmons. Found, just like that after all this time. He'd grilled Dean but the young pianist didn't know the details. Just that Quincy had been found playing piano in a Gospel Mission in Los Angeles, a refuge for homeless men, a place to feed their spirit and their bodies.

"It was in the paper today, I guess," Dean had said.

Wilson wanted to see for himself. He packed up his horn and walked down Columbus Avenue to an all-night coffee shop and bought a paper out of the machine. Inside, he took a booth, ordered coffee and a sandwich and scanned through the *Chronicle*. The story was in the back pages, between a bunch of ads. Wilson folded the paper and read and reread the story several times.

LOST JAZZMAN FOUND

Quincy Simmons, once prominent on the jazz scene, was recently discovered at a homeless shelter and church, playing piano and living in a small room in back of the shelter. Simmons disappeared almost 25 years ago, following an arrest for drug possession and an illegal hand gun. Simmons was released on bail but when it was thought the gun had been used in a convenience store robbery, bail had been revoked pending further investigation.

Simmons had jumped bail and was never seen again until now. At the time of his arrest, he was appearing with saxophonist Wilson Childs at the Jazz Workshop in San Francisco. Sources say Simmons has little memory of the arrest and subsequent flight, or how he got back to playing piano again.

"Oh Quincy," Wilson said to himself. "You never knew and nobody could find you."

"More coffee?"

Wilson looked up at the waitress. "What? Oh, yes, thank you."

"Something wrong with the sandwich?" she asked, looking at his untouched plate.

"No, guess I just wasn't as hungry as I thought," Wilson said. He picked up the sandwich and took a small bite and nodded at the waitress. She shrugged and walked away.

Wilson looked at the article again. There was no writer listed, just Times Staff Writer. He grabbed his horn and the check and went up front to pay and get a handful of quarters.

He found a pay phone and dialed information for the *Los Angeles Times.*

"City Desk," a gruff voice said.

"Hello," Wilson said, not quite sure what to ask. "I'm calling about a story you ran today, Quincy Simmons, the piano player."

"Who?" The man sounded annoyed.

"Quincy Simmons. The story was on page 27. It says 'Lost Jazzman Found.'"

"Hang on," the voice said. Wilson could hear paper being rattled and shuffled. "Yeah, I got it. What about it?"

"Can you tell me who wrote it? It just says staff writer. I need to talk to the writer. It's important."

"Hang on," the voice said again. "Let me check the assignment sheet."

Wilson waited, desperate for a cigarette.

"Okay, here it is. Anne Carson, but she won't be in till morning, and no I can't give you her home number. Call back then."

"Thanks," Wilson said, but the voice was already gone.

Wilson waited till nine the next morning to call. He was switched around several times, then finally he heard, "Anne Carson."

"Hello," Wilson said. He'd rehearsed what he was going to say but now his mind went blank. "This is Wilson Childs. I . . . "

"Oh my God," Carson said. "I was just pulling your bio. Are you in L.A.?"

"No, but I wanted to talk to you about the story you wrote."

"I'm doing a follow-up, or will if I can convince my editor." She sounded excited, urgent to Wilson.

"Did you see Quincy? Is he . . . is he okay? I need to talk to him."

"Physically, yes, but he's pretty foggy on things. It's like he's missing twenty-five years or something. He seemed nervous talking to me."

"He never knew," Wilson said.

"Never knew what?"

"The gun charge, about it being dropped. That's why he jumped bail."

"Oh, Jesus," Carson said. "Jesus."

There was a long pause while they both listened to their thoughts.

"Look, Mr. Wilson, I know this is a dumb thing to say but I've been a fan of yours for a long time. I even found a record you made with Quincy Simmons, *Childs Play.* Do you remember it?"

Wilson smiled. "Yes," not surprised at the question. He'd recorded a lot and sometimes the sessions got mixed up in his mind like with a lot of musicians.

"Oh, it was wonderful, well, still is," Carson said. "Look, can you come to L.A.? I could meet you, take you to see Quincy, and—"

Wilson cut her off. "Don't tell him I'm coming. I want to be the one to tell him, okay?"

"Sure," Carson said, "I understand."

Wilson knew she didn't but was grateful to her for saying so. "I have one more night here. I can come down Sunday morning."

"Great!" Carson said. "I'll meet you. Let me know the flight time and airline."

"I will. Miss Carson?"

"Yes?"

"Thank you."

Wilson walked out of baggage claim at LAX, carrying a small bag and his horn. He stopped, looked around and saw a young blond woman, leaning on a Honda, waving at him and arguing with a security guard.

Wilson walked over. "Miss Carson?"

"Yes," she said, putting out her hand. She was maybe 30, Wilson thought, the same age as his daughter, dressed in jeans and a sweater and running shoes. "It's a pleasure."

Wilson put his bag and horn in the back and got in the car. Carson started the engine and pulled away while punching in numbers on a cell phone. "You're early enough for the service," she said glancing at Wilson.

He noticed the ashtray, the pack of cigarettes on the dash board. "Do you mind?" he said. He pulled out his own from the leather jacket pocket.

Carson nodded and spoke into the phone. "Reverend Stiles? Anne Carson. He's here, in my car. Uh huh, uh huh. Just tell Quincy he's going to have a visitor. Okay, see ya then." She closed the phone, cut off two cars and turned down Lincoln Boulevard heading for the Santa Monica Freeway, Wilson guessed.

She cracked both windows as they lit cigarettes and relaxed a little, smiling at Wilson. "So you haven't seen Quincy since . . ."

"I visited him in jail, but no. Not since then."

Carson nodded. "He looks almost the same. Well, hell, so do you," she said, smiling at him. "It's just so . . . so weird. How does a guy like that just disappear for so long?"

"How did you find him?" Wilson asked.

"I didn't," she said. "Reverend Stiles, he runs the mission, called me. I'd done a story on the shelter and he knew I was a jazz fan. Quincy mentioned something about playing piano with you once, so I went down to check it out, and *whoa*. There he was. Quincy Simmons, playing hymns and gospel songs for a bunch of guys who were just waiting for a hot meal. I couldn't believe it."

The Sunday morning traffic was light and they made good time. The radio was on low and tuned to a jazz station. Wilson shook his head, recognizing *Miles at the Blackhawk,* and wondered how close he'd come to being on that record.

Carson took the Harbor Freeway to downtown and exited on Sixth Street. Wilson hadn't been to L.A. in a long time but he remembered the area. They drove down Sixth, past boarded up storefronts, liquor stores and men standing on corners or stretched out sleeping in doorways. Carson turned off 6th and pulled up in front of a building with a sign that read: ALL SOULS MISSION & CHURCH. ALL ARE WELCOME HERE."

They got out of the car. "Let's put your bag and horn in the trunk," Carson said. She unlocked the trunk and Wilson put his bag in. "I'll take the horn with me," he said.

Carson smiled at him. "I hoped you'd say that." She stuffed a camera in her shoulder bag and led Wilson inside.

Reverend Stiles, a small wiry black man in rimless glasses, was at the pulpit, reading from the Bible as they slipped in and sat down in the back row. He finished the passage, closed the Bible and addressed the audience of shabbily dressed men of all ages. Wilson suddenly felt uncomfortable, then he saw Quincy, rising from a chair and seating himself at an old upright piano.

"And now with brother Quincy's fine help we'll all sing and then have ourselves a hot breakfast. Praise the Lord."

The men murmured along as Quincy played the chords for some old gospel tune Wilson vaguely remembered but played somehow differently by Quincy, making it almost a blues.

Wilson listened for a minute and then unzipped his bag and put his horn together and walked up the aisle next to the wall. He watched Quincy, head down, his hands outstretched on the keyboard, oblivious to the voices of the reluctant men singing behind him.

Wilson waited for the next chorus, then began to play as he walked closer to the piano. Quincy's head jerked up and he looked around and for a moment their eyes locked. Wilson watched recognition wash over Quincy's face, saw a slight smile forming as Wilson reached the piano. He played a line, repeated it and Quincy fell right in, as if twenty-five years was only yesterday.

Wilson looked out over the audience as he and Quincy segued into a more modern blues, their own kind of gospel. Quincy was smiling now, feeding Wilson chords, comping behind him like they were back in the Jazz Workshop.

Wilson played two more choruses, then took it out. As the men filed out to the dining room, he put his horn on top of the piano. Quincy stood up and came toward him. They looked at each other for a long moment, then hugged. Wilson held Quincy by the shoulders. "I missed you, man," he said. "Where the hell you been?"

"Oh, around," Quincy said. "I'm not so sure about all of it, but I'm glad to see you. Yes, I am."

Reverend Stiles and Anne Carson looked on. She snapped a couple of pictures and then finally Stiles said, "We have a nice breakfast if you two gentlemen would like to join us."

In the dining room on rough wooden tables and benches, Wilson and Quincy talked over ham slices and eggs. "How long you been here?" Wilson asked.

Quincy shrugged. "Oh, about six months, I guess. Before that it's all kind of hazy. All over, you know. I just lost track, lost myself, I guess. Then I walked in here one afternoon, saw that piano and everything sort of came back." He sighed and looked away, nodded to Reverend Stiles and Anne Carson who sat nearby, stealing glances at them. "I just couldn't make that jail scene, man. I just had to get away."

"Can we smoke in here?" Wilson held up his cigarettes to Reverend Stiles, who nodded yes. Wilson got one going and looked at Quincy. "Look, man, there's something I have to tell you."

Quincy looked at him. "What?"

"The gun charge was dropped, man. All you would have done is time served. It was dropped." Wilson took a deep drag on his cigarette and watched Quincy, saw the realization in his eyes.

"I tried to find you, man, I really did. But you were gone."

Quincy nodded. "And you put up the bail, didn't you? Got stuck when I took off."

"Oh, that was nothing, man," Wilson said. "Forget it." He studied Quincy. "You know, about ten years ago, *DownBeat* said you were dead."

"Yeah, I know," Quincy smiled. "That lady from the newspaper told me." He smiled again. "Guess it was just as well. People stopped lookin' for me then, huh?"

"I never believed it," Wilson said. "Quincy Simmons dead? No way."

"Hey," Quincy said, "did Miles ever call you?"

"Naw, he got Hank Mobley for the Blackhawk gig, and then Wayne Shorter after that. You ain't heard the shit he's playing now?"

"Don't know if I want to," Quincy said. "I haven't heard much music lately. Tell me about you, man. You doing all right?"

Wilson shrugged. "I went with Basie for a while, then all that fusion rock shit hit. Now we're in style again. There's a young cat, Wynton Marsalis, trumpet player, got famous and so did jazz again. Bunch of young bloods. They call them the young lions." Wilson shrugged and grinned. "I'm too old to be a young lion and not old enough to be an old veteran. Record companies tell me, 'Wilson Childs, you play good, but we can't market you.' Ain't that a bitch. But everybody is playing bebop again, and that's something I know how to do."

They talked for a long time. Telling stories, remembering the good times, and finally reached that point old friends do who have been apart for a long time. Reunited, caught up on things, and the future looming in front of them. But the big question still hadn't been answered. Wilson suddenly realized Quincy might as well have been in prison all this time.

"Can you talk about it, man?" Wilson asked, looking into Quincy's eyes. "What happened?"

Quincy held up his hands. "I don't know. A lot of it's hazy, but it was starting before I took off. I know we were doing well, but I couldn't shake feeling lost, depressed. I don't know what you'd call it. That's why I bought the gun. I kept thinking somebody was coming after me. Sounds crazy, but I guess I was a little crazy.

"I saw this doctor for a while. He gave me these pills, supposed to make me feel better, but, I don't know, just seemed to make it worse. That's why I was hoping Miles would take you on. I just wanted to quit playing, go away for a while, but I knew you'd never let me do that."

Wilson shook his head, knowing Quincy was right, but also knowing Quincy would never have let him turn Miles down if he'd called.

"I just kind of drifted," Quincy continued. "For a while it was nice, not having the pressure, worrying about gigs, how I was playing, where the money was going to come from." He looked up at Wilson. "You understand what I'm saying?"

Wilson nodded. He knew. You choose this life, all those things Quincy said came with it. Only you don't choose the life. It chooses you. But the rest of it, he could only imagine. Years of nothing odd jobs, living hand to mouth, nobody knowing who you were or where you were, maybe not even knowing yourself.

"What about now?" Wilson asked. "Whatever you want to do I'll help you." Wilson grinned at him. "You're going to be famous now, you know, now that you're found again. I'm going to have to hit on you for a gig." Wilson studied him. "Do you want to play again? I heard you out there, man." He nodded toward the church. "It's still there."

Quincy nodded. "Reverend Stiles has been letting me practice, but until you walked in today I wasn't sure."

Wilson grinned. "Well, motherfucker, let's go on the road, then."

DownBeat picked up the story courtesy of Anne Carson's followup profile in the *Times,* and then the phone never stopped ringing. The following month, Quincy Simmons and Wilson Childs were on the cover of three jazz magazines, and Anne had written the stories. Several record companies, including the one that had told Wilson they couldn't market him, were interested. Now, it seemed, they could.

A month later, a reunion gig was arranged at the Jazz Bakery in Los Angeles that sold out a week in advance. When they took the stand to an ovation and opened with one of the bop tunes they'd played years ago, Wilson could feel the adrenaline rush as Quincy's rich chords, like a lush carpet that makes you want to walk barefoot on it, filled the room. Wilson felt a great weight lifted from his shoulders as he walked to the microphone.

It was Wilson Childs who played better than ever.

24

The Shrimp Peel Gig

James Reed

We were easy to find. A poster board sign on an easel pointed up the stairs, and the ocean wave roar of two hundred people was no problem to follow. I stood at the door with my two cases and looked over the hall. It was an atrium, five or six stories of glass and black granite polished all the way to the top. Down here at floor level, the catering crew was distributing dessert.

I was part of the after-dinner music, two whole bands, one Dixie, one swing. The Dixie was an afterthought booked at the last minute. Somebody on the hospital board saw shrimp on the menu and decided there should be an extra taste of New Orleans. Hank said it would cost, and they said fine. He brought the charts and told the Starliters to show up late. They're the big band. I was subbing on second alto. In the Seven Ten Strutters, the Dixieland, I'm the clarinet, and that's turned pretty regular. We do a lot of ball games and little festivals. At Pioneer Days we usually follow the guy with the marionettes and hammered dulcimer act. He wears a coonskin cap and pretends he's a hillbilly, but he's got new jokes every year. Hank's are only new if he forgets how they go.

The audiences either don't notice or don't care, but I know some of them are repeaters. Hank has a following. He's been running bands in town for thirty years. These days it's mostly the Strutters and the Starliters, and with the big band he conducts far more than he plays. It's the Dixie that gives him a work-out. He takes the trumpet, and at the festivals he talks a lot between tunes, I think because he needs the rest. He gives the crowd a bit of history. He's got these facts he looked up at the library. They're written on recipe cards, but they must be disconnected snippets because they change every time he takes the mike. Or maybe his eyesight's going. Buddy Bolden played cornet or clarinet, you never know. And the audience generally doesn't. They nod politely and blink, their white hair ruffling in the breeze, or the younger couples with kids down front stare into space or dig out change for ice cream cones. Children dance like mad when we do play, and oldsters actually like us, but for people in between we're just whatever's up there for an hour.

Or three. Tonight it's Hank Leitner and the Starliters, with a 9:00 o'clock downbeat. At midnight we turn into pumpkins. And of course for that New Orleans sound so essential to tonight's festivities, the Strutters play first, a little Dixie to rev up the crowd.

That's the idea, but the diners seemed pretty settled. I threaded through the tables toward the stage and saw people were already leaning back in their chairs, looking stuporous, their bellies as round and tight as turtle shells. That was the men. The women sat like sculptures in sequins. A few still chewed. One woman in a ten-year-old suit and a hairdo even older was so slow and careful I wondered if her teeth hurt. It was fork to mouth to plate to mouth. She was working on the green beans and hadn't seen the dessert, but her husband was tracking the caterer's plates. His eyes bulged like golf balls when the cheesecake and chocolate pie appeared. Everyone received a wedge of each.

Not exactly a dancing crowd. They looked like candidates for a coma.

Hank was putting folders on the stands. Good man. Ever optimistic. The bandstand was a narrow set of risers, and I nodded as I passed. He looked puzzled that I carried two cases, so I reminded him, "I'm Nate for the night. He called on Tuesday. Didn't he tell you?"

"Alto. Second. Got it," said Hank. "I forgot." He pointed down a hall. "Case room's that way. Left at the exit sign, then a sharp right."

"Thanks," I said, thinking he looked pretty good tonight. He'd lost some weight since the bypass, which wasn't bad, but he'd lost too much, really. He seemed drawn and sickly, at least in the face, like any minute he expected some new pain. Tonight he was looking okay.

Me, I'm feeling pretty immortal. The ticker's fine and I go to gigs when I want. I don't have to cancel because my wife won't let me out to play.

Nate had said, "You'll be fine. You've played these tunes before, just not these charts."

"Oh, I know," I said, "but—"

"It's okay," he told me. "Please."

I propped the phone against my ear and watched Kelly finish loading the dishwasher. Our daughter, Stephanie, was running leftovers to the basement freezer. I was drying a big pot, and the towel felt damp and cloying in my hand the longer I stood there. "But don't you need the—"

"Quince," he said. "It would be a very difficult night."

Which meant this was a difficult night, as he talked to me on the phone.

Did I actually hear his wife in the background? Probably not. I didn't need to. I could imagine her scowl as she passed from one room to the next. I could see her sliding across the doorway while Nate, poor Nate, whispered into the phone.

Kelly smiled and said, "Saturday's fine. So you're out a little later. We'll rent a movie."

*

A couple of Starliters warmed up as I put together my horns. Murph walked in with his trombone and said, "Two tonight? Doing some Roland Kirk?"

"Just Nate," I said. "I'm him for the evening."

"Pray that you're not," he warned.

I laughed and said, "Now I lay me down to sleep."

"But not next to her, or my soul she'll keep." Murph shuddered from head to toe. "That woman's crazy." He flipped the latches on his case and said, "I bet Nate quits after this. You gonna be a Starliter?"

"Do I have a choice?"

"No more than anybody else." He clicked his slide in place and gave it a couple glisses. "I wouldn't walk in that house without a tranquilizer dart."

"You and Jim Fowler," I said.

"The mama armadillo protects its young. You can, too," Murph said, and started playing the theme song.

That's how he warms up. Always has. He picks a tune and plays variations. They get more and more Baroque, and I mean that literally. The guy improvises counterpoint that looks gorgeous in transcription. In fact, we first met on a gig with Nate. We were at some crossroad Elks' Club for New Year's Eve, a hundred miles from nowhere, and I heard this trombone playing "Caravan" like Bach had written the tune instead of Ellington. When he was done I asked if he knew the *Brandenburg "A" Train Concerto.*

"No, but I'm hell on *Two-Part Choo-Choo Number 9.*"

Nate was this bland fellow off to the side who looked at both of us like we'd just beamed down from Mars.

That's how Murph and I knew we were the normal ones. Nate was along for the ride but couldn't figure out his companions. He took it with good humor, though, or grace, at least. Or silence. He was a straight man to us, like some headmaster raising his eyebrows at the antics of the boys, but inside him was another straight man who couldn't play along, not because he disapproved, although he did, but because he didn't know how.

We liked him anyway. It was an early gig for all of us, over twenty years ago, and we weren't sure then you could really make a living this way. It seemed too good to be true, and it was, but those first gigs weren't all that good, either, only we didn't know it at the time. Getting a gig at all, at our ages, was like being tapped with a wand. We were breathing fairy dust, and it filled our lungs with magic, because we got all the same gigs.

"Keep this up, we should book ourselves as a trio," Murph said.

"More like a duet plus one," Nate told him.

"Who's the extra Mouseketeer?" I asked.

"Whoever's most out of place," he said.

And tonight I had his job.

One of the trumpets was playing long tones. Another was taking quick runs into the stratosphere. I'd fixed his horn a few weeks ago, mostly new springs in the valves and a thorough cleaning. I probably made a repeat customer there. We'd never met, but somebody recommended me to him. He kept saying, "I thought this one was supposed to stick," between lightning fast chromatics. He teaches at a junior high in some little town nearby.

I just barely escaped the school band routine myself. Ten years is borderline. You stay or break. I'd been fixing horns out of the basement and giving private lessons and decided another year of fifth and sixth graders was more than I could take. The kids were okay, but I had to drive from school to school and convince their parents that this was important, or that it wasn't. It wasn't the end of the world if Billy really wanted to play football instead because he sure wasn't doing himself or me or the other kids any good.

I couldn't see myself doing that until 65. I made my break. It's been six years, so I think I beat the small business odds. I've got a school district contract and do most of the symphony winds. One guy flies out to New York for every little thing, but nobody local would dare touch his horn. Not that he'd let them. That oboe costs more than my car. But I'm doing all right. The work is steady. I teach a few lessons. I play a few gigs.

All of us have day jobs except Hank and a couple others who've retired. He's got a trumpet buddy in the Starliters who says, "Howdy," and not much else. The guy stands six foot four and keeps his hands in his pockets except when he's playing. They met in the 50s, and that was that. His name is Arnold. He may be the last man alive who got a crewcut and stuck with it. There's a trombone player with a vibrato you could drive a truck through. He wears little half glasses on the tip of his nose, and his eyes water. His name is Benjamin, but he goes by Benj. "Like the trumpet," he says, "but I spell it out of my name." He worked forty years as an actuary and took the buy-out when it came. "Now all I do is play," he says. "Life couldn't be better, except my wife hates me always underfoot."

The rest of us are middle-aged, we're surprised to find out, all in our thirties and forties.

We haven't gotten over thinking we're young.

It's an out-of-date life, playing music fifty years old. I mean, I'm a legit player at heart. There just isn't much call for it, and time's running out on the dance bands. There's not a circuit like there used to be. You get your gigs in town, and everybody's back at work in the morning. Nate's barely hung on, and once he got married he started dropping anyway. Had to, but he tried to stay with the Starliters. It was his parents' music, and he liked imagining they might be swirling around a dance floor, and

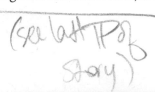

he might see them, which would never happen, of course, because when he was twelve they were killed in a car accident, coming home from a dance, in fact, a country club soirée. By then only the rich could afford a big band, or were even interested. It wasn't the radio sound. It wasn't in the jukeboxes, but Nate grew up with his very own World War II nostalgia. He never saw his parents grow old. He never fought with them about adolescence. They stayed handsome and beautiful and kind. And he provided the appropriate soundtrack every night he played.

Or maybe he just liked getting out of the house. He's another prisoner of the public schools. We met doing a Vikki Carr show, I think, or Andy Williams or somebody who'd come to town. Nate was a fusty old guy even at 28. Bebop struck him as a mortal error. "Those young modernists," he said, "they ruined everything," and he played within the limits of his impeccable taste. Then he'd go home. He didn't drink or smoke (anything). A piece of blueberry pie and black coffee was as much decompression as he needed. The next day he'd conduct the kids through their Hal Leonard arrangements.

Five years ago he got married. It surprised everyone he knew. Murph once said Nate lived in terror that a woman would say hello because he'd have to ad lib.

"The only thing he knew to say to a girl was, 'I do,' and look where it got him."

"Same place he always was," I said. "She moved in."

"And she hardly ever leaves the house."

She has taken to sobbing when he does. Even in the morning, when he leaves for school.

"He'll chain her in the basement someday," Murph says. "Those quiet guys always do. Nobody would blame him, either. I pulled into his driveway once. I needed to borrow a keyboard. You could hear her moaning outside the house."

✳

I took my horns out to the bandstand and saw Mylar balloons hovering over every table. They were silver on one side with shamrocks on the other, heart-shaped leftovers from St. Patrick's Day weighed down with lollipops tied to the ends of long, green ribbons. At the far end of the room, a pair of women in gold lamé were still handing them out. Maybe the balloons were supposed to be a doorprize, or a last minute attempt to be festive, but somebody untied a lollipop and a Mylar heart shot toward the ceiling. It was a little silver dot when it finally bumped to a stop six stories up. The crowd, of course, applauded while the man unwrapping his sucker looked sheepish. I set my alto on the stand but held onto the clarinet so I could keep warm air in it.

"Balloons," said Murph, "but I don't see any funny hats."

"No noisemakers, either," I said. "Except us."

"A one and uh two and uh. T'ank you, boyss."

Murph's divorced. It's easy to think of him doing schtick in his bedroom. It's harder to imagine he might stop.

Hank came over and patted my shoulder. "We're going to be a little delayed," he said. "They're going to have a speaker."

"Is he here?" I asked.

Murph said, "Is he sober?"

"'Yes' to question one and 'I don't know' to question two," Hank said. We surveyed the crowd, but anybody there could have been due up to the mike. It was a mass of genteel drunks. Hank said, "They want a drum roll when he's ready to speak."

So we stood around waiting. The desserts got finished. I thought about snagging one, but no go. The caterers were efficient. They scurried about in their white tops, black pants, and burgundy aprons while we milled around in our tuxes, looking lazy because we weren't on time.

Nate would have had a fit. "Punctuality is part of the job," he used to say, usually when a headliner was late and a crowd was growing restive.

I wondered how often his wife's weeping at the door had made him tardy.

Kelly was at home with Stephanie. We'll get a movie, she'd said. Go on. Go play.

Hank was telling Murph some joke. I'd lost track of the conversation but could tell he was nearing the punch line. I mouthed the words, "Where's the toast?" and Murph chuckled like it went right along with the joke he was hearing. I smirked back and looked at Hank's neck, rising from a collar it could no longer fill. His flesh looked loose and grey, and if I eased up on tiptoe, I could see the bend of his collarbone.

His doctor told him to watch it after the bypass. Exercise was a good idea, but maybe the trumpet should be cut back.

"Well, hell, what am I going to do?" he said one night at a Mardi Gras party. He pulled his calendar out and flipped through the pages. "I've got bookings two years in advance. You can make the 19th, right?"

Once upon a time he was a hot kid who tried the life. He went to New York in the '40s and played the clubs and hotels, even subbed occasionally with Guy Lombardo, but he had kids, and the dance bands were dying. A lot of jazzers got jobs in Vegas or films or television, or they were angry, like Miles, but guys like Hank couldn't find work, not steady work, not enough to raise a family. He came home and carried mail, did some administrative work as he got older, and played every chance he got. He bought the Val Behrents book when Val finally doddered into retirement and has kept a couple or three bands afloat, part-time, ever since.

The Seven Ten Strutters take their name from Hank's booking address for Leitner Productions, 710 Prairie Lane. His answering machine plays four bars of "Sentimental Journey." Then it beeps.

The Strutters were getting restless, especially Murph, whose smile was pasted in place to hear another joke, but we were still waiting on the speaker. A few Mylar balloons rose to the ceiling. I didn't see any way to retrieve them, but surely the light fixture crew had some kind of access. Meanwhile, the balloons nudged up there like bulbous mirrors on the inverted surface of a nighttime pond.

There was a drum roll, and we all snapped to attention, or at least attentiveness. Hank drifted toward his horn, and Murph muttered, "Finally."

A tall man with a rumpled nose lurched through the tables to our mike. When he arrived, he held on, steadying himself.

Murph whispered, "Have another drink, Senator."

Sure enough, our senior senator had a few words about the good work performed by the doctors and staff at St. Anne's and, of course, the generosity of people like those assembled tonight.

I'm paraphrasing. The Senator had a few words, but they were aslosh on a small sea of liquor. Or maybe beer. He bills himself as a populist.

He made some disjointed reference to St. Anne's night following St. Patrick's by two days. One or two balloons with shamrocks blew upward. The crowd tittered. People's cheeks rolled fat with lollipops.

"I am reminded," said the Senator, and he told a story he must have used in a filibuster.

Hank's favorite joke has this old couple, this elderly pair, he always says, sitting around one night when the gentleman has an idea.

"You know what sounds good?" he says to his wife. "An ice cream sundae."

"Oh," she says, "that does sound good. With chocolate sauce?"

"And whipped cream," he says. "And nuts sprinkled on top. And a cherry."

"That sounds just delicious," she says, "and I think I could make some. We've got all the ingredients," and she goes to the kitchen.

She stays there. She stays there a long time. The old gent settles back in his chair and enjoys the ball game on the radio, and maybe two or three innings pass. There's a pitcher working on a shutout, but he's got men on first and second, and the count is two and two. He tries a curve ball. The batter swings late. It's a foul tip, and the old man's wife returns from the kitchen. She's carrying a tray with a cup of coffee and a glass of orange juice. There's a plate with two eggs, sunnyside up, and three strips of bacon, done just right, silverware, of course, and a cloth napkin and a little vase with a flower in it.

The old man looks up and says, "Where's the toast?"

Our audiences like this joke. Hank tells it almost every gig, but sometimes he forgets how it goes. He'll get lost while the old man's describing the sundae or while his wife is in the kitchen. Sometimes the man is watching football. By then the joke is hopeless. In the band, we're rolling our eyes. Someone usually calls out the punch line. Hank ends up saying, "Okay, here we go, this is it," and he repeats a couple of lines and gropes his way to the end. And the audience laughs. They love this joke.

I don't think it crosses generations. It may be waiting for us on the other side.

The Shrimp Peel crowd wasn't showing much patience, but the Senator was obviously adrift. More Mylar lifted toward the ceiling. White sticks wiggled out of lips. People, men mostly, started heading for the bar. The Senator saw the traffic and something clicked. Maybe his thirst. He put in more compliments for the doctors and staff and even called the hospital board by their names, drawing some disciplined applause, and then he wished everyone a fine evening, knowing they were in the capable musical hands of the Seventy Ten Starliters. Then he handed over the mike, received his own applause, and made a swift, uneven beeline to the bar.

"Jesus," Hank said before counting us off. "Where's the toast?"

*

By the time I was twelve measures in, Kelly and Stephanie were probably near the end of their movie. It was a Saturday night, and I was out playing. What else was new? It's got to the point that at home I might even be in their way. This is their routine, and Kelly tells me it's comfortable. Worse, I think I believe her.

It's not that I'm unwanted, but three is something more than a crowd, at least if it's all the time. Stephanie's a fun kid. I never mind just going to the store with her or running her to the library, and on Saturdays it's a joy to have her in the shop. She's meticulous repadding a flute, and she's polite in the presence of customers. Let them leave, though, and she'll announce which ones are crazy. Or pompous. Or just stupid. The mom who believes her kid's trumpet was folded over like a taco "just like that, as soon as he opened the case, I don't know how it happened," is sure to get Stephanie's slack-jawed mutant look the second the door closes behind her. We'll get half an hour of horseplay out of people like that and love every minute, but somehow the jokes don't quite translate at home. They're her property and mine, and the Saturday night popcorn and movies belong to Kelly.

And the playing belongs to me.

With a little moxie, maybe I could turn into Hank and run two bands. I could do it till I drop. There's a dynasty for you, Val Behrents to Hank Leitner to me.

Then Kelly really could have me committed. She'd have every right.

She looked at me like I was crazy when I floated the notion of quitting the schools.

"What about your pension?" she said.

"We'll roll it over."

"How about the mortgage?" she said. "And groceries? And your car? It's already ten years old."

All these were legitimate concerns, and we ignored them. We assumed we'd scrape by. Money always turns up—that was our premise. Stephanie was two, and it took a year to get our legal and financial ducks lined up, but we figured it was now or never, or I did, and Kelly indulged my desperate whim, partially because Stephanie was so young.

"Get that bankruptcy over early," Kelly said. "And this counts as your mid-life crisis, too. No affairs just because you hit 40 or 45."

"I'll be fixing register keys and banging dents out of tubas," I said. "Who'd have the time?"

She considered my fate and said, "Who'd even be interested?"

"In me?" I asked. "You'd better."

We're easily entertained at our house. A couple snide remarks, and everybody's happy. We'd expect nothing else.

At Nate's wedding, Kelly took one look at his wife and said, "That woman isn't sane."

I said, "Of course not. She's getting married today."

But Kelly was right. That woman's breathing sounds like a growl.

I fretted the rest of the week after Nate's call. I can always get gigs. I don't need to be taking his. More to the point, he doesn't need to be giving them up. He can't afford it, not if he wants to play, because he's easy to ignore. He's a good reed man, but he's not sociable. He can't tell a joke, and he can't listen to one, and nothing that happens even strikes him as funny. Gigs are goofy, almost every time. You can always remember something stupid or strange. It's the audience or the band or the hall you're playing. Maybe you're supposed to wear ugly hats or some clown remembers he used to take piano lessons and thinks he should try again. And sometimes the night's even perfect. The charts are good and you're even better.

But Nate never sees that stuff, or never talks about it. He's a guy who brings peanut butter sandwiches for the breaks. Perfectly square slices of wheat bread with the skimpiest layer of peanut butter you've ever seen, creamy, of course, so he could spread it thinner, with some shimmer of grape jelly applied like shellac, and he'd call this supper. That's the baggie he kept in his case, along with a toothbrush and tube of Colgate. He even flossed. The whole time, he'd never say boo.

A guy like that, he stops taking calls, the calls stop coming.

He's probably still eating those sandwiches, except now it's at home, at night, maybe after his wife has gone to bed, and he stands in the kitchen with one light on over the sink and sees his reflection in the black glass mirror of the window pane and knows he'll see it tomorrow and the day after that as he chews his dry food in a house that is finally quiet.

*

The crowd was half gone by 10:30. We were the Starliters then, the big band. An hour after that a few diehards pushed themselves across the dance floor, and we kept playing, but took it as an open rehearsal, with wisecracks between tunes and no stiff smiling for our smattering of applause. We just hooted at missed changes and the breakneck tempos imposed when the drummer got bored. Or we laughed at our echo, which bounced around in all that glass and granite and sometimes played a full measure back to us after we stopped. There may be a song still caught among the balloons, our own lost chords stuck in an endless reverb. Murph figured they'd break loose someday and settle to earth like runaway Muzak.

"I think we lost the whole second set," he said. "We'll be our very own ghost band."

Hank said, "I don't like the sound of that. I'm not dead yet, you know."

"Let us know when you are," said Benj, misting his slide. "I might be, too, and just didn't notice."

"Check the obituary page," Hank said. "If you're listed, you can't make the gig."

"I'll be sure to call," Benj said, "so you can line up a sub."

Hank pointed at me and said, "Careful, we're already losing our saxes."

"Sure," said Murph, "but who says Nate was ever living?"

There I sat, one of the honorary dead.

Arnold shook his horn, emptying his spit valve. He caught me watching and said, "Howdy."

Would Kelly believe this was how I spent my time?

Murph told me once how he got divorced. "She got tired of the gigs, and I got tired of her."

"So now you're both happy, right?"

"No," Murph said, "but I get to play anyway."

I need to tell Kelly how grateful I am.

The Dixie part of the program went okay. The audience didn't care. We did some stomps and shuffles, Armstrong and Dodds, some Oliver, but we didn't sound authentic. Never do. The voicings are right except for no banjo, but the style is all wrong. Listen to the records, and that's not us. We're not even Bix Beiderbecke happy music clones who make their way to Davenport every year. Most of us learned swing thirty years after it was popular. It's as ambitious as we get. No bop, no genuine New Orleans.

The audience so thoroughly didn't care that we cut the Dixie portion short. We didn't even bother with "Saints." I think it was "Butter and Egg Man" and out. Then the Starliters joined us and I became Nate.

I'd played beside Hank, but I'd never seen him conduct. I wondered who his model was. Not Guy Lombardo. Maybe Jerry Lewis.

That's not fair. Hank took it seriously. He wasn't showboating, but he looked fake, like a parody of a frontman. He jabbed and kicked at every beat. The Starliter charts were big and brassy, in that Kenton and Basie mold, with lots of punctuation. *Ba-dop ba-dop bop!* with big accents. Hank punched out every one and did little swivel steps, but this was music as he meant it to be heard, for dancing. I was sightreading, so I kept my nose down and missed a lot of gyrations, but I'd glance up and see Hank squinting at us, and listening. None of us was really there. We were the sound we produced and nothing else. Hank was shrunken in his tux, a man whose heart was given extra time for beating by a doctor's hands reaching into his chest, but he actually listened to every night's performance. It wasn't just a walk-through. Hank had not let go of the time when this music mattered, when it had an audience, when it was the natural idiom.

This audience, the Shrimp Peel crowd, really wanted rock 'n' roll. They were in their thirties, forties, and fifties. They liked that throbbing motor sound of bass guitar. They heard, as Hank did, the music of their youth. The Starliters were the sputtering engine of another age, maybe an interesting mechanism, but nothing anybody would actually drive.

Of course, there's always some drunk idiot who wants to get behind the wheel. Sometimes it's a woman in spangles who thinks she's Billie Holiday, or more likely Patti Page. She climbs onstage and wants to sing. We're lucky if she doesn't knock over the mike.

Or throw up at our feet, which is what the fat man did after pawing Hank's bony shoulders and begging him to be a pal and play "My Wild Irish Rose." Hank winced at every swat, and even though we didn't have it, the tune wasn't in the book, the piano player fluttered out an intro arpeggio just so the guy would stop whapping him.

It worked. The fat man made some noise of recognition and pointed at the piano, then turned around and tucked in his shirt, at least in front. The back hung like a tablecloth under his suitcoat. He wobbled to the microphone and stood, suddenly struck dumb.

It could be he saw the audience and froze. Some people panic when they see the little round eyes of a crowd. What seemed a good idea with that last shot of liquor dissolves or gets murky and unmanageable once you're standing there, sweating, without a glass in your hand. Or it might have been the sight of his wife, that thin woman in the ten-year-old suit who'd grimaced every time she took a bite of green beans. Obviously she'd come directly from work, where she was probably a secretary or ran the payroll, and she'd left after putting in some overtime to come straight here, to be punctual meeting her husband at this benefit dinner-dance he'd committed them to attend, and now he stood weaving, disheveled and drunk, his mouth gaping around a microphone which only heard, and amplified, the clotted rasp of his breath, and he stood there hearing it and watching everyone else hear it, too.

But probably it was the column of liquor that hardened and clenched in his belly and poured back out. I think he felt it coming and couldn't sing a note. He felt it surge past the back of his throat and through his mouth and explode in the air. I don't know how he missed the microphone. It was a sickly beige stew of vomit. I saw the cheesecake and chocolate pie. I saw some chicken and beans and recognizable shrimp. I don't think the guy ever chewed.

Murph leaned over my shoulder while the man retched on his hands and knees and said, "It's probably a good thing Nate isn't here for this, you think?"

"It is a bit indelicate," I said. I watched the man's wife, her knees pinched tight, grab him under the arm to help him to his feet, and saw him slip on the wet floor as a mop crew approached and Hank was calling up our next tune, and I knew people would talk about this gig, when the fat guy spewed his supper across the floor, but Murph was right. Without Nate here not to laugh when we normally would, we weren't laughing, either.

*

As the crowd thinned, we started playing ballads, tunes with slow, thick chords that didn't take much reading. I appreciated the break. I'd done well enough for someone new to the book. If Nate were really quitting I had the job locked if I wanted, and sitting there under Hank's arm, under its slow churn of a beat, while Benj and Murph and the other bones played some lush harmony and Arnold muted his horn to take a solo, I hoped for the first time that Nate would stay at home. It made me feel small and mean. For one thing, I needed the money. Stephanie's dentist had started talking orthodontia.

But the money would be there somehow. That's still our premise, and it works. The real truth is, Nate is just gone. I can't see him any other way. He is trapped in that house. He got married because people do, because someone showed an interest, and it looked like his only chance. She was a teacher at one of his schools, someone else vaguely waiting for an exit, and now she lies in bed and tolerates no sound but hers, the moaning that spreads to every room in the house.

About a year ago he suggested we play some duets, no concert in mind, just for fun, just to play. He was down to the Starliters only and thought something legit would be a nice change.

"I'm not much on clarinet," he said, "but it is what I learned on."

We played some Krejci, Bach, and Mozart, or tried. I saw his wife, at least thirty pounds heavier than at the wedding, as she appeared at the door, then vanished. She glared as if we carried a grudge between us, but except at the wedding, we'd never spoken.

Nate and I ran through our duets, at least a few bars each, but upstairs his wife groaned at almost every note. The sound rolled down the stairs and vents. It rose, and soon she was wailing. I asked if we should stop, and he said no. But I couldn't play. He said she wasn't feeling well, and he grimaced, swabbing his horn. I was packing mine as fast as I could.

He said, "She has days that are painful," and his fingers attended to his horn in its case.

Nate was gone, and I was taking his place. I played second alto and clarinet when it was needed and looked up to a smaller audience as the night wore on, but once I saw a pair actually leave. Down the long hall to our case room, if you didn't turn left, there was an exit to the street. I had sixteen measures' rest and was looking around and saw a couple about my age, about the same age as Nate, huddled together like teenagers as they walked. He wore a grey suit, and she wore a dress of black and white sequins in swirls. Suddenly they took each other's arms, and they danced, by themselves, for ten or twelve bars, as if they'd heard this music all their lives, and then they left, taking the door I'd use myself in maybe half an hour.

25

The End of Bull Mácha

Josef Škvorecký

For Jan Hammer, Sr., in memoriam
and for Vlasta Průchová-Hammer, in fond memory

Das Spiel ist ganz und gar verloren,
Und dennoch wird es weitergehen.
(The game is totally lost, and yet it will go on.)

ERICH KÄSTNER

Bull Mácha was leaning against the pedestrian railing at the corner of Vodičková Street and Wenceslas Square. The thin mist of a dank afternoon was slowly falling into the streets, blurring the features of the people trudging past him. The streets were coming alive with the bustle of a Sunday evening in the big city. Through the silvery grey veil of a wet autumn dusk the lights in the store windows and cafés were coming on, and the faces of the girls Bull Mácha's impassive eyes were stalking in the crowd seemed to assume a new and mysterious charm under the misty, magic chiaroscuro of artificial lighting. Their hazy beauty touched him like a sudden pain, and in the depths of his heart he longed to draw close to them in a place where one could get closest of all: a café, one of the dance halls whose windows were already beginning to glow through the spidery mist that was slowly descending upon the city of Prague. It was the month of November in the year of our Lord 1953.

The figure leaning against the green railing, with his low, carefully combed coiffure turned to face the flaming entrance of the Soviet Book Shop, was in his own way a living human fossil. At the age of twenty-nine, František Mácha still referred to himself by his old nickname, Bull, in full "Gablik" Bull—Zoot-Suiter Bull—and he insisted that others do so too. And the vague notion of belonging to a grand conspiracy against something uncertain, a conspiracy he still felt a part of, was epitomized, even after all these years, by the title "Gablik." It was an expression that had stuck to him long ago, during the vogue for a popular American Civil War movie and its raffish, devil-may-care hero, Gable himself.

Now Gablik Bull Mácha was standing on the corner of Vodičková Street and Wenceslas Square, his heart lacerated by those winsome, cosmetically improved young faces, and by a strange, miserable nostalgia. He was alone, his hands stuffed into enormous pockets, and from the overcoat, cut strictly according to fashion with the sloping shoulders of a wine bottle and a collar as wide as an acolyte's, a small head emerged, with a painstakingly fashioned coif in front and the sides slicked back into a ducktail. From that face two watery grey eyes stared: dull, bored, desperate. Bull had the heel of his left foot hooked over the bottom rung of the green railing, with his leg swung over as far as he could to the left, and he had pulled up his narrow trouser leg to avoid making a bulge at the knee, so that all might remark on his black-yellow-and-green-striped socks and gaze in wonder at the Gothic upturned toes of his Hungarian winklepickers. He was especially proud of those winklepickers with their snow-white soles flashing in the descending fog like crown jewels, cared for with boundless love and worn only on ceremonial occasions.

But Bull Mácha's soul was sad. He stood erect and motionless above the crowds flowing from the square into Vodičková Street and back, like a solitary rock in the tide, alone, lonesome and rejected. And in the pain that gripped his heart, he remembered another age, and evenings like this, with the chiaroscuro lighting, the cold, the bright shop windows, when he wasn't alone, when crowds of people his own age, his cronies, would mill about together, and the strange, magic words of an exotic language no one had ever used before flew back and forth through the air, and from the Boulevard Café down below came the Dixieland sound of Graeme Bell, and up above in the Phoenix, Frankie Smith was singing and Leslie "Jiver" Hutchinson was blowing his horn and the sharp, bebop riffs of Dunca Brož drifting up from the underground wine bar tugged invitingly at his ears. Where had those times gone? Where was Kandahár, the tenor player with those tight black negro curls? Where was Harýk? Where was Lucie?

Gablik Bull Mácha was the only one left. He knew exactly where the rest were, and the question that had surfaced in his sad, nostalgic thoughts was only figurative, rhetorical. Kandahár the tenorman, whose real name was Nývlt, was now an architect with Stavoprojekt. He was married, and his wife went to chamber music concerts and was studying to be an opera singer. And that was the end of Gablik Kandahár. And Venca Štern, the trombonist with the magnificent, crackling, tailgating style? He was manager of some factory that made movie screens in the border district. Harýk was in the jug for an illegal attempt to cross the border. Lucie was determined to remain faithful to him, and worked as a secretary at the Central Council of Revolutionary Trade Unions.

He was the only one left, unmarried, unchanged, just as he had been back in the nylon age. He was still willing to bloody his knuckles to get into a public recording session by Karel Vlach's swing band, which—like him—was all that was left of those wonderful times. He was alone, the last of his clan, and when he wanted to find a spirit that was even slightly kindred he had to hang out with seventeen-year-old punks who didn't even know what the word *gablik* meant.

And so now he stood at the corner of Vodičková Street and Wenceslas Square, a historic site that was part of a faded, bygone world, and as his eyes flitted from face to face, he said to himself, "Shit, there's no one here, no one in the whole damn city of Prague." He had nowhere to go. He was beat, utterly beat.

Just then a familiar face appeared in the river of people flowing by. "Mack! Hey, Mack!" Bull called out. The familiar face looked up, searching for a moment in the mist. Then it broke out in a friendly grin.

"Well, if it ain't Bullsie," said the wilted young man in an army coat with black threadbare epaulets and no regimental insignia. He was pushing a beat-up baby carriage, and at his side slouched a peroxide blonde. Once she'd been a real dish—a luketa—but now her face looked wilted and royally fed up.

"Hey, hand me some skin, man," said Bull, in the familiar accent of the nylon age, all his vowels tight and flat, the words drawn out. "How's it stackin' up?"

The soldier took the proffered hand and replied in the same fashion. "It's stackin' up shit, Bullsie, pure shit."

Bull glanced quickly at the soldier's woman, but Mack's crude language obviously didn't faze her.

"The wife," said the soldier.

"Pleasure." Bull held out his hand. The wife looked apathetically into his eyes. "Like we've already met, right?"

Bull looked at her faded features and suddenly, in the light of memory, they began to change. He felt a chill come over him. "Hey, right!" he said. "You must be—you're Maggie Vančuříková, aren't you?"

"Didn't recognize me, didja? Quite a shock, eh?" she said mechanically. Her voice was unpleasant, and Bull had the feeling that she was mad at him, that she almost hated him.

"Ah shit, Maggie, it's been a hell of a long time since I seen you last. You was still carrying on with Jackie Petráček, so I figured—"

"You figured I'd wait for him, right? Fat chance."

"Anyway, what'd he pull down that time?"

"Six," she said curtly.

"Right. Well, that explains it. But jeez, it's great to see you both. Hey, I should congratulate you!"

"What the hell for?" asked the soldier.

"Like you're married, ain'tcha? I never heard about it when it happened, so better late than never."

"Congratulate us for the brat too, while you're at it," Maggie said. Her voice trembled with an echo of deep anger.

"So this here's the family future," said Bull as he bent over for a quick, obligatory admiring glance at the pale and also apparently faded infant sleeping under a smudgy blanket in a carriage that had seen better days. This is Maggie? he was thinking, that blonde-haired chick from the White Swan? The one who won the bugathon in the House of Slavs back in '46? There's gotta be a mistake.

"Still in the army, Mack?" he asked quickly, so he wouldn't have to think about it.

"You got eyes, haven't you?"

"Yeah, but it's been a long time."

"Third f'kin year, man."

"Somebody slipped them a bum report, eh?"

"Believe it. But I got the bastard's number."

"Lemme know who the son-of-a-bitch is. We could have a heart-to-heart talk with him some night in a dark alley. I can get some people together—"

"Look after him myself," Mack interrupted.

"Suit yourself," said Bull. "But you're getting out soon, ain'tcha?"

"The word is, Easter. The word is they're gonna disband us," Mack said. "And how about you, Bull? Man, you're just the same as you always was. Nothing's changed, except you shit on everything."

"Bull always did that, didn't he?" said the wife. "Or maybe you're different now?"

Deep down, the couple's words made Bull feel good. Yes, he always shat on everything. Still did. Always would.

"You kidding?" he said. "Same as always. They ain't making me over."

"That's what you say," said the soldier. "You'd sing another tune if they shoved you in with the politicos."

"Hey, I did my stint, didn't I?"

"Not with the Black Barons you didn't. Real f'kin chain-gang stuff, I can tell you. And how long were you in, anyway, man?"

Bull Mácha laughed contentedly. "Three months, man. Pretended I wet the bed."

This made even the gloomy wife laugh. "Still a free man?" she asked.

"One hundred percent," said Bull.

"No plans to get hitched?"

Bull laughed again. "I ain't rushing it."

"Maybe you should," sneered the wife, "while there's still time."

That angry light flashed in her eyes again. Christ, said Bull to himself, it ain't my fault they went and made themselves a brat.

"Ever go dancing?" he asked, to change the subject. And also to find out—to reassure himself.

Mack looked surprised. "Dancing? We got other things to worry about, man. Take the brat, that costs something, doesn't it? And you make shit in the f'kin army."

The small flame that had flared up in Bull's heart when he saw his old pardner began to flicker and wane. "What I mean is, you still like jazz, dontcha?"

Mack shrugged his shoulders. "I got no time. Tell you, man, it's like licking shit from a liquorice stick."

"Mack, if we're gonna make that movie we got to move our bones," said the wife.

"Sure," said Mack. "Movie starts at five-thirty and we got to dump the brat at my mom's."

"If you gotta go, you gotta go," said Bull.

"Show up sometime," said Mack. "I'm usually home on Sundays. Made a deal with the brass."

"I'll do that," said Bull. "Take it easy."

"See you," said Mack, and shook his hand.

"So long, Bull," said the wilted girl who had once been Maggie Vančuříková.

"So long, Maggie," said Bull. "So long." The soldier gave the baby carriage a push and the couple blended into the crowd flowing down the street. Bull's impassive eyes followed them for a while. The wife was wearing an old coat. She'd lost weight, and it hung from her as if from a coat rack. Maggie! Shit, where had it all gone? Where? And Mack! In '46, '47, it was five nights a week, every week, in the Boulevard Café. Now he says he hasn't got time for it. Hasn't got time! What the hell else is your time supposed to be for?

Again Bull peered into the Sunday crowds parading through the thickening mist. Up there above the city it was night already, and the streetlamps were coming on. They hung like spheres of luminous honey dissolving in milk, with thin golden haloes forming around them in the mist. They've all given up, they've all just said to hell with it! It was like a betrayal. Maybe they're just scared shitless, who knows? They all used to be so wild about it, and now everyone's in such a goddamned hurry to drop it. All it took was closing down a few jazz gardens, slapping a ban on jazz in the cafés, and everybody says screw it. But ain't makin' me over. Never! Bull felt a wave of disgust and resistance rise within him. I can remember the beginnings. Back when I still wore my Gable moustache . I can remember when the Nazi cops used to chase us down Wenceslas Square because we had our hair long in the back and wore our shoelaces for neckties. I wore oversized fedoras and flat-brimmed hats and strap belts low in the back, and in '44 the cops hauled me in and shaved my head and then got me tossed out of school on my ear, and then shoved me into the Technische Nothilfe. Can't forget stuff like that. I ain't gonna forget it, anyway. They ain't makin' me over!

"Well, glory be to the Lord Jesus Christ! Bull Mácha!" The voice came from somewhere beside him, and he turned to see who it was.

There was a pale little hepcat in a double-breasted winter overcoat with narrow shoulders, a tie as loud as a fireworks display, and a brilliantined coif looping down over his forehead. He gave Bull a friendly smile.

"F'rever'n'ever, amen," said Bull.

"Hey Bullsie, why don't you tag along with me?" said the hepcat, still smiling.

"Where to?" Bull asked.

"National House up in Vinohrady. Jan Hammer's cookin' there tonight."

"No kidding?"

"Absolutely, man. They wangled the permish at the last minute. Never had a chance to poster."

"Seriously?"

"I kid you not. Come on, Bull! The joint'll be jumping."

Jan Hammer!

"Is he still hanging out with that bebop crowd?"

"Course. Rhythm Fifty-three. Vlasta Průchová's singing."

Vlasta Průchová! The wave of rebellion building up in Bull's soul now took on a concrete shape. Even if everyone else said to hell with it, he wouldn't!

"So let's move," he said to the hepcat, and quickly unstuck himself from the railing. The hepcat trotted along beside him, trying to keep up. They walked up Wenceslas Square, hands in their pockets, shoulders slouched, the misty golden spheres of the streetlamps reflected in their slicked-back hair.

"Workin' these days, Bull?" asked the hepcat, partly to be polite, partly out of curiosity.

"Got a job in a junk depot."

"How's the bacon?"

"Sliced pretty thin."

They were silent for a while. Then the hepcat said, "Hey, man, have you heard? Prdlas put a group together. They cook at his place every Thursday."

"What's the line-up?"

"Prdlas horn, Šmejda liquorice stick, Rathauskej bull fiddle, Bimbo skins. You could bring your git-box over sometime, Bull."

"I might." Bull was silent for a moment, then said, "They play hot?"

"They'll burn your ear off, Bull! Drag your git-box over some night 'n you'll see."

"Sounds good."

They turned into the park around the museum. The dusk was thicker there, and people were hurrying to get through the park and back into the illuminated streets. They walked through the park and quickly up the side streets to St. Ludmilla's. The hepcat opened the conversation again.

"Líza said she was coming."

"Which one's she?" said Bull.

"Works in Pearl's, remember? She got really blasted last New Year's Eve at Tubby's."

"She the one they had to carry out?"

"That's her. She was screwing Hekáč."

"You goin' out with her?"

"Not me," said the hepcat. "She treats me like a piece of shit. But she's class, eh?"

"Yeah, she's OK, she's OK," said Bull. OK, he repeated to himself, but she's nothing compared to Lucie. Or to what Lucie used to be. He remembered a different evening in the National House in Vinohrady, when Terš was playing and Lucie wore a yellow dress with a wavy fringe on the hem of her skirt and they danced the boogie together and he rolled her right over his shoulders.

Why had it all dried up? When did it happen? And how? It just sort of happened by itself, and no one even noticed. But it happened, and in the end, he was the only one left, alone. And he missed Lucie. It had been a long time since he'd been with a decent girl like Lucie. All he knew were gangs of young teenies. He was too old for them. There was a whole generation between them. A painful longing pressed Bull's heart. Where had all those jitterdolls gone? Where, goddammit?

They began walking faster. The windows of the National House shone brightly across the square. They walked towards it, two figures, one tall, one short, a large coif and a smaller one, shoulders slouched like a wine bottle's. As they came closer to their goal, the smaller one said, "Jeez, man, you know, it's strange they let this dance go on at all."

"Finally got it through their skulls people are pissed off," said Bull.

The hepcat chuckled. "Like where I work," he said, "they're always after us to join some goddamned choir, can you believe it? Want us to sing some stupid Russian shit, stuff like that. I mean fuck that."

"You in the Youth League?"

"Yeah. Collective membership, like nobody even asked us if we wanted to join or not; they just signed us up. They expect us to play their little games, but like everybody's saying fuck that."

"What else they expect?" said Bull, but he felt the touch of doubt. They ain't makin' me over, he said to himself again. Not me. That'll be the day, when they get me to go to a bunch of meetings. Screw 'em; they'll never change me.

The windows on the second floor of the National House poured bright shafts of light down into the square, which by this time was quite dark. The walls of the church stretched blackly towards heaven, and they could hear the faint sounds of an organ. Black figures stood around the entrance to the National House, and the puffs of breath that came from their mouths merged with the evening mist. They went through glass revolving doors into the lobby, and as the door gently swept them into the building, their ears picked up the distant riffs of wild, delicious music.

"Hear that? They're already blowing a storm," said the hepcat excitedly. "Hammer's really belting it out!"

Bull stopped and listened. The crisp, metallic halting tones of a vibraphone came tumbling down the stairs.

"Great!" said Bull, and both of them ran eagerly up the stairs. The music mingled with the hum in the crowded hall, that familiar, ancient backdrop to pleasure. They put their coats in the cloakroom and then, despite their hurry, stopped in front of the mirror. Beside it hung a poster displaying a caricature of an antediluvian zoot-suiter, and underneath this were the words Zoot-Suiters Not Welcome!

"Hey, man," said the hepcat. "Get a load of these wise guys."

"Screw 'em," said Bull.

The diabolically beautiful music was drawing them inside, but the magnetism of the mirror was powerful. They appeared in its shiny, smudged surface, a big and a small coif, and they pulled out enormous combs and began grooming their hair. Bull's jacket, reflected in the mirror, was first-class English cloth, from which the tailor—who still had a private shop—had produced a loose-hanging garment with rows of buttons down the side and a collar that dipped down to a point midway between his shoulder blades. Bull Mácha put the finishing touches on his coif and pulled out his tie. In the past, he had worn his hair long at the back, and then in a crewcut; now it was coiffed in front, with long sides slicked back. Over the years, his tie had grown from a tiny knot that resembled a shoelace knot to a super-wide American windsor that he had to use the end of a fork to tie properly. It was this type of knot that now sat resplendent beneath his chin. He straightened the knot, jerked his arms forward to free his sleeves, then hooked his thumb under his collar and adjusted the slouchy jacket on his shoulders. Finally, he ran the palm of his hand over his coif, then turned around to look at himself from behind. He was ready to go. He was ready to enter a ceremony which—though he had never thought about it—he felt contained the meaning of life.

No longer paying any attention to the little hepcat still trotting along at his side, he entered the hall. He positioned himself in one corner, and the first thing he did was take a good look around. His eyes were no longer impassive, but bright and eager as he watched the band on the podium. The smile that washed over his small face was almost happy. The vibraphone, Jan Hammer standing over it waving his sticks like a magician over a metal stove-top, bobbing his head to the rhythm, grinning like an ecstatic idiot as a wild foxtrot tumbled off the podium, Vlasta beside him in a blue dress, rotating her beautiful hips and clapping her hands to the rhythm, and Kyntych, his head bowed over his trumpet, the bell pointed towards the ceiling, Rocman with his glasses and clarinet, Tiny Vondráš with a tenor sax in his face. They played and played—man, how they played! Behind them, Poledňák pounded the drums furiously, then gently; then there was a sudden off-beat break, a roll of rim-shots, and he slipped back into the groove again and on they played, man, how they played! Bull felt a wonderful mood blossom inside him, and without thinking, he started stamping the parquet floor with his Gothic Hungarian winklepickers and staring intently, his eyes now alive with worshipful delight, at the sticks of the swaying vibraphonist. The desperate rebellion that had been building up inside him all afternoon, right until he had heard Hammer play, gave way to a victorious sensation of certainty that all this would last, that they wouldn't manage to suffocate it after all, that it was the same jazz it had always been, sounding just as sassy as it always had, with the same crowd of people dancing to it, and that no one in the world could wipe out this music, this world, the only one he had ever wanted to belong to.

Then, feeling the urge to dance, he started looking around at the girls. He wanted to have it all, the music and the women, because jittermolls belonged to this musical worship service too, girls who felt the dirty syncopated tone of the swinging tenor-sax player travelling through their nervous systems just as it did through his.

It looked as though Lady Luck was with him. A luketa was just sidecarring past him, with some donkey pushing her back and forth. To those magnificent thundering riffs and swinging rhythms, these two were dancing, if that was the word for it, like a couple of hicks at a tea dance in the outer boondocks. He watched them for a while, a contemptuous smile on his small face. He saw the geek step on the luketa's foot, and the luketa looked fed up. What else? She wore a black, close-fitting skirt, a wide black nylon belt, and a blouse with big flowers on it. Her face was like a beautifully painted Easter egg. The geek's clothes were strictly John Farmer. Bull felt that fate had brought this woman across his path. She reminded him of Lucie in her best years. Class. You could see the kind of class in her that was missing in the women who went with the cats he hung around with now, for lack of anything better.

The band finished and the scarecrow led the luketa back to her table. He bowed, she thanked him coldly and sat down to her glass of lemonade. A fellow in a black suit and a nowhere tie sat down beside her.

The vibraphone started playing again. Bull kicked himself into gear, and in a flash he was standing in front of the luketa.

"Take your bones for a strut, miss?"

She looked up at him with blue eyes. "I suppose so."

She got up. Bull put the palm of his hand against her nylon belt and led her onto the floor. They began with an ordinary foxtrot, but he could feel right away that this girl was a marvellous dancer.

"They're really socking it out, eh?" he said.

She looked at him again with her blue eyes. He expected some warm, enthusiastic response, some affirmation of his statement of faith. But instead she said, "I beg your pardon?"

It sounded almost hostile. Almost unpleasant. At least he had that impression. Like some goody-goody defending her reputation. But he didn't believe that.

"You like the way they play?" he asked uncertainly.

"So so."

He tried a more complicated step. She responded immediately. Maybe she just didn't understand what I said, he thought. It's okay. He held her out at arm's length and tried something more daring.

"No. Stop it!" she said suddenly.

"Don't you want to jelly the goulash, darling?"

"I beg your pardon?"

"You know: kick loose, introduce a little juice, show 'em we're alive to the jive?"

"No. Just dance the way you did at first."

"Aw, go on," said Bull desperately. "You dance magnif. It's a pity to waste your talent tromping down sauerkraut."

"It suits me just fine."

"But it's got no jolt to it, my dear! Come on!" he said, and again he tried to execute a variation that required more imagination than the standard foxtrot shuffle. But she just stood there and left him hanging. It was embarrassing. He stopped.

"Don't do that!" she said threateningly. "If you want to cause a scandal here, find someone else to do it with."

"Scandal, miss?" He took her around the waist again. She relented, but he felt the muscles of her back go tense under her blouse. "Scandal?"

"You know very well what I mean. I don't dance any of that jitterbug stuff."

Bull's heart almost stopped. He couldn't believe his ears. Again, he felt that pain deep in his soul.

"Don't tell me that, miss," he said. "You're a champ! Okay, so what dances do you dance?"

Her reply sounded like an article in the Youth Union daily. "All kinds, but it has to be decent. If you don't like it, you can take me back to my seat."

"But it's such a drag, miss. It's for cripples!"

"It's good enough for me," she said.

Hammer hit the vibraphone, and Vlasta's voice was clear, bell-like. "Rhythm, that's my kind of thing," she sang. "Rhythm, that's what makes it swing!"

It really got to him. The silly goose can't be serious.

"All right, here's a surprise for you," he said resolutely, and grabbed her firmly by the hand, hit the floor with his left toe crossed over his right, then did a quick reverse repeat, and again and again, at the same time tapping the parquet with his heels and toes, step-dancing beautifully to the rhythm. There was a lot of art to it. And suddenly he felt her tugging on the arm he was holding and trying to struggle free.

"Let me go, let me go!" she hissed, pushing him away. He stood there helplessly, his arms hanging loose, staring at her in amazement. Her eyes flashed with hatred again.

"Find yourself some—some jittermoll for that, not me!" she shouted. Then she turned around and disappeared into the crowd.

Bull was thunderstruck. Then he realized that several couples dancing nearby were scowling at him. He felt himself beginning to blush, so he turned around and walked out of the hall, his heart pounding. At first, he was stunned by the realization that she had made him look like a fool. But in the foyer he came to his senses and once more felt that malignant, miserable afternoon pain in the depths of his soul. How could she have done a thing like that to him?

He stood leaning against the banister and began to hate her intensely. The whore! I'll bet she's in the goddamned Youth League. Dumb, just like the rest of them. But the sweet image of that face could not simply be driven off by the insults which, in his mind, he heaped on the girl's head. It was as though he were reviving other faces from the past, and it hurt.

"Hey, Bull!" said a fellow who was just coming up the stairs.

"Hi, René."

"How come you're not inside?" asked the fellow called René. He'd been a Gablik and zoot-suiter too. Then he got married and said to hell with it. So what was he doing here?

"Taking a breather," said Bull. "Where's the old lady?"

"Went for a piss. Come on, let's check out the talent."

"Bugger all out there, I'll tell you that," said Bull. "Hammer's cooking, and that's about it."

"And he's not bad," said René, pricking up his ears. "Still tight as ever."

"Maybe. But Hammer and Vlasta's all that's left of the old Rhythm Forty-Eight. Rest are all new."

"They can still cut loose, though."

"That's a fact," said Bull. He felt a faint hope stir inside him. "So I see you haven't said to hell with jazz after all."

"Yeah," said René. "That's a fact. Always ready to listen to anything solid." He turned to Bull, half closed his eyes, and said didactically, "All the same, Bull, you know, the classics it ain't."

"No, you're right there," said Bull. He felt the hope dying stillborn. "The classics it ain't," he said ironically, but René didn't seem to get his point.

"Any floozies around?" he asked casually.

"Take a look, why don't we," said Bull. But his hope was dead. He didn't want to spend time with René.

They took up positions at one of the doorways and scanned the dance hall. Bull tried to see his luketa. He found her. She was with the guy who had first sat down at her table. They were dancing a neat, nowhere foxtrot. Enough to make you puke.

"Know that woman over there?" he asked René. "The one with the black nylon belt over by the edge of the floor? The blonde?"

René looked in that direction. "Never seen her before. But she don't look completely useless."

"No, she don't," said Bull. "What do you suppose she does?"

"Who knows? Maybe one of the sexual proletariat. At least she looks like it."

Bull laughed bitterly. "I think you're way off," he said, and then he greeted René's wife, who had just joined him. "Evening."

"Evening." Her lips were thin, like a corpse's, and her cheeks were painted with purple rouge. Her hair was done up in small tight curls, like a lambskin cap.

"Want to dance, Jarka?" asked René.

"Hmmm," she said coquettishly.

"You coming too, Bull?" René asked, out of politeness.

"Sure," said Bull. The couple drifted away. Bull looked around and saw a jittermoll type who had just come in. He knew her. She hung around with the beboppers. Called herself Evita.

"Greetings, Creamroll," he said.

"Hi, Apache."

"Want to polish the floorboards?"

"Why not?" she said. He led her onto the dance floor. Kyntych was just blowing a solo in the middle range, a diabolical, fast bebop solo. A deluge of short notes in foxtrot rhythm. Again, a desperate wave of defiance washed over Bull Mácha. If everyone else has shit on it, if they're all like that stupid broad, such a looker and yet so dumb, I ain't gonna change. They ain't makin' me over! And if the first one didn't want to, Evita certainly won't mind.

He took hold of Evita and started showing her everything he knew. Evita wasn't a bad dancer. They stayed in one corner of the hall and commandeered their own private dance floor, a space of several square metres where Bull really began to cut loose. Would zootsuiters please refrain from dancing excessive dances? Just watch. He spun Evita around until her skirt was flying high above her knees. That's how it's done! Hammer laid down a groove on the vibraphone and everyone settled into it. They howled, they bleated, they wailed, the drums thrashed, the cymbals sizzled. Bull really cut loose now. He felt that this was something big, what he was doing, that it was everything you could possibly do here, everything you could possibly accomplish in this lifetime—

Suddenly someone was tugging his sleeve. He swung around irritably and saw a waiter.

"What do you want?" he blurted out, without waiting to see what he had to say.

"Sir," said the waiter. "You can't dance that kind of dance in here."

He felt a rush of anger. "What the hell are you talking about?"

"It's forbidden. Otherwise you'll have to leave the dance floor."

"Well now, ain't that nice," said Bull. "Why don't you just take a walk. I paid for my ticket. I can do what I damn well feel like."

"I'm telling you, you can't dance like that here. Wild dances are forbidden."

"Is that so? Well, you can kiss my ass," said Bull, turning back to Evita. They began dancing again.

But the waiter held on to him. "Watch your language, sir. I'm telling you to stop that kind of dancing."

"Look," said Bull, talking to him over his shoulder. "Why don't you just drop out of sight?"

"I'll have to call the police," said the waiter.

That was all they needed! Bull was outraged. "Get lost! You're in the way!" he roared at the waiter, and then he and Evita danced their way into the crowd. He saw the waiter stand there uncertainly for a few moments, then turn and leave the hall.

"Just let him try," he said to the girl called Evita.

"You shouldn't have been so rude to him, Bull," said Evita. "He'll rat on you for sure."

"I don't care if he takes it all the way to the goddamned ministry!" said Bull. "I had the Germans on my back for dancing, and they couldn't stop me. Nothing to worry about, Evita."

He started dancing again, deliberately making wild figures on the floor, but he kept looking nervously over Evita's shoulders at the door. No one appeared. The number was over, Evita pressed close to him, and they followed the crowd off the floor.

The waiter was standing in the doorway, and beside him was a uniformed policeman with a revolver and a fur collar sewn to his tunic.

"That's him," said the waiter, pointing at Bull.

Bull tried to disappear, but the waiter caught him by the shoulder.

"Take your hands off me," said Bull.

"Come with me," said the cop gruffly.

"What's going on?" growled Bull.

"That's the one," said the waiter. "When I asked him politely to stop dancing that way, he started yelling at me and using very filthy language."

"Don't you know jitterbugging's not allowed?" asked the cop. "There's a ban on it."

"There ain't no such law," said Bull.

"But there's a ban," said the cop.

"Don't get your shorts in a knot!" said Bull. "I paid, I dance."

"You watch your language!" shouted the cop.

"I am," said Bull. "And what are you hanging on to me for, anyway?"

"Nobody's hanging on to you," declared the cop. "You were dancing forbidden dances and causing a public nuisance. I'm warning you to lay off. Otherwise I'm going to have to—"

"Introduce me to anyone who thought I was a nuisance," said Bull arrogantly.

"Shut up!" shouted the cop. "If you don't stop—"

"Well, this is just great, this is wonderful!" said Bull bitterly. "A guy forks over eight crowns and they don't even let him dance."

"You can dance all you want, but you can't make a public nuisance of yourself," repeated the cop.

"You're the public nuisance!" said Bull. All at once he didn't care what happened to him. He was only desperately angry. "You should be out chasing down some real public mischief. Leave people with regular jobs alone when they're trying to have some fun."

"That's it!" said the cop. "Leave the room at once!"

"You got no right! I ain't done nothing!" said Bull. He caught sight of Evita standing to one side, making herself small and watching him with wide eyes. A crowd of gawkers had gathered around them. A new wave of defiance washed over him. I'm not gonna let these assholes trim me back, he said to himself.

"Don't tell me what I have a right to and what I don't," said the cop.

"You think you got a right to everything," said Bull. "And just because somebody wants to have a little fun, you'd as soon lock him up as let him, right?"

"Shut up!"

"You'd like that, wouldn't you? You'd like us all just to shut our mouths!"

"You're coming with me," declared the cop.

"No I ain't. I ain't done nothing!"

"Let's go, then," said the cop, taking Bull under the arm. This guy has muscle, Bull realized.

"Take your hands off me!" he said, but the cop was already dragging him off towards the washrooms.

When they got there he said, "Show me your ID book!"

"You got no—"

"Open your mouth once more and you're going with me," the cop interrupted him. His face had hardened, and Bull saw that the fun was over.

"This amounts to police brutality," he said, pulling out his ID book. And when the cop took out his notebook and began laboriously taking down Bull's name and address, he added more quietly, "This is curtailing my personal freedom."

Then he said nothing, and merely watched as the cop struggled with his notes.

A long time passed before he finished and returned the ID book to Bill. "And now clear out, fast!"

"You're trampling on human dignity," said Bull, quietly now, almost to himself.

"There's the cloakroom," said the cop.

Bull looked around for Evita, but she'd made herself scarce. There were only a few gawkers left, staring round-eyed at him.

"Well, are you going or aren't you?" said the cop.

"Yeah, sure, don't get your socks in a knot," said Bull. They've all dumped on me. He went to the cloakroom, got his coat, and walked slowly down the stairs. The cop watched him go. They've shit on me. And now I'm in it all alone, he said bitterly to himself. They've all shat on it.

The revolving door spat him out into the raw night. Light from the windows on the second floor was seeping into the fog, and he could hear the faint tones of Hammer's vibraphone. A trolley bus was going past the church. There was a pre-Christmas quiet in the air, as though nothing at all had happened. Bull stuck his hands into his pockets and started walking. But he had nowhere to go. He couldn't go back, and there was nothing ahead of him.

"The bastards!" he hissed between his teeth, without having anyone in particular in mind. But they were somewhere around. Someone must be responsible for all this. "The bastards," he repeated quietly. "But they ain't makin' me over. They ain't makin' me over."

He walked down the square and soon was lost in the fog that seemed to be dissolving the streetlamps in misty golden globes of light.

Translated by Paul Wilson

26

You're Too Hip, Baby

Terry Southern

The Sorbonne, where Murray was enrolled for a doctorate, required little of his time; class attendance was not compulsory and there were no scheduled examinations. Having received faculty approval on the subject of his thesis—"The Influence of Mallarmé on the English Novel Since 1940"—Murray was now engaged in research in the libraries, developing his thesis, writing it, and preparing himself to defend it at some future date of his own convenience. Naturally he could attend any lectures at the University which he considered pertinent to his work, and he did attend them from time to time—usually those of illustrious guest speakers, like Cocteau, Camus, and Sartre, or Marcel Raymond, author of *From Baudelaire to Surrealism*. But for the most part, Murray devoted himself to less formal pursuits; he knew every Negro jazz musician in every club in Paris.

At night he made the rounds. If there was someone really great in town he would sit at the same bar all evening and listen to him; otherwise he made the rounds, one club after another, not drinking much, just listening to the music and talking to the musicians. Then, toward morning, he would go with them to eat—down the street to the Brasserie Civet or halfway across Paris to a place in Montmartre that served spareribs and barbecued chicken.

What was best though was to hang around the bar of his own hotel, the Noir et Blanc, in the late afternoon during a rehearsal or a closed session. At these times everyone was very relaxed, telling funny stories, drinking Pernod, and even turning on a bit of hashish or marijuana, passing it around quite openly, commenting on its quality. Murray derived a security from these scenes—the hushed camaraderie and the inside jokes. Later, in the evening, when the place was jumping, Murray kept himself slightly apart from the rest of the crowd—the tourists, the students, the professional beats, and the French *de bonne famille*—who all came to listen to the great new music. And always during the evening there would be at least one incident, like the famous tenorman's casually bumming a cigarette from him, which would prove Murray's intimacy with the group to those who observed. Old acquaintances from Yale, who happened in, found Murray changed; they detected in his attitude toward them, their plans, and their expressed or implied values a sort of bemused tolerance—as though he were in possession of a secret knowledge. And then there would be the inevitable occasion when he was required to introduce them to one of the musicians, and that obvious moment when the musician would look to Murray for his judgment of the stranger as in the question: "Well, man, who *is* that cat? Is he *with* it?" None of this lessened Murray's attractiveness, nor his mystery, no less to others, presumably, than to himself; but he was never too hard on his old friends—because he was swinging.

When the Negro pianist Buddy Talbott was hired, along with a French drummer and bass, to play the Noir et Blanc, he and his wife had been in Paris for only three days. It was their first time out of the States, and except for a few band jobs upstate, it was their first time out of New York City.

Toward the end of the evening, during a break, Murray went into the men's room. Buddy Talbott was there alone, in front of the mirror, straightening his tie. Their eyes fixed for an instant in the glass as Murray entered and walked over to the urinal; the disinfectant did not obscure a thin smell of hashish recently smoked in the room. Murray nodded his head in the direction of the bandstand beyond the wall. "Great sound you got there, man," he said, his voice flat, almost weary in its objectiveness. Buddy Talbott had a dark and delicate face which turned slowly, reluctantly it seemed, from the glass to Murray, smiling, and he spoke now in soft and precisely measured tones: "Glad you like it."

And, for the moment, no more was said, Murray knowing better than that.

Although Murray smoked hashish whenever it was offered, he seldom took the trouble to go over to the Arab quarter and buy any himself; but he always knew where to get the best. And the next evening, when Buddy Talbott came into the men's room, Murray was already there.

They exchanged nods, and Murray wordlessly handed him the smoking stick, scarcely looking at him as he did, walking past to the basin—as though to spare him witness to even the merest glimpse of hesitancy, of apprehension, calculation, and finally, of course, of perfect trust.

"I've got a box, man," Murray said after a minute, by which he meant record player, "and some new Monk—you know, if you ever want to fall by. . . ." He dried his hands carefully, looking at the towel. "Upstairs here," he said, "in number eight. My name is on the door—'Murray.'"

The other nodded, savoring the taste, holding it. "I'd like to very much," he said finally, and added with an unguarded smile, *"Murray."* At which Murray smiled too, and touching his arm lightly said: "Later, man." And left.

The hash seemed to have a nice effect on Buddy's playing. Certainly it did on Murray's listening—every note and nuance came straight to him, through the clatter of service at the bar and the muttered talk nearby, as though he were wearing earphones wired to the piano. He heard subtleties he had missed before, intricate structures of sound, each supporting the next, first from one side, then from another, and all being skillfully laced together with a dreamlike fabric of comment and insinuation; the runs did not sound either vertical or horizontal, but circular ascensions, darting arabesques and figurines; and it was clear to Murray that the player was constructing something there on the stand . . . something splendid and grandiose, but perfectly scaled to fit inside this room, to sit, in fact, alongside the piano itself. It seemed, in the beginning, that what was being erected before him was a castle, a marvelous castle of sound . . . but then, with one dramatic minor—just as the master builder might at last reveal the nature of his edifice in adding a single stone—Murray saw it was not a castle being built, but a cathedral. *"Yeah, man,"* he said, nodding and smiling. A cathedral—and, at the same time, around it the builder was weaving a strange and beautiful tapestry, covering the entire structure. At first the image was too bizarre, but then Murray smiled again as he saw that the tapestry was, of course, being woven *inside* the cathedral, over its interior surface, only it was so rich and strong that it sometimes seemed to come right through the walls. And then Murray suddenly realized—and this was the greatest of all, because he was absolutely certain that only he and Buddy knew—that the fantastic tapestry was being woven, quite deliberately, face against the wall. And he laughed aloud at this, shaking his head, "*Yeah, man,*" the last magnificent irony, and Buddy looked up at the sound, and laughed too.

After the set, Buddy came over and asked Murray if he wanted a drink. "Let's take a table," he said. "My old lady's coming to catch the last set."

"Solid," said Murray, so soft and without effort that none would have heard.

They sat down at a table in the corner.

"Man, that sure is fine gage," Buddy said.

Murray shrugged.

"Glad you like it," he said then, a tone with an edge of mock haughtiness, just faintly mimicking that used by Buddy when they had met; and they both laughed, and Buddy signaled the waiter.

"I was wondering," said Buddy after the waiter had left, "if you could put me onto some of that."

Murray yawned. "Why don't you meet me tomorrow," he said quietly. "I could take you over to the café and, you know, introduce you to the guy."

Buddy nodded, and smiled. "Solid," he said.

Buddy's wife, Jackie, was a tall Negro girl, sort of lank, with great eyes, legs, and a lovely smile.

"What we'd like to do," she said, "is to make it here—you know, like *live* here—at least for a couple of years anyway."

"It's the place for living all right," said Murray.

Murray was helpful in much more than introducing them to a good hash connection. Right away he found them a better and cheaper room, and nearer the Noir et Blanc. He showed Jackie how to shop in the quarter, where to get the best croissants, and what was the cheap wine to buy.

He taught them some French and introduced them to the good inexpensive restaurants. He took them to see *L'Âge d'Or* at the Cinematheque, to the catacombs, to the rib joint in Montmartre, to hear Marcel Raymond speak at the Sorbonne, to the Flea Market, to the Musée Guimet, Musée de l'Homme, to the evening exhibitions at the Louvre. . . . Sometimes Murray would have a girl with him, sometimes not; or on some Sundays when the weather was fine he would get someone with a car, or borrow it himself, and they would all drive out to the Bois de Boulogne and have a picnic, or to Versailles at night. Then again, on certain nights early, or when Buddy wasn't playing, they might have dinner in Buddy and Jackie's room, listening to records, smoking a piece of hash now and then, eating the red beans and rice, the fish, ribs, and chicken that Jackie cooked. The most comfortable place in the small room was the bed, and after a while the three of them were usually lying or half reclining across it, except when one of them would get up to put on more records, get a drink, or go to the bathroom, everything very relaxed, not much talk, occasionally someone saying something funny or relating a strange thing they had seen or heard, and frequently, too, just dozing off.

Once Murray bought a pheasant, had it cooked, and brought it up to their room, along with a couple of bottles of chilled Liebfraumilch, some wild rice, asparagus, and strawberries and cream.

Jackie was quite excited, opening the packages. "You're too much, baby," she said, giving Murray a kiss on the cheek.

"What's the grand occasion, man?" asked Buddy, beaming at him.

Murray shrugged. "I guess we'll have to dream one up," he said.

"I guess we will," said Buddy smiling, and he started slicing up a piece of hash.

Afterward they lay across the bed, smoking and listening to music.

"It's funny, isn't it," said Murray, while they were listening to Billie, "that there aren't any great ofay singers."

The others seemed to consider it.

"Anita O'Day is all right," said Jackie.

"Yeah, but I mean you wouldn't compare her with Billie, would you," said Murray.

"Some of the French chicks swing," said Buddy absently, ". . . Piaf . . . and what's that other chick's name. . . ."

"Yeah, but I mean like that's something else, isn't it," said Murray.

Buddy shrugged, passing the cigarette, "Yeah, I guess so," he said, sounding half asleep; but his eyes were open, and for several minutes he lay simply staring at Murray with an expression of mild curiosity on his face.

"Murray," he asked finally, "did you want to learn piano . . . or what?" Then he laughed, as though he might not have meant it to sound exactly like that, and he got up to get some wine.

Jackie laughed too. "Maybe he just *likes* you baby—ever think of that?"

"Yeah, that's right," said Buddy, making a joke of it now, pouring the wine, "that ought to be considered." He was still smiling, almost sheepishly. "Well, here's to friendship then," he said, taking a sip.

"You're making me cry," said Murray in his flat, weary voice, and they all laughed.

Then it was time for Buddy to go to the club.

"I'll make it over with you, man," said Murray, slowly raising himself up on the bed.

"Stick around," said Buddy, putting on his tie. "Nothing's happening there yet—you can come over later with Jackie."

"That seems like a good idea," said Jackie.

Murray sat there, staring at nothing.

"It's cool, man," said Buddy smiling and giving Murray an elaborate wink of conspiracy, "it's cool. I mean, you know—make it."

"Solid," said Murray, after a minute, and he lay back across the bed again.

"See you cats," said Buddy, opening the door to leave.

"Later," said Murray.

"Later, baby," said Jackie, getting up and going to the door and locking it. Then she went over to the basin and began brushing her teeth.

"That was a funny thing for him to say, wasn't it," said Murray after a minute, "I mean about did I want 'to learn piano, or *what*?'"

Jackie moved the brush in a slow, languorous motion, looking at Murray in the mirror. "Well, it's very simple really. . . . I mean, he *digs* you, you know—and I guess he would like to do something for you, that sort of thing." She rinsed her mouth and held the brush under the water. "I thought he made that part of it pretty clear," she said, then looking directly at him. She crossed over to the dressing table and stood in front of it, straightening her dress; it was a cream-colored jersey which clung without tightness to all of her. She stood in front of the glass, her feet slightly apart, and touched at her hair. He watched the back of her brown legs, the softly rounded calves, tracing them up past the cream-colored hem behind her knees into their full lean contours above—lines which were not merely suggested, but, because of the clinging jersey and the way she stood, convincingly apparent.

"That's a groovy thread," said Murray, sitting up and taking the glass of wine Buddy had left on the night table.

"Oh?" She looked down at the dress reflexively and again at the mirror. "Madame what's-her-name made it—you know, that seamstress you put me onto." She sat down on a chair by the mirror and carefully wiped the lipstick from her mouth with a Kleenex.

"Yeah, it's crazy," said Murray.

"Glad you like it, Murray." The phrase had become an occasional joke between the three of them.

"I was by the Soleil du Maroc this afternoon," he began then, taking a small packet out of his shirt pocket, unwrapping it as he leaned toward the light at the night table. "I just thought I would twist up a few to take to the club." He looked up at her and paused. "I mean, you know, if there's time."

Jackie's head was cocked to one side as she dabbed perfume behind an ear and watched Murray in the mirror. "Oh there's *time,* baby," she said with a smile, ". . . make no mistake about that."

When Murray had twisted one, he lit it and, after a couple of drags, sat it smoking on the tray, continuing to roll them carefully, placing them in a neat row on the night table.

Jackie finished at the mirror, put another record on, and came over to the bed. As she sat down, Murray passed the cigarette to her, and she lay back with it, head slightly raised on a pillow against the wall, listening to *Blue Monk.*

When Murray had rolled several, he put the packet of hash away and stashed the cigarettes in with his Gauloises. Then he leaned back, resting his head on Jackie's lap, or rather on what would have been her lap had she been sitting instead of half lying across the bed; she passed the cigarette to Murray.

"Has a good taste, hasn't it," said Murray.

Jackie smiled. "Yes, indeed," she said.

"Hadj says it's from the Middle Congo," said Murray with a laugh, "'*C'est du vrai congolais!*'" he went on, giving it the Arab's voice.

"That's just how it tastes," said Jackie.

With his face turned toward her, Murray's cheek pressed firmly against the softness of her stomach which just perceptibly rose and fell with breathing, and through the fine jersey he could feel the taut sheen of her pants beneath it, and the warmth. There was nothing lank about her now.

"Yeah," said Murray after a minute, "that's right, isn't it, that's just how it tastes."

They finished the cigarette, and for a while, even after the record had ended, they lay there in silence, Jackie idly curling a finger in Murray's hair. For a long time Murray didn't move.

"Well," he finally said instead, "I guess we'd better make it—over to the club, I mean."

Jackie looked at him for a minute, then gave a gentle tug on the lock of his hair, shrugged, and laughed softly.

"Anything you say, Murray."

That Sunday was a fine day, and Murray borrowed a car for them to go out to the Bois. Jackie had fried some chicken the night before and prepared a basket of food, but now she complained of a cold and decided not to go. She insisted though that Murray and Buddy go.

"It's a shame to waste the car and this great weather. You ought to make it."

So they went without her.

They drove up the Champs through a magnificent afternoon, the boulevard in full verdure and the great cafés sprawled in the sun like patches of huge flowers. Just past the Étoile they noticed a charcuterie which was open and they stopped and bought some more to put in the basket—céleri rémoulade, artichoke hearts, and cheese covered with grape seeds. At a café next door Murray was able to get a bottle of cognac.

At the Bois they drove around for a while, then parked the car and walked into the depth of the woods. They thought they might discover a new place—and they did, finally, a grove of poplars which led to the edge of a small pond; and there, where it met the pond and the wooded thicket to each side, it formed a picture-book alcove, all fern, pine and poplar. There was no one else to be seen on the pond, and they had passed no one in the grove. It was a pleasing discovery.

Together they carefully spread the checkered tablecloth the way Jackie always did, and then laid out the food. Buddy had brought along a portable phonograph, which he opened up now while Murray uncorked the wine.

"What'll it be," Buddy asked with a laugh, after looking at the records for several minutes, "Bird or Bartók?"

"Bartók, man," said Murray, and added dreamily, "where do you go after Bird?"

"Crazy," said Buddy, and he put on *The Miraculous Mandarin.*

Murray lay propped on his elbow, and Buddy sat opposite, cross-legged, as they ate and drank in silence, hungry but with deliberation, sampling each dish, occasionally grunting an appreciative comment.

"Dig that bridge, man," said Buddy once, turning to the phonograph and moving the needle back a couple of grooves, "like that's what you might call an 'augmented *oh-so-slightly.*'" He laughed. "Cat's too much," he said, as he leaned forward to touch a piece of chicken to the mayonnaise.

Murray nodded. "Swings," he said.

They lay on the grass, smoking and drinking the cognac, closing their eyes or shading them against the slanting sun. They were closer together now, since once Buddy had gotten up to stretch and then, in giving Murray a cigarette, had sat down beside him to get a light.

After a while Buddy seemed to half doze off, and then he sleepily turned over on his stomach. As he did, his knee touched Murray's leg, and Murray moved lightly as if to break the contact—but then, as if wondering why he had reacted like that, let his leg ease back to where it had been, and almost at once dropped into a light sleep, his glass of cognac still in his hand, resting on his chest.

When Murray awoke, perhaps only seconds later, the pressure of Buddy's leg on his own was quite strong. Without looking at Buddy, he slowly sat up, raising his legs as he did, sitting now with knees under his folded arms. He looked at the glass of cognac still in his hand, and finished it off.

"That sort of thing," said Buddy quietly, "doesn't interest you either." It was not put as a question, but as a statement which required confirmation.

Murray turned, an expression of bland annoyance on his face, while Buddy lay there looking at him pretty much the same as always.

"No, man," said Murray, then almost apologetically: "I mean, like I don't put it down—but it's just not a scene I make. You know?"

Buddy dropped his eyes to a blade of grass he was toying with; he smiled. "Well, anyway," he said with a little laugh, "no offense."

Murray laughed, too. "None taken, man," he said seriously.

Murray had risen at his more or less usual hour, and the clock at Cluny was just striking eleven when he emerged from the hotel stairway, into the street and the summer morning. He blinked his eyes at the momentary brightness and paused to lean against the side of the building, gazing out into the pleasantly active boulevard.

When the clock finished striking he pushed himself out from the wall and started towards the Royale, where he often met Buddy and Jackie for breakfast. About halfway along Boulevard Saint-Germain he turned in at a small café to get some cigarettes. Three or four people were coming out the door as Murray reached it, and he had to wait momentarily to let them pass. As he did he was surprised to notice, at a table near the side, Buddy and Jackie, eating breakfast. Buddy was wearing dark glasses, and Murray instinctively reached for his own as he came through the door, but discovered he had left them in his room. He raised his hand in a laconic greeting to them and paused at the bar to get the cigarettes. Buddy nodded, but Jackie had already gotten up from the table and was walking toward the girls' room. Murray sauntered over, smiling, and sat down.

"What are you doing here, man?" he asked. "I didn't know you ever came here."

Buddy shrugged. "Thought we'd give it a try," he said seriously examining a dab of butter on the end of his knife. Then he looked up at Murray and added with a laugh, "You know—new places, new faces."

Murray laughed, too, and picked at a piece of an unfinished croissant. "That's pretty good," he said. "What's the other one? You know, the one about—oh yeah, 'Old friends are the best friends.' Ever hear that one?"

"I have heard that one," said Buddy nodding, "yes, I have heard that one." His smile was no longer a real one. "Listen, Murray," he said, wiping his hands and sitting back, putting his head to one side, "let me ask you something. Just what is it you want?"

Murray frowned down at where his own hands slowly dissected the piece of croissant as though he were shredding a paper napkin.

"What are you talking about, man?"

"You *don't* want to play music," Buddy began as though he were taking an inventory, "and you *don't* want . . . I mean just what have we *got* that interests you?"

Murray looked at him briefly, and then looked away in exasperation. He noticed that Jackie was talking to the patron who was standing near the door. "Well, what do you think, man?" he demanded, turning back to Buddy. "I dig the *scene,* that's all. I dig the *scene* and the *sounds.*"

Buddy stood up, putting some money on the table. He looked down at Murray, who sat there glowering, and shook his head. "You're too hip, baby. That's right. You're a *hippy.*" He laughed. "In fact, you're what we might call a kind of professional *nigger lover.*" He touched Murray's shoulder as he moved to leave. "And I'm not putting you down for it, understand, but, uh, like the man said, 'It's just not a scene I make.'" His dark face set for an instant beneath the smoky glass and he spoke, urgent and imploring, in a flash of white teeth, almost a hiss, "I mean *not when I can help it,* Murray, *not when I can help it.*" And he left. And the waiter arrived, picking up the money.

"*Monsieur désire?*"

Still scowling, staring straight ahead, Murray half raised his hand as to dismiss the waiter, but then let it drop to the table. "*Café,*" he muttered.

"*Noir, monsieur?*" asked the waiter in a suggestively rising inflection.

Murray looked up abruptly at the man, but the waiter was oblivious, counting the money in his hand.

Murray sighed. "*Oui,*" he said softly, "*noir.*"

27

The Jazz Baby

Julian Street

Had a stranger seen Elsa Merriam sitting at the piano in her drawing room at dusk on this spring evening, with the lamplight falling on her cheek and her golden hair, he might have guessed her ten years younger than her actual age; but had he told her of his guess she would not have thought him sincere, for it was a part of Elsa's charm that when people spoke admiringly of her girlish figure, the fine texture of her skin, the delicacy of her coloring, or when on meeting her with the stupendous Lindsay they voiced amazement that she could be his mother, she saw in their utterances only efforts to be tactful.

Her fingers touched the keys softly; she was listening not so much to her playing as for the sound of the front door, for the Easter holidays were here and Lindsay was coming home this afternoon from college, bringing a friend with him.

"Chet Pollard's family's in Europe or some place," her son had written, "so he can't go home this vacation. He's a good egg, terribly smooth and talented musically."

When presently from the hall below came the dull sound of the front door closing, she stopped playing and rose from the piano, but, on hearing a sedate tread upon the stair, sat down again. The step was not Lindsay's, but her husband's.

"Hello, dear," he said on reaching the doorway. "Lindsay not home yet?"

"No, but I've sent the car to the station."

Her husband came in, kissed her on the cheek, and having performed this customary rite, turned to leave the room.

"Been playing?" he asked casually over his shoulder as he moved away.

"Yes, I've found a Grieg sonata with a nice cello part for Lindsay, and I've been brushing up on some of our old Beethoven duets."

"H'm, he likes Grieg and Beethoven, does he?" he inquired vaguely, heading for the stairs.

She was smiling as she resumed her playing. It seemed impossible that Hobart Merriam should not know that his son liked Grieg and Beethoven.

Again the sound of the front door, but this time a distinct concussion followed by a tumult of voices, boyish laughter, the noise of something scraping the banisters, then as she was halfway across the room, Lindsay in the doorway, wearing the shy, affectionate grin with which he always greeted her. He let his suitcase fall with a thud to the floor, but with a second piece of baggage was more careful, depositing it gently upon the carpet; then taking his mother by the shoulders he leaned far down and kissed her, while she marvelled, as she always did when he reappeared after an absence, that this gigantic college creature was identical with the helpless infant of a few years before.

"Mother," he said as he straightened up again, "I want you to meet—I mean, this is my friend Mister Pollard."

Mr. Pollard was a handsome youth almost as tall as Lindsay, with brilliant dark eyes and a complexion like a dairymaid's. Why, Elsa wondered, were the young people of this generation so much taller? Certainly in her girlhood, boys of this height were exceptions.

As she welcomed her son's classmate his manner was that of one overtaken by mirthful recollections.

"Huh-huh! I'm sure it was very kind of you—huh-huh—to invite me here for the vacation, Mrs. Merriam."

Lindsay also began to laugh in the same nervous manner; the two stood chuckling together as if at a secret jest. Desiring to help them regain their composure she spoke gravely of practical affairs. Had their train been on time? Had the chauffeur found them without difficulty? But though Lindsay became calmer his friend continued to laugh his replies. Trying to pacify him was like trying to haul down a captive balloon in a high wind.

"Lindsay tells me you're fond of music," she said.

The young man gurgled that he was, and she turned to her son.

"I didn't have time to write about it," she told him, "but there's a splendid symphony concert tonight with Lazlof playing the cello part of a Grieg sonata I've just bought for us to do. I got three tickets on the chance that you and Mr. Pollard would be able to go with me."

Abruptly the laughter ceased; a profound solemnity overtook the two boys; they stared at each other, evidently exchanging wireless messages which resulted in the nomination of Lindsay to be spokesman.

"Look, Mother," he began, "it certainly was good of you. We certainly appreciate it and everything. But now look—Chet thought—at least there's a girl—I mean a couple of girls—they were down at the prom—and this girl's mother is a friend of Chet's mother, and she wanted him to be nice to her when he came to New York, so we kind of arranged to take them to the theatre tonight—only we haven't called up yet, so of course they might not be able to go, and—"

Here Pollard seemed to think best to break in.

"Oh, they'll be able to go all right," he said with the air of one sure of his women.

Mrs. Merriam was quick to help them out of their embarrassment.

"I thought it likely you'd have an engagement," she said, "but I got tickets on the off chance. I'll probably be able to get Cousin Ellen and Aunt Fannie to go with me."

"Gosh!" said Lindsay sympathetically.

"I admit I wish Dorothy Hallock were at home," said his mother. "We went to lots of concerts last year. I always have a fine time with Dorothy, she's such a sweet girl."

"Yes," her son replied, "sweet's the word; sweet means dopeless."

"Indeed? And what does dopeless mean?"

"Just what Dorothy is—unsophisticated."

"I should hope so!" she said with a little baffled sigh. "Well, dear, hadn't you better be seeing about your theatre seats?"

"I'll call up Bea and Midge," Pollard said, and Lindsay forthwith led him to the telephone closet in the hall.

Mrs. Merriam was at the piano when her son returned alone to the room.

"Here's that Grieg sonata," she said. "Bring your cello and we'll run through it before dinner."

"Look, Mother," he answered uneasily, "I didn't bring my cello this time. You see, the vacation's so short, and it's such a job lugging it around."

It was the first time he had failed to bring his cello home, and she was keenly disappointed: perhaps he read her disappointment in her face, for he went on: "I would of brought it, Mother, but it's so darn bulky and I had two other things to carry."

"I suppose you couldn't, then," she said.

From early childhood Lindsay had loved good music and she prized the taste as his most valuable inheritance from her. As a girl she had dreamed of becoming a professional pianist; at fifteen she was sufficiently advanced to study under a great master; two years later, however, her mother had died, and just then, when she felt so alone, she had met Hobart Merriam and married him. At the time there was some talk of a resumption of her studies, but it was prevented first by Hobart's complete indifference to music, then by the birth of Lindsay. Lindsay more than made up to her for the loss of her career; he was worth a thousand girlish dreams; deep down in her heart she acknowledged to herself that, good and kind though Hobart was, her real companion was her son.

Early she had begun to give him rudimentary musical instruction; at seven he had a little cello, and within a few years he had so far progressed that she began to harbor visions in which her early ambitions for herself came to fruition in him; visions in which she saw him seated with his cello on a stage, playing to a hushed audience.

Because of the boy's talent she would have preferred to keep him at school in New York, where he could continue his musical education under the best teachers, but his father had other plans for him. His own parents had been poor, and he was determined to give Lindsay the advantages of boarding school and college, which he had been denied. Elsa fought off the selection of a school as long as she could and when compelled to decide, chose one in which the head master was musical. Occasionally she would go up and hear the school orchestra, in which Lindsay played, and all through the school year she looked forward to the summer vacation at Westfield, in the Berkshire Hills, where they had time to play together a great deal, working up difficult duets, and also trios—for Dorothy Hallock often joined them with her violin.

Summer residents were wont to speak of Westfield as unspoiled, by which they meant that the same families occupied the same houses every season, that the country club was simple, and that there was no flamboyant hotel to attract social gypsies. The automobile, of course, did tend to bring to the country-club dances young people from the smarter settlements near by, giving Westfield occasional glimpses of the genus "flapper," but such glimpses served only to heighten local conservatism.

The Hallocks were typical of the place: old New Yorkers whose residences in the city and the country dated from an era of architectural ugliness; but they were spacious, homelike houses, and their owner and his wife were old-fashioned enough to be attached to them, and moreover to have a family large enough to keep them comfortably filled. With her music and her quick intelligence, Dorothy, the youngest of the Hallock children, seemed to Elsa the most attractive girl in Westfield, and it flattered her that despite the difference in their ages Dorothy so evidently enjoyed being with her. It was nearly a year now since Dorothy had gone to school in Paris, and the elder woman had genuinely missed her.

Lindsay, too, had missed Dorothy, Elsa thought; for during the summer of her absence he spoke often of their need of a violin, and showed a restlessness she had never seen in him before. Until that summer he had always been satisfied to stay in Westfield, but he now began to take nocturnal motor trips to dances at neighboring resorts. Of course, though, he was at the restless age.

Often when they were playing she spoke of Dorothy.

"Sure I miss her," he once told her. "She's an awfully nice kid, but I wish they'd get some new girls in this place."

"Why, Dorothy isn't a kid. She's only a year younger than you are."

"Nearly two years," he corrected. "She's sixteen."

"She'll be seventeen this summer."

"Well, anyhow," he said, "I couldn't get interested in her; we know each other too well. Look, Mother, can I have the motor tonight? There's a dance over at Arlington. And I need twenty-five dollars."

In September he went away to college, and she was overjoyed when presently he wrote that he had made the college orchestra. During his Christmas holidays they played but little, most of his time having been given to social activities. She supposed it was only natural that a college boy should want a lively vacation, and she prized the more such odd moments as he spent with her.

And now, after what seemed a trifling interval, the Easter holidays were here. Time went faster and faster. After another little interval it would be summer and they would go again to Westfield; before long he would be out of college; then, presently, he would marry and she would lose him. She must make the most of the few remaining years. Ah, how she wished that he had brought his cello home!

II

Chet Pollard was still at the telephone when Mr. Merriam came downstairs.

"Well, Lindsay," was his greeting to his son, and the two shook hands, Lindsay giving a jerky little half bow. He always seemed a trifle ill at ease when he greeted his father; Elsa believed it was because both were conscious of the fact that two or three years ago they would have kissed.

"I believe you're taller than ever," Mr. Merriam said.

"No, I've stopped growing but I'm putting on some weight. If I can put on about twelve pounds I've got a chance for crew."

The father made no comment upon this, but remarked: "Your mother and I were pleased that you passed your uniform tests."

"Believe me, I was pleased!" said Lindsay, grinning. "I was half expecting to get on pro. Spanish and French saved me; they're gut courses."

"They're what?" his mother asked.

"Gut—soft—easy," he elucidated.

"H'm," said his father. "Better have your bags taken upstairs. I tripped over one of them in the hall."

"You did?" Lindsay looked concerned. "You didn't trip over that long black one, did you? Gosh, I wouldn't have anybody trip over that!"

"It might be a good idea, then, not to leave it in the center of the hall."

"Gosh! Did I leave it there? Well, I'll take it up to my room right now!"

He started for the door, but his mother interposed.

"Just ring for Wilkes," she said. "He'll take them up."

"Not on your life!" Lindsay answered with great earnestness, as he picked up the suitcase and the long black box. "Not this thing. I'll carry this myself."

"What you got in it you're so particular about?" his father asked.

"Well," replied the boy obscurely as he started for the stairs, "it's something I can't afford to have broken."

"But look here," persisted his father, "why are you so careful about that box? What you got that's so breakable?"

Lindsay, who was now halfway up the stairs, stopped, and looking over the balustrade laughed down at the anxious, upturned faces.

"Oh, it's not hooch—if that's what you mean. No, Dad, nothing like that. It's just something—something that I—well, I wanted to ease it to Mother, but I guess I might as well show it to you now."

He descended, let the leather bag plump to the floor again, and carried the mysterious black case to the drawing room, where he placed it carefully upon a couch. Then, without moving to open it, he turned and earnestly addressed his parents.

"Now look," he said, "in the first place, I want you to realize I got this thing at a wonderful bargain. Probably you could go from one end of this country to the other and you'd never see a bargain like it again. Probably there aren't five others like this one I've got here, in the whole country. I want you to realize, Mother, what a perfectly unprecedented—"

"You haven't told us what it is, yet," his father broke in.

"I was just going to tell you," the boy returned, "but first I want to make absolutely sure you understand what a wonderful bargain I've got."

"It seems to me," remarked his father dryly, "that you have succeeded in impressing that point upon us. What is it?"

"But first," continued Lindsay—"first you must realize that it's quadruple gold plate over triple silver plate. If you understood about these—these things, why, you'd know they don't *make* 'em that way—not except when they get a special order. And even then you'd have to wait weeks and weeks before you'd—"

"What you *got*?" demanded his father in the tone of one whose patience is being worn thin.

"That's what I'm trying to tell you," answered the youth, going to the box and undoing a catch at one end.

But instead of releasing the other catches and opening the box he turned and with all the impressiveness he could command delivered a final word.

"It cost two hundred and seventy-five new," he declared, "and what do you think I paid for it? Only one hundred and fifty dollars! That's all! Yes, sir, only one hundred and fifty! Why, if I hadn't of bought it it would of been a crime! Nothing less than a crime! I want you to keep that fact in mind, Dad, because—"

"For heaven's sake!" cried Mr. Merriam, "what—you—got—in that—*box*?"

Dramatically Lindsay threw back the lid, revealing in a velvet recess a shining, tubular, twisted, bell-mouthed something scaffolded with metal bars and disks.

"Oh, Lindsay!" cried his mother in an anguished voice.

"Quadruple gold plate over triple silver plate!" her son reiterated shrilly.

"You haven't mentioned what it is—not even *yet*!" commented Mr. Merriam with abysmal cynicism. "Is it a fire extinguisher or a home-brew outfit?"

"No—home blew," replied his son.

Seizing the gilded instrument and holding it as if to play, he began to shuffle, undulating his body in a negroid manner and singing:

When I blow those home-blew blues
    On my sexy saxophone,
I can get any gal I choose—
    Come, ma baby, youse ma own!
Bring yo' bottle, baby dear;
Fill it full of gin or beer;
Come and lap the home-made booze,
    While I blow those home-brew—

Hear me blow those home-brew—
Blues!

Having finished his song he blew upon the instrument, evoking from its golden throat sounds resembling ribald laughter ending on a dissonant note.

"Oh, Lindsay!" cried Mrs. Merriam again.

"That's a nice refined song!" said his father caustically. "I suppose that's what they teach you in college?"

At this juncture Chet Pollard came from the telephone closet.

"I had an awful time getting 'em," he said. "They had to page 'em all over the hotel. It's a darn nuisance!"

"Can they go?" Lindsay demanded.

"Naturally," replied Pollard.

Lindsay introduced him to his father; then: "We want to get theatre seats for tonight, Dad," he said. "I was wondering if you'd work your drag at the club."

"It would be nice if you could get seats for the new Shaw play," said Mrs. Merriam.

Again she sensed an exchange of wireless messages between the two young men.

"But look, Mother—"

Pollard, however, cut Lindsay short.

"That's so, Mrs. Merriam," he declared. "I understand the Shaw play is very—very clever. In my opinion Shaw is one of the cleverest playwrights there is; but you see, these girls we're going to take are musical—uh—they're very musical, and—uh—they thought they'd like to go to something—uh—something musical this time."

"There's a lovely little operetta called 'Mignonette'," the mother suggested. "Quite the daintiest thing I've seen in years. If you—"

"But look, Mother," Lindsay broke in, "we were planning—"

Here, however, the more adroit Pollard again took matters into his own hands.

"Yes, indeed, Mrs. Merriam," said he, "I hear 'Mignonette''s awfully dainty. But I guess these girls must of—uh—must of seen it, or something. Anyway, they were speaking of another musical show they hadn't seen, and—"

"So we thought—" began Lindsay.

"What's the name of it?" Mrs. Merriam asked.

"It's at the Apollo," answered the guest.

"I don't remember what's at the Apollo," she said, and turning to her husband, who had begun to read the evening paper, asked him to look it up.

At that, however, Pollard spoke up quickly.

"Oh, yes," he said, as if the name had just come to him. "It's 'Jazbo.'"

Mr. Merriam now became interested.

"'Jazbo'?" he repeated. "Isn't that the name of the show the police were—"

"It's quite all right now, though," his son interposed hastily.

"Who says so?"

"I was reading in the paper where they made those girls put on different costumes."

"Costumes?" said his father. "Was there trouble about costumes, too? I understood it was the dancing of this woman, What's-her-name, that—"

"Khiva," said Pollard. "But they say her manager paid the police to make a row, Mr. Merriam."

"Yes, just an advertising dodge," quickly supplemented Lindsay.

"The advertising dodge seems to have worked so far as you two boys are concerned," his father commented.

But this elicited immediate protests.

"No, sir, that's not it!" declared Pollard righteously.

"No, I should say not!" Lindsay added. "Why, Dad, the music in this show's knockout. Three big foxtrot hits in one show: 'My Raggedy Rose,' 'Sweet Cookie,' and 'You Gorilla-Man.' And besides, if you invite a lady to go to the theatre, and she expresses a desire to see some particular show, and you—"

"And they have Joe Eckstein and his Saxophone Six," urged Pollard.

At this Mr. Merriam became still more interested.

"Oh, those fellows?" he said. "They must be the ones I heard last year. They're very good." He smiled at the memory; then looking with dawning curiosity at his son's new treasure lying in the open case he asked: "Is that the same sort of thing they play?"

"Sure," replied the collegian, "a saxophone—but this one's quadruple gold plate over triple silver plate."

"Let's hear you play it, then."

Lindsay took it up, put the mouthpiece to his lips, and blew a stream of bubbling bursting notes.

"Can't you play us a tune?"

But the saxophonist shook his head.

"Needs other instruments—a piano, anyhow," he answered.

"There's your mother—she'll play for you."

But Lindsay shook his head again.

"Oh, Mother can't play jazz," he said.

"Your mother can't?" exclaimed Mr. Merriam. "I guess your mother can play anything anybody else can!" He looked questioningly at his wife, but she remained silent.

"No," said Lindsay, "jazz isn't like other music. It's very tricky. Maybe, if you'd like, we can get somebody in to play before vacation ends. Chet here's got his clarinet with him, and he's knockout on it."

Having won his father over to his instrument he now exhibited it in detail, showing how the stops worked.

"Gosh, I was lucky to get this one!" he said. "I never would of got it if Len Spinney hadn't been dropped out of college. You remember Len, Mother?"

She nodded. "You say he's been dropped? That's too bad."

"Yes, and he didn't need to be. But he kept going to New York to see a girl, and he took too many cuts. He didn't mind much, though. He'd been thinking of marrying her, anyway, so when he got dropped he decided to do it; but he hadn't any money, and that's how I came to get it so cheap. He had to have a hundred and fifty dollars."

"A classmate of yours—married?" cried his mother.

"On a hundred and fifty dollars?" demanded Mr. Merriam.

"Uh-huh," replied Lindsay with a nonchalance that both parents found ghastly. "That was all he really needed right away. His wife couldn't go on a wedding trip. She has to stay in town because she's in the Follies."

Mrs. Merriam stared at her son, thunderstruck, but the father was vocal for them both.

"My God!" he exclaimed.

"Well," said Lindsay, "she's knockout for looks and a wonderful dancer, and a fellow has to marry sometime, doesn't he? By the way, Dad, I need twenty-five dollars and—Oh, I tell you who we could have in to jazz up the piano—Bea Morris—eh, Chet?"

"None better," said the other youth.

"Who's Bea Morris?" Mrs. Merriam inquired.

"Girl 't's going to the theatre with us tonight. Say, Dad, would you mind 'phoning for those seats?"

"How many?" asked his father, moving toward the door.

"Four."

"Aren't these girls to have a chaperon?" Mrs. Merriam asked.

An expression of pain came over the boy's face. "Gosh, Mother," he sighed, "where you been all this time? If a girl's so dopeless she has to have a chaperon she doesn't get asked—that's all."

"Well, I'm thankful we haven't a daughter to bring up, the way things are," she said.

"Oh, I don't know," returned her son. "Just because there's no chaperon it doesn't necessarily mean necking."

"That's a comfort," Mr. Merriam said. "Then it's four, is it?"

"But really, Hobart," pursued his wife, "do you think it's proper for these boys to take young ladies to see a musical comedy the police were going to close?"

Again the look of pain swept over her son's face.

"Oh, Mother!" he protested. "Don't be a flat tire! You'd call the Hallocks proper enough, wouldn't you?"

"Certainly."

"Well, Mrs. Hallock took Bobby and a lot of young people to see 'Jazbo'—a big theatre party, and a lot of subdebs at that."

"I could telephone and ask her what she thought of it."

"Mother! What kind of a position would that put me in? Asking people what shows I'd ought to see or not! You seem to forget I'm practically twenty."

"It can't hurt to ask her what sort of show it is," his mother contended, "if I don't tell her—"

"Well," he said, still protesting, "I don't say she'd exactly *recommend* this show. Maybe she didn't know about the police and everything, but she took 'em, all the same. One of the girls came down to the prom, and she told me. She said she was kind of disappointed in the show, herself, after so much talk; said it wasn't so very rancid—just a little sour in spots."

"I'm not worrying about you," said his mother, "but about where you take these young girls."

But Pollard hastened to reassure her.

"Oh, don't worry about that, Mrs. Merriam," said he. "They're not young. Both of them are over twenty."

"But what will their mothers think if I—"

"As far as that goes," he told her, "their mothers won't know anything about it. Midge hasn't got any mother, and Bea's mother is in White Sulphur or some place. And anyhow, Mrs. Merriam, she's a very broad-minded woman—she lets Bea do just whatever she pleases."

"What do you think, Hobart?" the mother asked.

"Oh," said her husband, "I'd let 'em go. These girls aren't our daughters, and from what I hear, it's the way all of 'em are now." And as she interposed no further objections he went to telephone for the theatre seats.

Immediately after dinner the two boys, slim and clean-looking in their "tucs," rushed away in a taxi, and a little later Mrs. Merriam, having been unable to find any one to accept her belated invitation, left her husband reading in his library and departed alone in her limousine for the concert.

But tonight the music, whirling in great somber currents through the auditorium, made only a background for her thoughts. Her mind was full of Lindsay. She was troubled about him; he had not only left his cello at college but had brought home what an instrument instead! A saxophone! And it had belonged to a boy who had been dropped from college and had married a chorus girl.

Who were these girls Lindsay was with? What had come over her son that he wished to take them to a tawdry show? She thought of her incessant efforts to develop in him a fastidiousness, not only in music but in other things, which should be his aesthetic and moral safeguard. And was this to be the outcome?

During the intermission she found friends to talk with; then the orchestra reassembled and she was left alone again. Lazlof, the great cellist, entered at one side, carrying his instrument, and amid applause made his way to a chair at the center of the stage; the choir of stringed instruments softly played the prelude, Lazlof lifted his slender bow, and the miracle began.

The sound of the cello added poignancy to her thoughts of her son. How often she had secretly visioned him playing to just such a hushed audience as this! But alas, that dream, like so many others, must be relinquished.

III

"Did you hear those boys come in this morning?" her husband asked at breakfast.

"Yes."

"Did you notice the time?"

"Yes; I didn't sleep very well."

"Nearly seven!" he said, and she had a wanly humorous sense of his looking at her accusingly, as though the lateness of their homecoming were in some way her fault.

"I went into Lindsay's room before I came down," he continued gloomily. "I could have set off a bomb in there for all they'd have known! Room in horrible disorder—clothes all over the place. I stepped on a watch—don't know which of them it belongs to. What condition do you suppose they came home in?"

"Lindsay has always thrown his things around," she said.

"But what could they have been doing? Do nice girls stay out with boys all night?"

"I don't know," she answered. "I don't believe I understand these young people."

"Well, I've been reading a book about them," he declared, "a novel some young fellow's written. If they're what *he* says they are they're a pretty queer lot."

"What's the name of the book?"

"I don't remember. If you want to look at it you'll find it on the table by my bed; it's got a red cover. Do you know anything about these two girls?"

"No."

"I wouldn't be surprised if they were chorus girls," said he.

"Oh, *no*!" It was as much a prayer as a denial.

"Why not? Didn't Lindsay say a classmate of theirs married a chorus girl? Didn't he seem to approve of it?"

"Oh, I can't believe he was thinking of that side of it," said she. "I think he was just glad to get the boy's saxophone."

"Well," he said in a sinister tone as he left the room, "you just read that book!"

Having the morning to herself she did read some of it and skimmed the rest. The publisher's announcement on the paper jacket proclaimed it A Passionate Tale of Youth in Revolt, and described the author as A Fearless Young Iconoclast, Impatient of Literary Shackles. Except one drunken middle-aged woman, there were in the world with which the story dealt no grown-up people. It was a world of flappers, gin, and familiarities.

When about noon the boys came down to breakfast she looked apprehensively for signs of dissipation and was infinitely relieved to find them clear-eyed and in high spirits. Lindsay, kissing her, did not smell of gin, but of the sticky oily stuff called Oleaqua that made his hair so shiny.

"Did you have a good time?" she asked as she poured their coffee.

"Did we! Do you know what time we got in? It was darn near seven."

"How was 'Jazbo'?"

"Pretty peppy, and great music. We just naturally had to go around to the Prowlers' Club afterwards, and dance all night."

"A club?"

"Not a real club; just a restaurant—the joint where they have the best music in town. Gosh, I can hear Sinzy yet whanging out that 'You Gorilla-Man'!" He began to hum, bouncing in his chair.

"Sinzy?"

"Yes," said her son; and as she looked blank he continued: "Mean to say you've never heard of Sinzy? Why, he's one of the greatest characters in this town. He's a terrible little twerp to look at—got a face like bad news from home, but I guess he's the best jazz piano player in the world."

"And the young ladies didn't get tired?"

Lindsay laughed.

"If they had their way we wouldn't be home yet, would we, Chet?"

"No," and he explained: "You see, Mrs. Merriam, these girls are a couple of the busiest little pep artists this side of Cayenne."

"They both dance well?"

"A girl's *got* to dance well to make the grade these days," her son informed her. "She's got to be practically as good as a professional."

"Then these girls aren't professionals?" she asked quickly.

"For heaven's sake!" returned her son. "What would we be doing with professional dancers?"

"Professionals look good on the floor," said Pollard, "but they try to lead you too much. But you take Midge"—he was speaking now to Lindsay—"did you ever dance with anybody as light as she is?"

"I sure did!" the other answered almost indignantly. "Bea's every bit as light as Midge—except maybe above the ears."

"Oh," retorted his friend, "you think so 'cause Bea falls for you harder! She sure was handing you a heavy line last night."

"Aw, what you talking about! She was not!"

"Sure she was! Didn't I hear her saying how you were so cynical and everything?"

"I guess you're sore because she didn't shoot you a line," Lindsay returned. "Next thing, I s'pose you'll say she's got a wooden leg or something. Why don't you say that, too? Why don't you say she can't bang the box?"

"No, I wouldn't say that," conceded Pollard. "I got to admit she's some jazz baby."

"You just ought to hear her, Mother!" Lindsay said.

"I should like to. Do you expect to see her again this vacation?"

"Do we? We're going to see 'em this afternoon."

"And again tonight," Pollard added.

"And that reminds me, Mother—I'd like the car if you're not going to use it, and I need twenty-five dollars."

"What's on tonight?" she asked.

"Dance."

"But this is Good Friday, dear!"

"Oh, we won't begin dancing till after midnight. We can start kind of late, and eat along, and go to a movie or something."

She saw her opportunity and seized it.

"Why not ask them here to dinner? We can have some jazz afterwards."

Again the wireless went to work between the boys.

"Why, I think that would be fine," Pollard said in answer to his friend's unspoken question.

"Yes, if we could get 'em," Lindsay said, "but they might have a date for dinner or something. You know, Mother, they're about two of the most popular girls in New York."

"Oh, we'll get 'em all right," declared Pollard.

"Hadn't you better telephone and ask them?" suggested Mrs. Merriam.

"Way I look at it," said Chet, "if I was doing it I wouldn't ask 'em anything. Keep calling a girl up and you don't have her guessing. These dopeless birds keep calling their girls up, 'Can you do this? Can you do that?' and so forth; so that girl isn't guessing, 'cause she sees the bird's dopeless. But my way would be, I'd wait till I saw 'em this afternoon, and then I'd *tell* 'em. I'd just say, 'You're coming to dinner, woman.'"

"All right," said Lindsay, impressed, "you handle it."

"Well, I'll expect them at eight," Mrs. Merriam said. "If they can't come, telephone me."

IV

Without having definite knowledge of their plans she had supposed that the boys would return in time to dress for dinner, but when at eight they had not appeared she concluded that they would arrive with the young ladies.

In a few minutes, however, they came in alone, paused breathless in the drawing-room door to tell her that the girls would be along presently, and rushed upstairs to dress; but when at half-past eight they came down the guests had not arrived.

"Where's Dad?" asked Lindsay.

"He had to stay downtown on business. Where are the young ladies?"

"Oh, they'll breeze in pretty soon," said Pollard with the insouciance of one accustomed to hotel service.

"You asked them for eight?"

"Yes, but it was after eight when we broke away."

It was nearly nine when the girls arrived. Though much of the slang she heard the boys use seemed meaningless, the term "breeze in" struck Elsa Merriam as describing very accurately the manner of Miss Bea Morris and Miss Midge Ayres. Their appearance fascinated her. Their figures were slight and supple, their necks and arms round and white like young birch trees, and their filmy little evening gowns, continually agitated as they flirted their bodies about, called to mind the cloudlike texture of springtime treetops whipped by erratic April winds. She could hardly tell them apart. Their faces had a look of unreality, suggesting carved masks, very pretty and almost human in expression; eyebrows plucked to a narrow line, cheeks frankly tinted, lips like scarlet poppy petals, hair like shocks of yellow uncurled ostrich plumes. Shaking hands with them she heard a little clatter of gold boxes knocking against each other as they dangled from short chains attached to their wrists.

"Oh, Mrs. *Mer*riam!" panted Bea, hardly waiting for Lindsay to introduce her, "we've had a perfectly fantastic time getting here!" She clutched her chest like an emotional actress.

"Simply re*volting*!" cried Midge.

Whereafter they ran on together in gasping, broken sentences, noisily exclamatory, recounting the misadventures of the preceding hour. Mrs. Merriam gathered that they might, by implication, be apologizing for the tardiness of their arrival; at all events, it was the nearest thing to an apology that she received. Stripped of dramatics, their story was a simple one. They seemed to wish her to understand that there had been difficulties with the shoulder-straps of the new frock Bea was wearing, and that the chauffeur had driven them to a wrong address.

"These old *shoulder*-straps! And just when I was trying to hurry! And that fan*tas*tic chauffeur! I told him *West* Forty-eighth as plain as could be, didn't I, Midge? But he drove—"

"You don't mean West Forty-eighth!" shrilled the other. "You mean *East* Forty-eighth. You told him—"

"Yes, that's what I mean—*East* Forty-eighth! East Forty-eighth, I told him, as plain as could be! But he drove us to *West* Forty-eighth. Poor creature must be feebleminded!"

"And he stopped in front of a *tailor* shop!" cried the other.

"Yes, fancy! A *tailor* shop!"

So they ran on, their arms, shoulders, and fluffy bobbed locks continually in motion, while Elsa, bewildered, listened and watched.

Catching sight of her reflection in a mirror Bea turned suddenly and crossed the room, revealing that the back of her dress consisted, above the waist, of very little more than the shoulder-straps, which were of flesh-colored ribbon. Before the mirror she took from her hair a comb, with which she fluffed up her outstanding yellow mane. Midge followed suit; then the two flopped down together on a couch, crossing their knees, exhibiting the tops of rolled-down stockings. Elsa had hardly convinced herself that she saw aright when the entrance of Wilkes, with the announcement that dinner was served, caused the girls to open the little gold boxes hanging from their wrists, and gazing into the mirrored covers, freshen the color on their already tinted lips.

"Did I tell you," cried Bea to the boys as she took her chair at the dinner table, "that I'm going up to the prom at New Haven? I'm so thrilled I'm almost insane!"

"Huh—New Haven!" commented Chet; while Lindsay asked: "Who you going with?"

"Freddie Spencer." And in response to a contemptuous snort from her host, she added, "Why, what you got against Freddie?"

"Sofa specialist," said he.

"Oh, indeed! Well, a New Haven boy told me he was a wonderful athlete."

"Cozy-corner athlete," the boy muttered.

"Look, Bea," put in Chet in a fatherly tone, "I wouldn't advise any woman I cared about to go to a lot of proms."

"Well, I like that!" she exclaimed. "Why, the prom at Princeton was the first one I ever went to in my whole life."

"New Haven's a very different matter," Pollard declared.

"Oh, is it?"

"I'm simply advising you f' your own good," Pollard went on. "A woman doesn't want to get herself known as a prom-trotter."

"Specially with a bird like Freddie," Lindsay put in quickly.

"Prom-trotter!" she repeated pettishly. "Don't be fan*tas*tic!" And to Lindsay: "I certainly wish I'd known you didn't like Freddie, though, 'cause if I had I wouldn't have invited him around."

"Around here?" he repeated, surprised. "When?"

"Tonight, of course."

"What you do that for?"

"We need somebody to drum, don't we? Freddie drums like an angel."

"Oh, we could of got along without drums."

"Well, anyway," said Bea, "he wasn't certain he could come. He was just starting out from the hotel when we met him—going to some putrid party—but he said he'd get away if he could."

"He's a knockout dancer," Midge put in.

"Yes," said Bea, "and of course you've noticed how wonderfully his hair grows. I've never seen a boy with such divine hair."

Whereat Pollard, who had been gazing at her, shook his head, exclaiming as if with reluctant admiration: "Oh, you *woman*! You *woman*, you!"

V

As Wilkes failed to pass cigarettes to the young ladies with the coffee, they produced them from their own cases, which, together with their makeup boxes, they had laid beside their plates on reaching the table; and the butler, thus prompted, hastily brought matches.

"I'll have a cigar," said Chet, and when Lindsay remarked at this deviation from custom he explained, "I'm off cigarettes—they're too effeminate."

"Listen," said Bea, "if we're going to play, let's go to it," and though the hostess had not finished her coffee the two girls rose from the table.

"Hold on," said her son. "Mother hasn't finished."

"Oh, don't wait for me," she said, whereupon the four young people left the room.

Nor was she greatly surprised at this, for with the exception of Lindsay, who had tried to include her in the conversation, they had ignored her throughout the meal.

When a little later she followed her guests to the drawing room she saw no sign that her entrance was observed. Midge and the boys were standing at the piano watching Bea, who was beating out a syncopated tune with a rhythm that reminded Elsa of a mechanical piano. She sat down in a chair across the room and watched. A cigarette was dangling from the girl's lower lip and as it burned shorter she threw her head back to keep the smoke out of her eyes.

"Give us an ash tray, somebody," she said, blinking and addressing the room.

The boys began to look about for ash trays, but they were on a table near Elsa, so she carried one over and placed it on the shelf at the side of the music, receiving by way of acknowledgment a little nod from the girl.

Presently the music was interrupted by the arrival of the sleek Freddie Spencer with his two drum cases.

"Yay, boy Freddie!" was Bea's greeting. "Glad you made the grade."

"Got in wrong doing it," he said.

"Why, was she snotty to you?"

"Yop."

"She's that way. She was snotty to me once, too," Bea told him. "I never get invited there any more. *I should lie awake nights!*"

While Freddie adjusted his drums Lindsay ran upstairs for the saxophone and clarinet, and when he returned the little orchestra assembled around the piano.

"We'll play 'Sweet Cookie,'" announced Bea. "Everybody ready? Altogether, now—let's go!" And with a crash they began; the piano, drums, and cymbals beating out the rhythm, the saxophone belching the tune, the clarinet garnishing the composition with squealing arabesques. The music, moreover, was accompanied by physical activities. Bea at the piano and Freddie at the drums were dancing—if people sitting down may be said to dance; Chet, his body undulating, maneuvered in short steps upon the rug, while Lindsay swayed in what appeared to his mother to be a sort of negroid ecstasy, swinging his instrument about as he played, and occasionally throwing his head back like one drinking from a bottle.

With a feeling that Midge was temporarily left out, Elsa moved over and joined her on a couch where she was seated, but Midge had no intention of remaining in the background. As they finished "Sweet Cookie" she leaped to her feet shrieking a demand for "You Gorilla-Man," and upon their complying, began to shuffle loose-jointedly, her whole body shaking as if with palsy; and upon their reaching the refrain she added to the tumult by singing loudly through her nose:

Oh, you Gorilla-Man, I'm so in love with you;
  Come catch me if you can. It won't be hard to do!
Oh, you Gorilla-Man! Oh, oh, you hairy ape!
  You're such a thriller-man; I love you for your shape!
Oh, my Gorilla-Man, my love won't let me rest;
  I love each curly lock upon your great big chest!
Oh, swing me through the trees, beneath the moon serene;
  You're my Gorilla-Man and I'm your Jungle Queen!

"But she doesn't know what the words mean," Mrs. Merriam reflected in extenuation; and as an afterthought she added: "Neither do I."

Overwhelmed at first by the mere volume of barbaric sound she found herself after a time trying to analyze jazz. It seemed to her to be musical Bolshevism—a revolt against law and order in music. Apparently, too, the jazz Bolsheviks were looters, pillaging the treasure houses of music's aristocracy. One piece was based upon a Chopin waltz, another was a distortion of an aria from "Tosca," another had been filched from Strauss's "Rosenkavalier." Had something gone wrong with the mind of the world? Was there a connection between the various disturbing elements—free verse, futuristic painting, radicalism, crime waves, obstreperous youth, jazz music, jazz dancing, jazz thinking? She rose, crossed the room, and standing behind Bea, watched her hands upon the keyboard.

"How do you do that bass?" she asked the girl in an interval between pieces. "You seem to hit a lot of black notes with the flat of your hand."

"That's what a crash bass is," said Bea over her shoulder.

"How did you learn it?"

"Just picked it up. But there are lots of basses I can do that are more difficult than that; take the Honky-tonk, for instance, or the Hoochy." Nonchalantly she exhibited several of her left-handed accomplishments. "It's a gift," she explained. "One of the best jazz players I know can't read a note—picked it up from listening to records and watching the keys go down on a mechanical piano. And they say even Sinzy can't read very well. Anyway, people that play classical music can't play jazz; they ruin it trying to put expression in it."

"Then," said Elsa, "the idea of jazz is to—"

But she was cut short by Pollard, who had been wandering restlessly about, and who now, unable longer to control himself, remarked: "It's getting late. We've got to ease along pretty soon. Let's play 'Tag, You're It'!"

"No, I can't play any more," said Bea. "This fantastic shoulder-strap's cutting the arm off me." She pulled the ribbon aside, exhibiting a red mark upon her flesh.

"If you'll come up to my room," invited Elsa, "I'll try to fix it."

"All right," said the girl, and they went upstairs.

"I'll have to take off my dress," she said on reaching the bedroom. "Guess you better give me something to get into."

Mrs. Merriam brought a peignoir; then she undid the few catches holding the dress together in the back, and Bea stepped out of it.

Hastily Mrs. Merriam looked away, holding the peignoir toward her.

"And he's going to dance all night with this girl!" she thought.

During the three remaining days of the vacation Elsa saw Lindsay hardly at all. After their noontime breakfasts the boys would dash away, returning at nightfall to change into their "tucs" and disappear again.

On Monday night as he and Chet were leaving the house Lindsay said good-bye to her. "We're going to take our bags to the station now," he told her, "and dance till train time."

"When does your train go?"

"Six."

"You're going out on a morning train in evening clothes?"

"Sure," he returned debonairly; "and to an eight-o'clock class."

"Then," she said, too wise to let him see how the picture shocked her, "I hope it's a gut course."

As she kissed him good-bye at the front door she seemed to remember something.

"What's the name of that jazz piano player at the Prowlers' Club?"

"Sinzy."

"I thought that was it, but it's not in the telephone book."

He smiled, saying, "It's short for Sinzenheimer."

VI

Restlessness was apparent in the first few letters Elsa Merriam received from Lindsay after his return to college, and she observed with concern that as the term progressed he frequently came to New York for weekends. Shortly before the beginning of the summer vacation he wrote:

> Why do we always have to spend our summers in the same old place? I'm sick and tired of Westfield. Why can't we take a house at Southampton, where there's something doing? If we've got to go to Westfield I want to visit around. Bea's invited Chet and me to spend a couple of weeks at their place in Southampton.

In her reply she suggested that instead of his going to Southampton, Bea and Chet come up to Westfield immediately after college closed. In her letter she said:

> Westfield's going to be quite gay in June and July. There's the golf tournament, and I've already heard of several house parties. Dorothy Hallock will be coming back pretty soon, and they're planning to have the amateur vaudeville at the country club soon after we get up there. You'll be glad to know that I've engaged Sinzy's orchestra to play for the dance afterwards.

She had barely finished writing when Wilkes announced the arrival of the instructor, an acknowledged leader in his special branch of the musical art, who since the Easter holidays had been giving her three lessons a week at a fabulous fee.

She found him in the drawing room, a slight, dark, foreign-looking man, dressed in a black-and-white-striped suit much cut in at the waist. His buttoned shoes had gray cloth tops and his haberdashery was obviously expensive, but his face, which was all nose and mouth, looked, as Elsa remembered hearing someone say, like bad news from home.

"Well," he said genially as she entered, "how's d' little woman t'day?"

"Fine," she answered, and congratulated herself on having made the appropriate reply.

"All right," he said. "Go to it!" And she sat down and played "The Spinning Mouse."

"Swell!" said her professor when she had finished. "Take it from me, you won't find nobody can play that piece like you can. They're scared of it—it shows 'em up. All you gotta do now is keep on—agitate the ivories."

She did keep on, in New York, and later in Westfield, until Lindsay came home, though after his arrival she did not practice when he was in the house. But he was not often in the house—particularly after Bea and Chet arrived from Southampton in Bea's yellow roadster.

In the week that followed she found herself somewhat in the position of a roadhouse keeper, supplying meals to transient motorists who might arrive at any hour or might not arrive at all.

On the night of the vaudeville and dance she sent the three young people over to the country club for dinner, saying that she would dine quietly at home with Mr. Merriam, who had arrived from New York that afternoon.

"One thing's sure," Lindsay told her proudly before leaving, "Bea's jazz is going to be knockout at the vaudeville. I told 'em they better put her at the end of the program, 'cause if she played early she'd kill the other acts."

Outside the open door the yellow roadster was purring, and Bea in the driver's seat was impatient.

"Snap it up!" she called in to Lindsay, whereupon he hastened out, and his mother went upstairs to dress.

Tonight it took her a long time. When she came down her husband was waiting, and from his expression she was immediately aware that her costume interested him.

"My goodness!" he chuckled. "Why, I'd hardly have known you. You look about eighteen. How did you get your hair like that?"

"It's a wig." She spun around, making the fluffy mass stand out.

"My goodness!" he exclaimed again.

When they reached the club she said: "You go out and sit in the audience. I'm going in the back way."

As Mr. Merriam entered, the vaudeville was about to begin; the footlights were turned on, the lights in the assembly room were dimmed, and those who had dined at the club were hastening to find seats.

In the half darkness Lindsay caught sight of his father.

"Where's Mother?" he asked.

"Oh, I guess she's somewhere around," answered Mr. Merriam.

"Here's three places!" Chet called, and Lindsay hastened on.

As he made his way between the rows of chairs, followed by Bea and Chet, he perceived that the Hallocks were seated in the same row, and that a young lady, evidently their guest, was in the chair next to his. She was talking to Bobby Hallock, and her face was turned away from him, but he liked the way her dark hair was piled up on her head, and it struck him that her gown had, somehow, a very fashionable look.

As usual there were no printed programs; the names of the performers were displayed successively on large cards placed at either side of the proscenium. The first card announced George M. Cohan, the second Uncle Remus, and the third Signora Wilsoni, who was additionally billed as the Sweet Singer of Hillside Road. But the members of the Westfield Country Club were much too astute to be deceived by the names upon the cards, or the disguises worn by the performers. They recognized Ellen Niles, dressed in her brother's clothes, which were much too large for her, flourishing a cane and singing nasally from the corner of her mouth; Bud Smith in black-face, feigning to hoe the stage while he gossiped humorously in negro dialect about various members of the club; and young Mrs. Templeton Wilson singing ballads in a demure blue frock.

The cards for the fourth number announced The Painted Jazzabel, but when the curtains were drawn back the stage was empty save for a grand piano and a bench. Almost at once, however, The Painted Jazzabel strolled on, and the manner in which she did so might accurately have been described as breezing in. Her figure was slight and supple, her neck and arms round and white like a birch tree, and her filmy little evening gown, continually agitated as she flirted her body about, might have made an onlooker think of the cloudlike texture of springtime tree tops whipped by erratic April winds. Her face had a look of unreality, suggesting a carved mask, very pretty and almost human in expression;

eyebrows pencilled to a narrow line, cheeks frankly tinted, lips like scarlet poppy petals, hair like a shock of yellow uncurled ostrich plumes.

"Gosh!" gasped Lindsay. "It's Mother!"

The note of burlesque in the costume was accentuated by two large tin boxes dangling at the end of dog chains wrapped around the wrist of The Painted Jazzabel. At the centre of the stage she stopped, faced the audience, opened one of the tin boxes, took from it a large stick of crimson grease paint, and gazing into the mirrored interior of the lid, touched up her cheeks and lips. Then, closing the make-up box, she took from the other a cigarette, lighted it, and let it dangle from her lower lip while, with a gait suggesting a surcharge of vitality, she proceeded to the piano, her arms, shoulders, and fluffy bobbed locks continually in motion.

As, after a moment, Elsa was generally recognized, there was amused whispering throughout the room; then laughter and applause—in which, however, her son did not participate.

"Gosh!" he muttered again when, in taking her seat at the piano, she momentarily revealed the fact that her stockings were rolled down.

"How perfectly fan*tas*tic!" Bea exclaimed. "What's she going to do?"

"Darned if I know—in that get-up! She usually plays Chopin."

But this time she did not play Chopin. Detaching the dog chains from her wrist she flung the two tin boxes with a clatter to the bench beside her, and with her cigarette still dangling, began in an extremely efficient manner to agitate the ivories, playing a composition which, despite embellishments, was instantly recognized by those familiar with the music of the moment as "Booful Baboon Babe." The music, moreover, was accompanied by physical activities. Elsa was dancing—if a person sitting down may be said to dance.

Her final burst of pyrotechnics was met by a roar of applause, but she seemed unconscious of it. Putting down her cigarette she opened the tin make-up box, took out a comb, and gazing into the mirrored cover, fluffed up her bobbed locks amid increasing laughter. Then after adjusting her shoulder-straps and pulling up her stockings she played the eccentric foxtrot "Stub Your Toe," and modulated from that into "The Spinning Mouse." This performance drew a comment from Bea, for "The Spinning Mouse" was notoriously difficult, and was seldom attempted by pianists because, to quote the words of an authority, "They're scared of it—it shows 'em up."

"Why, I didn't know your mother could rag!" she said, during the tumult that followed.

"Neither did I, but—gosh! I think she's got Sinzy trimmed, don't you?"

She did not answer his question, but remarked: "Well, I never could see that 'Spinning Mouse.'"

Lindsay had his own views as to his mother's appearance, and was planning to express them to her at the earliest possible moment; but for this new accomplishment of hers he had only admiration, and the criticism implied in Bea's remark annoyed him.

"Do you mean you couldn't see it, or you couldn't play it?" he demanded.

"I mean," she replied stiffly, "that it's just a stunt to show off with."

"Anybody that can play like my mother can," he said, looking her pugnaciously in the eye, "has got a darn good right to show off." And he added: "I don't remember as I ever saw you showing off that way!"

Angrily she returned his gaze for a moment, then slowly pivoted and spoke to Chet.

"It's awfully stuffy in this place," she said. "It's given me a headache. Come on, let's get the roadster."

She rose and Chet followed.

"But look, Bea," protested Lindsay, "you can't go like that! They're expecting you to play."

"Then they're going to get fooled," she said scornfully. "They've got too much piano playing on their program. This whole place makes me sick abed, anyway! Come on, Chet."

Lindsay watched them to the door. All right, then! If Bea wanted to go like that, let her! He was pretty well fed up on Bea, anyway—and Chet, too, for that matter! Oilcans! It was one thing to go out to dances with them, but quite another to have them visiting for days and days in your own house. What did he care whether Bea played tonight or not? It made no difference to him. All he'd have to do was notify the committee that she'd changed her mind—a simple enough matter, since Mrs. Hallock, the chairman, sat but a few seats away from him.

During the intermission he rose and informed her of Bea's departure; whereupon the young lady at his side smiled up at him and ventured a remark:

"I'm not surprised that your friend doesn't want to play," she said. "Your mother's a perfect marvel."

Lindsay's eyes grew large as he looked back at her.

"Why, Dorothy!" he cried. "For heaven sakes! And I've been sitting right next you all this time!" He seized both her hands.

"I've been wondering how long it was going to take you to speak to me," she said.

"Believe me," he answered, gazing at her appreciatively, "I wouldn't of waited long if I'd recognized you; but how could I, in that grown-up dress, and with your hair done that way?"

"Do I look so much older? You know short skirts and bobbed hair aren't considered smart any more. They're *vieux jeu.*"

"In Paris, you mean?" he asked her eagerly. "Are they? Well, I'm mighty glad to hear it! I'm fed up with flappers, with their short skirts and their stockings at halfmast. I like a woman to be dignified, and her hair done up." He sank down in the chair beside her and continued: "You know, Dorothy, as a matter of fact, I don't think much of modern girls. What can they do? Nothing but dance. Or if they play it's only jazz. Their manners leave much to be desired, and they haven't got anything above the ears. In my opinion, your family did a mighty good job to send you to a nice conservative place like Paris. I tell you, if I had a daughter—" But at this juncture, catching sight of his mother, still in that outrageous flapper make-up, he broke off. "Excuse me," he said. "I've got to see about something. I'll be back."

VII

As he paused on the margin of the group surrounding his mother one of the older men spoke to him.

"Well, Lindsay," he said, "I didn't know your mother was such a siren."

"She isn't!" he returned shortly, and began to elbow his way toward her.

The young men were around her, too; they were congratulating her and she was handing them a line. He was beginning to feel a contempt for his own sex. You might think they were hoping she was going to keep on like this! Dumbbells!

As he was about to speak to her he found himself cut off by a small, dark individual wearing a tight-waisted "tuc."

"Well, little woman," Lindsay heard him say as he patted her on the arm, "you sure did put it across. I'll tell the world you're some jazz baby!"

Lindsay crowded in and put his arm roughly around her.

"Look, Mother," he said in a low, determined voice, "you come out of here!" And without regard for the maestro or the others he drew her toward the porch.

"What do you want, dear?"

"What do I want? I want you to go home and get some clothes on!"

"But I have to stay for the rest of the show, and the dance. I promised young Mr. Curtiss—"

Still with his arm around her he was propelling her down the porch toward the door of the ladies' dressing room.

"Look here," he said, "you don't dance with young Mr. Curtiss, or young Mr. Anybody Else till you get some more clothes on! The idea of your coming to a public place like that!"

"What you so snotty about?" she demanded.

"Mother!"

"Well, don't you want me to be up-to-date? I haven't had so much attention in years."

"Up-to-date!" he repeated with vast superiority. "If you kept really up-to-date you'd be aware that short skirts and bobbed hair aren't considered smart any more. They're *vieux jeu*—that's what they are!"

He thrust her through the door, planted himself outside, and waited until she reappeared in her light cloak; then taking her by the elbow he hurried her down the gravel drive and into the car, and drove her home. As they neared the house, they saw, disappearing down the drive, the tail light of another car, and Lindsay thought he knew what car it was.

"Did Miss Morris and Mr. Pollard just drive away?" he asked Wilkes, who let them in.

"Yes, Mr. Lindsay. They came home and packed in a hurry—got Sarah and me to help them—and from what they said I don't think they're coming back."

"Didn't they leave any word?" asked Mrs. Merriam.

"No, madam; but they were saying how they would make Southampton in time for breakfast tomorrow morning."

"Yes," said Lindsay to his mother, "and they'll stage a snappy entrance at Southampton—breezing in to breakfast in evening dress, and thinking they're the hit of the piece. If you want to know what *I* think, I think that kind of a performance is pretty juvenile."

"But they can't have gone without leaving a message," she said, incredulous. "That would be so rude."

"They think it's the thing to be rude," he told her, "and there are lots more like 'em. Park in people's houses, order their servants around, treat their hostess like a hotel keeper, and get up and go when they feel like it, without so much as saying 'Thank you.' There's modern young people for you! Nothing above the ears. I tell you, Mother, if I had a daughter you bet I'd get her out of all this kind of thing. I'd send her over to Paris, where it's conservative."

He had walked upstairs with her and they were standing at her bedroom door.

"Paris? Conservative?" she repeated, mystified.

"Yes. Now hurry, Mother, will you, so we can get over to the club by the time the dancing begins? I told Dorothy I'd be back."

"Ah!" she said to herself as she shut the door.

While she was dressing he paced the hall outside, occasionally shouting to her.

"Didn't you think she looked wonderful?" he demanded at the top of his lungs.

"Who?" she called back, laughing silently.

"Why, Dorothy."

"Of course," she shouted. "Dorothy always looks well." Then, with an amused sense of experimenting with words, she added: "And she's such a sweet girl."

This time he did not correct her, but heartily agreed, whereupon she asked: "You wouldn't call her dopeless, would you?"

"I should say not! Not since Paris. She's a very sophisticated woman. Look, Mother, let's get her over for some real music tomorrow afternoon."

"All right," Elsa called back happily.

When a little later she emerged from her room he surveyed her critically.

"That's more like it," he said.

They descended and got into the car, but after he had started the motor he thought of something and setting the brake, jumped out again.

"Wait a second," he said. "I want to get my saxophone to show to one of Sinzy's men. I bet he's never seen one that's quadruple gold plate over triple silver plate. I think maybe I can sell it to him."

28

'Round About Close to Midnight: A Fairly Fairy Tale

Boris Vian

Yodel . . . yodel . . . yodel . . . yodel . . .

GILLESPIE, *COLLECTED WORKS*

What is this bipop?

PAUL BOUBAL, *POETIC ANTHOLOGY*

(*Jazz Hot:* Christmas, 1948)

The doorbell rang like a fast Brownian lick. I listened more carefully. There was no doubt. Somebody was imitating the trumpet solo on Ray Brown's "One Bass Hit."

Sluggish with sleep, I got out of bed, slipped into my pants and a sweater and went to open the door. Who could it be at this hour? I tried to get my head together. Maybe a policeman had come to arrest me for outraging public decency under the covers of jazz magazines.

I opened the door. A man walked right in. He was small and shriveled, about fifty years old at first sight. He looked familiar except for his bulging stomach. He raised his right arm in the Nazi salute: "Heil Gillespie!"

He clicked his heels twice up-tempo like those two brass chords in "Stay on It." ("That must be hard to do," I muttered to nobody in particular.)

"Heil Parker," I responded automatically.

"Permit me to introduce myself," he said. "Goebbels—special propaganda delegate to the UN Musical Commission, Jazzband Department."

"Goebbels?" The name was familiar. I searched my memory. "You used to be thinner," I said finally. "Didn't they hang you?"

"And Ilse Koch?" he asked with a big smile. "Did they hang her too?"

"What? . . . "

"I did the same thing she did," he said, lowering his head, blushing. "I got pregnant in prison. The Americans freed me. I get along rather well with Americans, especially after they heard my 'Flight of the Bumblebee Rag' played by the Moscow Railroadman Jazz Band. When they needed a bebropagandist, I was the obvious choice."

"And Goering?" I asked. "What about Goering? Is he obviously anything?"

"He plays bongos in the UN bop combo."

We were still standing in my vestibule. "Come in," I said. "We obviously have important Things to Come together."

*

He lifted a glass of elixir of cannabis and toasted: "To our beloved Birdland." After eating a small opium cookie, he continued: "I'll explain why I've come for your help."

"But I'm not qualified to help you," I said.

"On the contrary," Goebbels answered, "nobody takes you seriously. That's Handy. It's a perfect cover. We must be prepared to spy for Herr Gillespie!"

He got up and clicked his heels like those two chords again: "All for bebop!" he exclaimed, sitting back down. "And now let's talk Buzzyness. Look at this, you will see how others have set an example . . . "

He handed me a piece of paper. It was a tract signed by the French Plumbers Union. It read: "The union requests all its members, as of

January 1st, 1949, to replace brass and steel screws with Zingleton. Vive Zutty! Long live Plumbers! Vive Mezzrow! Vive Ie Republic-o-reeny! Smrt fasizmu! Svoboda narodu."

"But this is Sabbytage!" I exclaimed, Furioso. I should have known it.

"Just camouflage, baby," Goebbels said. "And did you Getz the code at the end?"

"No. What's it all about?"

He laughed. (Bop.)*

✳

We sat down in a Chinese restaurant. "The do-re-mi of bebropaganda," he began, "is to infiltrate the language with our own jive. Dig!"

He called the waiter and ordered wild Reece with Steamin' pea-bop soup. Getting the idea, I asked for a pot of Tea-lonious. The waiter almost fainted. Goebbels pointed to him and shook my hand with a Spring of Joy: "That cat will remember this night for the rest of his life. Get the Groove, Holmes?"

"It seems obvious," I said.

"Maybe for you," replied Goebbels. "You've already Serged Miles Ahead. But for them, the squares, the straight studs . . . do you realize the Richies and Powell we can have?"

The waiter was writhing in agony on the floor. He did not seem well at all. I Lewist my appetite.

"Let's go someplace else," I suggested. "How about the Boiling alley in Phil Woods?"

"Fine. But first a bottle of Dexter Corton, 1942."

"I think I'd prefer soda-bop," I said. "I'm not feeling Wallington enough to go bar-bopping. I'd Rodney Stitt down for a while. Anyway we're getting Carneyd away. Let's try and be reasonnyble."

"No. The more unreasonnyble the better," he replied. We went outside: "You don't have a Basie understanding of propaganda. Aren't there people who have never understood one word in any article ever written by Andre Hodeir? Of course there are. But Hodeir writes books about

* "You'll see. Let's cut out and scarf some frim-fram sauce."

jazz, they're published by Larousse, a very serious company. And people who read his books generally consider him one of the best jazz critics. That's only one example."

"Zoot alors!" I exclaimed.

"There's no shortage of ideas in the UN Musical Commission, Jazz-band Department. We plan to publish a book about Urbie Greenbelts entitled 'Megabopoli.' Colonel Tom Parker is changing his name to Charlie. Jimmy Carter, a young politician in Georgia, will change his to Ron. Through our sophisticated long-term infiltration techniques, we are grooming Charlie's piano player Al Haig for Secretary of State. Dizzy Gillespie has decided to run for president so he can sing 'Salt Peanuts' in the White House. Now's the Time to get going before it Petersons out."

*

Approaching Boulevard Saint-Germain, we Passed a bookstore.

"Let's go in here," said Goebbels.

"I would like the complete works of Leon B. Bopp," he said to the clerk.

"I'm sorry, we don't stock that," the clerk replied, puffing on a musicians' cigarette. "But may I suggest 'Vian with the Wind' by George Mitchell instead?"

"No," said Goebbels, "and don't Purdie me on."

We left Pretty fast.

"Did you see him bebogarting that Roach?" Goebbels axed. "He's counter-revolutionary. We must brainMarsh him to the Max."

"Don't fight windmills," I advised. "Let's not make enemies in Groovin' High places. I get along quite well with the Archiedemie Francaise and they have agreed to replace the syllable 'van' by my name. It won't cost them much, and I need the publicity. We both need the publicity."

"That's not the problem," he replied, worried. "That book was written by *Blue* Mitchell, not George. Wait! Who's that Duking out the door?"

I recognized the bookseller. He was in a Rushing.

"Wow!" said Goebbels. "He's Something Else. He's Flyin' Home. We've got to find out what's Hamptoning."

"What if we take a Shorty cut?" I proposed. "It might be Tough, but . . . "

"Shorty?! White West Coast Shorty *Rogers*?" Goebbels looked at me, paling with anger. "And did I hear you say Tough? *Dave* Tough? Rhymes with Stuff? Another chalk-faced impostor."

I turned white with fear—Whitey Mitchell white . . . whiter, white as Stan Kenton. "Dave Tough's not all that Whiteman," I said.

Goebbels reached into the pocket of his Black, Brown and Beige jacket. He pulled a metal object far-out and then there was a loud "CLICK!"

*

The receiver clicked as I picked it up. The phone must have been ringing for five minutes. I came out of my round-Midnightmare and mumbled: "HiLow. Sleepy John Estes here."

"Hello," I heard. "It's Hodeir . . . Hello?"

"Hodeir? Which Hodeir? The Hodeir that rhymes with Brubeck?"

"What's wrong with you? It's Andre. Did you Wright your editorial for the Christmas issue?"

"No. You'd better do it this year," I sighed, awake by now. "My Dickie doesn't feel very Wells. I can't Garner enough strength."

"Come on," Hodeir laughed. "It's too late for you and me to change Erroles."

Translated by Mike Zwerin

29

Powerhouse

Eudora Welty

Powerhouse is playing!

He's here on tour from the city—"Powerhouse and His Keyboard"—"Powerhouse and His Tasmanians"—think of the things he calls himself! There's no one in the world like him. You can't tell what he is. "Negro man"?—he looks more Asiatic, monkey, Jewish, Babylonian, Peruvian, fanatic, devil. He has pale gray eyes, heavy lids, maybe horny like a lizard's, but big glowing eyes when they're open. He has African feet of the greatest size, stomping, both together, on each side of the pedals. He's not coal black—beverage colored—looks like a preacher when his mouth is going every minute: like a monkey's when it looks for something. Improvising, coming on a light and childish melody—*smooch*—he loves it with his mouth.

Is it possible that he could be this! When you have him there performing for you, that's what you feel. You know people on a stage—and people of a darker race—so likely to be marvelous, frightening.

This is a white dance. Powerhouse is not a show-off like the Harlem boys, not drunk, not crazy—he's in a trance; he's a person of joy, a fanatic. He listens as much as he performs, a look of hideous, powerful rapture on his face. When he plays he beats down piano and seat and wears them away. He is in motion every moment—what could be more obscene? There he is with his great head, fat stomach, and little round piston legs, and long yellow-sectioned strong big fingers, at rest about the size of bananas. Of course you know how he sounds—you've heard him on records—but still you need to see him. He's going all the time, like skating around the skating rink or rowing a boat. It makes everybody crowd around, here in this shadowless steel-trussed hall with the rose-like posters of Nelson Eddy and the testimonial for the mind-reading horse in handwriting magnified five hundred times. Then all quietly he lays his finger on a key with the promise and serenity of a sibyl touching the book.

Powerhouse is so monstrous he sends everybody into oblivion. When any group, any performers, come to town, don't people always come out and hover near, leaning inward about them, to learn what it is? What is it? Listen. Remember how it was with the acrobats. Watch them carefully, hear the least word, especially what they say to one another, in another language—don't let them escape you; it's the only time for hallucination, the last time. They can't stay. They'll be somewhere else this time tomorrow.

Powerhouse has as much as possible done by signals. Everybody, laughing as if to hide a weakness, will sooner or later hand him up a written request. Powerhouse reads each one, studying with a secret face: that is the face which looks like a mask—anybody's; there is a moment when he makes a decision. Then a light slides under his eyelids, and he says, "92!" or some combination of figures—never a name. Before a number the band is all frantic, misbehaving, pushing like children in a school-room, and he is the teacher getting silence. His hands over the keys, he says sternly, "You-all ready? You-all ready to do some serious walking?"—waits—then, STAMP. Quiet. STAMP, for the second time. This is absolute. Then a set of rhythmic kicks against the floor to communicate the tempo. Then, O Lord! say the distended eyes from beyond the boundary of trumpets, Hello and good-bye, and they are all down the first note like a waterfall.

This note marks the end of any known discipline. Powerhouse seems to abandon them all—he himself seems lost—down in the song, yelling up like somebody in a whirlpool—not guiding them—hailing them only. But he knows, really. He cries out, but he must know exactly. "Mercy! . . . What I say! . . . Yeah!" And then drifting, listening—"Where that skin beater?"—wanting drums, and starting up and pouring it out in the greatest delight and brutality. On the sweet pieces such a leer for everybody! He looks down so benevolently upon all our faces and whispers the lyrics to us. And if you could hear him at this moment on "Marie, the Dawn Is Breaking"! He's going up the keyboard with a few fingers in some very derogatory triplet-routine, he gets higher and higher, and then he looks over the end of the piano, as if over a cliff. But not in a show-off way—the song makes him do it.

He loves the way they all play, too—all those next to him. The far section of the band is all studious, wearing glasses, every one—they don't count. Only those playing around Powerhouse are the real ones. He has a bass fiddler from Vicksburg, black as pitch, named Valentine, who plays with his eyes shut and talking to himself, very young: Powerhouse has to keep encouraging him. "Go on, go on, give it up, bring it on out there!" When you heard him like that on records, did you know he was really pleading?

He calls Valentine out to take a solo.

"What are you going to play?" Powerhouse looks out kindly from behind the piano; he opens his mouth and shows his tongue, listening.

Valentine looks down, drawing against his instrument, and says without a lip movement, "'Honeysuckle Rose.'"

He has a clarinet player named Little Brother, and loves to listen to anything he does. He'll smile and say, "Beautiful!" Little Brother takes a step forward when he plays and stands at the very front, with the whites of his eyes like fishes swimming. Once when he played a low note, Powerhouse muttered in dirty praise, "He went clear downstairs to get that one!"

After a long time, he holds up the number of fingers to tell the band how many choruses still to go—usually five. He keeps his directions down to signals.

It's a bad night outside. It's a white dance, and nobody dances, except a few straggling jitterbugs and two elderly couples. Everybody just stands around the band and watches Powerhouse. Sometimes they steal glances at one another, as if to say, Of course, you know how it is with *them*—Negroes—band leaders—they would play the same way, giving all they've got, for an audience of one. . . . When somebody, no matter who, gives everything, it makes people feel ashamed for him.

Late at night they play the one waltz they will ever consent to play—by request, "Pagan Love Song." Powerhouse's head rolls and sinks like a weight between his waving shoulders. He groans, and his fingers drag into the keys heavily, holding on to the notes, retrieving. It is a sad song.

"You know what happened to me?" says Powerhouse.

Valentine hums a response, dreaming at the bass.

"I got a telegram my wife is dead," says Powerhouse, with wandering fingers.

"Uh-huh?"

His mouth gathers and forms a barbarous O while his fingers walk up straight, unwillingly, three octaves.

"Gypsy? Why how come her to die, didn't you just phone her up in the night last night long distance?"

"Telegram say—here the words: Your wife is dead." He puts 4/4 over the 3/4.

"Not but four words?" This is the drummer, an unpopular boy named Scoot, a disbelieving maniac.

Powerhouse is shaking his vast cheeks. "What the hell was she trying to do? What was she up to?"

"What name has it got signed, if you got a telegram?" Scoot is spitting away with those wire brushes.

Little Brother, the clarinet player, who cannot speak, glares and tilts back.

"Uranus Knockwood is the name signed." Powerhouse lifts his eyes open. "Ever heard of him?" A bubble shoots out on his lip like a plate on a counter.

Valentine is beating slowly on with his palm and scratching the strings with his long blue nails. He is fond of a waltz. Powerhouse interrupts him.

"I don't know him. Don't know who he is." Valentine shakes his head with the closed eyes.

"Say it agin."

"Uranus Knockwood."

"That ain't Lenox Avenue."

"It ain't Broadway."

"Ain't ever seen it wrote out in any print, even for horse racing."

"Hell, that's on a star, boy, ain't it?" Crash on the cymbals.

"What the hell was she up to?" Powerhouse shudders. "Tell me, tell me, tell me." He makes triplets, and begins a new chorus. He holds three fingers up.

"You say you got a telegram." This is Valentine, patient and sleepy, beginning again.

Powerhouse is elaborate. "Yas, the time I go out, go way downstairs along a long cor-ri-dor to where they puts us: coming back along the cor-ri-dor: steps out and hands me a telegram: Your wife is dead."

"Gypsy?" The drummer like a spider over his drums.

"Aaaaaaaa!" shouts Powerhouse, flinging out both powerful arms for three whole beats to flex his muscles, then kneading a dough of bass notes. His eyes glitter. He plays the piano like a drum sometimes—why not?

"Gypsy? Such a dancer?"

"Why you don't hear it straight from your agent? Why it ain't come from headquarters? What you been doing, getting telegrams in the *corridor,* signed nobody?"

They all laugh. End of that chorus.

"What time is it?" Powerhouse calls. "What the hell place is this? Where is my watch and chain?"

"I hang it on you," whimpers Valentine. "It still there."

There it rides on Powerhouse's great stomach, down where he can never see it.

"Sure did hear some clock striking twelve while ago. Must be *midnight.*"

"It going to be intermission," Powerhouse declares, lifting up his finger with the signet ring.

He draws the chorus to an end. He pulls a big Northern hotel towel out of the deep pocket in his vast, special-cut tux pants and pushes his forehead into it.

"If she went and killed herself!" he says with a hidden face. "If she up and jumped out that window!" He gets to his feet, turning vaguely, wearing the towel on his head.

"Ha, ha!"

"Sheik, sheik!"

"She wouldn't do that." Little Brother sets down his clarinet like a precious vase, and speaks. He still looks like an East Indian queen, implacable, divine, and full of snakes. "You ain't going to expect people doing what they says over long distance."

"Come on!" roars Powerhouse. He is already at the back door, he has pulled it wide open, and with a wild, gathered-up face is smelling the terrible night.

Powerhouse, Valentine, Scoot and Little Brother step outside into the drenching rain.

"Well, they emptying buckets," says Powerhouse in a mollified voice. On the street he holds his hands out and turns up the blanched palms like sieves.

A hundred dark, ragged, silent, delighted Negroes have come around from under the eaves of the hall, and follow wherever they go.

"Watch out Little Brother don't shrink," says Powerhouse. "You just the right size now, clarinet don't suck you in. You got a dry throat. Little Brother, you in the desert?" He reaches into the pocket and pulls out a paper of mints. "Now hold 'em in your mouth—don't chew 'em. I don't carry around nothing without limit."

"Go in that joint and have beer," says Scoot, who walks ahead.

"Beer? Beer? You know what beer is? What do they say is beer? What's beer? Where I been?"

"Down yonder where it say World Café—that do?" They are in Negrotown now.

Valentine patters over and holds open a screen door warped like a sea shell, bitter in the wet, and they walk in, stained darker with the rain and leaving footprints. Inside, sheltered dry smells stand like screens around a table covered with a red-checkered cloth, in the center of which flies hang on to an obelisk-shaped ketchup bottle. The midnight walls are checkered again with admonishing "Not Responsible" signs and black-figured, smoky calendars. It is a waiting, silent, limp room. There is a burned-out-looking nickelodeon and right beside it a long-necked wall instrument labeled "Business Phone, Don't Keep Talking." Circled phone numbers are written up everywhere. There is a worn-out peacock feather hanging by a thread to an old, thin, pink, exposed light bulb, where it slowly turns around and around, whoever breathes.

A waitress watches.

"Come here, living statue, and get all this big order of beer we fixing to give."

"Never seen you before anywhere." The waitress moves and comes forward and slowly shows little gold leaves and tendrils over her teeth. She shoves up her shoulders and breasts. "How I going to know who you might be? Robbers? Coming in out of the black night right at midnight, setting down so big at my table?"

"Boogers," says Powerhouse, his eyes opening lazily as in a cave.

The girl screams delicately with pleasure. O Lord, she likes talk and scares.

"Where you going to find enough beer to put out on this here table?"

She runs to the kitchen with bent elbows and sliding steps.

"Here's a million nickels," says Powerhouse, pulling his hand out of his pocket and sprinkling coins out, all but the last one, which he makes vanish like a magician.

Valentine and Scoot take the money over to the nickelodeon, which looks as battered as a slot machine, and read all the names of the records out loud.

"Whose 'Tuxedo Junction'?" asks Powerhouse.

"You know whose."

"Nickelodeon, I request you please to play 'Empty Bed Blues' and let Bessie Smith sing."

Silence: they hold it like a measure.

"Bring me all those nickels on back here," says Powerhouse. "Look at that! What you tell me the name of this place?"

"White dance, week night, raining, Alligator, Mississippi, long ways from home."

"Uh-huh."

"Sent for You Yesterday and Here You Come Today" plays.

The waitress, setting the tray of beer down on a back table, comes up taut and apprehensive as a hen. "Says in the kitchen, back there putting their eyes to little hole peeping out, that you is Mr. Powerhouse. . . . They knows from a picture they seen."

"They seeing right tonight, that is him," says Little Brother.

"You him?"

"That is him in the flesh," says Scoot.

"Does you wish to touch him?" asks Valentine. "Because he don't bite."

"You passing through?"

"Now you got everything right."

She waits like a drop, hands languishing together in front.

"Little-Bit, ain't you going to bring the beer?"

She brings it, and goes behind the cash register and smiles, turning different ways. The little fillet of gold in her mouth is gleaming.

"The Mississippi River's here," she says once.

Now all the watching Negroes press in gently and bright-eyed through the door, as many as can get in. One is a little boy in a straw sombrero which has been coated with aluminum paint all over.

Powerhouse, Valentine, Scoot and Little Brother drink beer, and their eyelids come together like curtains. The wall and the rain and the humble beautiful waitress waiting on them and the other Negroes watching enclose them.

"Listen!" whispers Powerhouse, looking into the ketchup bottle and slowly spreading his performer's hands over the damp, wrinkling cloth with the red squares. "Listen how it is. My wife gets missing me. Gypsy. She goes to the window. She looks and sees you know what. Street. Sign saying Hotel. People walking. Somebody looks up. Old man. She looks down, out the window. Well? . . . *Ssssst! Plooey!* What she do? Jump out and bust her brains all over the world."

He opens his eyes.

"That's it," agrees Valentine. "You gets a telegram."

"Sure she misses you," Little Brother adds.

"No, it's nighttime." How softly he tells them! "Sure, it's the night-time. She say, What do I hear? Footsteps walking up the hall? That him? Footsteps go on off. It's not me. I'm in Alligator, Mississippi, she's crazy. Shaking all over. Listens till her ears and all grow out like old music-box horns but still she can't hear a thing. She says, All right! I'll jump out the window then. Got on her nightgown. I know that nightgown, and her thinking there. Says, Ho hum, all right, and jumps out the window. Is she mad at me! Is she crazy! She don't leave *nothing* behind her!"

"Ya! Ha!"

"Brains and insides everywhere. Lord, Lord."

All the watching Negroes stir in their delight, and to their higher delight he says affectionately, "Listen! Rats in here."

"That must be the way, boss."

"Only, naw, Powerhouse, that ain't true. That sound too *bad*."

"Does? I even know who finds her," cries Powerhouse. "That no-good pussyfooted crooning creeper, that creeper that follow around after me, coming up like weeds behind me, following around after me everything I do and messing around on the trail I leave. Bets my numbers, sings my songs, gets close to my agent like a Betsy-bug; when I going out he just coming in. I got him now! I got my eye on him."

"Know who he is?"

"Why, it's that old Uranus Knockwood!"

"Ya! Ha!"

"Yeah, and he coming now, he going to find Gypsy. There he is, coming around that corner, and Gypsy kadoodling down, oh-oh, watch out! *Ssssst! Plooey!* See, there she is in her little old nightgown, and her insides and brains all scattered round."

A sigh fills the room.

"Hush about her brains. Hush about her insides."

"Ya! Ha! You talking about her brains and insides—old Uranus Knockwood," says Powerhouse, "look down and say Jesus! He say, Look here what I'm walking round in!"

They all burst into halloos of laughter. Powerhouse's face looks like a big hot iron stove.

"Why, he picks her up and carries her off!" he says.

"Ya! Ha!"

"Carries her *back* around the corner. . . . "

"Oh, Powerhouse!"

"You know him."

"Uranus Knockwood!"

"Yeahhh!"

"He take our wives when we gone!"

"He come in when we goes out!"

"Uh-huh!"

"He go out when we comes in!"

"Yeahhh!"

"He standing behind the door!"

"Old Uranus Knockwood."

"You know him."

"Middle-size man."

"Wears a hat."

"That's him."

Everybody in the room moans with pleasure. The little boy in the fine silver hat opens a paper and divides out a jelly roll among his followers.

And out of the breathless ring somebody moves forward like a slave, leading a great logy Negro with bursting eyes, and says, "This here is Sugar-Stick Thompson, that dove down to the bottom of July Creek and pulled up all those drownded white people fall out of a boat. Last summer, pulled up fourteen."

"Hello," says Powerhouse, turning and looking around at them all with his great daring face until they nearly suffocate.

Sugar-Stick, their instrument, cannot speak; he can only look back at the others.

"Can't even swim. Done it by holding his breath," says the fellow with the hero.

Powerhouse looks at him.

"I his half brother," the fellow puts in.

They step back.

"Gypsy say," Powerhouse rumbles gently again, looking at *them,* "'What is the use? I'm gonna jump out so far—so far. . . . ' *Sssst—!*"

"Don't, boss, don't do it agin," says Little Brother.

"It's awful," says the waitress. "I hates that Mr. Knockwoods. All that the truth?"

"Want to see the telegram I got from him?" Powerhouse's hand goes to the vast pocket.

"Now wait, now wait, boss." They all watch him.

"It must be the real truth," says the waitress, sucking in her lower lip, her luminous eyes turning sadly, seeking the windows.

"No, babe, it ain't the truth." His eyebrows fly up, and he begins to whisper to her out of his vast oven mouth. His hand stays in his pocket. "Truth is something worse, I ain't said what, yet. It's something hasn't come to me, but I ain't saying it won't. And when it does, then want me to tell you?" He sniffs all at once, his eyes come open and turn up, almost too far. He is dreamily smiling.

"Don't, boss, don't, Powerhouse!"

"Oh!" the waitress screams.

"Go on git out of here!" bellows Powerhouse, taking his hand out of his pocket and clapping after her red dress.

The ring of watchers breaks and falls away.

"*Look* at that! Intermission is up," says Powerhouse.

He folds money under a glass, and after they go out, Valentine leans back in and drops a nickel in the nickelodeon behind them, and it lights up and begins to play "The Goona Goo." The feather dangles still.

"Take a telegram!" Powerhouse shouts suddenly up into the rain over the street. "Take a answer. Now what was that name?"

They get a little tired.

"Uranus Knockwood."

"You ought to know."

"Yas? Spell it to me."

They spell it all the ways it could be spelled. It puts them in a wonderful humor.

"Here's the answer. I got it right here. 'What in the hell you talking about? Don't make any difference: I gotcha.' Name signed: Powerhouse."

"That going to reach him, Powerhouse?" Valentine speaks in a maternal voice.

"Yas, yas."

All hushing, following him up the dark street at a distance, like old rained-on black ghosts, the Negroes are afraid they will die laughing.

Powerhouse throws back his vast head into the steaming rain, and a look of hopeful desire seems to blow somehow like a vapor from his own dilated nostrils over his face and bring a mist to his eyes.

"Reach him and come out the other side."

"That's it, Powerhouse, that's it. You got him now."

Powerhouse lets out a long sigh.

"But ain't you going back there to call up Gypsy long distance, the way you did last night in that other place? I seen a telephone. . . . Just to see if she there at home?"

There is a measure of silence. That is one crazy drummer that's going to get his neck broken some day.

"No," growls Powerhouse. "No! How many thousand times tonight I got to say No?"

He holds up his arm in the rain.

"You sure-enough unroll your voice some night, it about reach up yonder to her," says Little Brother, dismayed.

They go on up the street, shaking the rain off and on them like birds.

Back in the dance hall, they play "San" (99). The jitterbugs start up like windmills stationed over the floor, and in their orbits—one circle, another, a long stretch and a zigzag—dance the elderly couples with old smoothness, undisturbed and stately.

When Powerhouse first came back from intermission, no doubt full of beer, they said, he got the band tuned up again in his own way. He didn't strike the piano keys for pitch—he simply opened his mouth and gave falsetto howls—in A, D and so on—they tuned by him. Then he took hold of the piano, as if he saw it for the first time in his life, and tested it for strength, hit it down in the bass, played an octave with his elbow, lifted the top, looked inside, and leaned against it with all his might. He sat down and played it for a few minutes with outrageous force and got it under his power—a bass deep and coarse as a sea net—then produced something glimmering and fragile, and smiled. And who could ever remember any of the things he says? They are just inspired remarks that roll out of his mouth like smoke.

They've requested "Somebody Loves Me," and he's already done twelve or fourteen choruses, piling them up nobody knows how, and it will be a wonder if he ever gets through. Now and then he calls and shouts, "'Somebody loves me! Somebody loves me, I wonder who!'" His mouth gets to be nothing but a volcano. "I wonder who!"

"Maybe . . . " He uses all his right hand on a trill.

"Maybe . . ." He pulls back his spread fingers, and looks out upon the place where he is. A vast, impersonal and yet furious grimace transfigures his wet face.

". . . Maybe it's you!"

30

The Silence of Thelonious Monk

John Edgar Wideman

One night years ago in Paris, trying to read myself to sleep, I discovered that Verlaine loved Rimbaud. And in his fashion Rimbaud loved Verlaine. Which led to a hip-hop farce in the rain at a train station. The Gare du Nord, I think. The two poets exchanging angry words. And like flies to buttermilk a crowd attracted to the quarrel, till Verlaine pulls a pistol. People scatter and Rimbaud, wounded before, hollers for a cop. Just about then, at the moment I began mixing up their story with mine, with the little I recall of Verlaine's poetry—*Il pleut dans mon coeur / Comme il pleut sur la ville,* lines I recited to impress you, lifetimes ago, didn't I, the first time we met—just then, with the poets on hold in the silence and rain buffeting the train station's iron roof, I heard the music of Thelonious Monk playing somewhere. So softly it might have been present all along as I read about the sorry-assed ending of the poets' love affair—love offered, tasted, spit out, two people shocked speechless, lurching away like drunks, like sleepwalkers, from the mess they'd made. Monk's music just below my threshold of awareness, scoring the movie I was imagining, a soundtrack inseparable from what the actors were feeling, from what I felt watching them pantomime their melodrama.

Someone plays a Monk record in Paris in the middle of the night many years ago and the scratchy music seeping through ancient boardinghouse walls a kind of silent ground upon which the figure of pitter-pattering rain displays itself, rain in the city, rain Verlaine claimed he could hear echoing in his heart, then background and foreground reverse and Monk the only sound reaching me through night's quiet.

Listening to Monk, I closed the book. Let the star-crossed poets rest in peace. Gave up on sleep. Decided to devote some quality time to feeling sorry for myself. Imagining unhappy ghosts, wondering which sad stories had trailed me across the ocean ready to barge into the space that sleep definitely had no intention of filling. Then you arrived. Silently at first. You playing so faintly in the background it would have taken the surprise of someone whispering your name in my ear to alert me to your presence. But your name once heard, background and foreground switch. I'd have to confess you'd been there all along.

In a way it could end there, in a place as close to silence as silence gets, the moment before silence becomes what it must be next, what's been there the whole time patiently waiting, part of the silence, what makes silence speak always, even when you can't hear it. End with me wanting to tell you everything about Monk, how strange and fitting his piano solo sounded in that foreign place, but you not there to tell it to, so it could/did end, except then as now you lurk in the silence. I can't pretend not to hear you. So I pretend you hear me telling what I need to tell, pretend silence is you listening, your presence confirmed word by word, the ones I say, the unspoken ones I see your lips form, that form you.

Two years before Monk's death, eight years into what the critic and record producer Orrin Keepnews characterized as Monk's "final retreat into total inactivity and seclusion," the following phone conversation between Monk and Keepnews occurred:

Thelonious, are you touching the piano at all these days?

No, I'm not.

Do you want to get back to playing?

No, I don't.

I'm only in town for a few days. Would you like to come and visit, to talk about the old days?

No, I wouldn't.

Silence one of Monk's languages, everything he says laced with it. Silence a thick brogue anybody hears when Monk speaks the other tongues he's mastered. It marks Monk as being from somewhere other than wherever he happens to be, his off-beat accent, the odd way he puts something different in what we expect him to say. An extra something not supposed to be there, or an empty space where something usually is. Like all there is to say but you don't say after you learn in a casual conversation that someone precious is dead you've just been thinking you must get around to calling one day soon and never thought a day might come when you couldn't.

I heard a story from a friend who heard it from Panama Red, a conk-haired, redbone, geechee old-timer who played with Satchmo way back when and he's still on the scene, people say, sounding better and better the older he gets, Panama Red who frequented the deli on Fifty-seventh Street Monk used for kosher.

One morning numerous years ago—story time always approximate, running precisely by grace of the benefit of the doubt—Red said, How you doing, Monk.

Uh-huh, Monk grunts.

Good morning, Mr. Monk. How you do-ink this fine morning, Sammy the butcher calls over his shoulder, busy with a takeout order or whatever it is that keeps his back turned.

If a slice of dead lunch meat spoke, it would be no surprise at all to Sammy compared to how high he'd jump, how many fingers he'd lose in the slicer if the bearish, bearded schwartze in a knitted kufi returned his *Good morning.*

Monk stares at the white man in white apron and white T-shirt behind the white deli counter. At himself in the mirror where the man saw him. At the thin, perfect sheets that buckle off the cold slab of corned beef.

Red holds his just-purchased, neat little white package in his hand and wants to get home and fix him a chopped liver and onion sandwich and have it washed down good with a cold Heineken before his first pupil of the afternoon buzzes, so he's on his way out when he hears Sammy say, Be with you in a moment, Mr. Monk.

Leave that mess you're messing wit alone, nigger, and get me some potato knishes, the story goes, and Panama Red cracking up behind Monk's habit of niggering white black brown red Jew Muslim Christian, the only distinction of color mattering the ivory or ebony keys of his instrument and Thelonious subject to fuck with that difference too, chasing rainbows.

Heard the story on the grapevine, once, twice, and tried to retell it and couldn't get it right and thought about the bird—do you remember it—coo-cooing outside the window just as we both were waking up. In the silence after the bird's song I said Wasn't that a dainty dish to set before the king and you said Don't forget the queen and I said Queen doesn't rhyme with sing and you said It wasn't a blackbird singing outside and I said I thought it was a mourning dove and then the bird started up again trying to repeat itself, trying, trying, but never quite getting it right it seemed. So it tried and tried again as if it had fallen in love with the sound it had heard itself coo once perfectly.

Il pleut dans la ville. Rain in the city. When the rain starts to falling / my love comes tumbling down / and it's raining teardrops in my heart. Rain a dream lots of people are sharing and shyly Monk thinks of how it might feel to climb in naked with everybody under the covers running through green grass in a soft summer shower. Then its windshield wipers whipping back and forth. Quick glimpses of the invisible city splashing like eggs broken against the glass. I'm speeding along, let's say the West Side Highway, a storm on top, around, and under. It feels like being trapped in one of those automatic car washes doing its best to bust your windows and doors, rapping your metal skin like drumsticks. I'm driving blind and crazed as everybody else down a flooded highway no one with good sense would be out on on a night like this. Then I hit a swatch of absolute quiet under an overpass and for a split second anything is possible. I remember it has happened before, this leap over the edge into vast, unexpected silence, happened before and probably will again if I survive the furious storm, the traffic and tumult waiting to punish me instantly on the far side of the underpass. In that silence that's gone before it gets here good I recalled exactly another time, driving at night with you through a rainstorm. Still in love with you though I hadn't been with you for years, ten, fifteen, till that night of dog-and-cat rain on an expressway circling the city after our eyes had met in a crowded room. You driving, me navigating, searching for a sign to Woodside you warned me would come up all the sudden. There it is. There it is. You shouted. Shit. I missed it. We can get off the next exit, I said. But you said no. Said you didn't know the way. Didn't want to get lost in the scary storm in a scary neighborhood. I missed the turn for your apartment and you said, It's late anyway. Too late to go back and you'd get hopelessly lost coming off the next exit, so we continued downtown to my hotel where you dropped me after a good-night, goodbye-again peck on the cheek. Monk on the radio with a whole orchestra rooty-tooty at town hall, as we raced away from the sign I didn't see till we passed it. Monk's music breaking the silence after we missed our turn, after we hollered to hear each other over the rain, after we flew over the edge and the roof popped off and the sides split and for a moment we were suspended in a soundless bubble where invisible roads crisscrossed going nowhere, anywhere. Airborne, the tires aquaplaning, all four hooves of a galloping horse simultaneously in the air just like Muybridge, your favorite photographer, claimed, but nobody believed the nigger, did they, till he caught it on film.

Picture five or six musicians sitting around Rudy Van Gelder's living room, which is serving as a recording studio this afternoon. Keepnews is paying for the musicians' time, for Van Gelder's know-how and equipment, and everybody ready to record but Monk. Monk's had the charts a week and Keepnews knows he's studied them from comments Monk muttered while the others were sauntering in for the session. But Monk is Monk. He keeps fiddle-faddling with a simple tune, da, da, da, da, plunks the notes, stares into thin air as if he's studying a house of cards he's constructed there, waiting for it to fall apart. Maybe the stare's not long in terms of minutes (unless you're Keepnews, paying the bill) but long enough for the other musicians to be annoyed. Kenny Clarke, the drummer, picks up the Sunday funnies from a coffee table. Monk changes pace, back-pedals midphrase, turns the notes into a signifying riff.

K.C., you know you can't read. You drum-drum dummy. Don't be cutting your eyes at me. Ima ABC this tune to death, Mister Kenny Clarke. Take my time wit it. Uh-huh. One-and-two and one-and-two it to death, K.C. Don't care if your eyes light up and your stomach says howdy. One anna two anna one anna we don't start till I say start. Till I go over it again. Pick it clean. All the red boogers of meat off the bone then belch and fart and suck little strings I missed out my teefs and chew them last, salty, sweet gristle bits till the cows come home, and then, maybe then it might be time to start so stop bugging me with your bubble eyes like you think you got somewhere better to go.

Once I asked Monk what is this thing called love. Bebop, hip-hop, whatever's good till the last drop and you never get enough of it even when you get as much as you can handle, more than you can handle, he said, just as you'd expect from somebody who's been around such things and appreciates them connoisseurly but also with a passionate innocence so it's always the first time, the only time love's ever happened and Monk can't help but grunt uh-huh, uh-huh while he's playing even though he's been loved before and it ain't no big thing, just the only thing, the music, love, lifting me.

Monk says he thinks of narrow pantherish hips, the goateed gate to heaven, and stately, stately he slides the silky drawers down, pulls them over her steepled knees, her purple-painted toes. Tosses the panties high behind his back without looking because he knows Pippen's where he's supposed to be, trailing the play, sniffing the alley-oop dish, already slamming it through the hoop so Monk can devote full attention to sliding both his large, buoyant hands up under the curve of her buttocks. A beard down there trimmed neat as Monk trims his.

Trim, one of love's names. Poontang. Leg. Nooky. Cock.

Next chorus also about love. Not so much a matter of mourning a lost love as it is wondering how and when love will happen next or if love will ever happen again because in this vale of Vaseline and tears, whatever is given is also taken away. Love opens in the exact space of wondering what my chances are and figuring the hopeless odds against love. Then, biff, bam. Just when you least expect it, Monk says. Having known love before, I'm both a lucky one, ahead of the game, and also scared to death by memories of how sweet it is, how sad something that takes only a small bit of anybody's time can't be found more copiously, falling as spring rain or sunlight these simple things remind me of you and still do do do when Monk scatters notes like he's barefoot feeding chickenfeed to chickens or bleeding drop by drop precious Lord in the snow.

I believe when we're born each of us receives an invisible ladder we're meant to climb. We commence slowly, little baby shaky steps. Then bolder steps as we get the hang of it. Learn our powers, learn the curious construction of these ladders leaning on air, how the rungs are placed irregularly, almost as if they customize themselves to our stepping sometimes, so when we need them they're there or seem to be there solid under our feet because we're steady climbing and everybody around us steady climbing till it seems these invisible ladders, measure by measure, are music we perform as easily as breathing. Playing our song, we smile shyly, uneasily, the few times we remember how high and wide we've propelled ourselves into thin air step by step on rungs we never see disappearing behind us. And you can guess the rest of that tune, Monk says.

You place your foot as you always do, do, do, one in front of the other, then risk as you always do, do, do your weight on it so the other foot can catch up. Instead of dance music you hear a silent wind in your ears, blood pounding your temples, you're inside a house swept up in a tornado and it's about to pop, you're about to come tumbling down.

When your love starts to falling. Don't blame the missing rung. The ladder's still there. A bridge of sighs, of notes hanging in the air. A quicksilver run down the piano keys, each rib real as it's touched, then gone, wiped clean as Monk's hand flies glissando in the other direction.

One night in Paris trying to read myself to sleep, I heard the silence of rain. You might call silence a caesura, a break in a line of verse, the line pausing naturally to breathe, right on time, on a dime. But always a chance the line will never finish because the pause that refreshes can also swallow everything to the right and left of it.

Smoke curls from a gun barrel. The old poet, dissed by his young lover, shoots him, is on his way to jail. Rimbaud recovers from the wound, heads south toward long, long silence. Standing on a steamer's deck, baseball cap backward on his head, elbows on the rail, baggy pants drooping past the crack of his ass, Rimbaud sees the sea blistered by many dreamers like himself who leap off ships when no one's looking, as if the arc of their falling will never end, as if the fall can't be real because nobody sees it or hears it, as if they might return to their beginnings and receive another chance, as if the fall will heal them, a hot torch welding shut the black hole, the mouth from which silence issues thick as smoke from necklaces of burning tires.

Monk speaks many languages. The same sound may have different meanings in different languages. (To say = *tu sais* = you know.) And the same sound may also produce different silences. To say nothing is not necessarily to know nothing. The same letters can represent different sounds. Or different letters equal the same sound (pane, pain, payne). In different languages or the same. A lovers' quarrel in the rain at the train station. The budding poet seals his lips evermore. The older man trims his words to sonnets, willed silence caging sound. Their quarrel echoes over and over again, what was said and not said and unsaid returns. The heart (ancient liar/lyre) hunched on its chair watching silent reruns, lip-synching new words to old songs.

Monk's through playing and everybody in the joint happy as a congregation of seals full of fish. He sits on the piano bench, hulking, mute, his legs chopped off at the knees like a Tutsi's by his fellow countrymen, listening in the dark to their hands coming together, making no sound. Sits till kingdom come, a giant sponge or ink blotter soaking up first all the light, then the air, then sucking all sound from the darkness, from the stage, the auditorium. The entire glittering city shuts down. Everything caves in, free at last in this bone-dry house.

Silence. Monk's. Mine. Yours. I haven't delved into mine very deeply yet, have I, avoid my silence like a plague, even though the disease I'm hiding from already rampant in my blood, bones, the air.

Where are you? How far to your apartment from the Woodside exit? What color are your eyes? Is your hair long or short? I know your father's gone. I met a taxi driver who happened to be from your home town, a friendly, talkative brother about your father's age, so I asked him if he knew your dad, figuring there would have been a colored part of your town and everybody would sort of know everybody else the way they used to in the places where people like our parents were raised. Yeah, oh yeah. Course I knew Henry Diggs, he said. Said he'd grown up knowing your dad and matter of fact had spoken with him in the American Legion Club not too long before he heard your father had died. Whatever took your father, it took him fast, the man said. Seemed fine at the club. Little thin maybe but Henry always been a neat, trim-looking fellow and the next thing I heard he was gone. Had that conversation with a cabdriver about five years ago and the way he talked about your dad I could picture him neat and trim and straight-backed, clear-eyed. Then I realized the picture out-of-date. Twenty years since I'd seen your father last and I hadn't thought much about him since. Picture wasn't actually a picture anyway. When I say picture I guess I mean the taxi driver's words made your father real again by shaking up the silence. Confirmed something about your dad. About me. The first time I met your father and shook his hand, I noticed your color, your cheekbones in his face. That's what I'd look for in his different face if someone pointed out an old man and whispered your father's name. You singing in his silent features.

Picturing you also seems to work till I try to really see the picture. Make it stand still, frame it. View it. Then it's not a picture. It's a wish. A yearning. Many images layered one atop the other, passing through one another, each one so fragile it begins to fade, to dance, give way to the next before I can fix you in my mind. No matter how gently I lift the veil, your face comes away with it . . .

James Brown the hardest worker in show biz, drops down on one knee. Please. Please. Please. Don't go. A spotlight fixes the singer on a darkened stage. You see every blister of sweat on his glistening skin, each teardrop like a bedbug crawling down the black satin pillowcase of his cheeks. Please. Please. Please. But nobody answers. Cause nobody's home. She took his love and gone. J.B. dies a little bit onstage. Then more and more. His spangled cape shimmers where he tossed it, a bright pool at the edge of the stage where someone he loves dived in and never came up.

Silence a good way of listening for news. Please. Please. Is anybody out there? The singer can't see beyond the smoking cone of light raining on his shoulders, light white from outside, midnight blue if you're inside it. Silence is Please. Silence is Please Please Please hollered till it hurts. Noise no one hears if no one's listening. And night after night evidently they ain't.

Who wants to hear the lost one's name? Who has the nerve to say it? Monk taps it out, depressing the keys, stitching messages his machine launches into the make-believe of hearts. Hyperspace. Monk folded over his console. Mothership. Mothership. Beam me up, motherfucker. It's cold down here.

Brother Sam Cooke squeezed into a phone booth and the girl can't help it when she catches him red-handed in the act of loving somebody else behind the glass. With a single shot she blows him away. But he's unforgettable, returns many nights. Don't cry. Don't cry. No, no, no—no. Don't cry.

My silence? Mine. My silence is, as you see, as you hear, sometimes broken by Monk's music, by the words of his stories. My silence not like Monk's, not waiting for what comes next to arrive or go on about its goddamned business. I'm missing someone. My story is about losing you. About not gripping tight enough for fear my fingers would close on air. Love, if we get it, as close to music as most of us get, and in Monk's piano solos I hear your comings and goings, tiptoeing in and out of rooms, in and out of my heart, hear you like I hear the silence there would be no music without, the silence saying the song could end at this moment, any moment silence plays around. Because it always does, if you listen closely. Before the next note plays, silence always there.

Three-thirty in the A.M. I'm wide awake and alone. Both glow-in-the-dark clocks say so—the square one across the room, the watch on the table beside the bed, they agree, except for a ten-minute discrepancy, like a longstanding quarrel in an old marriage. I don't take sides. Treat them both as if there is something out there in the silence yet to be resolved, as if the hands of these clocks are waiting as I am for a signal so they can align themselves perfectly with it.

I lie in my bed a thousand years. Aching silently for you. My arms crossed on my chest, heavy as stones, a burden awhile, then dust trickling through the cage of ribs, until the whole carcass collapses in on itself, soundlessly, a heap of fine powder finally the wind scatters, each particle a note unplayed, returned perfectly intact, back where it came from.

When Monk finishes work it's nearly dawn. He crosses Fifty-seventh Street, a cigarette he's forgotten to light dangling from his lower lip.

What-up, Monk.

Uh-huh.

Moon shines on both sides of the street. People pour from lobbies of tall hotels, carrying umbrellas. Confetti hang-glides, glittery as tinsel. A uniformed brass band marches into view, all the players spry, wrinkled old men, the familiar hymn they toot and tap and whistle and bang thrashes and ripples like a tiger caught by its tail.

Folks form a conga line, no, it's a second line hustling to catch up to Monk, who's just now noticed all the commotion behind him. The twelve white horses pulling his coffin are high steppers, stallions graceful, big-butted, and stylized as Rockettes. They stutter-step, freeze, raise one foreleg bent at the knee, shake it like shaking cayenne pepper on gumbo. The horses also have the corner boys' slack-leg, drag-leg pimp-strut down pat and perform it off-time in unison to the crowd's delighted squeals down Broadway while the brass band cooks and hordes of sparrow-quick pickaninnies and rump-roast-rumped church ladies wearing hats so big you think helicopter blades or two wings to hide their faces and players so spatted and chained, ringed and polished, you mize well concede everything you own to them before the game starts, everybody out marching and dancing behind Mr. Monk's bier, smoke from the cigarette he's mercifully lit to cut the funk drifting back over them, weightless as a blessing, as a fingertip grazing a note not played.

In my dream, we're kissing goodbye when Monk arrives. First his music, and then the great man himself. All the air rushes from my lungs. Thelonious Apoplecricus, immensely enlarged in girth, his cheeks puffed out like Dizzy's. He's sputtering and stuttering, exasperated, pissed off as can be. Squeaky chipmunk voice like a record playing at the wrong speed, the way they say Big O trash-talked on the b-ball court or deep-sea divers squeak if raised too rapidly from great depths. Peepy dolphin pip pip peeps, yet I understand exactly.

Are you crazy, boy. Telling my story. Putting mouth in my words. Speechless as my music rendered your simple ass on countless occasions, what kind of bullshit payback is this? Tutti-frutti motherfucker. Speaking for me. Putting your jive woogie in my boogie.

Say what, nigger? Who said I retreated to silence? Retreat hell. I was attacking in another direction.

The neat goatee and mustache he favored a raggedy wreath now, surrounding his entire moon face. He resembles certain Hindu gods with his nappy aura, his new dready cap of afterbirth in flames to his shoulders. Monk shuffles and grunts, dismisses me with a wave of his glowing hand. When it's time, when he feels like it, he'll play the note we've been waiting for. The note we thought was lost in silence. And won't it be worth the wait.

Won't it be a wonder. And meanwhile, love, while we listen, these foolish things remind me of you.

31

Jazz Wife

Xu Xi

You marry the music not the man.

Here's that intro no one sings. The old familiars stick to form—AABA, AABA, AABA, AABA. Here's the one to the B that goes *ba-doinnnng,* all wrong.

✳

She walks into that bar, that club, that jazz space and listens to the boys in the band. Comes to visit a bartender, is all.

1978. Jazz is dying in America faster than a doornail that *tings!*

Break.

Trumpet arrives first. Bandleader. Having scoped her out from on-stage, he plants himself on her left. "So, you like jazz?"

"Doesn't everyone?" she replies.

"You like musicians?" He's a stand-up comic in his spare time.

Now she swings 'round and scopes him out. *Not* her type, although if you ask, she'll say she has no type. Not at twenty-two, she doesn't. Sips her Scotch and soda. "Don't know."

In the empty room, an elderly couple asks loudly, above their hearing, for "String of Pearls." Pianist appears, singing, *Glenn's dead, forever.* He's Black and White, like she's Black and Yellow. Oreo and banana crumble.

Pianist tells the trumpet, "I'm blowing this gig, man. Screw the money."

"Hey pal. You promised."

"Didn't promise nothin'." His volume rises, pounding the lower register.

She slides off the barstool. *Inconsiderate bastards. Least they could do is take their anger elsewhere.*

Time she left anyway.

The pianist storms out behind her. Tall, skinny, straight ahead. Even mad, he's looking good. His car, blocking hers, doesn't start, here in the middle of—*fucking nowhere,* he shouts, into the still of the night.

✳

You don't sing in the shower, or anywhere, unless you have perfect pitch.

At her place around an ancient upright, she sings, *Someday, when I'm awfully low.*

"You're flat," he says.

"So how do I hear better?"

"You listen. Maybe tape yourself."

She plays the opening to "Misty," the only standard she knows.

He interrupts. "Your rhythm's off."

"Rubato," she replies.

"Wise guy."

"I ain't a guy," and stops playing to prove it.

But when he plays, she falls in love with the miracle of his touch, the sprawl of his octaves, the grace of his ballads and the speed of his bebop. The man can play. He's still a boy, though, like she's still a girl, when he finally stops playing to kiss her.

✳

They live together in Cincinnati.

Time is a half note, a quarter note, an eighth, a sixteenth.

"Demisemiquaver?" she asks, recalling foreign music theory. "Crochets and semibreves?"

He spits back jazz. "Modes," he says. "Dorian, Lydian. Modal like Bill Evans."

"Paganini was a wild man, like Dad." The story of her life is the accident of conception, in Hong Kong, between a Black American banjo player and a Chinese stripper in the bars of Wanchai. She, an immigrant daughter in her father's home town, searches for roots, writes about Paganini to get, belatedly, a bachelor's degree in something.

"*I'll* teach you about music," he says. "But first you have to marry me."

"I'm not a musician," she replies.

"You could be if you tried."

But she's not sure, has never been sure, whether or not to believe him.

To-*may*-to, to-*ma*-to. *Let's call the whole thing off.*

✳

You learn to feed the boys in the band.

Running out the door of their marriage in Cincinnati, he shouts up the stairs, "We're rehearsing at eight."

Their home in Clifton is old and rambling. Ivy clings. Hours spent scrubbing and vacuuming because he cannot abide the tiniest speck.

Today, though, she doesn't clean. When the guys rehearse, the aftermath is like a bar the morning after. Bass player smokes, drummer inhales. The front line rotates, depending on availability—trumpet, trombone, tenor, alto, flute—and, because tonight he's really desperate, the oboe. Too many bottles of beer. Empties line the wall of his studio.

They're guys now. Boys belonged to a quainter era.

What she does instead is season the wok to prepare for their midnight feast. *Don't ask, just cook.* Collard greens for the Black players, nothing too weird for the Whites. Yellow doesn't play, not in Cincinnati. When they smell it they break. This way he eats, keeps up strength for the next gig and the next, if and when one comes along.

Afterwards, the complaints. Trumpet too loud, bass doesn't swing, and there are *way too many reasons* an oboe does not belong in jazz. The oboist, a blond from the college orchestra, needs rides all the time—which he gives—because her car keeps breaking down. The one girl in the band. *Why doesn't she change her axe,* he groans.

But to change your axe is to change your life.

"Are oboes like trumpets?" she asks.

He snaps. "How would I know?"

Why is he angry? She only meant to make him laugh with that joke among the guys. About the trumpet player at the club, that gal with the mouth. A jazz wife in the audience doesn't count, except to listen to the path of his solos.

They don't have sex after rehearsals.

In time, the oboe moves on and he makes love to her again.

✳

It's the gigs you miss most. The real jazz gigs.

Sometimes, a cat blows in from New York. If he's lucky, it's not a piano man. Then he's in demand. Everyone needs rhythm.

Guys have become men.

A first-call jazz man. Blows his regular lounge gigs for these. Anything for a chance to play the real thing.

She is thirty. "I'm getting up there," she says. "Fertility's dying."

"Later," he murmurs his refrain. Sometimes, he forgets he has this wife, the girl to whom he once played "My Romance."

If it isn't music, it's later.

Yet every time he pounds a fist she flinches, afraid *only* for his hands, those precious, life-making hands.

But at the club that night, the real gig night, jazz wives congregate. Tonight, they're out catting. Silk stockings for New York, and even Chicago, but not L.A.

They know *everyone's* song.

On the bandstand, he's in a suit, out of respect, regardless. Tonight, New York is white and young in jeans, barely out of boyhood. A genius on tenor.

She is proud. The music is all.

Not a cough in the house, the half empty house.

✳

You get and keep steady work.

"So what're you doing this weekend?" her bachelor colleague has asked every Friday afternoon for over six months.

"Oh you know," she smiles. "Same old same old. He's working."

"Don't you go to all his gigs?"

"Not anymore."

Guys hover. Black and Yellow is exotic in Ohio. This one has thin lips and sexy gray eyes. Wait, she thinks, *are* gray eyes sexy? He's nice, though, asks about her, not him, her nearly famous husband, at least in Cincinnati.

Her colleague says, "Don't you get jealous of all those singers?" By now, her husband's a first-call accompanist in fancy lounges, as far north as Chicago, where he's playing this week.

"He's not like that," she replies. "He comes home." The oboe, she has surmised, was an aberration. In his book, the *only* singers are Billie and Betty.

"You're in love," he says, as he does every time, the standard bridge to eyes that invite, *anytime you're tired of being a good wife.*

✳

Music is the wife.

AABA, AABA, AABA, AA *ba-doinnnng.*

✳

Until she becomes famous for a day.

One Saturday evening, she rescues a child. He breaks away from pregnant Mom and runs headlong into traffic. Blind instinct sends her after the boy, pulling him to safety. The driver brakes hard. Cars collide. A total mess.

All she can remember, as she tells the TV cameras, is the boy's face looking up at her. Trusting, unafraid. Confident in his innocence, a belief in his right to life.

The Cincinnati Enquirer sends their newest hire. He waits till after the cameras depart, annoyed. It's his thirtieth birthday and drinks are on his friends.

In a nearby bar, they talk for over an hour. He catches himself asking more and more questions, long after the story, just to keep the conversation going. He eyes her legs, reminds himself, *this is work, she is married, I am . . . a man.* Afterwards, she thanks him for the drink, pausing to notice gray eyes and a mouth like her colleague's.

The headline reads: JAZZ WIFE SAVES CHILD.

Crescendo.

Music pauses.

✳

In time, the reporter moves on. Larger city, bigger paper. To write about music. She's been a good teacher, in and out of bed, elevating him beyond the news.

Jazz wife gives life. Her husband is none the sadder.

✳

Time after time. So lucky to be loving you.

The passing years unfold, childless.

✳

The night he plays "Nature Boy," she goes, uninvited, unexpected.

From onstage, he sees her arrive. Doesn't smile, doesn't break into "Our Romance" the way he used to, years ago, whenever she came to a gig among friends.

His solo begins.

The best performance of his life. It's in his face. His eyes gaze past all to music heaven. The boys in the band play hard, for him, with him, in him, caught up in the frenzy, in this, his moment of genius. In the empty house, she hears it too, feels his solitary flight.

Then, his face becomes one with that child. Trusting. Unafraid. Certain of his right to be saved, to survive. In her solitude, she knows. If it hadn't been her it would have been somebody else.

She leaves, at last, in the middle of his solo.

*

After he's gone, you live for the music.

32

A Really Good Jazz Piano

Richard Yates

Because of the midnight noise on both ends of the line there was some confusion at Harry's New York Bar when the call came through. All the bartender could tell at first was that it was a long-distance call from Cannes, evidently from some kind of nightclub, and the operator's frantic voice made it sound like an emergency. Then at last, by plugging his free ear and shouting questions into the phone, he learned that it was only Ken Platt, calling up to have an aimless chat with his friend Carson Wyler, and this made him shake his head in exasperation as he set the phone on the bar beside Carson's glass of Pernod.

"Here," he said. "It's for you, for God's sake. It's your buddy." Like a number of other Paris bartenders he knew them both pretty well: Carson was the handsome one, the one with the slim, witty face and the English-sounding accent; Ken was the fat one who laughed all the time and tagged along. They were both three years out of Yale and trying to get all the fun they could out of living in Europe.

"Carson?" said Ken's eager voice, vibrating painfully in the receiver. "This is Ken—I knew I'd find you there. Listen, when you coming down, anyway?"

Carson puckered his well-shaped brow at the phone. "You know when I'm coming down," he said. "I wired you, I'm coming down Saturday. What's the matter with you?"

"Hell, nothing's the matter with me—maybe a little drunk, is all. No, but listen, what I really called up about, there's a man here named

Sid plays a really good jazz piano, and I want you to hear him. He's a friend of mine. Listen, wait a minute, I'll get the phone over close so you can hear. Listen to this, now. Wait a minute."

There were some blurred scraping sounds and the sound of Ken laughing and somebody else laughing, and then the piano came through. It sounded tinny in the telephone, but Carson could tell it was good. It was "Sweet Lorraine," done in a rich traditional style with nothing commercial about it, and this surprised him, for Ken was ordinarily a poor judge of music. After a minute he handed the phone to a stranger he had been drinking with, a farm machinery salesman from Philadelphia. "Listen to this," he said. "This is first-rate."

The farm machinery salesman held his ear to the phone with a puzzled look. "What is it?"

"'Sweet Lorraine.'"

"No, but I mean what's the deal? Where's it coming from?"

"Cannes. Somebody Ken turned up down there. You've met Ken, haven't you?"

"No, I haven't," the salesman said, frowning into the phone. "Here, it's stopped now and somebody's talking. You better take it."

"Hello? Hello?" Ken's voice was saying. "Carson?"

"Yes, Ken. I'm right here."

"Where'd you go? Who was that other guy?"

"That was a gentleman from Philadelphia named—" he looked up questioningly.

"Baldinger," said the salesman, straightening his coat.

"Named Mr. Baldinger. He's here at the bar with me."

"Oh. Well listen, how'd you like Sid's playing?"

"Fine, Ken. Tell him I said it was first-rate."

"You want to talk to him? He's right here, wait a minute."

There were some more obscure sounds and then a deep middle-aged voice said, "Hello there."

"How do you do, Sid. My name's Carson Wyler, and I enjoyed your playing very much."

"Well," the voice said. "Thank you, thank you a lot. I appreciate it." It could have been either a colored or a white man's voice, but Carson assumed he was colored, mostly from the slight edge of self-consciousness or pride in the way Ken had said, "He's a friend of mine."

"I'm coming down to Cannes this weekend, Sid," Carson said, "and I'll be looking forward to—"

But Sid had evidently given back the phone, for Ken's voice cut in. "Carson?"

"What?"

"Listen, what time you coming Saturday? I mean what train and everything?" They had originally planned to go to Cannes together, but Carson had become involved with a girl in Paris, and Ken had gone on alone, with the understanding that Carson would join him in a week. Now it had been nearly a month.

"I don't know the exact train," Carson said, with some impatience. "It doesn't matter, does it? I'll see you at the hotel sometime Saturday."

"Okay. Oh and wait, listen, the other reason I called, I want to sponsor Sid here for the IBF, okay?"

"Right. Good idea. Put him back on." And while he was waiting he got out his fountain pen and asked the bartender for the IBF membership book.

"Hello again," Sid's voice said. "What's this I'm supposed to be joining here?"

"The IBF," Carson said. "That stands for International Bar Flies, something they started here at Harry's back in—I don't know. Long time ago. Kind of a club."

"Very good," Sid said, chuckling.

"Now, what it amounts to is this," Carson began, and even the bartender, for whom the IBF was a bore and a nuisance, had to smile with pleasure at the serious, painstaking way he told about it—how each member received a lapel button bearing the insignia of a fly, together with a printed booklet that contained the club rules and a listing of all other IBF bars in the world; how the cardinal rule was that when two members met they were expected to greet one another by brushing the fingers of their right hands on each other's shoulders and saying, *"Bzz-z-z, bzz-z-z!"*

This was one of Carson's special talents, the ability to find and convey an unashamed enjoyment in trivial things. Many people could not have described the IBF to a jazz musician without breaking off in an apologetic laugh to explain that it was, of course, a sort of sad little game for lonely tourists, a square's thing really, and that its very lack of sophistication was what made it fun; Carson told it straight. In much the same way he had once made it fashionable among some of the more literary undergraduates at Yale to spend Sunday mornings respectfully absorbed in the funny papers of the *New York Mirror;* more recently the same trait had rapidly endeared him to many chance acquaintances, notably to his current girl, the young Swedish art student for whom he had stayed in Paris. "You have beautiful taste in everything," she had told him on their first memorable night together. "You have a truly educated, truly original mind."

"Got that?" he said into the phone, and paused to sip his Pernod. "Right. Now if you'll give me your full name and address, Sid, I'll get everything organized on this end." Sid spelled it out and Carson lettered it carefully into the membership book, with his own name and Ken's as co-sponsors, while Mr. Baldinger watched. When they were finished Ken's voice came back to say a reluctant goodbye, and they hung up.

"That must've been a pretty expensive telephone call," Mr. Baldinger said, impressed.

"You're right," Carson said. "I guess it was."

"What's the deal on this membership book, anyway? All this barfly business?"

"Oh, aren't you a member, Mr. Baldinger? I thought you were a member. Here, I'll sponsor you, if you like."

Mr. Baldinger got what he later described as an enormous kick out of it: far into the early morning he was still sidling up to everyone at the bar, one after another, and buzzing them.

Carson didn't get to Cannes on Saturday, for it took him longer than he'd planned to conclude his affair with the Swedish girl. He had expected a tearful scene, or at least a brave exchange of tender promises and smiles, but instead she was surprisingly casual about his leaving—even abstracted, as if already concentrating on her next truly educated, truly original mind—and this forced him into several uneasy delays that accomplished nothing except to fill her with impatience and him with a sense of being dispossessed. He didn't get to Cannes until the following Tuesday afternoon, after further telephone talks with Ken, and then, when he eased himself onto the station platform, stiff and sour with hangover, he was damned if he knew why he'd come at all. The sun assaulted him, burning deep into his gritty scalp and raising a quick sweat inside his rumpled suit; it struck blinding glints off the chromework of parked cars and motor scooters and made sickly blue vapors of exhaust rise up against pink buildings; it played garishly among the swarm of tourists who jostled him, showing him all their pores, all the tension of their store-new sports clothes, their clutched suitcases and slung cameras, all the anxiety of their smiling, shouting mouths. Cannes would be like any other resort town in the world, all hurry and disappointment, and why hadn't he stayed where he belonged, in a high cool room with a long-legged girl? Why the hell had he let himself be coaxed and wheedled into coming here?

But then he saw Ken's happy face bobbing in the crowd—"Carson!"—and there he came, running in his overgrown fat boy's thigh-chafing way, clumsy with welcome. "Taxi's over here, take your bag—boy, do you look beat! Get you a shower and a drink first, okay? How the hell are you?"

And riding light on the taxi cushions as they swung onto the Croisette, with its spectacular blaze of blue and gold and its blood-quickening rush of sea air, Carson began to relax. Look at the girls! There were acres of them; and besides, it was good to be with old Ken again. It was easy to see, now, that the thing in Paris could only have gotten worse if he'd stayed. He had left just in time.

Ken couldn't stop talking. Pacing in and out of the bathroom while Carson took his shower, jingling a pocketful of coins, he talked in the laughing, full-throated joy of a man who has gone for weeks without hearing his own voice. The truth was that Ken never really had a good time away from Carson. They were each other's best friends, but it had never been an equal friendship, and they both knew it. At Yale Ken would probably have been left out of everything if it hadn't been for his status as Carson's dull but inseparable companion, and this was a pattern that nothing in Europe had changed. What was it about Ken that put people off? Carson had pondered this question for years. Was it just that he was fat and physically awkward, or that he could be strident and silly in his eagerness to be liked? But weren't these essentially likable qualities? No,

Carson guessed the closest he could come to a real explanation was the fact that when Ken smiled his upper lip slid back to reveal a small moist inner lip that trembled against his gum. Many people with this kind of mouth may find it no great handicap—Carson was willing to admit that—but it did seem to be the thing everyone remembered most vividly about Ken Platt, whatever more substantial sounding reasons one might give for avoiding him; in any case it was what Carson himself was always most aware of, in moments of irritation. Right now, for example, in the simple business of trying to dry himself and comb his hair and put on fresh clothes, this wide, moving, double-lipped smile kept getting in his way. It was everywhere, blocking his reach for the towel rack, hovering too close over his jumbled suitcase, swimming in the mirror to eclipse the tying of his tie, until Carson had to clamp his jaws tight to keep from yelling, "All *right,* Ken—shut *up* now!"

But a few minutes later they were able to compose themselves in the shaded silence of the hotel bar. The bartender was peeling a lemon, neatly pinching and pulling back a strip of its bright flesh between thumb and knife blade, and the fine citric smell of it, combining with the scent of gin in the faint smoke of crushed ice, gave flavor to a full restoration of their ease. A couple of cold martinis drowned the last of Carson's pique, and by the time they were out of the place and swinging down the sidewalk on their way to dinner he felt strong again with a sense of the old camaraderie, the familiar, buoyant wealth of Ken's admiration. It was a feeling touched with sadness, too, for Ken would soon have to go back to the States. His father in Denver, the author of sarcastic weekly letters on business stationery, was holding open a junior partnership for him, and Ken, having long since completed the Sorbonne courses that were his ostensible reason for coming to France, had no further excuse for staying. Carson, luckier in this as in everything else, had no need of an excuse: he had an adequate private income and no family ties; he could afford to browse around Europe for years, if he felt like it, looking for things that pleased him.

"You're still white as a sheet," he told Ken across their restaurant table. "Haven't you been going to the beach?"

"Sure." Ken looked quickly at his plate. "I've been to the beach a few times. The weather hasn't been too good for it lately, is all."

But Carson guessed the real reason, that Ken was embarrassed to display his body, so he changed the subject. "Oh, by the way," he said. "I brought along the IBF stuff, for that piano player friend of yours."

"Oh, swell." Ken looked up in genuine relief. "I'll take you over there soon as we're finished eating, okay?" And as if to hurry this prospect along he forked a dripping load of salad into his mouth and tore off too big a bite of bread to chew with it, using the remaining stump of bread to mop at the oil and vinegar in his plate. "You'll like him, Carson," he said soberly around his chewing. "He's a great guy. I really admire him a lot." He swallowed with effort and hurried on: "I mean hell, with talent like that he could go back to the States tomorrow and make a fortune, but he likes it here. One thing, of course, he's got a girl here, this really lovely French girl, and I guess he couldn't very well take her back with him—no, but really, it's more than that. People accept him here. As an artist, I mean, as well as a man. Nobody condescends to him, nobody tries to interfere with his music, and that's all he wants out of life. Oh, I mean he doesn't tell you all this—probably be a bore if he did—it's just a thing you sense about him. Comes out in everything he says, his whole mental attitude." He popped the soaked bread into his mouth and chewed it with authority. "I mean the guy's got *authentic* integrity," he said. "Wonderful thing."

"Did sound like a damn good piano," Carson said, reaching for the wine bottle, "what little I heard of it."

"Wait'll you really hear it, though. Wait'll he really gets going."

They both enjoyed the fact that this was Ken's discovery. Always before it had been Carson who led the way, who found the girls and learned the idioms and knew how best to spend each hour; it was Carson who had tracked down all the really colorful places in Paris where you never saw Americans, and who then, just when Ken was learning to find places of his own, had paradoxically made Harry's Bar become the most colorful place of all. Through all this, Ken had been glad enough to follow, shaking his grateful head in wonderment; but it was no small thing to have turned up an incorruptible jazz talent in the back streets of a foreign city, all alone. It proved that Ken's dependence could be less than total after all, and this reflected credit on them both.

The place where Sid played was more of an expensive bar than a nightclub, a small carpeted basement several streets back from the sea. It was still early, and they found him having a drink alone at the bar.

"Well," he said when he saw Ken. "Hello there." He was stocky and well-tailored, a very dark Negro with a pleasant smile full of strong white teeth.

"Sid, I'd like you to meet Carson Wyler. You talked to him on the phone that time, remember?"

"Oh yes," Sid said, shaking hands. "Oh yes. Very pleased to meet you, Carson. What're you gentlemen drinking?"

They made a little ceremony of buttoning the IBF insignia into the lapel of Sid's tan gabardine, of buzzing his shoulder and offering the shoulders of their own identical seersucker jackets to be buzzed in turn. "Well, this is fine," Sid said, chuckling and leafing through the booklet. "Very good." Then he put the booklet in his pocket, finished his drink and slid off the barstool. "And now if you'll excuse me, I got to go to work."

"Not much of an audience yet," Ken said.

Sid shrugged. "Place like this, I'd just as soon have it that way. You get a big crowd, you always get some square asking for 'Deep in the Heart of Texas,' or some damn thing."

Ken laughed and winked at Carson, and they both turned to watch Sid take his place at the piano, which stood on a low spotlighted dais across the room. He fingered the keys idly for a while to make stray phrases and chords, a craftsman fondling his tools, and then he settled down. The compelling beat emerged, and out of the climb and waver of the melody, an arrangement of "Baby, Won't You Please Come Home."

They stayed for hours, listening to Sid play and buying him drinks whenever he took a break, to the obvious envy of other customers. Sid's girl came in, tall and brown-haired, with a bright, startled-looking face that was almost beautiful, and Ken introduced her with a small uncontrollable flourish: "This is Jaqueline." She whispered something about not speaking English very well, and when it was time for Sid's next break—the place was filling up now and there was considerable applause when he finished—the four of them took a table together.

Ken let Carson do most of the talking now; he was more than content just to sit there, smiling around this tableful of friends with all the serenity of a well-fed young priest. It was the happiest evening of his life in Europe, to a degree that even Carson would never have guessed. In the space of a few hours it filled all the emptiness of his past month, the time that had begun with Carson's saying "*Go,* then. Can't you go to Cannes by yourself?" It atoned for all the hot miles walked up and down the Croisette on blistered feet to peek like a fool at girls who lay incredibly near naked in the sand; for the cramped, boring bus rides to Nice and Monte Carlo and St. Paul-de-Vence; for the day he had paid a sinister druggist three times too much for a pair of sunglasses only to find, on catching sight of his own image in the gleam of a passing shop window, that they made him look like a great blind fish; for the terrible daily, nightly sense of being young and rich and free on the Riviera—the Riviera!—and of having nothing to do. Once in the first week he had gone with a prostitute whose canny smile, whose shrill insistence on a high price and whose facial flicker of distaste at the sight of his body had frightened him into an agony of impotence; most other nights he had gotten drunk or sick from bar to bar, afraid of prostitutes and of rebuffs from other girls, afraid even of striking up conversations with men lest they mistake him for a fairy. He had spent a whole afternoon in the French equivalent of a dime store, feigning a shopper's interest in padlocks and shaving cream and cheap tin toys, moving through the bright stale air of the place with a throatful of longing for home. Five nights in a row he had hidden himself in the protective darkness of American movies, just as he'd done years ago in Denver to get away from boys who called him Lard-Ass Platt, and after the last of these entertainments, back in the hotel with the taste of chocolate creams still cloying his mouth, he had cried himself to sleep. But all this was dissolving now under the fine reckless grace of Sid's piano, under the spell of Carson's intelligent smile and the way Carson raised his hands to clap each time the music stopped.

Sometime after midnight, when everyone but Sid had drunk too much, Carson asked him how long he had been away from the States. "Since the war," he said. "I came over in the Army and I never did go back."

Ken, coated with a film of sweat and happiness, thrust his glass high in the air for a toast. "And by God, here's hoping you never have to, Sid."

"Why is that, 'have to'?" Jaqueline said. Her face looked harsh and sober in the dim light. "Why do you say that?"

Ken blinked at her. "Well, I just mean—you know—that he never has to sell out, or anything. He never would, of course."

"What does this mean, 'sell out'?" There was an uneasy silence until Sid laughed in his deep, rumbling way. "Take it easy, honey," he said, and turned to Ken. "We don't look at it that way, you see. Matter of fact, I'm working on angles all the time to get back to the States, make some money there. We both feel that way about it."

"Well, but you're doing all right here, aren't you?" Ken said, almost pleading with him. "You're making enough money and everything, aren't you?"

Sid smiled patiently. "I don't mean a job like this, though, you see. I mean real money."

"You know who is Murray Diamond?" Jacqueline inquired, holding her eyebrows high. "The owner of nightclubs in Las Vegas?"

But Sid was shaking his head and laughing. "Honey, wait a minute—I keep telling you, that's nothing to count on. Murray Diamond happened to be in here the other night, you see," he explained. "Didn't have much time, but he said he'd try to drop around again some night this week. Be a big break for me. 'Course, like I say, that's nothing to count on."

"Well but *Jesus,* Sid—" Ken shook his head in bafflement; then, letting his face tighten into a look of outrage, he thumped the table with a bouncing fist. "Why prostitute yourself?" he demanded. "I mean damn it, you *know* they'll make you prostitute yourself in the States!"

Sid was still smiling, but his eyes had narrowed slightly. "I guess it's all in the way you look at it," he said.

And the worst part of it, for Ken, was that Carson came so quickly to his rescue. "Oh, I'm sure Ken doesn't mean that the way it *sounds,*" he said, and while Ken was babbling quick apologies of his own ("No, of course not, all I meant was—*you* know . . . ") he went on to say other things, light nimble things that only Carson could say, until the awkwardness was gone. When the time came to say goodnight there were handshakes and smiles and promises to see each other soon.

But the minute they were out on the street, Carson turned on Ken. "Why did you have to get so damned sophomoric about that? Couldn't you see how embarrassing it was?"

"I know," Ken said, hurrying to keep pace with Carson's long legs, "I know. But hell, I *was* disappointed in him, Carson. The point is I never heard him *talk* like that before." What he omitted here, of course, was that he had never really heard him talk at all, except in the one shy conversation that had led to the calling-up of Harry's Bar that other night, after which Ken had fled back to the hotel in fear of overstaying his welcome.

"Well, but even so," Carson said. "Don't you think it's the man's own business what he wants to do with his life?"

"Okay," Ken said, "*okay.* I *told* him I was sorry, didn't I?" He felt so humble now that it took him some minutes to realize that, in a sense, he hadn't come off too badly. After all, Carson's only triumph tonight had been that of the diplomat, the soother of feelings; it was he, Ken, who had done the more dramatic thing. Sophomoric or not, impulsive or not, wasn't there a certain dignity in having spoken his mind that way? Now, licking his lips and glancing at Carson's profile as they walked, he squared his shoulders and tried to make his walk less of a waddle and more of a headlong, manly stride. "It's just that I can't help how I feel, that's all," he said with conviction. "When I'm disappointed in a person I show it, that's all."

"All right. Let's forget it."

And Ken was almost sure, though he hardly dared believe it, that he could detect a grudging respect in Carson's voice.

Everything went wrong the next day. The fading light of afternoon found the two of them slumped and staring in a bleak workingman's café near the railroad station, barely speaking to each other. It was a day that had started out unusually well, too—that was the trouble.

They had slept till noon and gone to the beach after lunch, for Ken didn't mind the beach when he wasn't there alone, and before long they had picked up two American girls in the easy, graceful way that Carson always managed such things. One minute the girls were sullen strangers, wiping scented oil on their bodies and looking as if any intrusion would mean a call for the police, the next minute they were weak with laughter at the things Carson was saying, moving aside their bottles and their zippered blue TWA satchels to make room for unexpected guests. There was a tall one for Carson with long firm thighs, intelligent eyes and a way of tossing back her hair that gave her a look of real beauty, and a small one for Ken—a cute, freckled good-sport of a girl whose every cheerful glance and gesture showed she was used to taking second best. Ken, bellying deep into the sand with his chin on two stacked fists, smiling up very close to her warm legs, felt almost none of the conversational tension that normally hampered him at times like this. Even when Carson and the tall girl got up to run splashing into the water he was able to hold her interest: she said several times that the Sorbonne "must have been fascinating," and she sympathized with his having to go back to Denver, though she said it was "probably the best thing."

"And your friend's just going to stay over here indefinitely, then?" she asked. "Is it really true what he said? I mean that he isn't studying or working or anything? Just sort of floating around?"

"Well—yeah, that's right." Ken tried a squinty smile like Carson's own. "Why?"

"It's interesting, that's all. I don't think I've ever met a person like that before."

That was when Ken began to realize what the laughter and the scanty French bathing suits had disguised about these girls, that they were girls of a kind neither he nor Carson had dealt with for a long time—suburban, middle-class girls who had dutifully won their parents' blessing for this guided tour; girls who said "golly Moses," whose campus-shop clothes and hockey-field strides would have instantly betrayed them on the street. They were the very kind of girls who had gathered at the punch bowl to murmur "Ugh!" at the way he looked in his first tuxedo, whose ignorant, maddeningly bland little stares of rejection had poisoned all his aching years in Denver and New Haven. They were squares. And the remarkable thing was that he felt so good. Rolling his weight to one elbow, clutching up slow, hot handfuls of sand and emptying them, again and again, he found his flow of words coming quick and smooth:

"... no, really, there's a lot to see in Paris; shame you couldn't spend more time there; actually most of the places I like best are more or less off the beaten track; of course I was lucky in having a fairly good grasp of the language, and then I met so many congenial ...."

He was holding his own; he was making out. He hardly even noticed when Carson and the tall girl came trotting back from their swim, as lithe and handsome as a couple in a travel poster, to drop beside them in a bustle of towels and cigarettes and shuddering jokes about how cold the water was. His only mounting worry was that Carson, who must by now have made his own discovery about these girls, would decide they weren't worth bothering with. But a single glance at Carson's subtly smiling, talking face reassured him: sitting tense at the tall girl's feet while she stood to towel her back in a way that made her breasts sway delightfully, Carson was plainly determined to follow through. "Look," he said. "Why don't we all have dinner together? Then afterwards we might—"

Both girls began chattering their regrets: they were afraid not, thanks anyway, they were meeting friends at the hotel for dinner and actually ought to be starting back now, much as they hated to—"God, look at the time!" And they really did sound sorry, so sorry that Ken, gathering all his courage, reached out and held the warm, fine-boned hand that swung at the small girl's thigh as the four of them plodded back toward the bathhouses. She even squeezed his heavy fingers, and smiled at him.

"Some other night, then?" Carson was saying. "Before you leave?"

"Well, actually," the tall girl said, "our evenings do seem to be pretty well booked up. Probably run into you on the beach again though. It's been fun."

"Goddamn little snot-nosed New Rochelle bitch," Carson said when they were alone in the men's bathhouse.

"*Sh-h-h!* Keep your *voice* down, Carson. They can *hear* you in there."

"Oh, don't be an idiot." Carson flung his trunks on the duckboards with a sandy slap. "I hope they do hear me—what the hell's the matter with you?" He looked at Ken as if he hated him. "Pair of goddamn teasing little professional virgins. *Christ,* why didn't I stay in Paris?"

And now here they were, Carson glowering, Ken sulking at the sunset through flyspecked windows while a pushing, garlic-smelling bunch of laborers laughed and shouted over the pinball machine. They went on drinking until long past the dinner hour; then they ate a late, unpleasant meal together in a restaurant where the wine was corky and there was too much grease on the fried potatoes. When the messy plates were cleared away Carson lit a cigarette. "What do you want to do tonight?" he said.

There was a faint shine of grease around Ken's mouth and cheeks. "I don't know," he said. "Lot of good places to go, I guess."

"I suppose it would offend your artistic sensibilities to go and hear Sid's piano again?"

Ken gave him a weak, rather testy smile. "You still harping on that?" he said. "Sure I'd like to go."

"Even though he may prostitute himself?"

"Why don't you lay off that, Carson?"

They could hear the piano from the street, even before they walked into the square of light that poured up from the doorway of Sid's place. On the stairs the sound of it grew stronger and richer, mixed now with the sound of a man's hoarse singing, but only when they were down in the room, squinting through the blue smoke, did they realize the singer was Sid himself. Eyes half closed, head turned to smile along his shoulder into the crowd, he was singing as he swayed and worked at the keys.

"Man, she got a pair of eyes. . . ."

The blue spotlight struck winking stars in the moisture of his teeth and the faint thread of sweat that striped his temple.

"I mean they're brighter than the summer skies
And when you see them you gunna realize
Just why I love my sweet Lorraine. . . ."

"Damn place is packed," Carson said. There were no vacancies at the bar, but they stood uncertainly near it for a while, watching Sid perform, until Carson found that one of the girls on the barstools directly behind him was Jaqueline. "Oh," he said. "Hi. Pretty good crowd tonight."

She smiled and nodded and then craned past him to watch Sid.

"I didn't know he sang too," Carson said. "This something new?"

Her smile gave way to an impatient little frown and she put a forefinger against her lips. Rebuffed, he turned back and moved heavily from one foot to the other. Then he nudged Ken. "You want to go or stay? If you want to stay let's at least sit down."

"Sh-h-h!" Several people turned in their chairs to frown at him. *"Sh-h-h!"*

"Come on, then," he said, and he led Ken sidling and stumbling through the ranks of listeners to the only vacant table in the room, a small one down in front, too close to the music and wet with spilled drink, that had been pushed aside to make room for larger parties. Settled there, they could see now that Sid wasn't looking into the crowd at large. He was singing directly to a bored-looking couple in evening clothes who sat a few tables away, a silver-blonde girl who could have been a movie starlet and a small, chubby bald man with a deep tan, a man so obviously Murray Diamond that a casting director might have sent him here to play the part. Sometimes Sid's large eyes would stray to other parts of the room or to the smoke-hung ceiling, but they seemed to come into focus only when he looked at these two people. Even when the song ended and the piano took off alone on a long, intricate variation, even when he kept glancing up to see if they were watching. When he finished, to a small thunderclap of applause, the bald man lifted his face, closed it around an amber cigarette holder and clapped his hands a few times.

"Very nice, Sam," he said.

"My name's Sid, Mr. Diamond," Sid said, "but I thank you a lot just the same. Glad y'enjoyed it, sir." He was leaning back, grinning along his shoulder while his fingers toyed with the keys. "Anything special you'd like to hear, Mr. Diamond? Something old-time? Some more of that real old Dixieland? Maybe a little boogie, maybe something a little on the sweet side, what we call a commercial number? Got all kind of tunes here, waitin' to be played."

"Anything at all, uh, Sid," Murray Diamond said, and then the blonde leaned close and whispered something in his ear. "How about 'Stardust,' there, Sid?" he said. "Can you play 'Stardust'?"

"Well, now, Mr. Diamond. If I couldn't play 'Stardust' I don't guess I'd be in business very long, France or any other country." His grin turned into a deep false laugh and his hands slid into the opening chords of the song.

That was when Carson made his first friendly gesture in hours, sending a warm blush of gratitude into Ken's face. He hitched his chair up close to Ken's and began to speak in a voice so soft that no one could have accused him of making a disturbance. "You know something?" he said. "This is disgusting. My God, I don't care if he wants to go to Las Vegas. I don't even care if he wants to suck *around* for it. This is something else. This is something that turns my stomach." He paused, frowning at the floor, and Ken watched the small wormlike vein moving in his temple. "Putting on this phony accent," Carson said. "All this big phony Uncle Remus routine." And then he went into a little popeyed, head-tossing, hissing parody of Sid. "Yassuh, Mr. Dahmon' suh. Wudg'all lak t'heah, Mr. Dahmon' suh? Got awl kine a toons heah, jes' waitin' to be played, and yok, yok, yok, and shet ma mouf!" He finished his drink and set the glass down hard. "You know damn well he doesn't have to talk that way. You know damn well he's a perfectly bright, educated guy. My God, on the phone I couldn't even tell he was colored."

"Well, yeah," Ken said. "It is sort of depressing."

"Depressing? It's degrading." Carson curled his lip. "It's degenerate."

"I know," Ken said. "I guess that may be partly what I meant about prostituting himself."

"You were certainly right, then. This is damn near enough to make you lose faith in the Negro race."

Being told he was right was always a tonic to Ken, and it was uncommonly bracing after a day like this. He knocked back his drink, straightened his spine and wiped the light mustache of sweat from his upper lip, pressing his mouth into a soft frown to show that his faith, too, in the Negro race was badly shaken. "Boy," he said. "I sure had him figured wrong."

"No," Carson assured him, "you couldn't have known."

"Listen, let's go, then, Carson. The hell with him." And Ken's mind was already full of plans: they would stroll in the cool of the Croisette for a long, serious talk on the meaning of integrity, on how rare it was and how easily counterfeited, how its pursuit was the only struggle worthy of a man's life, until all the discord of the day was erased.

But Carson moved his chair back, smiling and frowning at the same time. "Go?" he said. "What's the matter with you? Don't you want to stay and watch the spectacle? I do. Doesn't it hold a certain horrible fascination for you?" He held up his glass and signaled for two more cognacs.

"Stardust" came to a graceful conclusion and Sid stood up, bathed in applause, to take his break. He loomed directly over their table as he came forward and stepped down off the dais, his big face shining with sweat; he brushed past them, looking toward Diamond's table, and paused there to say, "Thank you, sir," though Diamond hadn't spoken to him, before he made his way back to the bar.

"I suppose he thinks he didn't see us," Carson said.

"Probably just as well," Ken said. "I wouldn't know what to say to him."

"Wouldn't you? I think I would."

The room was stifling, and Ken's cognac had taken on a faintly repellent look and smell in his hand. He loosened his collar and tie with moist fingers. "Come on, Carson," he said. "Let's get out of here. Let's get some air."

Carson ignored him, watching what went on at the bar. Sid drank something Jaqueline offered and then disappeared into the men's room. When he came out a few minutes later, his face dried and composed, Carson turned back and studied his glass. "Here he comes. I think we're going to get the big hello, now, for Diamond's benefit. Watch."

An instant later Sid's fingers brushed the cloth of Carson's shoulder. "*Bzz-z-z, bzz-z-z!*" he said. "How're you tonight?"

Very slowly, Carson turned his head. With heavy eyelids he met Sid's smile for a split second, the way a man might look at a waiter who had accidentally touched him. Then he turned back to his drink.

"Oh-oh," Sid said. "Maybe I didn't do that right. Maybe I got the wrong shoulder here. I'm not too familiar with the rules and regulations yet." Murray Diamond and the blonde were watching, and Sid winked at them, thumbing out the IBF button in his lapel as he moved in sidling steps around the back of Carson's chair. "This here's a club we belong to, Mr. Diamond," he said. "Barflies club. Only trouble is, I'm not very familiar with the rules and regulations yet." He held the attention of nearly everyone in the room as he touched Carson's other shoulder. "*Bzz-z-z, bzz-z-z!*" This time Carson winced and drew his jacket away, glancing at Ken with a perplexed little shrug as if to say, Do you know what this man wants?

Ken didn't know whether to giggle or vomit; both desires were suddenly strong in him, though his face held straight. For a long time afterwards he would remember how the swabbed black plastic of the table looked between his two unmoving hands, how it seemed the only steady surface in the world.

"Say," Sid said, backing away toward the piano with a glazed smile. "What is this here? Some kinda conspiracy here?"

Carson allowed a heavy silence to develop. Then with an air of sudden, mild remembrance, seeming to say, Oh yes, of course, he rose and walked over to Sid, who backed up confusedly into the spotlight. Facing him, he extended one limp finger and touched him on the shoulder. "Buzz," he said. "Does that take care of it?" He turned and walked back to his seat.

Ken prayed for someone to laugh—anyone—but no one did. There was no movement in the room but the dying of Sid's smile as he looked at Carson and at Ken, the slow fleshy enclosing of his teeth and the widening of his eyes.

Murray Diamond looked at them too, briefly—a tough, tan little face—then he cleared his throat and said, "How about 'Hold Me,' there, Sid? Can you play 'Hold Me'?" And Sid sat down and began to play, looking at nothing.

With dignity, Carson nodded for the check and laid the right number of thousand- and hundred-franc notes on the saucer. It seemed to take him no time at all to get out of the place, sliding expertly between the tables and out to the stairs, but it took Ken much longer. Lurching, swaying in the smoke like a great imprisoned bear, he was caught and held by Jaqueline's eyes even before he had cleared the last of the tables. They stared relentlessly at the flabby quaver of his smile, they drilled into his back and sent him falling upstairs. And as soon as the sobering night air hit him, as soon as he saw Carson's erect white suit retreating several doors away, he knew what he wanted to do. He wanted to run up and hit him with all his strength between the shoulder blades, one great chopping blow that would drop him to the street, and then he would hit him again, or kick him—yes, kick him—and he'd say, God damn you! God damn you, Carson! The words were already in his mouth and he was ready to swing when Carson stopped and turned to face him under a streetlamp.

"What's the trouble, Ken?" he said. "Don't you think that was funny?"

It wasn't what he said that mattered—for a minute it seemed that nothing Carson said would ever matter again—it was that his face was stricken with the uncannily familiar look of his own heart, the very face he himself, Lard-Ass Platt, had shown all his life to others: haunted and vulnerable and terribly dependent, trying to smile, a look that said Please don't leave me alone.

Ken hung his head, either in mercy or shame. "Hell, I don't know, Carson," he said. "Let's forget it. Let's get some coffee somewhere."

"Right." And they were together again. The only problem now was that they had started out in the wrong direction: in order to get to the Croisette they would have to walk back past the lighted doorway of Sid's place. It was like walking through fire, but they did it quickly and with what anyone would have said was perfect composure, heads up, eyes front, so that the piano only came up loud for a second or two before it diminished and died behind them under the rhythm of their heels.

Authors' Biographies

Don Asher (1926–). Born in Worcester, Massachusetts, Asher has had two overlapping careers, as jazz pianist and writer. He has credited his musical experience with influencing his writing style, especially dialogue. His novels include *The Piano Sport, The Electric Cotillion,* and *The Eminent Yachtsman and the Whorehouse Piano Player.* His collaboration with Hampton Hawes on the latter's memoirs, *Raise Up Off Me,* received an Ascap-Deems Taylor award.

James Baldwin (1924–1987). Baldwin was born in Harlem, became a Pentecostal preacher at 14, then rejected religion a few years later. He began his writing career in Paris where he had emigrated partially in response to his native country's repressive attitude toward blacks and homosexuals. He wrote in a variety of genres and is as well regarded as an essayist as a writer of fiction. His books of essays include *Notes of a Native Son, Nobody Knows My Name,* and *The Fire Next Time.* His short stories are collected in *Going to Meet the Man,* and his novels include *Go Tell It on a Mountain, Giovanni's Room, Another Country,* and *Just Above My Head.* He also published a volume of poetry toward the end of his career: *Jimmy's Blues.*

Toni Cade Bambara (1939–1995). Bambara grew up in some of the poorest neighborhoods in and around New York, and worked at a variety of jobs while trying to make her way as a writer. Active in both the Black Arts and black feminist movements, she edited the influential *The Black Woman,* an anthology of poetry, stories, and essays by black women. She published two novels, *The Salt Eaters* and *Those Bones Are Not My Child,* and several collections of short stories, including *Gorilla, My Love* and *The Sea Birds Are Still Alive.*

Amiri Baraka (1934–). Born and raised in Newark, New Jersey, Baraka has seldom been far from controversy. His voluminous writings have often been criticized for their depiction of women, gays, Jews, and whites. Among his best-known works are two collections of essays on jazz, *Blues People: Negro Music in White America* and *The Music: Reflections on Jazz and Blues;* a novel, *The System of Dante's Hell;* and two short, powerful plays, *Dutchman* and *The Slave.* He founded the influential Black Arts movement of the 1960s, won an American Book Award, served—very controversially—as poet laureate of New Jersey, and appears in David Horowitz's book *The Professors: The 101 Most Dangerous Academics in America.*

Frank London Brown (1927–1962). Born in Kansas City, Missouri, Brown worked at a variety of jobs, including associate editor of *Ebony Magazine* and jazz musician. At the time of his premature death he was finishing his doctoral dissertation in political science. His only novel, *Trumbull Park,* like most of his works, deals with the experiences of urban black Americans. An uncompleted second novel, *The Myth Maker,* was published posthumously. Brown is reputed to be the first writer to have read his stories to jazz accompaniment.

Michelle Cliff (1946–). Born into a mulatto family in Kingston, Jamaica, Cliff was urged from an early age to try to pass for white. She grew up in the Caribbean, the United States, and Europe, and has taught at several colleges and universities. Deeply concerned with racism and sexism, her works include such story collections as *Bodies of Water* and *The Store of a Million Items* and such novels as *Abeng, No Telephone to Heaven,* and *Free Enterprise.* Among her awards are Fulbright, MacDowell, and National Endowment for the Arts fellowships.

Wanda Coleman (1946–). Coleman grew up in the Watts neighborhood of Los Angeles during the turbulent 1960s. While working at an unusually wide variety of jobs, she began her voluminous writing career. Her claim to be the most prolific African American poet of all time is supported by the fact that she has written thousands of poems, given more than 500 public readings, and collected more than 5,000 rejection slips. Known as "the unofficial poet laureate of Los Angeles," she has also been active in recording with progressive musicians. Centrally concerned with racism, her many books include *Heavy Daughter Blues: Poems and Stories 1968–1986; African Sleeping Sickness: Stories and Poems; Bathwater Wine* (poems); *Mambo Hips and Make Believe: A Novel;* and *Native in a Strange Land: Trials and Tremors* (essays and criticism). She was nominated for a National Book Award, won an Emmy for Daytime Drama writing, won the Lenore Marshall Prize, and became the first literary fellow in the Los Angeles Department of Cultural Affairs.

Julio Cortázar (1914–1984). Born to Argentine parents living in Brussels, Cortázar moved with them at an early age to Argentina where he later taught school for several years before emigrating, for political reasons, to Paris where he lived for the rest of his life, working as a translator for UNESCO and producing a multitude of works in various genres. Some of his richly imaginative short stories (which are variously referred to as *surreal, postmodern,* and *avant-garde*) can be found in *Blow-Up and Other Stories, The End of the Game,* and *We Love Glenda So Much.* His best-known novel, *Hopscotch,* is generally regarded as a modernistic masterpiece.

Kiki DeLancey (1959–). Born Kiki Nicolozakes into a coal-mining family with close ties to the Greek community in Cambridge, Ohio, DeLancey worked for many years in the coal industry, starting as a permit clerk and working her way up to executive vice president of a coal company. She characterizes herself as a self-taught writer who learned her craft by reading such masters as Faulkner and Sherwood Anderson. Her stories are typically set in the hardscrabble communities bordering the Ohio River and focus on the marginal lives of their inhabitants. Her first collection of stories, *Coal Miner's Holiday,* was the 2003 Independent Publisher Book Award Winner for Short Story Fiction.

Ralph Ellison (1914–1994). Born in Oklahoma City, Oklahoma, Ellison attended the Tuskegee Institute to study music and later left for New York to study sculpture. Ellison published one novel during his lifetime—*Invisible Man*—which is still considered a landmark in American literature. Elected into the American Academy of Arts and Letters, Ellison received such prestigious awards as the Medal of Freedom, the Langston Hughes Medallion, and the National Book Award. He also published the essay collection *Shadow and Act.* Posthumous collections include *Flying Home and Other Stories* and the novel *Juneteenth.*

Rudolph Fisher (1897–1934). A physician as well as a writer, Fisher was born in Washington, D.C., and was prominent among the writers who generated interest in black literature during the Harlem Renaissance of the 1920s. Often focusing on prejudice *among* (rather than the more typical *against*) blacks, his works combine realism and satire in their depiction of urban black culture. His stories can be found in *The Collected Stories of Rudolf Fisher; The Short Fiction of Rudolf Fisher;* and *The City of Refuge: The Collected Stories.* His two novels are *The Walls of Jericho* and *The Conjure-Man Dies: A Mystery Tale of Dark Harlem.* His final work was an adaptation for the stage of *The Conjure-Man Dies.* It has been said that Fisher anticipated the "black-is-beautiful" movement by half a century.

Sam Greenlee (1930–). Born in Chicago, Greenlee became one of the first African American foreign service officers but quit when he grew disillusioned with his role as government propagandist. When no American publisher would accept his first novel, probably because of its controversial nature, it was published in England as *The Spook Who Sat by the Door.* It sold more than a million copies, was translated into six languages, and won the *Sunday Times* (London) Book of the Year Award. It is regarded as the first black-nationalist novel and is said to have inspired the "blaxploitation" movie genre of the 1970s. A second novel, *Baghdad Blues,* gained renewed interest after the overthrow of Saddam Hussein. Greenlee is also a poet and talk show host and has served as Illinois poet laureate. *Blues for an African Princess* and *Ammunition! Poetry and Other Raps* are two of his poetry collections.

David Huddle (1942–). Because Huddle was born and raised in Wythe County, Virginia, he is sometimes referred to as an Appalachian writer. His works in a variety of genres include the poetry collections *Stopping by Home, Summer Lake: New and Selected Poems,* and *Grayside;* the short story collections *Only the Little Bone, The High Spirits: Stories of Men and Women,* and *Intimates;* the novels *La Tour Dreams of the Wolf Girl* and *The Story of a Million Years;* and a collection of essays, *The Writing Habit.* He has twice been awarded fellowships from the National Endowment for the Arts and teaches at the University of Vermont, Burlington.

Langston Hughes (1902–1967). Born in Joplin, Missouri, Hughes became a central figure in the Harlem Renaissance of the 1920s. Representing a variety of genres, his works center on the lives of working class blacks and celebrate their resiliency, strength, and humor. He was awarded the Spingarn Medal for distinguished achievements by an African American by the NAACP. His first novel, *Not Without Laughter,* won the Harmon Gold Medal for literature; his short story collections include *The Ways of White Folks* and *Laughing to Keep from Crying;* his two autobiographies are *The Big Sea* and *I Wonder as I Wander.* He was also active in the theatre, on one occasion collaborating with Zora Neale Hurston on the play *Mule Bone.* Above his cremated remains at the Schomburg Center for Research in Black Culture in Harlem is an African cosmogram titled *Rivers* after the title of his signature poem, "The Negro Speaks of Rivers."

Phil Kawana (1965–). Kawana was born and raised in Taranaki, New Zealand, of Maori descent. He is a short story writer, poet, and performer whose works often limn the lives of young Maoris caught in the conflict between the new, urban culture of New Zealand and its more traditional, rural counterpart. He has twice won the Te Kaunihera Maori Award for best short story in English by a published Maori writer. So far, he has published two collections of short stories, *Dead Jazz Guys* and *Attack of the Skunk People,* and one of poetry, *The Devil in My Shoes.*

Yusef Komunyakaa (1947–). Komunyakaa was born and raised in Bogalusa, Louisiana, and served in Vietnam, for which he received the Bronze Star. His many poetry collections include *Warhorses, Taboo, Talking Dirty to the Gods,* and *Pleasure Dome: New and Collected Poems;* his selected poems, *Neon Vernacular,* received the Pulitzer Prize. His many other honors include the Levinson Prize from *Poetry Magazine,* the Hanes Poetry Prize, and the Morton Dauwen Zabel Award from the American Academy of Arts and Letters. He teaches at New York University.

Ellen Jordis Lewis (1964–). Lewis was born and raised in New York City, where she worked as an advertising copywriter. She now lives in Portland, Oregon. Her short works have appeared in such publications as *Quick Fiction* and *Brilliant Corners.*

William Henry Lewis (1967–). Lewis was born in Denver and grew up in many cities, most significantly Chattanooga. His fiction has appeared in many journals and anthologies, including *Best Short Stories of 1996.* He has produced two collections of short stories, *In the Arms of Our Elders* and *I Got Somebody in Staunton,* the latter of which was honored as a finalist for the PEN Faulkner Prize for Fiction and named as a Fiction Honor Book for 2005 by the Black Caucus of the American Library Association. The recipient of a 2008 NEA Fellowship, he teaches at the University of Maryland, College Park.

John McCluskey, Jr. (1944–). McCluskey was born in Middletown, Ohio, and has taught African American studies for many years at Indiana University. He has said that he wants his works "to heighten the appreciation of the complexities of Afro-American literature and life." He has served as editor and contributor to a number of books on black culture, including *Blacks in History, Volume 2* and *Stories from Black History: Nine Stories.* His two novels to date are *Look What They Done to My Song* and *Mr. America's Last Season Blues.*

Bill Moody (1941–). Born in Webb City, Missouri, Moody has been a teacher, disc jockey, jazz drummer, and freelance writer. In addition to writing a non-fiction book on jazz—*The Jazz Exiles: American Musicians Abroad*—he is in the midst of producing an ongoing series about a jazz pianist who becomes involved in detective work. In the first novel in the sequence, *Solo Hand,* the piano-playing protagonist, Evan Horne, becomes involved in solving a mystery after injuring his right (or solo-playing) hand in an auto accident. The other novels in the series so far are *Death of a Tenor Man, The Sound of the Trumpet, Bird Lives!,* and *Looking for Chet Baker.* He has said that for him the writing of fiction is like the making of jazz.

James Reed (1954–). Reed was born in Minneapolis and graduated from the University of Nebraska at Omaha, where he later served as both fiction and managing editor of *The Nebraska Review.* The first recipient of the Nebraska Arts Council's Individual Artist Fellowship Master Award in Literature, Reed has published short stories in a variety of literary magazines, including *Bat City Review, Brilliant Corners, Carolina Quarterly,* and *Epicenter,* and he has been awarded a National Endowment for the Arts Fellowship.

Josef Škvorecký (1924–). Born in Náchod, Czechoslovakia (now Czech Republic), Škvorecký spent two years as a slave laborer in a German aircraft factory during World War II. Because his early writings were improvisational and supported democratic values, they were censored by the Communist Party. With his wife, he founded 68 Publishers, which published banned Czech and Slovak works and provided an outlet for such dissident writers as Milan Kundera and Václav Havel. Although he still writes primarily in Czech, he is considered Canadian by the country to which he fled after the Soviet invasion of Czechoslovakia. Among his novels available in English are *The Cowards, The Swell Season,* and *The Tenor Saxophonist's Story.* Two novellas are *The Bass Saxophone* and *Emöke,* and his selected short stories are collected in *When Eve Was Naked.* His autobiography is called *Headed for the Blues.* Persistent themes in his work include the transcendent potential of music, especially jazz; the horrors of totalitarianism; and the expatriate experience. Among his numerous awards are the Neustadt Prize, the Canadian Governor General's Award for English Language Fiction, and the Czech Republic State Prize for Literature. He has also been nominated for a Nobel Prize.

Terry Southern (1924–1995). Born in Alvarado, Texas, Southern, in the fifties, participated in the Paris postwar literary movement and hung out with the Beat writers in Greenwich Village; in the sixties he was in the thick of the swinging London scene, and in the seventies he helped to change the tone and substance of Hollywood movies. His satirical essay "Twirlin' at Ole Miss" is credited with being a seminal work of "New Journalism." He contributed to the screenplays of *Dr. Strangelove, The Loved One,* and *Easy Rider;* selected essays and stories appear in *Red-Dirt Marijuana and Other Tastes;* and *Flash and Filigree, Candy* (with Mason Hoffenberg) and *The Magic Christian* are among his most famous (or infamous) novels, which are generally counter-cultural, absurdist, satirical, and even pornographic.

Julian Street (1879–1947). Street was born in Chicago and went to work as a reporter in New York City when he was just 17. He had a long, productive career as journalist, fiction writer, and author of books on food, wine, and travel. He was made a Chevalier of the Legion of Honor for his writings on French wine and gastronomy and won an O. Henry Memorial prize for a short story. Among his more popular books are *My Enemy the Motor, The Need of Change,* and *Paris à la Carte.*

Boris Vian (1920–1959). Born into an upper middle-class family in a wealthy suburb of Paris, Vian was a man of many parts: poet, writer, editor, critic, translator, musician, singer, songwriter, actor, and inventor. In Paris he served as liaison for Duke Ellington and Miles Davis and worked for a number of important jazz periodicals. His writings are characterized by fabricated vocabulary, word play, and surreal plots. Largely because of this, perhaps, few of his works have been translated into English. His best-known novel available in English is *L'Écume des jours,* whose title has been variously rendered as *Froth on the Daydream, Mood Indigo,* and *Foam of the Daze.* Of the novels he wrote under the nom de plume Vernon Sullivan, *I Shall Spit on Your Graves* has been translated, as have two collections of short stories and incidental writings: *Blues for a Black Cat and Other Stories* and *Round About Close to Midnight.*

Eudora Welty (1909–2001). Born in Jackson, Mississippi, where she lived most of her long, productive life, Welty published in various genres, generally setting her works in the Deep South. Notable among her short story collections are *A Worn Path, A Curtain of Green, The Wide Net and Other Stories, The Golden Apples,* and *The Collected Stories of Eudora Welty.* She received the Rea Award for her significant contribution to American short fiction and a Pulitzer Prize for her novel *The Optimist's Daughter.* Other novels of note are *The Ponder Heart* and *Delta Wedding.* One collection of her photographs is titled *One Time, One Place,* and her autobiographical series of lectures are collected in *One Writer's Beginnings.* She was the first living writer to have her works published by the Library of America.

John Edgar Wideman (1941–). Wideman was born and grew up in Pittsburgh, the Homewood neighborhood of which provides the setting for much of his work. The second African American to win a Rhodes Scholarship, he has received numerous literary awards and honors: he is the first writer to twice win the International PEN/Faulkner Award; two of his nonfiction works were nominated for National Book Awards; he won a Rea Award for the Short Story; and he is the recipient of a MacArthur genius grant. Among his novels are *Sent for You Yesterday, Philadelphia Fire,* and *Two Cities.* Many of his short stories can be found in *Fever, God's Gym,* and *The Stories of John Edgar Wideman.* Three of his notable nonfiction works are *Fatheralong, Brothers and Keepers,* and *Hoop Roots: Basketball, Race, and Love.*

Xu Xi (1954–). Xu Xi is the pen name of an Indonesian Chinese woman raised in Hong Kong who began writing stories in English as a young girl. Her story collections are *History's Fiction, Daughters of Hui,* and *Overleaf Hong Kong.* Identified by *The New York Times* as a pioneer English-language writer from Asia, she was the recipient of a *Ploughshares* award and had a work selected for an O. Henry Prize Stories collection. Her new novel, *Habit of a Foreign Sky,* was shortlisted for the Man Asian Literary Prize, and she is also the author of three other novels, including *The Unwalled City.* She teaches in the MFA program at Vermont College of Fine Arts.

Richard Yates (1926–1992). Yates was born in Yonkers, New York. Generally considered the principal novelist of the post–World War II Age of Anxiety, his seven novels include *Revolutionary Road, A Special Providence, The Easter Parade,* and *A Good School.* During his lifetime, he also published two short story collections, *Eleven Kinds of Loneliness* and *Liars in Love; The Collected Stories of Richard Yates* appeared posthumously.

Acknowledgments

"The Barrier" from *Angel on My Shoulder: Stories* by Don Asher, reprinted by kind permission of the author.

"Sonny's Blues" © 1957 by James Baldwin was originally published in *Partisan Review.* Copyright renewed. Collected in *Going to Meet the Man,* published by Vintage Books. Reprinted by arrangement with the James Baldwin Estate.

"Medley" from *The Sea Birds Are Still Alive* by Toni Cade Bambara, reprinted by kind permission of the author's estate.

"Norman's Date" from *Tales of the Out & Gone* and "The Screamers" from *Tales* by Amiri Baraka, reprinted by kind permission of the author.

"Singing Dinah's Song" by Frank London Brown, reprinted by kind permission of the family of Frank London Brown (Evelyn B. Brown-Colbert and daughters).

"A Woman Who Plays Trumpet Is Deported" is reprinted with the permission of Michelle Cliff.

"Jazz at Twelve" from *Jazz and Twelve O'Clock Tales* by Wanda Coleman. Reprinted by permission of Black Sparrow Books, an imprint of David R. Godine, Publisher, Inc. Copyright © 2008 by Wanda Coleman.

"El perseguidor" translated from *Las Armas Secretas* and "Bix Beiderbecke" translated from *Obras Completas* by permission of the estate. © Heirs of Julio Cortázar, 2008; and by permission of the translator, Sandra Kingery. "Bix Beiderbecke" is an unfinished story, found among the papers of the writer after his death.

"Swingtime" from *Coal Miner's Holiday* by Kiki DeLancey, published by Sarabande Books, Inc. © 2002 by Kiki DeLancey. Reprinted by permission of Sarabande Books and the author.

"A Coupla Scalped Indians" from *Flying Home and Other Stories* by Ralph Ellison, copyright © 1996 by Fanny Ellison; Introduction copyright © 1996 by John F. Callahan. Used by permission of Random House, Inc.

"Common Meter" by Rudolph Fisher, from *The City of Refuge: The Collected Stories of Rudolph Fisher,* edited and with an introduction by John McCluskey Jr., published by University of Missouri Press, 1991.

"Blues for Little Prez" originally appeared in *Black World* and is by Sam Greenlee, reprinted by kind permission of the author.

Tenorman: A Novella by David Huddle, reprinted by kind permission of the author.

"The Blues I'm Playing" from *The Ways of White Folks* by Langston Hughes, copyright © 1934 and renewed 1962 by Langston Hughes. Used by permission of Alfred A. Knopf, a division of Random House, Inc.

"Old Ghost Revives Atavistic Memories in a Lady of the DAR" is reprinted by permission of Harold Ober Associates Incorporated. Copyright © 1949 by Langston Hughes.

"Dead Jazz Guys" from the short story collection entitled *Dead Jazz Guys and Other Stories* by Phil Kawana, published by Huia Publishers, 1996. Reprinted by permission.

ACKNOWLEDGMENTS

"Buddy's Monologue" by Yusef Komunyakaa originally appeared in *Brilliant Corners* and is reprinted by kind permission of the author.

"Miss Brown to You" by Ellen Jordis Lewis originally appeared in *Brilliant Corners* and is reprinted by kind permission of the author.

"Rossonian Days" from *I Got Somebody in Staunton* by William Henry Lewis. Copyright © 2005, 2006 by William Henry Lewis. Reprinted by permission of HarperCollins Publishers.

"Lush Life" by John McCluskey, Jr., originally appeared in *Callaloo* and is reprinted by kind permission of the author.

"Child's Play" by Bill Moody, reprinted by kind permission of the author.

"The Shrimp Peel Gig" by James Reed originally appeared in *Brilliant Corners* and again in the anthology *Tribute to Orpheus,* and is reprinted by kind permission of the author.

"The End of Bull Mácha" from *When Eve Was Naked* by Josef Škvorecký, reprinted by kind permission of the author, and by the translator, Paul Wilson.

"You're Too Hip Baby" from *Red-Dirt Marijuana and Other Tastes* by Terry Southern. Reprinted by permission of SLL/Sterling Lord Literistic, Inc. Copyright © by Estate of Terry Southern.

"The Jazz Baby" by Julian Street, reprinted by permission of *The Saturday Evening Post.*

"'Round About Close to Midnight" from *Round About Close to Midnight: The Jazz Writings of Boris Vian* by Boris Vian, reprinted by permission of the translator, Mike Zwerin.

"Powerhouse" from *A Curtain of Green and Other Stories,* copyright © 1941 and renewed 1969 by Eudora Welty, reprinted by permission of Houghton Mifflin Harcourt Publishing Company.

"The Silence of Thelonious Monk" first published in *Esquire,* November 1997. Copyright © 1997 by John Edgar Wideman, reprinted with permission of The Wylie Agency, Inc.

"Jazz Wife" by Xu Xi originally appeared in *Brilliant Corners* and is reprinted by kind permission of the author.

"A Really Good Jazz Piano" from *The Collected Stories* by Richard Yates, published by Vintage. Reprinted in the U.K. by permission of The Random House Group Ltd. Reprinted in the U.S. by permission of Henry Holt and Company, LLC.

Sascha Feinstein received the 2008 Pennsylvania Governor's Award for Artist of the Year. His recent books include collections of essays: *Black Pearls: Improvisations on a Lost Year;* interviews: *Ask Me Now: Conversations on Jazz & Literature* (Indiana University Press, 2007); and poems: *Misterioso,* winner of the Hayden Carruth Award. The founding editor of *Brilliant Corners: A Journal of Jazz & Literature,* he teaches at Lycoming College and Vermont College of Fine Arts.

David Rife is Professor Emeritus of English at Lycoming College in Williamsport, Pennsylvania, where he taught American literature and modern fiction for thirty-five years. The author of *Jazz Fiction: A History and Comprehensive Reader's Guide,* he has published work in such publications as *American Literary Realism, Dictionary of Literary Biography, Annual Review of Jazz Studies,* and *Journal of Modern Literature.* He now divides his time between Pennsylvania and Florida.